THE
PLANET
OF THE
GODS

Books By: A.M. Johnston

The Planet of the Gods

THE
PLANET
OF THE
GODS

A. M. JOHNSTON

IC PRESS

Idea Creations Press

www.ideacreationspress.com

IC PRESS Idea Creations Press
www.ideacreationspress.com

Library of Congress Control Number: 2016956061

ISBN-13: 9780997890402
ISBN-10: 0997890401

Printed in the U.S.A.

Cover art and map created by Paul Johnston

For Madge Annalee Sorensen,

who first instilled my love of storytelling.

DATHERON WORLD MAP

NENTALIA

COLUXIA

MAJENRICH

NORSTAGG

THUGROD

HESTAROS

ELWYSH

ELWYSH

LEGEND

- ◎ VARDISTON
- ◉ ABENDROTH
- • MALACUS' CABIN
- ✛ WARP GATE

1

ALLEN

BRIGHT, VIBRANT COLORS filled his vision, igniting his chest with a surge of adrenaline as he scanned the horizon taking in the sights. Air ripped through his hair and tugged at his clothes as he threw himself into a nose dive. Far below him he could see rolling hills of trees, rivers leading into a large lake, and every snaking road the landscape had to offer. Wind whipped past his face with such velocity that his eyes began to tear up from the force of it. But he didn't care. He was flying, and enjoying every second of it.

Arching his back, and pulling his arms away from his torso at a forty-five degree angle, he abruptly ended his descent, using the momentum he had gathered from the nose dive to increase his speed through the open air. At the sudden change in direction, he brought his eyes up to look straight ahead—no longer focusing on the earth beneath him—and raised his arms, fists first, directly into his line of sight. A smile of pure elation covered his face as he barreled through a cloud, nearly sending a small flock of geese into a tailspin as he tore past them. Effortlessly, he twisted himself sideways and glanced down the length of his body, past his feet, to the geese already beginning to disappear into the distance.

"Sorry!" he yelled, doing his best not to laugh at the near miss. Not that they could understand him anyway. But the sky did belong to them first, he rationalized.

The freedom soaring through the heavens offered was indescribable and unparalleled. No one could reach him up here. Nothing else mattered. This was what it meant to truly be free.

Almost lazily, he pushed everything else from his mind, concentrating intently on the wind through his light-brown hair and the chill air leaking beneath his shirt to caress his thin, muscular frame. Even though the temperature was noticeably low at this altitude, he couldn't bring himself to feel cold. In his opinion, chilled skin and gooseflesh was a small price to pay for the exhilaration of aerobatics.

He tilted his head up and arched his back again, this time banking sharply upward and holding his body in position until he completed a full loop. He let himself go completely, performing one aerial maneuver after another. Time ceased to exist. There was just him and the open sky. He loved it up here.

Suddenly, as if from a great distance, he could hear someone calling his name.

"Allen . . ." the voice murmured.

He let his concentration break momentarily, doing his best to discern where the voice could have originated.

"Allen!" the voice called again, this time a bit more firmly.

Try as he might, he couldn't quite locate the voice's source. He knew he recognized the voice, but he was lost in the moment and having far too much fun playing in the air.

"Allen Hamilton!" the voice was much more authoritative and agitated this time.

The crisp smacking sound of a ruler against his desk snapped him back to reality. With great effort, Allen brought his eyes from a picture he had been drawing on the back of a test to see his history teacher, Mrs. Abram, standing over him with her hands on her hips and a glare in her eyes. She was a middle-aged woman with a body shape that reminded him of a pear. Mrs. Abram took her job very seriously, and as such always wore some sort of conservative attire and styled her hair in a bun. She kept the hair on her scalp pulled back so tightly, it looked as if her roots might lose their grip at any moment and he'd often wondered if that wasn't the reason for her cranky disposition.

"Time's up!" she proclaimed in her annoyingly nasal voice.

He saw her reach out to snatch the test from his desk and took one last look at the sketch he had nearly completed on its reverse side. He took in every last detail of it, nearly losing himself in his own imagination again as he appraised his work. On top of having a vivid imagination, he was also quite a talented artist; even if he did say so himself.

The fluid pencil lines created an image worthy of notice by even the most accomplished comic book artist's standards. The background was comprised of rivers, many different types of trees, and a lake; all of which were overlaid by clouds sparsely populating the foreground, creating shadow work he hadn't quite finished, on the landscape beneath them. However, it was the focal point of the picture that grabbed him the most, threatening to suck him back into his own imagination. There, in the center of the page, was a young man he had purposely drawn in his own likeness soaring through the air. His arms extended like a bird's wings as he passed through one of the clouds from the lower right corner of the page and into the center of the page. Just as in his daydream, streams of white fluff trailed from his limbs and a flock of geese scattered in his wake.

Allen let out a huff of frustration and disappointment as he watched Mrs. Abram work her way up the aisles between desks, gathering the remaining tests, carrying his unfinished picture with her. To him, it was more than just a drawing; it was an extension of himself. The way his art allowed him to express himself meant far more to him than just simple lines on a page. It was as if it opened his mind completely, leaving him in a sort of trance or transporting him to another world. Sometimes when he drew, he could lose himself for hours in overwhelming torrents of his imagination, making him feel as if he were actually there. He felt every sensation physically that he hoped others could see visually in his art.

Exhaling a deep sigh, he did his best to bring his thoughts back to his immediate surroundings. He stared out the windows to his left at the lush greenery that enveloped the school grounds. Leaves and branches were swaying in the wind, and he couldn't seem to stop a slight smile from creasing his lips as he saw several geese flying overhead in the shape of a V. The morning dew hadn't quite evaporated completely, and the sun was still inching its way into the sky, as if it were just as reluctant as he was to accept that a new day was already here.

Mrs. Abram continued her rounds, collecting the morning's quiz papers from the rest of the students. She liked to begin her class, nearly every day, with a pop quiz on the lecture she had given the previous day. She followed a strict curriculum and Allen assumed she felt that quizzing her students every morning allowed her to better gauge which students were paying attention and which were potential trouble-makers. While the rest of the class grumbled and complained about her methods, it had never really bothered him. He had a good memory and prided himself on his attention to detail.

Aside from having the naturally perceptive mind of an artist, Allen had learned quite a bit from his mother about scrupulous attention to detail. He had spent a significant amount of time in his youth watching his mother, a prosecutor for the state at the time, preparing case after case against thieves, murderers, and rapists. Most children would probably act out, throw tantrums, or create any number of other outbursts to gain the attention of a mother who so tirelessly shuffled through endless amounts of papers and case notes into the early hours of every morning. But not Allen.

Only once had he asked her why she spent so much time reading instead of playing with him or watching television like the mothers of his friends. It was obvious to him, even at that young age, that his question had upset her. Apparently unsure how to respond at first, she stared at him in bewilderment while tears slowly filled her eyes. She pushed herself away from her desk and scooped him up onto her lap.

"I wish I could play with you all the time," she had said to reassure him. "But mommy is the one who has to talk to judges, and lawyers, and other people and convince them to put bad men in jail. And that means that I have to do lots of homework to make sure that the bad men I put in jail, stay in jail."

"You have homework too?" he asked, staring up into her teary eyes.

She smiled down at him, letting out a laugh at his response. "I sure do. And I have to pay extra special attention to all the little details to make sure I don't get anything wrong. Because as much as I like putting bad men in jail, I also need to make sure that I don't put the wrong guy there instead. The littlest details can sometimes be the most important ones, Allen. Remember that."

That explanation had appeased him. After that, Allen spent almost every evening sitting next to her at her desk, or lying on his stomach on the floor of her office, doing his homework with her. When he didn't have homework, he would read other books that interested him or draw pictures for her. Sometimes, especially in his younger days, he would draw pictures of her with a briefcase in one hand, a bad guy in the other hand, and a cape on her back as she flew through the air toward a jailhouse. He could tell that she had been particularly proud to hang those ones on the refrigerator, or frame them and put them on the desk in her office.

As a result of having a lawyer for a mother, and all the time he spent studying with her and following her example, he had a strong moral compass and sense of justice, and greatly enjoyed the pursuit of knowledge and truth. It was this set of habits which taught him to excel academically.

Having finished the task of collecting the morning's test, Mrs. Abram marched to the front of the classroom, placed them in an orderly pile on the corner of her desk, and began the day's lecture. A cool breeze brushed his face from the small opening in the window next to him, bringing with it promises of gorgeous day to come as Mrs. Abram scratched names and dates on the chalkboard. She was going over some of the finer points of the industrial revolution, naming some of the most influential inventions borne of the era—such as the steam engine and the light bulb—and the stories of the individuals responsible for them. In his opinion the manner with which she presented the lessons was completely tedious and boring. He doubted she could keep him interested in the history of Stan Lee and the birth of Marvel comics.

Resigned to the fact that his second period of the day was going be monotonously long, he retrieved his sketch tablet and a pencil sharpener from his backpack at the side of his desk. He sharpened his pencil and blew the shavings onto the floor. Skimming through the nearly full sketch tablet, he finally reached a blank page, rested his head in the nook of his left elbow on his desk, and let his attention drift from the day's lesson back into the furthest reaches of his imagination as he contemplated what to draw.

Normally he was more than able to keep himself focused on his studies, but he had a 4.0 grade point average and was nearing the end of his senior year. This, he reasoned, was a good enough excuse to allow himself to quietly slip into a daydream on occasion during class—especially considering he had already acquired the necessary amount of credits to graduate. To him, the remaining two and a half months of school were more formality than necessity.

He touched the lead of the pencil to the paper and slipped into the deepest recesses of his mind.

The bell signifying the end of the period snapped him out of his daydream this time. All the other students gathered up their things and scurried for the door as quickly as they could. Allen stole a sidelong glance at the clock above the door, taking his time replacing his text book and sketch tablet in his backpack. If the day maintained its current slow pace, he knew it would be a long one.

***

By the time the lunch bell rang, Allen would have been ready to pull his hair out with impatient anxiety had he not continued to disappear into his art instead of actually participating in class. It also didn't help matters that he was positioned, in nearly every class, to see just how clear the sky was becoming as the day progressed. As much of a bookworm and a daydreamer as he was, he hated being cooped up when the weather was so welcoming.

As he entered the cafeteria, his nostrils were assaulted by the acrid odor of multiple types of food and cleaning supplies used to prepare for the imminent onslaught of teenagers. From the relatively large commons area, a cacophony of students talked over each other, utensils clanking against plastic trays and wooden tables. The constant patter of footsteps emanated well into the corridors beyond. From where he stood, a few steps inside the double door entrance, he noted the length of the line to be served was longer than he was willing to endure. Better to have a seat somewhere and wait for the line to dwindle, he decided.

He scanned the growing crowd, searching for a place to sit. The majority of seating was still being sporadically occupied, but it was easy to see a common theme among most of the tables. Allen never really felt like he belonged to any one, specific clique or group so he always searched for a place he deemed inconspicuous before sitting down. Jocks and cheerleaders were already in their usual spot near the exit in the south-east corner of the cafeteria; cheerleaders at one table, the jocks at the other. Immediately outside the windows behind them, a few empty picnic tables could be seen.

Allen noticed someone at a table near the center of the cafeteria doing his best to summon him without attracting the attention of the athletes at the next table. The portly young man had a sheepish look on his face. He was postured awkwardly, motioning insistently, nearly under the table, for Allen to come and join him. He purposely had his back to the table full of athletes. A look of satisfaction crossed the dull features of the boy's face when Allen's eyes finally settled on him.

The boy was Eugene Whitaker; a sophomore nearly two years younger than Allen was. He had arrived halfway through the first semester the previous year, and with his large build and disheveled appearance he had immediately become a target to many of the other students. Allen had noticed the poor boy's relentless harassment, but hadn't wanted to get involved at first, and Eugene seemed to take most of it in stride as far as he could tell. So, even though it bothered him to see such torment, he had kept his opinions to himself and stayed out of it, hoping that the hazing was a passing phase and not a precedent being set.

One day near the end of winter, however, he had happened upon an entire crowd of his peers hooting and hollering as they gathered around a spectacle of some sort. As he pushed his way through the mob—some cheering while others laughed—he could plainly hear a voice panting in frustration and the muffled crunch of snow underfoot. What he saw when he got to the center of the circle angered him to his core. Three members of the football team had taken Eugene's backpack and were tossing it back and forth amongst each other, tripping him occasionally as he ran back and forth between them in a desperate attempt to reclaim his belongings. Eugene's clothes were wet, his face red with effort, and he seemed on the verge of tears. When finally he stopped in the center of the three, completely out of breath, one of the bullies launched the backpack at Eugene's head. He went down like a pile of bricks.

Something inside him snapped; he had seen enough.

Rage completely inundated him as he ran into the center of the circle, swinging his own backpack—which was always full of books—with wild abandon. He bashed one of the assailants in the side of his head from behind, sending him sprawling unconscious to the ground before he even knew he'd been hit. It happened so fast that neither of the two left standing seemed sure what had occurred. Before either had a chance to react, he'd flattened a second target with his backpack, striking him directly in the face and filling the air with a sickening thud and blood-red mist as he, too, fell to the ground. The third antagonist anticipated his attack and ducked under the arc of the backpack, only to have his nose smashed in by Allen's left knee.

He knelt and helped Eugene to his feet, asking him if he was alright. When Eugene nodded that he was fine Allen turned his attention to the crowd of spectators.

"What's wrong with all of you?" he shouted. "This boy has done nothing to deserve the kind of aggression you've shown him! He doesn't retaliate. He hasn't complained. He hasn't even turned anyone in to the principal as far as I know, and still you harass him! And for what? What reason could any of you possibly have to treat anyone like this?"

Every eye in the crowd was on him; some with looks of disdain and contempt, others in complete shock at what they had just witnessed. No one said a word as he continued. While he wasn't yelling anymore, the heat in his voice was unmistakable. "You look down on him because he's different. You treat him poorly and call him names because he's overweight. Half of you probably don't even know his name. You're cowards. Every last one of you."

Allen took one last look at the three boys lying haphazardly in the snow before ushering Eugene away from the crowd. Nobody said a word, and nobody tried to stop them as they walked back toward the school's main entrance. He'd been suspended from school for the first time ever, and had gotten a stern lecture from his mother on fighting and the legal ramifications it could bring She'd also admonished him to control his temper, that his impetuousness would one day get him into trouble he might not be able to talk his way out of.

The bullying dramatically decreased after that for Eugene, but Allen found himself shunned by many he'd thought were his friends. From then on, Eugene shadowed him like a lost puppy. While he'd never held any ill-will toward Eugene for what had transpired, he wasn't in the mood to share the boy's company today.

Without acknowledging him, Allen made his way toward the exit beyond the table of jocks. Every person at the table noticed him as he walked past and weren't shy about casting glares in his direction. About six feet from the exit, as he neared the edge of the table, Bryce Holden, one of the three he had laid out in defense of Eugene, stuck his leg out in an attempt to trip him. Allen, on his guard for such a thing, noticed it and swung his left leg hard, in an exaggerated step, kicking Bryce's leg out of his way.

Bryce let out a yelp and sprung to his feet. "Why don't you watch where you're going, loser?"

Having reached the exit door, he turned around to face Bryce. "What makes you think I wasn't?"

Bryce took a step toward him, only to be halted by one of his friends grabbing his wrist. He jerked his arm free and pointed a threatening finger at Allen. "You're lucky, Hamilton!"

"Whatever." He shrugged as he walked away, stepping through the doors and inhaling a breath of fresh, spring air.

A million things ran through his mind as he moved across the grass toward the picnic tables set up on the exterior common area. His thoughts wandered to everything from teaching Bryce and his friends a lesson in humility, to the drawings he had started in his morning classes, to what he was going to do over the coming weekend. The tables were dilapidated and warped from years sitting out in the open weather and a lack of maintenance. Only a few sporadically placed sections of chipped paint still maintained the table's original color, leaving the rest an unsightly shade of dull gray, but at least out here he would find solitude from the chattering inside. The bench creaked as Allen sat down. He was extremely uncomfortable, but at least the weather outside was nice. He felt the warm mid-day sun gently caressing the back of his neck as he placed his backpack on the bench next to him. A smile crossed his lips when he remembered that he was going to see Sarah this evening.

Sarah Campbell, who was almost two years older than he, was one of his oldest and dearest friends. He had known her since he was ten years old, when his mother had dated her father for a brief time.

Carol—his mother—had met Sarah's father while on the way home from work, when he'd accidentally rear-ended her car. Things started out heatedly between the two, but the damage to both vehicles was minimal and Tony—Sarah's father—seemed to him, even at his young age, to be a very smooth talker. They discovered that they both were single parents, each with only one child. They had exchanged phone numbers before departing the scene of the accident.

As their relationship began to develop, Tony would bring Sarah over to play with Allen, while Tony spent time with Carol. Occasionally they would all go out to dinner, or a movie, but Allen quickly found himself really looking forward to the evenings his mother would go out with Tony because it meant he would get to see Sarah. She, like him, was very bright for her age and didn't seem to be intimidated by anything. He became infatuated with her. When things between Tony and his mother dwindled and finally fell apart, he and Sarah remained friends; often spending entire weekends together or going camping, despite objections from various boyfriends over the years. Allen always wanted to ask her out, or to be more than just friends, but the time never seemed right and rejection from her was one of the only things he truly feared.

Allen snapped out of his reverie when, from the corner of his eye, he noticed Bryce Holden, Eric Conrad, and Brad Schultz—the very same three from the incident the previous winter—guarding the entrance back into the school cafeteria, accompanied by two of the boy's girlfriends. Bryce had dark brown hair, which he kept cropped short. Eric had thick blonde hair, which came down past his ears, and Brad wore his rust colored hair slicked back into a pony tail. All three had roughly the same build—the stout frame of a young athlete—and were wearing their varsity jackets emblazoned with the school team's colors: red and silver; although, Eric was several inches shorter than the other two. It wasn't difficult for anyone to see that they were trouble waiting to happen, especially when all three were together.

They stood with their glares transfixed on him as they passed cigarettes among each other and began to light them. Allen could hear them mumbling, not once taking their eyes off of him. Rather than give in to their obvious attempt to intimidate him, he turned around on the bench, purposely facing his back toward them, noticing as he shifted, that there was a half-eaten apple on the ground at his feet. He tapped it slightly with his right foot, nudging it away from him a few inches.

Just then, Bryce, Eric, and Brad erupted in laughter. Allen glanced over his shoulder, feeling slightly paranoid. The laughter stopped abruptly when they noticed him leering at them.

"What!" Bryce shouted in a challenging tone. "Mind your business or I'll come over there and stuff my foot down your throat!"

Allen rolled his eyes, purposely letting them see his blatant gesture, and then turned his back to them once more. He found their bullying pathetic and refused to feed into their antagonism. A moment later, as he considered just getting up and walking around the school to the main entrance to avoid them, one of the three guarding the cafeteria entrance hurled their lighter at him, striking him in the back of the head.

Without hesitation, and faster than he would have thought himself capable, he reached toward the ground, grabbing the half-eaten apple from between his feet. Almost in one fluid motion, he was on his feet and had turned completely around; hurling the apple at the first target he set his eyes on. As it ricocheted off Bryce's forehead, it exploded into a sticky haze, sending small chunks of apple into the air. The three boys and the two girls with them could only stare in response; all of them sharing the same horrified, thunderstruck look.

As cognition began to return, Bryce's expression heated until he was red in the face. All three marched toward him in unison. Before they took more than three steps, the bell signifying the end of lunch rang. Allen couldn't help feeling a wave of relief flow through him.

"You're so lucky," Bryce growled, wiping apple fragments from his brow. "I don't have time to finish this right now. But after school, you're dead!"

"If you say so," he goaded.

As they stormed off, Allen turned to gather his things. He took a deep cleansing breath to calm his nerves, hoping that his brazen reaction wouldn't come back to bite him.

The rest of the school day went by much quicker for Allen than the first half. He continued to drift away into his imagination and fill in empty pages of his sketch book. Aggravating as the confrontation at lunch had been, he did his best to keep it pushed from his mind, but occasionally found his thoughts dwelling on it and wondered if he had handled the situation as appropriately as he had initially judged. He reminded himself that he wasn't afraid of them and that it was important stand up for what you believe in; even if he had to risk the occasional lumps and bruises to do so.

As he exited the building amongst the crowds of other students, Allen was surprised to see a familiar face smiling at him from the parking lot. There, leaning against the driver's-side door of her black, older model, sports car stood Sarah. Her long jet-black hair fluttered in the slight breeze, accentuating her gorgeous features, leaving him virtually breathless as he watched her hazel eyes following him. Even though he had long since memorized every detail of her supple beauty, seeing her lithe, curvaceous figure standing there was arresting. He had completely forgotten until that moment that she had offered to pick him up from school.

Allen smiled inwardly, doing his best not to appear overexcited to see her, as he changed course and began heading directly for her. His heart began to quicken, almost uncontrollably, and he found it difficult to keep his legs from following suit.

As he closed about half of the distance to her car, he noticed her expression abruptly change from pleasant delight to apprehensive consternation. Before he was able to ascertain what could cause such a sudden change in her countenance, a bright light filled his vision and he felt himself crumple to the ground. Sound muffled all around him and sharp, precise points of pain began to jolt him from a seemingly random source. The wind was violently driven from his lungs as he desperately tried to regain awareness of his surroundings. With great effort, he braced his knees to the ground underneath him just in time to see a foot flying toward his face.

Through instinct alone, Allen caught the foot and twisted it at the ankle as hard as he could. He saw Eric Conrad land with a thud in front of him. Rage completely swept through him as the realization of what was happening struck him. In a blind fury, he leapt on top of Eric and began to unleash pure animosity toward his aggressor. When one of his blows made impact on Eric's nose, the sickening snap of bone separating from cartilage filled his ears, sending warm blood splattering across his knuckles and on the front of his shirt. Before he could land another, he was pulled off of Eric and hoisted to his feet. He realized there were two arms wrapped around either of his, binding his movement, as his feet struggled to find purchase underneath him. Confusion swept over him when Bryce stepped up to began his assault anew and Allen realized both of his arms were still bound.

"You just couldn't leave well enough alone, could you punk!" Bryce wailed, pummeling his face and body in rapid succession. "I warned you! This is for the apple!"

Allen could feel his left eye beginning to swell as crowds of students swarmed in to watch the spectacle. Nausea swept through him in furious waves as his own blood began to fill his mouth. Students all around began cheering and shouting as they watched.

Just as he was about to give in to the sweet embrace of losing consciousness, he heard a sharp clanking sound. Bryce's eyes rolled back into his head and his crumpled body hit the ground hard in front of Allen. The two still holding him up released their grip and he sank helplessly to the ground next to Bryce. He spat, emptying the warm red blood from his mouth and attempted to catch his breath. His head spun wildly. Another sharp clank pierced through the ringing in his ears and he was only vaguely aware of the body landing almost directly behind him.

Allen rolled over onto his back, hearing another clank—followed by another thud—as he struggled to gather his wits and correct his blurry vision. After a few moments he noticed a silhouette hovering over him, resting something on its shoulder. When finally his vision became clear, he stared up in wonder at who had rescued him.

"I can't leave you alone for five minutes without you getting into some sort of trouble, can I Allen?" Sarah smirked.

He wiped the blood from his swollen lips onto the sleeve of his tee-shirt as she helped him up and into her car. The bitter taste of it lingered in his mouth and he couldn't seem to completely banish the ringing in his ears as they made the journey back to his house. He could feel his pulse announcing itself in undulating waves of pain where the injuries from the beating he had taken had broken his skin or had caused swelling. He ached all over. As much physical pain as he was in, however, he was more concerned about the look of disappointment and disapproval his mother would give him when she learned what had happened—not to mention the lecture he would certainly receive on the legalities such a situation caused.

As much as he knew he shouldn't, Allen couldn't seem to shake the feelings of guilt, shame, and helplessness he had experienced at the realization that it had been Sarah who'd rescued him. It was embarrassing to appear so fragile in her presence; although if she had thought any less of him for it, she hadn't let it show.

Now that the experience was over, he could feel self-doubt creeping in on him. She seemed to be the only one who could cause him to second-guess himself. He wanted nothing more than to see her smile at him, the way he saw her smile at other guys she dated, and relished every second he got to spend with her. But it was different being next to her and feeling this weak, this ashamed. He felt like he didn't deserve to even be in her presence at the moment—like he was less than a man and definitely less than she deserved. He knew such thoughts were irrational, but couldn't seem to escape them as he stared out the passenger window at the trees and gravel rushing past his vision. His mind once again drifted into his imagination as he leaned his head against the passenger window.

"We're here," Sarah said moments later, jerking him away from his brooding and back to reality. "Are you sure you don't want me to take you to the hospital?"

"No. I'm fine. Nothing is broken . . . except maybe my pride," he said jokingly, more for his benefit than for hers. He stared out the window thoughtfully, noticing storm clouds rapidly invading the bright sky from the distant horizon. It seemed to be an outward manifestation of how he felt about the direction his day had taken. Allen didn't dare test his voice again, at least not at that moment. He just sat there a minute or two longer, staring out the window in silence rather than making eye contact with her. He could feel her watching him and after a moment, decided to get out of the car and head toward the front door of his house; she was quick to follow suit and ushered him across the front lawn without a word.

The steps of the porch creaked underfoot as Sarah escorted him to the door of his house. She insisted on opening the door and holding it for him, although he had refused her assistance in reaching it. After all, he didn't want her to think he was weak; he could still walk on his own. His head pounded and his knees shook in protest at his efforts, but he refused to appear more helpless in her eyes than he already felt.

As they reached the kitchen, his thoughts were everywhere but where he was. Relieving the pressure of his weight from his legs as he sat in one of the chairs at the kitchen table almost seemed euphoric. He could hardly believe that he had sustained such a beating. It didn't seem real. It had all happened so fast that he couldn't seem to reconcile what could have caused it. He began to blame himself. If only he hadn't overreacted at lunch. Why did he always have to act so impulsively? Why couldn't he just let things go? Why did he constantly feel the need to test his luck and push others to their limits?

Allen took a deep breath, and choked back another wave of tears, as he stared out the picture-window beside the kitchen table. He did his best to swallow the painful lump in his throat as he watched the storm clouds continue to overwhelm the late afternoon sky. As irrational as he knew it to be, he couldn't help but wish he had super-human abilities. Everything would be so much easier if he had the kind of advantages that his favorite characters had. Surely he and all those who were truly important to him would be better off if he had the ability to make his imagination reality—the ability to avert any catastrophe through a sheer force of will.

He turned his focus back to Sarah, watching with great interest as she rummaged through drawers with familiarity in search of wash cloths, bandages, and whatever else she might need to clean him up. She was so beautiful. If he was distraught moments ago, he was now buoyant. Sarah had a way of making everything better for him. Just having her there with him seemed to somehow make all his worries fade; she was his best friend. He had long ago admitted to himself that he was in love with her, but he dared not tell her for fear of losing her friendship.

Finally, she seemed to have collected everything she needed. Allen caught a faint whiff of her perfume as she pulled a chair directly in front of his and sat facing him. She hooked her hair behind her ears and gave him an appraising look. Wetting one of the wash cloths, she leaned in so close that he could feel her warm breath on his chin. It was intoxicating. His heart hammered in his chest so hard and so rapidly that he was sure she could hear it. He didn't want her to see how intently he stared at her as she washed the dried blood off his face, but he couldn't bring himself to look away.

He sat quietly while she wiped away the blood with a warm rag, flinching when she wiped across the cuts under his eye and on his lip. After a moment, her eyes darted up to meet his and she hesitated slightly. Leaning back in her chair, she blushed.

"Well, it's not as bad as I thought," she said. "But maybe you should finish cleaning up in the shower."

For a moment, seeing her pull away from him so abruptly, Allen couldn't help feeling like he'd done something wrong. Rather than making an issue of it, however, he just nodded his head.

Sarah helped him up, gave him a gentle hug, and nudged him toward the stairs which lead to the upper floor of the house. "Go on," she said, "a shower will do you some good. I'll still be here when you're done."

The hot water from the shower hurt him almost as much as it helped; his external injuries screamed in turmoil under the pressure of the scalding water, adding new and unique waves of pain to the ones he was already experiencing; it also, however, relaxed his muscles and gave him a good opportunity to clear his mind.

As he made his way to his bedroom he heard voices coming from downstairs. He listened for a moment, wondering who Sarah could be talking to; he didn't think his mother could be home from work already. The voices were, however, both female and seemed to be enjoying the conversation. Curious to see who Sarah was talking to and anxious to see her again himself, he rushed to his bedroom to get dressed.

Getting dressed—even into something as light as the white cotton tee-shirt and charcoal gray sweat pants he had chosen—demonstrated to him just how sore certain parts of him actually were. Once he was fully clothed again he followed the voices back downstairs to their source. He stood in the doorway to the living room, feeling apprehensive as well as elated when he saw that his mother was home. She and Sarah were sitting next to each other on the black leather sofa, facing away from him and flipping through an old family photo album.

For several minutes he just watched them. His mother, Carol, was a handsome woman with the same wavy, light-brown hair as his; although hers nearly reached her shoulders. Although he couldn't see their faces at the moment, his Mom always wore thin-framed glasses over her dark brown eyes, which had creases in the corners etched from years of constant laughter. Allen noticed, as she pointed out another picture to Sarah, that his mother was still in her two-piece suit that she always wore to work underneath her judge's robes.

Noticing his own reflection in the large mirror on the opposite wall, he risked a couple of steps into the living room since he didn't dare announce himself just yet. The mirror had been there as long as he could remember. It had large, ornately carved golden borders and—according to his mother—had been a gift from his father. He had always thought that it looked very out of place in their living room. He was nervous to be back in Sarah's company and also about what his mother would have to say about his appearance, so he carefully inched his way toward them from behind to keep from being noticed.

Carol and Sarah were engrossed in the photo albums and reminiscing about some familiar pictures. There were others Sarah had apparently never seen; she asked his mother for the story behind them. With the two of them facing away from him as they rummaged through older volumes, neither of the women had noticed Allen peeking over their shoulders from the side of the couch.

Allen recognized several volumes of albums—most of which documented his childhood—strewn about the surface of the coffee table in front of the sofa and wondered just how long he had been in the shower, and how quickly his mother had gotten home from work. He could see pictures of himself at little-league baseball games in one at the edge of the table; there were various school pictures and old report cards in another.

"Are these wedding pictures?" Sarah asked. "I never knew you were married."

"Yes. I was married, once upon a time. But it didn't last long."

Allen, having completely calmed himself up to that point, felt his face flush in anger. "That's because he ran out on us," he blurted.

Both Sarah and his mother jerked their heads around. He hadn't necessarily meant to draw their attention in that way, but he now had their full attention, regardless of intent.

Sarah gawked at him, and he realized she had never heard him so blatantly condemn someone. "You shouldn't talk about your father that way," she said.

"Yeah . . . well, there's a reason you've never heard either of us mention him," he retorted in a heated voice. "He's a piece of crap who couldn't handle the responsibility of being a man and sticking around to raise his son!

"He walked out on us, without ever looking back, right after I was born! If I ever meet him, I'll knock him out!"

His mother's face was an amalgam of emotions. She looked as if she might burst into tears, as if she was both angry with his disposition on the subject and disappointed to hear it. She looked as if she wanted to slap him, but lowered her gaze and turned her head while she considered something. Allen had asked her once, when he was younger, why he didn't have a dad; she had simply said that she would tell him when he was older.

The grandfather clock, which stood against the far wall of the living room chimed several times, accentuating the already awkward silence hanging in the air.

Carol inhaled a slow, measured breath before she spoke. "You were far too young to remember him, Allen. You don't know what you're talking about."

"I know he ran out on us! I know he hurt you . . . I know I never had a father because he walked away without a second thought. What more is there?"

Allen could see the fading light of day shining through the windows, reflecting in his mother's glistening eyes. He hadn't wanted to upset her, but he felt nothing but resentment for men like his father. How could any man, regardless of their background or upbringing, fail to love their child enough to rise to the occasion? How could any father do that to their son? For that matter, how could

29

any husband do that to a wife he supposedly loved enough to spend the rest of his life with?

His mother set the photo album back down on the coffee table and drifted away in thought for what seemed like a very long time; the silence in the room—not to mention the sorrowful look on her face—was difficult for him to endure. Finally, after several minutes of consideration, she decided to speak.

"Your father," Carol began, "wasn't the bad man you make him out to be. I have many very fond memories of him."

"Then why haven't you ever told me much about him?" he asked.

His mother sat silent for another moment before answering. "Because it's painful to think about . . . and you were too young to understand. But I suppose now you're old enough to hear what happened and decide for yourself what to think."

Carol paused briefly before continuing, "Your father and I met many years before you were born. I was still young and he was strikingly handsome. My car had gotten a flat tire in the middle of nowhere on Highway 89 and nobody had stopped to help me out. I was there for hours before he came walking along the side of the road and saw me there. He walked right up to me, looking like he'd been out in the hot sun all day, and offered to help fix my tire. He didn't ask for anything in return, just offered to fix my tire for me.

"I didn't have a spare tire, I didn't have any money for one, and I had never been in a situation like that. I was panicking, but he was so cool and so confident. He told me to just have a seat in my car and let him fix it. I honestly don't know how he did it, but it didn't seem to take him that long and he had my tire fixed. He told me that the tire wasn't ruptured and that he had only needed to air it up. How he managed it though, I still have no idea.

"I offered him a ride into the city and we ended up talking a lot on the way; he was just as charming as he was dashing. He got himself established with a job and an apartment, and we started dating. It wasn't long before we were both very much in love with each other . . . it came on so fast. We were actually together for quite a while before we finally decided to get married.

"Everything seemed to be going so well . . . And then one night, shortly after you were born, he came home in a panic. He told me that he hadn't been completely honest with me about his past. He told me that he was from another country and that he was being deported home . . ."

"How could they do that if you were married?" Allen asked, the tone in his voice receding from heated contempt to one searching for answers. "I thought marrying a citizen gave you citizenship."

"That's not always the case; there's far more to it than that. It's a common misconception," Carol answered. She seemed to withdraw into herself for a moment, as if in search for the strength to continue her story. "He told me he was being extradited back to his country, that he was a fugitive of sorts and he had to leave . . . He said he was doing it to shield me, that he wasn't sure if he'd ever be able to come back. It was one of the longest, most difficult nights of my life.

"It was shortly after that that I decided to go to law school. I was desperate to find a way to get him back; I thought that if I studied hard enough, I could find a loophole in the law and bring him back. I wasn't really thinking rationally though; he never even told me what country he came from—"

"So, what you're saying then, is that, not only did he run out on you, but he was a criminal from another country to boot. Did he even ever write you, or call you from this mystery country he came from?"

Carol clearly didn't like the manner of his comment, but made no attempt to reprimand him for it. "No," she said in a composed voice. "He didn't. After that night, he was just gone. It was as if he disappeared off the face of the planet. I was never able to even find anyone who knew him."

"So then," Allen drawled, attempting more discretion with his disdain for the man who had sired him, "how do you even know the name he gave you was his real name? He could've easily been lying to you from the beginning. You just told me yourself that you met him on the side of the road. For all you know, from what you've told me, he could've been running from another woman he had left high and dry with more of his illegitimate offspring. Who knows? Maybe the night he freaked out and split town, he was running because that woman had finally found him. Maybe what he was shielding you from was the truth: that he's always been a cheat and a low-life, and he didn't want to be caught in a lie."

Allen felt a stab of pain as he took in his mother's reaction; part of him wished he hadn't spoken so harshly.

His mother looked as if she were in another world as she responded, "I don't know how to explain it, but I know there is more to it than you see on the surface . . . I know he loved me. I have long since considered everything you just suggested. But there are too many things that just don't add up. For one, he was frantic the night he left. I think that may have been the only time I ever saw him cry, or even lose his cool."

"Maybe he's just a good actor," he muttered.

Carol, seizing an opportunity to change the subject, let out an exasperated sigh as she inspected Allen's appearance. "Or maybe he's just a magnet for trouble, too," she teasingly accused. "Maybe that's where you get it. Come here; let me take a look at you."

Sarah, who had been noticeably quiet during the conversation, let out a slight chuckle at his mother's remark making him all but forget his apprehension of this moment. He sometimes felt as if his mother's scrutiny could intimidate a hungry mountain lion. He was, however, surprised that she hadn't immediately acknowledged his injuries.

After a brief inspection of his condition, she stood face-to-face with him, resting her hands on his shoulders. "You don't look as bad off as I imagined you might be from Sarah's account of things," she said.

Allen glanced past his mother at Sarah, still seated on the couch, and flashed a look of embarrassment and gratitude. He was glad he hadn't had to tell his mother the story. "What did she tell you?" he asked apprehensively.

"Just the important parts," she assured him. She paused for a moment and then gave him a sly look. "Like how she saved your butt."

Allen felt his face turn crimson as he gave his mother an indignant look. "I was ganged up on by four guys," he said defensively.

"Relax," she laughed, "I was only giving you a hard time. I'm actually very grateful she was there; it would've turned out much worse had she not been." Her expression turned grim, "You can count on me calling the school in the morning and talking to the principal about this though."

"I had already assumed as much." He rolled his eyes. "So what are you doing home so early?"

His mother gestured behind her with a tilt of her head, "Sarah called me. I wasn't in the courtroom when she called; I was in my office. So I just passed off my last couple of hearings to another judge. I told him I had a family emergency."

He arched an eyebrow at her. "You passed off cases? I didn't even know you could do that."

"Well, they can't expect us all to not have lives outside the courtrooms. Besides, they were just a couple of arraignments; nothing major."

She took a couple of steps toward the living room entrance and gave both he and Sarah a look of quiet appraisal. "I don't know about you two," she said, "but I'm starving. You guys up for dinner?"

He and Sarah exchanged a look and then Sarah answered, "Oh, yeah. I could definitely eat."

"Yeah, sure," he shrugged.

"Good," his mother said with a smile.

After much deliberation, they had eventually decided to order pizza from a local establishment called, simply: The Pizzeria. It had been a long time since they'd eaten dinner together, just the three of them. In his opinion it was a wonderful end to an otherwise stressful day.

The sun was almost completely hidden behind the horizon when Sarah finally announced that she had to leave, accentuating a dark royal blue sky with bright pinks and oranges which looked to be desperately clinging to the last vestiges of the day. The moon, already high in the sky, asserted its dominance as twilight faded away into the night. Crickets, owls, and various other nocturnal creatures could already be heard echoing their songs through the woods, which came up like a wall of vegetation along the far edge of his back yard, as he walked her out to her car.

As they moved toward her car, parked at the curb, Sarah glanced over her shoulder as if to see whether he was watching her or not. He was.

There was a slight chill to the humid evening air as they reached her car. A breeze sent a shudder up Allen's back, covering his flesh with goose bumps as they both leaned up against the passenger side of her car next to each other.

"I had a good time tonight," he said. He watched the leaves of the big oak tree in his front yard dance in the breeze, nervous to make eye contact with her.

"Yeah, me too," she said.

Allen stuffed his hands into his pockets when they began to shake. He wasn't sure if it was because he was nervous, or if he just found the evening breeze to be that chilly. Either way, he didn't want to risk her noticing.

After a couple of moments and probably about a thousand heartbeats, he gave Sarah a sidelong glance. "Thanks for saving my butt today," he said with a slight grin on his face.

"No problem," she giggled. "Just don't make a habit of it."

They both laughed.

Finally mustering up the courage to do so, he turned to face her. "So when do I get to hang out with you again?"

There was a sparkle in her eyes that Allen wasn't sure he recognized as she returned his focused stare. "I don't have to work tomorrow," she offered.

Allen's heart raced all the faster at her insinuation.

Before he had a chance to respond, however, a bright light briefly illuminated her features, casting harsh shadows across her face and the surface of her car. He saw Sarah shield her eyes from the luminous onslaught with her left arm before turning to see what could have caused it.

Dull light still danced from deep within the woods behind Allen's house as he and Sarah charged into his back yard. Birds scattered in all directions in the wake of whatever was emitting the soft glow coming from somewhere deep in the forest. The air almost seemed to be sizzling as a sharp, concussive gust of wind escaped the confines of the wall of trees lining the edge of Allen's yard. A barrage of leaves and twigs burst from the woods, littering his yard in the aftermath of the shockwave.

"What in the world was that?" Sarah gasped.

"I have no idea . . ." he muttered, almost to himself.

Then, just as quickly as it had begun, the wind stopped. Light faded back into darkness and all that could be heard was the frantic, raucous chatter of the forest.

He and Sarah looked at each other, both of their eyes wide.

"That was really weird," Sarah said after a moment of personal deliberation.

"You can say that again," Allen answered.

With their eyes still transfixed on the flora behind Allen's house, they stood in silence for several minutes. Neither one of them seemed to want to be the first to break the hush filling the air.

A shudder of trepidation crawled up Allen's spine when a thin streak of light shot skyward and into the distance from deep within the heart of the forest. It looked as if a shooting star had somehow come to land there, plotted its escape, and at that moment ascended back into the stars from whence it came.

"What do you suppose could cause that?" Sarah asked hesitantly.

"I don't know. But I think I want to go check it out." Allen grinned.

2

IMPETUS

HE HATED THEM ALL. He hated how highly they were regarded, despite the fact that they were nothing more than glorified bounty hunters. He hated the condescension he could see in the eyes of every single one of them that looked at him or any of his ilk. Most of all, however, he hated that he was left with no choice in this matter but to employ their services.

Krathantor; Gorrlock scum, that's what they were.

It was the bad blood between their races and the poor treatment his people suffered at the hands of Gorrlocks like them that had given him the strength to take the seat of power from his Gorrlock predecessor. Since then he had become a hero to his people; those who shared his ancestry, anyway. Like all Triclopians within the walls of the city of Vardiston, Luziaph had been a slave, a second-rate citizen prior to his rise to power through force. Now the tables were turned, at least in this city. He was the Proctus of Vardiston now, able to set the laws and ensure his people were no longer mistreated by the Krathantor and vermin of their like.

The God-King, ruler of the entire world, was also a Gorrlock. It was really no wonder He held the Krathantor in such esteem. Someday soon He, too, would answer to Luziaph for the crimes He had turned a blind eye to while Triclopians like Luziaph suffered at the hands of those belonging to the God-King's supposedly superior race. But for now, he would have to do his best to continue earning the man's trust, beginning with capturing the escaped convict the God-King didn't seem to want anyone to know about just yet. If accomplishing such an end meant employing the God-King's personal hunters, then Luziaph would just have to suffer the indignity.

It took great effort to keep the contemptuous snarl from his lips as he watched the three of them enter his throne room, moving toward him past the procession of the statues of his enemies which decorated so much of the Palace of Vardiston. He silently vowed to himself that they, too, would someday decorate a portion of his home.

At last they stopped in front of him, their countenances distorted with unhidden contempt for their superior. The one in the middle, presumably the one in command of the others, as they stayed a couple steps behind him to either flank, glared up at him with those malevolent black and red eyes all Gorrlocks shared. "For what purpose have we been summoned?" he asked in a demanding tone.

For the moment Luziaph decided to overlook the impudence in the Gorrlock's voice. He let all three of his eyes fall on the one who had spoken, holding him in his sight a long moment before responding. "To fulfill your duty," he answered simply. "A convict has slipped the bonds of servitude and escaped deserved fate in the pits. I would have him captured and deposited at my feet that I might present him as gift to the God-King."

The Gorrlock glared up at him unflinchingly, the light from the throne room reflecting sharply off his pitch-black armor. "And what weighs in the balance to prevent me from taking such glories from your grasp and claiming them as my own? Many seek to ingratiate the God-King in such a way as to present Him with gift."

The fool probably had no idea that Luziaph could cripple him with a thought. Doing so was a considerable temptation at the moment. Instead, however, he put on his most charming smile, hoping to disarm the hostility in the other. "The truth falls from your tongue in this," he replied. "However, I would urge great consideration toward returning the convict to me, as the sum I offer for such would be double that of your normal bounty. Each."

Surprise registered on the faces of all three Gorrlocks. "You would pay twice the normal bounty to each of us?" The leader of the three asked with shock in his voice.

"I would," Luziaph stated confidently.

Skepticism tainted the shock in the Gorrlock's eyes. "Who is it you would have us hunt, that his return would inspire six times the normal sum to spring from your pockets?"

"Learning such would spoil the hunt, would it not?" he said with a smile. The Gorrlock watched him thoughtfully for several long moments, testing his patience. "I would have answer to my generous proposition. Do you accept, or not? Choose!"

The Gorrlocks exchanged surreptitious glances. "We accept," their leader said.

The smile returned to Luziaph's lips. "Good," he said. "According to my source, your target has fled . . . to Earth." He watched recognition turn to fear in the eyes of the Krathantor, delighting in their hesitant reactions to the information. "A word of caution prior to your departure," he added a moment later. "He has slipped the bonds of his Triaga, escaped the Pits of Faustuum, and opened his own warp gate off this world. He is to be considered dangerous in the extreme." Luziaph let his words sink in for only a moment before adding, "I prefer that he be returned intact, the breath of life still swelling within his breast. Employ the alternative only if choice is removed from your grasp."

They acknowledged his warning only with a nod of their heads before turning their backs to him and leaving to begin their hunt.

Slits of light broke through the blinds of Allen's bedroom window. Dancing stripes of shadow moved their way across his still-blanketed body as the sun continued to rise outside. He stirred from his sleep, doing his best to stretch his muscles back to life and kicking his blankets off in the process. For a long while he just lay there, struggling to keep his eyelids open. He continued to drift in and out, groggily, for what seemed like an eternity, his mind still trapped somewhere between sleep and awake. Visions of the dreams he'd been having returned to him, beckoning him to resume his slumber.

Inhaling a deep yawn, Allen stretched his legs. He felt a sharp pain in his left eye and winced as he attempted to thumb away the sleep. Then he remembered what had happened yesterday and a wave of irritation settled upon him. He'd nearly forgotten about the black eye and other injuries he'd suffered at the hands of Bryce and his friends. He also remembered getting to see Sarah. That, at least, had lifted his spirits. Then something else about last night returned to him: the disturbance in the woods behind his house.

Allen had almost thought Sarah was going give him matching eyes when he had told her he wanted to inspect the cause of the disturbance.

"Are you crazy!" she'd exclaimed. "That was some kind of explosion! And you want to go check it out?"

"How do you know it was an explosion?" he'd protested. "I don't see a fire or any smoke. There wasn't a loud boom. In fact there wasn't a lot of sound at all; mostly just light show and a huge gust of wind. Besides, whatever that was practically happened in my back yard! I'm definitely going to go check it out!"

Sarah hadn't seemed pleased about that at all, but by now she knew how Allen got when he locked his tunnel-vision onto something. She had turned her gaze away from him, toward the forest, a look of disquiet distorting her features. "At least wait until tomorrow and go in the daylight, okay?"

"You know," he'd teased, "if you're that worried about me, you could always come with and protect me."

She'd given him a stiff jab in the shoulder in response.

"Ouch," he'd said, feigning injury; luckily for him she'd jabbed him in the shoulder that wasn't sore. He'd rubbed the shoulder vigorously, however, to accentuate the charade. "All right! Sheesh! You just told me you have tomorrow off. You know I'm going to go check it out. Come with me? We'll go after I get home from school."

Seeming to understand there wasn't really anything she could say to talk him out of it, Sarah had finally conceded. "Okay. But I get to pick what we do when you're done playing investigator."

"Deal," he'd smiled at her.

Allen lay in his bed, steadying his breathing as he mused over the events of the previous day. It had seemed so very long since he'd seen Sarah before yesterday, and now he was going to be with her two days in a row. A heartened smile grew across his face as the fog of his dreams continued to fade from his immediate memory. He was only slightly aware that the bruises on his ribs were already beginning to itch stingingly as they throbbed synchronously with his breathing.

Allen's attention was jolted from his lazy meditation when a hard gust of wind pounded sharply against his bedroom window. He abruptly sat upright, instantly wishing he hadn't as a sharp pain in his ribs threatened to steal the air from his lungs from the sudden effort. He recoiled briefly, slamming his eyes shut tightly as he attempted to banish the needles of pain coursing through his abdomen. After a couple of moments he was able to steady his breathing again, and stood up as quickly as the lingering, stinging remnants in his sides would allow. He closed the distance between his bed and the window in a matter of a couple strides. Using the thumb and index finger of his right hand, Allen spread the blinds open to gaze at the expanse of his back yard. He kept his left hand clutched tightly to his ribs for what little comfort it offered.

As he stared out his window, Allen was more than a little disconcerted at what he saw. The wooden bench-swing, which rested underneath a large maple tree several yards away from the house, was swinging violently in the aftermath of the raucous gale which had just pounded his window. But the maple tree, as well as the trees lining the border of his back yard, only danced slightly as if the amount of wind moving past was negligible. It didn't make sense.

Before he could culminate his thoughts toward a logical solution to what he was seeing, three separate streaks of light—one right after another—shot up from the forest canopy trailing away in the same direction as those from the night before. Even in the bright morning light, the effulgent streaks disappearing into the distance stood out as if the stars themselves had torn a path through the sky. The sight left three bright streaks burning afterimages in his vision when he blinked. Allen's eyes filled with tears as he continued to blink in an effort to cleanse the numbing effect which seemed to have scorched his retinas. As he regained his senses, he continued to stare at the woods bordering his yard. Try as he might, he was still just as baffled the second time as he was the first time he'd seen it—especially considering that it was broad daylight this time and . . .

Suddenly a sharp feeling of trepidation shot through him; it was bright already. He must have overslept. Immediately, Allen let go of the blinds and turned to face the alarm clock resting atop his dresser; it read 9:23 a.m. He cursed, realizing he must've forgotten to set it.

Frantically he moved to get dressed and ready for school. His mind raced. The exercise of changing into clothes appropriate for school was far more challenging than it had been to get dressed after his shower the night before. He was a little surprised his injuries hurt more now, leaving his range of movement very stiff. By the time Allen dressed and made it downstairs, he was already very late and irritated. He was once again forced to acknowledge with brutal clarity, as he lifted his backpack over his shoulders, just how sore he was after the previous day's encounter. More than just the discomfort of wearing the backpack troubled him, however. He realized that since he'd missed the morning bus, he was going to have to ride his bicycle.

He was in such a rush as he entered the two-car garage that he tripped over the door sill, landing face first on the concrete beyond and driving the wind from his lungs. His already bruised ribs felt as if they had cracked on impact and he struggled for what seemed an eternity to regain his breath. When air finally returned to his lungs, it was almost as painful as it was blissful. He lay there for several moments, gasping in every sweet, yet painful breath and trying to gather his wits enough to stifle the urge to vomit from the intensity of the aching in his chest. As he got himself up off the ground, his head was still spinning from the tumble and, even though he still felt a sense of urgency about being late, he couldn't make himself move faster than a limp as he approached his bicycle.

It had taken more effort than he had expected and nearly all his resolve to lift the garage door open. Due to the pain still reverberating through his ribs and his lungs, Allen justified leaving the garage door open; he wasn't sure if he could get it open again once he got home from school. His breathing was still shallow and labored as he mounted his bicycle and he knew that he would have to pace his ride to the school to prevent the need to inhale too deeply and further agitate his injuries.

Sarah had just begun shampooing her hair, barely bringing it to a full lather when she heard the phone ring. She had been so lost in thought that the ringing sound hadn't immediately registered in her mind. Initially it had seemed to be coming from far away, like a nagging noise from the deepest vestiges of her sub-consciousness, echoing its way to the forefront of her thoughts. After a couple of rings, however, it shattered through here reverie, demanding her attention. She muttered a silent curse at the timing of the phone call as she quickly dunked her head under the hot, flowing water emitting from the shower-head in a scramble to rinse soapy foam from it.

The night before, when she'd returned home to the one-story, two-bedroom house she shared with her father, she'd had a million things on her mind. Each thought had rushed through her mind all at once, as if each one was frantically petitioning her consciousness to be heard above all the others. The end result might have made Sarah think she was going insane, if it hadn't been a regular occurrence. Whenever her brain went into "overdrive", as she called it, she never got much sleep. Last night had been no exception. She'd tossed and turned, literally for hours, eventually giving up the battle to suppress her racing thoughts. Completely flustered she'd gotten up, made herself a light snack and put a movie on in an attempt to hopefully distract herself enough from her thoughts to drift to sleep. She was uncertain what time it was by the time she'd finally fallen asleep, but she was certain that she hadn't gotten much rest before her racing thoughts had woken her from a restless slumber.

Sarah hated nights like that. But they came so frequently that she was more than used to them.

She had really enjoyed spending time with Allen and Carol. Ordering pizza from The Pizzeria had been a wonderful, nostalgic indulgence. Her initial reasoning for going to visit Allen had been to try to get her mind off of Tommy–now her ex-boyfriend–and at the same time get back at him by spending time with her best friend since she was twelve. Many times over the course of their relationship Tommy had directly forbidden her from seeing Allen for no other reason than petty jealousy. This was one of the many things which had ultimately inspired her to leave him.

Her heart still ached over all of the drama and bickering she'd experienced because of Tommy. She knew that she'd made the right decision in dumping him, but for some reason she still had to fight off a lump in her throat whenever she thought of him. Even as she reflected on how poorly he had treated her sometimes, a part of her still missed him. She felt like an idiot for even having thoughts like these, or for ever being attracted to someone who constantly referred to her as "woman." He hadn't been like that in the beginning, though . . . or at least she didn't remember him being like that.

Sarah had wanted the chance to vent some of these frustrations to Allen the day before, but it just somehow hadn't seemed appropriate to her to open herself up like that after he'd been beaten up in front of her. Even though Allen had given her the opportunity to do so she had shied away from it, choosing instead to bottle up her emotions in some misguided attempt to protect her best friend's feelings. She wasn't sure now, nor was she at the time, why she hadn't just told him about it. If there was one thing she truly appreciated about Allen, it was that he always made her feel better about herself. He had this presence about him that just made her believe in herself. He had a way of making her believe anything was possible. All of these things and more had kept her up later than she wanted to be and had been echoing through her mind still when the phone started to ring.

The phone rang again.

"Hold on! I'm coming!" she yelled as if it could hear her.

Having completely rinsed the shampoo from her hair, Sarah cranked the water valves off, aggressively pulled the shower curtain open and reached for the folded towel she had rested atop the back of the toilet before getting into the shower. Water was tenaciously sluicing down her feminine form, dripping all over the bathroom floor and creating a trail of small puddles as she emerged from the shower in a quickened stride toward the doorway, leading to the hallway beyond. She hurriedly wrapped the towel around herself as she rounded the corner into the hallway, redoubling her efforts to reach the phone before it stopped ringing.

As she rounded another corner to her right, entering the kitchen, she heard her father's recorded voice begin the greeting message on the answering machine, saying the standard, "We're not home right now, so leave a message and we'll call you back as soon as possible." Sarah huffed an irritated sigh at not only having her shower interrupted, but not making it in time to see who was calling on the caller identification, much less answer it. She decided that, rather than immediately return to her shower, she would wait and at least find out who had been calling and why.

The answering machine beeped and Sarah heard a familiar voice.

"Uh . . . Hey, Sarah," Allen stuttered. "I got home from school early today. Long story . . . I'll explain when you call back. I was just calling to make sure you were still coming over today . . . I, uh . . . I've got a lot to tell you."

Sarah could hear in his voice that Allen was a little agitated and out of breath. She considered for a moment as she listened to him continue to stutter whether she should answer now or just call him back after she finished her shower. After a moment, however, she began to cross the kitchen, reaching down to tighten the towel around her as she made her way toward the phone.

Sarah could feel water still on the surface of her ear as well as in her ear canal as she pressed the receiver to it. The feeling of it made her wince slightly. "Hey, Allen," she said. "Are you there?"

"Yeah. Sorry, I didn't wake you. . . did I?" he asked.

"No, you didn't wake me. I was in the shower. What's going on?"

Sarah couldn't help but notice dead silence on the other end of the line for a moment. She could almost *hear* Allen blushing.

"Oh . . . um . . ." he stuttered. "Well . . . a lot, as it turns out. You're still . . . um, coming over to hang out today . . . right?"

"Of course," she assured him.

"Do you think you could come over soon?"

"Sure. Let me finish getting ready and I'll come right over. What's up?"

"You know . . . it's a lot to get into over the phone. And I think I need to take a shower, too. Why don't I just let you go and I can fill you in when you get here?"

"That works," she replied. "I'll see you in about an hour."

Sarah stood in silent contemplation for a few moments after returning the phone to its place on the wall. She wondered what might have Allen all worked up. It wasn't even noon yet, and already he seemed on edge about something. As selfish as it sounded to her, she actually hoped whatever it was had nothing to do with the disturbance in his back yard the night before. Sarah was hoping that he had all-together forgotten about going to investigate the cause of the disturbance. She didn't feel like cavorting around the woods behind his house in search of something potentially dangerous. Just thinking about it filled her with an overwhelming sense of foreboding.

Knowing Allen like she did though, Sarah was pretty sure that he hadn't forgotten about it. Once he got something in his mind, he rarely let it go without satisfying his curiosity. Sarah could recall more than one instance in which Allen's curiosity had gotten him into trouble.

One occasion in particular had taken place in the very woods he was always intent on exploring. Once, when he was twelve and she was fourteen, they had been playing in the woods behind his house when they happened upon something which had grabbed Allen's attention. It was a warm summer day and they had traveled a bit further into the woods than they normally would have. They had been chasing each other, making a game out of following each other's path, which included climbing the same trees and jumping on the same rocks. When they stopped to catch their breath, Allen had heard an indistinct scratching noise. It was dull at first and Sarah hadn't heard it. Allen decided to follow it to its source.

When they located the source of the noise, it seemed to be coming from a small hole at the base of a maple tree. Ignoring caution, Allen stuck his face right up to the hole to get a better look. He told Sarah that he could see something moving in the hole and he was curious what it was. She had told him then that she didn't think it was a good idea to go poking around in strange holes, especially when you don't know what was down there. He reasoned to her that it was a small hole and couldn't possibly house a large or dangerous animal.

Allen broke a firm, but thin branch off the maple tree and started using it to dig some of the dirt away from the base of the tree. Being uncomfortable with his brazenness, Sarah had backed away several steps. After only a few moments of digging they heard an irritated screeching sound, and a badger came charging out of the hole. Allen had leapt to his feet so fast it took Sarah's eyes a moment to catch up. He had narrowly avoided being bitten by the badger and immediately turned in to a full sprint back toward his house. Grabbing her hand as he charged past, they ran side by side all the way back to his yard before they had stopped.

Even the memory of such a thing got Sarah's heart racing.

Only when she noticed how cold her hair felt against the back of her neck did she finally snap out of her reverie. Goose bumps crawled up her arms from a combination of the chill air in the kitchen against her still-wet skin and the nervous sensation she had about indulging Allen's curiosities regarding the disturbance in his back yard. She shuddered at what they might find and hoped that she was just overreacting.

Sarah had never been as openly ready to take risks as Allen, though. She often wondered how he could have such a keen mind, able to reason things out with wisdom that seemed to surpass his age, and still be so impulsive. She found him to be a walking contradiction at times. She mused to herself that perhaps that was part of what fascinated her about him. Allen was often able to think things through with absolute clarity and just as often seemed to take risks anyway; almost as if to spite the logic he was capable of using. Sarah couldn't recall one instance in which she remembered Allen being intimidated or afraid, though his temper did occasionally get the better of him. Whenever she was with him, that confidence seemed to immerse her and give her strength that she wasn't completely convinced she'd have were he not there with her.

As she walked back down the hallway toward the bathroom, Sarah was lost in thought. Now that she was off the phone with Allen, her mind was once again racing. She couldn't help certain realizations from dawning on her in hindsight as she contemplated how important her friendship with Allen really was to her. Admitting to herself that Allen had that affect on her—that he was able to make her feel more confident in herself—brought to mind certain aspects of her recently extinguished relationship with

Tommy. She recalled that the times she had argued with Tommy the most had been when she had stood up for herself by countering one of his opinions or demands. Each instance had taken place shortly after being around Allen, when she had been feeling strong enough due to Allen's influence on her to stand her ground with Tommy on a subject. That in turn had most likely been why he'd forbidden her from seeing him; he'd probably noticed the connection, too.

Sarah reminded herself that Tommy was no longer her problem, shook the thought of him from her mind, and turned back toward the bathroom. He had stopped her from spending time with Allen for too long. She told herself then and there that she was going to enjoy seeing her best friend, even if she had to follow him into the woods to do it.

Sarah had genuinely thought she could get ready and be at Allen's house in an hour. She had initially planned on finishing her shower, getting dressed in something simple and heading straight over there. As her mind continued to race, however, dwelling on everything from her friendship with Allen to her experience with him the night before, she had decided to spend a little bit more time preparing to spend the day with him. She recalled him agreeing to letting her pick what they were going to do once they had finished their trek into the woods and decided that she was going to make him do something away from the usual activities at his house.

Sarah found herself applying small amounts of make-up—not too much, but just enough to accentuate her features. She had never put on make-up specifically for Allen before, but it somehow just seemed appropriate to her today. She'd blown her hair dry, brushed it out, and pulled it back into a pony tail—purposely leaving her bangs free to hang against her cheeks, or be hooked back behind her ears. Sarah picked out her favorite pair of dark blue jeans that fit her perfectly and a deep red V-neck tee-shirt with sleeves so short they barely covered her shoulders. She had reasoned that particular outfit to be appropriate enough to wear into the woods and still look nice if she decided to take him some place public afterwards. In her preparations to see Allen, she had even applied a noticeable amount of perfume. All in all it had taken her nearly two hours, instead of the original one she had offered, to get completely ready.

Allen's garage door was wide open as she pulled into his driveway. She could hear the mating songs of birds echoing in the distance as she exited her car and started toward Allen's front door. The warm glow emitting from the sun felt good on the back of her neck as she stood on his front porch, waiting for him to answer her knock. The sun reflected off her windshield due to the car's slight angle in the driveway; it momentarily blinded her when she absently glanced over her shoulder at it.

She rubbed her eyes and knocked again.

When Allen finally opened the front door, as her vision was still coming back into focus, she noticed he wasn't wearing a shirt. The sight of it caught her completely off-guard. Her eyes, focusing first at his waist, drifted slowly up at his masculine form. The solid, firm tone of his muscles was something she had never really noticed before. As she stood there, gawking without realizing it, she wondered why she never had. He may not have been the biggest guy around, but he certainly was built well.

Sarah felt her face flush a little when she finally met his eyes.

As she stood there in mute embarrassment, frantically trying to think of something to say to make her feel less awkward, her gaze again drifted to Allen's toned chest and abs. It was then that she noticed the bruises he'd suffered on his ribs the day before at the hands of

Bryce and his friends. They were darker and much larger than she had thought they would be. The bruises stood out in stark contrast to the way the light gleamed off the definition of his wet torso; he looked as if he'd only just taken his shower. Suddenly she didn't feel quite so guilty at how long it had taken her to show up.

Alarm was still in her eyes as she met his gaze again. "Wow . . . those are bigger than I thought they'd be," she stuttered. "Your bruises, I mean."

She felt her face go completely crimson.

"Are you sure you shouldn't have a doctor look at you?" she added quickly, in an attempt to redeem her slip of the tongue. "I mean . . . they look painful."

"Yeah, my sides are a little tender," Allen admitted with a smirk. "But I'm sure nothing is broken. I'm just a little sore. Come on in."

Allen turned and headed back into the house and Sarah followed, closing the front door behind her as she entered. She shadowed him as he made his way through the familiar path toward the kitchen. Sarah watched as Allen grabbed a black tee-shirt, which he had apparently draped over the back of a chair at the kitchen table and started to slip both of his arms into it. She took a couple of cautionary steps toward him and found herself reaching out to lightly touch the bruises on his side. He winced slightly as her fingers made contact.

"Seriously," she said softly, "I didn't think he hit you that many times, or that hard. These bruises just look worse than I thought they would."

"Yeah, well . . ." Allen began as he slipped the shirt over his head and pulled it down his torso, "I've had an interesting morning, to say the least. That's part of what I was talking about when I said I'd fill you in when you got here. I tripped and fell, hard, when I went into the garage to get my bicycle."

"Your bicycle? You didn't ride the bus to school?"

"Like I said, I'm having one of those days where I really feel like I should've just stayed in bed," he said in an irritable tone. "I landed face-first in the garage, it knocked the wind out of me and I think that's what deepened the bruising."

Before continuing his story, Allen turned and walked over to the refrigerator. He glanced back over his shoulder at Sarah as he opened it.

"Are you thirsty?" he asked.

Sarah took a few steps toward him and hung her purse over one of the posts which made up the back of the kitchen chairs.

"No. I'm fine," she answered.

"Okay," he said as he poured himself a cup of orange juice. "Anyway, I forgot to set my alarm last night, so I overslept. I had to ride my bike to school and ended up getting called into the principal's office as soon as I got there."

"For what?" Sarah asked, unintentionally cutting him off.

"For getting my butt kicked yesterday," he answered irritably.

"I don't understand," Sarah leaned her back side against the kitchen table as Allen put the juice back into the refrigerator. "You mean you got called into the office to tell your side of the story?"

Allen turned around, taking a big swig of orange juice before he responded.

"Not exactly," he said. "I thought that's what he wanted from me at first, too. But as it turns out, I ended up basically getting expelled for it."

"What!" Sarah couldn't believe her ears. "How can they expel you for getting jumped? That makes no sense."

Allen downed the rest of the juice all at once and rinsed his cup in the sink. He set the cup down at the side of the sink and wiped his hands dry on the bottom of his tee-shirt.

"Tell me about it," the tone of frustration was evident in Allen's voice as he turned to face her. "I went through the whole story for Principal Bowden. He even told me he believed my version of the events. Afterwards he tells me that since I have a really good grade-point-average and all the credits I need to graduate, that he's decided to put me in 'exempt status.' Whatever that means.

"He basically ordered me to stay home from school for the rest of the school year because he didn't want a repeat of yesterday. He's worried about the football players you bashed being in good enough condition to play in the State Finals. He tried to sugar-coat the whole thing by telling me I should apply for some colleges and internships."

"That's total bullcrap," Sarah offered in an empathetic tone. She couldn't help but feel a small pang of guilt for bludgeoning Allen's attackers—as if it had played some part in his suspension. She reminded herself that he was outnumbered and she had done the right thing.

Allen chuckled at her remark. "Yeah, that's not even the part that upset me the most. He said he'd discussed it with my mom and that she was okay with it."

Sarah now understood why Allen had sounded so flustered when he'd called her earlier. Sure, Carol was overprotective, but the fact that she was okay with this particular course of events surprised even Sarah. She remembered a couple of instances in which Allen had received a C on an interim report and Carol had grounded Allen for it. His education was always of paramount importance in her eyes. The fact that she would approve the Principal's choice to suspend, or even expel, Allen was virtually incomprehensible. More than that, though, Carol had been a prosecutor for years. Now, she was a judge. She lived to bring justice to the eyes of the public. This disciplinary directive didn't seem just to Sarah at all. It made no sense that Carol would support it.

"I'm lost," Sarah admitted. "What was your mom thinking? Why on Earth would she agree to that?"

Allen's gaze turned serious. He fixed Sarah with that penetrating stare of his which she was certain could see into her soul. "Oh, believe me," he said, "I'm going to ask her that myself when she gets home tonight."

As intense as Allen's eyes were at that moment, Sarah found herself shrinking away from them. She wasn't really sure why, but it made her nervous when he got that look in his eyes. As Sarah glanced around, attempting to control her insecurity of being under his scrutiny, she caught a furtive glance at the swollen knuckles of his right hand. When she brought her eyes back up, she noticed he was still watching her.

"What happened to your hand?" she asked, gesturing to his swollen knuckles.

"Oh," Allen brought his hand up and looked at it as if seeing it for the first time. He began to laugh a little as he explained. "When I left Principal Bowden's office, Bryce—he's the one who was punching me while the others held me yesterday—was sitting in the office. I was so upset by what Principal Bowden had just told me that . . . I don't know. I guess I lost control. Bryce made a snide remark and I punched him in the face. The principal wasn't too happy about it, but what do I care? I'm basically expelled anyway."

Sarah's jaw dropped. She was beginning to see Allen in a completely different light. Hearing him say that he'd aggressively stood up for himself and had openly disregarded authority to do so, left her in complete awe.

He had never done anything so blatantly aggressive before, not even when defending her to Tommy. Added to that was the fact that she had noticed his toned physique for the first time only moments ago. Sarah couldn't help suddenly feeling like she was truly seeing him for the first time. The feeling was alien to her; she'd never really looked at him that way before. It was like she was noticing for the first time that the boy that had been her friend for most of their lives was more of a man than she'd ever realized.

Allen began to laugh a little harder at seeing her reaction and then winced in pain, apparently unable to endure the discomfort it brought. As if in response to her thoughts, he said, "Yeah, I didn't know I had it in me either."

Sarah, hoping to use Allen's injured condition to dissuade him from searching the woods, at least for a couple of days, took a couple of steps closer to him and lifted the side of his shirt. She stood there staring at the bruise on his right side for a moment before meeting his eyes.

"Are you sure you're up to walking all the way into the woods? We can do it some other time," she offered.

Allen let her look at the bruise a moment longer before he removed her hand and lowered his shirt. "Yes. I'm sure. Speaking of which, it happened again this morning . . . right after I woke up."

Sarah hesitated a moment. "What happened again?"

"Whatever it was we saw last night," he said, "it happened again this morning; that same concussive burst of air, followed by the streak of light. Except this morning, instead of one streak, there were three."

Sarah was speechless. She hadn't known what to say to talk him out of it before. This would surely make him more curious and determined.

As if to make her point for her, he added, "I want to go check it while the effects of whatever happened are still fresh."

Allen walked past her, sat down at the kitchen table and began putting his shoes on. She hadn't even noticed his shoes under the table.

"You can bring your baseball bat if you want," he said sarcastically while he tied the laces of one of the shoes.

"Why? Do you think I'll need to save your butt again?" she sniped back at him.

Allen sat up holding his side as he tried to stifle a short-lived burst of embarrassed laughter. "Good one," was all he could manage to say in response.

"Remember," Sarah said, "You told me I get to pick what we do once you're done playing in the woods." It wasn't a question.

"I know." Allen stood up and headed for the back door, down the hall from the kitchen. "Does that mean you're ready to go?"

"As ready as I'm going to be," she retorted. "Do you mind if I leave my purse here in your kitchen?"

Allen gave her a sardonic look. "I seriously doubt you'll need anything in it while we're in the woods. Besides, it's not like we're going to be gone that long. We'll be back before you know it."

"All right," Sarah said in a sardonic tone of her own, "then let's get this over with and go find out what's exploding in your back yard."

3

BOUNTY

TREES BLURRED PAST their vision as the three hunters stalked their prey. The rhythmic swooshing sound the trees made as they flew by was as thrilling as it was mesmerizing. One of the hunters—the leader—stayed in full view ahead of the others as he ducked under some branches and over others with practiced precision, methodical purpose guiding his every move. The second, taking up the rear, stayed roughly ten meters behind the leader and off to his left flank. The third was high above, leaping from tree top to tree top and covering the leader's right flank. All three were here for the same, solitary purpose: to find their target and bring him back, alive if possible. The alternative, however, was also acceptable.

The first thing any of them noticed when they arrived was just how acutely different the atmosphere of this planet was by comparison to their own. There was a hollowness to the very air that left them speechless, their senses taking several moments to readjust to their new environment. The gravity was far less dense than what they were accustomed to. Their bodies were able to move much more fluidly and quickly. At the same time, since they were used to far more intensive surroundings, they found themselves needing to use a level of restraint none of them were very familiar with. Fugitives rarely escaped their planet, so they didn't often hunt them outside their own domain. They all felt as if they were much stronger here in some ways, and much weaker in others. The sensation was very disorienting.

Once their uncanny senses had finally readjusted enough for them to be relatively comfortable, they began pursuit without pause. There was no way for them to know how much time they had lost chasing him through the warp gate. Time moved at a different pace on their home world than it did elsewhere, leaving it more than difficult to gauge how long the jump had taken them and how much of a head start their target had because of it. They were, however, after a brief scan of the area, able to discover in which direction he had gone.

As they followed that trail now, all three focused their concentration into heightening their senses. The one high in the trees stole a sidelong glance to his left when he heard birds over a hundred feet away squawking, scattering in the hunter's wake as they burned past at dizzying speeds. He could hear the hammering heartbeats of every frightened animal for a mile all around them, at the intrusion of their sovereignty. So far, it seemed as if their target had a bigger lead on them than they realized.

The one bringing up the rear left flank systematically cycled through every visual spectrum he'd learned in all his years of training. He zoomed his vision as close as he could, examining the bark of every maple and balsam that flew past, as well as the ground below, searching for any tale-tell mark possibly left behind by their intended target. He found none. Casting his gaze straight ahead of himself, he scanned the entire horizon, occasionally switching his sight for a thermal view of the landscape. Their newest objective was proving to be more resourceful than the usual scum they chased. But they knew going into it that he had also been well-trained. That's why these particular three had been chosen. They were the elite hunters: The Krathantor.

The hunter in the lead stretched out with another sense in search of whom they hunted. It was a sense he had trained long and hard to master. As challenging as it was to adjust to his new hunting-grounds, he found manipulating this one of his senses to be just as easily accomplished as it was anywhere else. Reaching out with his mind, he could feel every nook, cave and gopher hole in his immediate vicinity. He stretched out slowly at first, eventually expanding his reach until he could sense the worms tunneling far beneath his rapidly moving feet. He knew which trees housed small birds and termites and which were just as solid as they appeared to be. Yet he could only sense the dimmest trace of a trail this particular fugitive had left behind. Whoever he was, he was quite talented.

As gifted as their mark appeared to be, these three would not be denied. They were a finely honed unit. Less than twenty active Krathantor even existed on their home world. They were the best; the elite guard to the original God-King of their planet . . . or so legends told. If the origin stories of their group were not exaggerated, they had, in ancient times, been personal guards and generals to his Lordship. Whatever their true origins were, however, they had, over time, evolved into mercenaries and assassins-for-hire. The Krathantor were no less deadly for the beliefs and practices they now followed, though. These three in particular were especially good at what they were bred into.

Still following the remote traces left in the air by their bounty, they came to an abrupt halt as a small clearing in the woods opened to their view. The hunter who had been bounding through the trees landed to the leader's right with thunderous force. All three stood in mute contemplation, bordering on amusement, as they reached a split in the trail they'd been following. The ripples in the air which had been leading them abruptly separated, going in three different directions just as they reached the clearing.

The leader, standing between the other two, took a step forward to closer inspect the trail. He stood a little shorter than either of the others, but what he lacked in height he made up for in girth. The traditional, form-fitting black and gold armor worn by the Krathantor, as bulky as it was in some places, left little to the imagination. With his hulking size, his pointed ears, and wearing the armor which was feared on sight where they were from, he cut an imposing figure. Long, jet-black hair draped nearly to the bottom of his jaw, over the pale-blue skin of his clean-shaven face. From under a fierce brow, he focused his black eyes, with red irises, intently on the trick their target had intentionally left for them.

With an unseen prompting from their leader, the other two stepped closer to his side to assess the situation. Both had the same pale-blue skin and pointed ears, the same black and red eyes most other races of their home world referred to as malevolent-looking, and wore the same black and gold armor. The taller of the two on his right was bald, while the other had hair much longer than their leader. Both leaned in for a closer look of their own.

The mercenary to the left of the leader swept his long hair away from his face as he stood upright. He looked as if he wanted to say something.

The leader of the three reached out with his mind, reinforcing the mental connection between all of them. It was the preferred method of communication while on the hunt, in order to maintain anonymity and keep surprise on their side. Through the telepathic link he could also give commands and relay information, such as clues one of the others may have overlooked, without drawing any unwanted attention their way. To any who may have seen the three, it looked as if they were simply standing there exchanging looks with one another.

"What is it, Sepharus?" the leader asked the long-haired hunter to his left, with his mind.

"Luziaph was correct; this man is exceedingly gifted. He is certainly more capable than the usual bounty we hunt," Sepharus echoed back.

"All the more entertainment for us," said the bald hunter to the leader's right.

"I am inclined to agree with Borograth," the leader said, indicating the bald mercenary to his right, never once taking his eyes away from the broken trail in front of him. "We rarely get opportunity to test the full depths of our skills. We are Krathantor. This one man is no match for us."

"We were cautioned not to underestimate him, Pythor," Sepharus reminded the leader. "I think it an error in judgment to approach this particular mark with overconfidence."

Pythor stood, silently examining each individual path before him, as he considered his colleague's words. No matter what method, or how many different types of probes he used, he just couldn't discern which was the real path and which were false. Finally, he turned his gaze to both of his subordinates.

"Perhaps you speak truth, Sepharus," he admitted. "It seems he has gone to great lengths to separate the three of us. Never have I seen tracks covered in this manner, nor this effectively. He undoubtedly believes he stands better chance if he can part us from one another's side."

"He would be mistaken."

"But you are not. It would be foolish for us to approach this with arrogance. If his talents are as they appear, as we were cautioned they would be, then he has been on our world for quite some time. One does not acquire skills of this magnitude any other way. This means he must know of the Krathantor and just how deadly a reputation we have earned. If this man actually believes that by separating us he stands better chance, then he is either stronger than previously cautioned or a complete fool."

Pythor turned away from the others, back toward the choice before them. He examined it for a moment longer before looking over his shoulder at Sepharus, a grim smile creasing his thin lips. "But that alone is not cause enough to cast aside enjoyment," he echoed into both of the other's minds.

Pythor signaled, through his mental link and hand gestures, for Borograth, on his right, to follow the path which split off to the right. He conversely gave the same mental prompting for Sepharus to follow the path to the left, leaving the one in the middle for himself, admonishing them all to stay on their guard.

Whoever they were chasing, they would play the game his way. For now.

Staying mentally linked with Pythor, Sepharus darted left onto a path leading deeper into the woods. Using his magnificent eyesight to guide the search and his finely tuned reflexes to steer him, he cut a path through the thick flora maze in front of him at a blinding pace. The ripple-like trail he was following lead him on a vertiginous path through the forest. At some points he bounded high into the trees, at other points he cut sharply at ninety degrees one direction or the other, or plummeted back to the ground. It seemed to Sepharus that whoever was leading the chase was purposely delivering a message of how capable he was by taking such a path.

A couple of times the trail he followed cut into a pair of pathways, but Sepharus was quickly able to discover the right path and put himself back on track.

After a while Sepharus reached an area of the woods predominantly populated by large oak trees. He noticed the path again turn abruptly at ninety degrees, only this time it went straight up one of the oaks. Sepharus wasted no time hurtling branches, one after another, as he raced up the tree's massive trunk. When he got about half way up the tree, the trail suddenly came to a dead stop. It seemed as if his target had just disappeared . . . or teleported. Sepharus whispered a silent curse to himself at that possibility.

He instantly reached out through the telepathic bond with Pythor to inform his leader of the discovery.

"Be on guard, brothers," he projected into the other's thoughts. "Our target appears to possess the ability to teleport. The trail I follow ends abruptly with no clue left behind as to where it reemerges."

"Understood," echoed the reply from both.

As Sepharus stood there, surveying his surroundings, looking for any sign that the path might pick up somewhere close by, a muffled whisper of a noise caught his attention from behind. He turned around just in time to witness the tree which was flying toward him as it impacted his chest. Completely stunned by the aggressive maneuver he plummeted backward, through limbs and branches, all the way to the ground. He struck the earth with such tremendous velocity that it drove him several feet into the thick dirt below.

As he grappled to regain cognition and pull himself to the surface, his sight filled with a blinding light. A brilliant arc of liquid light, as big in circumference as the tree which had just stunned him, ripped its way through the air toward him from above in desperate search of purchase.

The last thought to cross his mind before everything went black was, "Dangerous, indeed."

The instant he felt the link to Sepharus break, Pythor slid to a halt, kicking up dust and debris as he slowed his momentum. The sudden separation from his connection to Sepharus forced him to pause, drawing his attention away from his immediate objective. He let his eyes go out of focus as he put more energy into expanding the diameter of his sixth sense in search of his brother of the armor.

Sound all around Pythor dimmed as he diverted all his effort into probing the forest around him for any sign of Sepharus. Time slowed to near a standstill while Pythor mentally shadowed the last trail on which he recollected sensing Sepharus. All he could feel was a void where his fellow hunter should be. As a matter of fact, the entire area seemed to have gone blank, as if there was something shrouding reality of its existence.

"Something is wrong," he called out to Borograth through telepathy. "I sense a disturbance in place of Sepharus. He appears as if removed from existence. I fear we may have underestimated our adversary."

"I feel it also," Borograth's voice whispered into Pythor's mind.

"Fall back to where the path split and regroup. Immediately."

"As you command."

Moments later they both reached the clearing, immediately setting down the path Sepharus had taken. Pythor took the lead on foot, Borograth close on his heels, if far above him. Removing their restraint to contain the potency of their abilities, the two Krathantor hunters ripped through the forest in front of them with wild abandon, leaving a clear path of destruction in their wake.

As they reached the first fork in the path, Pythor signaled for them to stop. As he examined the new split in the trail, Borograth pounced out of the trees to land directly beside him.

"It seems our bounty is intentionally trying to split us again," Pythor said.

"So it would seem. How would you have us proceed?"

Pythor turned to Borograth, fixing a grimly condescending look on him for a moment, as if considering how to explain something to a child. Finally, after a long pause, he spoke. "I think the solution obvious. It is clear we made a mistake in allowing him to dictate our route of pursuit. A mistake that will not be repeated; we stay together."

Just then, as if in response to Pythor's proclamation, a subtle burst of light, followed by a violent ripping sound, came from behind them. A fraction of a second passed as they turned around to face the intrusion. There, before them, was a large oak tree split in two, straight down its middle, looking as if the core itself had just been ripped away from reality. An instant later a long magnificent-looking double-pronged pike burst forth, seemingly from nowhere, heading straight for Borograth. Catching his throat between its two prongs, the pike drove Borograth back with explosive force, pinning him to another large tree by his neck.

That's when he struck. Leaping from the shadows with lightning quickness, the man they had been sent to capture drove his knee deep into Borograth's abdomen with enough power to rip the tree to which he was pinned in half on impact. Chunks of bark and wood exploded onto the thickly vegetated terrain. Splinters and chunks of wood littered the air as Borograth landed unconscious several meters away. By the time the dust settled, the man had once again disappeared into the shadows.

But not before Pythor got a good look at him.

Pythor stood acutely assessing his surroundings, intently focusing his senses on locating his prey. "Well, well, well," he said in an arrogant tone as he scanned the area. "Luziaph told us the man we chase is to be considered dangerous. He did not inform us the man we hunt is the Arena Champion, himself!

"Dangerous, indeed," Pythor laughed aloud. He crouched into a ready position, a new sense of thrill heightening the excitement for him. The Krathantor, Pythor in particular, considered themselves the finest warriors of their world and as such lived to prove their mettle.

"I fear, however, your time as Champion will be all too brief," Pythor taunted. "Next year I shall finally be of age to compete! Then everyone will know that I am the strongest! What will they all say when it is learned that I, Pythor, have defeated you now, today? What will be my reward when the God-King Himself learns that one not yet even old enough to enter the Arena Games has utterly defeated its current Champion? I will become legend!"

Pythor continued his attempted goading of the man in the shadows as he stalked through the woods in search of him. He couldn't help but notice how patient, or tolerant this man must be. None of his taunting was working. The man seemed content to stay hidden and pick his moment to strike. Realizing that this only made him more dangerous, Pythor admonished himself to stay on guard.

"Remove yourself from the cover of shadow and fight me, Champion!" Pythor mocked. "Surely the legendary Zorthos does not fear the likes of me, one nearly half his age? Do you hear me? Face me, coward!"

Getting no response from his prey and unable to narrow his target's location to a specific point, Pythor decided to search for his fallen comrade. As he cautiously made his way through the debris and greenery he couldn't help notice how eerily quiet it had gotten. Not even the local creatures of the forest were making as much as a sound. What little light broke through the small openings in the forest canopy above him, danced their way across Borograth's body in odd shapes as Pythor stepped closer to him.

Kneeling down, Pythor was relieved to discover that Borograth wasn't seriously injured; he'd just been knocked out. Pythor hoped he would find the same true of Sepharus.

As Pythor stood up, his silent brooding was answered when something large struck him from behind. The object was hurled at him hard enough to send him sprawling several meters across the ground, kicking up dirt, moss and other debris as he skidded hard into the base of another tree. It only took him a moment to throw the object off himself and leap to his feet. As he stood there, silently probing his surroundings for the next attack, Pythor stole a sidelong glance at what he'd been struck with.

It was Sepharus.

Pythor couldn't help being taken aback by the sight. He wasn't expecting to find his fellow hunter in this manner.

Almost without thinking, he knelt down to check on the condition of Sepharus. He rested his left palm on Sepharus' chest and the other on Sepharus' forehead. He was alive, but only just.

Before the rage over such a discovery could even register in him, Pythor was struck hard enough to see a bright light. He could feel several things, which he could only assume were trees, bursting apart on his back. Wind blew his hair across his face and into his eyes as he flew through the air from the force of it.

The world was still spinning when his feet finally found purchase once again underneath him. He stumbled backward a couple of steps as he struggled to gather his bearings. At the last possible instant, as Zorthos' foot was only inches away from his face, Pythor side-stepped the attack, hooking an arm around his opponent's leg and using Zorthos' own momentum against him to launch him hard into the ground behind them. Not one to waste such an opportunity, Pythor leapt atop his adversary, pummeling him with flame-charged fists. One after another, his glowing green fists rained down on Zorthos, decorating the front of his own black and gold armor with spatters of red and singeing Zorthos' beard and chest hair.

Gathering the very air around them, Zorthos cast Pythor away from him with a condensed burst of wind aimed directly at his pitch-black chest plate. Pythor landed next the unconscious form of Sepharus. Standing up to his full height as he glared at Pythor, Zorthos wiped the blood from his nose and mouth. Strings of crimson temporarily painted lines into his disheveled, dark brown beard. He brushed the leaves out of the mane of long brown hair on his head and out of what remained of the hair on his muscular chest as he took a step closer to Pythor. He was wearing only a tattered pair of pants and some plain looking boots. He may not have been wearing a suit of armor, or much of anything for that matter, but Zorthos was as intimidating a presence as Pythor had ever come across. The air was virtually crackling with his energy.

As Pythor pulled himself up to his hands and knees, Zorthos stepped up right behind him. Pythor glanced over his shoulder, momentarily meeting the other's intense gaze. His violet eyes looked as if they could pierce a hole through anyone. As subtly as he could, Pythor slipped his hand toward Sepharus, removing something from his friend's belt. If this was going to work, he may only get one chance. He had to get it just right.

Pythor waited on his hands and knees for Zorthos to begin his next attack. Watching Zorthos approach in his peripheral vision, Pythor gathered his strength for the counterattack. He could feel the gathering energy behind Zorthos' raised fist, making the hair on the back of his neck stand out. Just a moment longer . . . he had to do this just right.

The instant Zorthos' fist began its decent toward him, Pythor moved on the ball of his heel, spinning around the attack as he stood up. As he spun past Zorthos' arm, Pythor drove his knee into his adversary's sternum, immediately driving an elbow into Zorthos' spine at the base of his neck a fraction of a second later.

Without hesitation he made his move. He slammed the item he had procured from Sepharus' belt firmly to the back of Zorthos' head, letting it clamp down hard around his cranium. A smile of victory covered Pythor's face; he knew that Zorthos was feeling his ability to harness and control his masterfully honed skills drift away into a fog at the back of his mind; still there, but just out of reach. The beating Pythor gave Zorthos following the loss of his powers was horrific. By the time he was satisfied, Pythor had left Zorthos a bloody mess, with his hands bound together by manacles in front of him.

After taking a few minutes to catch his breath, Pythor immediately set to work reviving his fallen partners. The easiest to bring around was Borograth. As soon as he had revived him, before Borograth even had a chance to stand, Pythor went straight to work on Sepharus; leaving Borograth to complete the journey toward cognition on his own.

Rather than go straight to his leader's side, the first thing Borograth did once on his feet was examine their bounty, which Pythor had dispatched on his own. He glanced over for a moment at Pythor as he stood over their bloody target, long enough to notice that he had at least also found Sepharus. He knelt down and wiped some of the blood from the face of the man who had bested him.

Borograth stood up with a jolt when he recognized who it was at his feet. "Our mark this time was Zorthos!" he exclaimed. Borograth looked over at his leader with a look of newfound respect and fear crossing his features. "How is it that you were able to best the Arena Champion?"

Pythor fired an icy glare over his shoulder at his bald counterpart. "Remove it from your concern and return your thoughts to more pressing matters," he hissed. "Come help me tend to Sepharus! I fear he is not long for this world . . ."

Borograth knelt next to Sepharus and watched for a moment, observing the technique with which Pythor was rejuvenating him. After a moment he'd apparently decided, rather than interrupt the process, just to focus his energies on amplifying Pythor's efforts.

"I must know, Pythor. How did you accomplish such a thing as to defeat the Arena Champion?" Borograth asked while they worked. "I bore witness to his performance in the last Arena Games, as well as other many accomplishments outside its walls. His power is extraordinary."

"He was nothing," Pythor stated blankly. "And he is lucky we do not return him to Luziaph absent breath! I should have killed him for offenses committed against a brother of the armor!"

After a brief, if awkward, silence Borograth looked up from their work again. "Luziaph did say he preferred our target be returned still breathing, to use more excessive means only if warranted."

"Our target received less than was deserved. Be certain of that," Pythor retorted bitterly. "Besides, my true allegiance is not to Luziaph. Nor is yours."

By the time they had stabilized Sepharus enough to travel, Zorthos was conscious. Sepharus was still unconscious, but Pythor had isolated the attack Zorthos had used to incapacitate him and countered it as best he could. He didn't like admitting it to himself, but he didn't have the required level of skill to completely undo what Zorthos had done. There was little more he could do at the moment. It was just going to take a while for Sepharus to regain consciousness.

Borograth threw Sepharus over his shoulder and set out at the silent command Pythor gave him.

Pythor reached down and ripped Zorthos up off the ground. "Move," he ordered aloud.

"And so I am to be returned to Luziaph?" Zorthos asked.

"As it should be," Pythor answered. "We move toward the warp gate to Datheron. I would see you answer to Luziaph for your crimes."

4

DISCOVERY

"DID YOU HEAR THAT?" Allen asked. He held a finger to his lips to hinder a response from her, seemingly trying to focus on the background noise of the woods around them. Shafts of light danced among the oaks and pines while Allen continued to listen. Whatever noise he'd heard was apparently gone. All she could hear was the reticent opus of various bugs and a few small animals which populated the timbered maze surrounding him.

"Hear what?" Sarah replied after a moment. She hadn't heard anything and silently wondered if he was playing a game with her; they'd already been out here far longer than she would've liked.

Clearly not pleased that she hadn't heard it, but seemingly noting the irritable disposition she was exuding, Allen began moving again. When they'd first set out over an hour ago, Allen had seemed sure of which direction he would lead her. They had followed a relatively straight path toward what Allen had judged to be the epicenter of the strange phenomena from the night before, and he'd explained to her that he'd gotten a better look at the spot earlier that morning from his bedroom window. That, he'd done his best to convince her, had given her a good look at just how far away from his house it appeared to be. Of course, he'd also originally projected it taking them only a half an hour to reach their destination. So it was only natural she was feeling a little grumpy about their excursion. She didn't even want to be out here.

It was obvious to her at this point that Allen was just being stubborn, not wanting to admit defeat or that he was wrong and looking for any possible sign to prove whatever theories he'd devised its origin to be.

For the first mile or so both she and Allen had remained familiar with their surroundings. Neither had said much until they reached a stream some distance away from Allen's house. For several minutes they just stood there watching the water flow past them. It occurred to Sarah that this was the furthest either of them had dared travel from his house when they were younger. She plainly recalled neither of them being brave enough to cross it in their youth and hoped that the same caution they'd both experienced in the past would be enough to dissuade Allen from continuing his newest obsession today.

Those hopes were dashed, however, a few moments later when Allen had pointed out a tree several meters upstream which had fallen across a narrow section, creating a bridge to the other side. If they were going to find a way across though, Sarah was glad that Allen hadn't decided to wade to the opposite bank; she was pretty certain he'd considered it.

They had made a little small talk after crossing the stream, although neither one seemed to have much to say. Allen had apparently gotten the majority of his frustrations out by relaying the events of his morning to her. Sarah on the other hand was spending most of her time trying her best to not fall or step in any mud. She didn't want to have to change her clothes again before she took him out later. She wanted to say a lot, but decided that it would be more appropriate and better-timed if she waited until he wasn't quite so distracted by one of his curious obsessions to do it. At this point though, she was beginning to get the feeling that they were going to be out here much longer than she had bargained for. That was the way Allen was sometimes. He just refused to let something go until he felt satisfied.

"I really don't think we're going to find anything out here," she pleaded. "Can we, please, go back now?"

Allen stood silent for another few moments, his eyes shifting amongst the foliage in every direction. "There is something out here," he said, almost more to himself than to her, "I can feel it." After a short-lived pause, he brought his eyes to meet hers. "I'm sorry . . . We have been out here longer than I thought we'd be. But we're close now. I know we are."

Sarah gave him a skeptical look, "Because you can feel it?" she asked, sardonically. "You're acting really strange, Allen. What's going on?"

Once again his gaze shifted from her to their surroundings, "I'm not sure. But there's something big out here and we're close to it." He took a step closer to her as he seemed to be considering his next words, fixing that penetrating look of his on her—the one that made her knees go weak any time he used it. "Just give me a little longer to search? If I'm not able to find it soon, we'll head back. I promise."

"And if you do find it?" she regretted the words before they had completely left her lips.

"Hey," Allen gave her a coy smirk, "it's me. I'm not going to let anything happen to you. Besides, I just want a good look at it. Once I've seen what I came to see, we'll leave."

"Okay," Sarah conceded after a moment's hesitation as they continued their trek deeper into the woods, "but I want you to know I'm following you under protest at this point. I have a bad feeling about this."

"Dually noted," Allen replied as he turned to set out again.

As much as she hated to admit it, even to herself, just hearing Allen say that he wouldn't let anything happen to her made Sarah feel better. She realized that there was nowhere she felt safer than when she was with him, even when they were doing something as potentially dangerous as seeking out the source of an odd explosion. As they ventured deeper into the forest under the pall of a thousand branches, Sarah noticed the raucous gale of the nearby creatures was little by little diminishing to a hush. She wondered inwardly if the eerie silence was where her overwhelming sense of foreboding was originating from. She decided that she needed to find something to divert her anxieties elsewhere, lest she have a panic attack before they reached a point far enough to satisfy Allen.

There were many things about which she wanted to talk to Allen. But she still didn't want to talk about those things out in the woods, especially when his attention was so diverted by something else. It just didn't seem an appropriate setting to indulge her own curiosities. Rather than let her anxieties overwhelm her, Sarah resolved to bring up a different topic and still have some of her own curiosities sated. She recalled a short-lived discussion from the previous evening which had filled her mind with questions about Allen's past.

"So, can I ask you a question?" she asked without looking up as she stepped over tree stump which had long since grown over with moss.

Allen seemed to recognize the tone and gave her a suspicious look. "Sure," he hesitated. "Go for it."

Sarah paused a moment herself, in response to Allen's reaction. Finally she just decided to blurt it out. "Why haven't you ever told me about your dad?"

An irritated look settled into Allen's otherwise pleasant features. "Oh," he sighed. "He's just not an important part of my life, that's all."

Sarah could plainly tell by his reaction and the irritable shift in his countenance that she had touched on a sore subject. She recalled how quickly he'd gotten defensive over it the night before; as if his anger on the subject were sitting on a shelf in the corner of his mind just waiting for someone, daring them even, to give it an excuse to be loosed. She wondered if there was more to the story than what she'd been privy to.

"I don't think that's it at all," she countered. "Everyone needs to know their parents. Both of them. I'm sure, deep down, there's a part of you that really wants to get to know him, to ask him why he really left . . . to give him a chance?"

"Not really," he replied defensively, without looking at her.

"I don't buy it." Sarah knew that she was on the brink of stirring up a debate, which could ultimately lead to an argument, but she persisted anyway. One of the many things about Allen's company which she so enjoyed was how confident, even in his explanations of his own opinions, he was. Sometimes she found herself purposely stirring up debate with him because she liked how he made her think about things, how he was often able to convince her to see things from a new perspective.

"You don't buy it?" he echoed.

"No. I don't. This is something I think we have in common. We both have a parent we don't really know.

With you it's your dad; with me it's my mom. Even though my mom wasn't there to help raise me, that doesn't stem my curiosity to know who she was, to wish I'd gotten to know her. You must feel the same way about your father. Maybe you just can't admit it."

"My situation is a little different than yours," Allen explained in a tone of measured patience. "If I were in your shoes, I'd want to get to know your mother, too."

"But you don't want to get to know your own father?" Sarah countered. "That makes no sense. I don't see how our situations are different."

Allen paused for a moment, seeming to carefully consider his words. "What makes our situations different," he said with obvious care, "is that your mom didn't make the choice to leave you. She died. I'm sorry . . . you never got a choice in the matter and neither did she. I'd be willing to bet that she would've stuck around, though."

Allen turned away from her, beginning to take a new direction in their exploration. "My dad just left," he said over his shoulder. "He could've chosen to face the consequences for what he did, whatever he felt he had to run from, and still be in my life, even if the time would have been minimal or limited. He chose instead to walk away and never come back. He apparently even told my mom that he knew as he was leaving that she probably wouldn't ever see him again. Why would I even care what his reasons were? His actions have already proven his intent."

Even though she knew he meant no offense, Sarah couldn't help feeling a little stung by the blunt manner in which he worded his argument. She withdrew into herself momentarily, feeling a pang of sorrow for Allen. She realized that he couldn't possibly be this defensive over anything if it wasn't important to him, even if only in the past. She knew this must be a subject on which he'd spent countless hours analyzing and overanalyzing, trying to determine what motives could possibly justify his father's choice to leave. She wondered if he blamed himself in any way, or if that thought had even crossed his mind. She wondered, too, if he held so much anger toward his father solely because of the pain he'd caused Carol. Sarah knew just how important Allen's mother was to him. The thing that bothered her the most though, was that she hadn't ever imagined Allen harboring such hatred toward anyone. He was typically very compassionate and kind toward most anyone he met.

"But what if he had good reasons behind those actions?" Sarah swallowed the lump in her throat. "You're condemning a man you've never even met and you're not even willing to hear an explanation for the choices he's made. How noble does that make you?"

Allen let out a frustrated sigh. "What possible reasons could he give to justify walking out like that?" he retorted, his words becoming a little heated. "What words could ever make his decision okay? More than that, how could I even trust his word? That type of guy would probably just make up something and lie anyway."

Allen stopped his progress and leaned against a tree, folding his arms over his chest and looking away from her as he spoke. "What explanation could possibly be good enough to redeem him from abandoning his own family?"

"What if he really was doing it to protect you and your mom?" she offered sheepishly.

"To protect us . . ." he echoed. Allen fixed an intense stare on her for a moment before looking away again. "If he was so interested in protecting us, why didn't he spare our feelings by at least telling my mom where he was going, or what he did that made him need to leave? Why else would he be scared of the truth, unless he's just a coward?"

"Maybe he didn't have enough time to tell her," she said meekly, feeling more defensive by the moment.

"He was with her for over a decade. He had plenty of time."

Allen's comment left Sarah feeling thunderstruck. Until yesterday she hadn't even known Carol had been married, or anything about Allen's father for that matter; it was something he just never talked about. Sarah was beginning to understand why Allen was so upset. She hadn't considered the possibility that Carol's relationship with Allen's father could have been anything but brief. He was, after all, long since out of the picture by the time Sarah met Allen.

Before the conversation could begin anew, however, Allen pushed himself from the tree he'd been leaning upon and quickly strode away. She knew she'd upset him with the subject she had chosen to discuss and hoped he understood that she was only curious about his past. How could he be angry with her for that?

They walked in silence for the next quarter of an hour. Even though she knew that her words had at the very least been partially responsible for the shift in Allen's mood, Sarah hated to see him in any kind of pain. She followed behind Allen as closely as she dared. As they walked past a couple of rather large maple trees to their left, a particularly large spider's web spanning the distance between the two trees sent a sudden shudder racing down her spine. She couldn't help feeling like there were eyes stalking her from the shadows of the forest floor. She nearly jumped out of her skin when a shrill howling sound echoed from the distance to her right. Struck still by the sound, she stared into the shadows, frightened by the idea of what she mind find if she looked too close. When she finally returned her focus to the path ahead, Allen was several meters away from her and still walking. Frantically, she quickened her pace to catch him.

"Allen," she breathed when she'd finally caught up to him, "I don't want to be rude, but I really don't want to stay—"

"I'm sorry," he said, cutting her off. He stopped walking again and turned to look at her.

"Sorry for what?" She'd completely forgotten what she was just going to say to him only a moment before when their eyes met.

Even though the sun was high in the sky, it did little to illuminate Allen's features beneath the shroud of the forest as he considered her for a moment. Ravens cawed through the distant reaches of the woods behind him as he took a step closer to her.

"I shouldn't have made it seem like I was upset at you for asking questions about my father," he said in a gentle voice. "You can ask me anything you want."

"Anything I want . . ." she repeated, her thoughts drifting momentarily to something of a more personal nature.

As she stood there, staring into his eyes, Sarah felt like there were a million questions she wanted to ask him. This boy she'd known for half of her life, who had never been more than just a friend, yet had been her truest friend in times of need, seemed only more captivating to her for the fact that she knew him so well and still had so many things she wanted to know. When it came right down to it though, she only dared ask a question about his father; the others she decided could wait for another time.

"Do you really hate your father?" she asked in a meek voice.

"Honestly," he answered, "I don't know. I mean . . . I turned out just fine without him. I like who I am, despite not having a father's influence. But I do want him to hurt for the pain he caused my mom. There's just something missing from her since he left her . . . left us."

"I thought he left shortly after you were born. How could you remember what she was like before he left?"

"As long as she still believed there was a chance to find him when I was younger, she still had that certain spark of life there, hiding just below surface of her sadness. She didn't completely give up the possibility that she'd ever see him again until I was almost ten years old; a few months before I met you, as a matter of fact. I still remember the transition my mother went through when she had given up hope, yet before she had completely accepted it as the truth. The depression she went through changed her.

"She still loves me to no end. She's still my mother . . . but she's different, now. After she finally accepted that he was really gone, she became more overprotective. She barely let me out of her sight for a while, as if she didn't want to lose me because I was all she had left of him. There's just something missing from her since she accepted that he's gone . . . and that part wouldn't have left her if not for him."

"I see," Sarah answered; it was all she could think to say before turning her gaze from him.

A chill breeze came from deeper in the woods and Sarah folded her arms beneath her breasts in an attempt to suppress a cold shiver. She could feel him watching her as tears began to gather in her eyes. He took a small step toward her and pulled her into a soft embrace. The smell of him filled her nostrils and his arms felt warm around her.

"I'm sorry," he offered. "I didn't mean to upset you."

"It's okay," she replied as she rested her head against his shoulder. "I'm not upset at you for confessing your animosity toward your father. It's just . . ."

When she hesitated for a moment, Allen gently pushed her away from his shoulder and met her gaze with a concerned look of his own. "What is it?" he asked. "It's okay, you know you can tell me anything."

"Do you mean that?" she asked, staring into his eyes.

A slightly suspicious look muddled the concern in his countenance. "Of course," he assured her cautiously. "What is it?"

Sarah's eyes became noticeably wet as she hesitated another moment. She knew he could tell that there was something she wanted to say to him, but he stood patiently awaiting her response rather than attempting to pressure her into it. She lost herself in his eyes as she considered all the things she'd neglected to tell him for so long, while she tried to muster the courage to translate them from thought to reality. That was yet another thing she truly appreciated about him; his seemingly endless patience with her. As the seconds turned into minutes, she wondered where to begin and how much she should say . . . and worried about what sort of reaction he would have to the truth.

As the moments passed, standing there with his arms around Sarah, Allen's imagination began to get the better of him and he could once again feel self-doubt creeping in on him. He wasn't sure how she was able to do it, but seeing that look in her eyes all but made his defenses crumble. Even though he knew he couldn't be responsible for what she was about to say, it was eating away at him to see her eyes glazed with tears as she decided how comfortable she was with telling him. The look on her face almost seemed guilty, as if she were about to confess something that might upset him. That particular thought made him feel as if he might go insane. He could think of nothing she could tell him for which she should feel any guilt. She'd never wronged him as far as he could recall.

Finally, after what seemed an eternity, she spoke in nigh above a whisper, "There's something I've been meaning to tell you for a long time . . . something I should've said to you ages ago . . ."

Another moment of apprehension passed and Allen's heart couldn't decide if it wanted to race uncontrollably or stand still out of fear of what was about to be said.

Before she could say anything, Allen noticed a dull light cover her features, becoming much brighter with each passing second. At first he'd assumed that it was light finally breaking through the ever-shifting canopy above to illuminate her face. After a couple of moments, however, the light had grown far too bright for that to be the case and they both found themselves shielding their eyes with their arms. He could feel an eerie quality to the air he just couldn't quite place as wind began to kick up twigs and dirt from beneath them. A very distinct and disorienting pulse of energy was resonating through him, filling the pit of his stomach with the odd sensation of falling at high speeds. Sarah tried to shout something at him, but the wind was beginning to get too violent to carry much sound.

Something struck Allen hard in his side, sending him to his knees. Whatever had been riding the violent torrent of air had been driven directly into his bruised ribs, forcing the air from his lungs. Allen began to feel a slight twinge of panic and irony that there was so much air being blown around him and he suddenly found himself unable to get any inside him. As Allen struggled to regain his wits, he forced himself to look around. The light, which had been blinding only moments before, was now coming in pulsating waves, sending sympathetic waves of nausea coursing through him. As he struggled to regain his breath, he found himself trying just as hard to subdue the urge to vomit from a combination of the pain in his ribs and the unseen energy undulating through him from somewhere nearby. He could see Sarah's hair whipping violently in the air as she slowly attempted to lower herself to Allen's side on the ground.

Then, as Allen felt the energy reach its zenith, a colossal burst of wind tore past them, taking their legs out from underneath them both. They were sent sprawling several feet away from where they had been. Allen felt air rushing into his lungs at long last and struggled to regain his composure as the world around him continued to spin. Slowly, he was able to bring himself to his feet. The first thing he noticed as he stood was that the burst of wind had been violent enough to tear the fabric of his clothes. The seams of his blue jeans were torn in places and his shirt had been completely ripped away from his right shoulder.

His next immediate thought was for Sarah's welfare. He frantically scanned the area for her. After a moment he saw her several yards away from him, not moving. Without wasting time to even consider what that might mean, Allen dashed to her aid.

Allen came to an abrupt halt when he finally reached her, both relieved and shocked by what he saw. He was grateful to find that she was breathing. He could clearly see her chest heaving as it took in oxygen. But he found himself unable to take his eyes off of her as she lay there. The gust of wind had torn her clothes apart, too, as it had sent her flying. There were gashes in her blue jeans, the left leg of which had been torn all the way up to the bottom of her hip, exposing her left leg in its entirety. There were some scrapes and minor bruising beginning to appear. What caught him most off guard, however, was that the left seam of her shirt had also been torn from her waist all the way to her armpit. As she lay there unconscious, Allen couldn't help but notice her shirt had been thrown across her torso exposing her stomach and the bra over her left breast. He'd seen her in a bathing suit before, but had never seen her exposed in this manner. He felt like a deer caught in headlights.

Snapping himself out of his current state of shock, he began to feel guilty for dragging her out here with him. He hadn't thought either of them would get hurt on this little expedition of his. Quickly, he knelt down beside her and pulled her shirt back down over her torso. He couldn't stitch it back together, but at least he could let her keep her dignity.

He knelt closer, lightly patting her cheek. "Sarah," he prodded, "Are you okay? Wake up. I need you to wake up."

Her eyes began to drift open lazily, then burst open all at once. She sat up with a jolt, immediately assessing the damage to herself and her clothing. "Oh, great," she griped in a weary tone. "This was my favorite pair of jeans!"

Hearing that she was more concerned with her outfit than anything else put Allen's mind at ease and caused him to chuckle.

At hearing his laughter, Sarah gave him an accusing look. "What's so funny?"

"Nothing," he assured her, resting his hand on her shoulder. "I'm just glad you're okay."

He stood up and offered her his hand to help her up. She accepted. When they had both finished brushing themselves off, Allen fixed her with a gentle, if apologetic, stare. "I'm sorry I dragged you out here. I didn't think either of us would get hurt. We can go back now, if you want."

She fixed him with a gaze of her own, which to Allen seemed more irritated than anything. "Are you kidding me? We get our clothes torn up, our skin scraped up, and the air knocked out of us, and now you're ready to go back? You're going to turn around when we're this close?"

Allen was just as amused as he was flabbergasted by her reaction. He had expected her to thank him and just start walking back. "First of all," he explained, "I don't want anything else to happen to you. I promised that nothing would, remember? Second, I honestly don't have any clue how close we actually are and I'd really rather not risk you getting any more scraped up than you already are."

Sarah gave Allen another look he wasn't quite able to interpret and she grabbed his chin, turning his head almost completely around. His eyes followed her arm as she pointed at something behind him.

And then he saw it, too.

There, not fifty yards away from where they stood a dull glow was emanating from, what looked to be, a clearing in the woods. Allen couldn't tell exactly what the source of the light was, but he could clearly see just how close to their objective they had gotten.

"It's right there," Sarah said in an irritated, yet determined tone. "Whatever that is ruined one of my favorite outfits because you had to come have a look at it. Now, it's right there . . . within reach. It'll only take a few minutes to walk over there. Then you can have your look at it, your curiosity can be sated and we can go to the mall so you can buy me a new outfit! Got it?"

The only response Allen could manage was laughter. Yet another thing he truly appreciated about her was how she could catch him so off guard at times, without evert upsetting him too much. Rather than argue the point, Allen simply took her hand and began marching once again toward their destination.

As she said, it had only taken them a few minutes to close the distance to the clearing. As they approached it, the hair on Allen's neck stood straight up. It felt as if the air itself were alive. Nothing could have prepared him for what he saw as the source of the strange energy finally came into view.

There, standing at least eight feet tall and several feet wide in the center of the clearing was a magnificent looking arch, comprised of a material Allen didn't recognize. It almost looked as if it were made of marble in some places, and of crystal in others. The surface of the arch seemed to be ever-shifting and it didn't appear to have anything holding it upright. From the center of the arch came the dull glow they had seen from so many yards away. Now that they were this close to it, the light wasn't so much dull as it was mesmerizing. As they stood there just staring, it looked to be a giant doorway of some sort. Whatever Allen was expecting to find, this was not it.

"What in the world is that, Allen?" she said, drawing his attention.

"I have no idea," he answered.

"But you want to get a closer look, don't you?"

Allen nodded at her appraisal and she motioned for him to go ahead.

As he cautiously approached the arch keeping Sarah in tow by holding her hand, Allen kept his mind as sharp as he could. The whole thing was beginning to feel very surreal, as if it was all some amazing dream he were going to wake from at any moment. Somewhere in the back of his mind Allen wondered if it was just some elaborate trick being played on him. He might have believed that he was dreaming if not for the overwhelming feeling of déjà vu he was experiencing as he neared it—not to mention the closer he got to the arch, the more the unique energy being emitted from the opening was causing his abrasions to ache and pulsate. He wasn't sure which concept was more haunting: that he somehow felt like he recognized the strange energy coming from the doorway, which was now compelling him to move ever closer to it, or the possibility that his mind was playing tricks on him and he could wake up from a daydream at any moment.

As he got within a few feet of the arch, he let go of Sarah's hand and moved closer to it, trying his best to make sense of what he was seeing. Getting as close as he felt comfortable without actually touching it, Allen became lost in what he was witnessing. The surface of the arch looked as if it were smooth in some places and rough in others, as if the very structure of it were in a constant state of fluctuation. He followed the surface of it all the way to where it met the ground. Kneeling on the ground for a better look, Allen was startled to discover that the base of it, which at first glance had seemed to be protruding from the ground, seemed to actually be part of the ground. Allen's mind struggled to understand how that was possible, as he examined it closer. But the more details he learned about this phenomenon, the more confusing it became.

Finally, after examining at it for a good while, Allen stood up and turned to face Sarah. She had a faraway look in her eyes as he took a step toward her.

"Allen," she asked in a small voice, "What is that thing?"

Allen turned his head for another look at it as he answered her. "I don't have the foggiest idea," he admitted. "It may sound strange, but I feel like I should know what this thing is . . . I feel like something is calling to me from within it. But whatever it is, I don't think we should keep it a secret. If it did this much damage in an instant," he continued, gesturing to the torn up foliage around them and to their clothes, "who knows what could happen if we just leave this thing out here without telling somebody about it.

"Let's go," he added with a slight grin, "We'll call somebody about this thing and then I can buy you some new clothes."

"It's about time," she said with a sigh of relief.

That relief quickly died, however, as they turned to leave. They hadn't taken two steps toward the edge of the clearing when three figures, two of which were blue-skinned, emerged from the shadows carrying another on one of their shoulders.

5

PROPOSITION

THE TENSION IN THE AIR was almost palpable enough to be cut through with a blade. For several moments nobody moved. The new arrivals to the clearing, as fearsome as they looked, appeared just as shocked to find intruders as were Allen and Sarah. Time became insignificant as all present seemed undecided as to how the situation should be handled. Finally, without taking his eyes off of the massively-built men standing directly across from him, Allen took a single protective step toward Sarah. Dressed in elegant-looking black armor, accentuated with golden trim and other various ornate designs of gold, the blue-skinned men and the other—who appeared just as human as he or Sarah— watched as he moved defensively between them and Sarah.

As one of the aliens neared, Sarah clutched desperately to his arm. He knew she was feeling more than a little exposed. He certainly couldn't remember ever feeling as much fear or uncertainty as he did at that moment.

The taller of the two blue strangers shot a questioning look to his short-haired companion. There was a brief, nonverbal exchange and the bald alien gently lowered the cargo he'd been carrying over his shoulders to the ground. As he stood back up, he seemed to catch the startled look of recognition on Allen's face: of the four who were now before him, three were blue-skinned and wearing the same black armor. That one of them was unconscious did nothing to lower Allen's sense of trepidation.

As Allen brought his eyes up from the unconscious alien, he shifted his gaze among the three still standing, trying to soak in every detail. Two of them wore menacing looks upon their faces, and Allen got the distinct impression they were sizing him up. The third, while not blue-skinned, appeared to be just as dangerous as the others—although the look in his intense violet eyes seemed to be one fueled more by curious shock than malevolent intent. To Allen, the man looked more like a caged animal than anything else, and he wondered inwardly, as he assessed the device on this man's head and the shackles on his wrists, if he was the reason the one on the ground was unconscious. Based on his appearance and the manner in which he was bound, it was obvious to Allen that he was a captive of the others. Allen also noted the dried blood which was matted in his beard and chest hair and realized that, even though this man had ultimately been captured, he must have put up quite a struggle.

Allen's mind couldn't seem to make sense of anything else he was seeing. He continued to let his eyes wander pointedly in search of anything that could explain this chance meeting in the middle of the woods; anything that might help him get Sarah and himself safely away. As of yet none of the three had made a solitary move, hostile or otherwise, toward him, but Allen didn't want to wait around to find out what these men were capable of.

Deciding he needed to at least try something, Allen gently reached behind himself, removing Sarah's grasp of his arm and slid his hand into hers. He clutched it firmly in a gesture of reassurance and slowly began to walk toward the edge of the clearing to his right and away from the others. After only a couple of strides he heard a deep voice say something in a language he didn't understand. Without breaking pace he risked a glance over his shoulder and was shocked to find that only two of the three men were still standing there; the bald, blue-skinned alien was gone.

The alien which remained raised his hand toward him and Sarah in a gesture which looked to Allen like nothing more than he was about to point at them as he shouted something else. Before his arm could complete its journey, however, the bearded man in shackles grabbed the arm and began speaking frantically in another tongue to his captor. They bickered back and forth for several moments and Allen found himself unable to use the opportunity to continue his escape. He was nervously captivated by the scene. Something inside was telling him that he needed to see how this exchange ended. He almost felt as if his fate hung in the balance of its outcome and was somehow silently determined to see whether or not it augured in his favor.

Sarah on the other hand apparently didn't share his appraisal of the situation and was desperately attempting to nudge him forward. When her silent attempts failed, she began to whisper his name.

"Allen," she whispered urgently. "Allen, let's go." After only a couple of promptings, she was able to bring his attention back to the present. "Let's go," she repeated.

He replied with a single nod and began calmly walking away from the two men, if a little reluctantly. Once or twice and without breaking pace he'd risked another glance over his shoulder to make sure neither of the men had noticed them moving again. With each step he could feel the pace of his heart quickening. The nervous sweat beginning to accumulate on his palm was making his grip on Sarah's hand flimsy. Of all the things now frantically fighting their way to the top of Allen's mind, one thought stood out above all the others: his curiosity had put Sarah within harm's reach. He was silently chastising himself over his foolishness.

Determined to rectify his mistake, Allen slowly but deliberately quickened his pace. The only thing he wanted now was to get her to safety; even answers to his curiosities were taking a back seat to his new objective. When they were approximately two or three yards from the entrance back into the forest, his anxiety began to rise. He tightened his grip on Sarah's hand and began to run for the protective cover of the shadows almost directly in front of him. He could hear alarm in the voices behind him and realized they must've seen him sprinting away. This made him run all the faster.

When they reached what couldn't have been more than a couple of feet from the first tree marking the entrance to their possible salvation, a dark figure plummeted from above, landing directly in front of them. Allen hadn't anticipated their path being blocked and was unable to adjust his momentum accordingly. He and Sarah barreled directly into the missing, bald-headed alien. It felt to him as if he'd collided with a brick wall. Once again he found himself on the ground clutching his aching sides, fighting to maintain consciousness. He struggled to see past the stars which were dominating his vision.

Sarah's screams brought Allen's focus back to the present. Ignoring pain and fatigue, he forced himself to his feet. The alien with whom they had just collided was standing several feet closer to his companions, holding

Sarah by her wrist in a vice-like grip. A momentary assessment of the situation revealed that the others had abandoned their bickering to witness how this new turn of events would play out.

All eyes were on Allen.

Allen's instincts took over. Without even taking the time to consider the outcome and ignoring the burning in his sides, he sprinted toward Sarah's captor. A contemptuous grin formed across the lips of the demon with black and red eyes as Allen got within arm's length of Sarah.

The only thought to cross his mind as he finally reached his goal was that he must protect her. He didn't care how he accomplished the task; only that he did. The blue alien began to pull her away and Allen decided to use the movement to his advantage. In that moment he stepped between the two and snatched the wrist being used to restrain Sarah, digging his fingers as hard as he could into the tendons just below the man's palm. Applying all the torque he could, he twisted the blue man's wrist, loosening his grip on Sarah and shoved the man away from her with all his strength. Allen then aggressively pulled her away from the immediate threat and made sure she was behind him before turning his attention to the reactions of the other witnesses. The aggressor stumbled backward several steps and it seemed that the only one present not caught off guard by his accomplishment was himself. The look on both of the blue faces rapidly changed from shock, to insult, to anger. While the bearded man appeared to be just as stupefied as the rest, his expression didn't turn as dark as his companion's; he simply looked bewildered.

As he slowly backed away, Allen kept his eyes focused on the silent exchange in front of him. No one present seemed prepared to make any more sudden movements, so he backpedaled with caution toward Sarah and the edge of the clearing. Through the eerie calm, he heard a strange voice echoing in the back of his mind urging him to flee. He considered for a moment that it must just be his own urgent desire to be away from this confrontation voicing itself in his mind, but then it got louder. "Run!" the voice echoed in his head. Still hesitant from his last attempt at running, Allen continued to back away slowly. He desperately wanted to listen to the voice, but his injuries were throbbing through the adrenaline and he wasn't entirely convinced he could get much of a lead in his current condition.

Then, in one swift motion, the alien had Allen in his grasp. The blue behemoth wrapped his arms around Allen's torso, pinning his own arms to his side. The blue man lifted him from the ground in a bear-hug and proceeded to squeeze the air from his lungs. The audible pop of one of Allen's ribs silenced the screaming from his mouth and forced a torrent of tears to escape the confines of his clenched eyes. He couldn't breathe. His chest was burning with a pain he'd never before experienced and he could feel his face turning purple from lack of oxygen.

Allen's vision was fading to black when he felt a hand on his shoulder. He could barely make out who it was at first. Then, suddenly, his vision corrected itself and he was able to see that the bearded man had a firm grip on both his shoulder and the alien's shoulder. Had Allen not been pinned against his captor, the manacles the bearded man wore would've prevented him from grasping both of them at once. He was, nonetheless, grateful for the intervention.

The bearded man's eyes were closed and he looked to be in a state of extreme concentration. A warm, soothing sensation enveloped Allen and the aching began to leave his sides. He could see excruciating pain beginning to register in his captor's eyes. After another couple of moments, the pain became too much for the other to withstand and he released his grip around Allen. They stumbled backward as they separated and Allen noticed the aching in his ribs was drastically diminished.

He glanced past the two directly in front of him. The other blue-skinned man slowly picked himself up from off the ground. Allen guessed that the bearded man had knocked him down and wondered if he was using the distraction of Allen's presence to bolster an escape of his own. Before he had a chance to completely gather his thoughts, however, his attention was brought back to the man who had just rescued him.

The man's thick mane of brown hair swayed behind his motions as he kicked the bald alien in his aching torso, sending him sprawling on the ground several feet away and then he abruptly turned toward Allen. The look in the man's violet eyes was fierce enough to make Allen's breath catch in his throat.

"Allen, Run!" the man ordered in a heavily accented voice. Allen hesitated and the man raised his tone. "Make haste or see your life stripped away!" the man bellowed.

That was all Allen needed to hear.

He turned from the spectacle before him, sprinting at full speed and grabbing Sarah by the arm as he flew past. Whatever the man's motives were, he had afforded Allen and Sarah the opportunity to escape and Allen was not going to sqander it.

In a matter of moments he and Sarah disappeared under the shroud of the forest canopy.

After making sure the two innocents had a head start, Zorthos brought his attention back to the two conscious Krathantor before him. The presence of the two Earth children had been an unexpected turn of events, but it had given him an idea and an opportunity to put it into action. If he could somehow force his stalkers through the gateway, closing it behind them, he would be able to get enough of a head start to accomplish what he had initially set out to do in the first place. Even with the energy-suppressor attached to his head still inhibiting his skills, he was beginning to like his odds of success—after all, one of them was already unconscious, another was now injured and the gateway stood open before him. Had he not been prepared for Pythor's counterattack earlier, he would not have been able to partition a portion of his power away, which would have left him unable to access any of his abilities at the moment. He smirked to himself at just how much the Krathantor had underestimated his skill.

The technique he had used to force Borograth to release the boy, Allen, had been extremely taxing, but Zorthos judged it to be more than worth the effort. He glanced down at Borograth, who was writhing in agony only a few feet to his left.

"How do your ribs feel?" he taunted.

Borograth's response was choked off by a fit of coughing as he stared up at him contemptuously, still struggling to take in air. Zorthos silently commended himself over his accomplishment, not even trying to hide the smile it had brought to his face.

"How very altruistic of you," Pythor called in his native language from across the clearing. "I never knew you had such a soft spot for the creatures of this planet. Ultimately, however, your efforts will come to no good end. It surprises that access to skills remain, encumbered as you are. However, with the level of exertion required to overcome the Triaga I placed upon your head, energy cannot possibly remain. I shall not be so easily dispatched as my companions. I bested you once; I can do it again."

Even as he stood there gloating, Zorthos realized that Pythor was right. It had taken a great deal of effort and concentration to complete the matter-exchange he had performed on Borograth and the Earth boy. If he was going to have the chance to bring his plan to fruition, he was going to need to stall Pythor long enough to rally his strength for the grand finale.

"My disposition toward them comes not from compassion, but from their innocence," he proclaimed. "They bear no concept of our capabilities, nor have they done anything to warrant aggression toward them. I am not like you, Krathantor; I am no assassin. I value the sanctity of life. They do not deserve to have theirs stripped from them."

"And who put words toward intent to remove life from them?" Pythor countered with a laugh. "Perhaps we intended only to put fear of the God-King into them. Besides, Zorthos, you know the laws as well as I do. Travel through any gateway is monitored in earnest, to the purpose of keeping the existence of our world secret. Dealing with such a security breach is sanctioned and well within our right to pursue."

"An excuse as flimsy as your spine, Krathantor," Zorthos spat with a glare in his eyes. "In times past far bigger breaches than eye-witness accounts of two children have been given life; all of which have been afforded zero recourse and you know it. You know as well as I that no one on this planet, or any other in the cosmos, would believe a story such as the one with which we leave them. Not a trace of the gateway will remain once we pass back through to Datheron. You justify your own excess."

Pythor walked slowly toward him as they continued to goad each other. In response to his approach, Zorthos moved away from Pythor to the other side of the warp gate, kicking the fallen Borograth in the sternum once more for good measure before stepping over him. Borograth screamed in agony. They traced each other's footsteps in the path of a tight circle around the gateway, never once taking their eyes off one another. The air began to crackle, alive with energy and deadly intent as they both prepared themselves for what they knew could only end in another epic struggle of wills.

Pythor considered his adversary for a moment before responding. "I find it interesting that you, of all people, preach the importance of proper procedure to me. After all . . . it is you which is branded fugitive here, not me."

"Justify it to yourself however you will," Zorthos sniped back. "But those two do not deserve death and there is nothing to be gained in their torture. You are correct on one matter, however. I do possess knowledge of the law. The most commonly sanctioned procedure to deal with a threat of such little import is to simply remove it from memory, or render them unconscious. They would awake thinking it no more than a dream. You Krathantor are nothing more than savages! Your ancestors would hide their faces from view were they to learn what you have done to their good name."

They continued to trace each other's trail around the arch in the center of the clearing. A cool breeze swept past them, carrying with it the scent of a dying season. Twigs crunched under Zorthos' boots as he continued to inch his way toward the fallen Sepharus. He knew the unconscious warrior only a few feet to his left would be the easiest to force through the gateway, but if he played his hand too early it would make getting the other two through considerably more difficult . . . and he was still trying to tap into his reserves. The Triaga was making it more than difficult to do so.

So intently were his eyes locked onto Pythor that he nearly tripped over Sepharus' limp form. Carefully and without looking down, he stepped over the body at his feet. He hadn't fully formed his plan, but he wasn't sure if he dared to traverse the clearing another time. He had no idea how long he could keep Pythor's attention side-tracked with his subtle goading. He had to act.

Slowly but firmly Zorthos wedged his right foot under Sepharus' abdomen. With a mighty effort, he kicked his right foot up and toward the opening of the warp gate, launching Sepharus directly at the light that was the doorway to another world. A sickening thud echoed through the woods as the alien's head deflected off the left-most upright of the archway. A brilliant flash of light filled the air and then Sepharus was gone. Zorthos burst toward Borograth with incredible speed, hoping to repeat the process before Pythor realized what he'd done, or do anything to prevent it.

Just before he reached Borograth, however, when he was mere inches away, Zorthos saw the world tilt out of perspective. Only when he had to spit out dirt, did he realize that he was lying on the ground. He stared up at the dancing trees as another small gust of air made its journey through the clearing overhead. A violent wave of nausea swept through him and he was forced to roll himself over, pushing himself to his hands and knees in a desperate attempt to prevent himself from choking on the bile rising in his throat. Zorthos vomited. His vision spun. He had almost convinced himself it would work. Now, as he struggled to breathe through the convulsions which were emptying the contents of his stomach, he almost laughed at his own foolishness. Almost.

Pythor did laugh . . . was laughing.

Zorthos spat the rest out of his mouth and stood erect, if on his knees. He stared across the clearing at Pythor as he wiped his mouth clean. The smug look spread across the Krathantor's features made his blood boil. He had risked it all on his little gambit and failed. He told himself it was okay that he had failed; at least he had prevented two innocent lives from being taken. Even if he hadn't accomplished what he'd initially set out to do, it was still okay. He would have another chance. He had escaped once and could do it again. After all, he was the Arena Champion—easily one of the most powerful men on Datheron. By all accounts he was what most in the universe would consider to be a god. None of that mattered at the moment, however. Pythor had him and he knew it.

"A valiant attempt, Zorthos," Pythor taunted. "But you should have known it doomed to failure from the start. Through the Triaga I can leave you absent cognition, with little more than a thought. Control and punishment are but an instant from reality as long as it remains firmly attached to your scalp. But you knew that, did you not?"

Zorthos didn't respond. It was still taking nearly all his concentration to remain upright.

"I shall make a suggestion," Pythor continued. "Let us make sport. I am going to afford you another chance to best me."

Pythor held his right hand out toward Borograth. Borograth let out a small grunt of displeasure when the pressure on his ribs changed as he began to float into the air. Slowly, through Pythor's mental command, he levitated past Zorthos and toward the gateway. The strain in Borograth's eyes was evident as he hovered there, fighting to maintain consciousness. Pythor smiled at the look of confusion on his companion's face. Then, suddenly, Pythor cast Borograth into the light with a mental prompt.

Zorthos stood the rest of the way up, completely stunned by his opponent's actions.

"It is done," Pythor said. "Now we are all that remain. Is this not what you wanted? Did you not think yourself to have a better chance absent their presence, that you might also force me through the gateway when unencumbered by unfavorable odds? Well I stand before you now, Zorthos. Alone."

Zorthos just glared at him.

"What holds you back?" Pythor continued to taunt. "Oh . . . I see. The spinning in your head yet lingers?"

"Enough. I am of no mood for games, nor am I of a condition to take part. Let us be away from this planet quickly, lest those two Earth children have the time required to alert authorities and return. You win. I shall follow, absent further protest."

Pythor's cocky smile faded. "No. I think not. Upon return to Datheron, I shall have no option save your return to Luziaph. Your punishment will be removed from my hands. Two of my brothers lay gravely injured due to reckless aggression on your part. I would see you suffer more before I relinquish control of your fate."

"Do what you will to me, but reason and will to fight give way to fatigue. I am defeated. With my skills inhibited as they are, I stand no chance. We both know the truth of that. Extinguish rage upon my flesh if you must, but I would think enough of my blood has been seen this day. It will be you who answers to Luziaph, should you return me to him absent breath."

After considering his threat for a moment, a slight smile creased the corner of Pythor's lips. "Let us strike a bargain, Zorthos. If you can best me, even through simple act of forcing me through the gateway, I shall return to

Luziaph absent your presence and inform him presently that choice was removed from my hands in the taking of your life; that nothing yet remains of you. I shall face the consequences willingly. If, however, you refuse to put your all into it, fail to best me, or refuse the attempt, I shall remove consciousness from you and hunt the two children you seem so intent on protecting. No quarter will be given them. I shall watch Mystica flee from their crippled bodies by my own hand, prior to dragging you to judgment. Choose."

Zorthos' brows knit together in anger. He knew he didn't actually have a choice in the matter. Pythor was toying with him. Too, he knew that Pythor was not bluffing. He would hunt the Earthlings and kill them. He didn't stand a chance and yet if he did nothing the two he had just spared from death would be back within its grasp before they got a mile from the gateway. He had to do something. An idea came to him, albeit a slim one.

"Another option yet remains," Zorthos offered. He hadn't wanted to mention it, but he deemed it better than the alternative.

"Enlighten me," Pythor mocked.

"Their lives need not be forfeit. They could be made to join us."

"Take them with us?" Pythor laughed. "Why, in the name of Paragus, would I entertain such a notion?"

"You bore witness to the boy's capabilities when confronted by Borograth. He should not have been able to remove Borograth's hand from the girl, nor should he have been able to cause loss of footing . . . yet he did. You must have sensed in him what I did . . . the boy has great potential. You could earn more of Luziaph's favor if you brought him a new champion."

Pythor's glower changed to a look of genuine intrigue. "Tell me . . . why do you care what becomes of them? Were I to take your advice, it would be the second time you have prevented me from ending them; the third time you have stayed Sythika's hand on their behalf, if the attempt by Borograth is to be included. What concern is it of yours what fate has in store for them?"

"I have already given voice to my concerns," Zorthos replied evenly. "They do not deserve to have their lives stripped away for the simple crime of being in the wrong place with unfortunate timing and I think you revel in the dealing of death more than is necessary. Life is sacred to me. Try to view the situation from this vantage point: should you choose to take them with us, should you return with me and the promise of a new champion, it can only serve to increase your renown. You will be known as the one who took glory from the legendary Zorthos and the one who brought Datheron a champion to be remembered long after our passing. Fear, as well as reverence, shall be your reward.

"If, however, you force them to accompany us and they both fail to learn our ways, the result would be no different from current desires. Dead is dead. You spoke of intent to become Champion, yourself. In doing things my way you increase the odds to your purpose. One way or another, your name would be synonymous with title of Champion! You win either way and I remain able to prevent their immediate demise. Choose."

Pythor's countenance remained interested, if a little suspicious. Zorthos watched silently as his adversary considered the offer.

"I did bear witness to the boy's capabilities," Pythor said at last, "But what reason is there to include the girl? What should prevent me from simply killing her and taking the boy?"

"Do not be a fool, Pythor. You saw his desire to protect her give life to unforeseen ability. And you know
106

the law; he must be made aware of what you offer, of what it means to pass through the gateway. The choice to return among us must be of his own volition, or it could destroy him. Absent her presence I fear his refusal all too certain."

For a long moment Pythor just stood there, not saying anything. He knew he had his captor's attention. He only hoped this gambit worked better than the last.

Finally, Pythor spoke. "Both must go of their own volition, Zorthos. Convincing the boy might prove as easy as you say, but how is it you think to convince the girl?"

A slow smile spread across Zorthos' face. "I believe the solution simple . . ."

Allen's ribs felt almost completely healed. Only a slight residual echo of pain still teased him as he desperately sucked air into his lungs. His legs and lungs alike were burning with the effort of running. He had momentarily worried about hurting Sarah's arm as he'd grabbed it in the clearing, but she'd moved with him as he'd torn past her. Before they had gotten more than a few yards from . . . whatever that was back there, she'd pulled herself right up next to him. He was only briefly surprised that she was able to run as fast as him. A moment later he'd received a bit more of a shock when she had slipped her hand out of his, given him a terrified side-long look, and then taken the lead in their escape. He followed her now, ducking under flying branches and hurdling large roots protruding from the moss-covered earth. She was several long strides ahead of him. He might've even laughed at her accomplishment, or his inadequacy to keep up, were he not so concerned they were still being pursued.

The pace at which his mind was racing dwarfed the speed of his legs as he moved. He had done some foolish things in the past, even reckless, which had put her at risk before, but never anything close to matching this. He wasn't even sure exactly what they were running from, why the skin of those men was blue or what language he had briefly heard them speak, but the pain the bald one had dealt him had been more than enough warning to prove their intent and how dangerous they were. His mind was reeling, trying to make sense of what had just happened. No matter how hard he tried, or in what light he tried to view the incident, he couldn't make sense of it. The entire scenario seemed to defy logic.

Allen pushed himself harder when he noticed Sarah was pulling away from him. She was weaving between trees, disappearing then reappearing, with a fluid motion he hadn't known her to possess. It occurred to him that he shouldn't be that surprised. She was always doing something which amazed him. He watched as she altered her course slightly, disappearing behind another tree. When he didn't see her emerge on the other side, he assumed she must be as winded as he was and had finally decided to catch her breath. He was glad at the prospect of resting for a moment. His lungs were burning so fiercely he thought he might begin to hyperventilate. Allen deliberately slowed his pace as he approached the tree. His heart was hammering in his eardrums from the exertion and he couldn't seem to get enough oxygen in his lungs with each breath as he pulled himself to a stop.

For several moments he just stood there, hunched over with his hands on his knees, clenching his eyes shut as he gasped deep, frantic breaths. He felt on the verge of vomiting. Rivers of sweat flowed freely from virtually every pore of his body, some fat drops trailing down and escaping the tip of his nose. He was shaking violently from effort. In a voice broken with deep inhales of air, he said, "First . . . you beat up four guys who . . . overpower me. Now you're . . . outrunning me. You can stop . . . showing me up . . . any time you'd like."

When she didn't comment on his sarcasm he looked up, intending to tell her he was only joking. She wasn't next to him. She was nowhere to be seen.

Allen stood up. Deep concern creased his features as he clutched a knife of pain in his left side. "Sarah?" he called. There was no answer.

Panic began to overwhelm his weariness as he continued to call her name with no response. Over and over he called out to her, roaming back and forth between the trees, on rubber legs. Still, there was no answer. After several minutes he leaned up against a large oak, deciding to put all his effort into calming his spinning head so he could think more clearly. Still feeling extremely nauseated from pushing himself so far past his limits, he rested against the tree, his eyes tightly shut, gasping for air and searching for understanding.

Then he heard a noise and a glimmer of hope sparked through his mind; his first inclination being that Sarah must be closer to him than he realized.

Allen rose from the oak and fervently scanned the area. He was still weak from exertion, but he forced fatigue to the back of his mind. He could plainly hear what the noise was now. Leaves were being rustled, as if by a slight breeze or by an animal moving past a bush with little regard for staying clear of the foliage. Then, as if from nowhere, the short-haired, blue-skinned alien plummeted from the branches above Allen and was suddenly upon him. He stumbled desperately backward to avoid the alien's advances and found himself on his back.

No sooner had he hit the ground, than the large malevolent-looking aggressor stopped in his tracks. He stood at Allen's feet, staring down at him with those sinister black and red eyes of his. "So . . . you put injury to my brother and think to escape judgment?" he sneered in a deep, heavily-accented voice.

Sarah tried to scream. A large, meaty hand had grabbed her from behind and clamped her mouth shut. Futilely she struggled against it. It was no use; whoever had her was in complete control. She cried out in terror, realizing exactly who must have grabbed her as the manacles on the man's wrists came into view. But what startled her even more was how gentle the tone of his voice was as it whispered into her ear.

"Calm yourself, girl." His voice was oddly accented. "I intend you no harm, but you must heed my words. Danger seeks out your friend, Allen. Acknowledge your understanding with a nod."

She nodded and he went on: "Good. While we exchange words he is being removed from this world, through the gateway to another. Absent your help . . . absent our help, death will find him in short order. Do you wish to help him?"

Sarah nodded again.

"Good girl. I shall release my grasp on you now. A few things of dire import must be explained and you must heed my warning as if life weighs in the balance. Then we must move with all haste if we are to stay the hand of fate."

Slowly, he released his grip on her and stepped away. Fear must have shown on her features as she turned to face the rugged-looking prisoner before her. If not for the ferocity in his violet eyes and the bonds on his wrists she might have found him to be handsome, but the fear his appearance inspired far outweighed any other emotion she was feeling. She blinked sweat out of her eyes as she took another step backward, away from the man. "Allen's in trouble?" she managed to ask in a weak, breathless voice.

"I fear it so," he answered. "And time conspires against us. But if you are to aid him, the words which spill from my tongue must be treated as if spoken by God, Himself. I hail from a world very far away from your own. Truth be told, it does not even share the same galaxy. My world holds wonders beyond your wildest dreams and dangers from which there is no escape. If we do nothing, death will surely have him."

"How do I know you're telling the truth?" she asked cautiously.

"You witnessed the men in black armor, bearing a complexion which matches the color of your sky?" The man replied calmly.

"Yes."

"Have you ever seen their like on your world before today?"

"No . . ."

"Then it is settled," he said with finality. "Trouble awaits your friend absent our help. We must hurry."

She responded without hesitation, her fear quickly beginning to diminish, "What is it you need me to do?"

"It is not I who require aid; it is Allen. If you wish to save your friend, you must agree to return with me to Datheron."

"Then what're we waiting for?" She turned away from the man in the direction of the clearing, determination to help her best friend taking immediate precedence over any fear she had previously been experiencing. She surprised even herself with the quickness of her response to such a ludicrous situation.

"Take pause," he said. "There is more you must know before a proper decision can be made. The choice to travel to Datheron would likewise put you at great risk. The benefits to living upon Datheron are great in number, but once there you may never again leave its surface. You would be forsaking your life on this world to the purpose of saving a trusted friend. Aspirations toward the self on this world would be lost forever. Sacrifice of this magnitude must be born only of careful consideration. There is no guarantee success would favor us."

Sarah considered his words for a moment. "But it is a guarantee he will die if I decide to stay here?" she asked.

The bearded man's reply came without hesitation, "Yes."

"Then why are we still standing here? Let's go."

He chuckled at her audacity and then his expression turned more somber. "He is lucky to have a friend such as you. But there is still more you must understand."

She turned to him and arched an eyebrow. "Then tell me while we walk. And as long as I'm going to be traveling with you, you should at least tell me your name."

He smiled at her. "I am called Zorthos."

"I'm Sarah."

Allen stood next to Pythor, high on a branch overlooking the clearing and the warp gate to Datheron. Only minutes before, as he had been lying before him on his back, Pythor had told him that the man with the restraints on his wrists was a fugitive from justice, that he was a killer. The blue man seemed to only marginally understand English and his speech patterns were strange to Allen. It had taken a great deal of effort to understand him correctly. He explained to Allen that the man in the shackles was unbelievably powerful and far more dangerous than he appeared to be. He told Allen that the man's name was Zorthos and that he had again escaped captivity and had gone after Sarah. Allen listened as the Pythor explained that Zorthos had a sick fascination with young and attractive women and that he was going after Sarah to lure her back to Datheron where he could do with her as he pleased. He didn't need to use much of his imagination to understand what Pythor was insinuating. When he asked Pythor why the other blue man had attacked him, Pythor had apologized, telling him that he had only ordered his subordinate to apprehend him and Sarah, adding that Borograth had turned aggressive of his own accord.

Allen had continued to listen as Pythor offered him the option to return to Datheron with him and save Sarah from the clutches of a madman. It hadn't taken him even a moment to consider his answer. He immediately stood to his feet and thanked Pythor for offering to help him save his best friend.

From the moment they arrived back at the clearing he could plainly see Sarah standing next to the gruff-looking alien criminal. He watched as Zorthos led her by the hand toward the gateway. Extreme anxiety assaulted him as he stood over the scene, unable to do anything but beat himself up for being the cause of what was about to befall the woman he cherished more than even his own life. Allen wanted to shout her name, to let her know he was there, but he didn't want to risk her life further by panicking her captor.

A brilliant light ignited the air, followed by a sound resembling a hundred torrents of wind colliding in mid-stream when the two below passed under the arch. After only a couple of moments the light dissipated and they were gone. Allen's heart sank. He'd been hoping to reach her before they even reached the gateway. Now, he would have to sacrifice his life on Earth to rescue his best friend.

With a firm grip around Allen's waist, Pythor leapt nimbly to the clearing below where they had been standing in the tree. Allen felt as if he were living in a bad dream. Nothing made sense. Here he was, about to travel to another world—one in which, he had been told, Gods were born—and all he could think of was how he wished he had just listened to Sarah and ignored his stupid curiosities.

He approached the majestic looking arch, gathering as much resolve as he could. He turned his head slightly, looking over his shoulder at Pythor for reassurance. Pythor, who stood a few feet behind him, nodded his approval and told him to hurry into the light. He swallowed his fear and took another cautionary step toward the door to the world he had been told was called Datheron.

The first thing he felt as he got within arm's length of the energy being emitted from within the arms of the archway was warmth. He shuddered with delight and the hairs on his arms stood out on end as he reached toward it. He felt as if he were somehow being summoned to the other side; it was as enchanting as it was haunting. Abandoning all reservations about passing through the light, he took a long stride into the white-hot doorway before him.

And then a wave of agony took him.

Crushing pain cascaded through his skin. He felt as if his body was being torn limb from limb and being compacted at the same time. It felt like he was burning in the middle of a star and buried deep within a glacier. Every inch of him wanted nothing more than for the unrelenting torment to stop. He would have given anything to make it end. So dominating was it that he was no longer sure if his vision was filled with nothing but white from being surrounded by the light of the gateway, or if he was in so much distress that he had simply been blinded. He struggled to breathe. He wanted to scream, but he couldn't. All that was left now was the pain.

6

CAROL

CAROL'S HEAD THROBBED. She had spent the last several hours listening to details of a case she would rather forget. The things some people were capable of made her sick to her stomach. But try as she might, she couldn't force the images, or the lame excuses the defense attorney had provided, from her mind. Cases like this one forced her to remind herself that her duty was to uphold the law; not choose sides.

She stopped in front of her car, closing her eyes and rubbing her temples with her fingers before finally opening the door and getting in. She mused that the stress this job was sometimes capable of inducing was enough to trigger migraines in the most patient and tolerant of people. How she was able to endure it on a daily basis was more than she could even answer for herself. There was almost no solace in knowing that her shift was over; tomorrow it would all begin again.

The cool stream of air coming from the air-conditioner felt luxurious against her palms and face minutes after starting her car. She sat for several minutes taking in what little peace and quiet she knew she was going to have today. She knew all too well that Allen would not be happy about his "exempt status" and would demand her reasons for accepting it the instant she arrived home. Basking in a fleeting moment of true quiet, she considered how she would respond, how she could help him understand the reasons which, ultimately, had been motivated almost solely through selfishness. She knew the decision was less than ideal, but she also hadn't told him just how much it had scared her to hear Sarah tell the story, to consider the possibility of what might have been had Sarah not been there. Although she hadn't shown an outward reaction to them, to see his injuries staring her in the face had tied her stomach in knots.

She had considered it all evening and had even strongly leaned toward filing lawsuits against the parents of the other boys involved, as well as the board of education. In the end, after calling the principal directly the next morning, she had decided that his suggestion to excuse Allen from the rest of the school year couldn't do that much harm. If anything it could prevent further aggression against her only son, the light of her life. After all, he already had the necessary credits to graduate and there were only a couple of months left until the graduation ceremonies. Allen, as strong as he was, had always struggled a little with bullies, and she knew her son well enough to know that he was likely just daydreaming in his classes instead of paying attention anyway. He would survive the injustice of being excused from attendance.

Now, as she shifted her car into reverse to begin her short drive home, she realized those reasons weren't going to be good enough for Allen. He would demand the truth and he had an eerie way about getting it out of her sometimes. No, she would just have to face the issue head-on and share her insecurities with him. Somehow she was just going to have to make him understand where she was coming from.

She recognized that she was overprotective of him, especially since his father, Zachary had left her. She also knew that it was irrational to assume that a scuffle with some boys in his school would steal her son from her. Allen was so much like his father and constantly reminded her of him that she would often find it difficult to punish him. Conversely, those same traits Allen shared with Zachary would often fill her with bitterness toward her wayward ex-husband and she found it difficult at times not to take that anger out on Allen. She tried to convince herself that wasn't what she was doing this time, it wasn't some misguided attempt to be overprotective or to project pain from the past on her son; it was for his own good. If it came right down to it, like it so often did with Allen, she would just have to put her foot down as his parent and tell him this is the way it was going to be. She hated it when he left her no other option.

Her palms were sweating, and her heart raced as she turned onto her home street. Soon she would be forced into a conversation she had no desire to participate in. She really hated openly confronting her son, especially when his feelings on a subject were justified. It was somehow different to face conflict in the courtroom than it was with her child. She could handle one far easier than the other. Tonight was going to border on torture for her.

But before she'd even reached her house, she noticed Sarah's car parked in the driveway. "Great," she muttered to herself, "It looks like we'll have an audience for our showdown . . ."

She pulled her car into the driveway, bringing it to a stop opposite Sarah's. Genuine confusion assaulted her. Genuine confusion swept through her when she noticed the garage door was open and his bicycle was on its side. Normally he left it chained and he never forgot to close the garage door. Casting a dubious glance between the garage and Sarah's car, she made her way to the front door of her house. Finding the front door unlocked increased her feeling of concern. Something definitely wasn't right.

She strode all through the house, calling Allen's and Sarah's names. There was no answer from either. As she passed through the kitchen, she noticed Sarah's purse hanging over the back of one of the chairs next to the table. A solitary cup sat next to the kitchen sink, water still pooled around the base of it from being rinsed out. Her caution quickly turned to trepidation as she tried to fit the pieces of what she was seeing together in her mind. It didn't add up. If Sarah's car and purse were both still here, they couldn't have gone very far. But then, why had both the garage and front door been left unlocked and open?

There had to be an explanation, and she did her best to calm her nerves. Stepping over to the sink, she stared out the window into the back yard, letting her mind wander in search of answers. Then an idea came to her.

Racing out the back door, she entered the expanse of her back yard, calling out1 to them once again, this time as loudly as she could. As she surveyed her surroundings, crying out their names, she was distraught to find that they were not answering, nor were they anywhere to be seen. Something was definitely not right.

For a long while she stood, lost in concern. There was something eerie in the air, although she couldn't place it and she was reminded of the anguish she had experienced years ago when Zachary had left her. From her peripheral vision, something caught her attention. She turned toward the forest lining the yard and for a moment, lost her breath. Far in the distance, rising slowly above the shroud of green, a pillar of black smoke dominated a portion of the evening sky. A pall of dread enveloped her when she recalled Allen mentioning that he wanted to go exploring in the woods after school today. It was something both Allen and Sarah had enjoyed when they were younger and they had always come back safely before; although, there were occasions when they had worried her by being gone too long or coming home with scrapes and bruises. So why did this time feel so different to her, so wrong? She decided it must be the smoke emerging in the distance.

Carol made her way back inside, doing her best to not let her concern overtake her. She glanced back at the smoke coming from the woods and couldn't keep a deep feeling of trepidation from forming in the pit of her stomach. She truly hoped those two weren't the cause of the smoke, and that they had the good sense not to go anywhere near it.

She really didn't think that Allen was reckless enough to start a fire in the middle of the woods. He wasn't a trouble-maker. But he was always doing something to catch her off guard. She couldn't count the number of times she'd thought him out of his element, only to have him shun his limits. When he'd asked to play baseball, she had initially wanted to say no. But after long consideration, not to mention the look of hope in his eyes when he'd asked, she'd eventually given in. To say that she was both surprised and impressed with his performance would be an understatement. None of the other parents, or his coaches, had said it aloud, but she knew her son to be the most talented boy on the team. His second time up to bat at practice he had knocked the ball clean out of the park. In her mind's eye she could still plainly see the look of excitement on his face, the booming grin covering his features, as he ran across every base, still holding the bat in his little hand.

She hoped he was okay.

Now, as she stood in front of her stove cooking a dinner big enough to feed all three of them, a knock came at the front door. Her heart skipped a beat. For an instant she thought it must be Allen and Sarah coming back from their little expedition. A moment later she let the notion drop when she realized that, not only would Allen have had his keys with him to let himself and Sarah back in, they would've entered through the back door. They certainly wouldn't have knocked.

It felt to her as if time stopped when she opened the front door. Her heart fell into her stomach. Standing before her was a police officer, a look of regret on his face. She barely heard him when he spoke.

"Ma'am," he said, "I'm afraid I have some bad news for you. There appears to be a fire growing in the woods to the east of here, just behind your house, and I'm afraid we need to evacuate the neighborhood. I assure you that everything is being done to contain the fire, and we don't anticipate it getting much further, but I need you to stop what you're doing and evacuate your house. We suggest going to a friend's or a relative's, as long as they're not in the immediate area."

Dread filled her being before she spoke, her voice coming out in a hollow tone before she had a chance to consider her words. "My son and one of his friends are in those woods. I can't leave without them."

The police officer spoke something into the chorded walkie-talkie clipped to his collar, although Carol was in such a trance she didn't hear what he said. A moment later, another officer appeared behind the one already on her porch.

The first officer said, "We're gonna need you to come with us and answer a few questions. We'll inform the emergency teams to keep an eye out for your son and his friend. What are their names?"

"I have dinner cooking," she answered mechanically, ignoring their question. "I need to turn off the stove."

She walked back into the kitchen, followed closely by both of the officers. She turned off the burner, and thought about her only son and his friend all alone in that burning forest as she stared out the window at the pillar of smoke rising from forest in the distance. It was starting to get dark and she wouldn't be here when the two returned. Why did she feel such an overwhelming sense of déjà vu?

It was just like the day she'd lost . . . Zachary.

Suddenly, she felt a gentle touch on her shoulder and started at the contact. The officer was telling her that it was time to leave. She could only nod her head as she took one last look out her back window, toward the smoke billowing up from the woods.

7

DATHERON

PURE, UNADULTERATED ANGER was the first thing to ignite in Allen once his vision finally corrected itself. He was still in tremendous pain, but it didn't compare to the rage sweeping through him at what he saw. Spread out before him, lying flat on her back, was Sarah . . . and she was stark naked. Towering over her, holding the shredded remains of her clothing in his hands was Zorthos. Sarah's eyes were closed and by the expression on her face, he couldn't tell if she was in pain or simply unconscious. He could hardly believe it. Not only had Pythor told him the truth, but Zorthos had wasted no time beginning his lecherous ritual. Shock registered on the man's face and Allen could only assume it was because he hadn't expected to get caught.

For a moment, as the anger penetrated him to his core, Allen felt the strangest, most magnificent sensation he'd ever experienced. It felt to him as if he was waking up for the first time, feeling the heartbeat of the universe itself echoing all around and through him. He felt immensely invigorated; pain and fatigue forgotten. Then, as he took his first step toward Zorthos—wanting nothing more than to use this new burst of energy to rip the man's head clean off his shoulders—his knees buckled. He felt crushing weight all around him. It was as if he weighed ten times what he should and he didn't have the strength to even support his own weight. He fell face-first toward the ground, unable to do much to prevent his head from impacting the dirt. Stars shook his vision. Dust choked him and he felt pressure all about him, as if the very air conspired to keep him pinned to the ground. He couldn't move a muscle. The pain was terrible; it felt like he was being compressed or compacted by some invisible force.

Zorthos' boot landed gently right next to Allen's face. His voice came in a soft tone. "Relax, boy. Your eyes mistake the truth of the situation."

With the greatest of ease Zorthos rolled Allen onto his back. He tore the clothes from Allen, leaving them in a pile between him and Sarah. Shivers of trepidation ran through Allen moments later when he realized that he too was lying naked on his back in a strange new world.

Closing his eyes in what seemed to be deep concentration, Zorthos trailed both his hands down the length of Allen's body, keeping them a scant six inches above his flesh as he did so. The act made him feel dirty and nervous in ways he'd never experienced before. When Zorthos reached his feet, the pressure crushing him was diminished greatly. Allen breathed much easier and felt a huge weight had been lifted from him. Even through extreme effort he was still unable to get up, but at least the pressure had abated somewhat.

Once the apparent task of lessening his discomfort was complete, Zorthos stepped over him toward the warp gate back to Earth. There, he stood in a ready pose while he struggled to turn his head slightly in an attempt to follow

Zorthos' movements. After a moment, the light emanating from the gateway brightened and swirled, casting harsh shadows across Zorthos' back. Zorthos' muscles tensed in preparation. A deep silhouette could be seen emerging from the light. Showing little restraint, Zorthos threw a devastating front-kick toward the shadow, forcing it back from whence it came. Instantly he knelt down, slapping his hands to the ground near the base of the gateway. He felt the earth beneath him begin to shudder and the air was filled with an ominous-sounding howl. Light danced all around, touching every color of the visual spectrum. A deep rumbling replaced the howling sound and the giant arch quickly dissipated back into the ground. Moments later, he and Sarah were alone with Zorthos.

Strain was evident in Zorthos' eyes as he turned to face Allen. The man looked as if he hadn't slept in days. In a weak voice he said, "That should afford us more time, though the shift in time between worlds makes the precise amount impossible to determine."

Without another word, Zorthos made his way past Allen, picking up his and Sarah's tattered clothing as he moved. For a while Zorthos was somewhere out of his line of sight, and Allen wondered what he could be doing. A chill air passed by, casting waves of gooseflesh across his naked body. Silently replaying the events in his head, his choices which had led Sarah and him into this predicament, he cursed his curious mind. If only he hadn't been so insistent that they inspect the woods behind his house; if only he had listened to her warnings to turn back.

After an eternity, Zorthos finally came back into view. He was cradling a bundle of light-colored clothing. First he knelt to Sarah's side, shooting a watchful glance toward Allen as he did so. When his eyes met Allen's, Zorthos paused for a moment, just staring, as if something Allen was doing was either impressive or shocking in the extreme. It was difficult for him to tell, but Zorthos appeared to be even more drained then he'd been after closing the gate. He appeared to be a man nearly driven insane from fatigue. A moment later he began separating out the clothing, pulling from the bundle a pair of pants, and lifted one of Sarah's legs.

Allen tried to speak, but found his voice unwilling to cooperate. The best he could manage was a displeased grunting noise.

Zorthos looked up at him, his voice coming in an extremely cracked tone, "As previously stated, your eyes interpret the scene falsely." He looked back down at the task before him. "But I must tend to her first as she has endured the harsh climate longer than you, to the point of having consciousness stripped from her. By now it should have betrayed you as well. That it has not is . . . unusual."

He desperately wanted to say something, but his voice wouldn't come. He watched as Zorthos worked at dressing Sarah in the light-colored garb, mumbling to himself as he made progress. He paid particular attention to Zorthos' speech. He decided that if Zorthos could speak, there was no reason he shouldn't be able to. He mustered all his concentration and effort, and tried again. In tones severely broken by strain, he managed, "What . . . are . . . you doing . . . to us?"

Zorthos peered up from his task, speaking in nigh above a whisper, "Remarkable." Continuing to sporadically stare at him in astonishment, Zorthos completed the task of clothing Sarah, pulling a tunic down her torso, cinching it together at the waist, and resting her gently back on the ground. When he finished he stood, locking eyes with Allen for a long moment before gathering up the rest of the clothes and making his way toward him.

Zorthos knelt in front of him. "I am certain a great many questions plague your mind," he began. "But I fear I am only able to provide answers to a select few, as our time is short and I grow weak from strain. Firstly, know that you are now on the planet Datheron. Atmospheric conditions and gravity are . . . unique here. Gravity here is five times that to which you are accustomed. It is for this reason that I remove yours and your girlfriend's clothing; here they weigh far more than you can carry and would have crushed you in short order had I not done so."

Allen wanted to correct him—tell Zorthos that Sarah was not his girlfriend—but he was still unable to speak freely, and part of him actually enjoyed the misconception. It was nice, if only for a brief moment, to entertain the notion that she was his girlfriend.

Zorthos continued to explain things to Allen while he clothed him, "The unique atmosphere here is what makes it possible to learn and acquire a great many things beyond your imagination; this world is where Gods are created. Everyone on this planet bears capabilities which far surpass anything ever achieved on yours. There stand some which have only a few minor skills, by our standards. Yet it would take only one properly trained individual from this world to decimate yours; a task which could be seen to completion in a matter of days. Needless to say, that makes this world very dangerous for the both of you."

Zorthos pulled the tunic over his shoulders, down his torso, and fashioned a crude looking belt around his waist to hold the strange ensemble together. Instantly Allen felt the rest of the residual pressure leave his body. Relief washed through him and his entire body began to tingle. He could feel the flow of his blood returning to its normal pace, punctuated by invisible needle points dancing their way across him, leaving gooseflesh in their wake. The feeling was as unsettling as it was comforting. Slowly the awkward tingling dissipated and he could feel all of his faculties returning in earnest.

Able to finally control his limbs once more, he sat up. "If you weren't doing to her what I thought you were doing . . . why then were we brought here? I only came to rescue Sarah."

Zorthos stared at him hard for a long moment before responding, "Apologies, Allen. We offered false pretense to deceive you into passing through the warp gate . . . It was I who made the suggestion. Pythor stands an intergalactic bounty hunter, member of an elite brotherhood called the Krathantor." Zorthos paused for a moment before continuing. "You must understand . . . the existence of this world is considered to be the greatest secret of the known universe. To those who hold knowledge of Datheron, it is considered a sacred right. Sometimes extreme measures are required in order to keep that secret. Pride does not accompany my part in your deception."

"You mean he was going to kill us?" he said flatly, doing his best not to betray just how angry he was feeling at the realization.

"Yes," Zorthos replied without breaking his gaze from Allen's eyes. "He intended to kill you."

Allen lowered his head, closing his eyes, as he considered Zorthos' story. He had never felt so betrayed, and so helpless in all his life. Finally he looked back up at Zorthos, "Is it true then, that we can never leave this place?" He was as terrified of asking the question as he was of its answer.

"I fear it so, Allen. No deception lived within that piece of the charade."

Allen felt as if all reality were slipping quickly from his grasp. The pit of despair into which he was falling was enough to swallow him whole, leaving nothing but the shell of who he once was in its place. He couldn't believe this was happening. His life as he had known it was effectively over. He would never go to college; never pursue his dreams of being a published author or a comic book artist. All his favorite activities were now lost to him. Worst of all, he realized he would never again see his mother. And she would never know what happened to him. This, he knew, would crush her irrevocably.

His vision spun. He felt on the verge of vomiting. It was over. It was all over. And all because he couldn't let his curiosities go. He desperately, frantically, searched for reason. He wanted this all to be a bad dream, one from which he would soon wake. This couldn't be happening. It just couldn't. Everything inside him was spinning all at once, each emotion assaulting him in succession like a whirlwind from within. He desperately wanted to cry, realizing moments later that tears were already flowing freely down his cheeks.

Then he thought of Sarah.

He realized that her life, her dreams and aspirations, were now lost as well. And it was entirely his fault. She would hate him. That thought, more than all the others combined, made Allen wail in agony. He resolved at that moment to find a way to undo his mistake, even if he could send only Sarah back to Earth. He would gladly endure a life of solitude on this world if only he could give her life back to her. That's what he would do. Reaching down as deep as he could, he gathered the necessary strength to rein in his emotions; he would need to stay focused if he was to get Sarah home.

Allen wiped the trails of hot liquid from his face and stood up. He glanced down at Sarah, realizing this mistake would prevent her from ever returning his love. But he didn't care. Her life was all that mattered to him now. He would find a way to get her home.

Keeping his new goal in mind, he turned his attention to Zorthos. The man stood stoically several feet away, seeming content to give him the time he needed to come to terms with the enormity of that which he now faced. He stared hard at Zorthos; if he was going to be of any aid to Sarah he would need answers, and he was certain that this man had them.

As he considered which question he should ask first, a thought dawned on him: this man knew his name . . . had known it on Earth when he told him to run from the clearing. Allen's features contorted accusatorily, "How do you know my name?"

Zorthos' response came without hesitation, "As previously stated, it is possible to learn anything upon Datheron . . . I stand a competent telepath, among other things."

"You mean you can read my mind? Hear my thoughts?" he asked with incredulity.

"Yes."

Allen wasn't quite ready to believe him. "What am I thinking right now?"

"I fear myself incapable of providing answer to that question at the moment, Allen. The device on my head suppresses abilities, and any remaining pool of energy has all but faded."

"Then how did you read my thoughts while on Earth?"

Zorthos let out a long, but patient, sigh. "For those with great power, possibilities to bypass defenses of the Triaga exist. But even the most powerful have limitations, and I fear I have traveled well beyond mine in the closing of the gate to Earth and the generating of garments which you and your girlfriend now wear."

Allen decided to correct him this time. "She's not my girlfriend."

"Then she is an exceptional friend," Zorthos replied with no hesitation. "Her purpose in traveling here was solely to the advantage of your welfare, to save you from Pythor. How else could I have deceived her into parting with everything she knew?"

He was taken aback. She had come to Datheron to rescue him. The thought should've made him feel better about their situation . . . but it didn't. If anything, it made him feel worse. She had been tricked in the same manner he had. She had been duped into giving up everything she would ever have at the risk of trying to save him. Because of him she was stuck here without ever having the opportunity to have a life of her own . . . a family of her own.

It was taking a lot more effort for him to keep his anger in check. "Then you're going to help me get her home. I don't care what you do to me, but she deserves to live her life the way she wants to. You had no right to bring us here!"

Zorthos replied in a heated tone, "Firstly boy, your life was only spared through my intervention. You should take solace in that much of it. Secondly, the way home is gone forever. You would do well to remove the task from your thoughts and set your eyes to the path ahead. Your previous life is gone; accept it."

Allen cooled his temper a little before speaking again. "If it isn't possible to get back to Earth, then how did you get there? For that matter, how did the Krathantor get there? I just watched you close the warp gate; that tells me it is possible."

Zorthos seemed almost amused as he spoke. "You are an observant boy. But you understand nothing of the requirements to open or shut the gateway to another world, not to mention the laws I have violated in the undertaking. Why is it you think the Krathantor hunt me?"

Following the remark Allen glanced down, noticing for the first time that the shackles around Zorthos' wrists were gone. He looked back into the eyes of his would-be savior. "So you're a criminal . . . That should mean you don't have any qualms about breaking the law. You obviously didn't have any when you went to Earth in the first place . . . I don't care what it takes. You will help me get her home." In Allen's mind it wasn't a question.

Zorthos' response was cut short by the sound of Sarah moaning in discomfort. Instantly he was at her side.

"Allen?" she said in a weak voice, looking up at him. When he nodded, she sat up throwing her arms around his neck. "Thank heaven you're okay."

He just held her for a long moment, staring contemptuously up at Zorthos.

After a brief reunion, Zorthos removed himself from them, speaking as he moved. "Now that consciousness has found you both again, we should not linger. More time than can be afforded has already been lost. Pythor will succeed in the making of a new warp gate presently. Fortune will not favor us if we linger until his return."

He helped Sarah to her feet and they quickly found themselves in tow behind Zorthos. Before they were completely out of the clearing in which they'd arrived, Allen glanced over his shoulder and noted that two of the other Krathantor were on the ground at the edge on the other side; though whether unconscious or dead he couldn't tell. As they moved, Allen noticed for the first time how very similar the forests of this planet were to his own. There were many types of trees he recognized. There were also, however, many he did not. After a short distance he noticed a series of trees which were oddly linked together by their branches. They reminded him of the root system of the Aspen trees on Earth, except that they seemed to be interwoven above the ground instead. As he continued to examine his new surroundings, scanning what he saw in all directions, he began to feel eyes on him. He wondered how many of the "dangerous" things on this planet Zorthos had mentioned were in this forest. Almost instinctively, he cast a furtive glance at Sarah. Now that he knew for sure that she was okay, he didn't dare let her out of his sight again.

As they continued to move, Allen brooded on the predicament he and Sarah now faced, and how much of it he wanted to tell her. He desperately wanted to get some real answers from Zorthos, but he was afraid some of them might reveal to Sarah just how foolish he'd been, causing her to hate him instantly. He knew that it was only a matter of time until she found out, but he wasn't quite ready to see the look of pure disgust in her eyes he knew would come once she learned the truth. So for quite a while they walked in silence.

After what must have been at least an hour by his estimation, Sarah did something which surprised him. She reached out and took hold of his hand as they continued to follow Zorthos. He gave her a quick, reassuring smile and continued forward.

It wasn't much longer before Sarah finally broke the silence. "So where exactly are we going, anyway?" she asked.

Zorthos answered without turning his head, or breaking stride, "We move toward the purpose of removing this infernal contraption from my head."

"What is it?" she asked.

"It is called a Triaga," Zorthos told her. "It was designed to suppress the abilities of those who are considered to be dangerous on this world."

"You mean you actually do have special abilities?" Sarah prodded. "You weren't just making that part up?"

Allen was confused by her question for a moment, ultimately assuming Zorthos must have already told her a little bit about himself and this world as part of the story he had used to coax her into coming here with him.

Zorthos glanced over his shoulder at her, but still didn't slow his pace. "No, such details were not exaggerated. As I was telling your boyfriend, prior to your regaining consciousness, everyone on this world bears at least one or two minor abilities. Such is the way life works upon Datheron."

"So then, the people of this planet are born with powers?" Sarah asked; to Allen it sounded more like a guess than a question.

Zorthos stopped and turned around. "No. Abilities are not simply granted at birth. A unique atmosphere, or aura if you will, envelops the whole of this world. It is this special aura which provides the possibility of learning any ability or skill desired. It unlocks the dormant parts of the brain, releasing one's inner potential and offers access to the life energy of the universe. Ours is the only planet in the universe to bear such an energy signature, and therefore the only planet in the universe on which gods can be created. But do not think the learning of an ability to be easy. Nothing could be further from the truth. Anything in life which holds true value will always bring struggle, and will certainly be difficult in the obtaining; even here upon Datheron."

Allen still refused to take part in the conversation, for fear of triggering the wrong response from Zorthos. But he was paying close attention, and was glad for Sarah's inquisition.

"What abilities do you have, then? And how long does it take to learn them?" Sarah asked.

Zorthos began walking again and Allen wondered how he could maintain such a pace if he was as exhausted as he claimed, and appeared to be.

Zorthos spoke over his shoulder as he moved, "For all who make the attempt, the learning of a skill takes a very long time. I am considered master of many and am proficient in many more. I stand among the most powerful on this world."

"If you're so powerful," Sarah asked, "why can't you just take off the Triaga now?"

"Firstly, none can remove their own Triaga," he replied, almost derisively. "And I fear I have beyond exhausted all remaining energy in the protection of you and Allen. It was one of my mastered skills which forged the clothing you now wear, and the energy required to complete the task was siphoned from my own life force."

Sarah glanced down at the ensemble she was wearing for the first time. A look registered on her face which bordered between disgust and fascination, followed by one of complete shock. "What happened to my other clothes?" she asked in an alarmed tone.

"Technically you still wear them . . . or rather what remains of them," Zorthos explained. "As I was explaining to your boyfriend—"

"Why do you keep calling him my boyfriend?" she interrupted.

"Is he not your friend?" Zorthos challenged.

Sarah appeared confused, "Of course he is . . ."

"Is he not a boy?"

"Well, yeah . . ." Sarah answered, if hesitantly.

"Then I fail to see the harm in addressing him as such," Zorthos stated, giving him a meaningful look as he did so. "Now, as I was saying, limits do exist regarding our capabilities. Not all who reside here can be referred to as godly. Only those who wield supreme talent, those expertly trained, can negate the effects of the Triaga. Those who can are exceedingly rare, and a tremendous toll is required for all who can even claim such skill. Now that I

135

am absent my reserves, I am unable to call upon any of my skills until this skriffing thing is removed from my head. My ability to regenerate the energy required is inhibited while I still wear it. And absent the aid of someone else in its removal, I fear I shall ever be burdened by the absence of that which has already been spent."

"Oh," was all Sarah said.

Zorthos, apparently pleased that his point had been made and understood, turned his eyes forward and picked up his speed.

Sarah gave him a tentative gaze, followed by a weak smile, and suddenly withdrew her hand, using it to comb her hair behind her ears. After a second glance, he noticed her face turning slightly crimson just before she started after Zorthos.

A short while later the sun began to recede behind the horizon, filling the air with a slight chill. Again, he felt eyes on him from somewhere within the shroud of the forest. An overwhelming sense of foreboding came as a violent shudder ran down his spine. Something was following them; he wasn't sure how he knew this, but he was certain of it. He was apprehensive about how she was going to react, but he took Sarah's hand in his anyway. Glancing over at her, he was pleased to see that the contact had brought a smile to her face. She gave his hand an affectionate squeeze.

They quickened their pace when they noticed Zorthos was beginning to move a little faster still.

"It is imperative we reach the edge of the forest before nightfall," Zorthos said, as if he anticipated their unspoken question.

"Why?" Sarah asked. "What happens after nightfall?"

"With my powers depleted as they are, we will most likely die," he stated bluntly.

"What?" she and Allen said in unison.

Instead of acknowledging their shock, Zorthos picked up his pace, yet again. All he said as he began to increase the distance between them was, "Hurry!"

They were now moving at a steady jogging pace. For a second time, Allen noted just how quickly Zorthos was able to move considering his exhaustion. It was beginning to get darker and, although he was still hesitant about asking Zorthos something which could end up being incriminating, his curiosities were getting the better of him again. He decided this situation warranted indulging his curiosities, considering his life could hang in the balance.

"What happens if we don't reach the edge of the forest?" he asked. "What's in these woods that can kill us?"

"The list of things that cannot kill us would require much less time in the telling," Zorthos replied over his shoulder.

He and Sarah exchanged worried glances as they continued their attempt to keep pace with Zorthos. Somehow the distinction Zorthos made didn't make him feel any better about their current situation.

Deciding Zorthos was being secretive with his response, he tried a different approach. "So then, how is the edge of the forest going to protect us?" he asked. "If there are things here that can kill us, why won't they be able to hunt us past the forest's perimeter?"

"Along the eastern edge of the forest lays a river of considerable width. The creatures we flee will not dare traverse it; they fear water," Zorthos explained. "They also fear fire, and along the opposite bank lay a series of large torches; a preventative measure to the purpose of staying their desire to continue chase beyond the boundaries of forest and river."

This reassured him, if only a little.

"In that case," he probed, "how much further is the edge of the forest?"

"To be honest," Zorthos answered, "such an answer is difficult to gauge absent my abilities. I do not think it to be much further, though I do believe us to be cutting fine hair in the attempt."

A strange, ominous rumbling sound emanated from the shadows causing Zorthos enough alarm to slow his pace. As he turned to them, a look of genuine fear registered in those violet eyes of his. "RUN!" he bellowed suddenly.

Allen's heart felt as if it had sunk to the pit of his intestines and leapt into his throat all at once upon hearing that solitary word. He tightened his grip on Sarah's hand and took off after Zorthos with a speed unknown to him. Weaving in between the massive trunks of trees all around, he pushed himself harder even than when he'd been escaping the Krathantor on Earth. There was no way he was going to let anything happen to Sarah. Not this time.

Moving at a rate which seemed impossible, he caught up with Zorthos in short order. They were all now sprinting as fast as they could. After a short distance, he noticed the tension building between him and Sarah through his grip on her hand; she was falling behind. He slowed just a little, glancing over his shoulder at her. She appeared to be pushing herself as hard as she could, and she was still gradually pulling further away. He found this most curious considering how easily she had broken ahead of him in the forest on Earth. He did his best to urge her forward, but she was becoming extremely winded. For whatever reason, she seemed unable to run any longer and was dragging him to a stop through his grip on her.

Panic rose within him, but he refused to leave her behind. Not knowing what else to do, he cried out to Zorthos for assistance. Zorthos, who had gained a significant lead on the two of them, pulled himself to a stop. Turning completely around, he began running back toward them.

Zorthos had only taken a few long strides in their direction when a massive blur burst from a low branch of a nearby tree, tackling him in the process. Sarah screamed as they hit the ground in a tumbling mess of limbs. Before the creature—whatever it was—could gain control of the struggle by pinning Zorthos to the ground, he used the momentum of the collision to hurl it over his head with his legs, sending it crashing violently into a bush.

Before the creature had much time to respond to the counter which had sent it flying, Zorthos sprang to his feet and leapt toward one of the lower branches of a nearby tree. He latched onto a vine and ripped it from the bark, landing gracefully next to the base of the tree. In what seemed to him to be one fluid motion, Zorthos had fashioned a crude slip-knot into the vine, forming a lasso, and turned his attention back to his attacker just in time to side-step another attempt on his life. The creature landed a few feet away from Zorthos, rebounding quickly and crouching into a ready position. It was now in full view, and Allen found himself almost more amazed than he was terrified by what he was seeing. The creature moved on all fours and was barrel-chested, resembling a large amalgamation of a gorilla and a hound. Its front paws were enormous—much larger than the rear—and bore six long, curved, razor-sharp talons. The ears were elongated and pointed, ever shifting as if constantly surveying its surroundings, and a trail of spikes followed a straight line from its scalp to the tip of its long, whip-like tail. But what grabbed his attention the most, before it turned to face Zorthos, were its intense eyes, which glowed a solid, bright red.

The beast pounced toward Zorthos again, but he was ready. As he dodged the attack, Zorthos looped the lasso around its neck and jerked it tight. The creature yelped and crashed awkwardly into the ground at Zorthos' feet. He kicked it viciously in the ribs several times before launching the other end of the vine over a high branch in the same tree from which he'd retrieved it. As the beast struggled to pull itself to its feet once more, Zorthos pulled rapidly on the vine until the creature was swinging from its throat several feet off the ground. Zorthos promptly knelt down and tied the opposite end of the vine to a root protruding from the earth at his feet.

Allen stared in wonder as the creature swung helplessly, lashing and flailing its limbs in violent, desperate attempts to free itself.

Zorthos immediately turned to the bewildered duo. "We need to be away from here quickly!" he barked. "How feel you, Allen?"

It took him a moment to divert his eyes from beast dangling in front of him before he could respond. "Uh . . ." he stuttered. "Um . . . I'm fine. Why?"

"Then remove Sarah's feet from the ground and keep pace! Quickly!"

Without another word, Zorthos turned and was away. A moment later, he had Sarah in his arms and was dashing after Zorthos.

As he pulled up next to Zorthos, he chanced a sidelong glance at him. "What in the world *was* that thing?" he asked in fascination.

"They are called skriff hounds. They are as fearsome as any hunter on Datheron and always hunt in packs. The one I dispatched was scout to the rest; the others will not be far behind. We should be safe upon reaching the river. They almost never risk submersion in water."

"Almost never?" he asked, bracingly.

"Swimming is a skill they lack," Zorthos said almost casually. "Though their adherence to caution would depend greatly upon level of hunger, and desire to feed younglings."

They had only been running a few minutes when he could hear a deep, throaty howling coming from somewhere behind them. He didn't need Zorthos to tell him that the rest of the pack had found the scout and were now on their trail.

Moments later Zorthos pointed straight ahead, almost excitedly. "Look!" he said. "The river is within reach!"

He glanced down at Sarah, who had her arms wrapped tightly around his neck and was looking to where Zorthos had pointed. He brought his eyes up to see that they were in fact nearing the edge of the woods. His heart swelled with excitement. They were going to make it.

As they passed through the last lines of the forest, he risked a look over his shoulder, instantly wishing that he hadn't. Through the darkness he could easily see several pairs of glowing red lights rapidly approaching.

Allen looked down at Sarah anxiously. "You're going to have to swim." She nodded her understanding and he set her down as carefully as he could without breaking stride.

They were only a few yards from the river now, and Allen could see just how large it truly was. Zorthos had said it was a wide river, but Allen hadn't expected it to be as wide as this. By his estimation it had to be at least two hundred fifty yards across, and the water was such a dark blue-green in the center that he wasn't sure just how deep it might be. On the opposite shore he could see the large torches Zorthos mentioned standing protectively a short distance from the water-line. As he took them in, he didn't think Zorthos had adequately described them. They were enormous and reminded him more of the torch lit at the beginning of the Olympic Games than anything else. He had somehow pictured something different. The base of each looked to be easily as wide as the trunk of a large tree and extended into a bowl shape which housed the flames. Fire was replacing the fading light of day with a firm red-orange glow, casting noticeable reflections off the surface of the water.

Allen had been staring so intently at the torches that he hadn't noticed they'd reached the water-line. Zorthos wasted no time diving straight in. Sarah was only a brief moment behind him and he was up to his waist in the water when he finally allowed himself another glance over his shoulder. The skriff hounds were skidding to a stop a mere ten feet away at the edge of the water pacing back and forth as he continued into the river. He could see their muscles quivering and their mouths salivating furiously.

Allen turned his attention back to the task of getting across the river. As he swam, he kept a watchful eye on Sarah's progress; he wanted to make sure she wasn't struggling from too much effort like she had been from the running only minutes before. It relieved him to see that she seemed to be doing fine.

A large splash came from behind them, followed by another, and his curiosities got the best of him again. He stopped swimming long enough to see what had caused it. Panic erupted inside of him. Two of the skriff hounds had leaped into the water and were attempting to swim after them. Zorthos was right about them not being excellent swimmers, but the fact that they entered the water at all worried Allen in the extreme.

Zorthos yelled, castigating him for slowing. He focused again and several laborious minutes later they were all nearly halfway across. Allen kept as much of an eye on their pursuers as he could without stopping again. They seemed to be making it across the river just fine, even if they were moving a bit slowly. Two more skriff hounds joined them and were now paddling their way awkwardly toward their prey.

Allen's heart nearly stopped when he heard Sarah scream. He turned toward her just in time to see her head pulled under the water.

"NOOO!!" he screamed.

Before he'd even had time to react, Zorthos yelled for him to keep moving and dived under the water after her. He felt lost; he didn't know what to do. The skriff hounds were closing the gap between them, Sarah had been sucked under the surface of the water by something unseen, and they were just barely over midway to the other bank. Unable to decide what to do, but unwilling to stay in one spot and allow the relentless creatures time to catch up to him, he paddled backwards slowly toward the opposite shore while keeping a watchful eye on the last place he had seen Zorthos and Sarah above the water.

The next several moments were pure agony. He wasn't covering nearly as much distance as he had been and the skriff hounds were getting uncomfortably close, but he didn't want to go too far from where he'd last seen Sarah. The combination of panic and the severely cold water made him shake.

Just when it seemed he was about to be swallowed by despair, and likewise the skriff hounds, he heard a commotion coming from the water behind him. He turned himself around in the water to face the opposite shore, immediately feeling relief wash through him; Zorthos and Sarah had breached the surface of the water and were several yards ahead of him toward their destination.

"Allen, you fool!" Zorthos bellowed incredulously. "What are you doing? Hurry or be lost to your own fate!"

143

Allen put all his effort into catching them. They were nearing the opposite bank when he heard frantic yelps, accompanied by a lot of splashing coming from behind him. He didn't dare risk another glance over his shoulder, didn't dare stop, but it wasn't difficult to understand what he was hearing. The skriff hounds had run into some sort of obstruction or had finally reached the limits of their capabilities and were fighting to stay above water. He felt great relief that the persistent beasts chasing them wouldn't continue their pursuit any further.

Coughing up water and gasping for air, he finally dragged himself onto the shore. He took a moment to gather his wits and fight off a fit of shivers before he looked up to make sure Sarah was okay. The alien outfit Zorthos had made for her was clinging tenaciously to her feminine form. Allen had seen her in a swim suit before, but somehow this seemed to leave less to the imagination and he found himself struggling to look away. She looked up at him and gave a weak, forced smile. He smiled back and pulled himself to his feet.

As they trudged their way toward the torches lining the bank, Allen noticed for the first time just how much more enormous they were up close; the sight of them took his breath away. A moment later, he was snapped out of his reverie when Sarah began to speak.

"I don't know how much further I can go," she panted. "Can we at least rest for a few minutes?"

Zorthos seemed to be genuinely considering her request for a moment as he looked back across the way they had come. With twilight approaching and the torches unable to cast light all the way across the river, Allen could only vaguely make out the shadowy shapes of the remaining skriff hounds as they stopped pacing the shoreline and retreated back into the woods.

After a long silence Zorthos said, "I fear not, Sarah."

Before they had a chance to ask the reason behind this, there came a light show deep within the woods across the river, followed by a huge concussive burst of air.

Neither he nor Sarah needed Zorthos to tell them what such a display signified.

8

INFECTION

"WE MUST MOVE QUICKLY," Zorthos stated flatly. He cast a sympathetic look at Sarah. "Rest would be well appreciated by all, yet I fear it a luxury we cannot presently afford. A great distance yet stands before us and events already conspire to keep us from our destination."

"How far away are we from our destination?" Allen heard himself ask. He was still hesitant about pursuing any line of inquiry which could ultimately backfire on him in front of Sarah.

Zorthos turned his gaze from Allen while he considered his response, as if staring at something in the distance. After a short-lived pause he brought his attention back to them. "Far," he answered. "Two days, minimum, through current method of travel and with current level of fatigue."

A look of consternation mixed with dread contorted the features of Sarah's otherwise beautiful face. For a moment that look made his heart sink; he pictured much the same reaction on her face when he imagined her finding out the truth of what his curiosities had really cost her.

Sarah let out a groan of disapproval. "Are you serious? There is no way I can walk for two days straight! I'm beyond exhausted now!"

Zorthos turned to him, as if ignoring Sarah's protest. "How feel you, Allen? Do your faculties betray you? Is a moment required before continuing the journey?"

Allen glanced at Sarah who was watching him expectantly. It seemed to him that there was a silent plea in her eyes, begging him to say that he was tired and he too needed to rest. But to his surprise as he turned his concentration inward, gauging his own faculties, he realized he felt fine. His adrenaline still had his heart hammering uncomfortably in his chest, but otherwise he felt great.

Zorthos continued to stare at Allen so intently it seemed he was trying to bore a hole straight through him. For a moment he recalled how uncomfortable he'd felt when he'd Zorthos ripped the clothes from his flesh. The man was a wanted fugitive on this planet; it sent a brief chill up his spine.

"Speak," Zorthos urged.

"Actually," he said, not daring to look at Sarah's reaction as he did so, "I feel fine. I feel better than fine, as a matter of fact. I mean . . . I should probably be just as winded as Sarah, but I'm not."

Zorthos' lips pursed, as if considering something. "Good. Then it is settled. For now we shall take proper turn removing burden of weight from her." He turned to Sarah and said, "Once exhaustion gives way to second wind, responsibility to keep pace will fall to you."

Zorthos took a step toward Sarah, but before he could grab her Allen took her hand, guided her arm around his shoulder, and began to hoist her onto his back.

Clutching Sarah's legs with his respective arms, he gave Zorthos a nod indicating that he was ready. Sarah wrapped her arms around his neck, gripping them together at the elbows and resting her head on his left shoulder as they began moving at a brisk pace away from the river. As they marched, he couldn't keep a guilty feeling of longing from creeping up inside him. Sarah had her arms and legs wrapped around him and seemed grateful that he had offered his back to her before Zorthos could. He suppressed the feeling almost as quickly as it came, reminding himself not to get his hopes up over such desires. He was sure she would hate him when she found out the truth.

They hadn't covered much distance when Sarah once again began asking questions which Allen had been hesitant to ask himself. If he didn't know better, he would've thought she was doing it purposely.

"Why is it that I'm the only one who's completely drained, here? I mean . . . how is it Allen isn't as winded as I am? Neither of us has ever been to this planet, so why does he have enough energy to carry me after all that running and swimming, and I feel like I've pushed myself beyond my limits?"

Allen kept his eyes forward and his grip on her legs firm, doing his best not to betray just how curious he was for the answer to her question. His focus, however, was entirely on Zorthos' response.

"Actually," Zorthos explained, "several reasons could exist for this. Firstly, you arrived on this world well in advance of Allen, and therefore have had to endure the gravitational fluctuation longer. That alone could easily offer explanation to present circumstances.

"The possibility also exists that his body simply compensates adjustment in better time. There are those throughout the universe whose potential alone are enough to grant selection to join ranks to those already here."

"I thought the knowledge of this planet's existence was some great big secret?" Sarah interjected.

"And so it is," Zorthos replied.

"But you have to explain to the person where they'd be going, what their options are; they have to agree to come back with you."

"Correct."

"So . . ." Sarah hesitated. "What happens to the ones who refuse the offer to return here with you? Are they hunted and killed too?"

Allen thought he caught the briefest glimpse of a smirk cross Zorthos' lips before he responded.

"No," Zorthos said. "In most cases removal of memory is sufficient to abate future problem. Rejects continue life, absent knowledge that the offer ever occurred. However, more drastic measures are occasionally required to stay catastrophe and keep knowledge of Datheron secret."

Sarah looked appalled. "So you just kill people for not wanting to leave their loved ones behind forever, for refusing your offer? Is that what your crime was? Is that why you were bound up and being brought back here . . . because you killed someone for denying you?"

There was no amusement in Zorthos' expression this time. "No," he said curtly, "Such is not the reason I am hunted. And you would do well to mind your tongue here, girl! Accusations such as that will not be offered the same level of tolerance I exhibit if placed to others."

"What about us?" she asked in a much lower tone. "Are Allen and I going to be killed if we're caught by that Python, or whatever his name is?"

Again, Allen was a bit taken aback by how much Sarah already knew. Just how much had Zorthos explained to her before bringing her here with him?

"He is called Pythor," Zorthos corrected. "And yes . . . the possibility of that end does exist. However, doubt lingers as to whether that will be his immediate recourse. Far more likely is the possibility that you be proffered as a gift to the man who purchased his services: Luziaph."

He hopped a step and readjusted his grip on Sarah's legs, effectively repositioning her; she'd begun to slide down his back a little.

"And what is it you think this Luziaph will do to us once he has us?" she asked coolly.

Zorthos considered her for a moment before responding. There was a breeze which carried with it a sweet scent that Allen didn't recognize, and Zorthos turned to Sarah once more.

"His immediate desires would most likely be to have you tested, to see if potential exists for you to succeed on this world," Zorthos said thoughtfully.

This time it was Allen who responded. "Succeed at what exactly?" he asked.

Zorthos stopped in his tracks for a moment. "Luziaph is one who will bend circumstances to his benefit whenever possible. If you earn his approval, his desires will turn toward training you to use skills to his purpose. You would forever be in his service."

Zorthos turned and began walking again. "If great potential lives in you he may have you trained in many skills that you might be presented to the God-King; either as gift or as combatant in the Arena Games, to fight under his banner."

"You mean we'd be his slaves," he said; it was a statement, not a question.

"Apologies . . ." Zorthos said in a distant voice. "But, yes."

"Oh, I am liking this planet more all the time," he said, the sarcastically. "I'm so glad we came here!"

"Would the alternative have been preferential?" Zorthos asked in a sardonic tone. Neither Allen nor Sarah said anything. "I thought not."

For a short while they followed the trail away from the river. He glanced over his shoulder and noticed it was a goodly distance behind them now. He could barely make out the torches lining its shore. He shifted his grasp on Sarah's weight again, noticing that his muscles didn't really burn all that much despite the fact that he had been carrying her for a while now.

Finally, he decided to break the silence. "So . . . tell us about this Luziaph character. Who is he exactly?"

Zorthos must have been in deep thought as he jerked his attention to Allen with a start. "Luziaph," he began after a moment, "stands Proctus of Vardiston. It is a city not all that far from here. There, supreme power is his constant ally; he answers only to the God-King."

"So," he reasoned aloud, "A Proctus is like . . . a political leader or a ruler of some sort?"

Zorthos nodded. "The entirety of the realm of Thugrod, surrounding Vardiston, is his to govern in the stead of the God-King."

"What's a God-King?" Sarah asked.

Zorthos cast a glance at her that resembled a teacher looking down at a child who had asked what color the sky was.

"It is exactly as it sounds, Sarah," he said. "He stands the most powerful on our planet, and therefore holds supreme power over all others. He is ruler over the whole of Datheron and a goodly portion of the surrounding star system."

"Would this God-King be able to send us back to Earth?" Allen asked; the words had escaped his mouth before he could stop them.

Zorthos let out a bark of a laugh that caught Allen off guard. "Is He capable of the task? Yes. But willing to do so . . . ? This is a different question all together."

"But you said yourself," Allen said, almost pleadingly, "he could just erase our memories of being here. He could make it seem as if it never happened."

"He could," Zorthos said in an understanding tone. "However, I fear convincing Him to do so would be an unachievable task. He is absolute in His laws, and you now stand a citizen of Datheron. You chose to come here. Apologies Allen, but you can never return home. Remove it from your thoughts or see yourself driven to insanity."

Allen felt the panic well up inside of him. This is exactly what he had been trying to avoid letting Sarah hear. To his surprise, she didn't say anything. In fact, she showed virtually no reaction at all. For a moment he wondered if this was yet another thing Zorthos had told her in preparation to bring her here. If that was the case, and she already knew, did she already hate him? If she did hate him, why then did she seem grateful to have had him offer to carry her first? Maybe, he thought, she was more afraid of Zorthos than she was angry at him. His mind was spinning with worrisome thoughts. He wanted to confront the issue and just find out the truth of what she knew and how she felt, but he was too afraid of what she might say and how she might feel to dare tread that ground yet.

He decided instead to keep the conversation going, if in a different direction, before Sarah had the chance to comment on what Zorthos had said. "Who are going to see?" he asked. "And what happens once we get there?"

"We move toward . . ." Zorthos hesitated, as if considering his words before continuing, ". . . someone I hold as closest friend, someone whom I have known for a great many years. I would have him remove this skriffing Triaga from my head. Once this task has been completed we can find a safe place to keep you hidden while I put my mind toward a proper solution."

He wondered what sort of plan Zorthos could be concocting. Was he planning to ditch them and go back to Earth to finish what he started without them? Would he turn them over to Luziaph himself in an attempt to earn some sort of pardon for whatever crimes he committed?

Allen's mind continued to wander to places he knew to be dangerous while they moved ever forward. He understood it was less than smart to jump to conclusions or create problems which weren't even there, but with everything he had been through over the last couple of days he was having a difficult time clinging to reason. He wondered inwardly for a moment what would happen if Pythor caught up to them before they reached Zorthos' friend. An idea came to him . . .

"Zorthos?" he said from a faraway place as he brought his thoughts back to the present.

"Yes?" Zorthos answered.

"You said you're one of the most powerful men on Datheron . . ." he probed.

"I am."

"And you said on this planet one can learn anything they want, that gods are created here . . ."

Zorthos eyed him suspiciously, "True. What are you getting at, boy? Come to plain words."

"Why don't you teach me, teach us, what you know? You could teach me everything you know . . . then I'd at least be able to protect Sarah and myself from any danger on this planet. And if I work hard enough, you could teach me how to open a warp gate back to Earth."

As Allen watched Zorthos, waiting for his answer, he couldn't keep a rush of excitement from sweeping through him. If Zorthos said yes, he just might be able to stop daydreaming about flying and actually learn how to do it.

Zorthos' expression was virtually unreadable. He seemed to be weighing Allen's request for a moment and then turned stoic. "No," he answered flatly. "Absolutely not."

"What!" Allen was incredulous. He had been certain that Zorthos was going to say yes. After all, the man had helped he and Sarah a great deal since they'd first met.

"Why not?" he bellowed. "If you're as powerful as you say you are, and are planning to remain in hiding anyway, why not teach me? If I'm to learn how to survive on this planet, who better to teach me than you? You've already helped me plenty up to this point. Why would you not be willing to help me with something this crucial?"

"Allen," Zorthos began; his voice was patient as he spoke, almost tender, "Most humble apologies. True grasp of the way things function here yet eludes you. A very large price already lingers above my head. That alone stands reason enough not to offer instruction. Consequences for being discovered in my presence would be severe for all present. Were you found consorting with me, even standing at my side absent protest, guilt and punishment would be harsh and swift. I refuse to put you or Sarah in the face of such risk."

"What did you do that was so terrible?" he asked in a calm voice of his own.

"I cannot offer answer to that question. However, I can tell you the God-King himself wants me delivered to Him . . . as does Luziaph. I have forged many enemies and you would do better to find your own way here. To be discovered in my presence would only worsen things for you. Which is why once we have reached my friend,

Malacus, you shall remain in his care for the foreseeable future. He will know what to do. You will be safe there."

He began to protest more over the issue, but was cut off as Zorthos raised his hand and shushed him. Zorthos closed his eyes and inhaled a deep breath through his nose. Assuming the man had smelled something, he mimicked Zorthos attempting to smell whatever it was that had his attention. For a moment, he didn't smell anything. Then another breeze blew past and Allen caught a whiff of the same sweet scent he'd smelled earlier but hadn't recognized. He couldn't place the smell, but it seemed to him a hint of it resembled the aroma of vanilla mixed with some sort of sweet berry.

"What is that?" he asked.

"Relief," Zorthos answered, simply.

Zorthos picked his pace up to a jog and moved off the trail a little to the right, cutting across his path to do so. They continued until they reached an area where the grass was nearly waist high. Night was in full swing and Allen could hear Sarah's breathing slowing to an even pace. He assumed she must be getting tired and was beginning to fall asleep on his shoulder. Finally Zorthos stopped and he could see several bushes gathered in an area together. They were nearly as tall as he was and had a plethora of leaves covered in some sort of light fuzz. The smell was much stronger here and Zorthos moved closer to one of the bushes, glancing over his shoulder and indicating that Allen should follow his lead. As he drew near, Zorthos held up his hand halting Allen's approach, signaling that he had come far enough.

Zorthos began sifting through the leaves in search of something, stamping his feet in an awkward pattern as he did so. It only took him only a couple of moments to find what he was looking for. He picked something off a stem, walked over to Allen and handed it to him.

"Dendegayra seeds," Zorthos said.

Allen stared down at the seeds in his hand. They were about the size of an Earth pea, although he couldn't tell what color they were in the dark. He looked up at Zorthos questioningly.

"Just one of those," Zorthos said, "holds enough healing properties to cure any Earthly ailment with which you may be familiar. When ingested they can heal anything from severe disease to gaping flesh wounds." Allen stared at him in disbelief, his eyes wide as he listened closely to what Zorthos was saying.

"They do not hold power to cure everything you could contract on this world," Zorthos continued, "but what they will not cure forms a very short list and they remain of great value nonetheless. Ingest one presently and see stamina elevated well beyond the requirement to see us through the night."

Allen stared down at the seeds in his hands again. He could hardly believe that something so small could heal so much. It just didn't seem possible. As he glanced back up, Zorthos was shuffling through one of the other dendegayra bushes searching for more seeds. As he searched, he sporadically lifted his feet from the ground and stomped them back down in an odd dance. He wondered how that could possibly be helping Zorthos harvest the seeds. After several minutes the man seemed to have finished looking and came back to stand in front of him.

"Well, why do you hesitate?" Zorthos asked in an almost accusatory tone. "Place one upon your tongue. You will find the taste equals the pleasant aroma. Be sure to chew thoroughly. Do not swallow it whole."

Allen nudged Sarah awake and slid her easily to the ground. Once he was sure she was awake and able to stand on her own, he turned back to Zorthos. "What happens if I swallow it whole?" he asked.

"Nothing to cause concern," Zorthos assured him. "But help offered from the seed will blossom much quicker through proper mastication."

Allen briefly explained to Sarah what the seeds were and their supposed capabilities. He placed one of the Dendegayra seeds in her hands and told her to chew it up. He put one in his own mouth and began to grind it between his teeth. As they chewed, Zorthos reached out and grabbed his hand. He dropped several more seeds into his palm.

"Place these in your pocket," Zorthos said.

Allen did as he was instructed, noticing he already felt a little bit of his energy replenished by the seed he swallowed. Within a matter of a few minutes he felt immensely better and could tell by Sarah's posture she was, too. He could feel the slight stiffness in his joints diminishing by the moment, and his muscles felt taut and responsive. He inhaled a deep breath. The air even seemed to taste cleaner, better to him. He felt completely invigorated. Allen stared down at himself in awe as the wave of energy surging through him engorged every fiber of his being. He felt as if he could run for miles without the need to stop.

"Those seeds are amazing!" he said to no one in particular. Sarah nodded her wide-eyed agreement when he looked over at her.

"Be cautioned," Zorthos said firmly. "Do not rely on aid from these seeds unless the need be great; if life weighs in the balance."

"We weren't in dire need of healing just now," he retorted. "Why do we need to be conservative with them? Are they addictive or something?"

"Not in the way you think. But ingesting them with frequency can cause one's immune system to become dependent. So thoroughly do the seeds heal that one's body can be deceived into diminishing its own antibodies. So, to a certain degree, the possibility exists that they become habit-forming absent choice. There have been many a Datheronian who learned this lesson far too late."

Zorthos looked at Sarah. "How feel you?" he asked.

"I feel tons better!" she said enthusiastically. "In fact I feel better than I can ever remember feeling! I have energy to spare!" She looked thoughtfully from Zorthos to the dendegayra bushes. "I think I should put some in my pockets, too."

Sarah took a couple of strides toward the bushes from where she and Allen stood. An instant later, Zorthos bellowed at her. Instinctively, Allen reached out and grabbed Sarah around the waist and jerked her hard away from where she stood, tossing her behind himself. As she flew through the air behind him, he lifted his foot with reflexes he was sure were related to eating a dendegayra seed. With a speed matching his newfound reflexes he slammed his foot down on top of something slithering through the deep grass. Allen could feel it—whatever it was—squirming mightily for freedom beneath his foot.

"Whatever you do, Allen," Zorthos said in an urgent tone, "Do not remove your foot until I give instruction. Are we of a singular mind?" He nodded that he understood, and Zorthos ran somewhere off to his left for a moment. When Zorthos returned he had a rock the size of his abdomen in his hands.

Zorthos moved right up next to him, staring down at the shaking grass beneath the sole of his heel as he lifted the rock over his head. He began speaking in another language again; the same language Allen had heard him speaking in the forest clearing which had hidden the gateway on Earth. Whatever he was saying, he was doing so in a threatening tone. Zorthos finished talking, continuing to eye the ground beneath him. The rock was still raised over the man's head. A moment later Zorthos said something else, something brief, and Allen felt as if he had almost understood the words himself.

The grass beneath his foot stopped moving. Whatever he'd stepped on to prevent Sarah from being hurt had stopped moving as well. After another moment or two of silence, Zorthos nodded to him.

"Okay. Remove foot from snake, but do so slowly. Once it recedes to shelter, we will need to be away from here quickly. Ready yourself."

Allen did as he was told. There was a sharp movement past his leg before it jutted away from him back toward the bush.

Sarah screamed in his ear. He hadn't even noticed that she was right next to him again.

Zorthos cursed in the other language. Allen wasn't sure how he knew Zorthos had cursed. Perhaps it was the inflection with which the man had spoken the words, or perhaps Allen was somehow beginning to understand. Zorthos had told him a person's dormant potential was unlocked on this planet. Either way, it was only an instant later he rushed past Allen, snatching Sarah into his arms as he moved.

"Run, you fool!" Zorthos barked over his shoulder.

Allen ran. He caught up to Zorthos and ran alongside him. He looked down at Sarah, who was bouncing uncomfortably in Zorthos' arms. She was unconscious.

"What's happened to her? What was that thing back there?" he asked.

"It is called a vehectra snake," Zorthos answered. "It is protector of, and symbiote to, the dendegayra bush. It burrows its home beneath the ground, among roots of the bush. Because seeds are both pleasant to the tongue and likewise breed addiction, people and animals alike are easily drawn to them. The bushes lack thorn—or any other proper protection for that matter—so the vehectra snakes dwell beneath, allowing alluring scent from the bush to draw prey within distance to strike. The two work together, each one ensuring survival of the other. The vehectra snake is known to grow large, their venom unbelievably lethal."

Allen's heart skipped a beat. Unbelievably lethal. He was only able to keep stride with Zorthos and prevent his knees from buckling through immense effort. Unbelievably lethal. Sarah couldn't die. That though was worse than death to him. She couldn't die. She couldn't. He refused to believe it.

". . . which was why I gave instruction to stand well clear of the bush while I gathered the seeds," he heard Zorthos say as he drifted back to the present.

"How lethal?" Allen asked.

Zorthos gave him a sidelong glance. "Had she not just eaten one of the seeds, death would have already claimed her," he stated flatly. "As it stands now, we have less than twenty-four hours to reach Malacus lest he be unable to remove the poison and undo the damage."

Less than twenty-four hours! Zorthos had told them that their destination was easily two days away! Allen's mind spun at the implications.

"How the are we going to get her there in twenty-four hours?" he yelled in a panicked tone.

"If we run the entire distance," Zorthos responded, "we should arrive with time to spare."

As good as the seed made Allen feel, he wasn't entirely convinced he could sprint for twenty-four hours. In fact, he'd never been able to run for long periods of time. He'd always felt a burning stitch of pain in his side after five to ten minutes of running. How was he ever going to get her there in time?

"Couldn't we just suck the poison out of her leg and give her another seed?" he asked in desperation. "Wouldn't that at least buy her some time? You said to use them when in a dire need to heal."

"Unfortunately not," Zorthos answered again. "You lack understanding of the venom's potency. Were you to attempt siphoning the poison from her, I would be left to carry the both of you. Consciousness would escape you the moment the venom touched your lips, leaving you to travel death's road alongside her. And giving her a second seed would likewise do no good; the seed already aids her as much as is possible. Her health was already at its pinnacle when she was bitten."

Allen's hopes sank. But he wasn't about to give up. He didn't care what it took; he wasn't going to let her die. Even if he had to eat every last Dendegayra seed in his pocket to keep replenishing his strength as they ran, he would get her to Malacus's in time to save her.

The hours passed as they ran with everything they had. Not once did either of them slow their pace. They ran in silence. Even though they had taken turns carrying Sarah, they hadn't slowed to exchange her; they simply tossed her to the other, letting him catch her in mid-stride. Allen felt he couldn't move fast enough. Every time he looked down at her, he feared he might find her dead in his arms. As fear welled up inside him, he found himself pushing harder, well past what he believed his limits to be. Amazingly, Zorthos had somehow been able to keep up with him. As exhausted as the man had been, Allen knew he must've eaten one of the Dendegayra seeds also.

The horizon was beginning to change to a subtle shade of pink in the distance slightly to Allen's right. Dawn was approaching and he was surprised to realize that he had run all night, not only without stopping but without ingesting another seed as well. Somehow he hadn't needed to stop to rest. He hadn't even needed to hydrate himself.

As the sun rose higher in the sky he was able to see just how beautiful the landscape of Datheron truly was. They were running through rolling fields of greenery. He could see a vast mountain range in the distance. They were so massive that the peaks disappeared behind the clouds in the sky, which made it impossible to tell just how far away they actually were. The fields through which they were running were comprised of grass that came halfway up his shins, which did nothing to make the constant sprinting any easier. It looked very similar to the grass on Earth up close—thin green strips growing very tightly together—but it had a purplish hue to it the further away it was. Trees grew sporadically among the hills, just as they might on Earth; some even being clumped together, forming small groves. The thing that caught his attention the most, however, was the color of the sky. It wasn't the same blue as that on Earth, which he had mistakenly thought it had been when seeing it through the shroud of the forest canopy the previous day. It was a dull turquoise, getting more vibrant as the sun rose higher still and the day progressed.

As they ascended a steep incline, Zorthos slowly fell behind. Allen was beginning to worry if Zorthos was going to pass out from exhaustion. The man had seemed tired yesterday before they'd even begun their trek out of the woods. Allen glanced over his shoulder as he cleared the top of the large hill and began his descent to the other side. He noticed another steep incline directly ahead and wondered if Zorthos would even make it over the first. As he peered back toward the top of the hill he had just overtaken, Sarah held tightly in his grasp, Zorthos did something which amazed Allen yet again. No sooner had the man's hair come into view, when he sailed through the air over Allen's head. He followed the movement as Zorthos soared past, landing gracefully at the peak of the corresponding hill a goodly fifty or sixty yards away, in front of him. Even from the distance between them, Allen could make out a grin on Zorthos' face as he turned to face him.

Zorthos stood silently, seemingly catching his breath, while allen advanced toward him. By the time he'd finally breached the top of the other hill he realized the muscles in his legs were beginning to burn slightly. The wind whipping past his face had begun to feel refreshing and he realized he must be sweating. Zorthos began running an instant before Allen reached him, and all at once they were running alongside each other again.

"How did you do that?" he asked as they moved.

"As previously stated, Allen, anything is possible on this world."

"No." Allen shook his head. "I mean, I thought your ability to harness your skills was depleted. You said your powers were completely spent. How did you fly through the air like that if your abilities are gone?"

Zorthos chuckled slightly. "That was not some special ability you just witnessed," he said assuredly. "It was simple physics; momentum and inertia. Such are easier to manipulate here, even with the severe gravity."

He eyed Zorthos skeptically. "How do you figure that?"

"I gathered speed prior to reaching hill in effort to make incline easier to traverse, just as I am certain you did," Zorthos explained. "You had taken the lead from me, after all. As I reached the top I simply thrust my body upward rather than allowing gravity to pull me to the other side of the slope. Momentum carried me over the depression between the hills."

"So, then . . ." he hesitated, "you're saying that I could've done that, too? It wasn't some trick or ability?"

"Yes. Your speed alone was enough to create sufficient momentum to carry you to the other side."

Allen contemplated what Zorthos told him as they continued their journey. He wondered if it was true, if he could actually have accomplished the same feat. The way Zorthos explained it made perfect sense to him. He found himself acutely aware of the terrain as he searched for an opportunity to recreate what he'd just seen.

The sun's rays were beating down on them from directly above the next time Allen glanced down at Sarah to check on her condition. He winced in fear when he noticed her saliva frothing at the corners of her mouth. His heart raced faster, but not from the pace at which they were still running.

"Is that normal?" he asked Zorthos frantically, indicating what he saw.

For the briefest moment Allen thought he caught a startled look of awareness in Zorthos' eyes when he saw the foam on Sarah's lips.

"She has little time," Zorthos said in an uncomfortably even tone as he fixated his eyes back in the direction they were running. "The venom is acting much faster than I would have thought possible. Only a couple of hours yet remain before she departs from this world."

That was exactly what Allen had been afraid of when he noticed it. The panic he had been suppressing all night was beginning to rise to the surface. He didn't know what he would do if she died. He felt as if his world would end if that happened. He had worked so hard; he had run far longer and far faster than he ever dreamed possible. He had pushed himself beyond his limits ten times over to make sure she would live. He refused to believe he had come so close only to fail. It all seemed like a bad dream.

He wished he could wake from this nightmare. There was nothing he wouldn't give to find himself in a cold sweat in his own bed right now.

"Remove it from your concern; our destination quickly approaches. We have made good time," Zorthos said, as if in response to Allen's thoughts.

"How much farther?" He was finding it difficult to fight the tears welling up in his eyes.

"There," Zorthos said, pointing at something in the distance.

He tried to locate what it could be Zorthos was pointing to. They were on another downward slope and Allen had a decent view of a large valley below them. All he could see was a lake that seemed to still be miles away in the center of the valley. There was a very large tree in the exact center of the lake that seemed as if it must be rooted underneath the water, as there was no land at its base.

After several discouraging moments of scanning the scenery Allen turned to Zorthos. "I don't see it," he whined.

"Upon the lake's opposite shore," Zorthos assured him. "We will have to run its perimeter; to swim the waters is dangerous and would waste precious time."

Allen nodded.

The next quarter of an hour was pure anguish for Allen. Sarah's mouth continued to foam more profusely, and his muscles and lungs were beginning to burn with intensity. He was desperate to make it to Zorthos' friend, Malacus. Whoever he was he was Sarah's only hope. If he couldn't help her like Zorthos had said . . .

At last, as they followed the shore around the lake a house came into view. It was a simple-looking home and reminded Allen much of the cabin he had once accompanied Sarah and her father to when he was twelve.

The house's walls appeared to be built with logs, much like any other cabin he had ever seen. The cracks between them were filled with some sort of mud or clay. The roof was sloped and appeared to be covered in some sort of massive tangle of vines. It even had a round chimney protruding through the roof near one of the far walls.

Allen's body shook with relief when he finally brought himself to a stop outside the front door of the house. He couldn't it take any more; he collapsed to the ground, setting Sarah down as gently as he could.

Zorthos was through the front door of the house and yelling his friend's name before Allen's knees even touched the ground. There was no answer. Zorthos continued to call out Malacus' name as he ran through the house, eventually resurfacing in the doorway. He pounded the base of his hand against the doorframe as he emerged. For a moment time stopped as Zorthos began shaking his head slowly. This couldn't be the way it ended. He felt his heart breaking along with his resolve, his will, and the rest of his body. He slumped down over Sarah's body. She was beginning to convulse.

Zorthos knelt down next to him and eased Sarah away from him, rolling her onto her side. "We do not want her to choke," the man offered in a weak tone.

"Where is he?" Allen sobbed. "You said he'd be here! He's her only chance! You said so!"

"A debt of apologies, Allen. His absence is most unexpected. As long as I have known the man, he has only seldom left this house. He should be here."

Allen let out a wail of anguish and did something which even shocked himself; he threw his arms around Zorthos and buried his face into the man's shoulder. This couldn't be real. But it was. He cried louder.

Allen heard someone yelling something from several yards away. He couldn't quite understand what was being said, but whoever it was seemed agitated. He tried to calm himself enough to see through his blurry vision. When he looked up at Zorthos, the man's eyes were fixated across the lake. Allen followed his gaze and stared in utter confusion for a moment as he wiped the tears from his eyes. Was he really seeing this, or were his eyes so full of tears that they were playing tricks on him? There, walking toward them across the surface of the lake was an old man dressed in loose-fitting garb, a heavy cloak billowing in his wake.

9

MALACUS

TEARS RAN DOWN ALLEN'S CHEEKS. He wiped his eyes clean on the sleeve of his tunic and struggled to clear his vision to confirm what he thought he saw. He was still shaking, not only from the test of endurance his body had been subjected to, but also from the racking sobs which he was only now beginning to master.

He looked again at the old man approaching them across the surface of the water. His flowing, silver hair hung just past the nape of his neck and a beard of nearly the same length trailed down his chest, bouncing with each step he took. The old man appeared to be as human as either Allen or Zorthos, and he wore a loose fitting grey tunic which looked much the same as the one Zorthos had fabricated for he and Sarah. The man had the same intense violet eyes as Zorthos and wore a heavy-looking black cloak with a deep cowl which, at the moment, was not covering his head. Draped over his left shoulder, trailing down to his right hip, was a small tan satchel which looked to be full of something. As the speed of the old man's gait increased with each step, Allen couldn't help but think he looked like a wizard.

As the old man approached, he continued to jabber something in the alien tongue Allen was beginning to get used to hearing, directing all of his consternation at Zorthos. The two of them seemed to be bickering back and forth for a couple of moments, until Zorthos said something which made the old man's eyes go wide as he turned his gaze to him, then to Sarah. He distinctly thought he'd heard the word "dendegayra" mentioned. When the old man took in Sarah's condition he immediately knelt to her side, shoving him out of his way. Quickly and deliberately he pressed his left hand, palm down, across her forehead and shoved his right down the front of her tunic, placing it between her breasts.

"Hey!" Allen objected protectively. But before he could do anything to separate the old man from Sarah, Zorthos was next to Allen, holding him back.

"Be still, boy," Zorthos whispered sternly. "Must you always assume the worst? He does not what you think. This man stands a Grandmaster of the healing arts; he knows how best to return her to health. If Sarah stands any chance at survival, it will only be through his intervention. You must let Malacus do what he will."

Allen glanced down once again at the old man. "That's Malacus?" he asked.

"Yes. Now silence further protests and allow him to give proper focus to the task at hand."

Allen watched intently while Malacus hovered over Sarah as if in a trance, his eyes shut, his brow furrowed in deep concentration. He mumbled something in his alien tongue and Zorthos knelt down, pulling Sarah's right pant leg up over her knee. Allen leaned in as close as he dared for a better look. He could see where the snake's fangs had punctured the skin just above her ankle—which was extremely swollen—and the weaving pattern of every vein coursing through her leg; they were all a sickening black color. It appeared to be covered by tiny black, infected lightning bolts as they trailed away from a deep reddish-purple lump just above her foot. Allen thought he might be sick at the sight of it.

A moment later, a thick black liquid began oozing from the contusion at a rapid pace. For several minutes he just watched in wonder at something which he'd never before witnessed, but somehow understood; the venom was being expelled from her body.

When the black ooze finally stopped, Malacus came out of his trance and placed both of his hands over the puncture wound. When he removed his hands a moment later, the wound already appeared to be scarred over. Allen couldn't explain how he knew, but he realized Malacus only intended to seal the puncture, not heal it entirely. Urgently, Malacus looked up at Zorthos speaking once again in his foreign language. Zorthos gave a short response and Malacus began speaking again, holding a closed hand out, and opening one finger at a time as he apparently listed off something to Zorthos.

Without another word, Zorthos was on his feet and through the door into the cabin.

When Malacus stood a moment later, Allen had expected him to pick Sarah up in his arms, or at least request Allen's help in carrying her inside. Instead, Malacus held his hand in the air over her and she lifted gently away from the ground as if being pulled up by invisible strings. Her hair drifted, looking almost suspended underwater. Malacus rotated her hovering form to fit easily through the door, then turned to Allen and tilted his head toward the cabin, indicating that he should follow them inside.

The inside of the cabin looked much different than Allen had expected it would. The interior walls didn't appear as if they belonged to a log cabin at all; they were all covered in the same plaster-like substance which sealed the creases on the outside, and had been smoothed out to create flat walls. Every doorway he saw had been constructed in an arch and the floors a smooth marble-like material. He could see a faint reflection of the other's feet and the flickering lights of the torches dancing across its surface. There was a large round table supported by a single round post protruding from the center of the main room, which appeared to be made out of the same substance as the floors. It actually looked to him as if the table was somehow part of the floor, as there was no discernable separation between the floor and the table's base. Nearly every wall was lined with shelves, most full of old tomes and scrolls. A few shelves held intricately designed artifacts and knick-knacks. Allen had no idea what they could be for. Through an elongated picture window with rounded edges, he could see Zorthos' back to him as he worked on something out of sight. The man's head was down as he worked and it almost sounded to Allen as if he were mixing something together.

Allen followed Malacus into another room and couldn't help feeling amazed when, with a flick of his hand, the torches on the walls flickered to life; appearing to have done so of their own accord. With another flick of his hand, Malacus lifted a chunk of the floor away to reveal a hidden stairway, down which they proceeded to a secret underground room. It smelled dank and musty, and stretched the entire length of the cabin above. No one had been down here in a long time, it seemed. There wasn't much to note in the room except that every wall was lined with yet more shelves, which held what appeared to be jars of ingredients, more scrolls and books, and various other artifacts; all arranged in haphazard fashion. Against the opposite wall, barely recognizable in the shadows, was a bed.

Torches decorated the breaks in the shelving and sprang to life at Malacus's gesture. He guided Sarah through the air toward the bed and rested her gently on top, which in the light, seemed nothing more than a large stack of blankets bound together at the ends and in the middle by strands of fabric.

Malacus turned to him. "Remain here with her," the old man said in plain English, if heavily accented. "I must aid Zorthos in completion of the antidote. Keep close watch on her; beckon immediately if her breath ceases."

Allen was thunderstruck. He hadn't expected the possibility that anyone else from this planet, other than Zorthos, spoke his language; especially after hearing him conversing with Zorthos in the alien tongue of this world.

Before Allen could regain his senses, Malacus held out his hand to him. "Relinquish the seeds from your pocket," he demanded.

"What?" Allen stammered.

"The seeds in your pocket; give them to me. Now, boy!"

As he stood there in mute shock, Malacus grabbed him by the shoulder. "Now!" Malacus barked. "Time is a factor! If the antidote is not administered presently, she will perish!"

He dumbly reached in his pocket and discarded its entire contents into Malacus' hand. Without another word, Malacus marched up the stairs. Once he was out of view, he immediately turned back to Sarah. She lay there on the bed, looking more ashen than he had ever seen her. If not for her shallow breathing, he might have thought she was already dead.

He stood, gaping. He couldn't make his mind function the way he wanted it to. With everything else that had happened in the last twenty-four hours he simply couldn't think straight. Awareness of how angrily his muscles were burning slowly pushed to the forefront of his consciousness.

Allen leaned over her and wiped the stray hairs which were pasted to her forehead and cheeks away from her face. Her skin seemed much cooler than he thought it would, yet she was sweating profusely. At least, he thought to himself, she seems to be breathing much easier and the rabid-looking foam is gone. Watching her, a sharp swelling filled his chest, feeling as if his heart might burst from within at any moment. He felt a lump rise so strongly in his throat it threatened to choke him as the realization of how truly close she was to death sunk in.

"She will survive," he heard a voice say from behind him.

Allen turned to see, through blurry vision, Zorthos standing there. He hadn't heard Zorthos' approach.

"I thought you were helping Malacus with the antidote," he said in a shaky voice.

"My aid is not actually required to see the task to completion," Zorthos explained. "He simply had me begin the process. The anti-venom takes time in the making. I began the process to see none wasted."

"Oh . . ." was all Allen could manage in response.

Unable to think of anything to say, Allen directed his attention back to Sarah. He watched her chest rise and fall laboriously with her breathing, and wished there was something more he could do. He couldn't recall ever feeling as helpless as he did at this moment. The strain of waiting for someone else to complete the antidote, her only chance at survival, was overwhelmingly unnerving. If only he had gotten her here quicker. If only the snake had bitten him instead.

Realizing he was slowly driving himself mad with this line of thinking, he decided he needed a change of scenery. Allen stood and began pacing the room, taking time to skim the contents of the shelves which lined the walls. Zorthos watched him stoically from the corner of the room, next to Sarah's bed.

"What is all this stuff?" Allen asked.

"It is Malacus' library. Most of it, anyway. These tomes hold a great many teachings of this world. The learning of specific skills, the history of our world, and journals containing tales of Malacus' own exploits reside among these shelves. Granted, what is seen before you is his own personal collection; the numbers here paling in comparison to the complete works of our culture. But a vast amount of knowledge can be found here, nonetheless."

Allen looked around the room. There were at least twenty partitioned sections of wall down here, all of which held numerous shelves of information. It would have taken Malacus an entire lifetime, possibly longer, to obtain all of this on his own.

"How many of these are his journals?" he inquired.

"Well," Zorthos drawled, "in all honesty, the term 'journals' may not give proper description; not by your interpretation anyway. Some document personal experiences, while others he has transcribed contain words of instruction."

Allen cocked his head toward Zorthos. "Others he's transcribed?" he questioned skeptically. "How much of this has he written?"

Zorthos' expression was very matter-or-fact as he responded. "All of it," he stated flatly. "All, save the historical volumes," he corrected himself. "Those,
174

however, are also written in his hand. The acquisition of the historical volumes among this library was exceedingly taxing. He had to first memorize information and then re-document it in his own hand. Nearly all here are duplicates of volumes which are housed solely at palace of the God-King."

Before Allen had a chance to voice just how flabbergasted he was by such a notion, Malacus appeared at the bottom of the staircase. He didn't acknowledge either of them; he just marched over to where Sarah lay.

Allen didn't hesitate. Within a moment of Malacus kneeling at Sarah's side he was hovering over the man's shoulder, watching as the healer tilted her head back and began slowly dumping the antidote down her throat. Once she had completely ingested the thin-looking light green liquid, Malacus stood, brushing Allen away in the process.

Malacus turned to Zorthos and spoke in what Allen had come to assume was the native tongue of Datheron. Allen paid deliberate attention to the conversation, hoping that he might somehow be able to overhear what was being said. He understood just how ridiculous a thought like that should be, but somehow he felt as if he might understand what was being said if he just listened closely enough. Malacus seemed to be questioning Zorthos.

The conversation, which seemed to rapidly be turning from interrogation to debate, went back and forth for several minutes, unabated. He was sure Malacus had just asked another question a moment later, to which Zorthos responded by tapping the device wrapped around his head to apparently accentuate his point as he spoke. Malacus seemed to consider Zorthos' words for a moment and then asked another question, gesturing toward him as he asked it.

Zorthos' answer was short, but it seemed to shock Malacus in the extreme. Malacus turned his gaze toward

Allen and simply stared, his mouth agape. Malacus seemed to be considering his options for several minutes as he paced the room. When he finally turned his attention back to Zorthos, he had apparently decided to drop all pretexts of conversing in his alien language.

"Does he know?" Malacus asked.

Zorthos' eyes opened wide at the question being asked in a way Allen could understand.

"Do I know what?" he asked, suddenly desperate to be included in the conversation. He found himself jumping to all sorts of conclusions as to what a question like that could mean. Were they talking about Sarah's condition? Was she going to die, after all? If she lived, would she be a permanent vegetable, or mentally handicapped from prolonged exposure to the toxin in her system? With great effort he reigned in his frantically swirling thoughts.

"Do I know what?" he repeated. "What's going on?"

Zorthos glared at the old man and responded in his own language. His expression was as serious as Allen had seen it in his brief time with the man. By his tone, he seemed to be warning Malacus of something.

Malacus considered Zorthos for a moment or two before responding in kind. "He is deserving of the knowledge, Zorthos," he said in a hard tone of his own. "If cowardice prevents the telling on your part, then the task shall willingly fall to me."

Zorthos let out an exasperated sigh. A long, tense silence filled the room while he apparently considered how to respond to Malacus' ultimatum.

"As you wish," he said in a defeated tone. "First, remove the Triaga from my head, then I will part lips and divulge truth to the boy."

"Tell me what!" Allen yelled. Neither of the the others paid him any attention.

"Part your lips and give voice to truth," Malacus commanded. "Then, and only then, will I remove the Triaga."

Allen thought the air between the two men might catch fire. They glared at each other for what seemed a very long time before Zorthos' shoulders finally slumped in resignation. All the tension completely left him when he finally turned his gaze back to Allen. For several more agonizing moments Zorthos just stared at him; his eyes filling with what Allen could only interpret as sorrow. Finally Zorthos spoke.

"Allen," he said in a remorseful tone, "you are my son."

10

CONTRITION

TIME STOPPED MOVING. Allen couldn't breathe. He wasn't entirely sure what he expected Zorthos to say, but it hadn't been this.

Slowly, he brought his world back into focus. He turned his gaze to Malacus to see if this was some sort of practical joke they were both playing on him. Malacus' head nodded slightly in grim confirmation.

Allen felt the bone in his hand, between the pinky and the wrist, fracture with the impact it made on Zorthos' jaw. Zorthos hit the floor with a sickening thud near the foot of Sarah's bed. He didn't seem the slightest bit angry or shocked at Allen's reaction; he just lay there passively, rubbing his jaw as he stared up at Allen.

Allen screamed at the top of his lungs from all the years of pent up aggression, all the anguish his father had caused . . . that this man had cause him and his mother. As the anguish took him, he realized his heart ached more than his broken hand. He had never let his anger slip its bounds before; certainly not this ferociously. But he lost himself in that moment as pieces of a puzzle over a decade old slipped into place. He desperately wanted to believe they were playing him for a fool, but something deep inside told him they were speaking the truth. Zorthos was his father.

Zorthos stood, but remained where he was. He watched him calmly as Allen tried in earnest to regain his composure.

Allen was clutching his right wrist so hard he was beginning to cut off the circulation in his hand. He could feel the dizzying warmth the rage left behind in his face, and he was having great difficulty slowing his breathing. He was only vaguely aware that Malacus had taken his hand and had begun to heal it. He could feel hot relief sweeping through his fingers, but he never took his eyes off of Zorthos. All of the times he'd cried himself to sleep as a child; all of the times he'd felt completely worthless or like he'd done something wrong to chase this man away; all the missed birthdays, and all the torment he'd received for being a "bastard child" from cruel children he'd gone to school with came flooding to the forefront of his mind. He couldn't help it. He was drowning in hatred for this man.

"I understand sour feelings felt toward me, Allen," Zorthos offered at last.

"Do you?" he bellowed back. "Do you know also how much I suffered, or how worthless you made me feel? What about how much it hurt my mom when you left? Do you know that, too? Do you have any idea how badly you hurt us?"

Zorthos' countenance paled, and Allen found himself hoping that he was causing this man pain; he hoped it hurt twice as much as it had hurt him and his mom.

"True understanding of the situation yet escapes you," Zorthos said weakly. "The choice was far removed from my hands."

"You're saying you didn't have a choice?" he yelled angrily. "There's always a choice! I would think on the planet of the gods, of all places, this would be a concept you'd understand!"

"Allen . . ." Zorthos, who'd seemed in complete control from the moment Allen first met him, now looked a broken man, a man who had suffered great loss in his life. "If you would allow explanation to be offered . . . It might not quell your anger toward me, but true understanding of what was lost that night would be reward for an open mind."

From a seemingly great distance, Allen reigned in his hatred, his anger for his would-be father, if only marginally. He decided if there was a reasonable explanation, he would hear it. He highly doubted that anything Zorthos said would change the way he felt about him, but he would listen, nonetheless.

"So talk," he said contemptuously, his jaw grinding in anger.

"First of all," Zorthos began, "you must understand that I loved your mother. I love her still. My life has been a hollow shell of what it once was, absent her presence. And you may not believe my words . . . but I love you, too. It has never been otherwise. When I first escaped this world, intention was never to return. I believed my remaining years would be spent on Earth. Even believing as I did, your mother was held at arm's length for many years prior to my taking her hand in marriage.

"As already explained, it is not permitted for anyone to part from this world absent the God-King's consent. I asked permission to leave, begged it of Him. He refused my request. Regardless of His command, my mind was firmly set in place on the matter, my will firmly set to purpose. I no longer wished to reside here. Seasons passed as I devised a plan to accomplish my goal of exodus. Once a plan was adequately formed, I departed this world; hoping with all in me never to return. Meeting your mother was not part of those designs, nor was falling in love with her, yet when fate offered companionship it was well-received and I was glad to have her. Hesitation prevented us getting close too quickly. I knew discovery of my betrayal would yield devastating results, putting her well within harm's reach; payment for my transgressions to be paid with her blood.

"After many years, when discovery of my absence seemed distant a memory, I believed myself safe in my new life. Comfort gave way to complacency. Your mother and I married. It remains, to this day, the happiest time of my life. You were conceived nearly two years later. To say that I was ecstatic over having a son would have been a great understatement. The two of you were the whole of my life . . . a life in which I had believed myself safe."

Zorthos stared into space for a very long time before he continued. "One day, as I walked the wooded area behind our house one of the Krathantor found me. He ordered my return to Datheron, told me payment for my crimes had come due. He was a telepath, as most of them are. The searching of my mind betrayed that I had taken a wife and we had a child. I refused to allow harm to come to either of you, so I killed him. I knew my location had been compromised, that time between my discovery by another Krathantor was limited; they excel in their purpose with unmatched ferocity and devotion. I did the only thing I could think to protect you and your mother: I left Earth to give myself over to the God-King's punishment. It may seem differently to you, Allen, but I did the only thing I knew could protect the two of you from certain death, or a life of suffering on this world. Neither were things I would allow to befall the ones I so loved. I chose exile from a life I cherished to protect you from one you would not."

For several minutes, he said nothing. He simply stood there, silently considering Zorthos' words; the heat he was feeling still tainting reason. If what Zorthos said was true, it meant that he had indeed sacrificed a great deal to protect him and his mother.

He wanted so badly to continue being angry with his father. For most of his life he had been looking forward to exacting some sort of revenge on the man, if he ever had the chance to meet him. This however, was nowhere near how he had imagined this encounter unfolding. Try as he might, the reasonable side of his mind was finding it difficult to continue hating this man for his choices. But that didn't mean he couldn't still be angry at him, or the situation his choices had wrought.

"So, tell me then," he said in a composed voice, albeit still tainted with anger, "if you did all of that to protect us, why couldn't you tell my mom the truth about where you were from? Why didn't you explain to her exactly what you were doing and where you were going, why you had to leave? She might not have suffered the heartbreak you left her with if you'd told her the truth."

"Allen, had I returned home," Zorthos replied in a tone of measured patience, "absent any warning whatsoever, saying, 'Apologies for my extended absence, but continuation of the life to which you are accustomed requires that I leave you behind, returning to a world of gods lest the God-King Himself kill us all,' . . . would such words have inspired belief? Would Carol have taken solace in them, or do you think it more likely that she consider me absent sanity and holding her own in similar regard?"

"I suppose you're right," Allen admitted, unable to remove the edge from his voice entirely. "You could've proven it to her, though. You could've showed her a couple of your abilities and proven where you were from."

Zorthos considered Allen for a few moments before he responded. "I believe suspicions of the truth danced among her thoughts," he said at last. "And honestly, Allen, the less your mother knew about this world, the better her chances of escaping the life to which you now find yourself condemned. So long as she remained absent knowledge of who I really was, or from where I truly hail, even the most gifted telepath could search her mind with nothing to show for their efforts."

"Plausible deniability," he said thoughtfully, more to himself than anything else. He considered everything he'd just been told, but continued to search for a way to debunk Zorthos' justifications for being absent most of his life.

"So, why didn't you ever come back?" he asked. "Couldn't you go to the God-King and tell him you had a family? Wouldn't He understand if you told Him you'd made a life somewhere else?"

Zorthos let out a tired sigh. "Allen, you act as if you hear, yet my words fall upon deaf ears," he said, irritably. "The God-King is nothing like the way you picture Him. He is not the all-loving, all-forgiving deity your culture believes a god should be. Had I confessed to having a family, the reward would have been one of two things: either you both die at the hands of the Krathantor, or life on your planet would have been stripped from you, quickly replaced with one of servitude upon this one. Either option, in the end, would have borne the same result: death would have taken you both long ago."

"Well, you obviously found a way to come back," Allen accused bitterly. "Why were you gone for so long?"

Zorthos exhaled a patient sigh. "Time moves far slower upon this world than it does upon yours. What was nearly two decades for you translated into only a couple years for me. This reason, above all others, bears the truth of what I spoke yesterday: those you care for on Earth will be long dead by the time you gain power enough to create your own warp gate home. Should the impossible come to pass and you find a pathway home opened to you in even a year's time, your mother will still have aged a decade in the waiting."

Allen didn't like admitting it to himself, but the more he learned about why his father had never been there for him, the more he found himself understanding why Zorthos had done what he'd done and why he couldn't have been there. The anger and resentment he'd felt for this man for so long was still there, but hearing his story knocked the wind out Allen's sails. He also found himself liking the idea of living on this planet less and less. More than anything else, he hated the idea that a year from now, his mother will have aged to the point she should be when he was supposed to be having children of his own.

Rather than let the despair he was feeling control him, he considered what all of this meant in relation to his primary objective: getting Sarah home to Earth. If approaching the God-King with a request to leave hadn't worked for Zorthos, how could it possibly work for him? He decided the first step in achieving his goal would be learning enough about how the abilities of this world functioned to be able to create his own warp gate back to Earth. Now that he knew Zorthos was his father, the man couldn't possibly refuse a request to train him.

"So, *Dad.* . ." Allen said, purposely putting an inflection on the appellation as he spoke it, "now that I finally know who you are . . . when do we begin my training?"

Zorthos appeared to be amused by the request, but quickly returned his countenance to a serious one. "Apologies, Allen. I stand beside my previous statement. I cannot train you."

"What? You can't be serious! Why not?"

"Allen," Zorthos soberly began, "you must understand: I am a known fugitive on this world. Simple association could bring the worst of fates upon you. Society of this world functions differently than that of Earth. Discovery that you aide me, that you share my blood, can come to only one conclusion: death.

"I cannot remain here at your side while Sarah recovers. Eventually, someone will turn up here in search of me . . . it is imperative that you not be seen at my side when that happens. Of even greater import is it that no one discovers the truth of who fathered you. Were that to happen, it is a certainty you would find yourself before the God-King; ever at His mercy. And I assure you He has none where the challenging of His laws is concerned. I fear the results of such an encounter would completely undo all I have sacrificed in the protection of you and your mother.

"Lastly, it is of the greatest importance that no one discovers that you hail from Earth. Were that to be uncovered, I fear there are those who would enslave you, or make attempt at your life."

"Why does my being from Earth matter?" he asked irritably.

"That is something to be addressed another time. You will just have to trust in my words," Zorthos said cryptically. "Promise me you will keep that secret close to chest."

Allen ignored the request; if Zorthos wasn't going to give him the answers he wanted, he would just have to get them another way. He looked around the room at Malacus' library, at all the things that the old man had written himself, and an idea came to him.

He directed his attention back to Malacus, who had been quietly listening to the conversation. "If he won't teach me," he said pointedly, "then maybe you will. How about it? Teach me how to survive here?"

Malacus shook his head, "I refuse. The downfall of our society will not rest upon my shoulders."

"What is that supposed to mean?" Allen demanded.

He was becoming increasingly frustrated. He was more than a little tired of all the secrecy and the childish manner in which he was being treated. His entire life he'd dreamed of being like the heroes from his favorite fantasy novels and comic books. He'd daydreamed about having supernatural abilities ever since he was a child. Now, here he was, with an actual opportunity to learn how to do some of the things he'd always dreamed of—his absentee father was even from a planet where such things were commonplace—and he was being denied the opportunity, denied even the option of learning without even being offered a reason why. Coupled with that was the emotional stress he was feeling over losing the life he'd had on Earth, and the possibility of Sarah's demise; he just couldn't take anymore. Something inside him snapped.

He glared at the old man with the intensity of a growing storm. He desperately wished he could direct some of his anger at either one of these men for denying him what was, more or less, his birthright. He pictured in his mind what he would do to them if he actually had the ability to do so. He envisioned slamming Malacus against the wall of shelves hard with his mind, pinning him there so he couldn't move. He imagined himself applying so much pressure to the old man that he couldn't breathe.

No sooner had he envisioned it then it actually happened. Malacus was lifted from his feet and slammed hard into the shelves behind him. For several moments he remained pinned to the wall, unable to move. A look of terror and utter disbelief contorted the wrinkled features of his face. He struggled for air.

When Allen realized what had happened, the shock of it brought him back to reality. Malacus slid to the floor, keeping his widened eyes focused intently on Allen as he gasped for air. Allen had no idea how he'd done that to the old man, but he was certain it was he who had flung Malacus against the wall. He turned his gaze toward Zorthos, who was staring at him with the same awe and consternation on his face as Malacus. No one in the room spoke for several minutes. They seemed to all be wondering the same thing: how had he accomplished that with absolutely no training?

After a long silence Zorthos looked at Malacus and spoke; once again in the alien language of Datheron. For whatever reason—possibly due to the frame of mind he'd invoked to achieve the mental body slam he'd performed on Malacus—Allen was able to completely understand the conversation this time. Realizing, as the others began to converse, that his mind was somehow translating words he couldn't understand moments ago, was jarring. An odd tingling ran down his spine and made his knees weak. The gravity of everything hit him all at once and he couldn't help it; he had to sit down.

"*The boy has great potential, does he not?*" Zorthos said with a smirk. "*He is definitely of my blood.*"

"*Indeed he does. I fear the prophecy is upon us.*"

"*Malacus, he must be trained. Life on this world would be dangerous in the extreme for him should he remain completely ignorant of his true capabilities. He will become a target to all once his presence on this world is discovered.*"

"*I will not knowingly train he who prophecy claims will bring our entire way of life to an end!*" Malacus countered aggressively.

"*The prophecy claims nothing of the sort. You, of all people, should know the truth of that. It states only that he will change the way of life for Datheronians. It speaks nothing of him ending life on Datheron—"*

"It states that life as we know it will end!" Malacus interjected, heatedly.

"That does not mean we will all die by his hand. It could simply be that the lives of all here change for the better. Therein lays the trouble with this particular prophecy: no one knows its precise meaning. Besides, he is not the first to be thought of as the child of prophecy . . . there have been others. Not one of them was proven to be the chosen one. Why should we believe otherwise of my son?"

"They were all killed or exiled before catastrophe could follow in their wake," Malacus replied pointedly.

"You speak of my exact concern. Perhaps he is fated to be no more a threat than they, but I would rather he not be killed absent good reason. It could very well be that, given proper chance, he will simply become another ordinary citizen of Datheron. That he is from Earth could yet be just another coincidence."

"It could be as you say, but I would rather not place faith in that chance. I would not like it should I be remembered as the man who facilitated the destroyer of Datheron."

Zorthos hesitated for a moment, as if considering his words carefully. *"The prophecy states also that it will be he who restores balance to the universe. It speaks not of precise meaning, but is balance not a primary tenet in the teaching of our unique abilities? Perhaps you would be remembered, instead, as the man who facilitated the restoration of balance."*

Malacus stood silently for a while, seeming to consider what Zorthos had suggested. He appeared hesitant to speak his mind on the subject. *"I remain unconvinced . . ."* he finally said.

"Malacus . . . of all who call this world home, you are among the most knowledgeable. You also stand his great grandfather. Who better to offer instruction our ways?—"

"You're my great grandfather?" Allen shot to his feet.

Zorthos and Malacus stared at Allen in bewilderment. After a moment, Zorthos burst out in laughter.

"Do you not see?" Zorthos said through his mirth in English, "He grasps hold far too quickly to let potential be ignored. Concede, you stubborn old man. Train your great grandson."

Malacus still didn't appear to be convinced, but conceded anyway. "I will teach him only how to stand an honorable member of our society," he offered. "I will give proper instruction as to the importance our culture bears and how to read our language. Should any abilities be learned along the way, such things will rest entirely upon his shoulders."

Zorthos turned to Allen. "You will receive no better offer from the stubborn old man."

Allen looked around the room at the expansive library before him. "Will I have access to all this information?" he asked.

Malacus considered his answer before responding. "Yes. Once proper grasp of the language has been obtained, as well as proper grasp of infrastructure and the importance our laws hold, I shall grant access to all you see before you."

"Deal," Allen smiled.

Zorthos approached Malacus. "I have completed my end of the bargain," he said. "It now falls to you to make good on yours; remove this skriffing thing from my head!"

Malacus seemed reluctant, but finally acquiesced, telling Zorthos to kneel before him. Zorthos did as instructed and both men closed their eyes as Malacus went to work. Malacus placed his hands on either side of Zorthos' head, directly on the Triaga. There was a faint humming in the air, and all of the torches lining the walls dimmed slightly. The process took several minutes; Allen could see Malacus beginning to perspire from the effort of it. The light in the room dimmed further and there was a slight gust of wind sweeping through the room. He could feel an echo of the energy Malacus was using reverberating throughout his entire body.

Suddenly there was muffled, metallic snapping sound and the Triaga fell away from Zorthos' skull. Both men let out a tired sigh of relief as the light in the room returned to its normal brilliance.

"You have my gratitude," Zorthos said. He stood up and reached into his pocket. As he removed his hand, Allen recognized the dendegayra seed a moment before Zorthos popped it into his mouth. Zorthos chewed it up before swallowing and moments later appeared completely rejuvenated.

Malacus gave him a look of disapproval. "I thought I had given better instruction than to ingest dendegayra seed with frivolity."

No sooner had Zorthos completed his convalescence than he turned and moved toward the stairs. "Apologies," he said as he walked, "but I need to be away and I have not the time to gather my strength through proper practice."

A sudden wave of irritation settled in the pit of Allen's stomach as the man who'd let him down for so long readily moved to abandon him again. "Hey! Where are you going?" he asked.

Zorthos turned at the bottom of the staircase, looking him in the eyes. "As previously stated," he said simply, "I cannot be found here; Pythor surely seeks me still. That he has not yet located me offers little refuge and even less consolation. He either closes in as we speak, or has decided upon taking his colleagues to Luziaph to the purpose of healing. Either way, it will not be long before he returns his mind to the hunt."

Allen felt more than a little dejected and offended to have just gotten his father back, only to have him leave again. He frantically searched for a way to convince Zorthos to stay and hide her with him and Sarah; or, at least stall his exodus. Though a part of him deep down wondered why he should bother; walking away from him seemed to be what the man was best at.

"Who exactly is this Luziaph?" he asked desperately. "Is he the God-King?"

Zorthos laughed at his question. "No, he is not the God-King," he assured Allen. "But he is dangerous, nonetheless. As previously stated, he stands Proctus of Vardiston and is one of the God-King's most favored servants. It is only a matter of time before he discovers my location, and I would not have my presence incriminate you when that comes to pass."

"Why exactly does he want you so badly, anyway?" Allen asked, unable to hide his wounded tone.

"In all likelihood, he desires sole credit for my capture to the end of gaining more of the God-King's favor. It is the God-King who has called for my arrest."

"So what will you do to change the fact that Pythor is chasing you?" he asked in an attempt to stall Zorthos further.

Zorthos gazed at him with the utmost intensity and answered his question matter-of-factly. "I shall turn events to my advantage, and teach him the meaning of being hunted. Then, I will kill him."

Without another word, Zorthos turned and disappeared up the stairs.

11

LUZIAPH

THE ELITE ROYAL GUARD formed a tight circle around Luziaph as they marched through the illustrious courtyard toward the entrance to the Palace of Vardiston. The morning light rising over the mountains to the southeast hadn't quite broken the boundaries of their jagged peaks, casting orange-pink hues and harsh shadows across the top of the palace's spires and stone statues which lined the walk to the palace. Even though the royal elite surrounded him as they moved, anyone could have seen who they were guarding. Standing well over a foot taller than any of the guards, Luziaph was difficult to miss, even from a distance. Normally their presence was an indulgence he could tolerate, but their protection wasn't something he'd ever really needed. Today, however, he was returning to Vardiston from a rather unpleasant visit at the palace of the God-King and was not in a particularly tolerant mood.

He had ventured to the palace with standard updates required of any Proctus about how his region was faring, as well as a report on the search for Zorthos. His primary goal, however, had been appropriating assistance from another member or two of the Krathantor. But he'd been turned away by that infernal mistress of the God-King. Luziaph wasn't sure exactly what real authority that witch, Divina, held, but she always seemed to be by the God-King's side and had a tremendous amount of influence over Him.

She had sent him away without even allowing him to meet with Rhenngoth.

With his third eye, located in the lower-center of his forehead, Luziaph glanced up at the splendor of his palace in the morning light. Purposely constructed in an ostentatious design and containing well over one hundred fifty rooms, it was easily the largest building in Vardiston, partitioned away from the rest of the city by a large wall. Normally, seeing the morning sunlight glinting off its exterior would have filled him with a certain sense of pride or, at the very least, satisfaction in knowing the authority that came along with this palace was his command. But as he reflected on the previous day's events he realized just how limited that authority, and his power, truly was. He had been reminded that the Palace of Vardiston paled in comparison to the grandeur of the God-King's palace in Nentalia.

Having had as much of their "protection" as he could tolerate, Luziaph ordered the guards to disperse and resume their posts. They were within one hundred paces of the palace's entrance now, and he decided he would rather finish the journey on his own. The guards hesitated, appearing unsure if they should follow the command to leave his side before they'd reached their destination, but only for a moment. They knew the penalty for defying a direct order and none were willing to test his patience.

As they broke rank and moved away from him, Luziaph's full form came into view. He had the cowl of his deep purple cloak draped over his head, as was customary while traveling on Datheron. Orange and pink highlights danced across the silver breastplate of his armor as he moved. As was also customary on Datheron, that armor marked him for who he was: the Proctus of Vardiston. While most other Proctus wore full suits of armor, Luziaph wore only a sleeveless breastplate, knee-high boots, and gauntlets over his wrists. A simple, yet elegant-looking black tunic completed his garb. Even though he moved with the gait of a man well over seven feet tall, his hands never strayed far from the weapons at his side; which he only felt the need to carry with him while outside his home. Being Proctus of one of the regions of Datheron meant being powerful enough, and ambitious enough, to earn such a station. With the natural abilities he wielded and the extra skills in which he'd trained himself, he was a force to reckon with even without the weapons.

Many who ruled a region of Datheron had earned the rank, and proved themselves by becoming Arena Champion in the Arena Games and thereafter swearing unwavering fealty to the God-King in return for the honor to serve under him. Luziaph had not. He had never even really had a desire to compete in the Arena Games. In his opinion, they proved little other than an opportunity to showboat one's skills and gain attention; he preferred results, not attention. No, his ascension to Proctus of Vardiston had come from proving himself capable outside of the Arena.

Luziaph's predecessor, Krylath, like the God-King and His Krathantor, had been a Gorrlock—blue-skinned, with pointed ears, and those malevolent-looking black and red eyes—and had enjoyed abusing the authority of his station. He had harnessed the ancient, mutual hatred between Gorrlocks and Triclopians, such as Luziaph, by reducing them in stature to no more than slaves within the walls of Vardiston. The hatred between the two races had existed for countless centuries since the original God-King's reign but only seldom was it publicly exploited in such a way.

For years the torture of Triclopians went on unabated under Krylath's rule. They were forced to do anything and everything demanded of them, many even dying to accomplish their tasks. None dared voice protest because none believed petitioning the God-King would do any good since He, too, was a Gorrlock.

It wasn't until Luziaph had lost his parents, his brother, and his wife to Krylath's cruelty that he'd decided fight back. At the protest of some, and with the blessing of others, he'd left for Nentalia to speak with the God-King and ask for something to be done to stop the needless death of his kind. He had decided, with nothing left to lose, that if the God-King would not grant his request, he would kill Him or die trying.

Before even reaching Nentalia, however, he'd been accosted by Krylath and some of his royal elite. He remembered well the anger and frustration he'd felt at being so near his goal, only to be surrounded by those who'd enslaved him, taken his lovely Lhymea from him. He swore he would not be taken alive and had fought his way through the elite to get a shot at Krylath, himself. By the time he'd finished, none were left alive save Krylath, on his knees begging for mercy. He'd showed no restraint, leaving Krylath immortalized in his supplication and his minions where they lay and had continued on to Nentalia.

When finally granted an audience with the God-King, Rhenngoth, he'd delivered a different message than the one he had originally set out with. He knew full well what it could potentially mean for a slave to kill a Proctus on the planet of the gods, but he no longer cared. Expecting to be killed for his confession, he was surprised to find Rhenngoth showed no anger over the death of a subordinate. On the contrary, Rhenngoth told him that He had been watching the battle and was impressed; Luziaph had, after all, just defeated an Arena Champion and several of his best men with no help. Rather than punish him for his actions, Rhenngoth had rewarded him for his accomplishment by offering him the position of Proctus of Vardiston; a reward he'd previously believed unbefitting for a Triclopian slave such as himself. As Proctus he would be able to change the laws he had originally intended to bring to the God-King's attention. It was then he'd decided he would settle for no less than one day becoming God-King Himself, giving him the authority to turn the tables Gorrlocks worldwide, once and for all.

Luziaph mentally shook himself from his reverie as he approached the front entrance to the palace. He glanced back over his shoulder, making sure his royal elite were all back at their posts. As he reached the entrance, he turned completely around and took a final look at the royal courtyard. All along the borders of the walkway were a series of statues; statues he had collected himself. They were all intricately detailed, and stood in poses of fear or shock. As he took them in, a small, proud smile stole across his lips. It had only been two days since he'd been here, yet he was relieved to be back. He knew this palace and everything in it; and those under its roof had to obey his every command. He was still silently fuming over being virtually ignored by the God-King the day before. With the mood he was already in, he was itching for anyone to give him a reason to snap.

Gazianna had only just begun preparing for Luziaph's arrival when, through one of the windows on an upper level, she noticed the royal escort marching through the courtyard toward the entrance. Luziaph was clearly visible in the center of the procession. She had not been expecting him to arrive so early. Panic struck her like a punch in the gut. She was his most prized personal handmaiden, at his beck and call no matter the time, and the recipient of his aggression whenever she failed to please him. The fact that she was not informed of his arrival would be no excuse in his eyes for not being prepared. He was constantly berating her and beating her. Sometimes she knew she deserved what she got for failing him. Other times his abuse just seemed to be a way to pass the time, a vile amusement for him.

Being a Gorrlock, Gazianna understood she could never hope for more from her life, not while she was in service to a Triclopian. She had been a mere girl, barely on the doorstep of womanhood, when he'd risen to power by killing her father. For a long time she wanted to kill him herself. She tried contacting the God-King to aid her in destroying the man who had taken her father from her. She had received no response to her pleas, however, and had been forced into the role of Luziaph's slave for nothing more than the crime of being a Gorrlock, daughter of the former Proctus, Krylath. She assumed Luziaph derived a certain amount of pleasure from turning the daughter of an enemy into his personal concubine. In the beginning, he had forced her to do the most vile things she'd ever done for the sake of amusing himself as much as humiliating her.

She hated him.

It wasn't long, however, until he'd broken her spirit completely. With his supreme mastery of telepathy, he could make her do things against her nature, whether she wanted to or not. It seemed the harder she struggled, the more he enjoyed it. Now, years later, she knew her role and dared not oppose him. Gazianna knew she had no control over her life, or even her own actions. Not anymore. Hers was not to reason why; hers was but to do, or suffer his wrath.

Frantically she raced through the corridors of the resplendent palace, and toward the main entrance to greet her master in a desperate attempt to not face that wrath now. She may be ill-prepared for his arrival, but that was certainly no excuse for not being present as he entered.

Her shoulder-length black hair swayed behind her as she rounded the corner into the entrance hall. Upon realizing she was moments too late to greet him at the door, she slid to a stop and threw herself at his feet.

"Most humble apologies, Master," she implored, her forehead to the floor. "Please forgive my tardiness."

"RISE AND MEET MY GAZE!" echoed violently through her mind and she found herself on her feet before she realized she had risen. At these moments Gazianna was unsure if it was of her own accord or through his telepathic grip on her, that she responded.

Desperately trying to reign in her terror, she stared into his cold grey eyes—all three of them—as he appeared to be deciding what to do to her for her failure.

A bright flash of light shook her vision and Gazianna found herself twenty yards away from her master, slumped against one of the eight marble statues which followed the walkway through the entrance hall. Judging by how badly her jaw ached, she assumed he must have backhanded her; though whether it was for being late for his arrival, or for speaking out of turn, she was uncertain.

Gazianna felt a miniscule part of her hatred slip through its bounds as she stared through blurry vision past the horrifying statues at her master. Before she'd even had a chance to mentally retract the instinctual response to his abuse, a searing pain shot through her head all the way down her spine. It felt like a bolt of lightning had struck her from the inside and was melting her brain. The pain was so severe she was only vaguely aware of something else striking at her from outside her body.

As badly as it hurt, she knew she deserved what she was getting this time. She knew better than to even think ill of her master. This was her fault for not controlling her vile Gorrlock prejudice.

As the pain began to recede and her vision began to return, she realized her left arm was wet. He was speaking to her, but through the ringing in her head it was no more than muffled noise. Apparently not responding as quickly as he wanted her to, he lifted her from the ground by her throat. Her vision roamed as she desperately fought to regain control of her senses.

Blood. That was why her arm was wet; it was covered in blood. Her blood.

At last she was able to regain her composure, and support her own weight, if only on the tips of her toes. Luziaph had her pinned to the western wall by her throat. She caught a glimpse of the entrance hall behind him and the mess he had made punishing her this time. There was a spider web-like crack in what remained of a statue across the hall where she had first impacted; the rest of it had shattered and crumbled to the ground. How and when she'd ended up on the other side of the room eluded her. There was blood everywhere. It trailed across the floor. It dripped down the statue, and was spattered on a couple of portraits.

Luziaph's tightening fist around her throat forced her to bring her focus back to him.

"You Gorrlocks are all of a singular nature!" he spat. "Even after all these years, after everything I have done for you, you refuse to sheath your hatred of me and my kind! Not even the Gorrlock who pronounced me Proctus of Vardiston bears any true respect for me or my capabilities!"

He pulled her face so close to his she could see her battered reflection in his eyes. He still had a tight grip on her throat as he spoke in a lowered tone. "The sight of you is enough to turn my stomach!" He released his hold on her and gestured to the open area behind him, "Leave nothing of this mess you have made and stay hidden from sight until the sun removes itself from the sky and returns once more."

As he took a step back from her, she surveyed the damage behind him. Inwardly, she wondered if he would allow her to have her injuries healed or if she was to suffer them while they healed on their own.

"Assistance in the healing of deserved wounds will come only when the entrance hall bears its original beauty," he answered to her silent request.

"Gratitude, my Master," she said through a swollen lip, lowering herself into a deep bow. She knew it would be a difficult task cleaning up all the blood, especially while she was still bleeding. She also knew that detail didn't matter to him. She would have to find a way to complete the task set before her, or receive further punishment.

After taking a few moments to wipe the blood from herself, Gazianna began the all too familiar, onerous chore Luziaph had given her. She had only been working a short time when, from the corner of her eye, she noticed someone else approaching the palace through the large entrance. She couldn't quite make out exactly who it was, but he was carrying two people; one on either shoulder.

Pythor was silently fuming over his failure to capture Zorthos as he lugged his two fallen comrades through the gates of Vardiston. Added to that, he was about to admit his lack of success to a Triclopian. It was humiliating enough being forced to serve the whims of that three-eyed pile of garbage. Admitting failure would be torture. Pythor knew, however, Luziaph's gloating would be insignificant compared to the shame he would feel when news reached Rhenngoth's ears. Having the God-King learn he had failed again was the last thing he wanted.

As he hiked the massive staircase toward the entrance to the palace, one of the two Triclopian guards stationed at its doors held up a hand to stall his progress when he reached the top. "What burdens your friends?" the Triclopian guard taunted. "Did they imbibe too much drink, or are they simply too lazy to walk of their own accord?"

The other guard snickered at the comment. Under other circumstances Pythor would have gladly risen to the bait and taught these two inferior creatures the meaning of respect, but he didn't have time for that just now. He'd forced himself to ignore their goading and had pushed past them without even making eye contact. Too much was at stake to give in to such a petty act as bickering with idiots. He told himself it didn't even matter that he hadn't taken a good look at the disrespectful vermin, since all Triclopians looked alike anyway; all completely bald with the same ignorant three-eyed countenance.

What Pythor saw as he made his way through the entrance hall gave him pause and irritated him in the extreme. A beautiful Gorrlock woman, whom he'd seen only a couple of times before, was cleaning up what appeared to be the sight of a minor battle. Her tunic was covered in the blood she was cleaning from the walls, and judging from the way her lower lip and right eye were swelling it very well could have been her own. Pythor also noted a blood-stained bandage wrapped around her left shoulder. He knew Gorrlocks were second-rate citizens inside the walls of Vardiston, but it made his blood boil to see the results of a beating he was certain Luziaph had administered.

"Where is Luziaph?" Pythor demanded the instant she looked up and noticed him. Fear plainly showed in her eyes as she took him in, considering his request.

"He has only just returned," she answered meekly.

"Returned from where?"

She hesitated a moment in answering and he briefly considered breaching her surface thoughts for the answer. "Apologies, master Krathantor," she finally responded. "He does not deign to share the details of such things with me. I am but a humble servant to his Lordship."

"Fair enough. I have business with the man. Please inform him of my arrival." Pythor tried not to sound too threatening in his request, but by the way she reacted he almost felt as if he'd threatened her life; her countenance had paled considerably and she began trembling. Her eyes widened and Pythor noticed for the first time that they were not the same color as all other Gorrlock's; hers looked human and were a bright shade of green.

"What part of the request troubles you?" he asked her.

When she didn't answer this time, Pythor decided to get the truth from her by listening to her thoughts. Fortunately, unlike most slaves within the palace, she had not been fitted with a Triaga.

"Please do not ask that of me," her thoughts echoed into his mind. "I was ordered to remain hidden from sight while the light of day still shines. Disregarding such a command will warrant severe recourse . . . He would kill me. Or worse."

Probing a little deeper confirmed Pythor's suspicions about the origin of her bruises. If there was one thing he couldn't stand, aside from a disrespectful Triclopian, it was seeing a Gorrlock woman treated in such a way; especially at the hands of a Triclopian. Pythor desperately needed to get a master healer for Sepharus and Borograth, but he wasn't willing to risk the well-being of another Gorrlock to do so.

Deciding to take a different tack, Pythor calmed himself and approached the woman. Even though he was moving slowly, she still seemed alarmed that he was moving toward her.

After setting his friends carefully on the ground next to him, Pythor lifted her chin with a finger and looked into her eyes. "What name do you go by?" he asked in as gentle a voice as he could summon.

"Gazianna," she answered shakily.

Pythor placed both of his palms to her cheeks. "Gazianna, I want you to relax. Do not fear my touch."

"What are you doing?" she asked, her eyes full of apprehension.

"Nothing that will bring you to harm," he assured her. "I shall seek out Luziaph myself. But allow me to first lighten your suffering, to remove the bruising and surface lacerations from your face . . . and I shall require something in return for such kindness."

She didn't respond, so Pythor set to work. He wasn't near expert enough to heal the injuries of his two comrades, but wounds as minor as Gazianna's should prove little challenge for him. In a matter of a few moments her skin had healed, restoring her features to their original beauty. She offered him a smile, albeit a weak one, as thanks for his kindness. Despite the shyness of it, Pythor found it to be beautiful.

After a moment she asked, "What is it you would have me do?"

Pythor motioned toward his two fallen brothers of the armor Sepharus and Borograth: "My brothers require the aid of a master healer. Should such service fail to reach them soon . . ." He couldn't bring himself to finish the thought aloud.

Gazianna nodded her consent.

"Gratitude, Gazianna. I would not ask this of you, but I fear Luziaph cares little for those of our kind and would use current injuries as a weight to be held over my head. They would surely perish in the waiting."

Gazianna assured him that she would see to it personally.

Satisfied that his fellow Krathantor would be taken care of, Pythor marched away from the entrance hall in search of Luziaph.

The sun was rising higher in the distance now outside the palace walls, causing angled pillars of light to cut through the hallways from the high corridor windows. Through his own skill in telepathy he could sense Luziaph wasn't far away. Another moment of probing and Pythor knew exactly where to locate him: the throne room. He knew Luziaph could sense him as well, possibly even already scanning his mind in preparation.

As he rounded the corner and entered the throne room, Luziaph came into view. The three-eyed lunatic stood in front of his throne, staring at one of the grotesque statues he so loved, which decorated nearly every hall in the palace. It seemed to Pythor that the ones Luziaph kept in the throne room were his favorites.

He came to a stop ten paces away from Luziaph, standing just below the dais upon which the throne sat.

Luziaph, who was standing with his back to the entrance of the room, spoke without turning to face him. "Why is it you have returned? Has your task been seen to completion?"

Pythor hesitated a moment, uncertain how to respond. Certainly Luziaph already knew the circumstances which brought him back prematurely. Perhaps Luziaph just wanted to humiliate him by forcing him to speak of his failure aloud. Pythor let the question hang in the air several more moments; he wasn't about to give this Triclopian vermin the satisfaction.

Finally Luziaph turned to face him. "Not only do you return absent success, you have allowed the unsanctioned arrival of two other-worlders upon the soil of Datheron, and they yet escape your grasp as well! So again I ask: Why is it you feel return to the Palace of Vardiston warranted?"

Taking nearly all his resolve, Pythor bit back his counter to Luziaph's accusatory tone. "It is not my intent to remain longer than is necessary," he answered, doing his best to restrain the anger he was feeling. "I come only for the purpose of gaining respite for Sepharus and Borograth, so the original task might be seen to completion."

"Failure is not something I tolerate; especially from the likes of you!" Luziaph barked. "Your allies are forfeit!"

Pythor knew the God-King wouldn't let any Proctus on Datheron knowingly dispose of a member of the Krathantor without His consent. But hearing the insolent words spill from Luziaph's lips nearly sent him into a blood-rage. Only his faith in Rhenngoth, and the knowledge that Gazianna was already searching for a healer, kept him from giving in to his anger.

One side of Luziaph's mouth twisted into a derisive grin. "Unless, of course, the mistake is rectified presently."

Still shaking from the effort of controlling himself, Pythor answered in as level a voice as he could muster. "What would you have me do?"

"What should have already been done!" Luziaph sniped. "You will receive no respite, nor shall your friends, until Zorthos and the two brats you allowed to cross over at this side stand before me! I have already given Gazianna command toward the ignoring of your request. And should you ever countermand one of my punishments again, you shall find yourself reunited with Krylath in short order! Are we of a singular mind?"

All Pythor could manage was a nod.

"Good," Luziaph said. "Then return to the task set before you lest you join your allies in the infirmary."

Livid over the confrontation, he turned his back on Luziaph and began his way back to the entrance hall of the palace. As he set out to complete his quest, he was certain of only one thing: one way or another, Luziaph would pay the price for his actions.

12

INCOGNITO

ZORTHOS WAS BEGINNING TO FEEL like the worst father in the history of the universe. He genuinely hated walking away from his only son for a second time. It had been different when Allen was a baby, when Zorthos wasn't able to see the look of resentment and disappointment in those azure eyes of his. But Allen was old enough to understand this time, old enough to see things for himself. Even though he was accustomed to time-shift between worlds, it was still strange seeing a full grown son which, for him, had only been born a couple of years ago. Allen had grown up without him, into a fine young man from what he could surmise from their brief time together. And the intelligence behind those eyes . . . Zorthos couldn't be more proud of his son.

He had done his best not to let it show outwardly, but it nearly crushed him to turn his back on Allen a second time. That calculating gaze Allen had acquired reminded him very much of Carol and how much he missed her. He knew, however, that as much as he missed her, she must miss him more. After all, he'd only had to deal with her absence for a couple of years; for her it had been nearly twenty. He wondered if she did miss him anymore, if she even still loved him. The thought occurred to him that she may have long ago moved on and remarried. Allen could have half-brothers or half-sisters in their teens by now.

He hated what life on this planet had cost him. What the God-King had cost him.

More than anything, he wished he could go back and change things. He would even be willing to give up all his powers, and the knowledge behind them, if he could just go back to his family. He knew, unfortunately, that he never could. This above all else steeled his resolve for what he had to do.

Zorthos knew all too well what the Krathantor were capable of, how ruthless they could be. Each of them expertly trained in several special skills, they were as fierce in their attacks as they were in their loyalty. He refused to leave Allen's fate to any one of them. Even as young as he was, Pythor in particular was exceedingly dangerous. He was an expert hunter, able to track anyone with his heightened senses across the galaxy. It was going to take some real ingenuity to cover the trail they'd left behind. Even if Pythor was taking his fallen brothers to be healed before he continued the pursuit, Zorthos had little time to spare. He could only hope he was able to move quickly enough. Even with the Triaga off his head, and able to take advantage of his full power, he wasn't sure he would be successful.

Knowing he wouldn't be able to accomplish everything he was setting out to do on his own, Zorthos decided he would have to risk a visit to an old friend. He didn't know if his company would still be welcome, especially since it was common knowledge he was now considered a traitor to the God-King, but he had to try. He closed his eyes in concentration, preparing to shift himself a great distance in an instant. He was nowhere near an expert at teleportation, but he didn't have time to run to his intended destination. Besides, what better way to test his newly replenished reserves than to attempt a particularly taxing skill? Calmly, carefully, he cleared his mind's eye, erasing everything he had seen before he closed his physical eyes. He called forth his memory of where he needed to go, every miniscule detail. If he didn't do this perfectly, he could end up with a severe headache at best, destroying his own mind or body at worst.

Knowing what was at stake, he committed himself to the task. He felt the air pressure shift around him, displacing itself to compensate for a presence which, only a moment before, hadn't been there. Cautiously, he inhaled a deep breath, letting it out slowly, and opened his eyes.

He found himself at the top of a large hill, overlooking an agriculturally rich valley. It was a large farming community which produced crops and livestock for the entire crown city of Nentalia, as well as much of Vardiston. From his vantage point, Zorthos could see a multitude of people and creatures all working in service to the God-King in his extensive gardens. Here, plant-life from many different planets was cultivated and harvested entirely for the well-being of others. Very little of what was grown here stayed here. They were only allowed to hold onto enough to keep them nourished and working; everything else belonged to the God-King.

Zorthos knew very well, with his status as a fugitive, he couldn't just stroll down into the valley through fields teeming with laborers. He would surely be recognized. But if he disguised himself as an ambassador of the God-King's vast empire, most wouldn't dare make eye contact. Without even taking his eyes from the bustling activity below him, he pressed his palm to a large boulder protruding from the earth at his side. His hand began to glow from his efforts, causing a trail of shimmering light to course from the rock up the length of his arm. As it enveloped him, the light began to take shape leaving a gaping hole in the boulder from the minerals and molecules he was commandeering to complete his task. As a master of alchemic reformation, he was able to take the very matter which made up an object and reshape it to suit his own needs.

After several moments the light began to dissipate. Steam drifted off him as his new uniform cooled from the heat such a transaction created. Briefly, Zorthos stared down at himself, inspecting his work. He needed to make sure it appeared authentic. He now wore loose-fitting white pants and boots which were intricately trimmed in silver; the pants being tucked into the boots at shin height. His white tunic was plain, except for the silver insignia on the chest representing subservience to the God-King. He wore silver, fingerless gloves over the sleeves of the tunic. Over top everything else was a long, solid white travelling robe with a deep hood and the same symbol etched in silver across his upper back, branding him a member of the Nyjaric Order. It seemed a good fit and hadn't cost him much energy to produce.

Pleased with his efforts, Zorthos lifted the hood over his head and began his march down the hill toward, quite possibly, the only friend he had left on the planet.

Grendolus was a Voldehyde, a race of beast-like men in appearance. Both male and female Voldehydes had fur all over their bodies except on their faces, chests, and abdomens. Their noses and jaws were primal in appearance, drawing outward, almost into a peak, resembling a monkey-feline hybrid. Known for natural strength and reflexes, not to mention ferocious tempers,

Voldehydes weren't normally ones to make friends with anyone; sometimes even among their own race.

Zorthos, however, had been able to bridge the gap in his youth by helping the beast-man out of some trouble with the local authorities of Nentalia. He was still working in direct service of the God-King when Grendolus had attacked a city guard in defense of another Voldehyde; his brother. Before the rest of the guards could swarm in and overwhelm him, Zorthos, who'd witnessed everything transpire, jumped in and saved Grendolus from being killed on the spot. With his smooth tongue he had also gotten Grendolus' brother out of trouble.

That, though, had only been the beginning of their friendship. Several more times over the next couple years, he had proven himself to be a friend worth having to Grendolus. If anyone would risk helping him now, he hoped Grendolus would.

As he made his way along the trail through the fields of crops, Zorthos noticed several people of various races glance his way briefly. As soon as they saw the robes he wore, their eyes went immediately back to their work. Pleased his disguise seemed to be having the desired effect, he proceeded toward the large building in the middle of the valley which sheltered all the workers. That was where he was most likely to find Grendolus.

As he entered the large, one story estate Zorthos' nostrils were assaulted by a pungent odor. It was a mixture of many different types of plants and vegetables, fertilizers, sweat, food being prepared and wet animal fur. The smell was nauseating.

He furtively glanced around, hoping he wouldn't have to search for long before he found who he was looking for. Grendolus was the caretaker of the entire project. Certainly one of the field workers would have rushed ahead to tell him one of the God-King's spiritual leaders and advisors was approaching.

To his left, a large silhouette filled a doorway. "What brings an enlightened one such a distance from comfort of Rhenngoth's sacred palace this day?" a deep, gravelly voice said from the shadows. "Here to check on progress of the latest crop, or does the God-King require something of a more specific nature from me?"

"I come on a private matter of grave importance," Zorthos answered, hoping that Grendolus would recognize his voice. "I would have words with you, away from prying ears."

From the pause and stiff body language, it appeared Grendolus had recognized his voice. His friend barked a couple of orders, and several workers and residents scurried frantically past Zorthos into the fields, none of them daring to make eye contact as they fled.

Once the building was clear of possible eavesdroppers, Grendolus said, "Then allow me to put concerns to rest, Zorthos."

Zorthos stepped closer to his old friend, concealing himself in the shadows. He reached up and drew back his hood. "Grendolus," he said with a warm grin, "The sight of you brings warm feelings to my heart."

"A sentiment I wish could be returned in kind," the beast-man answered. "Your presence here risks all I have, even in the entertaining of a simple conversation. And in the guise of a member of the Nyjaric Order no less! Does your brazenness know no bounds?"

"I know. Most humble apologies, old friend. I would not have come were it not of the utmost importance."

Grendolus hesitated for a moment, "I cannot promise the fulfillment of your request, but I will listen."

"I fear I need you to do more than offer a sympathetic ear," he said, trying not to betray the fear in his own voice. "I require the use of your special talents to cover the scent left in my wake from discovery by the Krathantor."

The answer was almost instantaneous, "No. Such an act would surely cost me everything. Apologies, old friend. I know I owe you much, but you ask me to betray Rhenngoth, Himself. This is something I cannot do."

Zorthos had been expecting such a reaction. "All I ask is that you listen to the circumstances and let reason guide your response. I assure you I ask you to keep nothing from the ears of Luziaph or Rhenngoth."

Grendolus hesitated once more and let out a huge sigh of resignation, "So be it. I promise only to hear your words. I offer nothing of the sort in the granting of further requests."

"You have my gratitude, old friend," he replied.

For the next half an hour Zorthos recounted everything he'd been through over the last few days. He told Grendolus the truth about Allen and Sarah being duped into coming to Datheron in a desperate attempt to save their lives. He told them about the battle he'd had with the Krathantor on Earth, about how he'd seriously injured two of them and Pythor was likely taking them to a healer, leaving a very small window of opportunity to put his plan into action. He explained how Sarah had been bitten by the vehectra snake and about leaving Allen and Sarah with another friend while she healed. When he finished his story, he waited while Grendolus digested the information.

"I can see the motives are pure in your desire for my help, Zorthos," Grendolus said after a long silence. "But understanding of the necessity to cover your trail from Krathantor's discovery yet eludes me. Why is protection of these two of such import?"

"Because of the prophecy," he answered, cryptically.

"You believe the coincidence of their heritage, that they hail from Earth, to mean one of them is the chosen one spoken of by Paragus in distant past; the one who will bring all life as it is known on Datheron to an end?"

"Certainty of such a claim yet remains inconclusive," he said. "But I believe the possibility in its truth lives, yes."

"Zorthos, you know as well as I that truth in such a claim would require one of them to have been sired by a citizen of Datheron," Grendolus said skeptically. When Zorthos only stared at him in response, Grendolus bore a look of grave concern. "Which one?" he asked, almost hesitantly.

Zorthos knew he was taking a dire risk divulging this piece of the puzzle, but he needed Grendulus' help. He had to take that chance. "The boy," he said. "He is my son."

The beast-man's jaw dropped. His eyes wide, he whispered, "Great Paragus . . ."

"Now you see the urgency in my request and the asking of it?" he pleaded. "I will not let them have my son. I need only to keep them away from him long enough—"

"Long enough to let the prophecy come to pass?" Grendolus accused.

"No," he countered immediately. "Long enough to return him to Earth so it cannot."

Grendolus stood to his full height of nearly seven feet and began pacing the room. "By the gods, Zorthos. By the gods! What you ask of me could be considered no less than high treason!"

"I know," he answered calmly; he had expected this reaction too. "That is why, upon completion of assistance, you will travel to Vardiston and confess."

"What!" Grendolus bellowed. "Has sanity fled your senses? You expect me to commit high treason, and then stand before Luziaph offering confession?"

Zorthos turned from where he'd been peering out the window and gently took Grendolus' forearm in his hand. He needed to calm him and stop his pacing. Before he continued he needed to be sure he had Grendolus' full attention.

"Listen to me," he said in a patient voice. "I would never purposely ask you to jump blindly in harm's way. You know the truth of this." When Grendolus nodded, he continued. "I ask that you use your ability to influence the weather to the purpose of creating a storm large enough to wipe away all trace of my reentry upon Datheronian soil. The location of my son must remain well-hidden. Pythor's talents, good as they are, will divine the proper origin of the storm and it will lead him here, to you. In this way, I can force him to come to me.

"While I remain here in wait, you will travel to Vardiston; admitting only that your part in the events was pressed by my hand, absent your own choice. You will offer proper explanation that the task was not done of your will and, upon my departure, you felt it your civic duty to inform him of my coercion straightaway. Tell him of my plans, that I lead Pythor into an ambush. Admit everything. He knows how powerful I am; you will not be punished. Please, Grendolus . . . This task cannot be accomplished absent your assistance."

Grendolus looked panicked and incredulous. For what seemed the longest several minutes of his life, Grendolus just stared blankly at the wall. His posture slumped as he considered Zorthos' request.

Finally, once again, their eyes met. "My participation demands but two conditions," he said in near a whisper.

"Give voice to them."

"Firstly," Grendolus began, "swear to me that you will send both Earthlings back from where they came."

"You have my word," Zorthos nodded. "What is the second?"

"The second," Grendolus said, his expression turning grim, "is that you must go with them, never to return. Sincerest apologies, old friend. I know I owe you much, but doing this risks all that I have labored so hard to build. I must know you cannot cause me any more trouble . . . and you will be with your son."

Zorthos smiled at his long-time acquaintance, "Nothing would please me more." He gestured toward the door, "Come. Let us bring our words to purpose. Time is in short supply."

13

COERCION

PYTHOR GRIMACED AS HE held his eyes closed in concentration. He searched unsuccessfully for Zorthos and the earthlings he'd harbored for far longer than he would have liked to admit. He knew hunting, distracted as he was, would be difficult for him, but he fumed as he left the Palace of Vardiston where his brother Krathantor lay at the mercy of that arrogant Triclopian. He knew Luziaph probably heard his thoughts of aggression, but he didn't care. Someone needed to put that insolent tyrant in his place and he hoped when the time came, Rhenngoth would award the privilege to him.

Pythor began his search returning to the location where Zorthos had shut the warp gate on them. Distracted as he was it took him a good long while to understand why he couldn't pick up their scent or locate a trail left behind, finally deciding that it had been washed away by a violent storm. Any hope of finding their track was long gone. He cursed his luck, unsure what his next move should be.

As he stood surveying his surroundings, he noticed something. Through his extremely heightened senses, he was able to determine that the storm seemed to have an alien point of origin; it had been generated to throw him off the trail.

"Clever," he mused aloud, though no one was there to hear him. Influencing the weather wasn't an ability he thought Zorthos to possess, but he knew the fugitive had to be behind it somehow.

Pythor quickly scanned the area for any trace of an energy signature which might have been left behind by the one who created the storm. He continued to scan diligently as he moved through the vegetation of the humid forest, stalking his way past large trees, through small clusters of bushes, and over thick roots protruding from the ground. The ground was still soggy from the storm and mud splashed his boots, covering them in little brown flecks as he moved. As he continued his search, pushing a branch out of his way, he came upon a skriff hound hanging from a tree by its neck. Pythor didn't need to wonder how such a thing had come to be.

It was nearly half an hour more before he finally found what he was looking for. He didn't know how to manipulate the weather either, but he knew something as powerful as that storm must have been would leave behind traces of the energy used to conjure it. Though he'd reached the origin point of the storm, there was something strange about it . . . it hadn't been Zorthos after all.

In the area where the storm had been instigated, Pythor detected the echo of an energy signature left behind by its creator. He was surprised to smell traces of Voldehyde. Apparently Zorthos did have a friend or two left willing to help him. Pythor grinned inwardly. He at least had a place to resume his search. He would track down this Voldehyde traitor and force him to relinquish Zorthos' location. He silently hoped he would find a challenge in it, but wasn't about to get his hopes up too high; most on Datheron didn't dare take on an Elite member of the Krathantor. Most likely, he would corner the culprit and get the information he sought without any real effort.

He followed the path left behind by his new target and exited the woods near a river bank. The trail led west along the river's edge for quite a while before it crossed the river and began to run north. There was a split in the path, as if the one who'd left the trail had somehow gone in two directions, but Pythor was too good at what he did to be fooled by such a tactic. The energy signature that headed north across the river was stronger, if only slightly, meaning it was the true path. Whether the Voldehyde he followed had gone further and circled back, or had been trying to deliberately confuse any who would follow him, he couldn't tell. But the echo which led north was definitely stronger, and he wasn't about to waste time chasing the wrong ghosts; he needed to end this game as quickly as he could. He wasn't sure how much longer Borograth and Sepharus could hold out without the attention of a master healer.

Pythor took a short running start and, in a single leap, cleared the expansive distance across the river. He landed gracefully on the opposite bank with little effort.

Now that he didn't have to traverse the harsh conditions of a forest as he hunted, he moved much quicker. He was nearly sprinting as he continued to follow his course. Wind and grass whipped past him in a rush, and he could feel himself gaining on his target. It wouldn't be long now, and he would be back on Zorthos' trail. He would be one step closer to exacting vengeance on Zorthos and getting the help his two friends needed.

Almost before he realized it, he reached his new target. Ahead in the distance he could see a lone Voldehyde making his way north; cutting through fields, leaping small hills, and ignoring the path completely. The Voldehyde didn't appear to be trying to hide; he appeared to be running with purpose.

Pythor sprinted in full force. In short order, he closed in on the beast-man who might deliver the Arena Champion to him. As he came within a few meters of his target, he leapt high in the air, twisting his body as he flew, and landed directly in the Voldehyde's path. He stood there, his arms crossed as his target slid to a stop before him.

The beast was as large in girth as any Voldehyde he had ever encountered, if a little taller. Panic covered the furry features of the Voldehyde's face.

Pythor grinned wickedly at him. "What carries you at such a pace?" he taunted.

The beast-man hesitated a moment, as if unsure how to respond. "I travel to Vardiston."

Pythor mentally stumbled. If this creature had been the one who helped cover Zorthos' tracks, why would he be heading directly for Luziaph's city? For the moment, he decided to ignore that particular quandary.

"Where is Zorthos?" he demanded.

"He hides at my plantation, among the workers," the Voldehyde offered freely.

Again he was halted in his line of questioning; he hadn't been expecting such a direct answer. This was quickly becoming a confusing encounter. "Give way to your meaning."

"My meaning is as it sounds," the Voldehyde said sardonically.

Rather than rise to the bait, Pythor realized he needed to extract more information from this beast-like creature. He could punish him for his flippant tongue after he learned what he needed to know. "Explain!" he barked angrily.

"No."

Pythor was stunned. It was unheard of to refuse the direct request of an Elite Krathantor. "What?" he demanded.

"Explanation will be given to Luziaph alone," the Voldehyde said assuredly. "You are welcome to offer escort if you so wish. But if Zorthos remains the objective, then duty should find you at the plantation south-west of Vardiston. He awaits your arrival in the large building near the center of the crop fields. He has dressed himself in the garb of one of Rhenngoth's chosen spiritual leaders."

Pythor gawked skeptically. "What name do you go by?"

The Voldehyde glanced around, as if nervous there were more Krathantor surrounding him. "Grendolus," he offered at last. "But nothing more will part from my tongue until I have reached Vardiston. I have provided the location of your target. Now leave me be. I need to see Luziaph."

"To what purpose, might I ask?" he challenged.

Grendolus hesitated before responding. "Urgent matters of business lend speed to my efforts in reaching him."

He continued to eye him suspiciously. "What urgent matters? Of what do you speak?"

Grendolus stared blankly in response.

Limited though his talents in telepathy were, he attempted to retrieve the information directly from Grendolus' mind. After only a couple of moments, he felt his consciousness being thrust back. Grendolus had blocked his advance.

"Attempting to breach the walls of thought?" Grendolus said, tapping a finger to his temple as he spoke. "I fear you have yet to obtain the level of skill required to accomplish such a task on me. I share knowledge of telepathy; enough, at least, to keep your pathetic attempts at bay."

Fuming over his failure to breach Grendolus' mind, Pythor silently considered his options. If this creature was telling the truth, he knew right where to find Zorthos. Voldehydes, however, were not renowned for their amiable nature, especially toward other races. Were he to head directly to the plantation, he could very well be walking into a trap. Or it could even be that this overgrown fur-ball was purposely giving him a false location so he could tell Luziaph where Zorthos really was, claiming a reward for himself. If that were the case, Luziaph would have no more need to keep Borograth and Sepharus alive; nor would he hesitate in eliminating them.

"Have it your way," he said with contempt. "I shall take you to Luziaph myself." His best course of action was to take Grendolus back to Luziaph and turn him in for aiding Zorthos' escape.

***

Grendolus, who had seemed just as eager to get his confession over with as he was, slowed his pace as they entered the grand courtyard to the Palace of Vardiston. Pythor gaped at the gruesome statues which adorned the walkway to the palace doors. There didn't seem to be any rhyme or reason to the type of statues on display. There were several depicting humans, several others resembling Voldehydes and various other races found on Datheron. Even the material used seemed to be random. Some were ordinary looking stone, while others appeared to be made of obsidian or marble, though all of the statues shared the same horrified expression.

Pythor urged his charge forward. "Keep moving," he ordered.

Grendolus nodded and began moving forward again.

As they approached the two guards stationed outside the palace entrance, the Triclopian who had taunted him before bore an expression of amused contempt. He appeared to have another snide comment in the works. Before he could share it, however, Pythor gave him a look that would have melted the stone statues they passed, letting his left fist begin to glow with the emerald flame of his kin. The Triclopian seemed to think better of his prepared remark and averted his eyes back to the courtyard.

When they entered the main hall, he noticed that the mess Luziaph had made punishing Gazianna had been cleaned with the exception of the damaged statue. Small bits of rubble still rested at its base, the statues around it appearing aghast at witnessing one of their brothers in pieces.

Grendolus missed a step when he noticed that the procession of sculptures continued past the gardens into the main hall. "I had forgotten his obsession with these macabre works of art," he said, his voice nearly a whisper.

"They are in no way art," he retorted. "Keep moving."

They had only taken a few steps forward when Pythor heard a voice he recognized as Luziaph's emitting from the shadows.

"You return sooner than expected," Luziaph said, emerging from a shadowed doorway. He was no longer wearing his purple cloak, but that didn't take away from the menacing edge his presence lent the room. "Your task has once again fallen short of completion. Concern for your fellow bounty hunters appears lacking as your hands upon arrival are without Zorthos, offering another in his stead."

Pythor felt as if he tripped over something that wasn't there. He hadn't sensed Luziaph in the room. He knew

Triclopians had a natural affinity for telepathy, but to cloak one's self completely required total mastery. He hadn't realized just how skilled Luziaph was in his native craft until that moment.

"The search for Zorthos is precisely what has forced premature return," he said. "This Voldehyde claims knowledge of Zorthos' current location, yet refuses to—"

"If such knowledge has already been uncovered," Luziaph interjected, "then why does your presence burden me instead of his?"

"Because," said Grendolus, frankly, "he does not trust the information proffered; prejudice taints his reason. He fears I send him into an ambush."

Pythor scowled at Grendolus. "This Voldehyde conspired to cover the trail left by Zorthos through means of casting the entire area beneath a pall of a massive storm, refusing to offer explanation for such action," he added.

Luziaph seemed not to have heard him. His gaze never left Grendolus. After a long moment, seemingly assessing the beast-man, Luziaph's lips contorted in a tight grin. "And does the Krathantor walk into ambush?"

"He does," Grendolus answered quickly; Pythor was shocked at the admission. "My presence here is to the purpose of offering explanation to you, Lord Luziaph, not this bounty-hunting scum. I offer assurances that my actions to cover the trail of Zorthos came at his command, through direct threat against me. Coercion his purpose; remaining alive long enough to inform you of such things, mine. He hides now at the plantation I patron in the name of Rhenngoth, for Nentalia and Vardiston. He awaits not only my return, but Pythor's arrival as well, to the purpose of catching Pythor off balance when he arrives."

Something about Grendolus' story didn't seem quite right to him and Pythor was feeling edgier by the second.

He knew he hadn't told Grendolus his name and wondered how the furry oaf had gotten it. Perhaps he'd learned it through their brief telepathic encounter earlier. It could be that while he had failed in retrieving anything from Grendolus' mind, the beast of a man could have possibly been probing his mind at the same time and succeeded. Though he felt certain he would've noticed such an intrusion. He wasn't completely sure why, but something about Grendolus' story was sounding alarms in the back of his mind.

"Such admission could be considered treasonous," Luziaph said smoothly. "Why would you risk it?"

"Please," Grendolus said, raising his hands in supplication. "I seek no trouble, nor reward. The choice was removed from my hands. I did only as I thought I must to survive long enough to make explanation. Also to request that his presence be removed from my plantation to the purpose of seeing Vardiston's needs once again well-filled."

Luziaph placed his hands behind his back as he considered Grendolus. The armor of his station reflected little glinting points of light from the sun-filled windows. Luziaph's third eye twitched in his direction while the others remained on Grendolus; a talent Pythor had always found unnerving. At last Luziaph exhaled a slow, deep breath and spoke:

"I sense your capabilities in the ways of telepathy," the Triclopian Proctus said. "I offer you one chance for amends . . . Submit to search of mind, that I might ascertain the truth for myself. Make no mistake; I stand a Grandmaster in the craft and will have the information I seek, regardless of acquiescence. But offer entry willingly and see the situation resolved with haste, and minimal pain to you."

Grendolus' eyebrow twitched. He hesitated.

"Unless, of course," Luziaph added, "you are lying, or fear discovery of other improper intent."

"I have nothing to hide," Grendolus said defensively, "But I refuse the surrender of my mind to you when I came willingly offering the truth."

Luziaph's eyes—all three of them—squinted slightly, but otherwise his face showed no reaction. "Then I fear your services are no longer required."

In a fraction of an instant, Luziaph had Grendolus' snout clamped firmly in the palm of his hand. As quick as he was, Phythor could barely see Luziaph's movement. The speed of it was dizzying. Grendolus struggled mightily, but Luziaph must have gripped his mind too. The beast's size didn't seem to matter, even though Luziaph only had him with one of his hands.

Grendolus let out muffled shrieks of terror or pain; Pythor couldn't tell which. The sound Voldehydes made in the throes of death was horrifying. His entire body went rigid, as if stricken with rigor mortis, and slowly his voice began to sound as if it was coming from a great distance. All at once he stopped moving, and the fur all over his body began changing pigment. There was an audible crackling, mixed with a sound which seemed to be stones scraping together. It was then Pythor finally understood Luziaph's fascination with his grotesque sculptures. They weren't molded from stone; they were actual citizens of Datheron who must have displeased Luziaph, being turned to stone for their apparent crimes.

That Luziaph had then decorated his palace with them spoke volumes to Pythor about Luziaph's perverse, Triclopian perspectives. It also offered explanation as to how he had bested Krylath. He had known the previous Proctus of Vardiston and knew him to be quite formidable.

At last Luziaph removed his hand from the now stone-solid Grendolus, and turned his three-eyed glare on Pythor. For several long moments, he said nothing.

"Such a fate awaits Sepharus and Borograth should you fail me again," Luziaph said at last. The menace in his voice alone could have turned someone to stone.

Pythor forced himself to sound more confident than he felt. "What purpose caused you to petrify him before you had the truth from him? Punishment of this nature, absent validity of one's guilt, could likewise be considered treasonous."

Luziaph laughed. "I had the truth from him before the two of you even entered my palace. He was lying. He was counted as trusted friend to Zorthos and did as he did out of cowardice, not altruism."

Not being a master of telepathy, Pythor had no way to know for sure if Luziaph was telling the truth about Grendolus. Luziaph probably knew that, which was why he seemed to be having so much fun with the declaration. An odd smile covered Luziaph's face as he took a few steps toward him, making him more than a little uncomfortable.

"Now," Luziaph said, "make haste to the plantation of which he spoke, and do not return again without Zorthos."

"I thought you said he was lying," he said, his eyes still resting upon the look of fear immortalized on Grendolus' furry face.

"Only about his motives. The part about Zorthos' location remains true."

Pythor turned to leave. He suddenly couldn't wait to be away from this wretched Triclopian's presence. He hadn't made it ten paces when Luziaph spoke again.

"Pythor . . ." Luziaph said airily.

He flinched and turned his head slightly, without turning completely around, to show he was listening. He couldn't see Luziaph behind him in his peripheral vision, and was shocked when he realized the man's voice next came from directly in front of him. He wasn't entirely sure how Luziaph had gotten in front of him so quickly.

"Do yourself a favor," Luziaph said venomously. "Do not fail me again. And remove the thought from your head that you ever stood a chance against me. Take six of my best men with you and bring me Zorthos."

"I do not require your help," he said as he pushed his way past Luziaph. "Nor do I want it. I can bring back Zorthos on my own."

"Yes, your level of success up to this point offers clear evidence of such a claim," Luziaph said contemptuously. "It was not an offer; it was an order. Take six of my royal guard with you. This time there will be no mistakes upon which to lay your failure."

Pythor wanted to protest further, but after the display he'd just witnessed thought better of it. He would do his brothers no good if he was dead.

14

DECEPTION

MOVING WITH PURPOSE, Pythor led the six soldiers away from the palace of Vardiston. He hadn't been at all pleased he wasn't given a choice in the matter, but he'd decided to stifle his objections for the time being. After all, Luziaph had told him to gather six troops to take with him; he hadn't told him which he specifically needed to take. Therefore, he had just grabbed random guards as he made his way toward the palace doors. It wouldn't be his fault if they couldn't keep up with him once outside the palace gates.

As he exited the palace, he had purposely made sure to recruit the Triclopian guard who had felt it necessary to goad him—someone of higher station. If ever there was a legitimate chance of teaching the piece of vermin a lesson in proper manners, it would be an excursion away from the palace and away from Luziaph's prying eyes. To his surprise, most of the guards he'd chosen had been able to keep up with his swift pace; only two lagged behind.

The sun arched its descent toward the western horizon as they began their trek, forcing him and those behind to squint slightly as they moved. It continued to set as they raced on, almost in silent challenge of their efforts; as if it was lowering to guard their destination.

Pythor couldn't recall having been to the specified plantation before. Being a bounty hunter for the God-King had taken him to some interesting places to be sure—often to one of the moons circling Datheron and occasionally to other worlds—but there were many places he'd never had to tread. He'd always considered it beneath him to concern himself with the matter of slaves, or the fields in which some of them worked. He found it amusing that Zorthos would choose to hide himself at a plantation, since he would most likely end up working in one after facing Rhenngoth's judgment, if he wasn't condemned to death for his transgressions.

As much as Pythor ached to claim the glory of besting the Arena Champion, he found himself distracted from the task. While Zorthos was the one who had incapacitated his colleagues, Luziaph was the one who was using their injuries as a means to control him. It was Luziaph who would end their lives, turning them to stone, if he didn't do exactly as commanded. The thought brought his blood to a boil. With the brand of manipulation he'd chosen, Luziaph was only proving the vile nature of his kind.

Thoughts of Borograth and Sepharus suffering swirled through his mind, causing his anger to swell from his thoughts to his very soul. He could feel the constricting rage clutching at his chest, begging for release. With thoughts of vengeance consuming him, his gait dragged. The soldiers keeping pace with him slowed to a stop just behind him. He felt on the verge of exploding.

To his right, the Triclopian guard drifted up behind him. He turned all three eyes on Pythor condescendingly. "What is wrong?" he taunted. "Do you need one of us to show you the way?"

"Mind your tongue, Triclopian," Pythor spat without returning the other's gaze. "Lest you see it removed from your head!"

The Triclopian guard gave him a grin that sorely tested his restraint. "You would not dare such a thing, surrounded as you are by six of Luziaph's most loyal," the three-eyed man taunted. "Even if you were that stupid, you would quickly be dragged before Luziaph to face judgment for crimes committed."

Pythor was quickly losing his grasp on self control.

"That would, of course, be after he has disposed of the other two Gorrlock scum he holds back at the palace as leverage," the Triclopian added with a smug grin.

Faster than the Triclopian could respond, Pythor slammed the heel of his boot into the other's sternum. The three-eyed pest bounced off a tree fifteen feet away with a sickening thud. In an instant he was standing over the arrogant antagonist. Slowly, but deliberately, he brought his hands in front of himself, cupping them horizontally across from one another. Reaching deep within himself, he called forth the energy of the one skill he had truly mastered. The air around his fingers began to heat drastically as it gathered and compressed between his palms. With a thought, he ignited the compressed energy, bringing to life a violent looking ball of fire. It burned an intensely bright green, casting emerald glares across the black body of his armor.

He extended his right arm toward his helpless victim, aiming the living, liquid flame directly at his face. The fireball, floating mere inches away from his extended fingertips, made a low hiss, as if begging to be released. Emerald sparks dripped from the living flame.

From the corners of his eyes, he could see the other royal guards swarming in around him. A couple of them had swords pointed in his direction, one held a spear level with his head, and the others seemed to be attempting to gather energy of their own to counter his threat against their colleague.

The Triclopian at his feet no longer looked sure of himself; he stared up at Pythor, all three eyes wide with fear.

"Make another remark such as that," Pythor said venomously, "and find yourself reduced to ashes!"

Pleased with the results of his assault, and without saying another word, he extinguished the flame, denying it the satisfaction of being loosed. He took a couple steps back from the guard he'd nearly destroyed, and gave one of the others the opportunity to help the fallen Triclopian to his feet. He had desperately wanted to relieve that Triclopian villain of his life, but he didn't want to risk doing anything to upset Luziaph . . . at least not until he'd secured the release of his brothers.

Pythor took several more steps from the six royal guards of Vardiston, carefully watching their movement over his shoulder. As he turned back around to face them, all of their eyes were watching him with disdain. Two of the guards were Saurothians; a race of lizard-like men with sharp minds and fangs to match. Saurothians, while fiercely loyal once their allegiance was earned, weren't ones to offer it willingly to anyone, of their race or not. However, once a bond was established with one, it was far more difficult to break than it was to earn it.

Two of them among Luziaph's royal guards had made Pythor curious enough to select them to come along. The rest of the guards, aside from the one Triclopian, were human; one with a darker pigment to his skin, the other's pale. They all looked as if they wanted to tear his heart out.

"Let us come to common ground," he commanded. "The six of you may have sworn allegiance to Luziaph, but out here you answer to me. A task has been set before us and my command alone gives life to your action while it remains incomplete. Our mission is the locating and capture of current Arena Champion, Zorthos."

At that proclamation several of the guard's expressions paled considerably, the loathing expressed toward him disappearing with the announcement of their task. They took a collective breath, as if hesitant to continue their quest. A look of genuine uncertainty passed among them.

"And let me assure you," he continued, "Zorthos is dangerous in the extreme. If any hope of survival yet lives for any one of you, it will come only through deference to me! You will follow any order given you! And I do not recommend the testing of my patience again! Are we of a singular purpose?" He glared deliberately at the Triclopian guard as he spoke the last sentence.

Without another look and not awaiting their agreement, Pythor turned and marched away. "Then let us press forward," he said over his shoulder.

***

Breaching the top of a steep hill, Pythor and his followers were able to see the lush valley below them which showcased a vast array of crops. Storm clouds were moving in from the North West, almost as if in mourning over the loss of the caretaker of these fields. As he stood overlooking the plantation which offered Vardiston and Nentalia the grand majority of their respective food supply,

Pythor's thoughts momentarily went to Grendolus and the horrifying end he'd suffered for wanting nothing more than to help a friend. He knew it was a fate he would share, for the same reasons, unless he could find a way to bring Zorthos back to Luziaph alive.

Knowing what Grendolus' mastered ability had been, he could only assume the beast had been put in charge of these fields for a reason. After all, what better way was there to regulate the environment for the specific purpose of growing plants than to be able to control the climate in which they are grown? The ability to manipulate weather would guarantee they would always have the right amount of rain, there would never be floods to overrun the crops, and they would be able to grow year-round. Pythor silently wondered if Luziaph had even taken that into consideration before torturously ending the Voldehyde's life.

He pointed to the large building in the center of the fields, "That building is where our target awaits us."

"What is your meaning in saying he awaits us?" One of the Saurothians asked in a raspy, guttural voice. "He knows of our approach?"

"Most likely," he answered without turning to face him. "Actions leading to our arrival here were set in motion by his hand, though he most likely expects me to be absent accompaniment. I am sure he did not anticipate the odds being seven to one in my favor."

"Then we have at least that much on our side," the other Saurothian said in a similar guttural voice.

"Do not delude yourselves into thinking this will be easy, or that our numbers offer advantage." He said as he turned to face them. "Zorthos is incredibly dangerous. He is not the only one born of his bloodline to bear the title of Arena Champion. His mother, Divina, stands one of a select few among history to be crowned Arena Champion twice. Zorthos comes by his abilities naturally, and has

234

been trained exceptionally well. Do not underestimate him."

All six guards exchanged worried looks as they considered his words.

Finally, after a long moment of uncertainty, the Triclopian guard stepped forward and spoke for the rest. "Tell us then, of what does your plan consist?"

***

It hadn't taken Pythor long to come up with a plan and explain it to the others. After a very brief conversation, he learned one of the Saurothians had the ability to blend in with his surroundings, becoming virtually invisible. The lizard-like creature wasn't a master, but had been proficient enough to sneak out ahead of the rest and take stock of the building's layout.

Once he knew how many entrances there were, and roughly where Zorthos could be found inside the building, he'd quickly laid out his plan to the others. There were four entrances to the building; two on the northern side, one on the south, and one on the east. Those entry points didn't include windows, but he didn't see Zorthos as one who would jump out a window to get away. Zorthos was powerful enough, and arrogant enough in his ability, he probably assumed he would just walk out the front door once he was done with Pythor.

Pythor explained that the last time he'd seen Zorthos, the man had had a Triaga clamped to his scalp. He also told them it hadn't prevented Zorthos from closing a dimensional gateway. The others exchanged a look of confusion at hearing this. He made sure they knew that just because Zorthos had a Triaga affixed to his head the last time he'd seen him didn't necessarily mean that he still did, or that he was any less deadly were that still the case.

The Saurothian confirmed that Zorthos had apparently found a way to remove the burden of the Triaga, as he hadn't seen it on the man's head while scouting ahead. He had nodded at the information, once again assuring those with him that Zorthos was as resourceful and cunning opponent as they had ever faced.

Once he was sure they were all clear on their parts, and on which exits they were to cover, he led them quietly down the hill and into the fields. The sky overhead had become completely shrouded in storm clouds, casting their surroundings into a surreal darkness. If he hadn't known better, he would have thought Grendolus had come back from the grave to offer Zorthos one last bit of assistance in his plan to escape.

Pythor stayed back, ducking behind a tree as he watched the others silently move to their designated places. He mentally steeled himself for the conflict he was about to face. For the sake of Sepharus and Borograth, he had to defeat Zorthos and bring him back to Vardiston. For a moment, he foolishly wondered if he would be able to convince Zorthos to join him in his revenge on Luziaph. He knew Zorthos had no love for the Triclopian Proctus. After brief consideration, however, he dismissed the idea; if anything, Zorthos hated the Krathantor as much as he hated Luziaph. The man would never willingly join him, even to reach a common goal.

Still . . . it couldn't hurt to make the proposal. If Zorthos did say no, their situation would be no different. If he was going to attempt it, however, he would have to do so in a way none of those with him would understand. He found himself reflecting on a time he'd known the Arena Champion as an ally and silently thanked Zorthos for offering instruction in the native tongue of Earth, as well as a few others from the immediate star system.

Once the others were in place, he stood and walked purposefully toward the main entrance of the large, one-story building. He furtively glanced at the Triclopian guarding the front entrance as he moved past. He stopped roughly ten feet shy of the building and bellowed Zorthos' name.

Without warning a large chain burst from the doorway, missing Pythor's head by inches. Had his reflexes not been what they were, he very well might have been decapitated by such an attack. An instant later the chain began rapidly retracting back through the open door. He turned with the motion of the chain, barely having time to note that the end of it held a large, double-pronged hook. The hook latched onto him, the prongs digging deep into his ebony chest plate, pulling him toward the building and through the doorway with blinding speed. Once inside, he ricocheted off the opposing wall with bone-shattering force. Splinters and dust exploded all around him at the impact.

As he lay on the ground trying desperately to bring his surroundings into focus, he could hear Zorthos taunting him. He couldn't quite make out the words, but the tone used was clear enough.

Finally able to bring his eyes into focus, he looked up at the silhouette standing over him. "Wait!" he said in English, hoping to forestall Zorthos' advance and knowing the others with him wouldn't be able to understand it. "I beg pause of you, Zorthos."

"Hesitation can only bring death," Zorthos replied in their native language, bringing the chain over his head with violent intent.

Pythor felt chunks of wood rain across his back as he leapt to escape impact of Zorthos' chain on the wall where he had just been.

Rage threatening to consume him, he rounded on Zorthos bringing a large yellow-green fireball to life in the palm of his hand. He leveled the flame at Zorthos, aiming for the man's head. Emerald highlights danced across the features of Zorthos' face. Through the new light added to the room by his will, he saw Zorthos spinning the chain wildly behind him, hesitating. He noticed the Saurothian had spoken the truth; Zorthos was no longer encumbered by the Triaga he had been captured with on Earth.

"Just pause a moment to hear my words," he demanded, still speaking in the tongue of Earth. "If after that you still wish to fight, I will take pride in obliging."

Zorthos eyed him cautiously and slowed the spinning chain. "Speak."

Pythor pulled himself to a standing position, never once losing aim. "You left quite the mark on Sepharus and Borograth," he began. "They may not be graced with recovery."

"Stop wasting my time, Krathantor," Zorthos replied, finally following his lead in the language he used.

"Luziaph holds them as leverage, to bend me to his purpose," he said quickly. "He refuses to offer healing until I deposit you at his feet."

"That is none of my concern," Zorthos stated flatly.

"Perhaps not, but it could offer salvation to your current predicament."

Zorthos squinted suspiciously, "Bring yourself to plain words or see this conversation ended!"

Pythor began walking, ever so slowly, toward the exit as he continued. He wanted to have a clear way out in case things got physical again before he could finish his proposal. "You see, I know there is no love lost between you and that Triclopian filth; your feelings against him rivaling that of me and my kin. And at this point, my only concern lies with their convalescence. We could find common ground in this."

Recognition dawned in Zorthos' eyes. "You cannot be serious."

"I have never been otherwise when it comes to matters of brotherhood. As much as it would please me to gain reward for your capture, I long even more for that three-eyed waste of flesh to be shown his true place! With our combined level of skill, victory would be assured, and my brothers would receive much needed aid."

Zorthos abruptly caught the end the spinning chain. "What in the name of Paragus fosters belief in such a course of action or that I would even consider taking part?"

Pythor lowered his hand, extinguishing the liquid flame, as he considered Zorthos. He wanted to make sure the man was listening closely. "You offer help to my purpose, and I will return favor in kind. Those Earthlings you care so much for will be forgotten, as will your whereabouts. In years past we worked alongside one another. Memory has not completely faded of a time when trust yet lived among us, when we Krathantor called you brother. Lend me your trust once more and see both our desires well satisfied."

Zorthos tilted his head toward the entrance, "And what of the six who arrived at your side, and yet await outcome to current conversation?"

He was only momentarily surprised that Zorthos knew about the guards he'd brought with him. "We kill them all. They yet remain loyal to Luziaph and would give effort to hindering our purpose, but none stand a match for either of our abilities."

"Allow me to probe your mind," Zorthos blurted after another moment's consideration.

"What?" Pythor retorted incredulously.

"Surface thoughts only," Zorthos added quickly, "so I might divine the truth of such an offer."

Pythor paused. Opening one's mind to another willingly, required a certain level of trust. Zorthos was asking him to take the first leap of faith, to trust him first. He was putting him in a very precarious position. Doing this could easily prove his intent, but it could also deliver Zorthos certain victory. Once inside his mind, Zorthos could incapacitate him with minimal effort; it very well could be the last thing he ever did.

"No?" Zorthos began spinning the chain again. "Then prepare to become one with Sythika!"

"Wait!" he pleaded. "If I prove the truth of my intent, do you promise to help me destroy Luziaph?"

"On the condition that passage back to Earth is provided for me and the children, and memory of the last few days is removed, word of them never to part your lips again."

Pythor hesitated a moment longer. He would be committing treason, himself, by opening a warp gate back to Earth. Not only would he be breaking the law by letting the Earthlings leave with knowledge of Datheron, he would be aiding the escape of a fugitive; one he had been charged with capturing. He hoped he was doing the right thing. He knew he would likely be put to death when the God-King found out about his involvement in Zorthos' escape. Ultimately, he decided his life was a small price to pay to save the lives of two others. But mostly he didn't really feel like he had a choice.

"So be it," he said. "Bargain struck. However, the responsibility of future pursuit will not fall upon my shoulders. You know Rhenngoth's appetite for vengeance knows no bounds."

"Understood," Zorthos said, once again catching the hook to stop the chain from spinning.

Reluctantly, Pythor closed his eyes and opened himself to Zorthos. He knew it would only be a matter of moments before Zorthos would ascertain the validity of his intent. Then, at long last, he would have his revenge on Luziaph. He would be able to get the help Sepharus and Borograth needed.

As he stood there, eyes closed, waiting for the process to begin, he felt a sharp agonizing pain take him. His entire body, down to the marrow in his bones, felt as if it was on fire. He crumpled to the ground, furious at himself for trusting Zorthos. He heard an ear-splitting scream as he fell, only realizing after he'd impacted the floor that it was his own voice. He struggled through the pain enough to open his eyes. He wanted one last look at Zorthos, wanted to curse him for betraying his trust.

That's when he saw him. There, crumpled in a convulsing heap on the ground in front of him, was Zorthos. He seemed to be in as much shock and pain as he was. Zorthos stared at him through the torment of it with the same loathing. It didn't make sense. If Zorthos wasn't the one doing this to him, then who was?

Through the agony enveloping him, he watched as Zorthos lost consciousness. Though he was no longer awake, his body didn't stop convulsing violently. Pythor glanced down to see his own body shaking in much the same fashion, despite his best efforts to regain control.

After what felt like an eternity of torture, the pain finally abated. Pythor's entire body felt like mush. He could barely roll his head from side to side. As he lay there, desperately trying not to vomit, and fearing his body couldn't handle any more physical strain, he heard a voice he recognized burst into soft laughter.

He rolled his head to the side enough to see Luziaph standing over him, an arrogant smile dominating his features.

"Somehow I knew you would not follow given command," Luziaph said condescendingly. "Fortunately experience, as well as skill, reveals the treachery beneath your miserable Gorrlock exterior. And such formalities have been appropriately accounted for."

At that moment, Pythor wanted nothing more than to melt the flesh from Luziaph's bones. Unfortunately, as it was, he could barely move his eyes to watch the three-eyed dictator standing over him. It hurt tremendously to even do that. Though he couldn't reach up to check, he was sure blood was oozing from his ears.

Luziaph took a step closer to him. The smile left his face, replaced by a scowl of such intensity it almost made him flinch. "It appears your services are no longer required!" Luziaph spat.

And then Luziaph brought his boot down toward Pythor's face.

15

STUPEFACTION

FOR THE NEXT SEVERAL days, when he wasn't sitting at Sarah's side, Allen spent his time trying to make sense of the tomes in Malacus' basement. Although he wasn't quite sure how he'd done it, he knew he'd slammed his great-grandfather against the wall with his mind the day he arrived. He desperately wanted to recapture the sensation he felt when he realized he had actually used telekinesis. But it seemed no matter how hard he tried, or how many different ways he attempted it, he couldn't figure out how he'd done it or how to recreate it.

Malacus, true to his word, gave him a few lessons in Datheronian infrastructure and the delicate balance it took to maintain it. He explained there were six major continents, each with a Proctus. The largest continent was Thugrod, where Vardiston, the capitol city of the region, was located. Allan also learned that it was proper to address the Proctus for the capital city from which he reigned, rather than the region. They each had direct command over their continent, while the God-King had dominion over the entire planet. There were originally six sentient species on the planet, but over time the civilization had invited other races to the planet and now there were over one hundred.

Allen was reminded that the gravity on this planet was five times that of Earth's, which was why he'd nearly been crushed before Zorthos had clothed him in the specially fabricated garb. He'd also learned that the unique aura enveloping the planet of the gods was responsible for more than just the opportunity to learn any ability one desired; it was likewise the reason for the flow of time as well as the sky's color according to Malacus.

It was a lot to take in. From what he could tell, there were a lot of corresponding similarities between the way the government on this planet functioned and the way a monarchy on Earth functioned, but there were also a lot of differences. Everyone had to have a specific skill—which on this planet was a supernatural ability of some sort—in order to provide a living for themselves and their family. Everyone had a duty to perform, and no one was above the God-King's law.

There was no need for a judicial system on this planet, since telepathy existed here. If the guilt of someone was in question, they were simply presented to a Grandmaster telepath who would search their mind for the truth. Seekers of this particular brand of truth evidently belonged to a group called the Nyjaric Order. If the crime was severe enough, the consequence was death to be administered immediately, or to fight as a gladiator on the sands of the Arena in front of a crowd. Only very seldom were citizens incarcerated for a crime, and even in such cases it was typically only until further punishment could be decided upon. Usually, if a crime didn't constitute a death sentence, there was a penance mandated by one of the Proctus. More often than not, that meant paying a steep fine, becoming an indentured servant for a time, or worst of all, sent to the Pits of Faustuum to mine the minerals used in the currency of this world. If one was unfortunate enough to be incarcerated, odds were there would be much pain before they were released, if ever that happened. Occasionally citizens were given the choice to fight in the Arena to earn enough money to repay the debt, but since such a fate needed to be requested by the condemned it rarely occurred. It horrified him the way life seemed expendable on this planet, and the more he learned about the way things functioned here, the more he wondered why Malacus was so reluctant to want them to change.

Malacus hadn't begun teaching Allen how to read the language of Datheron yet, but that hadn't stopped him from sifting through some of the books at his disposal anyway. The way he saw it; if he could understand the spoken language it shouldn't be too difficult to learn how to read it. It wasn't nearly as easy as he'd hoped. Without some basis for comparison, he was completely lost.

When he wasn't helping Malacus with some mindless task or learning the intricacies of the way life on this planet functioned, he was keeping a constant vigil at Sarah's side. She hadn't woken up yet, but the color had at least returned to her face and she was breathing normally. Twice a day, Malacus would visit the basement to administer a concoction he assured Allen would keep her on the road to recovery. Sometimes Malacus would let him give her the proper dosage, instructing him not only in how to administer it, but how to make it as well.

Whenever he instructed Allen, Malacus made him speak in the alien tongue, which he had learned was called Ancient Olyphitarian. Apparently it was the language of the original God-King, and had survived as the common language learned by all who came to the planet for thousands of years. Malacus was more insistent that Allen become fluent in the language than he was about anything else he taught him, explaining to him that almost no one spoke the language native to Earth; it was considered taboo. He hadn't been able to get Malacus to tell him any more about the prophecy he'd been discussing with Zorthos, or why being from Earth was such a bad thing, but the last thing he wanted was trouble. Rather than create a debate over it, he just did his best to appease the old man.

As one day drifted into another, Allen wondered how his mother was doing without him. It still broke his heart that he hadn't gotten the chance to say goodbye to her. He missed her terribly and wished there was some way to at least let her know that he was all right. It hadn't even quite been two weeks yet on this planet, but he knew it had to be far longer than that on Earth since he'd disappeared. Still, he refused to believe there was no way to reach her. He clung tightly to the words his new-found father had told him about being able to learn to accomplish anything on this planet. Even if he couldn't give her back the time she'd lost with him, Allen vowed to himself he would find a way to let her know that he was alive and well.

The sun was high in the sky one afternoon as he took in as much of his surroundings as possible while following his great-grandfather away from the cabin he'd slowly been trying to accept as home. Malacus hadn't yet told him where they were going; only that it would be the first step in his physical training. They walked about two hundred yards away from the cabin before Malacus came to a stop in front of him and turned around.

"This should be distance enough," Malacus said, more to himself than to him. He gazed over Allen's shoulder toward the cabin. "Yes, this will offer good first trial."

The old man hadn't explained to him where they were going or what they would be doing, so naturally Allen was confused when he looked around and saw nothing. They were standing in the middle of a field of the same shin-length grass he and Zorthos had traversed to reach this place the night Sarah was bitten. There was nothing else near them. The closest tree was nearly a hundred yards to his left, he could see no workout equipment, and they'd brought nothing with them.

"This is it?" Allen asked in English. "This is where you were leading me?"

Allen found himself on the ground before he realized what had happened. His head was spinning and his backside was tingling with a sharp new pain.

"In the native tongue!" Malacus admonished in Ancient Olyphatarian. "How many times must I remind you of this? You are no longer on Earth, boy! English is a dead language to you now."

Allen could feel his anger welling up at the admonition, but stifled it nearly as quickly as it had come. "Apologies," he offered, doing his best to keep his voice from sounding sassy and switching his words to the native language of Datheron.

After picking himself up off the ground and brushing himself off, he stood before his great-grandfather, feeling the man's gaze nearly penetrate him as he seemed to consider something. After a long moment Malacus' posture slackened, if only a little and he nodded. "Are you ready to begin?" he asked.

Allen nodded and took another look around him. "What exactly is it you ask of me? What task brings us to such a distance away from the house this day?" he asked.

"The task does not bring us anywhere," Malacus said with a slight smirk. "It is you who will be doing all the work."

Allen wasn't sure if he necessarily liked the sound of that, but he reasoned that it couldn't be that strenuous since there wasn't really anything around them. "I see," he said as flatly as he could. "In that case, what is it you would have me do?"

Malacus gave him an even more sly-looking grin, "I would have you walk back to the house."

"What?" He was sure he'd heard the old man wrong.

"I would have you walk back to the house—from here," *Malacus repeated,* "wearing naught but the lower half of your protective tunic."

Allen considered the task for a moment. He didn't think it sounded that hard, but he wasn't sure how much protection from the intense gravity of this planet each piece of clothing offered. "As you wish," he said at last. "Can I first ask question of you?"

"No," *Malacus stated quickly.* "Questions will be given answer only upon completion of the task presented."

Before Allen had a chance to protest, he felt his arms lift of their own volition and the tunic slipping over his head. Malacus was already past him as the garment leapt into his hands. "And I shall not be returning to aid in the effort," he added, "So I caution you against wasting time, and encourage the placing of all effort toward the task set before you. Reach the house under your own merit or find yourself sleeping among the elements this night."

The weight of his own body began to crush him. He suddenly found himself extremely top-heavy. Before he could master the new weight, he felt himself toppling backward, and landed with a hard thud directly on his back. The impact sucked the wind right out of his lungs. For what seemed an eternity he struggled with what should have been the simple task of reclaiming his breath. Mild panic began to set in. How in the world did Malacus expect him to make it all the way back to the cabin if he couldn't even stand up on his own? It occurred to him, as he felt his face change color, this was perhaps the point of the exercise.

Infuriated at the way Malacus had introduced him to his task, and determined not to fail in his first actual training challenge, he pushed against the ground with all his might. At first, laying on his back, he was unable to gain more than a couple inches onto his elbows before being sucked back to a completely horizontal position. He still hadn't managed to get his wind back yet, which was only making the task more difficult. After a moment he tried again, only to find himself in the exact same position.

Frustrated, but not defeated, he decided the first thing he needed to do was relax. He let himself calm completely and concentrated only on breathing. After another several rapid heartbeats, he was able to suck hot relief into his lungs at last. The minor achievement felt like a major victory as he lay gasping in the life-giving air. He felt his face return to its normal pigment. Every sweet breath tasted good and brought his vision a little closer to focusing.

When he finally felt composed enough, he decided to give standing another try. He steeled himself, took another deep breath, and pushed against the oppressive force pinning him to the ground. As he pushed, he noticed something: his legs were still able to move relatively easily. Using this discovery to his advantage, he pressed the heels of his feet to the grass and lifted his lower half up above his torso. With a mighty thrust, he kicked against the earth with his right foot using the momentum to flip him over onto his stomach. He hadn't really gained much, but he felt a definite sense of accomplishment with his face firmly planted against the long grass beneath him.

Now, in a better position to manipulate his weight, Allen planted the palms of his hands out to his sides as he prepared to do the most difficult push-up of his life. Knowing he wouldn't be able to accomplish this maneuver without the aid of his legs, he brought his knees underneath him. Using all the strength and resolve he had, he lifted himself into a crouched position. For a long time he just knelt there, his upper body weight teetering back and forth, as he struggled to maintain his balance. Something as simple as sitting upright, without the protection of the shirt Zorthos had given him, was one of the most strenuous things he could ever remember doing. Because he weighed so much more than he had on Earth, he wasn't able to lift his arms to help him take control of his balance; attempting it had nearly deposited him face-first back onto the ground.

Allen wasn't sure how long he sat before he finally decided he needed to attempt standing. Scared he would fail, and nervous he might momentarily find himself tasting dirt again, he shifted all his weight to either leg, one at a time, as he planted his feet beneath himself. With his legs having near complete control, and his upper body weighing well over twice what it normally did, lifting himself to his full height was a massive weight-lifting squat. It was the most awkward sensation he could remember enduring.

At long last he was standing upright. He had his feet braced underneath him a shoulder's width apart. He couldn't believe how intensely oppressive the gravity was on this planet. It was going to take him all night, at least, to hobble his way back to Malacus' cabin, if he was even capable of doing it.

Remembering Malacus' words, that he would not be helping Allen back to the cabin, and determined not to let this chore best him, he cautiously took his first step. Lifting his leg as much as he could, he moved forward as far as he dared. He could feel himself already sweating from the exertion. He didn't even need to check his feet to know his

250

progress was minimal; only a few inches. His breath quickening already, he forced himself to keep moving. After a few more steps he could feel all the muscles in his legs beginning to shake in protest. He only made it another couple of steps before they buckled and Allen found himself barreling face first toward the ground. He knew he'd only made it a few feet, at best, from his starting point, and he was already completely spent.

As he lay there, panting heavily from his efforts, he wondered inwardly how he was ever going to accomplish the goal Malacus had set for him. His head was spinning and, as he struggled to catch his breath, he realized his abs hurt easily as much as his legs did. He hadn't even noticed how much he was using them as he was pressing forward, but they were on fire with the strain of his short-lived work out.

"This is . . . impossible." he panted.

Allen continued his progression through the rest of the afternoon and evening, and on into the night. As the sun set and the sky darkened, he hadn't even made it quite half way. He'd had to persist in shifts, making it only a scant foot or two at a time before he collapsed again. Sometime in the middle of the night, after he was sure he'd passed the half-way mark, he decided he needed rest. He'd reasoned that perhaps a nap would bolster his strength enough to finish the journey. It wasn't long, however, before he gave up on that idea; trying to sleep in such intense gravity was pointless and virtually impossible. Completely exhausted, and beyond uncomfortable, Allen forced himself back to his feet and continued the torturous ordeal. He vowed to give his great-grandfather a piece of his mind. If he ever made it back.

By the time he'd finally reached the cabin, it was late morning the next day. To say he was completely drained would've been a massive understatement. His entire body was sore to the point of being numb. He couldn't keep himself from shaking all over. He wanted to collapse inside the doorway, forcing Malacus to pick him up and carry him the rest of the way to a bed, since he had technically made it back to the cabin on his own. But through his own stubborn pride, he expelled the idea. He wanted to see the look on the old man's face when he saw Allen still standing, not defeated as he was sure Malacus was expecting.

As he made his way into the common room of the cabin, the largest of the small domicile, he was more than a little irritated to find Malacus hovering inches from the ground, with his legs crossed beneath him and his eyes closed.

The old man was snoring lightly.

His great-grandfather was sleeping. He'd left Allen outside, to basically fight for his life, and this crazy old coot was in here taking a nap? Had Allen the energy, he would have exploded across the room and kicked the unconscious old man square in the teeth. As it was, he wasn't sure he had the strength to scream. After several very long moments of letting his ire build, he opened his mouth to at least attempt it. If he couldn't make Malacus feel guilty for the manner in which he had treated him, then he hoped to at least startle the old man awake. He took in as much air as his lungs would allow and prepared to bellow something foul . . . but nothing came out. He tried again. Still nothing. He was somewhere between wanting to laugh at the irony and wanting to cry from exhaustion. But he didn't even have the energy for that.

With no fight left in him, he crumpled to the floor.

When he finally regained consciousness, his vision was blurry at first. He could scarcely recall where he was. Nothing else was real except for the excruciating physical pain he was in; his muscles convulsed violently as he lay there. He heard a voice speaking to him from a distance. At first he wasn't sure what the voice was saying.

"Drink this," the muffled voice said, once he could finally understand it.

Allen wasn't sure if he could even swallow. Every muscle in his body ached. His head felt as if it could burst at any moment. He could feel a thick liquid trickling down his throat. It hurt so much to even attempt swallowing that all he could do was let it ooze past his tongue into his stomach. He wanted the liquid to stop coming, but it seemed to pick up speed, pooling in his mouth. Finally after several torturous minutes which felt like hours, it ceased. He could feel sweat cascading from his forehead across his temples. He moved his head ever so slightly to the left to see who was standing over him.

But the movement told him nothing. Before he could bring his eyes into focus, the blackness took him again.

Allen's muscles still ached when he came to again but he was no longer debilitated. It took a tremendous amount of effort to sit up, sending hot lines of pain rushing through his abdomen as he did so, but he managed it. It was getting dark outside and he found himself wondering how long he'd been out. He looked around, searching for his great-grandfather and any memory of how he'd gotten into his bed. He glanced down at himself and found that he once again wore his protective tunic. Allen felt a huge wave of relief and gratitude come over him at the realization.

With great effort he stood, his legs like rubber beneath him. As he slowly walked toward the entrance to the common room, he noticed a light flickering around the corner. He poked his head through the doorway, resting his weight against the door frame. Malacus, who was once again hovering cross-legged a few inches from the ground, looked up from the book he was reading.

"How do faculties greet you?" the old man asked, with seemingly genuine concern.

"Like death," he answered, not even attempting to speak the appropriate language.

"The answer does not surprise. Only luck yet finds you among the living," Malacus said.

"No kidding." Allen retorted sardonically. He pushed his weight off the door frame and trudged toward Malacus. It was all coming back to him, now that the physical pain wasn't dominating his cognition. He brought himself within a few paces of the crazy old man who had nearly killed him, and sat down facing him.

"I think true understanding yet escapes you," Malacus said. "To make it back on your own should have been impossible to accomplish"

"But I did," Allen interjected. He couldn't help feeling a certain sense of pride at hearing the old man admit he'd surpassed his expectations.

Malacus had a look as serious as Allen had ever seen on the man, "Your body had fallen to shock, near to the point of seizure when I found you. It had most likely been so for some time as I knelt to your side." He paused, as if making sure what he was saying was sinking in. "Had fate seen you fall any further from your final destination than you did . . ."

"It was your crazy idea to have me do that stupid training exercise," he said defensively. "Why are you getting after me for it?"

Malacus paused before he responded. He had a haunted look of astonishment on his face. "I am not, as you say, getting after you, Allen. I simply did not expect you would make it further than a few paces at best. The sun was low in the sky as I approached to check your progress. Allen, you have my sincerest apologies, but when I saw the distance travelled in the time allotted, I was

254

taken aback. My level of surprise gave way to desire to see your true limits. My intent was not to see you lose consciousness to the point of seizure."

Allen wasn't sure what the old man was trying to say. His mind raced at the possible implications in Malacus' apparent confession. He still had many questions, but something told him he needed to remain silent and hear what had to be said.

"My original intent was to retrieve you, regardless of distance travelled, upon completing the preparation of supper," Malacus' eyes were distant as he spoke. "When I checked your progress again several hours later, you had traveled further still. Curiosity once again overpowered caution. Then when you at last collapsed before me, I had to work with haste. You must understand. You should not have been able to traverse the distance presented. The potential that lives in you is remarkable. It is unprecedented."

Allen still wasn't sure what Malacus was trying to get at, but he was growing impatient, so he prompted the response he wanted. "But I did make it," he repeated. "So what does that mean?"

Malacus shook his head slowly, "The answer continues to elude me."

Abruptly Malacus stood and walked to the area Allen would have considered the kitchen. It didn't have a stove or any other appliances Allen was used to seeing in a home, but it had several cupboards which all contained ingredients, and it was where Malacus prepared everything—meals, potions, poultices, everything. When he returned, he offered Allen a goblet.

"Drink this," Malacus commanded. "It will help with the aching which currently claims control of your muscles."

Allen thanked him and downed it with a quickness that surprised even him. His arms burned with the strain of lifting the goblet to his lips, and he hadn't realized just how parched he was. Once the beverage was gone, he wiped his chin clean and set the goblet on the floor to his left.

"So, which part of my making it surprises you the most?" he asked apprehensively. "I mean, why shouldn't I have been able to make it?"

Malacus considered him for a moment. "To begin with, the gravity of this world far exceeds that to which your body is accustomed. Your body has yet to be given the proper chance to acclimate to current surroundings. I put the task to you to the purpose of learning your reaction, to gauge response to a given command; to see if *will* lives among your other attributes. I did not anticipate that you would succeed."

"I see."

"Tell me, Allen. How did you fare such success? Without anyone to show you how to adapt to such drastic change in your environment, how did you come about completing such an onerous task?"

Allen thought it a silly question. "Well," he answered honestly, "you told me you weren't coming back. You lead me to believe if I didn't make it back, I would be stuck out there. I knew I had to get back here to . . ."

"To Sarah," Malacus finished for him, the words coming in English this time.

Allen lowered his gaze from his great-grandfather's. "Yes. I need to be here when she wakes up, that's all."

Malacus spoke softly, "She means a great deal to you."

He met Malacus' eyes again. "Yes."

"You worry for her."

"Yes."

"Do you love her?"

Allen hadn't been expecting such a direct question. He could feel his ears heating. "Yes, but . . ."

"She does not know," Malacus finished for him again.

"No," he confided. He knew it was silly, but he was beginning to feel a little embarrassed now that the truth was out there. He hadn't said it in front of Sarah, but his heart was racing all the same at having admitted it aloud to someone else.

He decided to change the subject and gave Malacus a serious look of his own; the same penetrating gaze he always employed when searching for the truth of the matter. "You told me I could ask you questions only once I made it back to the house. Well, I made it back, and I still have questions. I'd like answers."

Malacus pursed his lips. "So I did. Very well, you have earned such a reward. I shall give answer, should it be within my power to do so."

Allen's thoughts returned to his mother. He was hesitant, if only slightly, of asking questions which could have answers he might not like. Deciding he needed the truth no matter what it was, he steeled himself. "I've been here for several days now, which I'm sure equates to several weeks on Earth."

Malacus nodded.

"And I'm sure that my mom is more than a little worried about me. Malacus, please, if there's any way I can at least contact her to let her know I'm alive and well, I need to know."

The old man appeared all the more old as a look of regret creased his features. "Most humble apologies, Allen. Even if such a way existed, it would be impossible to see to completion. Contact with any other world is explicitly forbidden. Permission to even attempt such a thing can be granted only by the God-King."

The answer was crushing, but Allen expected it. He'd been thinking about the problem for a while and had another idea. After all, with anything being possible on this planet his imagination could now, hopefully, become reality.

"What about time travel?" he asked. "Couldn't I learn how to manipulate the flow of time and return myself to moments after I left once I'm finally able to return to Earth?"

Malacus seemed slightly surprised by the question, and apprehensive to answer it. He considered Allen for several minutes before finally responding. "Time travel is dangerous business, Allen," he stated flatly. "Mistakes caused by such tampering can yield repercussions beyond anticipation. The ripples of such repercussions would be felt to the limits the universe, not just on the world from which they originate. It is for that reason that it, too, remains illegal."

The response was disheartening, but it hadn't been an answer to his question. Not a directly, anyway.

"But it is possible?" he pressed.

Malacus sighed deeply. "Yes. Anything is possible," he said with finality.

Allen wasn't sure how he would accomplish it, or even if he could, but knowing it was possible gave him a thin thread of hope upon which to cling. He decided that would be his answer to this particular problem, at least for the time being. Having this new goal would give him something else to work toward once he was able to get Sarah home to Earth. He had been slowly preparing himself for the eventuality that she would learn the truth of his responsibility for her being here, and the resulting spite he was sure she would feel once she realized it. This would keep him going once he was able to give her life back to her.

Malacus' voice snapped him out of his reverie. "Was that all you wished to know?" the old man asked.

"No," he said timidly. "Sarah is in a coma isn't she?"

"Yes."

"Do you know how much longer she'll . . . be like this before she wakes up?"

The question was another which potentially held an answer he wouldn't like. But he needed to know. He needed to know she would wake up. He needed to know his choice in coming here hadn't cost her everything, if only to ease the guilt he felt over it.

"It is difficult to speculate," Malacus said. "We have seen her through the most difficult part of her journey; the vehectra toxin has been completely removed from her system. Final result rests entirely upon her shoulders. Desire to wake must come from deep within the subconscious. She must fight alone for victory in this."

That hadn't exactly been the answer he was expecting, or hoping for. But it did at least offer some hope. "I wish there were some way for me to make her hear me," he said, thinking aloud.

"There may yet be," Malacus said.

Allen's attention was immediately brought back to the present. "What?" he asked incredulously. "What was that?"

Malacus grinned. "I said only that you have finally made request to which I can offer assistance, however minimal. I cannot promise results of such a request will match your desire, but we shall divine such an answer together."

"Then what are we waiting for?" Allen stood up abruptly. As he did so, he noticed his muscles were no longer as sore as when he'd sat down. They still hurt, but it was a fading, tingling pain—reminiscent of a bruise that was nearly healed.

Malacus looked up and down the length of Allen's body as he, too, came to his feet, apparently noticing the auspicious effects of the concoction he'd given Allen.

Once they were in the basement at Sarah's side, Malacus turned to face him. "Understand success in establishing such a connection to her mind may take ample time in the attempt. I need you to remain calm and patient."

"Okay."

"Also understand that extended connection to her mind can prove detrimental to the both of you. We will need to keep our effort brief; our intent is not to force her from this coma. It is about offering a guiding hand, not pulling her from quicksand."

"I understand."

Seemingly satisfied with his comprehension of the situation, Malacus fixed his eyes on Sarah once more. "I am going to place my fingers to her temples. Place yours upon my forearm." Malacus pulled back the sleeve of his tunic and Allen did as instructed. "You may hold her hand if you so wish, but it is not vital."

Allen nodded that he understood. He kept a firm grip on his great-grandfather's right forearm with his left hand. With his other Allen took hold of Sarah's right hand. She didn't grip his in return; her hand would've felt dead if not for the warmth of her flesh.

Without looking at him, Malacus said, "My eyes close in preparation. Bring yours to follow suit."

Allen closed his eyes.

Through the darkness he heard Malacus say, "When the time is right you will need to reach out to her. Do not push with excess. We attempt only in the hope that she takes strength from our presence, to bolster the fight from within."

"I understand."

With those final words spoken, Allen felt his great-grandfather begin focusing all of his energy toward this single purpose. With his eyes closed, he wasn't sure how he knew it, but he knew the process had begun.

With his eyes locked shut in concentration, he could feel Malacus reach out to Sarah with his mind. He could somehow sense every miniscule thing the old man was doing. He could feel him probing her thoughts as if standing right next to the man, inside her mind with him. The sensation was as alarming as it was illuminating.

They continued to search, side by side—Allen somehow understanding completely each step they made through her subconscious—for what seemed a long time before they finally heard another voice. It was faint; sounding like it was coming from a great distance. But Allen knew they had reached Sarah at last.

"Sarah," he called out to her. His voice had an eerie echo to it, sounding almost ominous. He heard her respond, but he couldn't make out what she'd said.

"Sarah?" he called again. "Sarah it's me, Allen. Can you hear me? Sarah?"

Again her response was unintelligible. He wasn't sure why, but it almost felt to him as if her voice were receding from his presence.

Allen wasn't about to give up so easily.

He continued calling her name as he chased her voice through the recesses of her mind for what felt like hours. Every time he felt like he was getting closer, the voice would move further away, as if repelled by his presence. He was becoming increasingly frustrated, but refused to break the connection before he'd told her he was sorry and that she had to keep fighting.

He moved faster, more frantically, in a desperate attempt to get close enough to the voice for it to hear him. When it finally became evident he would not be able to accomplish this feat, at least not through his current methods, Allen stopped chasing it.

"Sarah," he called out as loudly as he could. "Sarah if you can hear me, you can't give up! You have to fight! I'm right here, and I'm not going anywhere! I need you to hear me . . . Please hear me! Sarah! Sarah, you need to fight this! Come back to me! I'm right here!"

Allen listened for a response for what felt like an eternity. Finally, when he realized he couldn't even hear the echo of the presence he had been chasing, he decided it was time to stop, at least for now. With an overwhelming pang of guilt gnawing at his heart, he began to recede from her mind. He heard his last words to her echo through both their minds, "Sarah, please don't die. I need you."

"Allen . . ." the voice had come from nowhere, a mere whisper.

Before he could lock onto its point of origin, he found himself spiraling away from it. He fought desperately to reclaim his ground, but it was too late. He was too far away now.

The light burned his vision, and his head throbbed miserably as all of his senses came back into focus at once. The ordeal had left him completely drained, if in an entirely different way than his task the day before. He felt nauseated.

He let his weight shift from his knees and fell onto his backside on the floor next to her bed, noticing he still had a firm grip on her hand, but Malacus wasn't next to him. Slowly, Allen scanned the room for the old man. When he finally came into view, Allen was surprised to note he was nowhere near him. Malacus was standing half-way across the room, gawking like a child.

"What are you doing all the way over there?" he asked. Even to Allen, his voice had sounded cracked.

Malacus shook his head in pure bewilderment, his mouth hanging agape. "Never, in all my years, have I witnessed such a thing."

"Such a thing as what?"

Malacus spoke softly, his voice full of wonder. "Allen, I was able to establish only a perfunctory link to her mind. She receded from our presence the moment first contact was made. I removed my grasp of her almost immediately. Somehow you were able to maintain the link of your own accord, even after my arm was pried from your grip."

Allen was stunned. Unsure what else to say, he asked, "How long have I been sitting here?"

"Nearly three hours."

Allen could plainly see that Malacus was haunted by the accomplishment. "I heard her voice . . . I tried chasing it," he offered meekly. "I wasn't able to catch it, but I did hear her call my name right as I was exiting her mind. But by then it was too late."

Malacus just stared at him. Unable to handle the look in his great-grandfather's eyes, he lowered his head, feeling the same sort of confusion, mixed with pride that he'd felt when he'd accidentally used telekinesis his first night here. He was more than frustrated to prove he was somehow capable of these amazing things, but had no idea how to replicate them, to master them.

He was suddenly feeling very run down.

When he met Malacus' gaze again moments later, Allen saw a curious look covering the old man's withered features. He had a slight grin and a wild look in his eyes.

"What?" he asked. "Why are you looking at me like that?"

"Come," Malacus said excitedly. "It is time for you to get some much needed rest. Tomorrow, training begins anew, in earnest."

16

COLLATION

ALLEN QUICKLY REALIZED his great-grandfather was a difficult taskmaster. Malacus had once again been true to his word, and the next day they began an intensive training regimen. It just hadn't been what he was expecting or hoping for.

When Malacus said they would be training in earnest, Allen assumed he would finally begin learning a special ability or two; he had, after all, already proven himself capable. He just needed to learn how to control it. Malacus, however, apparently didn't share his assessment of the situation. Rather than learning how to replicate the abilities he'd already shown a propensity for, he was spending a great deal of his time learning to read the language of Datheron. When he wasn't studying Olyphitarian conjugation, Malacus insisted he relive the first training challenge he'd been given.

Malacus marched him out to the same spot after lunch each day, and Allen made it as far as he could by dinner time. The first couple of days had been the worst, had almost felt more difficult than the first time; his muscles feeling so torn and useless he was sure he'd never use them again. But Malacus fed him the same healing elixir with dinner, and by the time he woke the following morning, his muscles felt tremendously improved.

After about a week, Malacus switched the garment he was required to remove. He was allowed to keep the undergarments Zorthos had fashioned for him, but he had to traverse the distance without his pants. Embarrassed at first, he had asked his great-grandfather what the purpose of the exercise was. Malacus told him that, when trying to get stronger, only a fool works out just one portion of their body. This didn't really make him feel any better and it wasn't exactly what he'd been asking, but he supposed the old man had a point. So, rather than create a pointless debate over it, he'd acquiesced, deciding to just suffer the indignity.

It wasn't long before he was able to perform either exercise with relative ease. He wasn't able to sprint, but he was finding it increasingly easier each time. His muscles no longer felt ripped from his bones when he made it back to the cabin. Allen had hoped making such impressive strides in his training would warrant some sort of congratulations, or a break from the old man. Instead, one day as he made it back to the cabin in record time, Malacus ripped off every layer of his clothes—with the exception of his undergarments—and told him to turn around, walk back out to the starting point then return or he would get no dinner. By the time he'd made it back to the cabin that night, he was too exhausted to care about food. His muscles, once again, had that all-too-familiar numbness to them. He hadn't even sought out Malacus to tell him he'd done it. He'd just gone straight to bed.

When he awoke the next morning, Malacus greeted him with a warm breakfast, the same healing elixir, and a new set of clothing. The design of the new clothes wasn't all that dissimilar to the ones he'd been wearing up to this point, but they looked somehow nicer. They were made of a lighter material, had finer stitching, and were the same dark grey color as Malacus'. He even had new leather boots and gauntlets to complete the ensemble.

Malacus explained to him that he'd received the new garb for two reasons: so he would look more like a proper citizen of Datheron, and because he no longer needed the protection of the uniform Zorthos had crafted. He was getting used to the intense gravity.

It was difficult for him to say how long he'd been on Datheron. He knew it had to be at least four weeks, possibly more. The days all seemed to blend together after a while. He was slowly getting better at deciphering the text in some of the scrolls and tomes in Malacus' hidden basement, and he no longer had any trouble speaking the language; he was now fluent. He could feel himself gradually getting stronger, both mentally and physically. And yet Sarah remained in her coma. He was beginning to wonder if she would ever wake up.

He spent as much time as he could at her side, doing most of his studying in the basement so as to be near her, in case she woke. He had even begun eating some of his meals down there as well, once or twice trying to recreate the link he'd established between their minds with Malacus' help all those weeks ago. But it had the same result as his futile attempts to duplicate the mental assault he'd made on the old man his first night here. It completely eluded him why he had been able to do those things with ease as they were happening, only to fail so miserably each time he tried again. It was as if he'd merely daydreamed doing it.

Finally, once he'd mastered the gravity of his new environment, and not feeling like he was learning anything useful, he decided to confront Malacus. After all, he was on the planet of the gods; he should be learning some supernatural abilities, not wasting time learning to translate a language which would be of no use to him if he ever made it back to Earth. Allen was tired of wasting time. He had already been able to call forth powers that he'd had no previous experience with or training in. How hard could it be to learn how to reproduce it on command?

One morning, after completing his daily journey in a matter of a few minutes, he stormed into the cabin, all but running back the entrance to Malacus' abode. As he came to a stop in front of his great-grandfather, sweating more from how warm day than from the exertion of a workout, he yelled: "I wish to learn a super power!" he demanded in the native language of Datheron. Now that he was fluent, Malacus no longer tolerated English from him.

There; he'd said it. It was out there now. Considering how much potential he'd shown, he didn't see how Malacus could possibly refuse his request.

Malacus cast a look on him which appeared to be a mixture of mild amusement and irritation. "Is that so?" he asked quizzically.

"It is," he answered firmly. "Why should I not? I have already proven myself to have a quick mind and capacity for such things. You, yourself, have spoken words toward the high regard by which you hold such potential. When training was offered, it was assumed I would be learning something of use. Instead you have me placing effort toward the study of Datheronian sentence structure, leaving one foot free to roam while keeping the other firmly fixed in place. When am I to learn something of real interest?"

Malacus set down the book he'd been referencing as he stood over some experimental-looking concoction before him on the kitchen's work table. He gave Allen a patient, if challenging look. "Tell me Allen, what ability is it you think to take precedence from the original bargain?"

Allen didn't even need to think about it. "I want to learn how to fly," he said in his most committed tone.

"Ha!" Malacus barked. "I thought you said you wished to learn something of use." Malacus fell to a mild fit of laughter.

"What is it you find amusing in the request?" he asked, feeling wounded by his great-grandfather's reaction.

"To begin with, for the level of usefulness offered, flight stands one of the most difficult abilities to learn. It is a foolish place to begin one's journey toward acquiring mastery of abilities only offered on this world."

"I do not understand your meaning," he replied, doing his best to retain the resolve with which he'd entered the conversation. "Why is it such a poor place to begin? It cannot possibly be as difficult as you claim. I have witnessed you levitating, hovering well above the ground beneath you, on many occasions."

"True. But levitation stands something all together different from flight. Have you ever beheld me soaring through the sky, among the birds to which such a domain belongs?" Malacus countered.

"Not in such a fashion. But—"

"That is because flight is exceedingly dangerous even in the attempt; of no use at all unless you have first mastered the corresponding precautionary abilities," Malacus interjected firmly.

Allen was more than confused. He hated the cryptic way in which Malacus often spoke. He seemed to like to allude to something and then stop, forcing Allen to ask a question which would ultimately leave him feeling stupid or inferior once the old man finally answered it.

"Precautionary abilities?" he asked, knowing he would almost certainly regret the question.

"Yes. Let us suggest that you had approached the subject from different direction, demanding that I teach you pyrokinesis; you want to learn how to create fire in the palm of your hand. What is it you would expect to learn of me first?"

Allen thought it a simple question with an easy answer. But he knew things were never quite as simple as they seemed with Malacus. "Uh . . . how to make fire appear in my hand?" he chanced.

"All right," Malacus' left eye squinted slightly as the hint of a lopsided grin began to form on his lips. "So now your hand is ablaze. Tell me, what becomes of flesh so touched by flame?"

"It burns," he offered, feeling dumber and more annoyed by the second.

"Correct. So if you do not wish the flesh of your hand to melt from the bones, what might you deign to learn first?"

Allen exhaled a frustrated sigh. "I know not. How to heal yourself, I would wager."

Malacus nodded. "That would be one such place to begin. What about learning a skill that would shield flesh from flame in the first place?"

Allen thought he understood where Malacus was coming from, but he said nothing.

"The same can be said of flying," Malacus continued. "With exception being that flight requires the taking of far more into account. Absent such precautions you would find yourself with far worse than blackened fingertips. If proper consideration is not given to every eventuality— wind current, oxygen levels presented by higher altitudes, possibility of landing prematurely due to loss of control . . ." Malacus paused thoughtfully and Allen couldn't help but feel that it was so he could grasp some deeper meaning in the old man's words. "Allen, such a skill demands a high price in the learning. A single miscalculation could mean your life in the balance. Without proper training, loss of concentration during such a feat would find you plummeting to your demise. For one such as you, whose potential appears to know no bounds, the attempting of such a skill might prove successful quickly, only to prove fatal at the first mistake.

"It is the same with virtually every skill you would place consideration toward; countermeasures must be taken into consideration. Rules must first be properly learned before consideration can be placed toward the breaking of them."

What Malacus was saying made sense, but he still felt as if the old man was holding back, not telling him everything. "I see," he said, putting all his effort into remaining patient with the lesson. "Then I would have you teach me an ability easier than flight. What lesson can you offer toward an ability requiring less in the area of precautionary measures?"

Malacus let out a patient sigh, as if he were explaining something complex to a child who wasn't quite getting it. "Again, as stated but a moment ago, rules must first be properly learned before one can place thought toward the breaking of them. Before true potential can be harnessed, you must first have a firm grasp of the basics. You must learn the reason behind such skills being possible. First, dedicate the primary tenet to memory, then learn what gives function to such lessons."

Allen let out a patient sigh of his own. He was almost regretting making the demand. "Primary tenet?" he asked, unable to keep the annoyance from his tone.

Malacus held up a finger to note the importance of what he was saying, "Life and existence, in all the universe, from the furthest reaches of space to the ecosystems which make the plane of terrestrial existence function, operate solely upon the basis of one principal: balance. The whole of life is balance; without it we could not exist."

When he said nothing, Malacus continued. "A force exists among the elements of the universe which cannot be seen, a force which controls the very fabric of life. Even though most throughout the known universe cannot feel its presence, it still gives sway to all that occurs everywhere; balance left in the wake of its flow. When one learns what you refer to as a 'super power', they are learning the harnessing and manipulation of this invisible force. This force is called Mystica."

Allen was vaguely familiar with the word. He'd seen it in several of the texts he'd been trying to translate for the past couple of weeks. "So were I to bend the laws of physics, moving with speed that rivals light, or learn to pass physical form through solid objects, or to fly . . . such things are only accomplished through manipulation of this Mystica of which you speak?" he asked skeptically.

"A crude interpretation at best, but truth lives among the words," Malacus nodded firmly.

"What is Mystica exactly?" he asked.

"Mystica," Malacus began, "simply put, is the energy of life. It is what gives breath to all that live, its touch reaching every living thing. Only through Mystica do younglings of any species come into the realm of life. Only through it are trees and other plants able to flourish.

"On this planet, enveloped as it is by unique atmosphere, learning to sense, harness, and manipulate Mystica is how one is able to bend the forces of nature to that of will. When creatures of any kind die, it is Mystica their body expels; it is that distinct lack of Mystica that stands so readily evident in empty eyes."

Allen didn't know what to say. This was not at all how he'd imagined this conversation going. Something

Malacus was saying gnawed at the back of his mind; something didn't quite make sense. "So, if harnessing Mystica is the only pathway to such abilities, how did I accomplish such things absent knowledge of its existence?"

"That, my dear great-grandson, is what makes such demonstrations so dangerous and equally impressive. That you had never heard the word 'Mystica' spoken is immaterial. Lack of knowledge of a subject makes such things no less dangerous. Sarah was, after all, bitten by a snake of which she had no prior knowledge, yet she remains ever in the tenacious grasp of the resulting coma despite her ignorance of its existence.

"The most important and elusive aspect of your capabilities remains that you were somehow able to give them life absent any training at all. Such things can only be obtained through laborious training, supreme dedication. Learning to manipulate Mystica in such a way as to achieve desired effect has only ever been accomplished through the most intense of dedication to one's studies."

The mention of Sarah and the incident which had put her in a coma left Allen feeling a little heartsick. None of this was what he wanted to hear the old man say. Realizing how long it could potentially take to learn how to harness Mystica the way he wanted left him feeling hopeless. He recalled watching Zorthos destroy the warp gate they had travelled through from Earth. It had appeared Zorthos was struggling immensely, and he'd had a lifetime of training. Allen wondered how he would ever be able to reach that level of skill while his mother was still alive. He wondered if he even could.

Feeling completely overwhelmed, Allen sat down and braced his back against the nearest wall. "Where is it then that you would have me begin?" he asked in resignation.

Malacus smiled. "At last a properly formed question. But original discussion has yet to be concluded." He waited for Allen to look up before he continued. "What is the primary tenet?" he asked in a slightly animated tone. Despite his initial objections to train Allen, moments like these made it evident the old man enjoyed passing on his knowledge.

"Life can only function through balance," he answered.

"Correct," Malacus said with a proud smile. "Tell me, if Mystica is the energy of life, what do you suppose lays in the balance?"

"The energy of death?" he guessed.

"Precisely!" Malacus replied in an excitable tone. "And such energy bears its own name. It is called Sythika."

"Sythika?" he scoffed. "Must I learn to manipulate it as well?"

Malacus' expression turned very serious. "No. Sythika cannot be manipulated. But recognition of it and respect for it is critical to any who would undertake training in the use of its counterpart. It is the balance to life; death. That death exists is what gives life meaning. It cannot be stopped. Eventually everything is victim to its path of destruction. You must not live your life in fear of it, but respecting death does give life proper perspective."

All of what Malacus said made at least some sense to Allen. He did already believe very firmly that life was precious. He knew some day he would die, and that he needed to make the most of what time he had. Too, he understood the importance of keeping life in its proper perspective. Yet he couldn't help but feel as if he was missing some grand point his great-grandfather was trying to make.

Not knowing quite what Malacus wanted him to say, yet wanting to assure the old man he was paying attention, he decided he needed to offer something to the conversation. "Tell me then. How is it I achieved such things absent the knowledge to manipulate Mystica?"

Malacus eyed him with a curious expression for what seemed a long time before he answered. Allen wasn't sure, but it seemed like there was an answer dancing on the tip of the old man's tongue and he was just reluctant to spit it out.

"I wish I could form a proper answer," was all Malacus said.

Malacus wasn't giving up any more information. He just sat there, seemingly letting him ponder what had been said up to this point. Unsure what brilliant deduction he was supposed to be making, he decided to redirect the course the conversation seemed to be heading.

"Tell me of the prophecy about which you spoke to Zorthos. What are its words?" he asked, trying his best not to sound demanding.

Malacus' countenance paled slightly. "Allen, if you truly are the one of which the prophecy speaks, to divulge such information at present, if at all, could prove unwise."

"Unacceptable! You keep truth from my grasp out of fear, not an interest to protect! If the words speak of me, the learning of them can only help, and choice to do so should fall to me alone!"

"Allen, many alter their destiny, regardless of desire, on the road specifically chosen to avoid it," Malacus said cryptically.

Allen was furious at the response he'd just been given. Couldn't this man ever answer a question directly?

"Avoiding the making of a decision out of fear is a fool's errand!" he snapped. "I refuse to believe that my life is predestined! I refuse to let fear dictate response! If results to such things have already been decided, then choices made in the present bear no meaning at all! If my fate has already been sealed, leaving my course unchanged regardless of choice, life itself becomes meaningless!"

Allen didn't even give Malacus the chance to retort. He stood from where he'd been leaning against the wall and stormed outside. He had entered that conversation with expectations completely different from where it had actually taken him. He could feel his anger slipping its bounds, and he didn't want an argument. He wasn't sure what he wanted at that moment. He hated feeling this way and couldn't help but feel as if it was happening more frequently since arriving on this planet. Everything seemed to be spinning out of control. He couldn't figure out how he'd gotten here. He'd gone into the conversation with one expectation, and left it with nothing but more questions. He was so tired of being treated like a child, being sheltered from things he was sure he could comprehend if only he were given the chance. He didn't know what to do. At that moment he just wanted to go home. He just wanted this nightmare to end.

As he stormed away from Malacus' cabin, Allen wasn't really paying any attention to where he was going. He desperately needed Sarah to wake up. He ached to see his mother, to be in her arms while she caressed his back and told him everything would be all right. He knew that no matter how badly he wished it simply wanting things to change wouldn't make it happen.

He had never felt as alone as he did in that moment.

Anger welled up inside him. How could everything go so wrong? White hot rage cried for release. He ran with all his might. Tears stung his face as he sprinted away. He didn't care where he was going; only that he was burning off his repressed energy.

He came to a steep hill and pushed himself to pick up speed. He recalled seeing Zorthos soaring from one hilltop to another. Zorthos had claimed it hadn't been any special ability, simply inertia and momentum which had carried him across the gap. He'd even told Allen that he could do it, too. But could he?

With anger fueling his acceleration, he breached the top of the hill, pushing from the ground beneath him the way he'd seen Zorthos do it. He let his momentum carry him away from the earth at his feet. The wind tore through his hair as he soared higher and higher into the air. He could feel his clothes rippling in protest as he continued gain altitude.

He closed his eyes and inhaled a deep, cleansing breath. He may not have been flying, but this was closer to it than he'd ever been before. He spread his arms, feeling the air part between his fingertips. His anger wasn't gone, but it was dwindling. This was what it felt like to be free.

Too late he opened his eyes.

With fear he realized he'd overshot the hill he'd intended to be his landing pad and was hurtling toward the ground at an alarming rate. There was nothing he could do; he couldn't slow his descent.

His last thoughts before he impacted were of Sarah.

17

PROPHECY

ALLEN ACHED ALL OVER. As he opened his eyes, he was surprised to see Malacus hovering over him. He remembered being angry at the old man, losing control of his emotions and his momentum, and flying toward the ground at what felt like fifty miles per hour. Despite how upset he was with his great-grandfather, that he was looking at Malacus at all meant he was alive; a fact for which he was very grateful.

In earnest Allen tried to lift himself to a sitting position. Malacus gently placed a hand on his shoulder, urging him back onto his pillow. Even if Malacus had not prevented him from getting up, he would likely have collapsed after another moment or two. His head throbbed. It hurt to breathe. He couldn't tell for sure, but it felt he might have broken at least one of his ribs, and possibly his left arm and ankle as well.

"Be still," Malacus said softly. Allen was surprised to hear the words spoken in English. "Consciousness has escaped you nearly two days."

"How did I get back here?" His voice was weak.

Malacus offered a warm smile, "Upon sensing consciousness leave you, I moved quickly to your side. You were of battered condition upon discovery." His expression turned serious, almost scolding. "You are fortunate to yet be counted among the living."

Allen shifted his gaze away from Malacus. He was feeling foolish for the way he had overreacted to their last conversation. At least the old man wasn't making an issue that he wasn't even attempting the native language. "I know," he said. "I'm sorry."

"No, Allen," Malacus said, "it is I who should bear apologies."

Allen brought his eyes back around to meet his great-grandfather. The look in the old man's eyes told Allen he was sincere.

"Why are you sorry?" he asked.

Malacus took a slow, deep breath, as if steeling himself for what he was about to say. "Apologies are offered for my reaction to the request made of me. Wisdom in the words you spoke found me following your departure. There is truth in saying choices presently made bear no meaning if the outcome has already been determined. Truth in what you said forced me to admit that, though my years far exceed yours, error in judgment can still be made. If the day arrives in which I have nothing left to learn, purpose for living will part from my shoulders as well."

The smile stole back onto Malacus' face, and the frustration Allen had felt completely evaporated. He still felt like a child for running away, but Malacus' compliment, accompanied by his warm grin, made Allen feel it wasn't a big deal.

"You must understand information was not withheld due to lack of respect, nor from lack of confidence in you.

Rather, it was borne of a desire to keep such things from influencing future decisions. Foreknowledge can be dangerous." Malacus paused for several moments before he spoke again.

"I would share the words of the prophecy with you," Malacus offered. "But understanding demands the prophecy be put into proper context."

Allen lay there, watching Malacus apparently gathering the strength to begin, the words the old man had spoken moments before finally registered. Malacus said he had been out for nearly two days. Nearly two days, and he was still in this much pain. With how much Malacus knew about healing, he really must have been in bad shape. The lesson the old man had given him about preventative abilities briefly sprang to mind. More than anything, though, the realization brought Sarah to the forefront of his mind. He wondered if she had finally awoken.

"Is Sarah . . . Did she . . ." Allen stuttered. "I mean, how is she doing? Is she better yet? Has she woken up?"

Malacus appeared as if he was being pulled back to the present from a faraway place. He arranged the fabric of his clothing, staring meaningfully into his eyes before he spoke. "Apologies, Allen," he offered. "Sarah's condition remains unchanged."

"Oh . . ." he replied, lowering his eyes from Malacus' gaze.

Somewhere deep down, Allen knew it was too much to hope for anyway. As long as she'd been unconscious, he'd often found himself wishing he could get her back to Earth if for no other reason than to get her to a hospital. With her being in such a deep coma, he'd found comfort in the idea that if she were at a hospital she would have doctors and nurses watching over her day and night, hooked up to machines that could monitor her condition closely. He realized, though, machines wouldn't actually be able to help her out of her coma; they were simply for monitoring her heartbeat and her brain activity. Here, on Datheron, Malacus could monitor her improvement.

It was a slow, agonizing torture watching her day by day, trapped in limbo. He wished he could do more for her. He wished she would just wake up.

"In order to understand the prophecy," Malacus began, snapping him out of his brooding, "you must first learn of the one who first spoke its words. He stands a legend, the very first God-King of Datheron. He was called Paragus."

Allen actually recognized the name. Paragus had been referenced in several of the documents he'd been studying at Malacus' instruction.

"Paragus," Malacus continued, "was the single most powerful force ever to tread our world, some say the universe; none have ever seen His like, before or since. Upon His arrival, those already calling this world home were primitive in nature. He descended from the heavens, clad in His glorious, godly armor forever altering the course of history."

"How long ago was this?" Allen interrupted.

"Years passed number in the thousands, even by Datheronian standards. Your world may not have yet reached its infancy when first he set foot upon our soil."

"Oh." The thought was mind-numbing.

"Now," Malacus started again, "Paragus proclaimed unlimited dominion over this world upon His very arrival. Since nothing could be done to stop Him, very little resistance found Paragus in the proclamation. He was a force of nature, immovable through ordinary means and offering kind gestures in return for fealty.

"Paragus began to teach the people of this world the ways of modern infrastructure. Paths gave way to roads, small huts to much larger structures, leaving prosperity in their wake. Only one thing set Him apart from the people He had adopted: It is said that He was of a ruthless nature, offering little patience in return for any defiance given Him by the people."

Malacus eyed him, as if to make sure he was paying attention to the story. "After a time, once cities of this world had grown both in size and stature, obsession borne of conquest took Paragus."

"Wait," he said. "He already had complete dominion over this world and He became obsessed with conquest? That doesn't make any sense. If He was already the supreme ruler of this planet, what else was there to conquer?"

"The universe," Malacus answered darkly.

"I see." was all he could think to say.

"Such a task, however, required much in the completing. Paragus would have to share further knowledge to a chosen few, offering the very secrets which made Him God among men."

"That sounds a little risky," Allen interjected. He supposed the people of this world had to have learned their abilities somewhere. "Didn't He realize that if He showed them how to become god-like that they would eventually get strong enough to challenge His rule?"

Malacus held a hand up, as if to push the objection aside. "Of course, such possibilities did not elude Him. But that topic will move us beyond its proper place in events. There is yet more to tell before dissection of his reasoning can begin."

"Oh, sorry."

If Malacus heard Allen's apology, he ignored it. "Now, the path of thought seems to have escaped me. Oh, yes . . . While the task to educate closest advisors and servants in the ways of the gods took place, a crisis emerged, threatening the world over which He'd gained dominion: The six Orbs of Sythika."

"Orbs of Sythika?" Allen interrupted again. "You mean they were orbs made up of the energy of death?"

Malacus grinned slightly at Allen's recollection of the word, "Precisely. They arrived; six orbs comprised entirely of compressed Sythika, in essence, living death."

"Wait. I thought you said no one can manipulate Sythika?" he challenged.

"That is correct," Malacus answered, placing his hands together in his lap.

"So then, where did the Orbs of Sythika come from? Who made them?"

Malacus leaned back as he appraised Allen's curiosity. "Do you not wish to hear the story behind the prophecy?" he said as he folded his arms. "Your interest is well appreciated, but the telling of a story is taxing in your presence. Have you ever been told such a thing?"

Allen felt blood rush to his face. "Sorry," he offered. "I'm trying to piece all this together in my head. It doesn't make sense to me that there could be orbs made entirely of Sythika without somebody being able to manipulate it."

Malacus raised an eyebrow. "Why must they have been brought to be only by someone's hand? Do you not recall my statement of such cosmic forces existing outside the limits of control? Sythika is one such cosmic force, Allen. Death cannot be manipulated, bargained with, or otherwise controlled. It exists of its own accord. Since there are none who can wield it, there are none who know true origin of the six Orbs of Sythika."

Allen was feeling more lost by the second.

"Now, bringing our topic back to point, the Orbs of Sythika emerged, threatening to engulf everything, carrying the fate of our entire world. Only Paragus understood the true magnitude of the situation, leaving Him to stand alone against their danger.

"It is said that many attempts were made toward their destruction to no avail. Panic enveloped Datheron, a great many losing faith in our God at witnessing His lack of success. In the end, however, a solution was administered, threats banished and faith restored. But such success came at great cost to the God-King, cutting short His remaining years. Some believe the Orbs of Sythika poisoned His mind, His very being, in return for victory over them."

Malacus paused for a moment. Allen wasn't sure, but it looked as if he were taking a mental inventory of what he'd said thus far. Either that or he was trying to remember the rest of the story. He realized he had no idea how old Malacus actually was.

"His reign," Malacus began again, "stretched the span of a thousand years, ever remembered for His brutality. As He lay upon His deathbed, with only moments of breath remaining, He spoke words of prophecy that echoed through the ages and are known still to all on this world."

Malacus eyed him closely, his look deadly serious. "The prophecy states: 'When the one born both of this world and of another called Earth arrives upon our soil, so shall begin the events to facilitate my return. He will free the Sword of Sythika from its slumber and reunite my broken soul. His choices will alter life on Datheron for all time. In his hands lay the fate of the universe.' "

Allen felt a cold chill rush up his spine. It definitely had an ominous ring to it. He now understood why they seemed to think it could be him the prophecy spoke of. He had, in a sense, been born of both worlds. His father was from Datheron, his mother from Earth, and he was now on Datheronian soil. He had no idea what the rest of it could possibly mean, but it was all too evident why his great-grandfather and his would-be father believed that the prophecy was about him.

"So wait . . . Does that mean I'm supposed to somehow resurrect Paragus, to bring him back to life? Is that why you're so nervous about the possibility I'll fulfill the prophecy?"

"That is but a small portion to a larger problem," Malacus said. "Prior to His passing from this world, His ultimate goals would have been well served in the sharing of His godly knowledge. The level of knowledge gained and progression in skill would have been solely at His discretion. As it now stands, several millennia have passed; the populace given ample opportunity in the balance to evolve into present condition. None yet remain who do not bear a special ability of some sort. Doubt lingers as to whether any here could survive daily trials absent abilities which have become way of life to all. There stand a great many among us who train constantly, far surpassing the level of skill which would have been permitted had His rule never ceased.

"I fear His reemergence into the world of life would bring imbalance to the whole of the universe, civil war almost certainly at its heel."

Allen was shocked and confused. "Do you really think one man could have that kind of impact, that just His presence would send the world into war?"

"There lives no doubt in my mind as to what the resurrection of Paragus would mean for life as it is known," Malacus replied in a grave tone.

Allen attempted to pull himself up again. The pain in his side was intense enough to take the breath from his lungs, but he was determined to at least prop himself against the wall behind his bed to stay alert.

"Well, I have no intention of being the catalyst that begins a war," he said. "I only want to find a way to get Sarah and me home. All I want is to get off this world and see my mother again. If I have my way, my presence will not be what brings the prophecy to life."

"I know," Malacus answered gently. "But where prophecy is involved, desires tend to fall to the wayside. The possibility exists that your quest to return to Earth could be the very thing which brings the prophecy to fruition. Sometimes the gravest consequences are borne of the best intentions."

Allen looked away from Malacus as he ran the words of the prophecy through his mind again. He wanted to find some way to discount the possibility that it could be referring to him. He'd read plenty of stories and seen plenty of movies in which the hero was mired in the tendrils of prophecy. Some of his favorite characters had become heroes by fulfilling a prophecy which centered on them. He'd always found those stories to be exciting and fascinating in a vicarious way. But reading stories and living them were two very different things. He didn't find the prospect of actually being the center of a prophecy at all exciting; he found it frightening. He didn't want to be remotely responsible for the lives of so many people. The very thought of it had him so anxious he thought he might be sick.

Allen brought his eyes back up to find the old man watching him with great interest. Considering a specific line from the prophecy, his thoughts reverted to a question he'd previously asked Malacus about manipulating Sythika. "What's the Sword of Sythika?" he asked. "Is it also made up of compressed Sythika?"

"Apologies, Allen. Proper answer cannot follow the question," Malacus replied. "None still live who know of its current location, the knowledge lost along with Paragus' life."

"And yet I'm somehow supposed to find it and 'free it from its slumber'?" he asked, doing his best to keep the question from sounding like an accusation.

"If you are truly the one of whom the prophecy speaks, then you will be the one to find it," Malacus said cryptically.

Allen exhaled a calming breath. "What can you tell me about the Sword of Sythika?

Malacus considered the question for a moment before answering. "Upon His arrival, Paragus carried but two things: the Sword of Sythika and His godly armor. Accounts of the sword being used, even by His hand, do not exist. In truth, its existence is only remembered due to its mention among the words of prophecy. Paragus had no need of such an ominous instrument of death, not when He donned His godly armor."

"What was so special about His armor?" he asked, almost fearing the answer.

Malacus looked at him as if he'd said something ludicrous. "It was His armor which gave Him such great power."

"His armor gave him His godly powers?" he repeated.

"No, not His abilities." Malacus corrected. "But powers possessed were greatly amplified in the wearing of the armor. True potential presented by the armor remains unknown, as none since Paragus have ever worn it. Yet it remains to this day coveted by all those who seek power, the sight of it feared by all who know its legend, even those not of this world."

"So then, you know where His armor is?" Allen guessed.

"Of course," Malacus scoffed. "Everyone knows where to find the Armor of Paragus. It stands ever on display at the Arena in Nentalia."

Allen was confused. "It's on display? Right out in the open? So what's stopping anyone from stealing it and using it to take over the world?"

Malacus arched an eyebrow. "Are you of the belief that, in the thousands of years since His demise, none have attempted such a thing?" He paused, as if to give Allen a moment to absorb what he'd just said. "All who have tried to don the Armor of the Gods have lost their lives in the attempt."

Allen wasn't sure he'd heard his great-grandfather right. "They all died," he repeated. "You mean just putting on the armor killed them?"

"Yes," Malacus said flatly. "In fact, it is believed by most that Paragus stands the only one who will ever wield its power, as none have been capable of the task since His passing."

The thought that simply trying to put on a suit of armor would kill a person made the hairs on the back of Allen's neck lift. He was glad the prophecy, if it was about him, didn't say he'd have to wear the armor. He briefly wondered how many had died trying, and why more people had tried after the first few failed attempts. It seemed to him that if someone died before your eyes, you wouldn't be eager to repeat the mistake that had just taken their life.

"What do you suppose it means when it says I'll reunite His broken soul?" he asked after a long moment of pondering.

Malacus let out a long sigh. "I fear precise translation of the words elude even my knowledge. Prophecy, by its very nature, gives way to speculation. It may seem straightforward on the surface, but perspective dictates interpretation. It is that vague nature which makes prophecies so dangerous, and what breeds such debate over their meanings. This prophecy has been debated since the day it was given.

"Nearly everyone of this world knows its words, hence the caution given against allowing any to learn you hail from Earth. If this truth was learned, motivation to target you would surely follow. You could be forced into slavery, made to serve another's wishes, have life stripped from you . . . or worse."

"Worse?" Allen puzzled. "What's worse than death?"

"Many things exist which can be counted worse than death," Malacus said, his eyes glazing over a little as he spoke. "Only the living can feel pain. And the very fate of the universe could weigh in the balance."

Allen turned his head away from his great-grandfather. "No wonder you didn't want to train me," he said in a weak voice. "I wouldn't want that kind of responsibility resting on my shoulders either."

At that moment, Allen wanted nothing more than to just give up. Maybe if he could just close his eyes and never open them again, the prophecy wouldn't be able to be fulfilled. If it was about him then his death could save a lot of people, possibly save the entire universe. That was a sacrifice he'd willingly make. His life was very precious to him, and he wanted desperately not to lose it, but he didn't want to be the source of such widespread effects either. If he really was the one at the center of this prophecy he was going to have some difficult choices to make in the days to come.

A thought occurred to him. "Why did you save my life?" he asked, once again facing the old man. "I mean, wouldn't it have been easier to just let me die? If the prophecy truly is about me, wouldn't my death have, in effect, saved the universe?"

Malacus' eyes became slightly watery. "You are my great-grandson, the only one I possess. It has yet to be proven whether the prophecy speaks of you or of another. You are not the first born of Earth to set foot upon Datheron. I would not risk losing you out of fear of what has not yet come to pass.

"Besides," he said, a hint of a smile ghosting the corners of his lips, "such an approach would only be taken by a coward. To let you die absent proof of guilt would have been very selfish. Do you not agree?"

Allen couldn't help smiling. He considered for a moment asking Malacus about the others from Earth he had referred to, wondering if they were possibly people of historic note among the culture of his home world. In the end he decided it was a topic best saved for another day.

"Yeah," he said at last. "I agree. So what happens now? Are you still going to train me?"

"For now," Malacus said, standing up from his chair, "you should get some much needed rest. I will continue to give lesson in all that is necessary to survive on this world. As always, the rest falls entirely upon your shoulders."

"Deal," Allen smiled.

Malacus turned and began walking to the doorway. "My stock of certain supplies runs low. A few days hence, when your injury has given way to renewed mobility, we shall travel to a nearby town in the interest of seeing them replenished. The trip will offer education, as well as a much needed change of scenery. You will see for yourself how things upon this world function. It will do you good to be away from this place, if only briefly."

As the old man walked away, leaving him to brood on all he'd just learned, Allen couldn't help smiling. Malacus was right; a change of scenery would definitely do him some good.

18

EXCURSION

AS MALACUS PROMISED, Allen was soon feeling like his old self. He was up and moving around, back to the same regimen of studying. Malacus hadn't even waited until he could get out of bed before he'd forced him to continue his studies. Right after dinner, Malacus had brought the materials up from the hidden basement where Allen had previously been working. Allen would have been upset about being forced to continue his studies so soon, but had been eager to focus his concentration away from the prophecy.

Allen silently wondered if Malacus knew that.

As soon as he was able, Allen went to the basement to check Sarah's condition. She was still unconscious, and her once fitted clothing draped over her body like a shroud. The sight of her losing so much weight only increased the intensity of the pit consuming his stomach. It concerned Allen she'd been lying there for as long as she had with no sign of improvement. He knew her muscles could get weak pretty quickly without use, which would make things more difficult for her when she finally woke. He wished she was back with him. Malacus was growing on him, but he missed Sarah. Much had happened since she was bitten by the vehectra snake, so there was much to discuss when she regained consciousness.

As leery as he was about leaving her to get supplies, he looked forward to a change of scenery. He'd been stuck in one place far too long and was beginning to feel a little cabin fever, and Malacus had assured him more than once that he would give her enough to sustain her in their absence. He'd been on this new world for well over a month now, and had't seen much of it. Not everyone could say they'd been to another world, and Allen did not intend to waste his chance.

As he stood watching Sarah, he heard footsteps approaching from behind him. Still, Malacus' words made Allen start.

"She will be fine, my boy," the old man assured him. "Are you ready to depart?"

Allen looked from Sarah to his great-grandfather. "Yeah, I'm ready. I just wanted to see her for a few minutes before we left. That's all."

"In the native tongue," Malacus admonished.

"Apologies," he responded in the alien language.

"No harm will come to her while we are away," Malacus said. "I have given her all she needs and we will be gone but a day."

"I know," he replied, once again looking down at Sarah. "But a strange feeling overwhelms the senses; as if my eyes will never again take sight of her should I choose to leave the comfort of these walls this day."

"A notion set on edge through caring for her as you do; one I would share if found in a similar position. She will be safe here. Place trust in my words and ready yourself for departure. The journey we undertake is a long one, our goals falling short of completion should we continue to delay."

A large part of him knew Malacus was right; he was just being overly anxious about leaving her alone. Malacus told him the trip would take most of the day and they would likely end up staying in the small town overnight before returning first thing in the morning. Still, he didn't like the idea of leaving Sarah alone. He felt like he abandoning her. But when would he have this opportunity again? The logical side of his mind told him he was stuck here and had the rest of his life to get to know this new world. But, at the same time, he knew sitting at her side wouldn't wake her, either.

Steeling himself, a deep sigh still on his lips, Allen nodded and followed Malacus to the stairs. He turned at the bottom for one final look at Sarah. She looked so gaunt, and yet somehow so majestic. Knowing Malacus wouldn't wait forever, he turned and made his way up the stairs, leaving Sarah to suffer her silent torment alone until he returned the next day.

***

As they left the cabin Allen had learned to call home, Malacus handed him a travelling cloak and briefly explained the custom. The hooded garb was worn as a public display of noble intentions. Wearing a traveling cloak was a sign of humility seen from a distance. The hood was removed only when the journey was complete. If one was seen travelling without their hood, or not wearing a cloak at all, it was assumed that his ill-intent was in the open for all to see. Allen found the custom very strange; many holes were in the logic behind it. He had, nevertheless, taken the cloak and thanked Malacus for the instruction.

It was late afternoon by the time the town came into view on the horizon. They had skirted the lake in front of Malacus' cabin and travelled in the same direction from which he and Zorthos had first arrived. Though in a frantic hurry his first time through the terrain, Allen recognized certain landmarks as they made their way toward their destination. It still fascinated him that the grass could look so normal up close, yet have a purple hue to it the farther into the distance it got. Somewhere along the way they reached a road he didn't recognize and followed it north.

They continued toward the town of Abendroth, which, according to Malacus had been named for a powerful wizard from the time of the original God-King. Abendroth had suggested the idea of a tournament, the Arena Games, to choose a successor for the only ruler the world had known for over a thousand years. Malacus also gave him a quick lesson in the economics and trade on Datheron and tested him several times along the way. In the end, however, he told Allen to just observe and let him do the talking.

Malacus had also given him a cover story, just in case they were somehow separated and he was questioned for any reason. Allen found it both interesting and disconcerting that Malacus felt the need to take such precautions when they were basically going to the store for groceries.

The cover story was that he was a ward and caretaker for Malacus. He had only been with the old man for a short time and hadn't trained in any special skills since being brought to Datheron from the distant, remote, world of Shennigar. Shennigar, Malacus told him, was one of the few worlds in the immediate solar system on which humans like he and Allen could be found. He informed Allen that being from Shennigar would raise very little suspicion, as there were a select few from that world who knew of Datheron and were occasionally brought from there to learn abilities. Most stressed by Malacus in their brief trek to Abendroth, however, was that Allen was to, under no circumstances, speak in his native language of English. While virtually none would correlate the language with Earth, it was not a language which would be understood and would most definitely raise suspicion.

Somewhere along the way Malacus had picked up a large stick of some sort and molded it into a walking staff. Allen had never seen the old man use one and silently wondered if he needed it or if it was another precautionary measure. The old man seemed extremely nervous about their simple excursion into town.

Even from a distance Allen could tell this town was different from any he'd experienced on Earth. The buildings appeared compressed together and gradually got taller the closer they were to the center. It didn't appear to cover a vast amount of land, but it did almost look as if they would be walking through the bowels of a very large hill once they got into the town.

As they continued their journey, Allen found himself absorbed in his thoughts. He'd thought the old man silly for being worried about something as simple as a trip into town, but as they drew nearer he couldn't help growing more nervous by the step. He reminded himself that he was going to be the only one in Abendroth who didn't have a special ability of some sort. He and Sarah were actually the only two on the entire planet who weren't trained in some sort of supernatural skill. He suddenly felt very exposed, very vulnerable.

A hand on his shoulder snapped him back to the present.

"Calm yourself," Malacus commanded. "You are too tense. You must appear at ease or people will think you to be of a dubious nature."

"Apologies," Allen offered. "My nerves yet remain on edge. I shall put effort toward regaining control of them."

"Good," Malacus nodded. "Heed my instruction and leave all discourse to me and we shall be on our way shortly. For you this excursion is about growing familiar with the sight of a new world and its people, nothing more."

Allen took a deep, cleansing breath. "Understood."

"You appeared to express excitement when first we left," Malacus observed. "What has changed upon our arrival?"

"Well," he began, considering his words carefully, "I stand the only one among the masses absent some sort of special ability, a condition which fills me with feelings of exposure. I would not see your efforts to keep me hidden fall short of intent should such a thing be brought to light." He didn't voice his concern that not having abilities might be all it took for someone to discover their ruse and determine that he was from Earth. Malacus had made it more than clear what would happen if anyone found out that detail.

Malacus nodded his head in understanding as he spoke, "Heed my warnings, keep eyes to observation and mouth free of words and no one will take notice of you. Appearance alone is not enough to betray your lack of abilities. Those of this world do not walk around flaunting such things for value of entertainment, or simply because we can. Though knowledge that such abilities can only be acquired of this world is common among the masses, such skills are honed only to the purpose of enhancing the value of life. I am certain such an example exists on your world, does it not? People of Earth do not walk the streets displaying prowess in skills possessed as they move simply to show that they can. Am I incorrect in the assumption?"

"No," Allen conceded. The reference brought a slight smile to his face. He briefly pictured what it would be like to see people walking the streets on Earth, painting portraits or playing instruments as they moved, or carrying things that they'd built by hand just to show they were capable. Thinking of it in such a way did make the notion seem silly.

"You will be fine," the old man assured him again. "Keep eyes and ears open to the surroundings and stay close at my side."

"As you command." He smiled, feeling comforted by Malacus' confidence.

Then a question came to mind that had been nagging him the whole time he'd been carefully listening to the old man's instructions.

"So, if my presence alone will not draw unwanted attention, why must I keep silent? Why go to such lengths to inform me of what to do and what not to do?" he asked. "From where is such concern spawned?"

Malacus glanced furtively at Allen from the corner of his eye. "Your talent for observation rivals the intelligence behind your eyes," he said. He let out a deep sigh before he continued. "Do you recall the man of whom your father and I spoke, the one who hunts him?"

"Yes," he answered. "He is called Luziaph, if memory serves?"

"Memory serves you well," Malacus nodded with a smile. "He is called Luziaph. He stands the Proctus of Vardiston. The level of authority he wields rivals that of his specially trained skills and his reach is wide within this region. He is not a man to be underestimated."

Allen nodded as he listened, trying to piece it together in his mind. "Go on," he said. "What about him? If we travel to Abendroth, why should the Proctus of Vardiston be cause for concern?"

"Because," Malacus said simply, "Abendroth stands the town nearest to Vardiston and is not beyond the reach of his influence. Luziaph is anything but careless. Agents under his patronage travel the countryside, ever watchful of anything to report to their master. That Abendroth sits in such close proximity to Vardiston makes risk of encounter all the more likely."

"Oh," he murmured. He now understood exactly where Malacus' desire for discretion was coming from. "So," he asked after a long moment, "You believe his agents already seek to find me?"

"They do not necessarily seek you specifically," Malacus answered quickly. "But he will stop at nothing to bring Zorthos before him once more. He stands a Grandmaster of telepathy and is likely to have already uncovered knowledge that Zorthos brought two with him upon his return. He might not yet know your names or faces, but capturing either of you would be an invaluable opportunity to lure Zorthos right to him. That does not even account for the fact that, with his mastery over the mind, he would quickly learn the truth of your origin should you fall into his grasp. Were that to happen . . ." Malacus paused, a haunted look briefly covering his features. "Well, we shall simply make certain that it does not."

"Such a thing should not pose problem," he said as confidently as he could. "I am here to observe and learn, nothing more. It is you who will bear the weight of conversation."

Malacus chuckled and clapped Allen on the upper back. "Good man," he said with a laugh.

The streets of Abendroth looked much different up close than they did from a distance. The pathways between buildings were much narrower than Allen had expected, teeming with all sorts of people, creatures, and activity. As he did his best to follow in Malacus' wake pushing through the raucous crowd, he was in complete awe at what he was seeing. Most of the buildings appeared to be constructed with some type of stone or rock, while others could have been petrified wood or clay. The architectural style in which most were built, as inconsistent as it appeared to be, was similar enough to that seen on Earth; a foundation, at least four walls, openings for doorways and windows; several had chimney-like vents to let smoke escape from what Allen assumed were fireplaces. But it was the people among the crowd that had drawn Allen's attention.

Humanoids of every type, shape, and size filled the streets as he continued to follow Malacus to their first stop. Allen certainly hadn't imagined it being so crowded that he would be virtually swimming through a sea of people, but what shocked him more was feeling as if he was living in a science-fiction movie. There were creatures that looked like they were half-beast, half-man fighting their way through the masses. Lizard-men, most of which were much shorter than the rest of the moving throng, cast their beady eyes about as they, too, slinked through the streets. There were gray-skinned creatures, which reminded him of the alien phenomenon that had become an obsession among the culture on Earth; blue-skinned men and women with pointed ears, like the ones he had seen chasing Zorthos on Earth, and a variety of others that seemed to be every color in between. He even saw a couple of creatures soaring overhead that appeared to be men with wings where their arms should be.

Sparsely dotted in the crowd were men and women who looked like he did. He reminded himself that appearing human didn't necessarily mean that they were. Among the humans he spotted, he was surprised and fascinated to see some who had a third eye in the middle of their forehead. He noticed that all who had a third eye, including the women, were completely bald; none appeared to have visible body hair of any type.

Here and there among the alien bustle Allen could also see things that, under normal circumstances, would have had him questioning his sanity. Down an intersection to the right he noticed a couple of three-eyed children which seemed to be playing "keep away" with another blue-skinned child's ball. Rather than tossing it back and forth between them, they kept the ball hovering just out of the other child's reach, letting it descend just enough for the blue-skinned child to almost reach it before causing it to levitate back out of reach. He found it disheartening and bewildering that even though there appeared to be countless differences here, something as simple as children tormenting each other remained the same.

As Malacus continued his course in a direct line, Allen noticed numerous things that would have been out of place on Earth. There was a fire pit under an awning on one of the clay-looking buildings which was being used to cook a powerfully built animal that very much resembled a boar. The human female cooking it kept it hovering and rotating over the fire with a flick of one of her wrists, while her other appeared to be fueling the flame, causing it to burn a little hotter. On the opposite side of the road, a little further away, a stout looking beast-man was sitting at a bench apparently repairing items by running them through his hands. Once finished with one, he reached down and grabbed another item from a pile at the base of his work table, clamped the broken item in his hands, ran a thumb over the broken joint, and the next moment set it aside as the repair was complete. He was so absorbed in watching all the interesting things around him, super powers that he had dreamed about for longer than he could remember, that, more than once, he nearly lost track of Malacus.

Being surrounded by so many examples, seeing that they truly did exist, that they were possible, had his heart hammering in his chest.

He couldn't wait to start learning how to do some of these things himself.

As he watched what would have been considered a supernatural phenomenon on Earth, he began to think it might not be so bad living on this world if he were actually able to learn some of these skills. He wondered if he would have enough time to learn how to effectively manipulate Mystica before he figured out a way to get home. He wished Sarah was here to see this.

The day seemed to be overcast in a sweltering heat wave. He hadn't remembered it being this hot at Malacus's cabin and wondered if it was possible for the climate of this planet to change so drastically so quickly, or if it was just due to being completely engulfed in a sea of people, some of whom were creating fires for various purposes adding to the heat.

Finally, after what seemed like hours, Malacus turned down an alleyway between two of the larger buildings somewhere near the center of town. The overhang of the roof on one of the buildings cast a small amount of shade over the alley. Allen was grateful for the momentary relief it offered from the heat. He felt a drop of sweat drip down the back of his neck and race all the way down his spine. Near the middle of the alley, Malacus descended a small staircase on the building to the right and approached a door.

Malacus reached out and rapped his walking staff on the door twice, then turned to face him. "Remember," he whispered, "Leave all discourse to me, even if question is directed to you. Should such an instance arise, defer to me."

He nodded to let Malacus know that he understood. The old man no sooner turned back around to face the door when it opened a crack. A golden-tinted beady eye surrounded by dark scaly skin appraised them through the opening for a moment before finally opening the door the rest of the way. Allen noticed as it did that the golden eye belonged to a lizard-man, similar to the ones he'd seen among the crowded streets; though his skin seemed to be a much darker pigment than those he had previously seen, and also a little more leathery. Allen wondered if this lizard-man was older than the ones he'd noticed before.

Before the lizard-man had a chance to greet them, Malacus began talking to him in yet another language— one he didn't understand. He wondered just how many languages the old man spoke, and why he was worried about Allen saying anything if the conversation was going to be held in a tongue foreign to him. Malacus gestured behind him, and Allen could only assume that the old man was introducing him. When the lizard-man glanced at him, he nodded in a way that seemed to be a greeting; Allen returned the nod.

After the brief introductions, he and Malacus were ushered into the lizard-man's home. Allen couldn't help but notice that Malacus didn't remove his hood as they passed through the doorway. The interior of the lizard-man's home didn't strike him as very homey; meager would be a better description. There was a workbench next to a sleeping pallet in the far left corner. The walls were lined with shelves stocked much like Malacus', and there was a bar stretched across the center of the room, partitioning one half from the other. There were no pictures or paintings on the walls and, by the shape the floor was in, it didn't look as if brooms had been invented on this planet yet. The lizard-man crossed the partitioned wall to stand on the other side of the bar.

As the lizard-man and Malacus conversed, he made his way to the window. Since he couldn't understand what was being said anyway, he wanted to see if he could catch a glimpse of more Mystica manipulation. The lizard-man must have noticed because the old man turned and addressed him in a harsh tone.

"Do not wander!" Malacus ordered, snapping his fingers and pointing to the floor directly beside him. "Stand here, and do not fall from my side again!"

Allen was momentarily offended by the way Malacus had seemingly demeaned him in front of this new acquaintance, but he realized that he didn't know all of the strange customs of this world and decided better of voicing his objections in present company. He adhered to Malacus' direction and scurried over to the spot the old man had indicated.

Once satisfied with Allen's compliance, Malacus went back to his conversation with the lizard-man. After another few moments the old man appeared to be listing off things and gestured to a shelf behind the bar. The lizard-man nodded and quickly shuffled off to retrieve what Malacus had requested.

When the reptilian vendor returned, he set three things on the counter and said something very brief to Malacus; Allen assumed it was the price for the items. The first was a very large vile containing a thick purple liquid; the second was a pouch containing a large quantity of what looked like mustard seeds; the third contained a fine white powder. Malacus appraised the items on the counter and, after a moment's consideration, reached into the front pocket of his tunic and pulled out a pouch of his own. Malacus fingered through the pouch briefly, eventually removing three round disc-shaped jewels. They reminded Allen of the coins he was used to on Earth, only they were slightly larger and appeared to be made out of some sort of crystal or colored glass. An odd symbol he couldn't quite make out protruded from the center of the crystalline coins.

Once the lizard-man was pleased with the transaction, Malacus scooped up his purchases and led him out of the building, up the alley, and back into the cramped streets.

As they pushed their way through the flowing constriction of people, Allen's curiosity got the better of him. "What sparked such an outburst back there?" he asked. "Why was reproach given with such ferocity?"

Malacus slowed his pace a little but didn't make eye contact with Allen as he spoke. "He believed you to be my caretaker," the old man explained. "On this world such a thing means that you are in my service at all times. It was a slight against me that you moved from my presence. Had I not, his suspicion would have grown as I failed to strike you for the transgression."

Though Allen found the reason stupid, he didn't voice his protest. It seemed that every time he found something he liked about this planet, or finally accepted an aspect of it, something new surfaced that challenged his composure. Rather than inquire further, he simply nodded and continued to follow the old man through the crowd.

Their next stop was at the corner of a large intersection near the very center of Abendroth. The buildings were much larger here than at the outskirts of town. There was a very large statue in the center of the square of a man in flowing robes, with a severe look on his face, his right hand outstretched toward the crowd below. His other hand turned outward at his side, and he wore a short but full beard and hair that cascaded past his shoulders. The crafted form had a very regal feel about it. He wasn't positive, but assumed it was a statue of the town's namesake.

The doorway of the building Malacus approached next formed a large arch at the top, but didn't have anything protecting it from the elements. At the bottom of the stairs below the arched doorway, Malacus told Allen to remain behind while he went in for the next item. He found it curious that Malacus didn't want him witnessing this transaction, but did as he was asked and stayed at the bottom of the steps, silently wondering if Malacus didn't want to risk repeating the scene at the lizard-man's shop.

Once the old man disappeared through the doorway, Allen immediately turned to scan the crowd for displays of abilities. The crowd here, at the center of town, was more sparsely populated than the streets they had travelled to get here. It seemed the citizens of Abendroth were purposely giving the statue in the center of the square a wide berth; though whether it was out of fear or reverence, he couldn't tell.

There wasn't much to see in the way of abilities. People seemed to be hurrying through the square, appearing to do their best to avoid detection. While there were a few who would occasionally stop to appraise the statue, most seemed oblivious to it.

Straight ahead, to the right of the statue, Allen noticed a disturbance among the crowd. Heads and shoulders shifted in an unnatural manner, as someone pushed violently through the river of people. The disturbance jarred more bodies, rippling toward the square where he stood. He followed the movement until it finally burst into the square, near the base of the statue.

A blue-skinned woman was being chased by what looked like law enforcement officers. While all the common citizens wore some type of fabric garb, these two were wearing light armor and carrying weapons.

The woman was frantic as she ran with wild abandon to escape her pursuers. She looked back over her shoulder to gauge her lead and for an instant met his gaze. He didn't think he'd ever seen anyone look so terrified.

Before she got halfway through the square, two guards stepped out from behind the statue right into her path. He did a double-take; he hadn't seen them in his initial assessment of his surroundings and he couldn't help but wonder how long they'd been standing guard there. On this planet he supposed they could have been there the whole time, watching invisibly from the shadows. Allen couldn't help wondering if that was actually the case, if perhaps that was why everyone seemed to be purposely skirting the statue.

The flow of movement trickled to a stop as the crowd swarmed in around the action. None seemed concerned or shocked by what was transpiring, only mildly curious. Allen noticed they still stayed well away from the statue's base as they watched.

"I have done nothing wrong!" the woman pleaded. "Please leave me be!"

Allen glanced back toward the entrance where Malacus was to see him appraising the disturbance from the arched doorway. He gave Allen a very serious look, told him to stay where he was, and disappeared back inside.

All four guards closed in around the woman, leveling their weapons at her. Two guards held ornately designed long swords; one of whom appeared human while the other was of the three-eyed race. One of the others carried a spear and likewise had three eyes, while the last had a short sword in either hand and was a lizard-man. The woman spun, eyeing not only the guards surrounding her but the crowd as well. She seemed to be looking for a way out of her current predicament. For a long moment, no one moved. Time stood still.

Then the guard holding the spear, ignoring her pleas, took an aggressive step toward her.

"Surrender, or perish!" the guard yelled.

Almost faster than Allen could register, the woman snatched the spear, forcing the point to the ground, causing the butt to crash into the guard's chin with bone-shattering force. Yanking it from his hands, she spun it, twisting her body to gain momentum, bringing the tip whistling around across the guard's throat. Blood sprayed the air as the guard toppled.

Allen could hardly believe what he'd just seen.

One of the other guards yelled, "Sarvato!" as the woman spun back into a defensive posture, pleading once again to be left alone. She seemed on the verge of tears as she leveled the spear at her aggressors. A guard with a long sword charged with lightning speed. Allen watched with rapt attention as the guard appeared to pass right through her, as if she were a ghost. Without even looking, the woman spun the point of the spear behind her, bringing it up through the guard's abdomen. He was momentarily staggered, but quickly regained his composure.

The guard grabbed the end of the spear protruding from his gut, which was still being tightly clutched by the blue woman, and twisted his own body, using the spear to throw her to the ground. Before she had a chance to get up, the lizard guard with short swords rushed in and sliced her stomach open. Then, as if nothing had happened, one of the guards scooped up their fallen comrade and began pushing through the crowd while the others urged onlookers to go about their business.

Allen was in complete shock. He'd never seen such violence before; not in real life anyway. Part of him felt as if he might be sick from the sight of it, another horrified that the guards would just cut the woman open and walk away rather than arrest her. His heart hammered against his eardrums.

He was appalled by the conflict he'd witnessed, and completely flabbergasted that no one else seemed to be. They all went back to what they had been doing, leaving the poor woman writhing in agony alone.

Allen didn't remember moving, but found himself kneeling at the woman's side, desperately wishing he knew how to manipulate Mystica the way Malacus did so he could heal this woman's suffering. She'd just wanted to be left alone.

As he he hovered over her, Allen watched the woman's eyes dart about, as if in search of anything to cling to, as if taking in everything one last time. Tears dripped down her face as her eyes met his, and he noticed for the first time that the parts of her eyes which should be white were black and her irises were red; the same as Pythor's. He offered the woman his hand, knowing there was nothing more he could do for her. She accepted it graciously.

One of the guards appeared over Allen's shoulder and ordered him to clear out, but he couldn't leave her. Instead he rested his free hand on the woman's stomach, just above the grievous wound, closing his eyes in sorrow, wishing he could heal her suffering. He recalled wishing he could do the same for Sarah when she was bitten by the vehectra snake. He remembered Malacus placing his hands on Sarah in a gentle way, the way he had his hands on this woman now, healing her. Closing his eyes, he let himself go, swept away with his desire to save this woman's life. He pictured in his mind how it felt to watch Malacus heal Sarah; how, at the time, it had almost made sense even though he'd never seen it before. Allen wanted nothing more than to take the pain from her eyes.

Suddenly, a painful vise-like grip clamped the back of his neck. As he was violently ripped away from the blue-skinned woman, he opened his eyes. The wound on her gut was nearly healed. Though the grip on his neck had his focus, he was elated that he had somehow, once again, harnessed an ability he hadn't been taught how to use.

The guard violently spun him around and planted a firm grip onto his throat.

"You were told to clear out," the three-eyed guard growled. "How dare you undermine the punishment dealt this woman?"

Panic set in as the hand tightened on his throat, constricted his breath. Tears stung his eyes. He needed air. Over the guard's shoulder Allen could see Malacus at the bottom of the steps, horror in his eyes. Under his arm he clutched a large package which appeared to be a picture frame wrapped up with thick cloth. Allen briefly wondered what it could be as he let his eyes once again find the old man's face. Malacus watched him with a whirlwind of emotion, appearing unsure what to do.

A dark-skinned human guard appeared behind him. He knew he probably shouldn't have interfered when he didn't understand the laws of this world, but he just couldn't leave the woman there to die. She had insisted that she'd done nothing wrong and they'd killed her anyway. Now the same guards had their attention on him, and he felt panic spread through his body at the thought that he might be about to die by their hand, too. He didn't want to lose his life for helping to ease someone's pain. He gazed pleadingly at Malacus over the shoulder of the three-eyed guard.

He was powerless. The old man had to do something.

Malacus gave him a desperate look, almost an apology, then clutched the package tighter and vanished, fading from reality in a matter of seconds. Allen could see people in the crowd being pushed aside as an invisible Malacus forced his way through them and away from him.

His great-grandfather was abandoning him, leaving him to suffer his fate alone! To say he felt betrayed would have been a vast understatement. He'd told Allen days ago that he didn't want to lose his only great-grandson, and now he was walking away, giving these guards the opportunity to end his life. As his vision started to fade, Allen recalled the worried feeling he'd had just before they'd set out that morning.

Now he was sure he'd never see Sarah again.

At long last, the guard let go of his throat. He collapsed to the ground, sucking in a much needed, life-giving breath. It tasted nearly as painful as it did relieving.

"On your feet!" the three-eyed guard demanded. "You are under arrest."

19

CAPTURED

THE RIVER OF PEOPLE parted willingly as the guards all but carried Allen from the center of Abendroth. The crowd watched with indifference as the three of them silently moved past. Allen desperately wanted to break loose and run, but the memory of what these guards had done to the woman was too fresh in his mind. Running would only get him killed. Hopelessness swept through him. He couldn't make his legs cooperate.

With frantic urgency his mind raced for a way out. His thoughts reverted to the story Malacus had given him should he be detained or questioned. He hadn't considered he would actually need it, but he could come up with little else to try.

"Please," he said, grateful he'd learned the language, as the guards dragged him away. "You must release me. Your eyes bore witness to misunderstanding, nothing more."

"Be silent," the human guard said.

"You mistake me," Allen pleaded. "I am not of this world; I did not know laws were broken in the act. I hail from Shennigar and am unfamiliar with the laws of this world. I have been here but a very brief time. I am the caretaker of that old man back there. You must let me go so I might tend to my duties."

The guards stopped moving. "What old man?" the three-eyed guard asked. "Of whom do you speak?"

Allen felt a renewed sense of hope; maybe this would work after all. He realized Malacus hadn't given him a false name to use for either of them. He hoped it wouldn't matter

"His is called Malacus," he offered, hoping it would make a difference.

"You speak with false tongue," the three-eyed guard scoffed, once again carrying him away. "Such a thing is not possible."

Allen couldn't understand what had happened. The guards had stopped; he'd had their attention. Then, at the mention of Malacus' name they'd discounted his pleas. He wondered if they knew the name Malacus and just didn't believe him or if they hadn't seen the old man he was talking about. Malacus had disappeared awfully quickly when he'd seen the guards had grabbed Allen. Maybe they'd wanted to arrest the old man and thought he was lying, giving them a fake name. Malacus did keep himself pretty secluded in his cabin in the middle of nowhere. Maybe it was both. Allen couldn't help feeling there was something more going on here than he realized.

Curious as he was about their hesitation, however, he knew he had more pressing concerns. He needed to get away somehow. He didn't want to be taken from Sarah without the chance to apologize for ruining the life she wanted on Earth.

"I beg of you," he protested, "You must hear my words! I speak the truth!"

"Be silent!" the human guard barked again, bringing the hilt of his short sword up toward Allen's face.

A bright light stole Allen's vision. The world spun. Warm blood filled his mouth and oozed down his chin. Only through monumental effort was he able to keep from striking back at the guard.

As Allen struggled to bring the world back into focus, he recalled what Malacus had told him about prophecy being out of the scope of anyone's control. It certainly seemed everything was slipping through his fingers; *everything* was out of control. Would something as simple as comforting a dying woman be the the catalyst that brought the prophecy to fruition? How could an act of kindness bring an end to the way of life for this whole world, possibly even the universe? The notion seemed ludicrous to Allen.

The fate of the universe couldn't be his responsibility.

Realizing he couldn't change events already in motion, Allen gave in to his fate; at least for the moment. Forcing his legs to keep pace with his captors, he moved despondently through the parting throng for what felt like hours, but was likely nowhere near. He ached with regret that he would not be there when Sarah finally woke. She would feel alone, abandoned.

In a way, she was alone . . . abandoned.

As much as he hated it, Allen knew all he could do now was try to figure out what to do next. It was the only way to help Sarah. He had to be there for her when she woke in a strange new world. Done was done; he couldn't change what had happened, but maybe he could find a way out of this.

"Can you at least impart knowledge of where it is you take me?" he asked, half expecting to get bashed in the mouth again for his curiosity.

The guard eyed him contemptuously with all three eyes for a moment, but answered the question. "Our commander will decide your fate."

"You will likely be escorted to Vardiston for sentencing," the other offered, if a little reluctantly.

Allen missed a step. "I am to be taken before Luziaph?" he asked.

"It seems you have been here long enough to know some of our laws," the human guard sniped.

Allen wasn't sure his heart had ever raced as it did in that moment. The cut on his lips pulsated with every rapid heartbeat. He felt the rise of a panic attack. This is exactly what Malacus had feared, what he'd tried to avoid.

"Why am I to be taken before Luziaph when it is you who killed that woman?" he asked, fearing the answer.

"She brought such retribution upon herself," the human guard insisted.

"How?" Allen pressed. "What was her crime? What did she do which warranted death in response?"

Both guards looked as if he'd said the dumbest thing they'd ever heard anyone say. "You really do come from off-world if such a thing escapes your understanding," the three-eyed guard said, a trace of annoyance and amusement in his tone.

"She killed Sarvato," the human guard stated, as if it should have been obvious.

"Sarvato?" Allen repeated, realizing he'd heard one of these men yell the name a moment after the woman had killed their colleague. "Was that the man's name, the one carried away upon the shoulders of the other guard?"

"Yes," the three-eyed guard answered.

"Oh," Allen said dumbly. "So prior to lethal action on her part, the intent was simply to arrest her?"

The three-eyed guard nodded. "We are not as unreasonable as you seem to think."

Allen wanted to point out that they'd arrested him for comforting a dying woman, but thought better of it. Somehow he didn't think they'd believe he healed her by accident. Admitting he hadn't done it on purpose would only raise questions. He was not looking forward to being taken before Luziaph. He knew he couldn't hide anything from a Grandmaster of telepathy. Too, he knew that if anyone started asking more complicated questions—like specific details about Shennigar—his story would crumble like a house of cards.

"What names do you go by?" he asked in an attempt to lighten the mood and get his mind off the hopeless path it was taking.

"Of what use could our names be to you?" the human guard asked; a little defensively in Allen's opinion.

"If you speak the truth about ushering me to Vardiston, I would think it preferable to have something to call you other than 'guard'," he answered, trying to make his remark sound offhand.

"Such determination has yet to be made by our commander. Until it has you would do well to close your lips and cease such ridiculous questions!" the human guard spat.

Based on the hostility in the guard's voice, Allen got the distinct impression it was going to be a long journey, if indeed he was to be escorted to Vardiston by these two.

Allen was taken to the far north side of Abendroth. As they had slowly moved toward the northern part of town, and away from its center, he'd noticed the same construction pattern. The buildings stood gradually shorter and closer together, with the exception of their command station. It was roughly four stories tall and stood out above the one-story buildings surrounding it. There were no windows on the upper portions of the outer walls marking new floors—like buildings on Earth—but it stood out in such contrast to those around it that he was sure it was at least two or three stories taller.

Allen hadn't noticed the building on his way into Abendroth with Malacus because they had approached from the south. The larger buildings in the center of town had blocked it from view. He'd noted that this was one of the buildings that appeared to be formed out of some sort of clay or brick. Light cracks trailed paths along the outer walls here and there and several guards, wearing the same style light armor as his captors, walked the perimeter, guarding the main entrance. None gave him more than a perfunctory glance as he was escorted to the entrance.

The inside of the building was nothing like he'd expected. While it did appear to have several floors, they weren't laid out in a fashion to which he was accustomed. A spiral staircase lined the outer walls and slowly coiled its way to the top, disappearing from view as it reached the ceiling. As they neared the center of the main floor, he noticed the ceiling had a large hole in it which appeared to go all the way to the top floor. Six pillars were laid out in a semicircular pattern surrounding the hole that led to the upper floors. Through the gap in the ceiling he could see that the pillars ran all the way to the top of the building, past the other floors.

Guards here and there were sparring with one another, while others adjusted their armor or moved up the staircase. Several others surrounded a fallen soldier and seemed to be in shock as they discussed his fate. Allen wasn't positive, but he thought it looked like Sarvato on the ground, the guard killed by the woman he had saved.

Suddenly, a beast-like humanoid guard approached Allen and his escorts from among the group surrounding their comrade. Both guards bowed as the beast-man reached them.

"Commander Thrax," they said in unison, their eyes still on the floor.

"Is this the one that killed Sarvato?" Commander Thrax asked, his eyes locked on Allen, awaiting a response.

Allen's heart leapt into his throat. It was one thing to be arrested for countermanding an execution, and quite another to be thought guilty of killing an authority figure. He wasn't sure these two guards would be completely truthful and didn't want to give them the opportunity to throw him to the wolves.

"I am not," he answered before either of the others had a chance. "They have already dispatched the woman responsible for that unfortunate act."

"Why does this prisoner speak out of turn, answering in your stead?" Commander Thrax bellowed at the two supplicant guards, without taking his eyes off Allen.

The two guards glanced surreptitiously at one another as they raised their heads. Before either had a chance to respond, Thrax began on them again.

"And why does he not yet wear a Triaga?" the Commander admonished.

The two guards scrambled to rectify their mistake. The three-eyed guard grabbed his right shoulder with one hand and gripped his forehead with the other. Allen knew struggling would only make it worse, so he tried to comply by going limp and letting his motions be guided. His head was pulled down toward his chest and something painfully clamped around the back of his head, near the base of his skull. The object wrapped itself around his head, under his ears on either side and up past the crown, nearly to his

THE PLANET OF THE GODS

forehead. He knew he was now wearing exactly what he'd seen on Zorthos when they'd met on Earth.

The instant it locked into place Allen felt as if he lost a part of himself. He couldn't quite explain exactly what it was, but he knew something was missing. He imagined it must feel similar to having the gift of vision, only to wake up without it the next day. The strangest thing about it was that, although he didn't know how to manipulate Mystica, something told him it was the distinct absence of Mystica he was sensing. Somehow that only added to the overwhelming sense of hopelessness he was already feeling.

"Now," Commander Thrax began again, "What did this one do?"

"He made attempt at healing the woman responsible for the death of our brother, Sarvato," the human guard answered with disgust.

The Commander looked genuinely surprised. "Why would you do such a thing?" he asked, directing his glare at Allen.

Allen, still struggling with the sense of loss he felt over having a Triaga clamped to his head, was a moment in responding. "I am not of this world," he answered meekly. "I am unfamiliar with most of your laws and customs. I did not realize what I did was wrong."

"From where do you hail?" Thrax asked.

"Shennigar," he replied, keeping his response simple.

Commander Thrax squinted slightly. "Shennigar," he echoed. "How long have you been upon Datheron, Shennigaran?"

Allen wasn't sure if there was a response that would jeopardize his story, so he decided to keep his answers as vague and truthful as he could without revealing he was actually from Earth.

317

"Apologies, the precise answer eludes me," he answered. "A little over a month, I think."

"He lies!" the human guard chimed in. "No one could learn healing of that magnitude in but one month's time!"

Allen silently castigated himself for not realizing that before he'd opened his mouth. He had to put all his effort into slowing his heart. He felt his knees might collapse at any moment. He frantically searched for a way to discount the human guard's objection.

Then it came to him. He would essentially be admitting guilt, that he had purposely tried to heal the woman, but he guessed it didn't matter, since he couldn't dissuade a notion they were all certain of anyway. He decided to risk it.

"I gave her a dendegayra seed," he said quickly. "I had but one in my pocket. I thought it would help her, but injuries sustained prior to ingestion must have been beyond the seed's abilities to rectify."

"Such a story does not match my recollection," the human guard mumbled under his breath.

Commander Thrax glanced at the guard who had spoken out of turn momentarily before turning his gaze back upon Allen. "I see," he drawled. "But reason yet escapes me as to why you would heal a woman who just killed a man wielding authority before your eyes."

Momentarily relieved that his gambit had worked, Allen answered as honestly as he dared while twisting things enough for the Commander to believe his words. "Where I come from life holds meaning. The taking of it is considered wrong no matter the circumstances. I simply did not wish to see another die. Had I a second dendegayra seed, such kindness would have been shown to Sarvato as well."

"And where was it that you learned to countermand such justice dealt by proper figure of authority?" Commander Thrax asked.

In Allen's opinion, killing wasn't justice. Murder was murder. He knew, however, the point wasn't up for debate and he had to answer the Commander's question somehow.

"Such was not my intent," he said, putting effort into keeping his voice steady. "My only concern rested with helping someone in pain, to spare her from the clutches of death."

The Commander barked a laugh and shook his head in wonder. "You are a strange one, Shennigaran. But I do not believe your tongue to be false."

A wave of relief swept over him at hearing the Commander's words.

"You do, however, have much to learn in the ways of life upon this world," Commander Thrax added. "Tell me. How came you to be on Datheron?"

"The choice was forced upon me," he answered quickly, purposely keeping his response vague.

"There must be more to it than that," Commander Thrax prompted after a moment.

Allen realized he wasn't going to be able to get out of this situation without divulging more. "I was brought here by one of the Krathantor. Chance found me where I should not have been, and he offered terms to part me from my home as opposed to knowledge of this world's existence . . . or my life."

"I see," Thrax said. "If such is the case, why were you not promptly delivered to one of the Proctus of this world, or to the God-King himself?"

Allen felt forced to dig himself into a hole he wouldn't be able to climb out of. "I feared for my life. Opportunity to escape presented itself and I took it. The severe gravity of this world prevented me from gaining ample lead. As I lay there, an old man happened upon me, offering convalescence in return for services as caretaker."

"Who is this old man?" Commander Thrax asked. "I would have his name."

Allen wasn't sure he wanted to say the name aloud again. When he'd mentioned Malacus' name last time, the other guards had all but called him a liar. Malacus hadn't given him cover names for either of them, and he wasn't sure what else to call the old man. He hoped they didn't ask him to lead them to Malacus.

When Allen didn't answer, the human guard answered in his place. "He told us the old man called himself Malacus."

"Malacus?" Thrax asked, incredulously. "Such a thing is not possible."

Allen was beginning to wonder just who Malacus truly was. The other guards had had much the same reaction to the name as did Thrax.

"The old man told you he is called Malacus?" the Commander asked.

"That is what he told me," Allen said. "The possibility exists that he gave false name. Why does it matter? Who is Malacus to you? Why is such a thing to be considered impossible?"

"Because," Commander Thrax answered matter-of-factly, "Malacus has been dead for a great many years. He once held the station of God-King, prior to Rhenngoth taking his life along with the title."

Allen's head spun with the proclamation. His great-grandfather was once the God-King of this world? He wondered why Malacus hadn't told him. It seemed to him the more time he spent on this planet, the more he was being lied to by those he was supposed to trust. Malacus had practically had to force Zorthos to admit that he was

320

Allen's father. And he had nearly killed himself before the old man finally divulged the details of the prophecy. Knowing that he'd kept his true identity a secret made him wonder if there had been pieces of the prophecy Malacus had purposely omitted. The old man was always speaking cryptically and trying to keep things from him . . . and Sarah was stuck there with him. . .

"After consideration, I do not believe you to be a danger to anyone," Commander Thrax said. "But elements of your story yet beg deference to one better equipped to deal with them. I fear I have neither the time nor the skill available to sort them out."

Thrax turned to the guards on either side of him. "Take him to Vardiston," the beast-man said with finality. "Luziaph shall be the one to find the heart of the matter."

20

CONFESSION

THE JOURNEY TO VARDISTON had taken nearly two days on foot. Although he realized that he didn't understand a lot about the planet of the gods, it seemed odd to walk everywhere they went. Even early settlers on Earth had horses and wagons and things to make traveling less strenuous. Allen marveled at how there could be so many close similarities between the two worlds, how this world could have so many things Earth could only dream of, yet it seemed somehow perpetually stuck in a futalistic period of cultural evolution.

Allen noticed as they'd left Abendroth, following the road north, that the guards had kept their hoods up, just as Malacus had told him. They refused to let him do the same with his hood. Evidently the manacles he wore weren't enough to brand him as a criminal; he was to leave his face shamefully in plain sight as well.

Along the way he had finally gotten the two guards to open up, if only a little. He learned the three-eyed guard belonged to a race called Triclopians, and his name was

Pendrik. The human guard had remained hostile toward him the entire trip, refusing to speak unless absolutely necessary. He had, however, learned his name was Brohm, though he'd been forced to ask Pendrik about it while Brohm had gone ahead to scout a camp that first night.

The first thing he'd noticed as Vardiston finally came into view after several days of walking wasn't its size, the sporadic height of the various buildings, or the large barrier wall surrounding it; it was the palace itself. The Palace of Vardiston stood much taller than the rest of the city, appearing as if a shepherd among his flock. The spires and turrets interconnected in some areas by massive walls and in others, a simple bridge. It was reminiscent of some of the more elaborate castles he'd seen in books on Earth and, at the same time, somehow very different. It was a sight he knew he'd never forget.

As they had moved through the city, he noted certain similarities to what he'd witnessed in Abendroth. There were plenty of examples of Mystica manipulation to be seen in the streets, which were filled with the same conglomeration of races—with a few additions. A very large creature, which appeared to have skin made of stone and eyes the color of midnight was carrying a massive marble pillar on his shoulder ahead of them and seemed to be heading for the palace as well. There were guards everywhere; though the armor these ones wore was distinctly different from the armor worn by his escorts. Some of the guards were riding creatures like a hybrid horse-lizard. Allen wondered, as he gazed at the mane that ran down the creature's back and at its elongated snout, why they hadn't ridden these to make their journey quicker. He chastised himself a moment later, however, realizing he was in no hurry to be questioned by Luziaph, possibly incarcerated . . . or worse.

Another large barrier wall within the city surrounded the palace entirely. Guards moved about the walkway atop the wall, vigilantly watching the crowds below. Several guards were posted at the entrance to the palace grounds and stepped aside after Pendrik explained the nature of their visit to allow them entry.

As they passed through the mouth of the barrier into the royal courtyard, the first thing Allen noticed was a procession of statues which followed the walkway to the main entrance. Though every single one was in some grotesque pose, as if they were all about to be slaughtered, Allen couldn't help marveling at the detail that had been put into them. He stared at them as closely as he could without lagging behind his captors. Having an artist's eye for detail, he was blown away by the pristine beauty of the workmanship. The sculptor had accounted for and added every hair, tooth, and minuscule wrinkle in the clothing, though each was carved in a different medium. He was completely entranced. The statues were obviously intended to make any outside aggressor wary as they entered the premises, but he found them mesmerizing.

As they entered the palace, he was almost sad to leave the statues behind . . . until he saw that they continued into the main hall. He was so enthralled by the craftsmanship he hadn't noticed a blue-skinned woman approach them from the other side of the room.

"Greetings," the woman said. "Please state your business here."

"We bring a prisoner to be judged by Luziaph," Brohm replied.

"Lord Luziaph has other business to which he must attend and as such will not be conferring judgment upon anyone this day," the woman told them. "Is the matter of an urgent nature?"

"No," Pendrik answered, before Brohm could. "He can be held in your custody until such time as Luziaph deems fit to see him. The issue is not of a personal nature."

Brohm appeared affronted, but said nothing to contradict Pendrik.

The woman nodded, turned, and walked down the hall. "This way," she said over her shoulder.

They followed the blue-skinned woman through a series of corridors, down several staircases, and further into the bowels of the palace. Somewhere along the way, the walls ceased to have windows; the only available light source coming from a series of glowing orbs which grew bright as they neared and dimmed as they passed. The effect left Allen feeling as if someone was watching them as they moved, marking their progress with a bright flashlight.

Though he knew he was being marched to some sort of holding cell, he couldn't make himself feel fear. He was passive, accepting his fate, watching events unfold. He didn't know what would happen to him, but he knew, regardless, he had no control. He put his mind to what he would say in his defense when finally brought before Luziaph. He hoped he would be able to convince the man that it was a misunderstanding and he needed to get back to his duties.

Somehow he doubted it would be as simple as that.

Finally, after walking for what felt like an eternity, they reached a very large room with high arched ceilings. Along the walls was a succession of odd looking pillars, which supported the mezzanine above. They were hollowed out and crescent shaped, appearing as if they would complete a full circle if the missing piece in the front allowed them to connect. Allen counted two dozen of these semi-circle pillars within the room. He noticed there were others, prisoners he assumed, intermittently occupying the spaces within the circular barriers.

The woman led the guards three-quarters of the way through the room and gestured to one such c-shaped pillar to her left. "This one will do," she said.

Brohm shoved him into the center of one of the columns. It took effort not to stumble to the ground. As he turned around, Allen watched the woman pressed her hand to the column on her right. There was a sharp pulse to the air, and a violent humming noise momentarily stole his hearing.

"He is new to this world," Pendrik told the woman. "You may find benefit in warning him about crossing the threshold." Then he and Brohm turned and left.

The blue-skinned woman eyed him with a newfound interest at hearing Pendrik's words. "You are in a holding cell," she told Allen; speaking slowly, as if in attempt to make the words easier for him to understand. "Defenses of the cell have just been ignited. Invisible barriers surround you. Should you attempt to pass through them, you will die a most excruciating death. Do you understand?"

"Yes," Allen replied. "I understand.

She appraised him silently for a moment then turned and left him to his thoughts. Allen wondered, as he sank down in his cell, just how long he'd be waiting before everything else was taken from him.

Zorthos couldn't believe his eyes. His world slowed to a standstill, his heart reverberating at a ferocious pace in his chest, as he watched his only son being escorted to a holding cell a few feet below him. He wondered if it was possible that Luziaph was presenting an illusion to torture him. If it wasn't, and Allen really was here, everything Zorthos had been fighting for, everything he'd done to protect his family, had all been for naught.

He wanted to call out to his son, but he didn't trust his voice. How could this have happened? Malacus was supposed to be taking care of him. If Allen really was here, what had happened to the old man? Zorthos realized, encumbered as he was by the Triaga, that it had to be real; Luziaph couldn't access his mind while Zorthos wore it.

After what seemed a very long time, he gathered the strength needed to use his voice.

"Allen?" Zorthos called out in English. For a long moment there was no response, so he tried again. "Allen, can you hear me?"

"Hello?" he heard his son say.

"Allen, is that really you, or do my senses deceive me?"

"Who's there?" came Allen's response.

"Allen, it is your . . . it is Zorthos."

There was another very long pause before Allen answered him this time. "So I guess that means Luziaph caught you, too?"

Zorthos' heard sank. He felt the world around him crumble. Lost in brooding thoughts as he was, it took him a while to respond.

"Yes, I suppose it does," he answered at last. "How did you come to be here?"

"I was arrested for accidentally healing a woman gutted by one of the guards in Abendroth," Allen said curtly.

"What in the name of Paragus were you doing in Abendroth?" Zorthos puzzled aloud.

"That's sort of a long story."

"Well, I do not believe time to be a factor, should you care to share the details," he laughed, mirthlessly.

It was a while before either of them spoke again. He wasn't sure just how his son felt about him yet and didn't dare push him too hard. He wanted to explain his actions better, to tell Allen how he really felt. But he knew words alone wouldn't be enough to quell the resentment he was sure Allen still felt.

While he awaited his son's response, Zorthos' thoughts drifted to visions of the past. He wondered how different life would have turned out for both of them, had that Krathantor not found him when he did all those years ago. He would be much older now, had he stayed on Earth, and would never have had to leave the love of his life agonizing over decisions for which she could never know the truth. He would've watched his son grow a man and been able to offer lessons Allen couldn't learn anywhere else. Neither of them would be in a holding cell, awaiting other men to determine their fate. He sincerely hoped his son wasn't the child of prophecy, but remained fixed in the idea that the only way to be sure would be to get him home; a task he knew to be virtually impossible.

"Why did you leave?" Allen finally asked, snapping him back to reality. That he had expected the question didn't make it any easier to hear.

"The reasoning behind my choices to leave Earth has already been explained." He replied, fighting to keep his voice steady. "I did so against my wishes, but—"

"I mean, why did you leave when we got here?" Allen interrupted. "Why did you turn around and walk away again the moment you got the Triaga off your head? You didn't stay and try to get to know me. You didn't even wait until the next day. You left me on a world I've never been to, with someone I've never met. I mean . . . were you even planning on coming back?"

Allen's words cut through him. He wanted to make his son understand why he had done what he'd done. But how could he explain that he hadn't planned on coming back? That he had believed he would be killed in his confrontation, if not by Pythor or Luziaph, then by Rhenngoth? He was sparing Allen more pain not letting him get attached to a father who would die before they had a chance to know one another. He wanted to say so many things, but none of them would make a difference, make his only son feel better. Worse, he knew he couldn't risk being incarcerated this close to Allen under Luziaph's patronage. To protect the secret—that Allen was his son from Earth—he would have to make another sacrifice and leave Allen hating him even more. Now, more than ever, Zorthos wished he could escape the hold this world and those who ruled it had over him.

"Allen . . . such things are of a complicated nature," he said weakly.

"Don't give me that evasive bull crap!" Allen shouted. "I deserve to know the truth!"

"Lower your voice . . . And place yourself in my shoes, Allen," he pleaded. "Sacrifices made to protect those I hold close were more costly than imagining could convey. I relinquished all I considered to be of import in that act; my life with you and your mother, the chance to watch you grow into a man, to be at your side always. For me only a few years have passed since your birth, yet you stand before me already a man. The opportunity to be a proper father was stripped from me. Where you have had ample time, nearly two decades, to grow hatred toward me, I have had less than two years to mourn the loss of my family.

"As previously stated, it is complicated."

"I don't think it is," Allen retorted. There was an obvious edge to his voice, though Allen kept it calm as he spoke. "And I don't think it's me who needs to see things from your shoes; I think it's you who needs to see them from mine.

"I watched my mom mourn the loss of a husband who never died. I grew up never getting to experience father-son outings, got made fun of for being a kid without a dad. I suffered the consequences of choices I didn't make! So don't you dare sit there and tell me, 'it's complicated'! I deserve more than that!"

"I know you do," he answered softly. "But I can give no more. Turning back time is not an ability I possess. Being counted among Luziaph's prisoners is a more pressing concern than family squabbles. How is your Olyphatarian?"

"I am fluent," Allen replied in the native tongue of Datheron.

"Impressive," he said, keeping his words in English. "You spoke of healing someone by accident?"

"Yes," Allen replied, reverting to English.

While he wasn't sure how one could 'accidentally' heal someone, Zorthos was both proud of, and scared for, his son. He recalled Allen slamming Malacus against the basement wall without realizing how he'd done it. He had an overwhelming and sinking feeling that Allen was indeed the child of the prophecy. In his selfish desire to have his own life, he may have unwittingly set the prophecy in motion.

"What other lessons of note have you learned in your time with Malacus?" he asked, steering his thoughts away from things he could not control.

There was a moment or two of silence. "The gravity of this planet is no longer an issue for me. And once, a few days ago, I telepathically accessed Sarah's mind to try and help her out of her coma. It didn't work."

Zorthos was genuinely thunderstruck. "You accessed her mind? What number of attempts yielded such results?"

"I was only able to do it the first time I tried it," Allen answered.

"You attempted it but once?" he exclaimed. "Such a thing is not possible!"

"Believe what you want," Allen said coldly. "Why do you want to know these things anyway?"

"Allen," Zorthos began, putting effort toward sounding sincere. "You may not believe my words to be true, or find comfort in them, but I am proud of you. And the sting of losing a father is not unknown to me. My father was taken from me, too, when I was but a boy."

There was a long pause before Allen responded. "If you know what it's like, then how could you do it?"

Zorthos was unsure how to answer, so he continued with what he needed to say. "Allen, I am of the hope you will someday find forgiveness in your heart. But I know it may never be so. And I would not see you face the same decisions which have left my life shattered, along with my heart. I pray you are never forced from your children; that you will know their embrace, their laughter. I pray also that truth and understanding of sacrifices made on your behalf finds you.

"It is far too dangerous for the two us to be held so near by a Grandmaster of telepathy. Your true origin will surely be revealed if action is not taken quickly. That is why I must yet make another unwanted sacrifice. I shall turn myself over to the God-King's will, prying myself from Luziaph's grasp once again. I shall offer persuasion that two Earth children were brought to Datheron by Luziaph's command, that he might ignite the prophecy to his own ends. With luck, such information will cause Luziaph trouble enough to afford you the opportunity to escape."

"Wait a minute—" Allen interjected.

"Allen, close your mouth and open your ears that you might hear the wisdom such a course offers!" he barked in a whisper, cutting Allen off. "Should Luziaph learn the truth about you, he will most certainly turn such knowledge to his advantage. There is a long-lived hatred between Triclopians and Gorrlocks. Luziaph is a Triclopian; Rhenngoth a Gorrlock. Luziaph would love nothing more than to be out from under the thumb of Gorrlock God-King."

"Which ones are Gorrlocks?" Allen asked.

"They are kin to Pythor; blue-skinned, pointed ears," he answered.

"Oh, Okay."

"In but a moment I shall have Luziaph summoned to see my plan set on proper path," Zorthos continued. "Refusal of such a request from me will not be an option; to deny me will bring the wrath of Rhenngoth raining down upon him. I know the sensation of a Triaga upon the head is strange and disorienting, but it must remain so while you take shelter here. Luziaph will be unable to access your mind while it remains fastened to your head. The wearing of one stands a double-edged sword. While you remain unable to access your abilities, he is unable to access your thoughts. Upon his arrival to hear given request, do not even acknowledge me. Are we of a singular understanding?"

"Yes, I understand," Allen answered, his voice calm, almost submissive.

"Good. Now, before my request is made, you must tell me. What in the name of Paragus found you in Abendroth?"

Allen's response was a moment in coming. "Sarah is still in a coma," he said quietly. "And a few days ago, Malacus and I had a bit of a disagreement. He seemed to think a trip would not only help with my education of how this world works, but the change of scenery would do me good too."

"I see," Zorthos said thoughtfully, more to himself than to his son. "I would wager the realization of that choice carrying potential of being what brings prophecy to fruition did not elude him prior to the making of it. It appears he may yet be known as the facilitator of destruction."

"He's done more for me than you ever did," Allen mumbled bitterly from his cell.

Zorthos thought the remark was as hurtful as it was unnecessary. He knew he would never be able to right the wrongs he'd done to his family from his current position. He would waste no more time and put his plan into motion.

"Guard!" Zorthos yelled, returning his speech to Olyphatarian.

They hadn't waited long before the blue-skinned girl, whom Allen now knew was a Gorrlock, responded to Zorthos' call. By how quickly she'd gotten there, she had to have still been in the room. It concerned him a little that she might have been listening to his conversation with Zorthos. Allen knew that she most likely didn't understand a word of it, but Malacus had constantly admonished him not to use English at all in the presence of others. He hoped that wouldn't create a problem for him.

"What is it?" the Gorrlock woman asked Zorthos, but watching both both of them while she waited for her answer. He realized her eyes weren't the same black and red that Pythor's were and silently wondered what the cause of that could be.

"I wish to see Luziaph," Zorthos told her.

"Luziaph is of a mood today, and is very busy," she answered, turning her gaze back to Zorthos. "He is not at the beck and call of prisoners."

"In this, he stands absent choice," Zorthos said with a smug grin. "I wish to turn myself over to the will of the God-King. Go and retrieve Luziaph. Tell him his prize has yet again slipped through clutching fingers."

The Gorrlock woman looked surprised at Zorthos' request, but turned and left without another word. With his cell placed as it was he could just barely make out Zorthos standing at the front of his cell watching her leave.

Once he was sure she was gone, Zorthos spoke again in English. "Such news will not be well received," he said with a chuckle. "Were I to venture a guess, I would say Luziaph will be down here in short order. Upon his arrival, be out of sight; tend to your own business. I would not have him even think that we know each other. And once you are taken before him for crimes committed, offer humblest apologies for transgressions made and assurances that you will rectify such things in any way he asks. Explain to him that you are new to this world and—"

"Yeah, Malacus already gave me a back-story," Allen interrupted. "He told me to say I'm from Shennigar and unfamiliar with the laws of this world."

Zorthos looked momentarily taken aback, but quickly continued. "Such suggestion strikes upon perfection," he said. "Should he press for further details, tell him you hail from a very small village by the name of Fornatyme. I have had occasion to tread there once or twice and know with certainty that the inhabitants are of the same species as we. Such a location is of obscure enough nature he should not require more information of you."

Allen nodded, considering Zorthos' words. He was exceedingly angry with Zorthos but he didn't want to see him go. With Zorthos here, he wasn't alone. Once Zorthos was taken away, he would be left in a cell to brood on his fate . . . he truly would be alone.

He reminded himself that there was nothing he could do to change the situation. He could only focus on the advice he'd been given by Zorthos and Malacus. While he sat, feeling increasingly isolated, something Zorthos had said brought a question to his mind.

"Zorthos," he asked into the silence. "You said while I wear the Triaga that Luziaph won't be able to access my thoughts, but I won't be able to access my abilities."

"Correct."

"Well, now that I've had one clamped to my head, I know just how disorienting it is," Allen continued. "So how were you able to use abilities with one on? You said there was a way around the effects of the Triaga?"

"That, Allen," Zorthos answered, "is also complicated. I shall do my best to see answer given, but it will be of no service to you under present conditions."

Allen nodded and Zorthos continued.

"The Triaga is a highly complicated and delicate piece of equipment. It was engineered by the first true masters of telepathy on Datheron: the Triclopians. Not all Triclopians are counted masters of the craft, but all are born with an affinity for it.

"Two things made circumventing of the Triaga Pythor placed upon my head possible. First, I am more skilled in telepathy than he is. That is not to suggest that no effect was felt, but I was able to form a path around defenses presented by inadequate skill. Second, the clumsy approach of my captor offered time to prepare for the binding effect. If one is quick enough and practiced enough, one can partition a portion of energy outside the device's reach to remain accessible should the need arise.

This likewise requires a high level of skill in telepathy, but it can be done."

"I see." Allen said, thoughtfully, realizing that Zorthos was right. That particular technique wouldn't help him in his current situation. But he found it interesting, nonetheless.

As Allen let his mind wander over all the things that had happened over the last couple days, he heard footsteps approaching. Zorthos eyed him severely from his cell, crossing his lips with a finger. Within moments a very tall Triclopian appeared in front of Zorthos' cell. He wore elaborately designed silver armor; sleeveless breastplate, gauntlets which covered his entire forearms, and knee-high silver boots. The tunic he wore beneath the armor was a deep, dark purple. Allen knew right away this had to be Luziaph.

As Luziaph came to a halt in front of Zorthos, Allen watched the eye in the center of Luziaph's forehead glance directly at him. It was a haunting sensation, seeing one eye focusing on him while the others remained on Zorthos. A shudder ran down his spine.

After a moment, Luziaph's third eye turned to Zorthos. "What is this nonsense?" he sniped in Olyphatarian. "Gazianna informs me you desire to turn yourself over to the will of the God-King? Since when has penitence become a quality you possess?"

"Since the desire sprouted to remove credit of my capture, and any punishment you might think to inflict, from your hands," Zorthos answered sardonically. "Besides, I have known the God-King since I was but a child. I have a feeling leniency will not be difficult in the convincing, or the acquiring."

"I see," Luziaph said suspiciously. "Then such penitence comes not from concern for this human boy, the one Gazianna informs me you have been conversing with in strange alien dialect?"

"Him?" Zorthos asked as he pointed in Allen's direction. "Of course not. Recognition of his is coincidental, from a mission undertaken in my youth while still in the God-King's employ and counted among the Krathantor. Such mission found me on Shennigar when this boy was but ten years of age. I merely offered words of comfort regarding incarceration, assuming such comfort would be found in hearing words spoken in a tongue with which he is familiar."

Allen was alarmed by just how smoothly Zorthos was able to lie. He wondered if he could ever trust the man.

"Is that so?" Luziaph asked in a smooth tone of his own. "Then you would not take issue with submitting yourself to my mind, that truth of the matter might be proven beyond doubt?"

Zorthos smiled at Luziaph. "By all means, make attempt. You know as well as I that such a thing will require the removal of my Triaga. Are you so eager for a repeat performance of my capabilities?"

Luziaph glared at Zorthos for a long moment, palpable tension in the air. Finally, Luziaph pressed his palm to a panel on the right side of Zorthos' cell. The plate glowed slightly while his hand made contact. A sharp pulse in the air made Allen feel as if he had suddenly changed elevations. He flexed his jaw in an attempt to relieve the pressure.

Zorthos stepped out of the holding cell and raised both his hands toward Luziaph. With an intense look of contempt covering his features, Luziaph snapped a set of manacles around Zorthos' wrists. Zorthos looked directly at him.

"Luck is with you, Araset," Zorthos said to him in Olyphatarian. "Heed my words and no harm will come to you."

Allen got the distinct impression that Zorthos was covertly telling him not to use his real name, to use this one instead. That the man had spoken the words in Olyphatarian must have been for Luziaph's benefit. He nodded to let Zorthos know he understood.

Luziaph eyed Allen suspiciously, then prodded Zorthos and told him to get moving. Though Zorthos had offered advice and given him an alias, Allen couldn't help feeling a certain level of betrayal as he watched them march away.

For the third time in his life Allen's father was walking away, leaving him to face the world on his own.

21

AWAKE

BLINDING LIGHT PIERCED HER vision as she struggled to open her eyes. It felt like a lifetime since she'd used them. Her head ached in an unnatural way. Her senses swam through a perpetual fog. She couldn't focus her mind on anything but the discomfort. It took monumental effort to even recall her name.

Sarah. Her name was Sarah.

As she struggled to piece together where she was and, more importantly, how she'd gotten there, Sarah heard a voice. It sounded as if it were talking to her from a great distance.

"Finally awake, I see," the voice said; it was heavily accented.

Through the swirl of memories and emotions that flooded her mind, one kept pushing its way to the forefront: Allen. She remembered going to his house to see him, and later following him into the woods behind his house. Something happened in those woods . . .

"Where am I?" she asked, her voice cracking in a way she'd never experienced before. Though no more than a whisper, it took tremendous effort to push those words past her lips. Through the swirl of memories and emotions that flooded her mind, one kept pushing its way to the forefront: Allen. She remembered going to his house to see him, following him into the woods behind his house. Something happened in those woods . . .

"Remove such concerns from your thoughts for now," the voice told her. "You are safe; that is all that matters."

She opened her mouth, wanting to ask if the voice knew where Allen was.

"Sshh," the strange voice said. "Make no attempt to speak. You have been absent consciousness for quite some time. Effort toward regaining faculties and finding comfort in new and unfamiliar surroundings would be better spent. There is yet a great distance to travel before your senses return to you fully."

Sarah noticed as she closed her mouth that it was extremely dry. Her tongue felt swollen. Her stomach hurt. Her muscles were weak. She wanted to know where Allen was. She needed to know he was okay.

She remembered then what had happened in those woods. She had been told Allen was in trouble and that only she could help him. She'd passed through a bright light and found herself in a strange new world. There was a man there who had helped them escape. She recalled a sharp pain piercing her ankle and everything going black.

But that was all just a dream. None of that could have been real.

"Water," she whispered with all her strength.

After a moment she felt something touch her lips. A cool fluid pushed its way over her tongue and into her mouth. She clenched her throat muscles, swallowing down the liquid relief. She could feel it slide all the way down her esophagus and coat the walls of her stomach. The sensation sent a shudder up her spine.

As she fought to bring her reality back into focus, she kept her eyes clenched tightly shut. Light was too much for her debilitated sight. Her head felt as if it was floating uncomfortably in some massive body of water. She realized then that the voice had told her that she had been out for quite some time.

"How long . . . ?" she began; the effort of finishing her inquiry had been too much.

After a pause, the voice answered, "Weeks. For a time, we thought you for the afterlife."

'We', the voice had said. It had to be referring to Allen. Why wasn't Allen speaking?

Sarah opened her mouth again in an attempt to ask where Allen was, only to find more liquid pushing its way down her throat.

"Drink this," the voice told her. "It will accelerate convalescence."

The new liquid tasted unpleasant, but it didn't stop coming until she began sputtering for air. Once she'd caught her breath, it poured down her throat again in earnest. Though she felt as if she wasn't swallowing much liquid, her stomach filled rather quickly.

At last the pouring stopped and she heard the voice say, "A couple more doses will find you on your feet in short order. It may taste of death, but it will return atrophied muscles to former strength. It also bears a sleeping agent which will keep you unconscious while it works; as such business is painful."

Utterly exhausted as she was, the last thing Sarah wanted to do was go back to sleep. The thought frightened her. What if she didn't wake up? What was the voice thinking?

"Cast worry aside," the voice said in answer to her silent fears. "It will be a restful sleep, from which I assure you will awaken. You will feel better soon. Until such time, worry for naught but recovery. I shall return in the morning to take stock of your condition."

Sarah felt the voice stand. She heard footsteps echoing away from her. Moments later she was drifting lazily back into the darkness.

***

When she awoke the next morning, Sarah noticed a dramatic change in her faculties. As her eyes slowly worked their way open, she immediately felt more alert. Her muscles still ached awkwardly, feeling almost bruised, but she was able to lift her arm enough to wipe sweat from her own brow. She nearly laughed aloud at that small victory.

Though the rest of her seemed to respond more readily, though strained, her eyes still had trouble adjusting. It took ages before she was able to make out shadowed shapes in the room around her. Only when her eyes had completely adjusted did she realize that the room was nearly shrouded in darkness. A solitary torch at the far end flickered lazily, as if keeping a silent watch. The walls were lined with shelves and a work table sat on the right side of the room. For a moment, as her mind grasped for cognition, she had thought she was in her own bed. Realizing she wasn't was very disorienting.

Once she was fully awake and aware of her surroundings, she realized she was starving. Her stomach felt emptier than she could ever remember it feeling. It seemed to be painfully trying to eat itself. If she didn't know better, she would swear it was succeeding.

With great effort she pushed herself to a sitting position, swinging her legs over the edge of the pallet on which she assumed she'd been sleeping for weeks. Even as dark as the room was, she could see she had lost a lot of weight. Her head swam with the sensation of being vertical for the first time in a long while. For a moment everything went out of focus again and she cradled her head in her hands. Hearing a noise coming from the opposite side of the room, she jerked her head up. The ceiling was shifting, lifting away from the room she was in, revealing a staircase she hadn't noticed in the dark. An old man in flowing, dark robes descended the stairs.

The man stopped when he'd reached the bottom, staring at her in a very curious manner. His gray hair and beard were highlighted orange by the torch to his left. Harsh shadows cut across his face. He appeared to be smiling, but in the darkness she couldn't tell for sure.

"I thought I heard you stirring down here," the man said, quizziacally.

Sarah wondered how he could have possibly heard her; she hadn't made more than a muffled groan as she'd sat up. She thought it more likely that he had hidden cameras watching her.

For several long moments he stood, staring at her. Then, as if to end the uncomfortable silence, he raised his arm and snapped the fingers of his right hand. Several more torches along the walls sprang to life. As new light flooded the room Sarah flinched, clenching her eyes shut against the intrusion. In the light, once her vision readjusted, she could make out the old man in his entirety. He looked at once pleasant and dangerous, lighthearted and intimidating, passive and commanding.

"Did you just—" Sarah tried to ask, watching the torchlight dancing along the walls.

"How feel you?" the old man asked in that same odd accent, not yet taking a step toward her.

Sarah was caught off guard by the question. She mentally stumbled, looking for an answer. All at once her mind was racing, absorbing all the new information the light had brought with it when it announced itself to the room. She had to force herself to look directly at the old man as she considered his words.

"I'm okay, I think," she answered at last.

Taking her answer with a nod, the man crossed the room toward her. With a flick of his wrist the stool which sat next to the small work table began to scrape along the floor, following in his wake.

Sarah went rigid. She decided she must still be asleep, dreaming.

The man halted his approach a few feet from her, the stool grinding to a stop just behind him. He sat down, leaning forward, and held up a finger, trailing it back and forth across her vision. She followed the motion for a moment before forcing her concentration to his intense, violet eyes.

"Where am I?" she asked.

"You are on the planet Datheron," the old man answered, taking her left wrist in his right hand and seemingly checking her pulse. "You were most unfortunate to have your ankle bitten by a creature greatly renowned for its lethal qualities; it very nearly succeeded in the taking of your life."

Sarah's mind swirled with the possibility that it wasn't a dream; that she wasn't dreaming now. She couldn't find a proper way to respond, so she said nothing.

"I am called Malacus," the old man offered. "You need not fear me, Sarah."

"How do you know my name?" she asked, completely taken aback.

Malacus chuckled. "It would impossible to not know such a thing after witnessing Allen bear silent vigil over your condition for such an extended period of time."

Allen's name brought her entire mind to a singular purpose. Her thoughts, if only for that moment, were no longer jumbled. "Allen?" she said, with almost frantic urgency. "Where is Allen? Is he okay?"

Malacus sat back on his stool and crossed his arms. He let out a deep sigh. "I fear Allen is no longer among us."

Her world spun. "He's gone?" she asked in a shaky voice.

"My apologies," Malacus said, nodding solemnly. "He was arrested two days past. I fear there is nothing to be done for him now."

She was confused and almost insulted at his response. "Wait," she said. "He was arrested? He's not . . . dead?"

"No," Malacus answered. "Not when last I saw him, anyway."

Sarah felt a momentary wave of relief. Arrested. Allen . . . arrested? She had to be dreaming; the Allen she knew would never do anything reckless enough to get himself arrested. Sure he'd been reckless sometimes, but he'd never engaged in anything that could be considered illegal . . . Coupled with that were the self-igniting torches and the stool that seemed to move of its own volition. No, she must still be dreaming.

"I wish for your sake it were so, but this is no dream. Of that fact I can assure you," Malacus said, seemingly in response to her confused thoughts. "Nor are you absent sanity. Other than minor malnutrition, health seems to yet favor you. I would wager you hungry. Am I correct in the assumption?"

As overcome as she was by the onslaught of new information she'd received since waking, she could only manage a nod.

Malacus stood and walked toward the stairs. "In that case, follow me."

At the bottom of the stairs he turned and faced her again, looking at her expectantly. After a long moment he said, "If you want to eat you will have to come upstairs. I serve no food down here."

With that, the old man turned once more and disappeared up the short staircase.

It took far more effort to reach the top of the stairs than Sarah had expected. Standing up, she felt like a child learning to walk. Her legs shook tremendously, voicing protest with fits of convulsions. It felt like she weighed much more than what she actually did. It was evident to her, as she fought to stand, that her legs were thinner than she remembered; they rubbed awkwardly on the fabric of pants she only vaguely recognized.

Once she'd finally negotiated herself into a standing position, she begain inching her way across the room to where she'd seen Malacus disappear. As difficult as the task was, she found herself taking stock of her surroundings when she needed to pause and catch her breath. The walls of the long room in which she'd been unconscious for so long were lined with shelves the whole way across. The room almost appeared to be a massive underground wine cellar, except books and tomes were on display instead of bottles. There was a work table to her right and that weird stool which had moved on its own, somehow, behind her. Sarah also noted a mirror resting at an angle in the middle of the room to her left. It was mostly covered with a blanket, but what she could see looked eerily familiar. The style of frame around the mirror looked remarkably similar to the one Allen's mom kept in her living room.

At last, after what felt an eternity, Sarah reached the other side of the room. Her exceedingly wobbly legs hadn't collapsed on her journey to reach the staircase, a fact for which she was grateful, but she'd needed several breaks before finally reaching her goal. She'd had to virtually crawl up the stairs, feeling completely embarrassed from the lack of control she had over her appendages.

The sight at the top of the stairs was one of the strangest she'd ever seen. The entire place, as small as it was, was all one room with the exception of a couple areas partitioned apart. It all appeared to have been molded into its current form; there were no seams or cracks in anything, not even where the table met the floor. These were also lined with shelves, all of which contained a wide selection of weird trinkets and books. Malacus sat cross-legged at the table in the center of the room, the surface of which wasn't far from the floor. Food had already been set out for her.

Malacus gestured to the place next to him, a grin creasing his features, "Your food grows cold."

Sarah felt a wave of embarrassment hobbling over to the table in front of him. She didn't want him watching her struggle to do something as simple as walking across the room.

"Embarrassment concerns you?" the old man teased as if once again reading her thoughts. "You have my word that I find no amusement in witnessing one struggle to adapt to a new climate. Now come, eat."

"How are you doing that?" Sarah asked, her curiosity momentarily overcoming her hunger.

"What is it that I am doing?" the old man asked without looking up from his own plate of food.

"You seem to know what I'm thinking."

"I stand a proficient telepath," the old man answered, taking a large bite out of a roll. He said it as if it should have been obvious.

With her mind still swirling from being truly awake for the first time in weeks, it took the comment a moment to register. She couldn't be sure she'd heard him right. Had he just said that he was telepathic?

"That is correct," the old man said through a mouthful of bread. "I am telepathic. If you wish to continue your stay here, however, proper manners must be observed as well as practiced, and your food grows cold. Now, please sit."

Deciding her hunger was the most pressing concern, she wobbled forward. To her great appreciation the old man kept his gaze focused on his own food while she made her way to the table. She wasn't sure what was in it, but it looked like a simple stew and it smelled better than she could remember any food ever smelling.

Finally, after what felt like an eternity of torture, she reached the table and knelt to eat. Her hands shook as she reached for the roll next to the bowl of stew. It felt far heavier than she'd expected it to; like lifting a rock. The task of eating seemed to be almost as much of a challenge as reaching the table had. The bowl was nearly too heavy for her to lift and the old man seemed to have forgotten to set out a spoon for her.

Once she finally finished the last bit of her stew—a tremendous task in and of itself—the old man set a goblet down in front of her. "Drink this," he said.

Without wasting effort to ask what it was or why he'd offered it to her, Sarah downed the entire thing. Her stomach was painfully full, but she felt much better knowing that she had food on her stomach at long last.

When she looked up, she realized the old man was watching her intently.

"Feeling a little better?" he asked.

"Yes, thank you," she replied.

"Good. On your feet," he said, rising from his place at the other side of the small table.

Sarah eyed the old man imploringly. "But I can barely walk!"

"Which is precisely the reason for such a thing, so up with you!" he retorted firmly, motioning with his hands for her to follow his instructions. "Your muscles are weak from lack of use. In order to undo the damage, proper time and effort must be put toward the task. So, up with you! You will attend my side as we take a walk."

She stared blankly at him, not wanting to move. It had taken so much effort for her to even come up the stairs and reach the table . . . the last thing she wanted to do was go for a walk with this grumpy old man.

"As I see it," Malacus said, more sternly this time, "you have but two options. You can either take advantage of hospitalities offered while you recover, or you can find yourself on your way. In this house there is no loafing about; your compliance and assistance is demanded in return for services rendered. For either to happen, your strength must first return to you. Now up with you, or find yourself left behind along with any opportunity of convalescence beneath this roof."

Feeling slightly indignant at the reprimand, Sarah reluctantly brought herself to her feet. For a moment or two her knees shook violently, threatening to drop her weight back to the ground. Once she finally felt somewhat confident in her posture, she brought her eyes back up toward the old man in front of her.

"Who are you exactly?" she asked. "How did I get here?"

"There will be time enough to explain such things while we walk," Malacus answered. And then he turned and marched out the front door without another word.

22

REHABILITATION

THE WALKS BECAME routine. Malacus had explained on that first walk, to the best of his ability, how she had arrived in his care. He told her about the time he had spent with Allen and how much Allen had learned. Sarah was informed that the day Allen had been arrested Malacus had taken him to the nearest town in an effort to lift his spirits, and acquire the ingredients he'd used to brew the concoction which had finally returned her to consciousness. He'd also confided in her that the mirror she'd seen in the basement of his cabin was intended to be a gift for Allen upon their return. Once properly enchanted the mirror would act as a portal of communication to Earth so that Allen could let his mother know that he was alive and safe. She found it bitterly ironic that Allen had been taken the day before she'd reawakened, on the very trip which had provided the necessary ingredients to revive her.

And now he was gone, and there was nothing she could do about it.

Sarah noticed her strength returning to her, if very slightly, in the following days. Walking was becoming much easier and her muscles seemed to adapt to the new atmosphere. She'd had to sacrifice her dignity, after being reminded about the extremely strenuous gravity of this world, allowing Malacus to help her out of her clothes in order to bathe her. Aside from Allen's absence, that had to be the worst part of her new life.

She was grateful, however embarrassed, that the old man never made a comment about her nudity and that he seemed to do his best to avert his eyes throughout the procedure. She desperately wished it didn't have to be that way, but she literally felt as if she were being crushed by the air around her with all her clothes removed. There was absolutely no way she could have bathed on her own. In fact, even though she had to wear the same grubby outfit every day, which she had learned was helping her adapt to the intense gravity, it was always a relief to have it back on.

The first time Malacus had explained the situation to her, she'd thought he was making a rather crude joke. When she'd accused him of being a perverted old man, he'd simply stared at her, maintaining the stoic gaze which so constantly dominated his weathered features. After a moment he'd offered her the opportunity to bathe herself before exiting the room. She hadn't even been able to completely remove her tunic on her own before toppling over and being forced to yell for his assistance. Upon his return, he'd quietly helped her through the process of removing her clothes without ever asking for an apology, or trying to make her feel guilty for doubting his word.

As he'd tossed her pants off to the side, she'd noticed something spill out of one of the pockets onto the floor. There were three of them; small, oblong, and tinted slightly green. When she realized what they were a lump formed in her throat and tears began to cloud her vision.

"I was unaware success to harvest seeds had come prior to the vehectra bite you received," Malacus had said, sounding genuinely surprised.

Feeling foolish for a decision she knew she couldn't take back, one which had ultimately cost Allen his freedom, she turned her head away from the old man as several tears escaped her control. "You can keep them," she'd bit out more angrily than she'd intended.

After a long moment Malacus' voice came soft, but firm. "No, the seeds should remain in your possession. Much was sacrificed in the acquiring of them. To gain nothing for your efforts would only add more tragedy to current circumstances. Besides, need of them may yet arise; this world, along with all the risks it presents, are new to you. As such, grave injury stands better chance of finding you than all else who resides here." With that, he'd stuffed them back into the pocket from which they'd fallen.

As extremely disorienting as it still was sometimes that she was no longer on Earth, Sarah did the best she could with what she had. The more acclimated she became, the more Malacus expected of her. She was cleaning up after herself, as well as Malacus, and found herself quickly slipping into her new role despite her longings to be home. She distantly wondered how her father was doing without her. It broke her heart that she hadn't had a chance to say goodbye and knew he was worried sick about her. She put on a brave face during the day, not wanting to show just how heartsick she was about being so far from home without anyone to relate to, and cried herself to sleep most nights. She supposed that Malacus, if he really could read minds, probably knew everything she was going through. But if he did, he never said anything.

In her mind she could see Allen rotting away, lonely and scared, in a jail cell somewhere. She wished she could do something to help him, and desperately hoped he was still alive. She knew it was entirely her fault he was there. If she hadn't gone closer to the strange plant that night, she wouldn't have been bitten by that snake; they would have never gone to town to help her; Allen would have never been arrested on a strange new world. It was all her fault and there was nothing she could do about it.

Every time the subject of Allen came up, she got the distinct impression that Malacus was keeping something from her. There were times when he seemed all too willing to answer her questions, trying to allay any fears she was having about what Allen's present condition might be; and other times when he seemed to clam up, as if there was something about Allen he just didn't want her to know. Any time she'd try to press the issue, the old man would give her more chores to do and leave her to them.

As the days pressed on, she became slowly more familiar with her new surroundings. In the mornings, after breakfast, the two would walk the valley in which Malacus' cabin was located; sometimes picking fruit from trees, or buds from a flower-like plant which she thought was absolutely beautiful. There had been many things about Datheron which she had first considered odd or creepy— such as the strange purplish hue to the grass, or the fact that the sky was more turquoise than blue. But the more time she spent on those walks among the elements, the more comfort she found in the sight of them. As they walked, Malacus would give her brief lessons about the things that could be found here. Any time he would tell her of a new danger she hoped never to face, her thoughts would turn to Allen and the same heartsick feelings would come rushing back to the surface. Malacus told her of a large plant, unique to this world, called the psyricka plant. Its buds emanated a melodic frequency to lure creatures close to it. Once one got too close, it would launch a tendril from the center of the bud which latched to its victims, allowing the plant to suck the life energy from its prey until it was full or its victim was dead. Such a thing terrified her to no end. She had, after all, been thrown into a coma for over a month by getting too close to a plant which had a symbiotic relationship with a lethal snake.

Upon returning from their walks, they would have a lunch of some type of stew and rolls. After eating they would go on another short walk, before returning to the cabin once more to begin her lessons in Datheronian culture. She often found her new home as appalling as she did fascinating. Datheron had no real judicial system to speak of, and she felt as if its society leaned more toward a dictatorship than the democracy she had grown familiar with at home. It offended her to learn that so many things on this world could result in a death sentence, or one that may as well be. Such realizations renewed her concern for Allen in earnest. But any time she would voice such concerns to Malacus, inquiring about any chance to remove Allen from his fate, he would tell her that there was nothing they could do and that it was best to drop the subject.

The lessons Malacus offered weren't all academic, however. He would sometimes catch her rifling amongst the things which occupied the shelves of both the upper and lower floors of the cabin she'd slowly learned to call home. Anytime he would find her someplace he evidently didn't want her to be, regardless of the reasons and explanations she would offer for doing so, she would receive a stern lecture and a difficult chore as punishment. It was like being seven years old again. She frequently found herself wondering if Allen had considered the old man to be as obnoxious as she did.

Malacus was slowly trying to teach her to speak the language most common among the populace of this planet, but she found the lessons exceedingly confusing and was flabbergasted to learn that Allen had apparently become fluent prior to being arrested. How anyone could become fluent in a foreign language in only a month's time was beyond her. But at least he was able to communicate with those who had him incarcerated, and was able to understand what it was they would sentence him to.

After a couple of weeks of fruitless effort toward learning the native language of Datheron, both she and Malacus were becoming increasingly frustrated. It seemed no matter how hard she tried, she just couldn't seem to get it. She found the sentence structure the old man employed, even when speaking English, to be confusing. She was able to make sense of it in her own language, but trying to translate it into a new one left her head spinning. It didn't make things any easier that he seemed to be holding her to the same standard Allen had exhibited while learning an alien tongue.

One day, when she'd simply had enough, she let out a scream of frustration. "I give up!" she yelled. "Why do I even have to learn this dumb language anyway? Can't we find a way to get Allen back? If we did, he'd be safe and he could just translate for me!"

Malacus expelled a flustered sigh. "As previously stated, such a thing is beyond our control; no amount of effort would make it otherwise. And you fail to see a larger problem. English is a tongue known to only a handful of this world. Yielding to frustration, continuing to use the tongue to which you are accustomed, will only bring unwanted attention upon you."

"What do you mean unwanted attention?" she'd asked in a heated voice. "Why is it so bad that someone here should hear me speaking English? I don't get it! What aren't you telling me?"

Malacus watched her for several moments, letting out another sigh before finally speaking again. "I suppose delay of the truth has reached its end," he said in a voice of resignation. "Come; there is much I would tell you."

She'd stood and followed him to the basement. It was a room she'd been in many times; the room in which she'd suffered the entirety of her coma . . . the room in which Allen had watched over her unconscious form. And even though she had seen it countless times before at this point, it still spooked her to see the old man shift the floor aside with a wave of his hand and cast light upon the room below with a snap of his fingers.

She shadowed him into the dank-smelling, gloomy room; watching as he scanned the shelves, tracing his fingers along each volume, apparently searching for a specific one. When at last he seemed to locate it, he pulled it from its confines and motioned for her to sit at the work table while he explained its contents to her. Her mind raced at what could possibly explain the need to abandon her native language.

He opened the book, skimmed its pages, and told her it was a book of prophecies. There was a specific one among its pages which had been around for thousands of years; known to nearly all on the planet, for it spoke of the end of life as it was known to all who lived here. While he continued to search for a specific passage, she wondered if this really even had anything to do with her inability to learn Olyphatarian or if it was another half-cocked lesson he was trying to teach her about patience or some other quality he assumed she lacked. The old man had an irritating way of turning everything into a lesson, and always seemed to make her feel dumb for not having seen the lesson herself.

When he seemed to find what he was looking for at last, he brought his eyes up to meet hers. A serious countenance consumed his features. "The nature of this prophecy is such that it has inspired fear and debate in its wake since its origin," he told her. "The weight of such words, when brought to fruition, shall affect more than just those of this world. The ripples it creates will stretch farther than any one man can realize."

"What does some ancient prophecy have to do with my inability to learn your language?" she asked, accusatorily.

"More than you can know, or will ever know if you do not hold your tongue," Malacus replied coolly. When she didn't respond, he cleared his throat and read the words of the prophecy: 'When the one born both of this world and of another called Earth arrives upon our soil, so shall begin the events to facilitate my return. He will free the Sword of Sythika from its slumber and reunite my broken soul. His choices will alter life on Datheron for all time. In his hands lay the fate of the universe.'

Hearing the words didn't clear up matters for her in the least. If anything it left her feeling more confused. But she had spent enough time with the old coot to know he wasn't done, so she kept her comments to herself and instead asked, "Are you telling me that if people find out that I'm from Earth that they'll somehow think I'm tied to this prophecy?"

Malacus simply nodded his head.

Sarah thought about the prophecy's words for a moment. "But . . . isn't it talking about a boy? Doesn't it distinctly say 'he'll' come from Earth and 'he'll' change the universe?" When Malacus just shrugged, she continued. "And what about the part that says he'll be born of both worlds? What does that even mean? That one of his parents is from here and the other is from Earth?"

"Much speculation comes from attempting to translate prophecy of any type. The nature of this one brings with it more than most. But such an assumption is

358

shared by many who have made attempt toward deciphering its meaning."

"Well then, it would just be stupid to assume that the prophecy has anything at all to do with me," she countered.

Then it hit her.

The old man thought the prophecy was talking about Allen. Recognition dawned in Malacus's eyes and she knew he'd been monitoring her thoughts again. He nodded his head at her unspoken realization.

"That's not possible . . ." she protested. "That would have to mean that his father came from this planet and . . . wait, that's why he was never in Allen's life isn't it? And why Carol was never able to find out where her husband came from! He wasn't deported to another country; he was deported to another world!"

All at once her brain went into overdrive, her thoughts swirling around in her mind with such ferocity that she could barely focus on a singular one. If this were true, Allen very well could be the boy this prophecy spoke of. More than that though, it would mean that he was in far more danger than she'd originally realized. All it would take was one fearful zealot finding out he was from Earth and he would probably be executed to prevent the prophecy from ever taking place. Her heart ached for Allen. Not only was he in a hopeless situation, surrounded by potential enemies, but somewhere on this planet his father might still be alive. Without realizing it he could be standing right next to the man. It could even be possible that his father was already executed for his crimes, or that he could unwittingly be the one to execute Allen.

And it would be all her fault.

If she'd just been more firm in protesting his decision to go into those woods, they wouldn't be here. If she'd insisted on taking him anywhere away from his house, none of this would've happened. She desperately wished she could turn back the clock, undo the mistakes which had put Allen so close to a potential death sentence. That thought hit her like a runaway truck. Had she gotten her best friend killed?

She felt sick at the realization. Tears welled in her eyes. Her entire reality was spinning and she didn't know if it would ever. . .

A soft touch pressed her shoulder.

"Calm yourself, child." His voice was soft. "All is not lost, nor does the fault rest at your feet. Foresight of such events could not have been known. Forfeiting will to tears and insecurities will not aid Allen or you. Strength and courage must be your ally if matters are to change."

With tremendous effort Sarah reined in her tempestuous emotions. The old man was right. What was done was done.

She brought her still wet eyes up to meet his, "How can you be so calm about this? Aren't you worried about what will happen to Allen if somebody finds out he's from Earth?"

"Such concerns are never far from my thoughts," he assured her. "Yet control over such things remains well beyond my reach. I fear all now rests upon Allen's shoulders. He must master his own destiny. Whether the words of this prophecy speak of him or of another is of no consequence. I have great faith in the boy and his capabilities. Take solace; if he is the child of prophecy, death will not find him easily."

Malacus' words did make her feel a little better, even if she was in a bad dream. She had never really been a fan of Allen's science fiction movies, but now she was living one. As she sat, pondering where life had brought her, she wasn't sure which she'd rather be the truth; that Allen was somehow a child of prophecy, destined to change the universe; or that he was the same boy she'd always known, who now sat in a prison cell awaiting his execution.

At that moment she wanted nothing more than to rescue Allen form his captors.

Malacus closed the book and placed it back upon the shelf. When he turned to face her, he held something small and sparkling. He extended his hand to her, revealing a small jewel encrusted amulet on a thin gold chain.

"This necklace," the old man said in a somber voice, "is an artifact of old. Construction of the relic is believed to have been at the hands of the original God-King. While it adorns the neck, foreign tongues become easy in the understanding. Such capabilities do not extend to the speaking of the language, yet comprehension of them will meet your ears."

Malacus placed the necklace in her upturned palm. "I yet hold expectation that you learn to speak Olyphatarian with fluency under your own merit. However, should unfortunate events part you from my side I would not have you absent understanding of it. Place it in your pocket for now, and upon your neck should you need it."

Sarah did as she was told, placing it in the pocket of her tunic. "Thank you," she said, her voice filled with awe. As she brought her eyes back up, another question danced on the tip of her tongue. She feared his reaction to it almost as much as the answer, but decided to ask anyway. "Do you know who Allen's father is?"

"I do," Malacus nodded.

She hesitated a moment before asking, "Does Allen?"

"He does," the old man nodded again, folding his arms.

Part of her was glad to hear that Allen finally knew who his father was. Part of her filled with sorrow that he'd had to learn the truth with no one to confide in. The revelation could only have left him feeling more isolated than he already felt. And now he was in prison somewhere on this godforsaken planet . . .

"Malacus," she implored, "are you sure there is no way for us to rescue Allen? I just can't help picturing him all alone in a jail cell; scared, with no one to talk to. I mean, you know an awful lot about how this world's politics function. Can't you plead for his innocence on his behalf?"

Malacus shook his head. "I fear such a course of action would raise questions we are yet unprepared to confront."

"What do you mean? What kinds of questions?"

Malacus exhaled another weary sigh, as if considering how much more he should tell her. "It is believed by this entire world that I departed the living a great many years past. Should otherwise come to light, I would be of no service to you or Allen. Great controversy would envelop the whole of Datheron at the proclamation, bringing with it the truth of Allen's origin. I fear no good would come of it. If I believed otherwise, Allen would already be sprung from his incarceration."

Sarah wasn't sure which part confused her more; his insinuation that everyone on the planet knew who he was or that it sounded like he had faked his death. She silently wondered if he had done so to escape a death sentence of his own. Either way, what he had just said could mean only one thing: there was nothing they could do for Allen.

Her heart sank, once again returning to a place it had so frequently taken refuge as of late.

"Come," Malacus said in a brighter voice. "Let us away from such dismal surroundings. I would have you join me for another walk."

Sarah groaned both inwardly and outwardly. She really didn't feel like taking another walk. "Right now? Do we have to?"

"Fresh air will brighten the senses, and turn mind from dreary thoughts," the old man insisted.

She really didn't think taking a walk was going to help anything. At the moment she didn't think there was anything on the whole planet that could. But she knew better than to argue the point, so she stood from the work table and followed her aging caretaker up the stairs for yet another walk.

23

CONDEMNATION

THE NEXT COUPLE WEEKS were hellish for Allen, alone in his cell for several days naught but his thoughts while he awaited Luziaph's judgment. The same Gorrlock woman who had escorted him to the incarceration chamber brought meals twice a day. There were several other slaves or attendants who brought food to the other prisoners; but only she brought his food. He couldn't help noticing her green eyes each time he saw her, since they were so different from any other Gorrlock he'd seen, he found the combination of her eyes and skin pigment bewitching. He'd tried to strike up a conversation with her on a couple occasions, only to have her meet his eyes for a moment and then quickly scurry off to whatever else was required of her. He hadn't intended on frightening her, he just wanted someone to talk to. After all, what good was learning the language if he wasn't able to put it to use?

He wasn't certain how long he'd been in his cell before he was finally brought before Luziaph. Thoughts of his wayward father, of Sarah's condition, and of his mother and how miserable she must be over his disappearance had been his closest companions, whispering in his ear hour after hour alone in the cell. After an unnatural amount of time, however, the same Gorrlock woman appeared at the threshold of his cell, looking down at him as he rested against the crescent pillar confining him. At first the sight of her had instantly made him hungry, as the only times he'd seen her she had come to serve him a meal. But when he noticed she didn't hold a serving tray in her hands, he became confused.

She pressed her hand to the plate which powered down the energy barrier to his cell, tilting her head to the side as she did so. "Lord Luziaph summons you," she said.

He made no comment; he simply brought himself to his feet, allowed her to place manacles on his wrists, and followed her down the gloomy corridor past all the other incarceration chambers and the prisoners within them. He couldn't even bring himself to look around as they moved, his normal curiosities blanketed by a sense of finality which was settling over him. As much as he didn't want to, he had to consider the possibility that this could be the day he died. Against all likelihood, he found himself almost welcoming the thought; anything had to be better than the solitary confinement he'd been forced to endure.

At the end of their long journey to Luziaph's throne room his eyes were once again assaulted by the hauntingly gorgeous statues he remembered seeing on his way into the palace. He marveled at them as he moved, only dimly aware of the large Triclopian's presence upon the throne ahead of him. Too quickly, the procession of statues ended and he stood before Luziaph. He sincerely hoped what Zorthos had told him about the Triaga protecting his thoughts from Luziaph was true. Upon coming to a stop, he noticed for the first time that the two guards which had brought him here were also standing before the Triclopian Proctus.

Luziaph kept his eyes on Allen as he addressed the two guards of Abendroth. "What was this one's crime?"

Brohm's voice remained noticeably silent for once. Instead, it was Pendrick who answered. "He was placed under arrest for countermanding sentence carried out upon a Gorrlock woman."

"In what way did such a thing transpire?" Luzipah asked his fellow Triclopian.

"The woman resisted arrest, bringing steel across a fellow guard's throat in the process," Pendrick offered. "This one," he continued, motioning to Allen as he did so, "knelt at her side, offering respite in the form of dendegayra seed."

Luziaph's eyes, all three of them, fell upon him once more. "Why would you do such a thing?" he asked in an elevated tone.

Allen cleared his throat, thankful for the lessons he'd received on Olyphatarian, "I am yet new to this world, and as such failed to comprehend the severity of your laws. My intent was merely to stay the hand of death from a mortally wounded woman, not to ignore laws of which I have yet to fully understand."

"Tell me, human," Luziaph said in a condescending tone, "from where do you hail that would teach such a thing as acceptance of removing breath from one in a position of authority?"

"The act of staying death was not an admission of condoning that which brought retribution upon her," Allen countered. "I believe all life is sacred, the taking of it wrong regardless of circumstance. I simply wished to prevent another life from being forfeit."

When Luziaph said nothing he continued, bowing his head slightly as he spoke. "Most humble apologies for fault in my actions. I offer contrition in any form you so choose."

Luziaph watched him for several long minutes before he spoke again. "Gratitude for testimonies given," he said to the two guards. "You may take your leave."

With that, the two turned and left the throne room, not even glancing in Allen's direction. He was only momentarily curious why Luziaph had thanked them for their words; what they'd offered was minimal in detail, and he had expected more to be said against him. Once they were gone, Luziaph continued his inquiry. "What name do you go by?"

The question caught him off guard. He'd been so nervous about this day arriving; had been kept in solitude for so long, that he hadn't been fully prepared for it. His mind raced, frantically searching for the name Zorthos had called him; a name he'd used in front of Luziaph. He silently wondered if such a question had been purposely posed as a test to see if Zorthos had been lying as Luziaph had escorted him away. After what felt like an eternity of deliberation, he answered, "Araset."

"Such a response required consideration?" Luziaph challenged immediately.

"Only the offering of it," he answered quickly. "Apologies, but I have never found myself in such a position. I am of rattled nerves at the thought of recourse for my actions."

"You claim to be new to this world," Luziaph said firmly. "Yet fluency of the language falls freely from your tongue. Explain."

Allen had to do some quick thinking to come up with a story which would appease Luziaph. He suddenly found it difficult to condemn Zorthos for the smoothness of his lies, and the reasoning behind them. If the man had truly done so for no other reason than to have a family free of this world's influence, to protect them, then who was he to judge?

"The bulk of my first days on this world were spent adapting to its unusual gravity and studying the native tongue," he began. "Such tasks were undertaken in complete seclusion, save the old man who offered respite as well as lessons. Upon finding my feet once again beneath me, I offered services as his caretaker toward the purpose of repayment for kindnesses shown. The day of my arrest found me in a populated city for the first time since my arrival upon Datheronian soil."

"I see," Luziaph replied, his tone composed. "Tell me how it is you came to know Zorthos."

"Who?" he asked, probably a little too quickly.

"Do not think me a fool, boy!" Luziaph spat. "The man who spoke to you from the opposing incarceration chamber upon your arrival."

Allen lowered his head in deference. "Apologies," he said in his most humble tone, "I was but a young boy when first my eyes met him. He came to my village of Fornatyme on Shennigar for the briefest of moments. Recollection of his name eluded me. I know not why he was there and had forgotten his presence until once again seeing him among your captives." Though he wasn't accustomed to lying, he couldn't help but feel pride in the way he had so smoothly offered an explanation to Luziaph's question.

Luziaph cocked his lips to one side, forcing his left eye to squint slightly. He seemed to be considering whether or not to believe Allen's story. After a very long pause Luziaph spoke again, apparently satisfied with Allen's words. "What skills do you possess?"

"None, save understanding of the spoken tongue," he answered quickly.

"That will not do at all," Luziaph said as he stood from his throne. "Punishment will be withheld until such time as you have completed training in a skill of worth. You now find yourself counted among my servants, ever at my beck and call while you take shelter within the walls of this palace. You will be required to pick a skill and become proficient in its use." He turned to his side and gestured with his right hand, "Gazianna will show you to your quarters and aid in the learning of desired skill."

Allen wasn't sure whether to be elated that he wasn't to be executed, or thrown into despair that he was Luziaph's slave for the foreseeable future. Either way, he found himself in a situation he'd been vehemently warned against by both Malacus and Zorthos. Two things, however minor they might be, had bolstered his spirits; he now knew the Gorrlock woman's name, and he was to be trained in a special ability by her specifically. He wasn't sure why the thought comforted him. There was just something about her presence he found soothing.

"Step forward," Luziaph commanded.

He did as he was told, unsure of the reasoning behind the order. Luziaph moved close to him, placing his hands on Allen's head. An odd vibration inundated his entire being. His ears filled with a strange humming sound. Then, a moment later, relief flooded his senses. He once again felt whole, as if a small part of him had just been returned. It wasn't until he saw the Triaga in Luziaph's hands that fear swept through him.

"If you yet possess no skills," Luziaph said to his unspoken question, "then control over you does not require such extreme measures as this. And the learning of a chosen skill will require that it be removed from your head."

He bowed his head once more. "Gratitude," he said, feeling as if any other response would have been inappropriate.

"Remove yourself," Luziaph told him. "But stray no further than a few feet beyond throne room's entrance. Gazianna will be with you presently."

Allen did as he was commanded. As he stood in the appointed place waiting for Gazianna to meet him, he wondered what reason Luziaph could have for speaking to her away from his ears. Could Luziaph be giving her specific orders regarding him that he didn't want overheard, or was it something else entirely? He still had a lot to learn about etiquette on this world, though he didn't need to wonder for long, as she came into view only a couple minutes later. He wanted to ask her what that was about, but was unsure if doing so would be considered inappropriate, so he kept silent.

"Come with me," she said in an annoyed voice. With a nod of his head he followed, fear of what his new life might entail flooding his mind.

The first several days following the removal of his Triaga had bordered on torturous. He shadowed Gazianna virtually everywhere she went, expected to complete the same chores as she and learn the layout of the entire palace. He tried his best to get her to open up to him, or even carry a conversation which didn't consist of duties and their explanations, but she was extremely withdrawn. Too, he couldn't seem to tell if she just didn't like him, or if she was simply upset at being made responsible for his training. Either way, she expected more out of him than he felt was fair and talked to him as if he was a burden.

The first time she told him to pick up a sack of grain and follow her to the kitchens with it he thought he might die; if not from the weight of the sack, then from embarrassment of his inability to lift it on his own. It was far heavier than it rightfully should've been in his opinion, and he had to remind her that he was still adapting to the gravity of this planet and the effects it had on his body.

She seemed to find that mildly amusing, throwing the sack over her shoulder with one arm, walking away from him with a grin on her face.

The palace was enormous. Everywhere they went, he lagged behind, unable to keep his eyes from wandering to his surroundings. Anytime he would stray too far from her side he would receive a swift, open-handed blow to the side of his head. The first time it had happened, he'd nearly struck her back. When he'd asked her what he'd done to deserve getting hit, she'd simply told him to stay at her side or he would get another.

Nearly every doorway had a large archway, some much larger than others depending on the grandeur of the room beyond. The entrances to the largest rooms contained massive, arched wooden doors which separated them from the corridors. Large paintings of various landscapes, as well as some of previous Proctus of Vardiston, adorned the walls of nearly every corridor throughout the entire palace. Some corridors also contained arched windows which displayed the courtyard below. More than once their duties found them in corridors, or the entrance hall, which were populated with the unique statues he so admired. Those were the locations in which he had received most of her strikes. He just couldn't help it; the more he saw them, the more they amazed him. Even up close the detail in them was astounding. If he didn't know better, he'd swear some of them were alive.

The 'living quarters' he'd been presented with could barely be considered such by his approximation. It was a tiny room with only three walls, which resembled a jail cell from Earth without the bars lining the missing wall. He was given a small sleeping pallet, much like the one he had last seen Sarah resting upon—the sight of it brought his concerns and longings for her rushing back to the forefront, but only for a moment.

His room also contained a small eating table which doubled as a work desk for his studies and the only recreation he seemed to be allowed: drawing. Every night before she left him, Gazianna would press her hand to a plate at the outer corner of his room, sending the same disorienting pulse through his body and locking him in for the night.

The first time he'd asked her for art supplies, she'd given him a look which made him brace for another strike. But when she'd seen his natural talent for drawing and painting, she had taken him, along with some of his work, before Luziaph. Upon seeing what Allen was capable of, Luziaph ordered him to paint a portrait of the Triclopian Proctus' likeness. The request had made him more than a little nervous. In a desperate attempt to get out of the request, he'd patiently explained to his new master that he'd never painted a portrait before, but found himself in Luziaph's presence, forced to work on it regardless of prior experience and pleas to the contrary a couple nights a week. Part of him wondered if Luziaph hadn't been so eager to have him around so that he could continuously try to gain access to his thoughts. On those evenings in particular, he paid close attention to keeping his thoughts in English, hoping with everything in him that Luziaph couldn't understand what he was thinking.

As far as his studies were concerned, Allen found Gazianna less than helpful. He had assumed that she would be giving him direct, verbal instruction in the learning of a special ability. Instead she simply asked him what he wanted to learn and handed books to him. The first thing that came to his mind when she'd originally asked him was learning how to fly. But remembering Malacus' admonishment of such a desire, and informing him of precautionary abilities, his decision became less clear to him. Having witnessed her using telekinesis on a couple separate occasions, he'd asked to learn that, hoping with everything in him that she wouldn't laugh at him or call him foolish for wanting to begin with a difficult skill. To his surprise, she'd just nodded and pulled a couple of books from a shelf in the palace's library.

He was given several hours in the afternoon to specifically dedicate to his studies. At first he thought that would mean a break from his chores and a chance to have Gazianna teach him hands-on. But he'd quickly realized that all it really meant was that he was left in a small room off one of the central corridors to read the text by himself. The entire experience seemed a bad joke compared to the way he'd learned at school on Earth. When he had difficulty understanding some of the words, or what they were trying to explain, he'd gone to track her down to ask her to explain it to him. The first time he'd strayed from where she'd left him, she'd struck him hard in the face and had taken him back down to the incarceration chambers and left him there for the night. After that, he just waited for her to come back to ask his questions.

He'd also quickly realized that taking food to the detention center was not one of her normal duties, and wondered if she had done so while he was there out of some sort of morbid curiosity, or if Luziaph had ordered her to keep an eye on him. More and more, he felt like he was under constant surveillance and wasn't sure if such fears were true, or if he just feared it to be true because the idea had been so firmly planted in his head by Malacus and Zorthos. Either way, it surprised him when she came to him one morning and told him that was where they would be beginning their work for the day. He followed her to the palace kitchens, putting particular effort into not falling too far behind, and helped her load several trays of food onto a cart with wheels. They were soon on the all-too-familiar route to the detention block of the palace, he pushing the cart as she led the way.

They passed the new trays of food out to the captives, following a pattern as they did so. Gazianna would press her hand to the plate which deactivated the energy barriers, exchanging trays with the inmate, handing the empty one to him in exchange for a fresh one. As they continued to follow this pattern, he noticed four guards stationed along the exit of the detention block. He wondered if they had always been there, of if they were only there as a precautionary measure because it was feeding time.

He was becoming more familiar with some of the native races of the planet, and could readily identify nearly every type he saw among the captives. He couldn't help but notice as they reached the last chamber there were still three full trays among empties on the cart. Allen was curious for only a moment, as Gazianna answered his silent question nearly as quickly as it'd come to him.

"There are yet more mouths to feed among the private incarceration chambers," she told him as they began moving back toward the exit.

"Private incarceration chambers?" he wondered aloud. He'd been following her around the palace for several days and had never seen any 'private incarceration chambers.' In fact, as he considered it he realized he didn't even know where they could be located; he was sure he'd been in every wing of the palace.

"Yes," she answered, giving him a dangerous glare. "Stay close to my side and say nothing of them or find your tongue removed."

As they moved through corridors he was quickly growing familiar with, he couldn't help reflecting on her comment. He was to tell no one about them. That made him wonder if anyone else even knew they existed, save Luziaph and his most trusted. He was curious why he was being trusted with their location, if in fact their existence was sheltered from even those among the regular palace staff. Of course, he could be making false assumptions, but why tell him to say nothing of them if not to keep them secret? He certainly didn't think he'd been here long enough or proven to Luziaph that he could be trusted such information. He couldn't shake the feeling that he was constantly being tested.

They hadn't gotten far from the normal detention area when Gazainna abruptly stopped. She turned to her right, briefly glancing around before pressing her hand on a normal-looking brick in the center of the wall. After a moment his ears filled with the sound of stone scraping on stone as the wall slid away from them, revealing a hidden passage. No wonder he hadn't known about it.

She ushered him through the doorway, quickly closing the entrance behind them. The sound of stone on stone echoed violently on this side of the hidden doorway. Once the wall was back in place, they began moving again. The new corridor sloped downward for quite a distance before finally leveling out. The only light was from a few, very sparsely situated torches lining the walls. By the time they reached the end of the secret hallway Allen wasn't sure how far underground they were, but he could see light clouds of vapor hanging in the air as he exhaled.

At last a heavily guarded doorway came into view in their dimly lit surroundings. The corridor expanded as they reached their destination to allow the extra room needed to station the guards. A quick count told him that he and Gazianna were outnumbered four to one.

As they stepped up to the door, one of the guards—a grey-skinned alien, looking very much like those popular among Earth culture—stepped in front of them to block their progress.

"Who is this?" he asked in a slightly high-pitched, grating voice, looking directly at Allen.

"He has been approved by Luziaph," Gazianna assured the alien. "Step aside."

"Lord Luziaph did not inform us of this," the alien countered harshly.

"I could convince him to come do so shortly, dragging him away from more pressing concerns, if such is your wish," she said firmly, "though I do not foresee his reaction to such a request as being favorable."

The alien's posture stiffened slightly as he considered her subtle threat. After a moment, he turned around and unlocked the door for them without another word. The alien led them into another tiny, well-guarded room containing yet another locked door. Such extreme measures left Allen feeling nervous about what type of prisoner could possibly warrant this type of security. The guards in the new room stiffened at seeing him, placing hands on their respective weapons.

The alien guard from the previous room assured them that he was approved, making most of them relax their posture, if only slightly.

The new door remained open, watchful guards at their backs, as he followed Gazianna into yet another tiny room. They had at last reached a very small holding cell of sorts. Hidden among the shadows of the poorly-lit room he could see three darkened figures slumped on the ground. Only one of them stirred at the intrusion to their solitude.

One of the guards grabbed a torch from the wall of the previous room, forcing Allen to squint and sending harsh shadows across the whole of the new one as it was brought into the small holding cell. Once his eyes adjusted, he froze at what he saw before him. Three

Gorrlocks—the three who had travelled to Earth in search of Zorthos—were sprawled out at his feet. They were without their black and gold armor, and each now wore their own Triaga, but Allen was certain it was them. He had to mentally force himself to draw a breath. The only one who appeared to be conscious was the only one who hadn't been when he'd seen them in the forest behind his house.

He hoped Gazianna hadn't noticed his reaction at seeing them.

The conscious Gorrlock looked up at Gazianna, "You again? Come to give us our scraps?" When she didn't respond, he continued. "Why do you yet serve the whims of that Triclopian scum?"

"Mind your tongue," she warned him. "Such remarks will not be met with tempered response should they be repeated in his presence."

"I care not what he thinks of my opinions," the long-haired Gorrlock man retorted. "You dishonor your kin in serving one such as him."

"The choice has long been removed from my hands," Gazianna said defensively.

"Yet services remain of your own volition," he sniped, indicating with a gesture toward her lack of Triaga.

"What would you have me do?" she asked in a cold voice.

"I would die before giving my services to the likes of him willingly," he replied in an icy tone of his own.

"It seems to me you were of a similar position not so long ago," she countered. "Your services given as freely as mine when balanced with offer of payment."

"And look where such a decision has landed me," the Gorrlock prisoner retorted sourly.

There was a long, awkward moment in which the two glared at each other. Though the tension in the air was thick, Allen was grateful for the distraction it presented. He sincerely hoped it had prevented her from noticing how nervous he was. Too, he was grateful that the two who could recognize him were both unconscious.

After a very long, silent exchange Gazianna at last turned around and grabbed the remaining three trays of food from the wheeled cart. She glared at the long-haired Gorrlock for another long moment before dropping the trays at his feet without a word. She then turned, grabbing hold of the cart and moving from the room with purpose.

"Come," she said to Allen over her shoulder.

He hesitated for only a moment before pushing himself to catch up with her quick pace.

24

DEFIANCE

AS HE RACED to catch up with her, Allen's heart was pounding in his ears. He wasn't sure which had caused her to be moving at such a pace; the fact that they had yet more chores expected of them and not nearly enough time to complete them, or that the long-haired captive had upset her with his words. Whatever the reason, he was glad to be away from the presence of those three as well, and made no complaint at moving away from them with such haste.

The long, dark corridor they had followed to reach the hidden incarceration chamber seemed much shorter on the way out. It could have been the rushed pace at which they were moving, or perhaps it was simply that his mind was racing quicker than his feet. Either way, he was momentarily surprised when they reached its end and the entrance began to open, announcing itself with a horrifyingly loud scraping sound.Once they had finally reached the warm corridor with which he was far more familiar, Gazianna stopped. She just stood there, hands trembling on the food cart while she seemed to gather her thoughts.

After several long minutes, he couldn't help himself. "Are you well?" he asked.

She shot him a severe look, "Of course I am. What would cause such a question to spring from your mouth?"

"Your hands," he offered gently, gesturing to them as he spoke, "they tremble."

"Mind your business," she answered defensively, jerking her hands from the cart.

He hadn't wanted to upset her, but wasn't all that surprised by her reaction; she seemed to have some pretty strong emotional barriers and had shunned every advance he'd made at trying to get her to open up to him. He realized, of course, that he couldn't force such a thing, but he also couldn't help caring about others and wanting ease their pain if it was within his power to do so; it was just who he was. He decided that he wasn't going to give up so easily this time, even if he did get struck again for it.

He gently placed his left hand on her right shoulder. He could feel her shaking slightly under his touch. "Apologies. I did not mean to offend. I simply wished to offer sympathetic ear."

She watched him for a moment, a look of uncertainty tainting the features of her otherwise beautiful, light-blue face. "Why would you care what troubles me?" she asked in an equally uncertain tone.

He considered his words for only a moment before responding. "I have come to consider you friend," he told her. "The only one I yet possess among a sea of enemies. How could I not care what troubles you?"

Her posture eased visibly at hearing his words. "You are unlike any I have ever met," she said in a tone barely above a whisper. She seemed to be considering telling him something for a very long moment, then her features reverted to the steeled look she always wore. "Remove such concerns from your thoughts, and turn them back toward proper task," she bit out, once again grabbing the cart and marching away.

Though not entirely surprised at her outburst, Allen was mildly irritated that he had gotten so close to convincing her to open up to him, only to have her shy away again. Something in him snapped. He had done nothing to deserve her hostilities and decided at that moment that he was going to give her a piece of his mind. No matter how angry she got, he would make sure that she could trust him once and for all.

Storming after her, he jumped in front of the cart, stopping her progress with his left hand. "Why do you speak to me with such hostility?" he challenged. "I open myself to you, offering sympathetic ear to friend only to have the gesture returned in the form of spit upon cheek! Tell me, what is it I have done to earn such reward for kindness offered?"

She looked apologetic for the briefest of moments before her features became firm once more. "You overstep," she warned him. "Remove your hand or find it broken and useless."

"Not this time," he challenged firmly. "You cannot threaten your way out of giving answer. I have kept a close eye on the way things work inside these walls. You are mistreated and abused by all with authority over you. I stand alone in considering you friend. Why would you turn from that? Do you not believe yourself worthy of such adoration?"

"Such is not the case," she breathed, her voice full of frustration. "Your words are well received, but I fear such talk will only serve to bring you to harm in the end."

"I do not understand." He said, genuinely confused. "Is friendship yet another thing forbidden under this roof?"

"Such is a luxury none bound by servitude can afford," she replied in a distant voice. "It can only lead to more pain, more loss. That is what makes it dangerous."

"That we have been condemned to endure such a fate as to serve the whims of another is what makes it a necessity," he countered. "How can any, even a slave, be expected to live life absent companionship of any kind? To force such solitude upon yourself can only add to the torture already experienced." He cast his penetrating eyes on her, hoping she could see the sincerity in them. "Please, give me a chance. You will not regret it."

Her eyebrows knit together, already showing the regret he'd assured her she would not feel. "I wish such a thing were true. But Luziaph knows my mind as he does his own. None can keep secrets from one with his skills. I am counted among his personal servants, and am only afforded what he deems worthy to grant me. Not even my thoughts are entirely my own. Such is my fate; to deny him or make choice absent his permission is tantamount to inviting death."

He released his grip of the food cart. "Apologies," he said with a sigh. "I do not wish to put you in harm's way. Know that I would not have it so. And that my offer remains, should you find the burden of solitude too much to bear."

She nodded her head, the same tortured look still upon her face. "Gratitude, Araset. Now bring your thoughts back to present, there is much yet expected of us this day."

They continued their path back toward the kitchens at a quickened pace, his mind a whirlwind of brooding thoughts. The encounter had not gone at all as he'd planned or hoped. He was beginning to see why his father wanted to leave this world in the first place, and where he had learned the deceptive ways through which he seemed to reach his ends. When he'd first been told that there was a planet on which gods could be made, a world where quite literally anything was possible, the thought of such a place had filled him with the wonder of endless possibilities. Yet now that he was here, learning just how backward their beliefs were, he was beginning to doubt that even the learning of superhuman abilities was worth such a price, such sacrifice. Trading his freedom for the ability to learn any power he wanted was like trading his fingers for the ability to read music; one would do him no good without the other.

He felt heartsick for Gazianna having grown up without knowing what it meant for her life to truly be her own. She had been here her whole life, not even knowing there was another way. He realized that his words must have seemed just as dangerous, possibly even as blasphemous, as they were romantic or intriguing. And even though he knew there was no immediate way for him to get home, that he may never again see Earth, he refused to adopt such beliefs as a way of life. His life was his own, and no one could make it otherwise. He hoped to someday be able to help Gazianna, and possibly the whole of Datheron, to see the truth of that.

And then the thought struck him: maybe that was what the words of the prophecy meant. Was it possible that he actually was the one the prophecy spoke of, that the way in which he would change life for Datheronians was to teach them the importance of independence and freedom? After only a moment's consideration, he decided that it didn't matter. He didn't care about some stupid archaic prediction of the future. Right was right no matter where you live or who you are, and he firmly believed that nobody had the right to another's life, or the choices they would make with it. And it wasn't his responsibility to convince a whole planet they were wrong in what they believed. How could the decisions made by one person so profoundly affect an entire world anyway?

As they reached the kitchens Gazianna handed control of the cart to him, telling him to take care of it and that she would meet up with him once she had gone to speak with Luziaph. He did as she asked, making quick work of the cart and dishes so that he wouldn't keep her waiting or force her to double back to retrieve him. Within a matter of ten minutes he found himself back in the palace corridors, on his way to Luziaph's quarters, hoping to surprise and impress her with the speed of his completion.

She was still speaking with Luziaph when he arrived outside Luziaph's private room. He didn't want to interrupt, so he waited at the threshold of the Triclopian Proctus' quarters, unable to prevent himself from overhearing what was being said. The conversation seemed to have only just begun, and he wondered if she had gotten side-tracked or simply taken her time in arriving.

"Were you able to learn anything of use?" Luziaph asked her.

Peeking around the corner, Allen noticed that her eyes never met Luziaph's as she spoke. "Sepharus showed no recognition of him," she offered. When he said nothing, she continued into the uncomfortable silence. "Pardon my curiosities, Master. But could you not just seek the answer for yourself within the boy's mind?"

"His thoughts remain of his native tongue," Luziaph said, thoughtfully. "I have yet to learn the deciphering of it."

"Forgive me if I speak out of turn," she said, her head still bowed in deference, "but he does not seem to be of a duplicitous nature to me. I do not believe he has been anything but genuine while in my presence."

Luziaph backhanded her hard across her face. "Your opinions matter for little and were not requested," he spat. "I know he is hiding something. Zorthos knows the

384

boy, and I do not believe the false statement he presented as explanation."

As Gazianna stood there, comforting her jaw with the palm of her hand, he was still trying to make sense of what he'd just witnessed. He had no idea why Luziaph had just hit her, and could feel anger swelling up inside him toward his new master. He desperately wanted to teach the Triclopian monster a lesson in manners, but knew that he stood no chance against him at the moment. If this was the kind of abuse Gazianna had endured her entire life, it was no wonder she was so cowed and emotionally withdrawn.

"Apologies," Gazianna said in a shaky voice.

"I must learn the truth," Luziaph muttered, ignoring Gazianna's comment entirely as he began to pace back and forth in front of her.

"What news from those sent to Shennigar toward the purpose of verifying Araset's origin?" she asked, still rubbing her cheek.

Luziaph shot a venomous look at her, and Allen expected him to backhand her again. But a moment later he answered without breaking pace. "There has been no word. But such things take time. The time shift between our world and others makes prediction of when such news will arrive impossible to determine."

Allen mentally stumbled. Had he overheard them correctly? Had Luziaph dispatched someone to Shennigar to find out if anyone there knew the name Araset? The security he had come to feel in his background story, however minimal it may be, was beginning to unravel. He silently wondered if she'd asked such a question for his benefit. Maybe she had spotted him and wanted to subtly warn him that he wasn't safe . . . or maybe it was just a huge coincidence. He made a mental note to look for an opportunity to ask her directly what kind of trouble he was in.

All at once Luziaph stopped pacing, backhanding her so hard it sent her sprawling to the floor. "No! I am certain of Zorthos' deceptive nature," he bellowed. "He is a traitor to the God-King, a traitor to the laws of Datheron, and should be punished as such!"

"I spoke no words to the contrary," Gazianna said. Her voice was shaky, pleading. He could see that it was taking tremendous for Gazianna to bring herself back to her feet; her knees shook in protest as he watched her stand.

"It was not required that you voice them aloud," Luziaph sniped. "It is but a simple matter for me to divine the truth lurking behind your eyes. Or have you forgotten so quickly my capabilities as well as your place?"

"No, Master," she said in an apologetic tone.

Luziaph eyed her intensely for another several moments before finally speaking again. "Tell me, has opportunity to broach the subject of the old man, whom he claims offered respite upon his arrival, presented itself?"

Gazianna hesitated. "No Master, it has not," she answered timidly.

"I wonder," Luziaph said, almost murmuring. "Is it that opportunity has not yet arisen or that you allow feelings for the boy to hinder action? Is it required that I demonstrate further lessons in obedience?"

"No Master," Gazianna pleaded. "I will—"

Her next words were strangled by the sound of a blood-curdling scream—her own. Clutching violently at her head, she collapsed to the ground. Allen watched in horror as Gazianna was thrown into an apoplectic fit at Luziaph's feet, writhing against an unseen assailant. For no other reason that he could see than to intensify the torture she was experiencing, Luziaph kicked her in the abdomen with such ferocity that it produced an audible popping sound.

He was utterly appalled at the scurrilous scene he was witnessing, certain that Luziaph was telepathically assaulting her, and quite literally kicking her while she was down. There was no point to this other than to cause her pain.

Allen decided he'd seen enough.

Rage coursed through him as he looked around for something he could use to bring an end to the horrific scene before him. There was nothing of use in the hallway in which he stood, so he quickly surveyed the visible contents of Luziaph's room. There, hanging on the wall next to Luziaph's large, luxurious bed was a long sword and a bladed spear. He concentrated as hard as he could, letting his need to help a friend in pain fuel his efforts. The same hot desire he'd experienced when he'd mentally body slammed Malacus rushed through him, and the bladed spear flew from its place on the wall straight for the Triclopian Proctus' head. At the last possible moment, Luziaph saw it speeding toward him. He dodged the spear with such speed Allen had barely seen the movement. He somehow knew, without understanding how, that Luziaph had slowed a moment in time to escape the fate Allen had thrust at him. The spear stuck in the wall, the free end reverberating wildly from the impact.

All three of Luziaph's eyes immediately found Allen standing in the doorway to his private quarters. "How dare you!" he bellowed.

Allen glanced down at Gazianna. She was lying on the floor in a fetal position, clutching at her ribs and wearing a look of both shock and gratitude. But at least the mental torture Luziaph had been imposing on her had come to an end. Her expression quickly changed to one of horrified recognition, and she frantically attempted to crawl away from her enraged master.

"You offer false statement regarding abilities possessed, then use hidden skill to countermand proper punishment being dealt?" Luziaph yelled. "I fear the truth of your innocence greatly exaggerated!"

"I fear your definition of punishment far exceeds 'proper' levels," Allen retorted coldly. He knew there was no way he could explain how he'd mentally thrown the spear, so he made no attempt to convince Luziaph that it hadn't been entirely purposeful.

"And who are you to tell me how to administer punishment deserved?" Luziaph spat. "You are but a slave, the same as she! And it is time you learn true meaning of the term!"

In the next instant, Allen's head felt as if it had been split open and dipped in acid. He was no longer aware of anything but the pain. Lightning bolts shot through his entire body; it felt as if his brain were melting out his ears. He wasn't sure if he was even still breathing; all he knew was that he wanted the pain to stop. His vision blurred, sound distorted. This must be what people meant when they said there are worse things than death.

Slowly the pain began to dim, the room gradually coming back into focus. He had to force himself to take a breath before he could deal with the urge to vomit. As his eyes began making sense of his surroundings once more, he saw Gazianna pinned to the wall, her feet dangling helplessly as Luziaph's right hand clutched her throat. It took tremendous effort, but he managed to put his feet beneath him and brought himself to his full height.

"Release her," he heard himself say; even to himself it sounded as if it had come from a great distance. The lingering effects of Luziaph's mental assault made the words of Olyphatarian come to him only with difficulty; he had to concentrate with intensity to form them in his mouth.

Luziaph turned his head, all three of his eyes once again finding Allen on his feet. A look of genuine intrigue covered his features. He tossed Gazianna to the side as if he no longer found her interesting and took several long strides toward Allen. Luziaph's lips were moving, but he was having difficulty making out the words. It still felt as if his entire world were spinning. Luziaph seemed to be asking him something, standing only a couple feet away and maintaining eye contact as he spoke.

There was a pause, and then Allen felt a sharp pain in the left side of his face and found himself looking up at his Triclopian master from the floor. How he'd ended up back on the ground eluded him. Luziaph shouted something else and kicked him in the gut.

Gazianna rushed to Luziaph's side, grabbing his right wrist and began pleading with him. A look of death followed, and Gazianna released her grip, taking a step backward. This had all somehow gotten out of control. What had he been thinking standing up to a Grandmaster of telepathy? Why couldn't he ever keep his nose out of troubling situations? He'd only wanted to help a friend, and ended up with nothing but pain of his own for his efforts. He had done her no real good at all.

Gazianna said something else, and Luziaph's eyes once again fell upon him. Allen was beginning to wonder if he'd ever hear anything properly again. A moment later he could feel Luziaph's presence once again in his mind. He wasn't entirely sure how he knew that was what he was feeling, yet it was unmistakable.

And then, all at once, his hearing corrected itself. The urge to vomit faded. The echo of the pain he'd endured, however, lingered heavily in the background of his consciousness.

A self-satisfied grin creased Luziaph's lips. "Tell me of the old man with whom you spent your first days among this world," he commanded. "Pendrick tells me you called him Malacus. Does he speak the truth?"

He didn't want to answer the question, but found it impossible to resist. "Such was the name he gave me."

"How can such a thing be possible?" Luziaph questioned. "Malacus has been dead for ages, since Rhenngoth claimed the glory and title of God-King from him in a battle to the death before the roar of the crowd at the Arena Games."

"I know nothing of which you speak," Allen responded, once again finding it impossible to keep the truth from spilling out of his mouth. "I only know that such was the name he offered me." He desperately wanted to ask why it was impossible that the Malacus he knew could still be alive, but found it too difficult to speak the words aloud. Was it that the name was that rare, or could it be something else. . . ? Surely he wasn't the only person on the planet with that name.

"That is where you are mistaken," Luziaph said with a smug grin, somehow responding to his unspoken question. "Upon this world, once one is crowned God-King, the name they bear becomes sacred; never again to be used by another. Even if he is not the man who was once ruler of all Datheron, to use the name is a crime in itself. I would have words with this 'Malacus.' Where might I find him?"

Terror flooded Allen's senses. Somehow Luziaph was aware of his thoughts, which meant that the Triclopian tyrant had either just figured out how to understand English, or his own diminished mental state had given Luziaph complete dominion over his mind, including what language his thoughts came in. He felt the same irresistible prompting to give his master the truth nudging its way through his mind. He didn't want to compromise Malacus' or Sarah's welfare, but he felt like he might die of shame if he didn't answer the question.

"He resides in a cabin, located in a valley some distance southeast of Abendroth," he heard himself say. "I know not its exact location."

Allen was heartbroken at the betrayal he'd just committed. How could he have so freely given away the location of those he cared for, especially to one as openly abusive as Luziaph? What had he done?

"At last," Luziaph said with a grin. "I knew there was more to your story than previously given, and now I shall have the truth! And along with it, leverage over Zorthos and quite possibly the God-King, Himself!"

Luziaph strode over to the spear protruding from the wall, and yanked it from where Allen had planted it. He examined the tip before turning back toward Allen. Without realizing it, Allen found himself pushing himself away from the floor. He stood erect, not quite understanding how he'd come to be so; his body seemed to be moving of its own volition.

Luziaph took a couple steps back toward him, speaking to Gazianna without removing his gaze from Allen's eyes. "Take him to the infirmary," he said in a smooth voice. "See his wounds properly attended. Then see him deposited in the private incarceration chamber, among the others tied to his deception. I would have them all together when I return with truth as my ally."

"Return?" Gazianna questioned. "Do you travel?"

"Yes," Luziaph said triumphantly. "To find the heart of Zorthos' deceit . . . and crush it!"

Allen wanted to ask what he'd meant by that. He wanted to ask what injuries he had suffered which were severe enough to require she take him to the infirmary; as much pain as he was in, it could be a number of things. He desperately wanted to take back everything he'd just divulged to this psychotic despot. But before he could take a single step toward reclaiming control of his mind, Luziaph brought the blunt end of the spear whistling through the air toward his face. A bright light shook his vision and then everything went black.

25

ABANDON

SARAH FELT LIKE DYING. Even though she had finally come to accept that she was stuck on this world, she still felt terrible about the direction hers and Allen's lives had taken. She knew it wasn't helping matters to dwell on that which couldn't be changed, but she couldn't keep thoughts of what might have been—what should have been—from swirling through her mind. She should be living on Earth with her father, going to work every day, and getting to know Allen as more than a friend. Instead she was on a strange world full of backward customs and violence, and her best friend was condemned to a life he hadn't asked for, quite possibly awaiting his execution . . . if he even still lived. She realized that she may never see him or anyone else she cared for again.

She was all alone, surrounded by those who could never truly understand her.

Sarah felt like dying.

To his credit, Malacus had been very kind and accommodating to her. He'd seemed very stern to her in the beginning, but the more time she spent with the old man the more he was growing on her. He was, after all, the only person she knew on this whole godforsaken planet. The amulet he had given her had helped in her studies of Olyphatarian. He didn't permit her to wear it all that often, but it had genuinely helped her make small strides in understanding what was to be her new primary language.

The first time she'd put the necklace on, the experience could only be classified as disorienting. She wasn't really sure how to describe it other than to say that it somehow did exactly what the old man said it would. She could hear the words spoken in the alien tongue, knew that she was hearing the other language, yet somehow her mind was able to understand it, as if the amulet were the missing piece of a puzzle.

Malacus had warned her not to rely entirely upon the amulet to learn the language, saying that doing so would only confuse her further in the end if she did. But he did let her wear it occasionally as he offered instruction, in order to help her over the hurdle of understanding the translation of sentence structure and conjugation.

She was definitely noticing a difference in her muscles now that she had been out of her coma for a while. Her legs were long since used to the walks they would take every day, and Malacus had even helped her other muscles adapt by giving her all the extra chores she'd been doing. She seemed to be able to move with relative ease in most everything she did . . . at least while she still wore the adaptive garments which had been given to her the day she arrived. But no matter how much she adapted to her new life, the emptiness she felt at being alone on an alien world threatened to consume her.

In an attempt to help keep her mind from falling to the threats of depression, Malacus had also begun training her in how to brew certain concoctions and prepare meals. She had never considered herself a good cook while on Earth and hadn't really ever enjoyed such domestic responsibilities, but found that the lessons had provided a creative outlet of sorts. The task of learning how to mix ingredients properly and, when necessary, cook them over an open flame had proven to be quite the challenge at first. But it quickly became one of the few things she was expected to learn which truly took her mind away from thoughts of depression, thoughts of Allen.

At night she would lay awake for what felt like an eternity, thinking about everything and nothing. She worried for Allen's mother, Carol, and how she must feel having lost both of the men in her life who mattered most. She considered it the cruelest irony that they had both been taken from her by a world she didn't even know existed; that, from her vantage point, it must have seemed as if they both simply disappeared off the face of the Earth. She realized that such a thought was far more accurate than Carol would ever know.

Her heart broke for her father. He must be enduring much the same torture as Carol; not knowing what happened to his only daughter, having had both of the women he cared for most stripped from his life before he was ready. She reflected on a time when she was a younger girl, when her father and Carol had dated for a brief time; she secretly hoped that they could find comfort with each other and at least find some measure of peace in one another's arms. She realized, of course, that it was a tragic way for them to end up together again; she just didn't want hers and Allen's disappearance to ruin the rest of their parents' lives, leaving them in misery for their remaining days.

She even found her thoughts occasionally drifting to Tommy. Even though things had been tense between them toward the end, and even though she now realized that they were wrong for each other, she wondered if he knew she was gone. She wondered, if he did know, what the knowledge did for him. Did he miss her? Was he worried for her? She chastised herself for even entertaining such thoughts, and realized it came more from missing her old life than it did from actually missing him. She knew they had no future together; she just wished she weren't trapped so far away from all of the things she used to so love, some of which would forever hold sway over her heart.

She realized, too, at this point that she no longer had a job even if she could go back to Earth today. Malacus had reminded her of the time fluctuation between this world and every other in the known cosmos, and she understood that she had most likely been fired long ago for job abandonment. She wondered if her boss had even cared what happened to her or if he'd just wrote up the pink slip and moved on with his day.

The thing which consumed her thoughts most frequently, however, was her concern for Allen. She refused to believe that he was gone for good. He wasn't dead; she could feel it in the depths of her soul. He had to still be alive. She knew Allen well enough to know that he had most likely already made some friends, and quite possibly some enemies. He was the type of guy who always seemed to know what was right, and never let anyone bully him into changing his point of view. He had a strength of character she considered as honorable as it was endearing.

She missed him terribly.

Malacus had told her that Allen had learned the truth of who his father was, though she hadn't asked him to share the man's identity with her. Part of her felt like it would be a betrayal to not let Allen be the first to tell her, to confide his feelings on the subject to her, so she had reasoned it would be better if she didn't know yet. It may be a small consolation, but it was one she held close to her heart in the hopes that she could finally offer the comforting shoulder she hadn't been able to while in her coma. Besides, it wasn't like the name of Allen's father would bring any semblance of recognition to her. She had, after all, only met a couple of people from this world and what were the odds that it was one of them?

Sarah trudged up the all-too-familiar staircase one morning after a night of restless sleep to find Malacus pulling some of the books and trinkets from the shelves which lined the walls of the cabin and stowing them away in a couple of large trunks. So consumed with his task was he, that he hadn't noticed her at first. He stood transfixed on a particular volume in his hand as if lost in a fond memory. She hadn't wanted to disturb him, so she'd just watched him silently for several minutes.

At last he turned around to place the treasured volume among the others in a trunk behind him, noticing her for the first time. "Good morning," he said when he saw her. "Apologies, I was unaware you had risen. I shall see to breakfast presently."

"It's okay," she said. "I just woke up." She gestured to the trunks at Malacus' feet, "What's all this about? Are we going somewhere?"

The old man hesitated for a moment before answering. "Indeed," he said, clearing his throat. "I fear our stay here has reached its end."

Her world stopped for a moment. He'd made it sound as if they were leaving fort good. If that was the case, where were they to go? What if Allen found a way out of his situation and came looking for them here? He'd be even more alone than he was now.

"Your concerns are understood and not unfounded," Malacus said, apparently listening to her thoughts yet again. "But a vision has come to me in the night. We must be away, or I fear terrible things will befall us."

"A vision?" she asked, suddenly more concerned than she'd even been a moment ago. "What terrible things? Has something happened to Allen?"

"I fear it so," he answered as he continued to pack. "I do not believe he has perished, yet I fear our location has been compromised. I had reservations it would be so as I saw Allen escorted away by the authorities of Abendroth, and should have set my mind to the purpose of remaining hidden much sooner. But I grow weary and complacent in my old age." He tossed a couple more books in the same trunk and turned toward the kitchen area of the cabin. "Come, we shall fix proper meal and then I shall have your hands join in the task."

Sarah followed in the familiar task of handing Malacus ingredients, grinding certain ones as instructed, and stirring others as he prepared the morning meal, a feeling of hollow numbness expanding through her as she did so. She had already lost so much since coming here; now she was to lose her new home as well. She could feel despair taking her. At the same time she felt insulted that she should have to give up the only thing of comfort she had left. The house may not belong to her, but it was all she knew of this world. It wasn't fair to take it from her too.

All at once she decided she couldn't take it anymore. She had to get some fresh air. Without a word she set the mixing bowl down on the counter and walked out the back door of the cabin. She stood there for only a few moments, breathing open air and staring up at the turquoise sky before she felt a hand on her shoulder. She started at the touch, realizing for the first time that her eyes had been filling with tears as one escaped its confines, cutting a warm path down the side of her face.

"I know your time here has come with less than ease and comfort," the old man said in a gentle voice. "I wish I could remove such burdens from your shoulders. You must believe me when I say that we both care greatly for Allen, yet we will do him no good if we are captured or stripped of breath. In this way we aid him by being absent when threat presents itself."

Sarah had to fight the lump in her throat to respond. "I just don't understand how any of this could have happened," she complained in a shaky voice. "One day I'm on Earth with my best friend, looking forward to the possibility of being more than friends, of making a life together, and the next I've lost everything important to me. I didn't even get to say goodbye to anyone before I left, and now you expect me to give up the only home I've known in this godforsaken new existence of mine . . . it isn't fair. I just don't know what I did to deserve this."

"I know, child." Malacus gave her shoulder an affectionate squeeze. "Yet fate seldom considers our concepts of fairness prior to thrusting itself upon us. The measure of a person comes not from what is handed to them, but from how they respond to fate's call. There may yet be a way to turn events to our advantage."

"How?" She whined, trying her best to keep the sob from her voice.

"I do not know. Yet I fear opportunity to discover such a way will be forever lost if we do not move quickly. Come. We should eat and return to task; we have little time."

She hesitated a moment longer, struggling to contain the raging storm of emotions threatening to overtake her. She exhaled a deep, cleansing breath before following the old man back inside. "What did your vision show you?" she asked as they moved back into the kitchen area of the cabin.

"That we are no longer safe here," Malacus responded cryptically.

"Oh, please," she said confrontationally. "There has to be more to it than that. If we're in danger, don't you think I deserve to know the truth?"

Malacus expelled a defeated sigh, seeming to consider her words. "I suppose you do," he said, meeting her eyes. "It is a skill I have yet to master, so details appear with little clarity. The premonition spoke of Allen's plight; I fear the discovery of his origin imminent and I am now certain that he is the true child of prophecy. The one who now holds sway over Allen's life knows of our location, and has intention to seek us out. We must not be here when he arrives."

"Why? What will happen if we are?"

"I fear such detail is hidden from view." He shook his head slowly.

Anxiety was overwhelming her. This was exactly what she didn't need right now. Part of her felt like giving up. Maybe, if she didn't fight it, the man who was coming for them would take her to where he was keeping Allen. At least then they could be together again, even if it was in servitude or death. After a moment's consideration, however, she decided that she just wasn't ready to face this world without the old man who had been her guide through learning to adapt. She steeled herself and hurriedly assisted Malacus in completing the morning meal.

Rushing through breakfast hadn't been smart. They'd eaten so quickly that indigestion was already troubling her as she began helping Malacus pack away the books and objects which decorated the old man's home. She moved with deliberate purpose, doing her best to handle the objects with care as she pulled them from the shelves.

They hadn't been working for more than an hour, when Malacus suddenly stood bolt upright. A look of panic consumed his rigid posture. "No!" he gasped. "It is too soon!"

In a flash the old man flew past her, snatching her wrist as he moved. It felt as if her arm had nearly been ripped from its socket as he dragged her across the cabin, toward the entrance to her basement bedroom. In one swift motion, he lifted the large tile covering its entrance and hurled her down the stairs. "Make not a sound," he barked. "And silence your thoughts, lest you be discovered!"

Withour another word, the tile slammed home, leaving her in total darkness.

Her heart pounded so fast and so hard she could scarcely hear anything else. She was sure she was on the verge of a panic attack. She struggled mightily to reclaim control of her senses. After an eternity of moments, she pushed herself up on to her knees. She could already feel where the bruises would be from where she'd impacted the cold, hard floor at the bottom of the steps—thankfully nothing seemed broken. In a state of confusion and panic, she crawled along the floor through the dark to where she knew her bed was and once there curled herself up against the far wall, wrapping her arms around her knees as she struggled to slow her breathing and racing thoughts.

For a long while, she could hear nothing above her. Then, all at once, she heard muffled shouting. She knew the conflict had turned violent when an explosion echoed violently from above. There were loud blasts she could only compare to gun shots or a cannon being fired. Another explosion. Terror consumed her; the man from Malacus' vision was here. She didn't need the old man to tell her that she was right; he was here and Malacus was fighting for his life directly above her. She desperately wished she could open her eyes to find this had all been a nightmare.

There was a final muffled crunching noise, and then silence swept through the room. It was over. The fighting had stopped. Remembering what Malacus had told her to do, should they ever be separated, she pulled the necklace from her pocket and draped it around her neck . . . just in case the old man hadn't been victorious. She hated herself for giving life to such a fear; she knew how important it was to think positively. But she also understood the merit in being prepared.

It felt as if she had waited in silence forever when at last she heard the door to her room being lifted from its confines. It didn't move with the same grace she was familiar with and she wondered if that meant that the old man had been gravely injured and was struggling to lift it free, or if he had lost the battle, leaving the enemy he'd been warned about attempting its removal alone. After a brief struggle, it slammed back into place. The room she was in filled with a strange grating sound that seemed to reverberate off every wall around her. A moment later, the ceiling over the stairs crashed down with explosive force, leaving her eardrums echoing wickedly and filling the small room with a cloud of dust and debris.

In the light coming from the entrance, Sarah could see the silhouette of a man looking down at her. It descended the steps with a regal grace she was unfamiliar with. Even without the torches lit, she could tell it was not Malacus that stood before her.

Her breath caught in her throat. Through the shadows it appeared as if the man she was looking at had three eyes.

"How very curious," the deep voice said menacingly. "Your thoughts are of the same tongue as his."

As the man began to move toward her, she noticed for the first time that he clutched something under his arm. He was holding the object the same way Allen would sometimes hold a basketball. As he got closer, he knelt down and firmly took hold of her wrist. She could feel his warm, rancid breath on the back of her hand.

"Do you understand my words?" he asked her.

She nodded, afraid to look him in the eye.

"Good," he said as he stood up, taking her hand with him. "If life yet holds value to you, come with me and give me no trouble."

She did as commanded, standing up on trembling legs and allowed him to usher her up the stairs into the light. When they reached the top of the stairs the sight that met her eyes took her breath away. The cabin had all but been destroyed. The wall which partitioned the main area from the kitchen stood in pieces, still crumbling. Books were scattered everywhere. The roof was missing. Only sections of the outside walls remained standing, looking very much like a bomb had gone off within the house. Sarah looked numbly down at the ground. Among the debris she saw what appeared to be the legs of a statue, surrounded by shattered bits of stone. She couldn't see Malacus anywhere.

As the tall, bald man dragged her away from the cabin—away from her home—she noticed for the first time what he held under his arm. It appeared to be the head of the shattered statue she'd seen among the tattered remains of Malacus' cabin. She suddenly had a terrible feeling about what had transpired above her while she'd cowered in the dark.

"Where are you taking me?" she asked her captor.

He stopped in mid-stride, turning to face her. She realized for the first time that she had not been mistaken; the man did have three eyes. It was one of the most disturbing things she'd ever seen. "What did you say?" he asked.

Sarah paused momentarily, feeling as if even repeating her words would only bring more trouble upon her. "I said, where are you taking me?" she repeated in a shaky voice.

"Interesting," he mumbled to himself, staring at her as if he'd just found a shiny new toy. "You understand the language, yet you do not speak it?"

She shook her head; certain he could see the fear in her face. She just wanted him to stop looking at her with those creepy eyes of his.

Then he began to laugh; a disconcerting, malevolent laugh. "How perfect," he said with a lecherous grin. "You shall have to wait for proper translation. Stay close to my side and keep your mouth shut, lest you receive the same as the old man."

And then she saw it. The three-eyed man held up the stone head for her to clearly see. There, frozen in a look of pain, was Malacus' face; a crack running across his forehead and down his nose. Flecks of his hair fell away as the man placed his trophy back underneath his arm.

Her heart broke. She had never been so afraid, or felt so alone in her life as she did in that moment.

Without another word, the man who had murdered her only companion on this world turned away from her, pulling up the deep purple hood of his cloak, still firmly clutching her wrist as he dragged her to a fate unknown.

26

ALLIANCE

THE ENTIRE WORLD EXPLODED as he awoke. The pain was so piercing, so all-consuming, that Allen found himself wishing he had never regained consciousness. As he struggled to ignore the pain and take in his new surroundings, the details of how he had lost consciousness eluded him. The room was spinning nearly as hard as his head was pounding. Nausea borne from the severe pressure enveloping his head threatened to throw him into a fit of dry heaves. At the same time he realized his stomach ached for want of food, yet the thought of eating anything made him feel even more nauseated than before; it was a vicious circle which kept him planted where he was for a long while.

The room he found himself in was nearly pitch black; a fact for which he was very grateful with the way his head throbbed. With great effort he reached his hand up to the left side of his face. His arm felt like jelly, as if it weren't even his own, but he had to check the stinging pain he felt there. As his left hand reached its destination, he fully expected to feel a large gash along his cheek. He was surprised to realize that there was none. It was extremely tender to the touch and most likely bruised, but there didn't seem to be an open wound. He noticed, too, that the whiskers on his face had blossomed into a full beard, and for a long moment he wondered just how long he'd been out. Then the realization came to him that he couldn't remember the last time he'd shaved; he certainly hadn't done it while in Luziaph's employ.

He groaned as he made his first attempt to sit up. His body seemed to be fighting vehemently against his efforts to rise from the cold, hard floor.

"So," he heard a voice say from the dark. "You yet live. For a while I thought you for Sythika."

Unable to sit up, he remained supine as he responded to a voice he didn't recognize. "Whose voice do I hear?" he asked, his own cracking under the strain of speaking aloud.

"I am called Sepharus," the voice said. "It was I you came to feed days past, accompanied by Gazianna. You now find yourself similarly encumbered."

At hearing Sepharus' words, Allen immediately realized where he was. His heart sank; he was in the underbelly of the palace with two of the only beings on the planet who could truly identify him. He didn't think things could possibly get much worse.

He rolled to his side, feeling for the first time something firmly clamped to his scalp. He groaned inwardly when he realized what it was, pushing himself up to a sitting position, feeling as if the act of movement had taken far more energy than it rightfully should have. As soon as he was able, he took stock of his new surroundings. The only light in the room came from a very small opening in the door to the chamber; he immediately recalled that the torches were kept among the guards on the other side.

"Gazianna offered tale of how you ended up among us," Sepharus said. "Tell me, what seized the senses in taking offensive action against your master?"

His head was still spinning, and he really didn't feel like defending his actions to someone he didn't know; someone who had chased his father to Earth for the purpose of capturing or killing him. After a moment of consideration, however, he admitted to himself that he had no idea how long he'd be stuck down here, and at least he had someone to talk to this time. "Protection of a friend," he offered, simply.

"Protection," Sepharus echoed. "Against he who holds dominion over the both of you?"

"None hold dominion over me," he protested. "I but find myself of a compromised position of late."

Sepharus fell to a fit of laughter. "You have spirit," he said through his mirth. "A trait to be admired."

"It pleases me that I could bring amusement to you," he answered.

"What name do you go by?" the other asked.

"Araset," Allen replied.

"That is not the name Zorthos called you upon the soil of Earth," he heard another voice say.

Allen's breath caught in his throat. He hadn't realized that either of the other Gorrlocks were awake. Panic began to flood his senses; he sincerely hoped that they hadn't had a chance to reveal his planet of origin to Luziaph while he was out. He scanned the darkness, struggling to make out which one had spoken; they both still lay motionless upon the floor. A moment later one sat up, propping himself against the wall.

"Welcome back," Sepharus teased.

"Save it," the other said. "This is the boy I told you of; the one Zorthos duped me into bringing back with us."

At hearing his words, Allen realized it could only be Pythor that had awoken. He rested his head against the wall behind him in resignation. He knew if he were trapped down here long enough that this would happen; he just wished it hadn't happened so soon. His head still spun, and the dank smell of the incarceration chamber was only adding to his sense of nausea.

"This is he?" Sepharus asked in an astonished tone. "This is the boy from Earth?"

"Say it louder," he said sardonically. "I do not think the guards heard you."

"Quite the flippant tongue on this one," Sepharus laughed. "Tell me, Earth boy, what difference would it make to me should your origin find its way into the light?"

Allen literally felt as if the walls were closing in around him. He just couldn't seem to catch a break. Things seemed to have progressively gotten worse for him since the day before he left Earth forever. He'd been expelled from school, then duped into forsaking his home world; the woman he cared for most in this life was probably still at the brink of death; he'd been arrested, beaten, subjected to slavery, told that he could be the crux upon which the fate of the universe hinged, and now he was trapped in a dark room among the ones who'd set these tragic events in motion. He'd often been told that things could always be worse, but he was having a difficult time imagining how at the moment. He had to find a way to convince these three to keep his secret, or he may yet be put to death.

"One of the first things I learned upon coming to this world," he began, "was the words of prophecy which speak of one coming to Datheron from Earth. The truth could very well warrant the taking of my life. I am aware that it could also mean yours, yet I would not have it so."

"You make but one proper assumption," Pythor interjected. "That it could mean your life; a consequence which holds absolutely no bearing over us."

"And what shall transpire when I let slip your part in my arrival here?" he challenged. "I could speak of desires overheard in my travels of three Gorrlocks wishing to ignite the prophecy, tricking me into accepting this world to further their own ends."

Pythor was silent for a very long moment before responding. "You would not dare such a thing when the truth is but a breath away. Have you already forgotten that you are captive to a Grandmaster of telepathy?"

"A skill he is unable to employ while I remain encumbered by Triaga," he retorted. "If it is truly believed that I am tied to the words of this prophecy, do you believe removal of such hindrance will be met with eagerness? Is it a risk you are willing to take?"

"No," Pythor admitted slowly. "Not yet, anyway."

Allen let out a sigh of relief. At least they wouldn't be seeking to divulge his secret immediately. That was one less thing amongst a forest of others that he would have to worry about; at least for now.

"Gratitude," he said, feeling as if it would be wrong not to.

For a long while they all just sat silently in the dark. Occasionally he would hear a brief conversation among the guards on the other side of the door. He hated the disorienting feeling which seemed to be consuming all of his senses, and couldn't decide if it was from having a Triaga back on, from the lingering effects of the beating he'd endured, or from the disgustingly musty air he was breathing. He had no idea how long he'd been down here or when he would eat next. It all seemed a bad joke at his expense. He'd been raised to believe that as long as he always did what was right, that things would even out in the end; that what goes around, comes around; that all good things come to those who are humble and patient, yet he now found himself in unforeseeable circumstances which could only yield catastrophic results. What had he ever done to deserve this? He supposed it didn't matter; all he could do now was move forward and make the best of the situation . . . if there was such a thing anymore.

When he could no longer stand the silence, he decided he'd at least occupy his thoughts with other things. "How long has that one been out?" he asked, gesturing to the only one whose name he didn't know.

"He drifts in and out," Sepharus answered. "As do we all while at the mercy of that Tricopian and this infernal Triaga."

"I do not understand," he replied, genuinely confused.

Sepharus looked to Pythor, who let out a frustrated sigh before explaining. "That Triclopian piece of filth delights in the torture of our kind, as do they all. We experience jolts through the Triaga at random which will often inflict enough pain to render us unconscious," he bit out; Allen couldn't mistake the bitterness in his voice.

"When I find myself free of this blasted thing, I will rid the world of his miserable existence," Pythor added a moment later, as if for good measure.

"Surely, not all Triclopians are of the same temperament toward Gorrlocks," he said.

"They are vermin—all," Pythor assured him.

Allen found it sad that he was billions upon billions of miles away from the planet he'd once called home, and somehow prejudice between races was still an issue. He let several long moments go by before he responded. "I do not believe such a thing," he said into the silence. "I met a

410

Triclopian by the name of Pendrick who showed me much kindness, all things considered."

Even in the darkness Allen could tell Pythor was glaring at him. "Such words do not come as great shock," he said defensively. "You are not a Gorrlock."

"Yet I still remain of the opinion that an entire race cannot be condemned by the actions of one," Allen retorted.

"Spoken like a politician," Pythor sniped, turning his gaze away from Allen.

"Believe what you will," he said. "I would not see any treated poorly for the crime of being born different."

"You are but a child," Pythor scoffed. "And have much yet to learn of the way things truly work."

"I understand well enough to realize life is but a commodity on this world," Allen said, not fighting the edge taking his voice. "A notion which sickens me."

"Yet such is the way it is," Pythor bit back. "Always has been, and forever shall be. A thing over which there is no control for any, save one: the God-King."

"Then perhaps He does not deserve the title," Allen retorted.

"You blaspheme!" Pythor bellowed. "How dare you speak in such a manner about that which you have no understanding, of he who has ruled over this world for nearly as long as Paragus Himself!"

Allen realized that things were getting away from his control. He hadn't intended to start a debate, or anger Pythor with his words; he'd only wanted to have more than just his thoughts to pass the time. He decided that it would be best if he just kept silent for a while. He really didn't want to give either of these two a reason to expose him to Luziaph.

Moments later, he heard a voice coming from the other side of the door; it could only belong to one of the several guards he knew to be stationed there. "What brings you to elevate voice?" the guard asked.

His heart pounded in his chest. He had no idea what the laws of this world had to say about speaking out against its supreme ruler; a man who was quite possibly the most powerful in the known universe. He genuinely hoped that he hadn't offended Pythor enough to cause him to reconsider his promise to keep Allen's secret.

"Nothing," Pythor answered, much to Allen's surprise. "A simple misunderstanding."

"Then keep your mouth clamped tightly shut," the guard said, giving the door a solid thump to accentuate his command.

Allen let out a low sigh of relief. "Gratitude," he said. "And apologies for any offense found in my previous statement."

"Save it," Pythor retorted.

Allen expelled a deep sigh of frustration. He didn't understand why he couldn't seem to get anyone from this world to drop their guard long enough to have a simple conversation. Every time he got close to success in his efforts, he ended up with the same result. Was he the only open-minded person on the whole planet? He considered the possibility that it might be best if he just stopped trying, but such a thought was extremely depressing to him. He didn't like the idea that, due to the time fluctuation of this world, he could possibly live several hundred Earth years in virtual solitude just because he thought things through differently than those who were born and raised on Datheron.

"Do you genuinely feel such a way, that all races should be considered of equal standing?" Sepharus asked, interrupting his brooding.

"I do," he replied, a little surprised by the question.

"You truly are not of this world," Sepharus said, seemingly marveled by the idea. "Tell me, where did you come by such a notion?"

Allen had grown so used to twisting the truth about where he was from that, for a moment, he considered how to word his answer without revealing too much. He had to mentally remind himself that these two already knew where he was from.

"Such a notion is commonplace where I am from," he said, thankful for the opportunity to openly speak of his old life on Earth. "There is great diversity among the populace of Earth, much like there is here. And there are those who do believe that one should hold supremacy over another, yet I count myself not among them. It has been my experience that one's genetic background holds absolutely no bearing on the type of person they will become. The sum of a man's actions is what defines character, not the color of skin."

"And what is it you believe Luziaph's actions speak of the man?" Sepharus asked.

He considered his answer for only a moment. "He is a pompous, abusive, shell of a man; a poor excuse of what a Proctus should be."

Pythor and Sepharus laughed loudly at his words.

"Perhaps there is hope for you yet," Pythor chuckled.

They continued to laugh for several more moments, and Allen found it difficult not to join in their mirth; it had been so long since he had genuinely laughed that he'd nearly forgotten how good it felt.

"I have questions I would have answer to, if you would be so kind as to oblige," he said once the laughter had died out.

"Speak them," Pythor prompted.

"How long have you been down here, among the bowels of this palace?"

413

Pythor sat silent for a moment before responding, and Allen found himself second-guessing his question, unsure whether or not he had offended Pythor yet again. "These two were stripped from my care and forced into such unfavorable surroundings the very day of our return," he said. "I found myself similarly betrayed many days later during confrontation with the criminal, Zorthos."

Having had time to cool toward the notion of his father being a criminal from another world didn't take away from the sting of hearing the words aloud. He still had strong opinions about Zorthos and the choices he'd made, but had recently come to understand some of the motivations behind the man's decisions; even if he didn't quite agree with them. The thought came to him that this might be an opportunity to hear Zorthos' story from another perspective.

"How much do you know of the man?" he asked.

"I am burdened with more than my fair share of knowledge on the subject," Pythor said with a touch of disgust to his voice. "He was counted among the Krathantor, an honorary Brother of the Armor, for a time."

A Krathantor? His father, a Brother of the Armor? He had no idea that Zorthos had once been counted among such an elite group. He realized, however, that there was quite a bit about the man that even his mother didn't know. He decided to see how much he could learn; after all, he didn't have much better to do with his time.

"Would you share such knowledge with me?" he asked, trying not to sound too desperate.

"What meaning would such knowledge hold for you?" Pythor asked, sounding very much like he didn't want to recount even knowing the man.

"Call it morbid curiosity," he said. "It was his attempted escape to my home world that forever altered my destiny, was it not?"

Pythor expelled a thoughtful sigh. "Very well," he conceded. "What is it you wish to know?"

"Anything that can be offered," he answered, still putting effort into not sounding overly eager. "Beginning with why he is considered fugitive."

"He is considered fugitive," Pythor began, "because he disobeyed a direct order from the God-King. He fled this world absent consent of Rhenngoth, remaining undetectable for well over a year before crawling back with his tail between legs, begging forgiveness.

"As previously stated, he was once counted among us, joining us on the hunt of those with whom he now shares title. His was a life of privilege, growing into manhood beneath the same roof as the God-King himself; a thing all of this world would consider a great honor. But not him. He saw it only as a burden, ever seeking a way to leave such glory behind him.

"Years past, he entered the Arena Games, the same as both his parents before him. On his first attempt he made it to the finals, earning the glory of being crowned its Champion, and still it was not enough. When one becomes Champion of the Arena they are afforded anything they wish, no matter how opulent. The God-King holds a ceremony for all to witness; it is a day remembered and celebrated by all in attendance, ever on the tongues of even those who are not. Such a thing is to be celebrated by all; the God-King granting any desire to one who has proven themselves to wield Mystica with skill and purpose! Yet when presented with such reward, Zorthos all but spat upon the feet of Rhenngoth, asking for naught but permission to leave the soil of Datheron for all time!"

"Where is the fault in such a request?" he interjected. "I thought Champion is granted anything, no matter how opulent."

"You fail to see insult where it should be obvious," Pythor replied. "Such a request may have been given consideration . . . had it not been asked for in the presence of an entire crowd. Once upon Datheronian soil, none are welcome to leave. To learn the abilities only this world can provide is a great honor, and Zorthos spat upon such tradition in front of all present in asking to leave this world behind him. He acted as if no more than a thief in the night, bringing shame to the title of Champion and his mother, Divina!"

"I did not realize that honor and glory were held in such esteem on this world that they could eclipse the personal desires of a man when weighed against the opinions of the masses," he replied, straining to keep the condescension out of his words.

Pythor had apparently not heard the bitterness in his tone. "Honor and glory are everything," he stated. "To win the favor of the crowd, of the God-King himself, is an achievement few ever obtain. I fear Zorthos does not see it this way because his has always been a life of privilege, every desire laid at his feet absent effort in the acquiring. Things come easily to the man, so he does not care to abide the same laws as the rest must follow."

Hearing Pythor recount some of the events of Zorthos' life brought the man's reasoning into perspective. If the entire population of Datheron felt as Pythor did, that honor and glory were more important than anything else, then it was no wonder Zorthos had wanted to leave in the first place. As much as Allen hated to admit it, he found himself understanding his father's decisions more and more; he just wished that his mother had been spared the heartache she'd suffered in not knowing the truth. All Zorthos had wanted was to live a life that was his own; to make his own choices, free of such severe laws and consequences. Despite himself, Allen was beginning to feel bad for the man and all he'd had to sacrifice.

As he sat there in the dark, contemplating what he had just learned about his father's past, Allen realized something; Zorthos' biggest dream was to be free of this world. When presented with the opportunity to have anything he desired, he didn't choose wealth, or power, or a station of note; he chose to be forever rid of shackles of a world on which one could learn to wield any special ability they wanted. A decision of such magnitude wouldn't have been made lightly. Such a decision could only have come from a tragic event in Zorthos' past. Why else would he have wanted to leave an entire world behind? Why else would he have wanted to run away from everything he had ever known? The decision had to have come from somewhere. Allen found himself wondering what had happened to his father to make him decide that the thing he wanted most was to desert his home forever.

"Is that all you wish to know?" Pythor asked, snapping him back to the present.

"No," he replied. "Apologies, I was but lost in thought. Tell me, if honor and glory are so revered on this world, what could make him turn from it? Why would he choose to leave this world behind the very moment of reaching its pinnacle of achievements?"

"That is a question for the fool, himself," Pythor responded. "The man is an enigma, holding none in esteem beyond himself. The reasons behind many of his decisions fall short of my understanding."

Allen hadn't expected much more of an answer than that, though he had hoped Zorthos' time among the Krathantor might have afforded Pythor a little insight into the situation. "You spoke of his mother, Divina," he said, recalling that Pythor had briefly mentioned her a few moments before, "and the shame he brought her with his request to leave Datheron. I would know more on the subject."

"Divina. . ." he began, the name dripping off his tongue as if it left a bad taste in his mouth. "She is a witch of extraordinary power. I do not care for the woman, but she is trusted advisor to Rhenngoth; her loyalty held as example to all. When her son spoke of disavowing citizenship, it cast a reflection of dishonor upon her before all present. The words spoken by her son were not met with pride or understanding. She suffered Rhenngoth's displeasure following the ceremony."

"How could she be held responsible for words spilling from her son's mouth?" he asked, mildly appalled by such a thought.

Pythor shook his head, seemingly in wonder of Allen's ignorance. "It was she who provided lessons to Zorthos; she who was responsible for molding him into the man he is; her tutelage, the stone from which his actions were carved. How could such a declaration not reflect poorly upon her?"

"Because the decision to speak the words was his alone," he replied. "None should be held accountable for the actions of another."

Pythor continued to shake his head, as if he simply couldn't understand where Allen was coming from. Silence consumed the room as Allen's mind raced, pregnant with information about his father he never would have considered possible. He had often dreamed in his youth, when he was still hopeful of his father returning, that he would learn that the man was some kind of hero; that the reason he had been away was because he had been off saving the world, earning renown in every country for his good deeds. To learn that his father actually was world renowned, even if on another world, was somehow unsettling. Pythor had even said that the man had grown

418

up under the same roof as the God-King. He wondered if that made his father royalty on Datheron.

"Tell me of Zorthos' childhood," Allen said. "For what reason did he grow beneath the roof of the God-King's palace?"

"Because his mother has been closest advisor to Rhenngoth for a very long time," Pythor replied. "Her achievements in the Arena Games, as well as her fealty to the throne, have ever been spoken of with reverence; earning her a firm place at the God-King's side. She stands one of the only Datheronians to ever be crowned Arena Champion twice. Her loyalty has always been unshakable, even upon command to destroy her own husband."

Allen wasn't sure if he had heard Pythor correctly. "Did you just say she killed her husband by order of Rhenngoth?" he asked.

Pythor nodded. "Doing so earned her the title of Arena Champion for the second time, and proved her fealty beyond question."

Allen wondered if Zorthos had been there to witness his father's death. Such a thing could easily be the reason the man wanted nothing to do with this world. He suddenly felt a horrible emptiness for the man who had sired him, and found himself wishing that he'd had more time to speak with him before he had been ushered away. Though there were still hard feelings toward him, Allen was beginning to feel as if he had approached such views unfairly. And now he might never get to see Zorthos again . . .

"How long will we be made to stay down here, far removed from prying eyes?" he asked no one in particular. He needed to get his mind away from such depressing thoughts.

Again, it was Pythor who responded. "Until Mystica flees weary body," he said, a touch of regret tainting the words. "Or until Luziaph tires of our presence and the pleasure found in our torture."

Those had been the exact words Allen had feared hearing the most. "I sincerely hope it is not so," he said, resting his head against the cold wall behind him. "I would not see any suffer such a fate."

"Then perhaps you would aid us in our efforts to flee this place," Sepharus whispered.

"Sepharus! Mind your tongue!" Pythor hissed.

"He is of the same position as we," Sepharus challenged. "The boy may be naïve, but I do not believe he will betray us to Luziaph."

Pythor glared at Sepharus for a long moment. Allen was beginning to feel awkward as the tension of the silence mounted. He realized that forming an escape plan and seeing it through could have severe consequences for all of them. The way things worked on this world, he wouldn't be at all surprised to learn that he would be held just as accountable even if he didn't participate. After giving it some thought he acquiesced, deciding that it couldn't bring him to more trouble than he was already in.

"I would be away from here," he announced in a low tone. "And I would not abandon you to suffer this fate alone, if given the choice."

"Then it is settled," Sepharus said with a grin, bringing his eyes to meet Allen's. "Here is what we will do. . ." He leaned forward, keeping his voice low.

Sepharus had only spoken a couple more words when a harsh light cut through the darkness, forcing them all to squint against the intrusion. The door to the chamber creaked in protest as it was forced open. Still struggling to bring his eyes into focus Allen looked toward the entrance, nervous that their intent to escape had been overheard and the guards were coming in to punish them. To his surprise he saw the silhouette of a woman standing against the harsh light of the torches on the other side of the doorway.

"Araset," he heard Gazianna's voice say, "Luziaph summons you."

27

ZORTHOS

THE JOURNEY TO NENTALIA had been an arduous one. Encumbered as he was by the Triaga Luziaph had placed upon his head, it had taken Zorthos far longer than normal to reach his former home. Having been locked in place by a true Grandmaster of telepathy, the Triaga prevented him from accessing even the most basic of abilities; Zorthos felt naked to the world. Coupled with the disorienting effects of the binding device on his head was the fact that Luziaph had sent over a dozen of his elite royal guards to accompany Zorthos to the world's capitol. Absent access to his abilities, he had no choice but to go through with his plan of submitting himself to the God-King's will.

With nothing else to occupy his time, Zorthos had found his thoughts drifting to moments from his past, events which had ultimately lead him to this point; realizing that he could very well be marching toward his own execution caused him to reflect upon a brighter time in his life. As the idea of his imminent death swirled through his thoughts, he decided that he would not change a thing. How could he regret choices which had led him to the woman he held dearer than life itself. Though the weight of her absence was a constant reminder of what he had lost, he couldn't bring himself to wish the pain away. Remembrances of the time they shared kept him warm during the cold nights, kept him strong in the face of adversity. He regretted only that their time together had been too brief, that it had ended the way it had.

He could still recall the very day he met her with exacting clarity. He had chosen Earth as his new home for a reason, hoping that fear of the prophecy would prevent the Krathantor from ever searching for him there. Though he had been to other worlds briefly during his time among the Krathantor, he recalled being marveled by the atmosphere of Earth. The buzz of activity which enveloped so much of the planet could be sensed even from great distances, and the gravitational fluctuation had been intoxicating. As he traversed the wooded area in which he had arrived, Zorthos had briefly contemplated the possibility of inserting himself as Earth's new God-King, able to reshape the laws he had found so unjust on his own home world. He had shunned such notions, however, giving heed to caution and the need to prevent discovery of his whereabouts, not to mention such a course of action would only turn him into that which he longed to escape.

After a while he'd come upon a strangely crafted road, populated by the most peculiar things he'd ever seen. He would eventually learn how such roads were paved, and that the things speeding past him were called automobiles, but he could never forget how disorienting the sight had been at first. It had been a warm, spring day and even from a distance he had thought Carol was beautiful as he approached her. Through his skill in telepathy he was able to surmise that she was in a state of panic, and that his name would seem odd to her. He had briefly scanned her mind for a suitable pseudonym, and a vague idea of what her dilemma was so that he might help her.

He hadn't needed to possess any skill in telepathy to see the fear in her eyes as he moved toward her, but he put on his most charming smile and asked her if she required assistance anyway; he realized that his thick accent and disheveled appearance couldn't have helped ease her concern. After accepting his offer he'd told her to just have a seat while he did all the work. Not wanting her to see just how he would fix the flat tire he had done his best to keep his tactics from her view; he may have broken several laws in his escape of Datheron, but he wasn't about to break its most sacred one of keeping its existence secret. It had taken him several minutes to determine just how such a task could be achieved-scanning her mind for clues and evaluating the molecular makeup of the tires through one of his perfected crafts-but he had eventually memorized the simplistic structure from one of the tires which was still intact and duplicated it to seal the ruptured one, filling it with air in the process.

When he was done, she had offered him a ride into town. At the time he hadn't been entirely sure what she'd meant, but had understood the kindness and sincerity in the gesture. He hadn't wanted to be rude, nor had he wanted to be free of her presence just yet, so he'd accepted her offer with a smile and a nod of his head.

Zorthos could still recall the feeling of uncomfortable excitement rushing through him as he experienced his first ride in a car. She had asked him many questions, for which he'd had to provide suitable answer. He genuinely hated all the lying he'd had to do to be with her, but it hadn't taken long to admit to himself that he would do anything to keep her safe and happy. Her mind was so full of curiosity, her heart so free of deceit, that he knew from the very beginning that he had never before met her like. The love that blossomed between them over the following weeks and years was like nothing he had ever experienced before, like nothing he even knew to be in existence.

He missed her more than words could ever properly express.

Zorthos often found himself reminiscing of silent moments in the past which had brought him the most happiness, but found them bittersweet as he continued the long trek to Rhenngoth's palace. He had told himself long ago that he would never, under any circumstances, return to the place which so haunted his past. But how could he not make such a sacrifice when his son's life weighed in the balance; there was nothing he would not suffer for Allen or Carol, even if it meant facing his wicked mother again or answering for his crimes.

His mother. Divina.

Of all that awaited him upon his reemergence to the illustrious palace of the God-King, a place he had once called home, the thing that he was looking forward to least was the imminent confrontation with Divina. He could scarcely recall a time when she wasn't utterly devoted to the Gorrlock who held dominion over the entire planet of the gods. There was a time when he had been proud of the statement. But that had changed the day she murdered his father to the roar of the crowd, Rhenngoth ushering the command with a wave of his hand from the comfort of his pulvinus in the God-King's private audience box.

He had been only eight years old when his parents had told him they would both be competing in the Arena Games. Such a thought had excited him as much as it worried him; he hadn't wanted to see either of them hurt the other. As the day finally arrived, his father, Sygrahm, had assured him that such was a worry he needn't concern himself with. With a somber smile, Sygrahm had ruffled his hair and sent him to find his seats among the crowd with two of his caretakers.

That was the last conversation he'd ever had with his father.

It had thrilled the young Zorthos to no end to witness both his mother's, and his father's victories in the arena. He knew that his mother had already been crowned Champion once before, and that his father was known to all as a competent gladiator, but witnessing their prowess for himself was an experience he knew even then that he would never forget. One by one they destroyed their opposition in a grand spectacle of Mystica mastery which was still spoken of with awe, until it was finally announced that they would face each other in the final match.

Anticipation mounted among the crowd to the point of palpability. The air was electric, the crowd erupting as the final match was announced and both of his parents made their way once again onto the sand of the Arena. To this day he found it difficult to say whether he'd been more excited, or nervous by the sight.

Then, at last, the match began and his parents fought each other with a ferocity the boy had not known them capable of. The display that met the crowd's eyes left the impression that they had both been holding back in the previous matches. His mother shot lightning from her fingertips; his father crafted weapons from the very sand beneath his feet. Blow after blow was delivered with explosive force, leaving him in fear for both for his parents.

At last it had appeared to be over as Sygrahm sent Divina sprawling across the length of the Arena, bouncing off the barrier walls with thunderous impact. Seeing her lying there, motionless, the entire crowd had thought Sygrahm to be the victor. He watched as his father knelt to his mother's side to help her up, only to be thrown back by an explosion beneath his feet. The sand came alive, wrapping itself around Sygrahm and binding his movement entirely. Divina heated the sand in place, hardening that which constricted Sygrahm's movements; the scream Sygrahm expelled as the sand turned to glass and bound itself to his skin haunted Zorthos still. Divina picked up a sword Sygrahm had crafted from the ground as she sauntered toward her immobile husband, casually glancing over her shoulder to gauge Rhenngoth's approval of her performance. Even from his seat in the crowd, Zorthos could make out the signal Rhenngoth gave her to end the life of her opponent.

A little boy's world stopped in that moment.

He had been unable to accept what he had just seen. He recalled not believing that his mother would heed such a command, yet even at that tender age he knew what defying such an order could mean. The aides who had accompanied him as he watched the entire tournament struggled to keep the act from his vision; part of him still wished they had been successful. The image of his mother sheathing a sword in his father's ribs was one that would wake him in a cold sweat for years following its occurrence.

In the act, Divina had killed more than just his father; she'd killed his innocence and any bond she'd ever had with him. From that day forward, he'd considered himself an orphan.

In the years that followed, he'd worked harder than any of the other children under the God-King's roof. He refused to suffer the same fate as his father, refused to allow his life to forever be at the disposal of Rhenngoth and his mother, Divina. He became devoted to his studies, seeking the knowledge of many of the techniques he had seen his father employ at the Arena Games, as well as many others which sparked his interest. Zorthos vowed that he would one day be free of the shackles of servitude, no more to bow and scrape at the feet of the man who had ordered his father killed. He devised a plan to force the God-King to grant him the freedom to leave it all behind: he would become Arena Champion and use his one wish to leave Datheron forever.

As they finally reached their destination, Zorthos shook the ghosts of his past from his mind. The palace of the God-King could be seen for miles, even from its place among the clouds, its spires towering as high and wide as a small forest. The palace itself could virtually be considered a city with its expansive size. Beneath its roof one could find any sort of respite they wished, any supply or training they could ever hope for. There were living quarters for visiting dignitaries and lesser citizens, galleries of art and culture, as well as shops containing any weapon, scroll, or ingredient one could want—or need. Having spent many years among Earth culture, Zorthos now considered such a conglomeration to resemble a museum or a shopping mall more than a palace. There was a very large section near the center of the expansive structure which belonged to the God-King and his private staff alone, but there was never a time when everything else around it wasn't bustling with activity. What most didn't understand was that, while his private portion of the palace was partitioned away by a barrier wall, the whole of Nentalia was the God-King's palace; which was the reason for it all to be constructed in the color gold, even the Arena.

The guards of Vardiston gaped at the grandeur around them as they moved ever onward toward their goal. He wouldn't have been surprised to learn that none of them had ever had occasion to come here before. They asked no questions, and he offered no resistance; the trip through the maze of corridors had reached its end before any of them realized it. Two guards, clad in silver chain mail armor, stepped forward, barring the way forward to the private portion of the palace.

"State your business," the Saurothian on the right demanded.

Zorthos pushed his way to the front of the group, purposely drawing their attention. "Stand aside, Ashiketh," he said in a confident tone.

Recognition dawned in the lizard-man's eyes as he came into view. The guard hesitated for several moments before responding. "Zorthos!" he exclaimed. "Have I lived to see such a day that the prodigal son returns, bound by the shackles of his deeds?"

"I am here to turn myself over to the will of Rhenngoth. Now stand aside, for I also bring troubling news he will be most eager to hear."

"Troubling news?" he heard a familiar, female voice ask. Divina had appeared behind the guards, parting them from her path as she came through the entrance they guarded.

Though he wasn't surprised that Divina had come to meet him at the gate, he had hoped to forestall their reunion until after speaking with Rhenngoth. "Greetings, Divina," he said with distaste.

"You will address me by title of Mother," Divina said sternly.

"Such is a privilege long since lost to you, Witch," Zorthos retorted.

"I see you have not yet come to proper senses," she replied, nonchalant arrogance tainting her words.

"I have come only to speak with Rhenngoth regarding my penitence, and to offer news of an urgent nature. I care nothing of your opinions toward me, woman!" he sniped.

The guards present cast uncomfortable looks amongst each other. Those closest to him and his mother took a step backward in an attempt to distance themselves from the mounting tension.

"Very well," Divina said with resignation. "I suppose I should expect no less from one who has brought such shame upon himself. You have always been of an obstinate nature." She glanced to the palace guards, and then to the guards of Vardiston. "I will take him from here. Gratitude for your assistance in his return."

The guards of Vardiston bowed their heads in deference and shuffled away through the throng of people behind them.

"This way, son," she called over her shoulder, leading him into the private portion of the palace.

He moved to stay in tow, unsure of how he would be able to convince her to be absent when he told the God-King of the events in Vardiston, yet refusing to accept her presence while he did so. He knew his mother well enough to realize that by addressing him as 'son' she was attempting to goad him into further verbal conflict. He remained silent as they moved, refusing to rise to the bait.

After a short while, he realized that she was leading him to the detention wing of the palace. "We do not move directly to Rhenngoth?" he asked, hoping to keep the conversation to a minimum.

"We do not," she answered.

He hesitated for only a few more steps before deciding he would need to hazard getting an explanation from her. "Surely Rhenngoth would prefer I be brought directly to him upon my return," he said.

"The world does not revolve around your actions, despite what you may believe," she replied, without looking at him. "Such is a decision to be made at his discretion alone . . . after I have informed him of your reemergence."

"He does not yet know that I return?" Zorthos questioned incredulously. "I find it difficult to believe that

430

his most trusted of servants would keep something of this magnitude from his ears."

"He has more pressing concerns at the moment," Divina said, nonchalantly. "I will inform him of your presence shortly. Until then you will wait to be summoned, among the other criminals."

Zorthos knew what his mother was capable of. One of her most useful abilities was that of precognition; the power to see things before they happened. He was certain that it was that ability which informed her of the precise time of his arrival. Usually such an ability was employed explicitly to keep Rhenngoth informed and out of harm's reach; the information her visions showed being brought to his attention openly. He wondered what sort of game his mother was playing that she would deign to keep his return from the supreme ruler of Datheron, the man she had chosen over her own husband.

As Zorthos stepped into the incarceration chamber, he decided that being forced to wait might not be such a bad thing; it would afford him the time to devise a way of keeping his information from her ears all together. He supposed that she would eventually learn what he had to say anyway, but he preferred to keep his son's existence from her as long as possible. Perhaps he should keep the fact of kinship out of it entirely, admitting only that two children of Earth had been brought to Datheron by order of Luziaph.

As Divina marched away from him, Zorthos realized he didn't need his mother's skill in precognition to know he was going to have plenty of time to dwell on the matter before he was summoned.

28

MACHINATIONS

TREPIDATION ENVELLOPED ALLEN as he followed Gazianna along the hidden corridor, away from Pythor and the other Gorrlocks. He found himself wondering just how far Luziaph's telepathy could reach; his imagination bringing fears to life of the man overhearing his whispered desires of escape through the ears of the guards stationed outside the private incarceration chambers. Then the thought occurred to him that Luziaph had made mention of travelling somewhere prior to knocking him unconscious and leaving him to rot alongside the Krathantor. The idea left him curious. Just how long had he been unconscious if Luziaph had already made his journey and returned? As they moved, he realized once again, that it had been equally as long since he had eaten.

The growling in his stomach began to rival the shaking in his knees.

As they reached the end of the hidden corridor, Gazianna hadn't yet spoken a word to him. She seemed content to make the entire journey in silence and he couldn't help wondering if she was ordered to remain silent, or if he had offended her yet again, somehow, in his attempt to stand up for her.

Once the secret entrance finished sliding home and the grating sound left his ears, he decided he could stand the silence no longer. "Do you know why Luziaph has summoned me?" he asked.

She cast him a furtive glance as they continued their progress through the palace hallways. "It is not mine to say," she answered without breaking pace.

Her response only served to make him more nervous. He felt like he was being marched to the principal's office all over again. Possibilities of what could await him were running amok through his mind. Was he about to be sentenced for throwing the spear at Luziaph with his mind? Was he to be reprimanded for his flippant tongue or disobeying his master? Or could it be that he was to be beaten again and sent back into the dark from which she'd retrieved him? Allen steeled himself, uncertain what could await him upon arriving before his master.

As they continued their progress, he couldn't help but feel as if this was his last chance to have a conversation with anyone, his last chance to convince Gazianna that he hadn't intended to bring more trouble to her.

He quickened his pace, stepping in front of her and gently placing his hand on her shoulder. "Gazianna, I feel I must apologize for any harm my actions may have brought you. Reason gave way to emotion at seeing him strike you. My intent was only to protect a friend from abuse."

Gazianna looked genuinely torn. She appeared to be struggling over whether to be more grateful or offended by the statement. After several long moments Allen realized that she either wasn't able to respond, or didn't know quite how to, so he released her and began walking again. As he pulled away from her she reached out to clutch his wrist. He jerked to a halt at the contact and brought his eyes to meet hers.

"I am grateful for your concern," she offered in a low tone. "But you must realize that you overstepped in attacking your master. What was it you thought to gain in such an act?"

"Your safety," he replied. "I would not see any treated as Luziaph treats you."

"And just where is it that you get such a notion that the choice falls to you?" she asked in a slightly more elevated tone. "You are but a slave, and forever shall be if defiance continues to mount offenses against the balance of freedom."

For a moment Allen considered telling her everything; that he was from Earth, that the weight of prophecy could very well rest upon his shoulders. Ultimately, however, he decided against it, reasoning that admitting it aloud to Luziaph's closest servant would certainly doom him. Instead he said, "Freedom . . . It seems to me that true definition of the term is known to no one of this world."

"You are a strange one," Gazianna stated as she began moving again.

In another time, in another place, he may have been offended by the statement. But he had too much on his mind to give it a second thought. Instead, he remained silent as he fell into step behind her.

He gave himself over to his fate, soaking in his surroundings as if it was the last time he'd be able to. The craftsmanship really was unlike anything he was accustomed to seeing on Earth. He could see similarities in the way some of it had been constructed, but there were noticeable differences, too; for instance, he had yet to see a door which moved on hinges, or glass in any windows.

The statues he so admired, could be seen through arched windows in the courtyard below as they moved. A brief sadness overcame him as he realized he might never learn how they were constructed.

The regret most dominant in his mind, however, was that he had let down the two most important women in his life, unable to ever explain to them where he'd disappeared to or what had happened to him. His mother had often told him that life was not always fair, but he thought the circumstances he now found himself in to be beyond ironic.

At last they reached the throne room. Allen couldn't even bring himself to glance at the statues lining the walls as he entered; his eyes immediately fell to Luziaph. The Triclopian Proctus sat in his throne, acutely aware of Allen's arrival; his three-eyed stare never wavering as Allen approached the throne. Allen noticed a large chunk of stone on the floor to the right of it, but couldn't make out what it was and had no idea why Luziaph would have put it there.

"At last I will put the lie to your charade," Luziaph grinned arrogantly.

Allen kept silent, refusing to say anything which could potentially make things worse.

"Have you nothing to say for yourself?" Luziaph taunted. "No flippant remark?"

He had to mentally force his knees to stop twitching from anxiety. Taking a deep breath and steeling his nerves he responded simply: "Apologies for my actions. I realize I overstepped. It will not happen again."

"NO IT WILL NOT!" Luziaph bellowed. "For you see, today I learn the truth! Today I cut through the heart of your deceit and bare reality for all to see!" Luziaph leaned forward in his throne, his tone turning dangerous. "Tell me from where you truly hail. Speak!"

"Shenniga—" His response was choked off before it could be completed by a pain so intense it momentarily stole his vision. As it slowly returned to him, he found himself lying on the ground. He struggled mightily to bring himself back to his full height.

As he stood there on wobbly legs, resisting the urge to vomit, Allen noticed that Luziaph had retrieved the stone block from beside his throne. When it was clear that he wasn't going to fall over, Luziaph tossed the block at his feet. The large rock bounced off the floor violently, a loud clunking sound echoing all around as it came to a stop in plain view.

Allen gaped at what he saw before him. It was the head of a statue, crafted with the same quality as the others he'd found so fascinating. But this one appeared to be . . .

"Greet the one you call Malacus," Luziaph gloated. "Or at least, what is left of him."

Allen refused to believe what he was seeing, what he had just heard. This couldn't actually be Malacus' head . . . could it? If that were true, it would mean that all of these statues had once been alive. He glanced around the room; recognition of how they had been made dawning on him for the first time. Suddenly he found the sight of them repulsive. He saw them for what they truly were: gravestones. His initial assessment had been correct; they were in place as a warning . . . a warning of what would happen to those who crossed Luziaph.

He was suddenly far more afraid of the man who held power over him. He glanced back up at Luziaph and then knelt down to inspect the head more closely, looking for signs that this wasn't just a trick devised to get the truth out of him. If it was a fake, it was crafted to perfection. It looked exactly like the old man who had given him his first lessons on Datheron; the man whom he had learned was his great grandfather. He felt sick to his stomach. The detail in the stone head was haunting; every strand of hair was accounted for, every wrinkle, even the eyes. . . If this is what had happened to Malacus, what had become of Sarah? If she was alone, and still in her coma, she would die without someone to keep her body nourished.

Allen's body was shaking with anger.

"What have you done?" he whispered.

His eyes met Luziaph's, the anger swelling in his chest beginning to overshadow his fear. "WHAT HAVE YOU DONE!"

A hint of a smile stole across Luziaph's lips as Allen rose to his full height. Luziaph looked to Gazianna and gave her a nod. Gazianna scurried away, apparently having been ordered to leave the throne room.

Once she was gone Luziaph arose from his throne and stepped closer to him, leaning down to bring his face within inches of Allen's. "I will have the truth from you," he said.

Though Allen desperately wanted to bash his fist against the side of Luziaph's face, to unleash all of his frustration on the man who had taken so much from him, he knew that he would most likely find himself writhing in agony on the ground before his blow had reached its destination, so he remained still.

Instead, he said in a dangerous tone of his own, "You will have nothing from me!"

"We shall see about that," Luziaph said smugly, standing to his full height and sauntering back to his throne.

Every time he thought things couldn't possibly get words, they did. Allen now genuinely understood why Zorthos had wanted to be rid of this world forever. He wished he could go back in time and unmake the decision which had placed him in the woods that day. He decided that no amount of power was worth what he'd had to sacrifice since arriving on this horrible planet.

He wasn't sure how much time had passed when he noticed Luziaph's eyes shifting to something behind him. A huge grin consumed the Triclopian's features. Instinctively, Allen turned his head, following his master's line of sight.

Allen's breath caught in his throat.

Time slowed to a standstill.

His eyes met hers and for a moment everything was right in the world. Somehow, Malacus had found a way to bring Sarah out of her coma. A great relief washed over him as he realized she hadn't been left to starve to death, trapped in her own mind. Then time began to move again, slowly at first.

Gazianna nudged Sarah to keep moving.

When Sarah recognized him she rushed forward, throwing herself into his arms. "Allen!" she wailed.

She clutched him so tightly he could barely breathe. If it meant her letting go, he wasn't sure he wanted her to.

Before he was ready, she was being pulled from his arms. Luziaph had a hold of Sarha's left forearm and was dragging her away. Allen reached out to snatch her and received a jolt through the Triaga for his efforts.

As his senses came back to him, Allen realized that he hadn't collapsed entirely this time; though he was on his knees. Everything was going wrong. His head was spinning so hard that he didn't think he could stand up; the woman he loved more than anything was in the clutches of the same villain who had stolen his own freedom, and the life of his great grandfather; worst of all, he was powerless to do anything to stop it.

"Now," Luziaph said menacingly as Allen came to his feet, "tell me where it is you come from or my collection of stone swells by one! And do not think to deceive me further or test my patience! I have already been made aware that Pythor and his ilk returned to this world with two from another. It is my belief that you and she are they. Tell me what world it is you come from and how it is you came to know Zorthos or she dies!"

He was trapped. He'd been vehemently warned against revealing his planet of origin, had been told doing so could very well be inviting death. Now if he did nothing, Sarah would pay the ultimate price for his inaction. Desperation for another solution swirled with frantic urgency through every corner of his mind. He found none. Ultimately his choice came down to whether he was willing to risk his life to save hers. When he thought of it that way, the choice became easy.

"Do I have your word no harm will come to her once I give the answer you seek?" he asked.

"You have my word she will die if you do not!" Luziaph barked.

With a sigh of resignation, Allen gave himself over to his fate. "I come from a world known simply as Earth," he said.

Luziaph's eyes, all three of them, grew wide with delight. "I knew it!" he whispered in excitement. "And Zorthos? What of him?"

Allen hesitated a moment before responding. "He is my father."

Luziaph let out a triumphant whoop. Allen noticed Sarah's eyes widen at hearing the statement and wondered if she'd understood him.

Luziaph released his grip on Sarah and she ran back to Allen's side. He took her in his arms once more. "Are you okay?" he asked her in English.

"I am now," she replied into his shoulder. "Allen . . . I was so worried about you. Malacus told me you were arrested, and that you might have been executed." She pulled herself back from him, still holding his shoulders in

439

her hands, and stared into his eyes. "Allen, why did you tell him where we're from?"

"You understood what I was saying?" he puzzled aloud.

Sarah nodded. "Malacus gave me an amulet that acts as a translator. He was trying to teach me to speak the native language . . . Allen he told me about the prophecy. Aren't you afraid we'll be put to death now that he knows we're from Earth?"

"Enough!" Luziaph yelled, drawing their attention away from each other. "The time of prophecy has reached Datheron at last, and fortune sees fit to favor me with position to hold sway over its outcome! You," he said, pointing at Allen, "will aid in ascending my position to the heavens!"

"I am aware of the words spoken in the prophecy," Allen interjected, reverting his speech to Olyphatarian. "And I give no concern toward the outcome. If given the choice I would return to Earth from whence I came, far removed from such perilous events."

"And so it shall be . . ." Luziaph replied. "Should you prove yourself in completion of one final required task."

"What would you have me do?"

Luziaph's mouth formed a wicked grin. "Bring to me the Sword of Sythika!"

"You ask the impossible," Allen answered immediately, his hopes deflating. "Even if truth reveals me to be the child of prophecy, I do not know where to begin the search. Nor would such a quest bring fortune to you. It is the chosen one who is to wield the sword, who is to change the fate of Datheron. What could you possibly do with the sword absent my presence to put it to use?"

"That is where I believe you to be mistaken," Luziaph responded smoothly. "The words of prophecy state specifically, 'His choices will carry enough weight to alter life on Datheron for all time'." Luziaph paused a moment, as if to let the words sink in. "Do you not see? It is the choices, not the man himself, which holds sway over the outcome of prophecy. You need only retrieve the sword of legend and turn it over to me. Such a choice will remove the burden of prophecy from your shoulders, return you to the home you so long for, and still prove its words true."

As much as he hated to admit it, even to himself, what Luziaph said made sense. If he could somehow retrieve the Sword of Sythika and hand it over to another, his choice to abdicate possession of the legendary weapon would still have a profound effect on the inhabitants of this world. He hated the thought of this monster bending prophecy to his will, becoming the new ruler of all Datheron, but he had to admit to himself that he didn't know enough of this world's customs to choose what was right or wrong for it. And he had to think about Sarah. He had made himself a promise, that he would get her home to Earth no matter the cost.

He looked to Sarah, knowing that she could understand the alien words he and Luziaph were speaking, a silent plea in his eyes.

"I want to go home," she said softly.

He nodded to her spoken request and turned his gaze back to Luziaph. "It will be so," he said to his Triclopian master. "Yet I know not where to begin such a quest."

Luziaph smiled in triumph. Even though Allen was certain it was a smile of pleasure, the wickedness of it could not be mistaken. "Excellent!" he exclaimed. "As it so happens, I believe myself to be in possession of the Sword of Sythika's hidden location."

Allen, curious to learn more, decided to entertain Luziaph's boasting. "How is it you have come by such knowledge?" he asked. "I was of the impression the sword's location had been lost to time."

"And so it has," Luziaph replied, clearly enjoying himself. "Tell me, what do you know of the legend of the sword?"

"Very little," Allen answered truthfully.

Luziaph clasped his hands behind his back and began to pace as he continued to speak. "I consider myself a student of its legend," he said. "I have read every text on the subject of which I am aware."

"Pause a moment," Allen interjected. "I was of the understanding that text of the Sword of Sythika existed in the words of prophecy only."

"There was precious little to discover," Luziaph agreed. "Yet I was able to learn bits of information regarding its origin, and how it came to be lost. You see, upon losing his mind, Paragus became known to make odd demands of his staff; one of which coming in the form of sheltering one of his most prized possessions: the Sword of Sythika. The sword itself—the blade of death—is said to rival the Armor of Paragus in potency of its counterpart. To even be scratched by the blade is believed to be certain doom.

"Paragus, knowing that his end was near, desired to keep the blade hidden from the hands of those untrained in its use; he feared the blade to be dangerous enough to threaten all life after his passing. Realization came to him that discovery of the blade would be but a matter of time if left on this world, yet those who could be trusted with its location numbered in the few. Paragus turned the Sword of Sythika over to his most trusted of guards: the Krathantor. Such is where my knowledge on the subject concluded until afforded the opportunity to probe the mind of Pythor and his companions."

Luziaph stopped pacing, fixing another self-satisfied grin on Allen as he continued his monologue. "What I discovered among his deepest thoughts was most informative. The Krathantor have ever been the trusted guardians of the secret; the only ones who yet know the sword's location. It is hidden well, on the larger of Datheron's two moons: Sythar. The very name given to the moon, a subtle clue as to what is hidden upon its surface."

"The moon?" he asked with incredulity. "You would have me travel to the moon?"

"I would have you do what is necessary to bring me the sword!" Luziaph shot back.

For a very long moment, Allen considered his options. He didn't like the idea of travelling to the surface of yet another world—even a moon. He had just gotten Sarah back, had just realized that she was okay, only to be ordered to travel who knows how many thousands of miles away from her; leaving her fate in the hands of this monster while he completed an impossible task. He would be completely alone, without anyone to turn to, if he travelled to Sythar. He decided that he would not undertake such a task alone, and resolved to make a few demands of his own.

"I would have conditions met if I am to do this for you," he said.

"You are not of a position to make such demands," Luziaph laughed.

"I believe that I am," he retorted. "You require my services to retrieve the sword. Absent my involvement, you will not have what you seek."

"Yet I hold the fate of you and this girl in my hands," Luziaph responded. "If you fail to meet the demands made of you, I will drain the Mystica from both of your bodies; beginning with her!"

"Do it," he challenged.

"Allen, what are you doing?" Sarah whispered harshly.

"I grow tired of this world and its backward laws," he said, ignoring Sarah's plea.

"Take the breath from my body. Add my corpse to your collection of stone. Do it knowing that you will never have the Sword of Sythika; nor will you have anything else you seek. You need me to complete this task, and I would have fair exchange for services rendered."

Luziaph paused for several minutes, seemingly considering Allen's words. "Speak then," he said with disgust.

Allen's thoughts turned to the Gorrlocks hidden several levels beneath him. He had told them that he would not leave them to their fate if he could help it, and perhaps he could secure their release and receive aid in his quest in one fell swoop.

"To begin with," he began, "I would have another join in my efforts."

"I shall command one of my elite to accompany you," Luziaph offered.

He shook his head. "No, I would have one of the Krathantor by my side."

"You jest," Luziaph sniped. "Why would I even entertain to such a request?"

He knew he had Luziaph's attention; there was no turning back now. "Think on it," he said. "You put voice to their knowledge of the subject. Who better to lead the way than one who already knows the location of the blade? And I do not ask for the release of all; one will prove sufficient."

"Done," Luziaph acquiesced with a scowl. "Is that all?"

"I would have but one more condition met," he answered with a shake of his head, and waiting a moment before speaking his final request. "I would have promise of freedom granted to more than just this girl and myself."

"Out of the question," Luziaph answered immediately.

"Then find yourself another puppet," Allen retorted.

Luziaph was clearly growing impatient with his brazen approach. After a moment's silence, however, he spoke again. "Who is it you would see removed from the bonds of servitude?" he asked.

"I would see the Krathantor released to resume their duties," he began, "so that they might open the gateway back to Earth. And Gazianna; I would see her be given the chance to live a life of her own choosing."

From the corner of his eye, Allen saw Gazianna start at his proclamation. He knew that his words had come as much of a shock to her as they must have to Luziaph. He hoped that his true intent behind the request was understood, and that she hadn't taken it as yet another slight.

Luziaph shot Gazianna a severe look before turning his attention back to Allen. "You overstep," he spat. "Release of the Krathantor is one thing; there is purpose behind the request. What could you possibly gain in securing Gazianna's release? You seek to add insult to other demands."

He shook his head again. "I seek no insult," he assured Luziaph. "Nor do I seek personal gain in securing her freedom. My intent is solely to her benefit. She has been friend to me and I would see her afforded the chance to forge her own path, free of the shackles of this palace."

When Luziaph said nothing, continuing to stare at him with skepticism, Allen added: "What need of her would there be once the Sword of Sythika is in hand? I bring the sword to you, freedom is granted to those deserving of it, and we return home to Earth. Victory finds us all."

After a moment's consideration, Luziaph's formidable exterior shifted: "It shall be so," he conceded. "Which of the Krathantor would you have at your side?"

"Whichever is most able," he replied.

Luziaph turned away from him, having risen from his throne during the previous exchange. As he sat back down, he appeared to be pleased with the way things were going. "As you wish," he grinned. "Yet it will fall to you to convince them to join in your cause. And until you complete the task set before you, this one," he added, gesturing to Sarah, "will replace you in performing duties at Gazianna's side."

Sarah looked scared. Allen wished he could have removed her from the equation entirely, but at least there was finally an end in sight to this nightmare. He turned his eyes to her and did his best to comfort her. "It'll be okay," he told her in their native language. "I will get us back home. I promise."

She nodded, quite obviously fighting to suppress the tears filling her eyes.

"Gazianna," Luziaph barked. "Return good Araset to the private incarceration chambers. Present him with food and any other supplies necessary for the journey set before him." Luziaph's eyes met Allen's, a self-satisfied grin consuming his features. "He departs for Sythar at the rising of the sun."

As Gazianna ushered him away from the throne room and Sarah, Allen felt as if he had just leapt a tall hurdle. Now all that remained was convincing someone who despised his father to join his cause, betray his oath to protect a legendary artifact, and aid in retrieving it from the moon. Whether Allen wanted to believe it or not, the jaws of prophecy were closing in around him.

29

SEPARATION

A SENSE OF HOPELESSNESS coursed through Sarah as she watched Allen walk away from her, following in the wake of the blue-skinned woman Luziaph had referred to as Gazianna. She felt glad to know he was still alive, grateful to have been able to see him again at last; yet she knew that it could be a long while more before she saw him again. She couldn't help but notice the same device Zorthos had worn upon their arrival on Datheron now decorated Allen's scalp, or how different he seemed in more than just appearance. She wondered inwardly why such a device was necessary. Zorthos had explained how the device was used to inhibit the special abilities possessed by those of this world. Could it be that Allen had mastered more than the alien tongue in his time here?

Hearing that Zorthos was Allen's father had surprised her at first. But the more she thought about it, the more it made sense. She could definitely see the resemblance between them—especially now that Allen had a beard—and recalled seeing pictures of Allen's father among Carol's photo albums; the man had been clean-shaven and much younger in the pictures, but there was no mistaking that it was him.

As Allen rounded the corner, disappearing from her view entirely, Sarah realized that she was once again all alone with Luziaph. Their journey to Vardiston had been just as emotionally taxing as it had been physically exhausting. Standing over seven feet tall, Luziaph moved with a gait she found difficult to keep pace with. The journey had taken nearly three full days of walking; Sarah's legs still ached in protest of the distance they had been forced to travel. Despite herself, she had silently thanked Malacus for all the walking he'd forced her to do; without the exercise she would have never been able to keep pace with her captor.

Along the way, they had made a stop in a city—if it could be referred to as such—called Abendroth. Sarah distinctly remembered Malacus telling her about the place after she had inquired about it. She knew that Abendroth had been the place where Allen was arrested and carted off to Vardiston, so naturally she'd had curiosities.

As she and Luziaph had entered the city, the throng of people parted willingly at the sight of her three-eyed captor; most people even bowing or groveling as they passed. Luziaph hadn't divulged much about himself—or anything else for that matter—during their trek, so she had wondered initially what about the man inspired such deference. It wasn't long, however, before Luziaph came to a stop in front of a large building with a stage decorating two of its outer walls. A crowd was gathering around the structure as half naked people of every size and color were slowly being paraded onto the stage, shackled by manacles and Triagas; there even appeared to be a couple of prisoners who were the same race as Luziaph. A large, furry man—looking very much to Sarah as if he were half man, half ape—emerged from the building clad in a suit of very worn-looking leather armor. At his left side was strapped a wicked-looking six-bladed mace, a whip gripped firmly in his right hand. The beast-man scowled at the prisoners, prodding a couple to keep formation. Once they were all in place he rounded on the crowd, appearing as a showman about to begin a spectacle for his audience.

Until the his eyes found Luziaph among the spectators.

Immediately, the beast-man lowered himself into a gracious bow. "Lord Luziaph," he said, bringing his eyes up as he continued to address the man. "I was unaware you would be in attendance this day. Will you be procuring more servants for the palace?"

That was when Sarah had made the connection to Luziaph and the reaction he inspired in the crowd. All at once she recalled hearing Zorthos mention his name when she and Allen had first arrived on this world. Zorthos had told the two of them that the man was the Proctus of Vardiston, that he was manipulative and ruthless. He had also warned that if Luziaph captured them, they would most likely be his slaves for the rest of their days.

In that moment Sarah had truly felt as if her life was over.

After a brief pause, Luziaph responded to the beast-man's question. "I require but a couple to swell the ranks of my servants," he said. "Tell me," he added, gesturing to the two three-eyed captives, "What crime finds these two in such a state?"

The two to whom Luziaph had just referred glanced past the prisoners between them, sharing a mild look of uncertainty. The beast-man regarded them for the briefest of moments before responding. "They were discovered standing over a fallen Gorrlock woman; her blood still wet upon their hands. They yet stand among the living

449

because no resistance was offered in their arrest when confronted by local guards."

"Remove their bonds," Luziaph ordered.

A look of genuine confusion came over the beast-man's face. "My Lord?" he asked.

"I gave command," Luziaph insisted. "Do it!"

Murmurs began to break out among the spectators in the crowd. The man on the stage shifted uncomfortably before hooking the whip in his hand to his belt and setting himself to the task. He pulled a strange-looking key from a pouch on his belt as he reached the first prisoner Luziaph had ordered released. Before unlocking the manacles on the captive's wrists, the beast-man turned back to Luziaph. "Are you quite certain? They stand guilty and submitted willingly to their fate."

"And I stand Proctus of Vardiston and master of all of Thugrod!" Luziaph shot back. "Their fate falls to my discretion! Question further the order given you and find yourself bound in their place! The Gorrlock woman must have given cause for such retribution; it is the way of their kind to torment Triclopians! Now move your key to purpose and see it done!"

The beast-man bowed his head in deference and turned back to his task. Sarah was incredulous at what had transpired. If she understood the circumstances correctly, Luziaph had just pardoned them for murder for no other reason than they shared a common heritage. She was appalled.

She knew her words wouldn't be understood, but found impossible to hold her tongue. "You've got to be kidding me!" she blurted out. "You're just going to let them—go? Just like that? That . . . creature just said they murdered a woman!"

Every eye in the crowd found her. Murmuring among the crowd began anew, much louder this time, as they continued to gawk at her. Luziaph glanced furtively around before casting his gaze on her; his deep, purple hood concealing part of his face from view. A look of pure hatred distorted his already unnerving appearance.

"Be silent!" he barked at her.

"But you're freeing killers!" she protested.

Sarah felt a sharp pain on her left cheek as Luziaph's hand impacted her face. "I told you to be silent!" he shouted. "Lose control of your tongue again and find it removed from your mouth!"

An overwhelming sense of embarrassment swelled over her as she rubbed her cheek. She was acutely aware of all the eyes on her, and the hushed whispers among the crowd. As the chattering continued, she began to feel more than foolish; recalling that Malacus had warned her against letting anyone hear her speak in her native tongue. She suddenly wished she'd had more time to practice her Olyphatarian.

Luziaph turned his eyes back to the stage as the two Triclopians were being ushered away from the other prisoners, rubbing their wrists and the backs of their heads. As they reached the edge and prepared to jump down from their elevated position with intent to join the crowd, Luziaph halted them with a command.

"You," he said, gesturing to the taller of the two Triclopians. "What name do you go by?"

The Triclopian stood to his full height, and replied without insecurity. "I am called Dhagorath," he answered. "This," he added, gesturing to the one behind him, "is my brother, Rexim."

Luziaph nodded at the man's answer. "Gather yourselves," he told Dhagorath. "I expect you at the Palace of Vardiston one day hence; I would have compensation for your release."

Dhagorath bowed his head. "As you command," he replied.

The beast-man, having completed the task of releasing two of his prisoners, pulled the whip from its place on his belt. He appeared to be agitated, but Sarah couldn't be sure. He looked uncertain whether or not he should begin addressing the crowd again. For several long moments he just stood there, his eyes firmly fixed on Luziaph. Finally, he apparently decided to speak his mind. "Forgive me," he said in a tone Sarah considered full of repressed anger. "But will compensation be given me for the cost of their release?"

Luziaph considered him silently for a moment, glancing around and taking stock of the other prisoners. After a short pause, he pointed to the only two women among the captives; one, appearing to be just as human as Sarah, the other with gray, leathery skin; her nose arched down the length of her face, looking very much like a beak between her large, watchful eyes. Her bright red hair was cropped very short, and her arms appeared to have strange growths protruding from her elbows. "I will take those two," Luziaph announced. "Couple their cost with that of the two Triclopians and bring the bill of sale to my palace. You will have your compensation."

The beast-man bowed his head once again, and ushered the two women from the stage. Sarah couldn't help but notice that he left the women shackled.

Over the remainder of their journey, the two women remained silent, though she could feel their eyes on her the entire way. Luziaph had appeared content with the silence, maintaining the same brisk pace he had employed since taking her from Malacus' cabin all the way to the palace. She felt as if she were in a movie when the palace came into view; its grandeur reminding her very much of something she'd seen on film. The statues which lined the walkway in the courtyard left her horrified; especially since she assumed that they had been crafted through the same means which had brought Malacus to his end.

She was terrified. The only hope she had left as they crossed the threshold of the palace's entrance was that Allen was still alive somewhere inside its walls.

The time she'd spent in solitude, hidden away in a room just down the hall from the throne room, felt like the longest time of her life. She felt as if it had been an eternity since she had seen Allen. The brief moments with him had been blissful; she had finally felt safe for the first time in a long while.

And now he was gone again.

Sarah didn't need to look at Luziaph to know he was watching her; she could feel his eyes moving up and down her form. A shudder shot all the way up her spine. Never in all her life had she felt this lost, this alone. All she wanted to do was wake up from this nightmare and find herself back on Earth in her own bed. She decided that, like it or not, she was just going to have to put her faith in Allen to complete the task he'd been given. She just hoped it didn't take him too long . . .

Allen could still feel Sarah against him—still smell her—as Gazianna marched him back toward the hidden incarceration chamber. He was so elated to see that she had finally regained consciousness that he found it difficult not to smile. Even though he knew he could potentially have a long, difficult journey ahead of him, he felt better than he had in weeks.

Sarah was alive. And if he completed his mission, they would be going home.

He felt a distinct pang of sorrow for the loss of Malacus. He couldn't believe that the old man who had taught him so much was gone, or that he had died in such a manner. Being turned to stone was something from myths and legends. He felt a shudder rush up his spine at the thought of suffering such a fate. He felt a great sadness for his great-grandfather and all those poor souls who had been transformed into statues at the whim of that three-eyed lunatic. He felt sick about ever appreciating their beauty. He knew now that it wasn't an act of artistic expression which had brought them to be; it was an act of lethal aggression.

Allen was snapped out of his brooding when the stone section of wall once again filled his ears with a grating sound as it revealed the secret passage behind it. He hadn't realized just how lost in thought he'd been until it occurred to him that the journey back to his cell was nearly complete. It dawned on him that Gazianna had once again remained silent for the whole trip.

"May I ask a favor?" he asked as they began their descent into the bowels of the palace.

Gazianna flinched at his words. She paused a long moment before responding. "I am to see you back to your cell; no more," she said, an edge of apprehension tainting her words. "And I fear delay will bring Luziaph's wrath upon me."

He was confused by her reaction to his request. It was true that she hadn't ever completely warmed to him, but he had felt as if some progress had been made in establishing a bond between them. Then the realization came to him that she had heard everything about his true origin. He realized that she was probably afraid of him now. He felt sad that the knowledge of his past could

454

inspire such fear, or that the fear spawned could completely alter her opinion of him.

With desperation he reached out and took hold of her arm, bringing her to a stop next to one of the few dimly lit torches in the dark corridor. Harsh shadows danced across her features as he pulled her to face him; her eyes remained fixed on the floor.

"Gazianna," he said softly. "Meet my eyes." He noticed that she trembled slightly, keeping her eyes firmly planted. He reached out and gently tilted her face upward with a finger. "Please?"

Her eyes met his and her trembling increased, if only slightly. "Why do you now fear me?" he asked. "Am I not the same man you have always known me to be?"

A conflict of emotions covered her countenance, made more haunting by the way the dim light played with her features. "You hail from Earth," she said in a shaky voice. "You have admitted to being the child of prophecy which will bring doom to all of Datheron. How could I not fear you?"

"Search your heart," he countered gently. "Do you truly think me capable of such an act? Am I not the man who stood at your defense when found on bended knee beneath Luziaph's raised hand?" Her emotions appeared to waver with the fluid motion of the flames on the wall beside her, so he continued. "Did you not hear my spoken word on your behalf in the interest of freeing you from servitude?"

Her eyes, which had been darting about in uncertainty, found their way back to his. "Why would you request such a thing?" she asked, the words sounding affronted.

A sorrowful smile crossed his lips. "You ask a question to which I have already provided answer. I consider you friend, and I would not see harm befall you any longer. I would have your life be your own; subject to the whim of no man."

The tears which began to fill her eyes glowed with the reflection of the torch light. "You honor me," she said, humbly. "Gratitude."

"None required," he assured her. "I treat you as you should have always been treated."

After another brief pause, she spoke again. "What is it you would ask of me?"

"I would have you keep a watchful eye on Sarah," he replied. "She is one I hold close to my heart. Please keep harm from reaching her if it is within your ability to do so."

"I do not know if I can make such a promise," she answered.

He nodded. "I ask only that you try." When she nodded to his request, he smiled back at her. "Gratitude. Now we should hurry, lest our momentary delay be noticed."

Allen took the lead as they continued on toward their goal. From the corner of his eye he caught her glancing at him in wonder a couple times along the way. He smiled inwardly, genuinely hoping she appreciated his efforts on her behalf, and looking forward to completing the task which would grant freedom to them both.

All too soon, he found himself once again locked in the dark among the three Gorrlocks who had begun the chain of events on which he now found himself. He sat down and leaned against the wall in the same place he had been before being summoned, before learning Sarah was still alive. A smile crossed his lips at the remembrance.

"The trip bore fruit, I take it?" Sepharus said into the dark.

Allen's eyes snapped up in search of the one who had spoken; his vision had yet to readjust to his current surroundings. "Of a sort," he replied. "Yet it was more disquieting than propitious."

"That foolish smile on your face would say otherwise," Pythor interjected. "Tell us, what did that Triclopian filth want of you?"

Allen had no idea how he was going to convince them to go along with the promises he'd made to Luziaph. Clearly there was no love lost for the man among these three. After a moment's consideration, he decided that he would just have to hope that securing their freedom would be enough to persuade them to be accommodating.

Rather than ponder the gentlest way to break the news to them, he chose to tell them the truth from the beginning. "There is much to tell," he began. "Yet I feel I must begin by offering confession."

"Let me venture a guess," Pythor interrupted, harshly. "You have struck bargain toward your own freedom at the expense of ours? What did he promise you?"

Allen felt mildly offended. "I made no such bargain," he retorted. "Confession comes in the form of my true identity." He paused a moment to let his words sink in. "I am the child of prophecy. Luziaph has asked me to obtain for him the Sword of Sythika."

"What!" the two Gorrlocks exclaimed together.

"That you come from Earth is not enough to support such a claim," Pythor said venomously. "And why should such a thing bring a smile to your face?"

"Zorthos is my father," Allen stated, ignoring the question. "During his time on Earth he met the woman who would become my mother. When he returned, 'with his tail between his legs begging forgiveness', he did so with regard to the safety of me and my mother."

Allen could scarcely believe that he was actually defending his father's actions to anyone. Hatred for the man had festered in him since he was a young boy. A year ago, if someone would have told him that he would one day be speaking words of defense on his father's behalf, he might have hit them or given them an irrational piece of his mind. Yet now he felt as if he genuinely understood what had motivated the man's decisions. While he still didn't entirely condone them, he realized that they had been made from compassion, not cowardice.

"His intent was to keep the two of us shielded from this world's existence," he continued. "I know not why he returned to Earth a second time, yet it is done. What has already passed cannot be undone. Know that I care nothing for the words of the fabled prophecy and would see myself home and away from this place."

There was a long silence as the two Gorrlocks who were conscious seemed to consider his words. He could feel the tension mounting by the second as they watched him intently through the dark.

When it was clear that neither of them were going to add to the conversation, he pushed forward with his proposition. "You asked what brought a smile to my face?" he asked. "I will tell you. It was two things; the first of which being that the woman I love yet lives. She and I will be awarded safe passage back to Earth should I prove myself to be the child of prophecy by acquiring the legendary blade."

"And the other?" Pythor spat.

"Your freedom," he replied. "All three of you to be released upon the task being seen to completion."

Pythor and Sepharus exchanged a startled look.

"How did this come to be?" Sepharus asked.

"At my request."

"You?" Pythor asked, appearing stunned. "You petitioned for our release? Why would you do such a thing?"

"Because none should die in the dark, absent the chance to see sun set on their final day," he answered. "As previously stated, I do not believe the color of one's skin to be proper motivation for hatred of another, and I see how Luziaph treats Gorrlocks. It would be unjust to leave you to rot down here, with none but him to know the truth behind your disappearance."

Sepharus appeared as if he wanted to thank Allen for his words, but remained silent upon receiving a severe look from Pythor.

"There is but one condition to the bargain which is yet unmet," Allen said.

"What condition?" Pythor asked; his red irises piercing through the darkness to focus on Allen.

"I require one of you to aid in the quest," he chanced.

Pythor barked a short-lived, derisive laugh. "And what makes you think you would find agreement in the request?"

"Should I undertake this quest alone, I will surely fall," he answered, truthfully. "You know the truth of this as well as I. Absent your help, I will die . . . Sarah will die." He gave Pythor a meaningful look. "And you will die, here among the shadows; never again to see the light of day."

Pythor huffed a sigh of resignation. "Even if agreement of our involvement were to be reached," he said, "where is it you think to begin such a quest?"

"On the moon of Sythar," he replied. Even in the dark he could see the startled look on Pythor's and Sepharus' faces. "Apologies," he offered, "but knowledge of the sword's location comes from Luziaph. He was able to obtain it from one of your minds prior to placing Triagas upon your heads."

"Great Paragus!" Pythor cursed. "How is it that things have come to this?" he mumbled to himself.

"Please," he begged. "I must have your answer. The fate of us all rests in your hands."

For what seemed an eternity, Pythor and Sepharus sat in silence. Every so often they would look at one another and shake their heads. Finally, Pythor turned his attention back to Allen. "I cannot help you. I refuse to aid in bringing such ominous power to the hands of that Triclopian piece of filth."

"Please," he begged, his heart sinking, "Do not condemn me to death out of your hatred for him; do not commit Sarah to the hands of Sythika. There yet remains time to find a way to avert such tragedy."

"I see none," Pythor retorted.

"If we could but find a way to remove the Triaga from your head, you could challenge him for ownership of the sword," Allen offered. "In that way my part in the bargain will be complete, and you can have your revenge on the man for crimes committed against you. If nothing else, agreement to help me will remove ill-favored conditions from your companions as well as yourself."

Pythor and Sepharus exchanged another look. This time Sepharus spoke. "The boy speaks truth. Once freed, even should you fail to keep the sword from Luziaph's hands, we will be able to bring events to the attention of Rhenngoth. There may yet be a way to avert disaster."

"Very well," Pythor sighed, after another moment of consideration. "But it will be I that accompanies the boy. You are not yet at full strength."

"Agreed," Sepharus nodded. "Besides, one of us must remain to keep a watchful eye on Borograth."

Pythor brought his eyes to meet Allen; his scarlet irises once again cutting through the shadows and sending a shiver up Allen's spine with their intensity. "There are things we must discuss at length prior to retrieving the sword," he said. "But I would do it far from here, on the surface of Sythar."

"Gratitude for agreement," he said with a smile.

"Save it," Pythor retorted. "I offer aid toward the benefit of my brothers, not you. When do we depart?"

Allen gave Pythor as serious a look as he could. "We begin our journey down the road of destiny at first light."

30

PREPARATION

IT WAS LUZIAPH who woke them the next morning, sending a sharp jolt into thier minds through the Triaga. Allen's world spun as he struggled to bring his vision into focus. Being woken in such a fashion left his heart racing. His stomach churned and his mind was sent into a panic from being awoken in such a fashion. He could hear the grumbles of discomfort coming from his cellmates and knew they shared his disorientation. He recalled thinking his mother was harsh when she would occasionally wake him by splashing water in his face; he now considered such a tactic to be mild.

As he surveyed his surroundings he noticed that the bald Gorrlock, who had previously been unconscious, was now awake.

"What is the meaning of this?" the bald one grumbled, his voice barely audible.

The spinning in Allen's head began to dissipate, and he realized for the first time that the cell to their incarceration chamber stood open. He glanced up through the shadows to see a tall silhouette occupying most of the doorway.

"Bring yourselves to attention," Luziaph said.

Allen was mildly startled at hearing the man's voice emanating from the shadow before him; he hadn't expected Luziaph to come to them. He glared up at his so-called master through the darkness, wishing that he would someday be able to return the favor, leaving Luziaph struggling for cognition on his knees. Propping himself against the wall closest to him, Allen looked to Pythor and the others to respond first. When none of them said anything, Luziaph reached behind him and pulled a torch into the small room, casting a harsh light on them all, forcing them to squint collectively against the sudden intrusion.

"Have you come to a decision?" Luziaph asked, looking directly at him.

"I have," he replied, the words coming to his mouth with great difficulty.

"Then tell me," Luziaph demanded, "which of the Krathantor will accompany you to the surface of Sythar?"

The bald Gorrlock looked alarmed as Pythor stood up, letting the act provide Luziaph with his answer. Allen silently wondered if Pythor's head was spinning as hard as his own; he didn't think he could have stood up as readily as Pythor had.

A huge grin slowly spread across Luziaph's lips. He had never before considered a smile to be ominous, but the way Luziaph was grinning sent a small shudder up his spine.

"Before I agree to this," Pythor said, "I would have promise made that you will keep your word regarding the release of my Brothers of the Armor."

Luziaph glanced to the bald Gorrlock on the floor as he grumbled something else, then brought his eyes back to

Pythor. "I give my word that the three of you will be released from the torment of imprisonment under my roof," he replied, with the same wicked grin still haunting his features. Luziaph turned to one of the guards at his back. "Bind them," he added, gesturing to Allen and Pythor. "I would have these two accompany me to the throne room to make preparation for departure."

Two guards stepped forward. As the manacles on their wrists snapped into place, Pythor glanced to Sepharus and gave him a small nod before they were ushered out of the darkness and away from the incarceration chamber.

As they followed Luziaph along the length of the dark, sloping corridor toward the main area of the palace, he began to feel apprehensive about the journey ahead of him. His favorite stories when he was growing up had always centered around a main character mired in the tendrils of prophecy. The protagonist would make a perilous journey; face seemingly insurmountable odds, only to emerge victorious and stronger for the trials he had faced. As he'd read those stories, he had never given much thought to how nerve-racking or difficult they must have been for the character. An unsettling sense of uncertainty inundated him as he followed Luziaph, about to begin his own quest foretold by prophecy. He didn't want the fate of so many to rest on his shoulders. He didn't want the responsibility of making decisions which could ultimately change life forever on this world. He wondered if he was making the right decision in handing the Sword of Sythika over to Luziaph. Ultimately, however, he decided to push such troubling thoughts from his mind; he had made a promise to himself, and to Sarah, that he would get them home. He would just have to go through with his part of the agreement and hope Luziaph was honorable enough to hold to his end of the bargain.

Before he realized it they had completed their journey to the throne room and he was once again glancing at the statues which decorated the room's outer walls. There were several human forms among them, as well as a couple Saurothians, a Voldehyde, and a Gorrlock wearing a suit of armor; the Gorrlock was on one knee, reaching up as if begging for his life. Allen found himself wondering what the stories behind these monstrosities could be, wondering what events had brought them to their end at the hands of Luziaph. Knowing that each one of these had once been a living, breathing being left him feeling heartsick; he genuinely wished there was something he could have done for them.

"Can you believe it?" Luziaph spoke ceremoniously as he sat on his throne before them, snapping Allen back to the present. "The time of prophecy is upon us, and you find yourself of a position to bring it to be." Luziaph was still wearing his smug grin, looking to Pythor for a response.

"I believe we will perish in the attempt," Pythor replied, which did little to inspire confidence in Allen. "That is what I believe."

"You will do everything in your power to prevent such outcome." Luziaph retorted, his grin fading as he spoke. "For your allies will remain where they lay until the task has been seen to completion!"

Pythor glared at Luziaph. "Very well," he said, finally. "There are supplies I would require to see our journey come to such an end."

"Speak them and see consideration given to the request," Luziaph answered.

Allen noticed for the first time, as he looked at Pythor to hear his words, just how proudly the man stood. His hair hung to the side of his face, looking as if it hadn't been cleaned in a long time; the lower half of his face was covered in dark stubble. He was wearing nothing but the Triaga upon his scalp, the manacles on his wrists and a loin cloth, yet his posture, as well as the look in those black and red eyes, said that he would not be intimidated.

"I would have my armor returned," Pythor demanded.

Luziaph let out a low, rumbling laugh. "I think not. I would not so blatantly hand over that which will heighten abilities to be used against my purpose."

Pythor's countenance remained firm: "More is provided by the armor than heightened abilities. It also displays me as elite Krathantor; an edge we will need to succeed in such an undertaking."

Luziaph considered Pythor for a long moment. "I fear it to be a risk with too great a cost," he said at last. "You will have to find another way to reach your ends."

Pythor's eyes squinted slightly, his eyebrows knitting together. His jaw tightened at hearing Luziap's denial of his first request. He seemed to be considering his next words very carefully. "Then perhaps I could convince you to remove other encumbrances? The surface of Sythar will present ample challenge even for ones not restrained as we currently find ourselves."

Luziaph expelled a mockingly derisive huff. "I think not, Gorrlock," he replied. "You attempt to gain edge against me upon your return. Do you think me a fool?"

"I think that absent my involvement you will not obtain that which you so desperately seek," Pythor countered smoothly. "In order for such outcome to be brought to be, either the armor which displays rank and station held, or ability to prove myself competent in battle will be required. I leave the choice to you. Give me one or the other, or send me back to shadows from which I was retrieved."

A look of pure disgust spread across Luziaph's features. "I grow weary of slaves presenting ultimatum!" he spat. "So be it," he added a moment later, his voice reflecting the look of hatred in his eyes. "Your armor shall be returned, but the Triaga will remain upon your head. After all, amplification of that which is suppressed will prove impossible while you remain so encumbered. Put words to your next request."

Though it wasn't clearly evident, Allen couldn't mistake the small look of triumph in Pythor's eyes at hearing Luziaph's acquiescence. "The boy will require appropriate battle armor," he said. "Something light, as he is unaccustomed to the wearing of it."

"Done," Luziaph replied. "One of my servants will see to it presently."

Pythor nodded. "We will also require equipment; a suitable sword and shield for the both of us, in addition to other provisions." When Luziaph nodded in agreement, Pythor continued. "And you must come to understanding . . . such a journey will not see its end quickly. We must be afforded ample time to complete the task set before us."

"Understood," Luziaph agreed. "Is that all you would ask in the interest of aid?"

"I would ask one thing," Allen blurted out. When Luziaph directed his gaze at him he nearly reconsidered what he'd been about to say. "I would ask to see the girl, Sarah, one last time prior to our departure."

Luziaph eyed him suspiciously for a moment. "I see no harm in such a request," he offered at last. "I will have Gazianna bring her to you once all other preparations have been seen to."

"Gratitude," he answered, bowing his head slightly.

With a wave of his hand, Luziaph dismissed them. "If that is all," he said, "see yourselves to Araset's old living quarters. I will have servants arrive shortly to remove bindings and meet other requirements. When you are ready, send word and I will have the warp gate opened for departure."

Allen and Pythor both nodded, before turning to leave. Apprehension once again overwhelmed Allen's heart as they moved through the palace corridors. Soon he would be embarking on a journey he had no idea he could even complete; he would no longer even be on the same world as Sarah. The thought depressed him.

They traveled the entire trip to his old living quarters in silence, a determined scowl dominating Pythor's features. Once or twice Allen caught the Gorrlock who would be his companion for the foreseeable future glancing in his direction. He found it extremely ironic that the man who had spoken the words to trick him into leaving Earth behind was the one who would be assisting him in his efforts to return. He hoped he could trust such a man, but realized there was little choice in the matter if he wanted to keep his promise to Sarah.

As they rounded the corner which led to his old living quarters, a servant and two guards stood at the room's entrance watching his and Pythor's approach. For a moment he wondered how they could have been notified of the situation already. After brief consideration, however, the thought occurred to him that Luziaph had most likely informed them of their new assignment without ever speaking to them face to face; he was a Grandmaster of telepathy, after all.

"Luziaph must be eager to have us on our way," he whispered to Pythor.

Pythor glared at him in response, but said nothing as they continued toward the three who were evidently to assist in providing them with the necessary equipment for their journey.

The servant, a frail-looking Saurothian boy with light, leathery skin, watched them with nervous eyes as they came within a few feet of the room. Without a word he turned and removed himself from them as they neared, the two guards following in the boy's wake. Allen looked to Pythor to gauge his reaction to the boy's abrupt departure, uncertain if they were supposed to follow him. Pythor maintained the same stoically bitter countenance he'd worn since they had been sent from the throne room.

"Do we follow them?" Allen whispered.

"Be silent!" Pythor hissed before falling in step behind their guides.

"A simple 'yes' would have proven sufficient," he mumbled to himself, quickening his pace to keep up.

As they continued their brisk pace, he couldn't help but note that they seemed to be moving toward the entrance of the palace. This made him nervous that Luziaph might be sending them on their way without meeting any of their requests. Though he admittedly didn't know where the palace's armory was located, he kept his eyes alert for Sarah as they moved, hopeful that if Luziaph was going back on his word that he would at least get to have some brief last words with her before he departed. When they reached the entrance hall and he still hadn't reached the armory or seen Sarah, Allen became more nervous and attempted to open his mouth in protest, only to be shot another severe look by Pythor.

As the main doors shifted to the side exposing the palace courtyard beyond, he was forced to jerk his head away from the bright light emanating from outside; all the time spent in the private incarceration chamber had made his eyes more than a little sensitive to natural sunlight. Upon reaching the bottom of the staircase just outside the main entrance, the lizard-boy leading the way abruptly turned left and continued to move quickly along the palace's perimeter. Ahead of them he could see a small room constructed into the far wall which surrounded the palace. Four guards flanked the entrance, two on either side. With no more than a nod of his head one of the guards, a Triclopian, acknowledged their approach and stepped aside to grant them entrance. Allen found himself both impressed and concerned at how far Luziaph's commands could evidently reach without needing to be in person to give them.

The Saurothian slave boy continued into the small armory and, after finally removing their manacles, immediately began sizing him up for his armor. He did his best to pay attention, but couldn't help looking around at all of the weapons and armor lining the walls. He saw ranged weapons he could only compare to crossbows, spears with long blades at their tips, swords of several lengths and varieties, even weapons which closely resembled nunchukus and tri-staffs from Earth's Asian cultures. Too, he saw weapons for which he had no comparison. There was a weapon with wicked looking short blades protruding in opposite directions from a common grip. He noticed what he assumed was another weapon which was shaped like the letter Y, the singular prong of which came to a spherical tip; he was unable to even ascertain how such a weapon would be gripped or what it could be used for. He realized as he looked around, it was no wonder he hadn't known of the armory's location; it evidently had but one entrance.

In short order, he found himself fitted with a set of armor which seemed to be made from some sort of stiff leather. He noted that the cuirass covered both his front and back, but left him exposed underneath his arms. After being asked which one was his sword arm, Allen was fitted with shoulder pads which attached to the cuirass and trailed half way down his arm on the right side, covering naught but his shoulder on the left. Next he was fitted with a battle gauntlet for his right hand and forearm and a cod piece to cover his groin. Finally, he was suited with greaves and a pair of boots with hard plates which ran along his shins. Over all, it certainly wasn't the most comfortable thing he'd ever worn, but it wasn't so heavy he couldn't move. He also realized that without the rigorous adaptive training he'd received from Malacus that he would likely have been crushed under its weight, rather than being able to move relatively freely. He couldn't help but notice that he hadn't been fitted for a helmet, but didn't say anything as he assumed that the Triaga on his head would prevent wearing one anyway.Once the fitting process had been completed, Allen caught Pythor looking him up and down. "That will have to do," Pythor stated in a tone of what appeared to be disappointed acceptance. Pythor held a sword out to him, hilt first. "Take stock of this," he commanded.

Allen glanced down at the blade for a long moment before taking it from Pythor. It had a short, stubby hilt with a rounded pommel and virtually no cross-guard. The blade itself, at first glance, appeared to be slightly shorter than Allen thought necessary. As he gripped it in his right hand, however, the weapon was heavier than he'd expected it to be. He slashed it carefully through the air a couple of times. "It will have to do," he said mockingly to Pythor.

Pythor rolled his eyes with obvious impatience, forcefully pushing a baldric and scabbard into Allen's chest. "Put this on," he said.

Next, once Allen had done as he was told and slid the sword home, Pythor began picking up shields one by one and testing their weight. With a slight grin he tossed a rather large metal one at Allen, unexpectedly. The weight of it forced Allen to the ground and nearly knocked the wind from his lungs. "Too much?" Pythor asked with a grin, looking down at him.

"Very amusing," he mumbled stiffly from beneath the shield.

After a moment, Pythor reached down and removed the shield, offering a hand to lift him from the ground as well. "Something a bit smaller then," Pythor said in a tone he would've considered playful, if he thought the man was capable of it.

After another moment's consideration Pythor reached for a smaller shield which, though rather large, was perfectly rounded with the exception of a chunk missing from the edge nearest to the hand grip. Allen couldn't imagine what purpose the missing section could serve.

"What of this one?" Pythor asked.

Allen, placing his left arm through the grips and lifting the shield a couple times, mimicked a blocking motion. "I think this one will do," he said thoughtfully.

In one swift motion, Pythor turned around, suddenly grabbing a fierce-looking long sword from the wall behind him, and swung it in Allen's direction. Through reflex alone, Allen lifted the shield just in time to deflect Pythor's attack. A sharp clang echoed through the small room housing all of the palace's weapons. All present stood in shock. The guards reached for their weapons. Allen's heart pounded in his ears.

As Allen brought his eyes up to look past the shield, Pythor was assessing the sword he'd just swung with a self-satisfied look upon his face. "So it will," Pythor mused. "And I shall have this blade. Now," he added, addressing the lizard-boy who had led them to the armory, "where is my armor?"

The boy bowed his head. "It is being gathered and will be returned by he who accompanies you on your journey," he spoke in a high-pitched, gravelly voice.

Allen looked to Pythor. "There will be another traveling with us?"

"You seem surprised by the news," Pythor replied, showing virtually no reaction. "A mission of such import is not to be taken lightly, especially by one as avaricious as Luziaph. He would not see us fail, even should success require that he send an army at our backs."

Allen glanced to the servant boy and then back to Pythor, nevousness setting in again. "Surely the acquiring of the sword will not require such extreme measures as to send an army?"

"The task is such that success will only be found by the child of destiny. Numbers will matter for nothing in reaching that end," Pythor replied cryptically.

"What if I am not the one spoken of by prophecy?" Allen asked, fearing the answer.

Pythor looked him directly in the eyes. "Then you will find yourself one with Sythika."

The words barely had time to register in his mind when, from the corner of his eye, he saw Gazianna and Sarah moving toward them along the palace's outer walls. Instantly, every other concern left his mind and he moved past the guards into the light. A look of genuine intrigue appeared on Sarah's face when she saw him emerging from the armory. It took him several moments, following her gaze as she looked him up and down, to realize that it was most likely the sight of him in a suit of armor which had inspired the shift in her countenance.

As soon as she reached him, Sarah's arms were around him and for a moment everything was right in the world once more. She was his and he was hers, and nothing else mattered. She pulled away and brought her eyes to meet his. "You look like a character from one of your fantasy movies," she said in English, a playful yet somehow sad smile dominating her features. Her eyes moved down his frame, noticing the sword at his hip. "You're not actually going to have to use that thing are you?"

"That remains to be seen," he answered in Olyphatarian, realizing only as he completed the sentence just how used to his second language he was becoming. He gave himself a mental prompt to speak in his native tongue. "I hope not, but it seems likely that I'll at least need to learn how to use it . . . just in case."

Her eyes drifted back to the hilt protruding from its sheath, and began to flood with worry. With a finger he gently lifted her chin, forcing her to meet his eyes. "I'll be fine," he assured her. "I promise. But I asked that I be able to see you before I left for a reason and I need you to listen to me for a moment." When she nodded he continued, "I need you to do your best to keep your head down and do what's asked of you while I'm gone. It isn't going to be easy, but I need you to stay safe until I return. Don't tell anyone about the amulet Malacus gave you, and don't give Luziaph a reason to discipline you. I don't know how long I'll be away, so I need you to be strong. Think you can do that?"

The way he'd worded his goodbye made Allen feel as if he were addressing a child and hoped she didn't find his words condescending. Her eyes continued to fill with tears, but after a moment she nodded and buried her face in his chest once more. "I'm scared," she said in a voice barely above a whisper.

"I know. . . me, too. But everything will be okay, I promise." Even to himself the words sounded feeble, desperate. He pulled away and put as much effort as he could into filling his voice with confidence. "Hey, it's me, remember?" he said with a weak grin. "How many times have we gotten into trouble together? And I always find a way out of it, don't I?"

Sarah's lips creased ever so slightly as she continued to focus on his chest. "Yes," she replied meekly. "But this is different." She added, bringing her eyes up to meet his. "This is life and death. Allen, if you can't . . . if you fail, we die."

"Hey," he said, allowing his voice to turn a little stern, fixating his calculating stare upon her. "That is not going to happen. I won't let it." He could tell she wasn't quite convinced, so he decided upon another approach. "Do you trust me?"

Sarah hesitated only a moment. "Of course I do," she answered.

"Good. Then do what I ask and keep your head down. Leave the rest to me. Trust me; I am going to get us home."

"Okay," Sarah nodded.

He took her in his arms, knowing deep down that this could the last time they ever embraced. The thought made his very soul ache. How could he be abandoning her to this fate? How could he leave her all alone on this world?

As he brooded on the events to come and leaving behind the woman he loved more than even his own life, Pythor spoke directly behind him. "It figures," Pythor said with disgust. "Luziaph sends one of his own to play custodian over our quest."

Allen turned his focus to see a Triclopian man approaching them, carrying what appeared to be a burlap sack full of something heavy. The man was wearing dirty, green travelling clothes and a light brown travelling cloak; the sight momentarily made Allen feel a bit overdressed. Knowing the natural hatred between Gorrlocks and Triclopians, he began to dread the task set before him all the more; the journey would be difficult enough without keeping the peace between natural enemies.

Sarah lifted her head from Allen's shoulder to see who was approaching. As she did, he felt her tense noticeably. She clutched his arm tightly and leaned in close to his ear. "Allen," she whispered, her voice consumed with anxiety, "that man is a murderer! He was arrested for killing some woman and Luziaph ordered his release just because they're of the same race!"

Her words caused Allen's concern to increase. He wondered how she could possibly know such a thing.

"I was there," Sarah whispered with urgency, as if in answer to his unspoken question. "Luziaph released that man and his brother. He did it in front of a whole crowd, pardoned them for murder for no other reason than they look alike!"

Allen brought his eyes back up in time to see Pythor violently snatch at the sack being carried by the man inspiring fear in Sarah.

The Triclopian's grip held fast.

"Relinquish that which belongs to an Elite Krathantor, you filthy Triclopian!" Pythor spat.

When the Triclopian man grinned wickedly at Pythor's words, a sharp thud filled the air as Pythor's right foot found its mark upon the Triclopian's chest sending him sprawling to the ground and gasping for air. The sack tore open, spilling the black and gold armor on the ground between them. Allen noticed too that the sack had evidently been packed with a couple of travelling cloaks. Pythor hadn't even retrieved the first piece of armor when the he was thrown viciously backward toward the walls of the armory. It was as if gravity had suddenly shifted and was sucking Pythor toward its new point of origin. Following the impact, Pythor remained pinned to the wall for several moments before finally sliding down to the ground.

"That will be quite enough," Allen heard a new voice say. As he turned his head to see where it had originated, he was surprised to see another man Triclopian standing just behind the other, who was still on the ground. The one who had spoken was wearing long, flowing white robes bearing the same insignia as Luziaph's armor across his chest. The sleeves of the outer robes were cut at the shoulders, exposing the long sleeves of the tunic beneath them. Knee high, white boots shown over top of the pants and light-weight looking gauntlets of the same color covered all but the man's fingertips. He noted that the hood of the man's outer robe was draped over his head. Allen's hopes sunk. If he was interpreting this world's customs correctly that could only mean that this man, too, was meant to accompany them to the surface of Sythar; now he would have two Triclopians to contend with.

Allen turned his head back to Pythor in time to see him picking himself up off the ground. In his opinion the look on Pythor's face as he did so could've melted steal. He fully expected Pythor to attack the robed Triclopian, or at least make an aggressive remark. Instead, Pythor silently walked over to his armor and began to suit up, never once removing his eyes from his aggressor. Once he was done, Pythor retrieved the sword he'd chosen from where it had landed when he'd been thrown backward, and continued to glare at the hooded Triclopian man while he moved back toward Allen.

"Are you okay?" he asked Pythor as he got within a couple feet.

"Be silent!" Pyhor whispered harshly. It was a long moment before Pythor finally diverted his glare from the Triclopian man for the first time since their exchange, and looked Allen directly in the eyes. "It will take more than a child's trick to bring harm to me. Be on guard, Earth boy. Regardless of opinions previously expressed concerning equality, these two are to be trusted at your own peril."

"Sarah tells me the one on the ground has been pardoned by Luziaph for giving a woman to the clutches of Sythika," he replied in Olyphatarian.

"The statement is not met with surprise," Pythor replied, his gaze shifting upon the other Tricopian, who was at last picking himself up off the ground. "A long journey yet awaits us. Be on guard at all times."

Allen nodded, bringing his own gaze to meet the two Triclopians whom Luziaph had personally chosen to keep an eye on their progress. There was a brief, muffled verbal exchange between the others after which the one not wearing robes nodded and moved toward the fallen travelling cloaks. After retrieving them from the ground he cautiously approached Allen and Pythor, a look of stifled distain on his face.

"Apologies," began the Triclopian criminal, though his words sounded forced to Allen. "I am called Rexim. I will be accompanying this trek at the request of Lord Luziaph. These travelling cloaks bear his mark upon them and are a gift for the journey."

Wanting only to be polite and hopefully keep the tension to a minimum, he gracefully accepted one of the cloaks, nodding his gratitude. Pythor, however, was not so gracious; he viciously snatched his cloak from the other's grip and immediately threw it over his shoulders, lifting the hood into place. The aggressive act left a nervous feeling in the pit of Allen's stomach; this might be more challenging than he thought. After another moment he followed suit, clipping the cloak to his armor and raising the hood onto his head.

Once all present were ready to travel, the white-robed Triclopian stepped forward to draw their attention. "I am called Ithaniel," he said. "It is I who shall usher Luziaph's will through the warp gate and to the surface of Sythar, a request which was given me with the greatest of urgency. Shall we begin?"

He and Pythor both nodded their acquiescence. Without another word, Ithaniel turned and marched away from them toward the gates of Vardiston. Allen moved quickly to keep up, giving Sarah a final glance over his shoulder. As he turned his attention back toward those leading the procession out of town, he heard her call his name. The look in her eyes as he brought his attention back to her was one of desperation. She appeared as if she wanted to say something, but hesitated as if afraid to.

After several moments, Pythor nudged him. "The time for farewells is past," he said in a low voice.

Allen slowly, ever so slowly, turned from Sarah. Before his second step had landed, her words came to him loudly, unbidden. "I love you!"

The words came as such a shock, he couldn't be certain he'd heard her right. The world slowed down while he attempted to confirm in his own mind that he had heard her correctly. His heart was suddenly hammering in his chest, his palms were wet, and his knees felt as if they might buckle under his own weight.

He realized, as he turned his gaze back toward Sarah, that his mouth was completely dry. As he gaped at her, wondering again about the words she'd just given him, he was only vaguely aware of the arm clutching his own and dragging him away.

31

SYTHAR

ALLEN WAS IN SUCH A STATE OF SHOCK from hearing Sarah's words, the trip away from Vardiston hadn't completely registered in his mind. His entire reality was spinning. The moment he'd daydreamed about for so long had come and gone, and he hadn't even had the presence of mind to reciprocate before being dragged away. He'd only been distantly paying attention as Ithaniel opened the warp gate, ushering the others into the light before passing through himself.

It could have been that he'd acclimated to Datheron, or it could've been the lingering effects of hearing Sarah say that she loved him, but passing through the warp gate for a second time seemed less painful to him. The first thing he noticed once the pain and disorientation of travelling through the gateway dissipated was how much different the atmosphere of Sythar appeared to be. He couldn't quite put his finger on what he was experiencing, but it almost seemed as if a tremendous weight had been lifted from him. This made no sense to him at first, as he could still plainly feel the armor pressing against his skin; armor which had only moments previously been more encumbering. After a moment, however, he realized that the gravity of Sythar must be less intense than that of Datheron.

As his senses began to return Allen found himself leaning against a tree in an unfamiliar jungle. He glanced around, momentarily taken aback and wondering if they had actually travelled anywhere. Vines wound their way around tree trunks and draped lazily from branches, the grass at his feet was lush and came half way up his shins. The air was extremely humid and he became acutely aware of just how unpleasant it was going to be to travel in this climate wearing leather armor. Being surrounded as he was by foliage only added to his disorientation; this was not at all how he had envisioned the surface of a moon.

"What skills do you possess?" he heard Pythor ask.

Allen brought his eyes up to see Pythor looking directly at Rexim, who, in the poor light of the jungle, bore a remarkable resemblance to Luziaph. If not for the definite difference in height, he might have thought the three-eyed Proctus had decided to join them after all. He mentally shook himself, realizing that his senses must not have fully returned to him yet.

"My skills are none of your concern, Gorrlock," Rexim replied indifferently, not even facing Pythor as he spoke; he appeared to be more shaken from passing through the warp gate than Allen was.

Pythor's jaw tightened at the response he'd been given. To Allen's surprise, however, Pythor composed himself as he approached the question again. "Listen well," Pythor said through clenched teeth. "Absent my abilities, gaining bearings in current surroundings will prove exceedingly difficult. Once proper direction is known, the path toward our destination will become clear. If abilities are possessed which can divine precise location of where we now stand, such would facilitate the journey coming to a quick and successful end."

For a long moment Rexim seemed to be considering Pythor's words, appearing as if he couldn't decide whether to be affronted or simply give an honest reply. Only when the tension seemed to have reached a boiling point did Ithaniel answer in his place. "We stand but one day's journey south of the northern edge of this oasis and the entrance to the Windavian desert."

Pythor grinded his teeth together, his black and red eyes still focused intently on Rexim, as he considered Ithaniel's words. A moment later he expelled a deep breath. "We must move with haste," he stated flatly. "Stay close at my back. I will lead us to proper destination."

Rexim, who seemed to have finally gathered himself, wore an indignant look as he glanced back and forth between Pythor and Ithaniel. In Allen's opinion the man seemed to be losing an internal struggle. "Why does leadership fall to you?" Rexim questioned accusingly. "The Triaga upon your scalp marks you as slave."

"And the armor upon my back marks me as Elite Krathantor," Pythor countered harshly. "It is my knowledge of Sythar which makes completion of this mission possible. You would do well to hold your tongue and defer to me while on its surface."

At hearing Pythor's tone Rexim balled his fists at his side, which almost immediately began to crackle with electric energy. A vicious glare filled his eyes. So quickly that Allen could barely follow the movement Pythor had knocked Rexim to the ground, drawn his sword, and had its tip held firmly under the Triclopian's chin. As impressive as the maneuver was, not to mention the speed with which it was performed, he couldn't help but feel frustrated with Pythor's impetuousness. It almost seemed to him as if the man possessed no tolerance, awaiting any excuse to demonstrate his aggressive side; especially where Triclopian's were concerned.

To his surprise Pythor hesitated only a couple of moments before removing his blade from Rexim's throat. "Do not provoke me," Pythor threatened in a low, deadly tone. "Despite what you may have been told, your presence is not required to see my objective completed, nor are abilities required to best you in combat. Now come; gather yourself. We move south." He slammed the blade home in its scabbard, and without even waiting to see if the others were behind him, Pythor began moving at a brisk pace, deeper into the jungle.

***

The sweltering humidity of their surroundings was enough to sap anyone's strength after only a short distance. Several hours of travel found Allen sweating profusely, his head spinning and his leather armor clinging uncomfortably to his skin. He wasn't entirely sure what he'd expected before they set out, but he certainly hadn't seen himself walking to the point of collapse through an alien jungle. Though the heat was oppressive, he couldn't keep his eyes from roaming as they moved toward an unknown destination. Most of the trees moving past him had extremely large trunks, bearing what he assumed were several different types of fungi, some of them also sparsely decorated with vines. It was almost eerie how close the scenery of Sythar resembled that of Earth. The air was filled with a cacophony of activity that seemed to somehow always stay just out of reach. He silently wondered if it was their presence the wildlife was avoiding.

Pythor had continued his exhausting pace without a word the entire trip, leaving the others little to do but follow his lead. In fact, not a word had been spoken by anyone since they had set out several hours earlier. In Allen's opinion the silence was nearly as difficult to endure as the heat. With the noteable tension between his forced colleagues, the silence had grown almost awkward. Rather than leave the awkward silence hanging in the air, he decided to ask the question bothering him almost as much as the heat. "How much further must we travel?"

Pythor cast an irritated glance over his shoulder, and turned his attention to the path in front of him. Before Allen had a chance to be offended by the response, or lack thereof, Pythor swept aside a swath of branches allowing a shaft of light to break through the looming darkness. Allen was glad to see there was still a little light left to the day, but was concerned how much hotter it would get if they were going to continue their journey under direct sunlight.

As his eyes adjusted to the intrusion, he was able to make out a clearing just past the forest wall; at the center was a large lake.

"Does this provide answer enough?" Pythor replied in a sardonic tone.

For a long moment Allen just stared at what lay before him. A strong gust of chill air blew off the surface of the water, past Pythor, hitting Allen directly. With how profusely he had been sweating, the breeze came as a shock, sending a cold chill through his entire body. As utterly exhausted as he was, the cool breeze reignited him with enough energy to burst past Pythor in a sprint toward the lake. In seconds he'd reached the edge of the water, ready to abandon the heat, and was suddenly ripped from his feet by the hood of his travelling cloak. He landed awkwardly on his side, his sword directly beneath him. Had the blade been unsheathed it might have inflicted a mortal wound.

As Allen rolled onto his back, trying to gingerly to move the sword from underneath him without hurting himself, Pythor mumbled something under his breath. Black hair draped over blue skin as Pythor appeared sideways across his vision from above.

"For what purpose did you impede me from respite?" he asked, looking up at the Gorrlock.

With one hand, Pythor easily lifted Allen to his feet. "Tell me," he said in a tone one might use to rebuke a child, "Is it common practice among the population of your world to run headlong into the unknown?"

Allen glanced over at the water, which looked so inviting he could hardly concentrate, then back to Pythor. "I fail to grasp meaning in the question," he replied.

"You ignore caution, ready to throw yourself into the water, unaware of what dangers such an act may present," Pythor admonished.

Allen was so light-headed, so dehydrated, that he wasn't even sure whether he should care what dangers lived in the water. "The water is unsafe?" he asked in an exasperated tone, looking back toward the lake.

Pythor sighed. "The point was missed by a wide margin," he muttered, shaking his head. After a moment of consideration, during which Pythor too stared out across the water, he brought his attention back to Allen. "How do you know the waters are not poisonous?" Pythor asked simply.

"Is the water poisonous?" he responded, dumbly.

Pythor shook his head in frustration. "Is the fate of our world truly at the mercy of such a simple mind?" he said, more to himself than to anyone in particular.

Allen felt as if he should've been insulted by the remark, but his head was spinning too hard for the words to register properly. He was only vaguely aware of the muffled laughter coming from the two Triclopians behind him.

After a brief pause Pythor began speaking again, attempting to approach the subject from a new perspective. "The water is not poisonous," he stated. "But such is far from desired intent. The point is that you lack knowledge of potential threats presented by immersing yourself recklessly. You must learn to heed caution when on an unknown world."

He nodded that he understood, but couldn't keep himself from staring longingly at the surface of the lake as Pythor continued.

"I can see we will make no progress until your thirst is sated, bringing with it the return of proper mental faculties," Pythor said with another sigh. "Go. Remove armor and see yourself cooled by water's embrace, but remain close to shore as you do so."

Allen only hesitated a moment before beginning the arduous task of removing his armor. As the chest-plate of his cuirass fell away, the air hit his torso with a force that sent another cold chill racing through him. For a very long moment he just stood there reveling in the relief that cool breeze provided.

After struggling to remove the gauntlets on his own for several minutes, Pythor graciously finished the process for him, dropping them on the ground next to the fallen cuirass. Once the entire suit of armor lay in a heap behind him Allen approached the water, noticing for the first time just how light he felt now that he was completely unencumbered. Glancing back at Pythor for just a moment, he turned and dived head first into the lake.

The water, though colder than Allen had anticipated, felt amazing. He wasn't sure just how long he spent dunking himself under its surface or swimming along the shoreline, but his fingers were wrinkled and he felt almost completely refreshed by the time he got out. The others had followed his lead, removing their own armor and garments in order to soak in the cool water as well, though none of them stayed in quite as long as he had.

As Allen emerged from the lake, Pythor stood to his full height and marched toward Allen's armor. He wasn't quite ready to dawn the cumbersome attire again, but the look in Pythor's eyes made him second-guess voicing his protest.

When the chore of redressing was done, Pythor took several steps away from Allen and drew his sword with a serious look in his eye. "Prepare yourself," he said.

Allen, uncertain what had inspired the sudden change in Pythor's countenance, looked around to see if he could gauge the situation from the other's reactions, noticing for the first time that Rexim was missing. After being unable to draw any clue from his surroundings, he brought his attention back to Pythor. "Where is Rexim?" he asked.

"That is not your concern," Pythor replied firmly. "Bring yourself to attention. It is time to begin your training."

Though he had never been easily intimidated, Allen found himself very nervous as he drew his sword and brought his shield up in front of him. He had never particularly cared for fighting, yet now found himself about to learn a method of fighting primarily intended to end the life of one's opponent. Pythor must have noticed the look of uncertainty in Allen's eyes because he lowered his own weapon and changed his approach.

"You have never before held blade against foe, have you?" Pythor asked in a tone more patient than Allen had ever heard from the man.

Allen shook his head in response.

Pythor exhaled a long breath. "Then the journey we begin today will be longer than anticipated," Pythor said in a tone of resignation.

With evident ease, Pythor threw his own sword at the ground, where it stuck at an angle. A moment later he was standing in front of Allen and to his left.

"Release your shield and raise your sword as if bringing it to purpose," Pythor commanded.

Allen did as he was told and lifted the sword, attempting to grip it with both hands. It only took a moment to realize that the hilt hadn't been designed for two-handed use, but that didn't keep Pythor from making a remark.

"Is that truly how you would grip a sword when faced with peril?" Pythor asked in a mocking tone. Without waiting for a response Pythor stepped closer to Allen and roughly repositioned his grip and stance. He left Allen standing there examining his work while he sauntered back to reclaim his own blade from the clay-like ground at his feet.

He looked up a moment later to find Pythor standing directly to his left.

"We shall begin by bringing familiarity to grip," Pythor stated. "Sword and body must move with fluid unison. Watch my movement and repeat."

Allen watched with great interest as Pythor cut the air in front of him with practiced precision. By the ease with which he moved, it was clear the man had been doing this a long time. Allen concentrated on every movement, every slash, every thrust, placing particular effort toward memorizing the deadly dance being demonstrated so expertly. He imagined himself replicating every fluid motion.

After repeating each step, each movement a couple of times Pythor turned to him and nodded to signify that it was his turn. For the next couple of hours they repeated the process with meticulous dedication. Allen was both surprised and impressed by the patience with which Pythor made minor corrections here and there to his execution. When Pythor seemed satisfied that he at least had the first set of motions down, they immediately began working on another.

The sun had nearly set by the time they finally stopped for the night. Allen wasn't even aware of how hungry he was, or how exhausting the training had been, until he spotted Rexim and Ithaniel sitting in front of a make-shift fire pit. A skinned animal resembling a boar or a large dog floated just above the flames, rotating by Ithaniel's mental direction. Allen hadn't even noticed Rexim's return and wondered if that was where he'd been; hunting dinner.

The aroma from the meat, though unfamiliar, wafted past Allen's nostrils, igniting in him a raging hunger. He was suddenly aware just how painfully empty his stomach was. When his stomach growled, rather loudly in his own opinion, the others turned mildly surprised looks at him. He considered making a joke about making sure the animal was dead before cooking it next time, but didn't think the others would appreciate his sarcasm. Instead he asked, "Is anyone else hungry?"

Much to Allen's surprise, Pythor began to laugh. The others turned to one another, quite obviously trying to suppress their own amusement and losing the battle a moment later. Allen wasn't quite sure how it had happened, but he'd made them all laugh and found it difficult not to join in their mirth.

It felt really good to laugh again.

The laughter brought pleasant thoughts racing back into his mind, casting aside the overwhelming feelings of despair which had been plaguing him of late. With the lighthearted shift in everyone's countenance, Allen found his mind quickly drifting to Sarah and her last words to him. She'd told him that she loves him . . . had actually spoken the words he'd longed to hear from her for most of his life. He genuinely wished he'd had the presence of mind to tell her exactly how he feels about her, and how long he'd been waiting for the right opportunity to do so. As disheartening as it was to think about their awkward goodbye, he absolutely couldn't wait to complete his objective so he could return to her and do just that.

He continued to dwell on what the declaration would mean for them once they could finally be together again, what it would mean when they finally returned home to Earth. He could see them being happy together for a very long time and found it virtually impossible to suppress the smile that was stealing across his lips as he stared into the dancing flames before him. He knew his mother would be genuinely happy for him and hoped that she will not have aged too much to see his dream become reality by the time they made it home.

Allen continued to allow his imagination to run away with him as he ate his meal, which consisted of nothing but the tough meat from an unknown animal. It had a mildly sweet tang to it and left him wishing he had something to wash it down, but it was good to eat to his capacity for a change. By the time he was finished he was so full he could barely breathe.

Afterwards, while he lay there staring up at the stars, he noticed a movement from the corner of his eye. He looked over his left shoulder to see Ithaniel tossing the remains of their meal to the center of the lake with his mind. Rexim stood right next to him; the men seemed to be conversing in purposely low tones.

"What do you suppose is the meaning of that?" he asked Pythor, nodding toward the two Triclopians.

Without even looking up from the embers he was stirring with a thin stick, Pythor gave a dark reply. "As previously stated, they plot against us," he said. "Vigilance must be our ally if we are to remain alert of their dealings."

Allen didn't like the idea that others were plotting against him and liked less that Pythor seemed convinced of it without any real proof. He looked over his shoulder once more to the others standing near the water's edge. They were definitely keeping their voices low, but in his opinion there didn't seem to be anything suspicious about their behavior—they could be merely *visiting* for all he knew. He felt genuine sorrow for the prejudice and hatred which so readily clouded Pythor's heart toward Triclopians. True, Sarah had warned him against trusting Rexim, but he saw no reason to make the same assumption of Ithaniel.

"You have said as much before," Allen remarked, keeping his voice as diplomatic as possible. "But reason behind the words has yet to present itself."

"Spoken like a fool," Pythor retorted.

"How are mine the words of a fool?" he asked defensively.

"You await personal experience to provide truth in the words from one who yet possesses it," Pythor answered in a tone of finality.

As Allen considered Pythor's words, Rexim and Ithaniel rejoined them by the fire. An awkward silence loomed in the air while the flames continued to dwindle. The others seemed content to keep company with their own thoughts as Datheron disappeared behind a wall of clouds above them. Normally Allen had difficulty abiding uncomfortable silences, but found the chance to be alone with his own thoughts after such an exhausting day to be relaxing. While allowing his mind to drift once again to Sarah, a particularly disturbing thought occurred to him.

491

"How does time flow upon Sythar?" he asked, turning to Pythor.

"Twice that of Datheron," the Gorlock answered without looking up from the fire.

The answer was more or less what he'd expected, but it brought with it other questions.

"You urged haste upon arrival," he said, "yet time moves quicker here than upon Datheron?"

Pythor nodded his head.

"Why then must we hurry?" he challenged.

Pythor cast a furtive and defensive glance at the two Triclopians before responding. "Because I do not trust the fate of my brothers to the will of Luziaph," he said, grimly. "Nor should you trust the fate of your woman to his graces."

The Triclopians shared a look of disgust at the remark. Rexim stood, focusing a particularly withering stare upon Pythor. "Mind your tongue, Gorrlock!" he spat. "Luziaph is a great man and an exemplary Proctus! He rescued me and my brother from a fate in the pits or worse!"

Before Pythor had a chance to respond, Allen decided to challenge the statement in his own way. "A fate deserved from what I hear told," he countered. "Did you not find shackles upon your wrist through act of ending the life of a woman?"

Rexim looked both affronted and surprised by his knowledge on the subject, but said nothing for several moments. Allen let his words hang in the air. All eyes were on Rexim.

"That Gorrlock whore got what she deserved!" Rexim said defensively.

Upon hearing the other's words, Pythor shot to his feet. Though his eyes never left Rexim, Pythor's words were directed at Allen. "Your woman spoke nothing of the victim being Gorrlock!"

Allen's first inclination was to correct Pythor's remark about Sarah being 'his woman', but quickly reconsidered choosing this moment to make that distinction. He could see this situation easily leading to violence, but could think of no way to diffuse it. Fortunately before either Pythor or Rexim could act on the growing hatred between them, Ithaniel rose to his feet as well, drawing their attention.

"This is neither the time nor the place for old grudges," Ithaniel said in a commanding tone. "Luziaph has provided directive; we have a mission to complete."

Ithaniel's interjection seemed to deflate Rexim. He sat down a moment later. Pythor, who appeared to be fighting an internal battle, refused to sit immediately. He stood there for several very long moments, his jaw grinding on something unseen, while he evidently contemplated an impossible task.

The tension in the air remained, even after Pythor reclaimed his seat. Allen had known before they left that the journey would be difficult to endure. He silently wondered just how long he would have to tolerate the hostility between his companions. As if prompted by Allen's brooding, Rexim asked the very question to which he'd wanted an answer.

"How long must we endure the company of these two?" Rexim asked, directing his question toward Ithaniel.

Before Ithaniel had a chance to respond, Pythor answered for him. "We remain in this oasis until I deem . . ." Pythor paused a moment, glancing at Allen as if considering his next words carefully, ". . . Araset ready to face the trials of Sythika," he finished.

Both of the Triclopians appeared insulted by the declaration and Allen definitely didn't like the sound of facing the 'trials of Sythika', but somehow found himself more concerned with training in the company of these three for an unknown extended period of time. He also couldn't help but notice the pause before Pythor said his name, or the fact that he had chosen to use his Datheronian pseudonym. He silently wondered what that meant.

"And just how long will that take?" Rexim questioned in an aggressive tone.

"That depends entirely on this one," Pythor replied, nodding to Allen.

No more was said the rest of the evening. As Allen lay on the cold ground next to the dying embers, his thoughts were alive with challenges yet to be faced and dangers yet unknown. He wasn't sure how long he stared up at the stars before he finally drifted to sleep.

32

FORSAKEN

SARAH HAD CRIED herself to sleep the night Allen had been taken away from her. Part of her felt very foolish for telling him how she felt, especially when she knew he had been given an impossible task to complete. She hoped the declaration wouldn't distract him, or lead to him being injured. More than anything, though, she hoped that she hadn't overstepped in telling him. It would crush her if she learned that he didn't feel the same, if he saw her only as a friend or worse . . . if he saw her as a big sister. She just wouldn't have been able to forgive herself if anything happened to him while he was away and she hadn't taken the chance to tell him.

The isolation of being on a strange world she didn't know, surrounded by things she'd only ever seen in movies, would have been crushing in its own right if not for Gazianna. The blue-skinned woman into whose care she had been placed had been at her side nearly every waking moment since Allen's departure. Even though they'd spent the majority of their time walking the palace performing onerous tasks, and there was a language barrier to overcome, she had come to find the woman's presence comforting. The only other comfort she had, despite how fervently Malacus had warned her against it, was the amulet the old man had given her; she knew without it she would have been even more lost.

In what little spare time Sarah did have she had managed to communicate to Gazianna her desire to learn to speak the native language fluently, though she didn't dare reveal the origin of how she could understand it and still not be able to speak it. The private lessons, however, had come to an end nearly as quickly as they'd begun once Luziaph learned of them. In a horrific display of abuse and control, the three-eyed lunatic had beaten Gazianna mercilessly, using methods which had shaken Sarah to her core, to exert his dominance.

Beginning by using his bare hands, Luziaph had sent the poor woman crashing into walls and those creepy statues right in front of Sarah. When the screaming had gotten louder she'd uncovered her eyes to see Gazianna clawing at her own face, quite obviously desperate to be free of a torment unseen. Once the appalling scene finally came to an end, while Gazianna lay there whimpering and clutching her head, Luziaph had cast a smile at Sarah she could only have described as demented.

After such a horrific display, she hadn't asked Gazianna to teach her Olyphatarian again.

Sarah would have thought after the abuse Gazianna had sustained that the woman would have at least been granted some time to recuperate. She was appalled to learn that her companion was sent to a healer and then expected to return immediately to her daily duties. The exterior wounds may have disappeared, but she knew that it would take more than an empathetic touch to heal the damage which so obviously still raged behind Gazianna's eyes.

Once the option to learn to speak Olyphatarian was taken away from her, she found it impossible to remove the amulet Malacus had given her. Though his warning had been clear about not wearing it for an extended period of time, she just couldn't bring herself to spend even a moment without it; doing so would have would've left her more naked to this crazy, backward world than she already felt.

The biggest drawback to being assigned to the care of Gazianna, other than all the abuse to which she bore witness, had to be all the time they spent directly serving Luziaph. Sarah had heard the term 'drunk with power' before, but this man took it to extremes she could have never conceived of on her own. Her only solace came from knowing that he couldn't understand her thoughts, though she knew that hadn't stopped him from probing her mind. She had yet to learn whether his limitation of comprehending her language impeded his ability to manipulate her in other ways. She hoped that it did and dreaded the thought that he could potentially torture her in the same way he did Gazianna. There were times when she was sure he was creeping around inside her head. The very thought induced a brand new feeling of violation, sending a cold shudder down her spine.

Though she knew Gazianna was considered Luziaph's personal assistant, Sarah got the distinct impression that all the extra time they'd been required to spend serving the Proctus of Vardiston had been to specifically keep her close at hand. The way she would catch him looking at her sometimes, and some of the random tasks he would have them perform left her feeling like the man considered her a pet or a trophy. Part of her wondered if he simply needed visual confirmation of her activities because he had no way of following her with his ability. It was during one such task which had been asked of them that she had learned that the painting of the Triclopian Proctus, which was hung on the wall directly behind the throne, had been painted by Allen. As much as she despised looking at the man, even in a painting, seeing something created by Allen's hand had been heartening in a way. She knew he enjoyed drawing in his spare time, but the detail in the painting of Luziaph was exquisite.

The restrictions her new life placed on her occasionally brought Sarah's mind back to the cautionary words Zorthos had spoken to her and Allen against allowing themselves to be captured by Luziaph. She remembered hoping that she would never even meet the man, let alone find herself at his mercy. She could scarcely believe that the choices she'd made had brought her here. Moments like these only became tolerable by thinking of Allen and the steeled look of resolve in his eyes when he had told her that he would get them home. She loved that look; the confidence in it had always given her strength, made her feel safe.

Among the many arduous tasks with which she and Gazianna had been charged, Sarah was expected to be present while Luziaph granted audience to the various inhabitants of Vardiston. She was not clear on why their presence was required when they'd first begun attending the sessions; she couldn't see how her being there would make any kind of difference. In one of their frequent attempts at communication, all of which took tremendous patience and effort from both women, Gazianna had told her that Luziaph didn't normally grant audiences to his subjects, adding that the sudden change led her to believe the man had a hidden agenda. While she had found the information both intriguing and worrisome, Sarah felt frustration at how long it had taken to get it out of

Gazianna; being the only one incapable of clearly verbalizing her thoughts left her feeling as if she were mentally challenged. There were times she was almost certain that others in the palace thought she was. She hated that feeling and the looks of judgment and pity which came with it.

Though much of Luziaph's attention was being demanded to resolve petty disputes over matters of money or honor among a couple individuals, it was becoming increasingly frequent that concerned citizens were requesting audiences to inquire about the rumors which had begun circulating concerning an off-worlder speaking an alien tongue having been sighted in the market of Abendroth, and the potential safety risk it presented to the populace. When Luziaph would confirm their concerns, pointing Sarah out as he did so, the reaction was always the same: the citizen would cast a wide-eyed, incredulous glare at her. Luziaph would then explain that there was nothing to worry about as he had her in custody, but would neither confirm nor deny that she originated from Earth as the rumors suggested. He would always sugar-coat the lack of a definitive answer by saying that he couldn't be expected to know her true planet of origin if he couldn't understand her language.

The problem with rumors, Sarah knew, was that they didn't necessarily need to be true for people to believe them or cling to them. All it really takes for a rumor to take a foothold in someone's mind was for it to sound real enough for people to fear it *could* be true. Sadly, on a planet where it was quite literally possible to make anything a reality, something as simple as Sarah coming from another planet was easily possible. In this case she knew their fears to be accurate and was glad, if only for that reason, that she couldn't confirm the truth with her own words. She wished that Luziaph would at least not point

499

her out when the question was asked. She quickly came to the assumption that pointing her out was the exact reason he wanted her there; it would place fear in both the citizens of Datheron and herself alike.

Quite possibly the thing which had Sarah the most concerned, however, was how much more frequently the subject of her origin was being discussed with the Proctus of Vardiston. It had only been a couple weeks since Allen's departure and word of her presence had already somehow spread far beyond the walls of Luziaph's city.

She and Gazianna were in the middle of preparing meals for the prisoners in the holding cells beneath the palace when they were once again summoned to take part in an audience with yet another concerned individual regarding the prophecy coming to fruition, this time in the form of a Proctus from one of the other realms of Datheron, called Hestaros. Sarah already didn't like being forced to endure these sessions, but hated more that they had been pulled away from feeding the prisoners. It was more than she just felt for those incarcerated; she was certain that one of the chambers had once been home to Allen and felt close to him while she was down there, though she never dared ask Gazianna which had been his.

Moments after she and Gazianna had taken their designated places at Luziaph's side, a large beast of a man, wearing a full suit of ornate silver armor, burst into the throne room, his entire body covered in fur. He marched with purpose toward the throne, glancing warily at the stone statues as he approached. He appeared to Sarah as if he must be the same species as the beast-man which had released the three-eyed criminals into Luziaph's care that day in Abendroth. He exhaled a deep breath through his snout as he came to a stop a few feet from Luziaph.

"Greetings, good Gharr," Luziaph said in his most placating tone. "To what do I owe the honor of your visit this day?"

"With talents such as yours, is the meaning not already clear?" Gharr replied, gruffly.

In all her time around the man, Sarah had determined Luziaph to be difficult to read and somehow still very temperamental. She would never have worded a response to the man in such a blatantly flippant manner, or in that tone, even if she were able to speak a language the man could understand. Gharr, however, was Proctus of another land and as such could likely get away with more than most.

Luziaph didn't answer for a very long moment and seemed to be thinking of how best to respond to Gharr's remark. Finally a small grin slowly crept across his face. "Of course," he said with a slight nod. "Issues of prophecy have reached your fair city and realm alike. Your journey to Vardiston was promised to the subjects of Hestaros toward the purpose of divining truth in the matter.

After another long pause Gharr snorted again. "Well?" he said in a demanding tone.

"Bring your mind to peace," Luziaph said, that sly grin still dominating his features while he raised his arms in a welcoming gesture. "Such is naught but rumors and conjecture; the whisperings of the weak-minded."

There was a low, guttural rumbling from Gharr following Luziaph's proclamation. The beast-man glared at Luziaph through squinted eyes, apparently considering the truth of his words.

"You are telling me," Gharr said slowly, as if questioning a child, "that word of a girl from off world, speaking an alien tongue is false?"

"I have said no such thing," Luziaph countered smoothly. "This girl here," he added, pointing yet again to

Sarah, "is the very one of which you speak. True origins, however, yet remain a mystery as I possess no way to translate her words."

Gharr's eyes immediately fell on her. He looked her up and down, his features betraying the fear and uncertainty in his heart. After staring at her in shock for quite some time, his head snapped back toward Luziaph. "Why does she yet live?" he bellowed.

The words alone nearly brought her heart to a stop. She looked to Luziaph in desperation, her mind suddenly full of worry that she might be executed before Allen returned.

Luziaph's eyes never left Gharr. "The sentence of death can hardly be enforced absent good reason," he reiterated in that smooth tone of his. "As previously stated, the ability to translate foreign words is yet unavailable. I cannot very well have her executed for nothing."

As repulsed as she was by Luziaph, Sarah found herself grateful for his words on her behalf. She was relieved that he hadn't simply agreed to have her slaughtered based on this creature's fear of ancient prophetic words denoting the end of life for those on Datheron. While she could understand the fear, she was thankful they had no way to translate her words lest they make good on the threat. Even though Malacus had warned her of this potential reaction to her presence, seeing it with her own eyes revealed the grim reality of it. She wished and hoped with everything in her that Allen would succeed as he'd promised and be able to take them far away from this awful planet.

As she brought her focus back to the present, she realized that Gharr was talking again; he didn't seem satisfied with Luziaph's decision to spare her.

"You realize it would be but a simple matter to circumvent your weakness and have her dealt with," Gharr was saying. "And you along with her for jeopardizing all of Datheron!"

"A petition to gather all of the Proctus of Datheron to convene and pass judgment could easily be arranged," Luziaph agreed. "If you find the presence of a girl with no abilities and a complete lack of knowledge regarding our customs to be that much of a threat, that is."

The fur on Gharr's head and neck rose a little at hearing Luziaph's challenging words. His eyes widened and he appeared to be suppressing a violent response. "Perhaps it is you who hold the safety of our world with little regard!" he barked.

Luziaph clasped his hands behind his back, his expression turning dark. "I have said all I will. You will do as you must, but my acquiescence will not be obtained with ease," he said in a firm tone.

"Your acquiescence will not be required!" Gharr retorted as he turned to leave. "Beware the next time our paths cross," he threatened over his shoulder as he stormed out.

Once Gharr was gone, Luziaph turned his three-eyed gaze upon her. "You had better hope your man, Araset, returns with my sword soon," he said, darkly. He turned his head back toward the exit and added, "For both our sakes."

Sarah shared a look of concern with Gazianna, and could only wonder why Luziaph had called Allen by a different name. The blue-skinned woman seemed to understand the silent plea in her eyes as she nodded for Sarah to follow her away from the throne room. With their limited capacity to communicate the two women had developed a natural understanding; Gazianna would lead the conversation in a way which would allow her to nod or shake her head in response. On rare occasions Sarah would use minor hand gestures to convey additional thoughts.

As they moved down the corridor away from where Luziaph still stood, she nudged Gazianna and nodded her head back toward the throne room.

Gazianna acknowledged the nod and continued forward. "Lord Luziaph plays a dangerous game," she said. When she gestured that she didn't quite understand, Gazianna continued. "It was he who sent word of your presence here to other realms, by way of discreet messenger."

Another look of shocked confusion prompted Gazianna to elaborate further. "The Triclopian, Dhagorath, was charged with travelling to other lands to whisper rumors of prophecy in the ears of any who will listen, as he has the skill of moving with great speed. His brother, Rexim, was sent with Araset and Pythor toward the purpose of ensuring delivery of the legendary blade of Sythika."

Sarah's mind spun with the implications of what Gazianna had just said. Why would Luzaiph call the attention of all of Datheron to the prophecy he believed to be about Allen when it had been he who'd sent Allen to ignite it? To Sarah it seemed a reckless path without proof of its validity, especially considering it could potentially prevent him from obtaining that which he so obviously desired. She shuddered to think of how this would play out; she couldn't see it ending well for her or Allen.

Grim thoughts dominated her mind as she and Gazianna resumed the duties from which they had been removed just a short while ago. She felt increasingly vulnerable the longer Allen was away from her, and with the direction events seemed to be moving she was uncertain she would ever see him again at all. Learning that he would have to be trained in combat with a sword had only increased her level of concern.

At night she would dream of him showing up to save her, carrying her off in his arms back home and away from this dreadful place; though more and more she found herself willing to accept her fate if only they could be together when it happened.

Allen had always seemed so strong, so confident. She could use some of that strength now.

She continued to follow Gazianna throughout the palace, letting her mind drift as they performed task after mindless task. So lost in thought was she that she hadn't even realized until much later that she had spaced out the entire chore in the detention block. Despite her best efforts not to dwell on it, she found herself counting the minutes of Allen's absence, hoping with each passing one that he would show up to rescue her.

33

GRADIUS

THE DAYS OF TRAINING WERE INTENSE and arduous as Pythor passed on his knowledge of combat to Allen. They began every morning as the sun was still rising and continued until the light of day was fading in earnest, only taking breaks to eat the food that Rexim had hunted and prepared for them. Neither of the Triclopians seemed pleased with the length of their stay at the edge of the lake, but kept their thoughts on the subject concealed most of the time. Pythor, on the other hand, left his thoughts out in the open as if daring either one of the others to prove his distrust of them to be accurate, as if challenging them to give him reason to prove his dominance in this mission. While the tension he had felt in the air that first night had never completely subsided, the training had been so all-consuming that he had barely noticed it since.

Allen had lost track of time as Pythor taught him not only to wield a sword and shield, but how to be aware of his surroundings as he put them to use. Both he and Pythor had been impressed by the speed with which he was learning; Pythor doing everything he could to accelerate Allen's progress. In the evenings after eating their final meal of the day, the Gorrlock would insist that Ithaniel use his minor knowledge in the art of healing, one of the Triclopian's many skills, to bring relief to his aching muscles so that they could start fresh the next morning. The way Pythor and Ithaniel would tend to him brought thoughts of Malacus to his mind. The old man had nursed his aching muscles back to health on more than one occasion during their brief time together, though his methods were wholly different. He could still scarcely believe Malacus was gone.

Even with the attention and effort Pythor would give him as they trained, it was clear he was learning quicker than either of them had anticipated. More than once he had surprised Pythor as much as he had himself by deflecting or dodging a maneuver which had previously caught him off-guard, allowing his blue-skinned insctructor to best him. When Allen had made comment that he must be a natural with a sword, Pythor had deflated his ego by explaining that the benefits of learning any skill one desired extended from Datheron to the surface of Sythar, if only fractionally so. He wanted to question the remark by bringing up the fact that he was still hindered by a Triaga, but thought better of it after only a moment's consideration.

As Allen improved in skill it became his responsibility to begin taking shifts watching over the others while they slept. The other three had been splitting the watch among themselves since that first night, allowing him to sleep without interruption. But when Rexim returned from a hunt one particular day, witnessing one of the few times when he'd been able to hold Pythor to a standstill for several minutes, the Triclopian complained that Allen seemed capable enough to begin joining in the responsibility. Though obviously offended by the way in which it had been presented, Pythor agreed and had assigned him first watch that very night; Pythor, whose distrust of the Triclopians was always evident, took his watch second. Allen often wondered if Pythor even attempted to sleep while it was their shift; it wouldn't be a stretch to say Pythor didn't trust them to wake him or Allen in the event of a crisis.

Allen had been nervous the first couple of nights, but quickly learned that the chore was more lonely than eventful. Only once had there been an incident, and it had taken place during Pythor's watch. The high-pitched, visceral cry of a beast had echoed across the lake, waking everyone. But by the time he'd grabbed his weapons and risen, the situation had been dealt with; a large creature, which closely resembled a gorilla fused with a wolf, bearing four eyes on its head and a long whip-like tail, rested unmoving at Pythor's feet.

In the beginning it had taken Allen nearly everything he had just to follow Pythor's movements; the man was capable of such fluid speed and precision that the task of mimicking what was being demonstrated, even at a slower pace, presented great challenge. However, a few short weeks had Allen in better physical condition than he'd ever been able to achieve while on Earth; capable of improvising and compensating his movements in order to adapt to his attacker with greater ease than he believed possible. With the length his hair was reaching, the shape his body was taking on, not to mention the full beard now covering his face, he doubted that even his own mother would recognize him anymore. The thought occurred to him that he probably very closely resembled his father in appearance now.

As the sun set on one of their more grueling sessions, sweat sluicing profusely over his entire form, he was able to catch the tip of Pythor's blade in the nook along the edge of his shield. He twisted the shield against

Pythor's momentum, at the same time bringing his left foot up underneath his attacker's legs, and slamming the hilt of his own sword into the Gorrlock's blue nose. The maneuver was so swift, so reactionary, that it caught even Allen off guard.

The two Triclopians rose from their seats next to the fire, looks of shock dominating their features. Pythor lay on his back, blood oozing lightly from his nostrils. For a brief moment panic rushed through him; fear of how Pythor might retaliate flooded his mind. Then the realization hit him: This was the first time he had bested his instructor in this way and he refused to squander the opportunity to capitalize on it. Kicking Pythor's sword away, he placed his boot on the black chest-plate, and rested the tip of his blade under Pythor's chin.

"Submit," he'd said, breathing heavily.

Pythor laughed so suddenly, so loudly, that he'd withdrawn his sword from its place against Pythor's throat. In an instant Pythor had clutched Allen's foot, twisted his ankle, and sent him sprawling to the ground several feet away. As he'd scrambled to reclaim his footing, he found himself in the same position in which he had held Pythor only moments before, a boot on his chest and Pythor's open palm outstretched toward his face.

"In a true battle upon Datheron and Sythar alike," Pythor admonished, his expression once again turning serious, "victory requires no blade in hand, nor does it require feet firmly planted upon the ground." He paused a moment, as if to let the words sink in, then shifted his palm to offer him a hand up from his back.

After helping Allen to his feet, Pythor dusted himself off, reclaimed both swords from the dirt, and extended Allen's back to him, hilt first.

He nodded his appreciation and understanding and took the sword in hand, slamming it home into its scabbard.

As they approached the others, who were still gaping at what had just transpired, ready for their evening meal, Pythor had surprised them all, declaring Allen ready and informing them that they would depart for their final destination immediately following dinner. The announcement surprised him more than it appeared to surprise the others, causing the pace of his heart to begin racing from more than just the exertion of the workout he'd just completed.

While they ate, Pythor explained that their destination lay on the other side of the vast Windavian desert, and that travelling at night would be the safest way for them to survive the journey ahead. He'd grown so accustomed to the daily training sessions, to his immediate surroundings, that he had pushed his main objective to the back of his mind. Now that his training was evidently complete, anxiety over the imminent dangers he would be facing slowly began to overwhelm him. Pythor had never elaborated on what the trials of Sythika would consist of, but Allen felt certain that his life would weigh in the balance if he failed.

Allen did what he could to shake the fear from his mind by reminding himself why he had embarked on this expedition: Sarah. Her last words still rang in his mind with clarity, giving him strength to do what he must to keep her safe, to earn passage back to Earth. He could only hope that she was managing on her own without him, that Gazianna was keeping her promise to watch out for Sarah while he was away.

Once their meal was finished they gathered their things in preparation. Allen, Pythor and Ithaniel wiped every trace of their stay by the lake away while Rexim gathered other provisions they would need as they traversed a sea of sand. Once they had everything they needed, they said goodbye to the beach which had been their home for the last few weeks. Allen was the only one who looked back over his shoulder before they reentered the jungle in the same place from which they had emerged weeks before.

***

The journey itself had presented new challenges to the four travelers. By the time they reached the edge of the desert on the other side of the jungle, night was in full swing and threatening to come to a close. They moved with haste and purpose as they exposed themselves to the elements outside the protective canopy of the wooded enclosure behind them. His legs burned from the effort, but he continued to lift one in front of the other, kicking sand away from him as he moved. Promises of a cave ahead in which they could shelter themselves from the coming heat were the strength behind his every footfall. The others didn't seem to be struggling with the sand quite as much as he was, but he refused to be left behind; he would do Sarah no good if he died before he could complete his objective.

For two full nights they trekked across the dunes and valleys of the desert, somehow always finding a cave in which to shelter themselves before the sun was too high in the sky. Pythor seemed to know exactly where he was going, causting Allen to wonder how many times the man had made this journey before on his own.

When they awoke on the third evening, they found themselves unable to venture out of the cave due to a severe sandstorm. Intense winds kicked millions of granules of sand past the exit and littered the first ten feet of the cave with dust.

Allen was forced to shield his nose and mouth in the nook of his elbow, squinting against the intrusion as he crouched in a corner with the others awaiting the end of the storm. By the time it was over they had all but been sealed away in the cave and only a sliver of the sky could be seen already turning a lighter shade of blue-violet through the gap between the wall of sand and the ceiling. It took a tremendous amount of work to clear the exit and they ended up spending another long day in the dark enclosure.

By the time they could finally see their destination in the distance a couple of mornings later, Allen's boots were full of sand again and he was already becoming overheated from exertion. When the peak of the mountain had first come into view the sun hadn't quite emerged from behind its rigid cap; bright pink and orange clouds painted the skyline surrounding it. He had allowed himself to feel relief when he'd first spotted it, not realizing how far they still had to travel to reach their goal. It wasn't until the sun was well past its zenith that they could make out the make-shift domiciles of the village at the mountain's base. He was so miserably overheated by the time they trudged toward the small desert community that his vision had become blurred and his sense of hearing had become muffled. His tongue felt swollen and cracked in his mouth. In that moment he would have given just about anything to dive into the lake he'd left behind a few days before.

As they approached the entrance to their destination at last, Gorrlocks could be seen exiting their homes and gathering in a cluster around a large statue which rested in the very center of the village. There was mumbling all around and all eyes were intently focused on the intruders emerging from the desert. Pythor took the lead when the crowd parted to reveal an old Gorrlock all in black, who was supporting his weight with a thick walking stick. Allen thought it far too hot to be wearing robes as thick as the ones on the old man, especially black ones, but was far too exhausted to offer a remark.

"Greetings, honored elder," Pythor began, bowing his head and holding his arms out to his side away from his body.

The old man looked Pythor up and down before he responded, as if trying to decide whether or not the black armor were genuine. "For what purpose do you bring outsiders to this most sacred of locations, Krathantor?" the elder retorted harshly.

"Events outside the measure of control have ushered me to this place," Pythor answered in a grave tone of his own. "I have been guided by the very hand of prophecy, to reclaim that which has remained under your protection since the time of Paragus."

There was a collective gasp from the crowd surrounding the elder, followed by worried murmuring. The elder Gorrlock was the only one who showed no reaction.

"Then it is as I feared," the old man said in a low tone. His black and red eyes fell on Allen and the two Triclopians; Allen thought he saw a look of distaste in those eyes while they lingered on Rexim and Ithaniel. "This must be the one," he said as his gaze once again found Allen.

"Indeed," Pythor answered.

"The sight of him falls short of expectations," said the old Gorrlock.

Allen might have been offended if he could focus on anything other than the debilitating effects of dehydration consuming him.

The old man drew much closer, looking Allen up and down as if to gauge his worth by sight alone. He poked at Allen's armor, clamped his hands around Allen's biceps, tilted Allen's chin in various directions, and walked a full circle around Allen as he continued to examine the supposed child of prophecy. Allen's knees were shaking from the journey he'd just completed and he desperately wanted to hydrate himself and lay down somewhere. He was feeling irritable and the last thing he wanted was to face any tests this soon, but he didn't have the energy to voice his protest.

The old man's hands found the Triaga upon Allen's scalp. "Why does he bear that which binds the use of Mystica?" he asked, the words directed at Pythor.

Before Pythor could offer any type of a response, Ithaniel stepped forward, answering in his stead. "Both of these men are captives of Lord Luziaph, Proctus of Vardiston. The Triagas are to remain upon their heads."

The elder Gorrlock cast a brief, icy look at Ithaniel and then turned his attention back to Pythor. "You bear the mark of a slave as well?" he asked with incredulity. When Pythor nodded, the old man shook his head in what Allen could only assume was disappointment. "This will not do at all," he muttered, bringing his eyes back to Allen.

The old man stepped close to Allen, reached his hands up and placed his fingers lightly upon the Triaga. He slowly closed his eyes in concentration. There was a low humming noise that was almost immediately interrupted by shouting and movement all around. He looked past the old man to see many weapons raised, as well as a few empty palms, all of which seemed to be full of emerald fire and aimed directly at him. It took him several moments to realize they were looking behind him. He turned to see Ithaniel frozen in mid-step seemingly reconsidering a previous course of action.

After a long moment of hesitation, Ithaniel turned his attention back to the Gorrlock elder. "Their Triagas must not be removed," he warned, though surrounded as he was the words sounded feeble, more like he was pleading.

"Your Lord Luziaph holds no authority over this place," the old, blue-skinned man stated flatly. "If this boy truly is the one spoken of in sacred words of old, then the use of Mystica must not be encumbered. To face the Trials of Sythika will require more than just skill with a blade."

Ithaniel seemed to be considering how to reply to the old man's ultimatum. "So be it," he said at last. "However, the Krathantor is to remain as he is lest I return with the wrath of Luziaph as my ally."

The elder's white hair danced lightly across his face as a breeze cut across them all. He glared at the Triclopian with intensity for several heartbeats before turning his attention back to Allen. Once again he placed his fingers along the Triaga on Allen's scalp. The same low humming sound filled the air with such force that Allen could feel the vibrations coursing through his entire body. His vision blurred completely. He felt so light-headed he thought he might pass out and would not have been at all surprised to find himself on the ground once the world returned to his eyes.

After what felt like a very long time he heard a distinct clicking sound and life returned returned to the world around him. He could feel the Triaga slipping off the back of his head, and as it did his senses were flooded with beautiful chaos. He was whole again in an instant; it was like waking for the first time in years.

As the world came back into focus around him, his senses were overwhelmed with a disorienting sensation. The air tasted better, colors seemed more vibrant, and pain seemed more intense. He watched as the ground moved closer to him very quickly, unable to do anything to prevent it. He clutched at the dirt beneath him while his body went into shock. His entire world shook. He was sure the intensity of it all was killing him.

But it couldn't end like this. He refused to let it.

Digging deep within himself, he focused his will on that which he knew could give him the strength to push through this pain. He couldn't understand why having a

Triaga removed would have this kind of effect on him; it hadn't been like this when Luziaph removed it the last time. But none of that mattered at the moment. Sarah needed him to succeed. For her he could endure anything and he would push through this. He still didn't like the idea that the fate of so many could rest upon his shoulders, that he may indeed be the child of prophecy, but he would even accept that fate if that's what it took to spare Sarah from the torment he was sure she now faced under Luziaph's patronage.

In an instant the storm raging within him was over. Bringing himself back to his full height, he somehow felt almost entirely refreshed. He had no clue how he had done it, or what had happened, but he somehow had even expelled most of the exhaustion which had been dominating him only moments before. Looks of genuine amazement were on the faces of all present as he inhaled a cleansing breath and once again took stock of his surroundings. Allen noted that the Triaga was still gripped firmly in the old Gorrlock's right hand.

"That is some skill you possess," the old man said.

Allen looked to Pythor who seemed far more impressed than anyone else present. "What skill?" he asked no one in particular. "What just happened?" He looked back and forth among the faces closest to him; they all seemed surprised by what they had just witnessed.

"Does the boy jest?" the old man asked.

Pythor shook his head. "He has little to no training in the art of manipulating Mystica. The boy hails from Earth."

"By Paragus," the old man whispered, a look of reverence covering his features. Pythor's words, coupled with what he'd apparently just done, seemed to have suddenly altered the old man's opinion of the situation. "Could this boy truly be the one for whom we have waited centuries?" he said with astonishment. After gaping at him for what seemed an eternity, the old man turned and walked back toward the crowd of Gorrlocks behind him. "Come," he called over his shoulder. "We have much to prepare if we are to begin the trials at the rise of the new sun."

Allen wasn't sure if he would be ready by tomorrow morning, but realized he had little choice in the matter at this point. He glanced to Pythor, who nodded that he should follow the elder's lead. Allen turned back toward the old man and rushed to catch up. "What must I do to prepare?" he asked as he fell in step beside the Gorrlock elder.

"You misunderstand," the old man replied, keeping his eyes in front of him. "It is not yours to prepare this night. Tonight we feast to celebrate your arrival . . . for tomorrow you face the very jaws of Sythika."

34

SKILL

PARAGUS STARED DOWN at Allen from the center of the Gorrlock village. The statue Allen had seen from a distance as he and the others approached from the desert had been crafted in the image of the original God-King of Datheron, whom the locals still evidently served. Though not quite as sharp in detail as the statues which decorated Luziaph's palace, and looking very much as if time had weathered its once vibrant features, it still cut an imposing image against the desolate backdrop of the village Allen had come to learn was known as Gradius. Coupled with that was the fact that the village rested at the foot of a very large, dangerous looking mountain, making the setting in which he would face the trials as forbidding as he could have imagined.

Allen gazed up at the carved figure of the man who had somehow foreordained his fate. Datheron's first supreme ruler appeared to Allen as if he must have been human in life, or was at least similar in features. His wavy hair came down to the nape of his neck. A stern-looking brow overshadowed severe cheek bones and a slightly elongated nose. A thick beard covered the man's strong jaw, and his body was adorned with an ornate, yet somehow simply designed, full suit of armor. Allen let his eyes wander down the frame of the sculpture. He took in every detail of that armor; it seemed somehow familiar to him, as if he'd seen it before in a dream. An intricate weave traced its way around the defining lines of what would be the muscles beneath the suit. The shoulders were covered in layered pads, the elbows and knees were likewise protected by padding which jutted from the edges of the boots and gauntlets. It looked at once to be regal and fierce, practical and elaborate. He couldn't take his eyes off of it.

Lost in thought as he was, he didn't notice when Pythor approached from behind to stand next to him. "This statue has maintained its vigil for thousands of years," the Gorrlock stated. Allen started when Pythor spoke, but was unable to remove his eyes from the haunting visage before him as the Krathantor continued: "It was Paragus who chose my kind to be His elite body guards. He is legend among all upon Datheron, for He brought with him civility upon His arrival."

Allen pondered Pythor's words as he began slowly moving around the base of the statue, taking in more of its elaborate details. What Pythor had just said brought a great many questions to his mind. "Paragus brought with Him civility?" Allen repeated. "Was He not originally from Datheron?" He of course recalled the story Malacus had told him about Paragus and his thousand year reign over Datheron, but something in him wanted to know how much honesty he could expect from Pythor . . . or Malacus, for that matter.

Pythor shook his head. "It is impossible to know from where Paragus truly hails," he replied, thoughtfully.

"Very little of His past is known by any. It is known only that He descended from the heavens, bringing with Him all concepts of modern infrastructure and government. There was a great crisis near the end of His reign which heralded the potential to learn His Godly secrets."

"You speak of the six Orbs of Sythika," he said, finally turning his gaze from the statue.

Pythor jerked his head toward Allen. "How is it you possess such knowledge?" he asked in amazement.

Allen watched Pythor's demeanor change at hearing of his knowledge on the subject. He wanted to trust Pythor, the man who had trained him in combat for the last month or more, but memories of how the Krathantor had tricked him into leaving Earth lingered in the back of his mind. Coupled with those doubts was the knowledge that his great grandfather, Malacus, a former God-King, had purposely remained in seclusion for who knows how long out of fear of being discovered by the Krathantor.

"I had the chance to meet my great grandfather shortly following my arrival," Allen said, resolving to admit the truth, while keeping his answers vague. "It was he who revealed the words of prophecy to me and the truth of events which led to its delivery."

Pythor seemed momentarily dubious while he considered Allen's answer, but nodded after a moment and continued his thoughts, bringing his focus back to the statue before him. "Legend speaks of Paragus exhausting His entire knowledge to remedy the crisis of the orbs. It was not until the crisis had abated that Paragus decided to share the knowledge of the Gods with His most faithful." Pythor paused a moment, as if lost in thought. "Some say the crisis revealed to Paragus a sense of mortality, inspiring the desire to not see His Godly secrets lost to time.

"Shortly before Sythika took Him, Paragus brought the very blade for which we have travelled to the surface of Sythar, entrusting knowledge of its location to only His most trusted Krathantor. Once He was gone . . . those most loyal to Him travelled here to join in the guarding of the legendary blade until time would finally choose to reveal the child of which Paragus spoke with His final prophetic breath."

Pythor once again brought his eyes to meet Allen's. "It is for this reason that my people prepare a feast this night. They celebrate the fact that the directive given by Paragus, Himself, has been successfully seen to completion. Your arrival brings with it the ability to rejoice in a job well done."

Allen looked around to the bustling activity consuming the village. The Gorrlocks didn't appear to be rejoicing over anything; their features remained expressionless as they carried dishes and food from one place to another, cooked the food, and finalized other preparations. The inhabitants of Gradius had not been particularly warm toward him or any of the others since their arrival, though he imagined centuries of isolation would make it difficult for anyone to be open with strangers. He felt a distinct pang of sorrow for his hosts at the realization.

Allen felt a hand on his shoulder and jerked his head toward Pythor.

"It is with this understanding that I implore you to reconsider your spoken agreement with Luziaph," Pythor said in a low tone. "In our time together I have come to consider you ally . . . and you have a natural talent which far exceeds previous expectations. You must not forsake the sacrifices my people have made to keep the Sword of Sythika from the wrong hands."

Allen could hear genuine desperation in Pythor's words; an emotion he had never before known the man to be capable of. He glanced down at Pythor's hand on his right shoulder, uncertain how to respond to the request given. "I consider you ally as well," he said, keeping his own eyes from meeting Pythor's. "And I do not wish to forsake that for which your people have so effortlessly given countless lifetimes. But what do you think will happen to Sarah, to your brothers who now stand trapped in the bowels of Luziaph's palace, should I fail to meet conditions of the bargain struck?"

Pythor removed his hand, a look dejection filling his black and red eyes. "My brothers would willingly go into the hands of Sythika to keep the blade from one such as he," he said with disgust. "You put far too much faith in the honor of that Triclopian vermin! He will betray the agreement with you the moment he has that for which he so willingly risks your life! Mark my words: you consign your woman and my brethren to death if you believe his words to be honest, if you hand over the blade spoken of in prophecy!"

Allen hated the idea of inspiring disappointment in anyone, especially one whom he considered to be a friend. But how could he willingly disregard his own word or the life of the woman he loved more than anything else? He turned his gaze from Pythor so he wouldn't have to endure that look of disappointment while he considered his options. No matter how hard he thought, or from which direction he approached the situation, he saw no easy way out. Every option seemed to end in its own distinct failure; some bearing consequences more severe than others. For a moment he wished once more that he could remove himself from the equation, but he knew that wishing alone was never a viable solution.

He brought his eyes back up to meet Pythor's. "I will remain open to other possibilities, should they present themselves," he told his blue-skinned companion. "But I can see no way out of the agreement at the present. If a solution finds its way to your mind, I will hear your words."

Pythor didn't seem quite satisfied, but nodded all the same. "Gratitude," he said after a moment's hesitation. With that Pythor left Allen to his own thoughts as he went to join his kin in the preparations.

Allen remained at the base of the statue for the duration of the day. He wasn't entirely sure why, but he just couldn't compel himself to leave its side. It was from there that he watched as the Gorrlocks prepared a large fire pit roughly twenty yards from where he stood, between the statue and the mountain. With a snap of her fingers, one of the Gorrlock women ignited the center of the pit, bringing to life a large green flame. Pythor nodded his approval to the woman and moved to where the Gorrlock elder stood, watching the preparations. Allen caught the two glancing his way as they conversed and couldn't help feeling as if he were the topic of discussion. He hoped Pythor wasn't revealing Allen's intentions to deliver the sword to another.

Allen likewise kept watch on Rexim and Ithaniel, who remained near the outskirts of the village not saying much to one another and speaking in hushed tones when they did. It could have been Pythor's influence, or some other sixth sense, but the more he watched the two together the less he trusted them. He had to consider that perhaps they just felt out of place in a village which consisted of a race known for its hatred of their kind. Such a thing could make anyone feel out of place. But something just didn't feel right about the distance at which they were keeping themselves. Perhaps it was the look in their eyes, or the spiteful expressions which seemed to so constantly consume their features; he couldn't be certain. But it did seem as if they were purposely remaining far enough away to prevent being overheard.

When at last the sun neared the horizon in the distance, the elder Gorrlock called for all present to gather around the fire to begin the festivities. As Allen drew closer, finally leaving the comfort of the statue behind him, six Gorrlocks, positioned at alternating points around the fire pit, began an interesting show of light. Each reached toward the green flames, pulling from it a ball of fire the size of a baseball and proceeded to pass it over the dancing light in the center to one another. Back and forth the glowing balls of liquid light flew through the air, from one hand to the next, sometimes going directly over the pit in the center of their circle and at other times being passed directly to the person to their left. With the fading light of day, the effect was as mesmerizing as it was haunting.

With each new fireball drawn from the pit the speed of their dance increased, as did the strength of their chanting, which Allen had not noticed at all at first. Faster and faster the balls of green light moved until the entire village was illuminated by an emerald glow. When the speed of their movements reached a point at which the light seemed but a blur of motion, the chanting became much louder and the flaming orbs began to be thrown skyward. With each one released, the word being chanted was expelled with fluid unity. As the lights reached a goodly distance above the gathered crowd, they burst in every direction at once. For Allen, it was like watching a fireworks display on the fourth of July. He couldn't help but smile at the memory.

Only when the bursting lights faded did he realize that the shroud of night had completely fallen over them. The chanting died all at once and he looked around to find every eye on the elder, who had his hands raised to the sky, drawing the attention of all in attendance.

"We gather this night to see our vigil over the Sword of Sythika come to an end!" the old man shouted. "For time has finally revealed to us the child of prophecy, the one for whom we have waited for countless centuries! With him comes the beginning of a new age: the return of Paragus!"

With the old man's proclamation, a wave of trepidation shot through Allen. He recalled what Malacus had said about the original God-King's brutality and glanced over his shoulder at the statue crafted in the man's image, suddenly reminded of the magnitude the consequences of his actions might bear. How could he be responsible for bringing that brutality back to life? His heart thudded in his chest as he brought his eyes back to the elder, still shouting his words into the night.

The old man's eyes found Allen through the dancing flames. "When the new sun rises fate will stand before you in a test of wills! You will face our finest blades master in a contest to the death, to prove your skill with a sword is sufficient to wield one of legend! Should you succeed; the second challenge will be revealed to you!"

It took several moments for the old man's words to register in his mind. "Wait!" Allen shouted over the elder's words, drawing attention to himself. "I am to face another in mortal combat?"

The old man nodded once, the flames between them casting emerald highlights across his weathered features as he did.

"What if I refuse?" Allen challenged. "I will not so willingly end the life of another!"

The elder's expression darkened. "Make no mistake," he warned, "Regardless of decision made, your own life weighs in the balance. To wield the Sword of

Sythika one must be willing to administer death. It is impossible to put the legendary blade to any other purpose. To be pierced by it, however slight, is certain doom."

Allen caught a look of warning coming from Pythor and decided to remain silent as the elder continued:

"The Trials of Sythika are a perilous journey! Only the true child of prophecy can face them and live; only he can wield the blade which once belonged to Paragus! Now! Let us feast on food this night, for tomorrow brings with it a feast of the eyes!"

With that, the Gorrlocks dispersed, some beginning to dance around the fire while others turned to filling their stomachs. Allen could see several Gorrlock children dueling each other with wooden swords and laughing. He could finally see mirth in some of the eyes which surrounded him, but felt no happiness in his heart as he considered what tomorrow would bring. How could they expect him to kill one of their own, and be eager to witness it? He had never before killed anything larger than a bug; the thought of ending another person's life was making him sick to his stomach. He knew Pythor had been training him for a purpose but he hadn't considered that he might be required to kill to obtain the Sword of Sythika.

A sharp nudge in his side woke Allen the next morning. With great effort he opened his eyes, the intrusion of light blurring his vision at first. Dreams of his mother being torn from him by Gorrlocks, or Sarah being put in compromising positions by a gang of Triclopians had haunted him all night. It wasn't until he'd pulled himself to an upright position, and his eyesight had adjusted to the light, that he'd realized that he was less excited to be awake than he was to escape such nightmares.

Pythor was looking down at him, his left hand extended in a gesture intended to help Allen to his feet.

"You meet your destiny this morning," he said. "How do your faculties greet you?"

"With great resistance," he replied, taking the Gorrlock's hand.

Pythor harrumphed. "Well, gather them to your aid, lest you find yourself permanently at rest." Though the words had sounded harsf, Allen nodded his understanding; more than just his pride rested on the outcome of the trials.

Allen stretched in an effort to banish the sleep from his aching muscles. The ground on which he had slept was unforgiving, leaving a lingering stiffness to his movements. Not much else was said as he followed Pythor to prepare for his first trial. He declined an offer of food, deciding he would rather spend his time warming up and work the stiffness from his muscles in preparation for what was to come.

He and Pythor sparred lightly while the rest of the village came to life. The clatter of their swords called to the children of the village, who gathered around them, looking very excited about what the day had in store for them. He did not share their enthusiasm. Rather, he placed all his effort toward focusing on Pythor's attacks, letting himself be completely absorbed in the task. He knew that very soon the moment for which he had trained so hard would be upon him and that it would test more than just his skill with a blade. The elder's words from the night before still rang in his mind with daunting clarity, "Regardless of decision made, your own life weighs in the balance." He could scarcely believe that he would quite literally be fighting for his life, that being proclaimed the victor would require him to kill. It seemed to Allen he would be losing regardless of the outcome; he didn't believe himself capable of taking the life of another.

Sooner than expected Allen heard the elder Gorrlock's voice calling for everyone to gather where the feast had taken place the night before. He couldn't stop his knees from shaking as he followed Pythor to the appointed place. And though he could see the anticipation in every face, feel it radiating in the air all around him as Pythor patted him on the shoulder in a gesture of encouragement, he could barely take it in. The entire village had gathered around him and the elder, enclosing them in a circle.

"The time has come," the old man announced, raising his arms above his head. A gust of warm air passed through the circle, causing his white hair to lift from his face, and his robes to ripple as if in a dance. "I offer one final chance to turn from this course before the door of prophecy closes at your back," he added, meeting Allen's gaze.

All eyes found Allen as they awaited his response. A very large part of him wanted to take the offer, to back away gracefully while he still could. But he had come too far and there was far too much at stake to turn away from the path before him now. He steeled himself. "I will not turn away!" he shouted.

The old man nodded his understanding and motioned for someone unseen to step forward. The crowd parted and a Gorrlock boy stepped into the center of the circle. He didn't appear to be quite as old as Allen was, and held a sword in either hand. The boy was slightly shorter than Pythor and was completely bald. The sight of the dual blades left Allen feeling more nervous than before; it was a style of fighting with which he had no training or experience. The boy appeared more resolute, but Allen thought he saw a hint of anxiety in those black and red eyes.

The old man placed both hands on the boy's shoulders, holding him at arm's length. "Fight well and go without fear into the arms of Sythika should you fail in the task set before you." The boy nodded and the elder of the

Gorrlock tribe released him and disappeared into the crowd of spectators.

Showing no hesitation, the blue-skinned boy charged at him, swinging both of his weapons with deliberate ferocity. Allen blocked and deflected each attack by a narrow margin and found himself being pushed back with every strike. He had not expected his opponent to begin so quickly or aggressively and chastised himself for being caught off-guard. At the last possible moment he was able to sidestep a thrust and counter by bashing his opponent in the shoulder with his shield; the maneuver afforded him the opportunity to gain some distance to regroup.

The boy quickly shook off the attack and fell into step as Allen began pacing the perimeter of their would-be arena in a tight circle. This time he decided to initiate the conflict, rushing forward and bringing the sword in his right hand down in an overhand slashing motion. His opponent deflected with ease every slash, swipe, and thrust he threw. The boy seemed content to let Allen press his attack, as if he were just toying with him.

With almost blinding speed, the Gorrlock boy spun past yet another thrust and in one fluid motion brought the pommel of his own sword crashing into the back of Allen's skull. A flash of light momentarily stole his vision, followed almost immediately by dirt filling his mouth. Purely on instinct, he pushed himself up off the ground and to the side as the blade of his opponent's sword was buried into the ground where his torso had been a fraction of a moment before. He threw all his weight down onto the flat side of the blade, twisting his body as he rolled across it toward the hand still gripping it. The maneuver forced the sword out of the boy's hand and allowed him to put all his momentum into his own strike as he forced the heel of his weapon to collide with his adversary's jaw bone.

The Gorrlock boy staggered backward. Allen leapt to his feet and slammed a front kick into the blue sternum with crushing force. While the other fell to the ground and attempted to regain his composure, Allen planted his blade into the ground, reached down for the boy's fallen sword, and heaved it with all his might over the head of every spectator present. He could hear it clatter to the ground somewhere in the distance as he reclaimed his own weapon.

As the boy found his feet once more, the realization of what he had just done registered in the boy's crimson eyes. A mild look of concern crossed his features. An instant later he was rushing at Allen with renewed savagery, his attacks coming almost recklessly . . . desperate. Again and again the boy slashed and stabbed at him; there seemed to be no end to his stamina.

A sharp pain shot all the way through Allen's right arm as his opponent's blade found its mark along his right shoulder, forcing his grip to slacken on the hilt. A moment later, he watched with terror as his own blade flew through the air into the Gorrlock boy's grip. Now he had nothing but the shield clutched in his left hand with which to defend himself.

The boy grinned wickedly at him. He began to show off, flourishing both weapons in every direction with grace and speed, taunting Allen. When he was through with displaying his skill, the boy held Allen's sword up for all to see and then tossed it into the distance with the other.

For what seemed an eternity the blue-skinned boy hacked and slashed at Allen's shield. The Gorrlock boy bashed at his only means of defense until Allen was certain he would cut right through it. He tried to reclaim any semblance of control to no avail. In short order he found himself on his knees, his shield raised above his head, and bleeding from multiple flesh-wounds on his legs and torso, matching the one on his right shoulder.

For a moment Allen saw the end coming. He knew he was about to die.

When the assault stopped for several seconds, Allen risked a glance over the top of his shield to find the boy walking a small circle, his arms raised in victory as he engaged the crowd. A moment later, in a flash of fury, the boy turned and rushed toward him for the final thrust. Time seemed to slow as the sword moved toward him in a direct line. He shifted his weight, repositioned his shield slightly, and let the blade slide into the notch along its edge. Twisting the shield as he stood up, he forced the blade from the boy's grip and sent it clattering away from them both. With tremendous force he slammed his shield against the boy's face in a back-handed motion, tossing him to the ground several feet away.

Almost without thinking he called the blade to his palm from its place at the feet of the crowd. Marching toward his fallen opponent, he slammed his foot against the boy's chest, and held the tip of the sword a scant inch away from his face.

"You are beaten," he panted. "Submit!"

A look of confusion crossed the boy's face. "This challenge can only end in death," he answered.

Allen took a deep, calming breath. "What name do you go by?"

"Senjin," the boy replied, confusion still dominating his features.

"Senjin," Allen repeated patiently. "Do you wish to die?"

"No," Senjin answered.

Allen nodded, "And I do not wish to end you. Submit and I will let you live."

The boy seemed torn by the offer. He looked over his shoulder at his peers, desperate for an answer to be revealed.

With a jabbing motion, he applied weight to his boot planted against Senjin's chest. "It is a simple matter to choose life over death!" he chided. "A choice which falls to you alone! So, choose!"

Tears slowly filled those black and red eyes as they gazed up at Allen, the look bordering hateful. "I choose to live," Senjin answered in a whisper. "I submit."

With that Allen tossed the sword and shield to the ground and offered Senjin his right hand. Now that he knew the battle was over, every knick and gash began to ache with renewed intensity as he helped the Gorrlock boy up off the ground. Senjin looked at Allen with shame as he reached his feet.

Allen patted him on the shoulder, offering a small reassuring smile, then turned to the crowd. "I have proven my skill with a blade to be true," he called in a raised voice. "I have done so absent the need to take Senjin's life!"

The crowd parted as the elder Gorrlock stepped forward. "The trials are in place for a reason," he said with outrage in his eyes. "To wield the blade of death one cannot shy away from the administering of it! You must end the life of your opponent!"

"I refuse!" he answered, allowing his own anger to flare to the surface. "The first trial was put in place to prove worth with a blade, not willingness to kill! I have done so! I will not end the life of another out of sport, nor will I do so to sate the requirements of some antiquated ritual! Death and the administering of it is not something which should be embraced with willingness!"

For a very long moment, the elder stood mute as he considered Allen's words. A scowl tainted his already severe features as he grinded his teeth. Finally the old man expelled a deep breath. "So be it. Gather yourself and tend to your wounds. The second trial will begin at the rising of the new sun."

The crowd was silent as the old man turned his back on Allen and marched away.

35

RESOLVE

THE FLESH WOUNDS LEFT BEHIND from Allen's battle with Senjin stung and itched as Ithaniel closed them with a slow wave of his hand. Numb to all else around him while the Triclopian worked his magic, he kept playing the events of the morning over in his mind, unable to prevent his nerves from shaking at the thought of how close he'd come to death. After an experience like that, being beaten up by Brad and the others in front of the whole school so long ago seemed almost laughable; though it had happened only a few months before, it seemed like a lifetime ago. It had been mortifying at the time, yet he now found himself wishing he could go back to those simpler circumstances. He realized that he would much rather be living his old, boring life than facing death head-on.

When Ithaniel was finished, Allen stood up and stretched his muscles. Phantom pains left in the wake of his injuries still tingled as he worked his limbs; the sensation was extremely awkward, bringing to mind the feeling of having an itch you just can't seem to scratch no matter how hard you try. He was so completely absorbed in his own mind that he didn't even notice that Pythor was standing beside him.

"Apologies," he said, stopping the momentum of his arm before it impacted his friend's nose. "I did not sense your approach."

"You appear shaken," Pythor said in response.

He nodded, walking past Pythor, allowing himself to collapse and rest his back against the exterior wall of a hut-like domicile. He expelled a long, deep breath. "Never before have I been required to earn the right to remain breathing by way of combat," he answered. "The task yet haunts me."

Pythor nodded his understanding and plopped himself down next to Allen. "You found success in the attempt," he offered, looking away from Allen at the villagers. "That is what matters. It will not do to dwell on what might have been; only on what is to come."

He knew Pythor was right. He put great mental effort into shaking the lingering anxiety still coursing through him. Doing so was far more difficult than the words made it seem. Coming as close to death as he had brought mistakes he hadn't considered in a long time rushing to the front of his mind and filled him with worry for Sarah and her current situation. He was suddenly very sorry he had left her behind at the mercy of Luziaph's will. His vision began to blur and a sharp aching filled his chest, forcing a lump up into his throat. How could he have left her alone and scared in the custody of a man who could turn her to stone on a whim?

In an effort to prevent Pythor from seeing the tears slowly filling his eyes, he cast his gaze at the base of the wall upon which he now rested, noticing for the first time that it was crafted the same way the inside of Malacus' cabin had been. The foundation appeared to be molded

535

directly from the earth beneath them, as if it had grown out of the ground like a tree.

"There is no shame in what you now feel," Pythor said in a low, gentle tone. "Shame will only come if you grant dominance to the emotion. You must steel yourself, for the second trial will require great focus."

Allen wiped the tears from his eyes and cheeks, but couldn't yet bring his eyes up to meet Pythor's. "What is the second trial?" he asked.

Pythor paused for a long moment before responding. "It is believed by those who dwell here that the child of prophecy will grasp the use of Mystica like no other," Pythor said, his eyes still straight ahead. "It is not known by any other upon the surface of Datheron, but Paragus had vision of your arrival long before Sythika threatened to take Him. Such is a secret known only to those descended from the original Krathantor, those whose fealty to Paragus never wavered."

Pythor clutched at the ground, drawing a small amount of clay-like dirt into his hand and eyeing it as it sifted through his fingers back to its point of origin. "Upon entrusting His sacred blade to those who remained here, words were offered regarding he who would one day reclaim the blade for his own. For most, even those born in Datheron's embrace, the mastery of Mystica comes only with great difficulty. It has been passed down that the Paragus spoke of such mastery coming with ease to a chosen one, that Mystica would flow through him as blood flows through all others."

Pythor turned his gaze upon Allen, a look of intense concentration consuming his features. "The second trial comes in the form of testing that connection to Mystica."

Allen's brow creased with concern. He had no clue how he could pass such a test. He had next to no formal training in the use of Mystica, and had only been able to manipulate it with sporadic success. He found himself wishing he had spent more time studying the tomes in Malacus' basement, that he'd had more opportunity to pick Gazianna's brain on the subject. "How will such a test be administered?" he asked Pythor.

"The knowledge eludes me," Pythor answered, simply.

"I do not believe I can pass such a test," Allen said. "The understanding of Mystica yet remains a mystery to me."

"And yet it bends to your will," Pythor countered. "I have seen it."

When Allen cast a look of confusion at Pythor's words, the Gorrlock continued: "Upon our arrival here, you healed fatigue in such a way that it came as surprise to even the honored elder of my people."

"I did?" Allen asked, taken aback.

Pythor nodded. "And the tale of how you found yourself incarcerated alongside myself in the bowels of Luziaph's palace is not yet forgotten."

Allen reflected on the moment in which he had thrown a spear at Luziaph with his mind. He had been consciously aware of what was happening, but had not quite understood how he'd made it happen. "It would seem I am capable," he said, staring off into space. "But such a thing did not happen entirely through purposeful intent. It just . . . happened."

When he looked at Pythor once more, the Gorrlock's eyebrows were raised and his eyes were full of awe. "Then you truly are the child of prophecy," he whispered. "By Paragus . . ."

Allen turned his focus from Pythor and let his mind drift from his surroundings. Since he first arrived on this world people had been telling him of the great and perilous destiny that lay before him. It seemed to him as if their beliefs on the subject were more responsible for choosing his course of action than he was. He wasn't even certain he believed in such things and found himself resenting that choice in the matter seemed to have been taken from him. Everyone expected amazing things from him and he was supposed to perform these miracles without knowing how he was to accomplish them. He didn't see how his ability to manipulate Mystica was impressive or beneficial to anyone; to him it just seemed like foolish luck.

More from anxiety than anything else he stood and began to pace in front of Pythor. "I cannot do this!" he shouted in frustration. "To pass a test absent proper training or preparation in the task is a fool's errand! Such a thing is impossible!"

Pythor stared up at him with knowing eyes. "It is if you make it so," he said in a patient voice. "But admitting defeat before the journey begins is the approach of a fool and will certainly condemn you to such outcome."

Allen stopped in his tracks and turned to face his Gorrlock companion. Though it had been worded differently, he recalled voicing the same belief to Eugene on his last full day at school. He had told his fellow student that it didn't take a great man to see his own faults, but a great man would find a way to overcome them. He realized that he was reacting to his current situation in the same manner that Eugene had to nearly every challenge he'd faced.

With new resolve he nodded his head and steeled himself. "How would you have me proceed?" he asked, though the question came out more defensive than he'd intended.

Pythor looked at him thoughtfully for what seemed a very long time. "What do you recall of occasions when Mystica heeded your bidding?" he asked at last.

After a moment's consideration Allen shook his head in frustration. "Nothing. Recollection of such things, as well as knowledge of the achieving escapes me."

"I did not ask if comprehension of method was known," Pythor replied. "What do you recall of the circumstances which found Mystica giving way to will?"

Allen drifted into his memories, searching for any clue which might reveal the secret of his accomplishments with the life energy of the universe. The first time he'd successfully used it he had been angry at Zorthos and Malacus for refusing to train him, causing him to slam the old man into a wall of shelving with his mind. The second occasion had come when, in an act of desperation, he had travelled into Sarah's mind in an attempt to bring her out of her coma. The third time, in which he had unknowingly healed the Gorrlock woman in Abendroth, had been what had gotten him incarcerated and later placed under Luziaph's patronage. In the fourth, he'd moved against Luziaph in the defense of Gazianna. Try as he might, he couldn't come up with a link between the incidents, save the emotional stress of them.

"Emotion dominated cognition," he offered, shrugging his shoulders. "Beyond that I cannot say."

"Perhaps such is the elusive answer we seek," Pythor replied, rising from his spot on the ground. When he offered only a blank stare in response, Pythor continued. "What were your thoughts in moments of such temperament?"

"The need to overcome current situation outweighed thought of any kind," he said.

Pythor grinned, if only slightly; something he had never before seen the man do. With that smile Allen's mind began racing. Could that really be all there was to it? Did he just have to harness that deep need into purpose? The concept seemed far too simple to be the real answer;

something told him there had to be more to it. He lost himself in thought, pondering how he could replicate such need for quite some time.

For a while, Pythor seemed content to watch the activity of the village while he waited for Allen to reach a conclusion, occasionally glancing at him or staring at the statue of Paragus as he did so. He wasn't sure when it happened, but he emerged from his reverie momentarily and noticed that Pythor had moved on to leave him with his thoughts.

Eventually a couple of Gorrlock children approached him with expectant looks upon their faces. One of the children, a small boy who seemed to be a little older than the other, congratulated him on his victory.

After he'd thanked him, the boy had told Allen that Senjin was his older brother and that he was grateful Allen had let him live. Then the boy asked if Allen would teach him and his friend how to perform the move which had bested his older brother. Allen smiled at the boy and politely declined, offering to do so another time. The two boys scowled at the response and ran off looking dejected.

A while later, as the sun was reaching its peak, Allen sought out Pythor who was standing next to the largest building in the village, speaking to the elder about something. As he approached the two Gorrlocks, the elder eyed him briefly and disappeared into the large structure, which resembled a very large clay igloo, without a word. Allen assumed it to be the elder's residence.

"I did not intend to chase him away," he offered.

Pythor waved away his concern with a small gesture. "Remove troubled thoughts," he replied. "What is it?"

"I would share words toward the purpose of making preparation for the next trial," he said. When Pythor said nothing in response, he continued: "Could you offer assistance in the understanding of harnessing my . . . gift in Mystica?"

Pythor shook his head slowly. "Even if the Triaga were removed from my head, one day would not prove sufficient for proper instruction. Besides, it is believed that the natural affinity you demonstrate can be understood only by the child of prophecy. You must turn to yourself for the answer."

Allen felt for a moment as if he were back in Malacus' basement, being denied by someone whom he believed he could count on. He realized a moment later, however, that he wasn't as upset by Pythor's refusal as he might have been. He almost felt relief, as the thought of using Mystica filled him with concern; every time he had accessed it thus far had brought him trouble in some form. And he couldn't see how this trial would be any different.

Rather than press the issue, however, he simply nodded and stood next to Pythor, joining him in watching the children of the village chase each other back and forth. The same boy which had approached him earlier was chasing several others, tossing flickering fireballs at them in some perverse version of tag or dodge ball. Allen watched as the emerald ball of light ricocheted off one of the other children's backs into the dirt, leaving minor scorch marks where it had impacted. The child that had been hit immediately retaliated by chasing the others, his right hand ablaze; the sight was as fascinating as it was disconcerting.

While they watched, Pythor did his best to explain to Allen what the boys were doing, how they were manipulating Mystica to create the flames. Although the explanation was more intricate than he could completely comprehend, there were some basic principals which he did understand. Pythor described in detail how the children were channeling Mystica through will, using it to compress and ignite the very air around them. He explained that doing so required not only slightly altering the chemical signature of the air to create the fuel the flame needed to spark to life, but also a certain level of skill in telekinesis to keep it from burning their flesh. It all seemed so convoluted that Allen wondered how he could possibly have accomplished even the small feats he had without years of training and study.

Pythor must have seen the look of discouragement on his face because a moment later he broke from his lesson to suggest that he approach the children for further instruction. When Allen gave him a puzzled look, Pythor reinforced the idea by saying that he could trade knowledge of his skill with a sword for theirs in Mystica since two of the boys were keen to learn from him anyway, adding that a lower level of experience might just be able to relate the methodology to him in a manner he would better understand. He nodded at the suggestion and left Pythor standing alone next to the elder's home.

It only took a couple of minutes for the children to notice his presence, and only a moment more for the child wielding the flame to hurl it at Allen's chest plate. He winced as it sparked off his armor. When he opened his eyes, several of the children had stopped in their tracks and were all watching him as if to gauge his reaction.

The boy who had hurled the flame looked up at him expectantly. "The task falls to you," he said after a moment. "You are the flame bearer now."

Allen glanced around to all the others who were watching him. He counted five boys and two girls, all of varying age, with their black and red eyes locked on him awaiting his response to the boy's challenge. "Apologies," he began. "I fear myself absent the ability to produce flames as you do. Can you teach me?"

The boy exchanged a brief, mildly amused look with a couple of the others. "Do you really hail from Earth?" he asked, bringing his gaze back to Allen.

"I do," Allen answered.

"What is it like there?" another child asked.

The question sent Allen into deep reflection about his home and everything he missed about it. For several long moments he stood lost in his memories, the ghost of a saddened smile upon his lips. "It is home," he answered in a low voice. "The differences between this world and the one from which I hail are great in number. Earth remains empty of the knowledge of Mystica and all conveniences provided in the understanding of it. An entirely different skill set has evolved in its absence, bringing with it structures far taller than most trees. Devices have been created to allow one to speak to another on the opposite end of the globe, absent sight of them."

The children all gathered around him as he continued to tell them of the marvels of his home world of Earth. They listened with rapt attention, their eyes wide as he explained to them how the people of Earth had created vehicles that moved without the need of anything to pull them. He did his best to explain the concept of computers, and television, and the wide assortment of other gadgets technology had bred into the world of man upon his home soil.

After a while even a few adult Gorrlocks found their way to the small group listening to him reminisce about the world which had sheltered him all his life, the world they had been taught to fear because it would one day produce a child which would end life as they knew it. Before he realized it nearly everyone in the village had gathered around him to hear what he had to say about the world spoken of in ancient prophecy. Even Pythor and the elder were in attendance, though at the very edge of the crowd.

Rexim and Ithaniel, too, were listening from a distance to the stories of his fabled home land. Allen, who had always wanted to be a writer or a story teller, couldn't help but smile inwardly at the thought that he had an audience listening to him speak.

"More than anything," he said, bringing his story to a conclusion, "I long to embrace my mother once more."

The boy who had hit him with the flame earlier sat at the front of the crowd, staring up at him with a puzzled look upon his face. "If Earth yet remains so close to your heart, what prompted the abandoning of it?" he asked.

Allen looked up to see all eyes in the crowd eagerly awaiting his response. He got the feeling that most of them were expecting him to say that he had specifically come to end them. He decided it was probably better to omit the details of how Pythor had tricked him into passing through the gateway. "I departed my home solely toward the protection of another I hold close to my heart," he answered simply.

"Protection from what?" the boy asked without hesitation.

The question came so quickly that it caught Allen off guard. "It is complicated," he answered.

The boy simply shrugged at Allen's lack of an answer. "Come," he said, standing up and taking Allen by the hand to lead him away from the crowd. "We will give lesson in producing flames."

Allen glanced over his shoulder at Pythor as the children separated themselves from the throng of adults, pulling him in tow. Pythor gave him a small nod, that same half-grin once again haunting his features.

For the next several hours the children crowded around him, each making their own attempt at teaching him how to generate the emerald flame they had been using for their game. When the lessons began he'd watched with

544

awe as each child in turn had produced a dancing green light in the palms of their hands. One by one they'd offered instruction as he attempted to replicate the effect to no avail. There were a couple of points in which he was certain he almost had it, when he could feel the heat beginning to grow between his palms. But every time he got that close the words of caution Malacus had given him about precautionary abilities kept springing into his mind, causing him to lose focus just shy of success. His greatest frustration came in knowing he had somehow accomplished other great things with Mystica without any kind of training at all, and now he couldn't even produce a tiny flame; something it was obvious came to these children with ease. He couldn't shake the feeling that it should have been easier than he was making it, that he was somehow over-thinking the whole process.

As he continued his apparent attempts in futility, the crowd of children slowly dwindled until only two remained at his side; the two which had approached him that morning asking to learn how he'd bested Senjin. In his time with them Allen had learned that Senjin's younger brother was called Theoxim. The other, who was a couple years younger and followed Theoxim around like a lost puppy, was called Anadar. To their credit, the two boys stayed at his side long after the other children had given up, despite their obvious boredom and frustration. He couldn't help wondering if it was because Theoxim wanted that lesson in swordplay in return for his efforts, or if the extra attention came as gratitude for letting his older brother live.

When the sun began to near the horizon above the desert and he still had yet to successfully conjure a tiny spark, he yelled in frustration. "I do not understand why failure finds me so easily in this!" he cried. He looked up hoping to find some sort of encouragement from the two boys, only to catch them playing another game involving the green flame which had eluded his every effort thus far. The new game appeared to consist of nothing more than passing the fireball back and forth, each boy engorging the flame slightly before sending it back to the other. The ease with which the two boys lobbed the flickering ball of light back and forth left him feeling both inspired and flustered.

Allen continued to watch them for a while before the emerald orb of light finally reached a size Anadar couldn't handle. The small boy fell backward, the flame flickering violently as it scattered and faded from existence. With a triumphant grin Theoxim stood over the other, offering him a hand up off the ground. When Anadar began to pout a little, Theoxim clapped him on the back and said, "Abandon emotion. You held the flame twice as long as ever before. Your skill yet improves!" Anadar nodded and wiped his eyes after being lifted to his feet.

Theoxim turned to him. "What troubles you?" he asked.

"The task set before me comes only with the greatest of difficulty," he answered, frustration still tainting his words. "I believe it impossible. I have no mind for such things. I fear Mystica shall forever elude my grasp."

Theoxim looked up at him with great disappointment and confusion. "I find the statement to be false. Just this morning my eyes bore witness to your ability in controlling Mystica." When Allen's eyebrows knitted together in confusion of his own, Theoxim continued. "You pulled sword to hand from great distance by thought alone! Such was the very thing which brought the defeat of my brother!"

Allen had been so immersed in his concern about the next trial that it had completely slipped his mind that he had called the sword to him to end the first. As he reflected on it, he realized he wasn't even sure he had done so consciously. It had just sort of . . . happened. He revisited the thought that perhaps he was just thinking too hard about how to do it, rather than focusing on making it happen.

Allen brought his eyes back down to meet Theoxim's. "I fail to understand how such a thing came to be. Need of the sword overcame all else in that moment. I believe that, perhaps, is how it sprang to my aid."

Theoxim shook his head slowly. "Then perhaps you are beyond my help."

With that, the two boys strode away, leaving Allen alone with his brooding thoughts of failure.

***

The next morning came far too quickly for Allen's liking. He had slept no better than the night before and awoke to find his back just as stiff. Troubling dreams haunted him once more as he slowly gathered his armor and began the process of putting it on. An overwhelming feeling of imminent doom loomed over him as he set to the task. He felt as if he were preparing himself for his own execution. He knew that it had been luck more than skill which had granted him victory in the previous trial and held no illusions that his chances of passing today's test were slim. Thoughts of Sarah's welfare crept into his mind and he found himself wishing the Gorrlocks would just give him the sword so that he could be away from here and back at home with her.

Pythor found him as he was preparing and helped fasten the cuirass into place. "You wear the look of one who has already failed," Pythor said in a firm tone.

"Your words are true," he replied, unable to meet Pythor's gaze. "I believe success to be an impossibility this day."

Pythor grabbed his chin and forcefully brought Allen's eyes up to meet his own. "Failure awaits all who refuse to try!" he admonished. "Wipe doubt from your mind and see it replaced with focus! These tests speak more about the man than mere skill in the tasks by which they are performed. You must face it, absent fear or see yourself before Luziaph with empty hands! More than just foolish pride weighs in the balance of the outcome. Steel yourself!"

Though Pythor's words had seemed harsh, Allen knew he was right. He had no hope of success if he couldn't shake the phantoms of fear from his mind. He was doing this for more than just simple bragging rights; he was doing this, ultimately, to gain his and Sarah's freedom, to gain passage back to Earth.

He expelled a deep, cleansing breath and looked at Pythor with renewed resolve. "Gratitude," he said. "I but lost myself for a moment. You words ring true, my friend."

With a final nod, Pythor clapped him on the upper back and led the way toward the next trial.

The tension in the air could be felt from a great distance as they approached. The entire village had once again gathered in the same place just beyond the statue of Paragus, and were all watching with great anticipation as the gap between them closed. The throng of spectators parted as he made his way to the middle of the circle again. He couldn't help but note that the area he'd been allotted seemed a bit wider than yesterday. Once in the center, he only had to wait a couple of moments before the Gorrlock elder emerged from the crowd and raised his arms to call for attention.

"The time has come," the elder called, looking around, waiting for the crowd to calm. After a moment the old man brought his black and red eyes to focus on Allen once more. "You now face the second Trial of Sythika. It is said that no knowledge comes from one path alone. To truly master any craft, one must find understanding in all aspects of it. Mystica is the counterpart to Sythika. You must, therefore, prove capabilities in its use not beyond your understanding."

The old man paused for a moment, as if to let these words sink in. "Theoxim," he called. "Step forward."

Great confusion filled Allen as he watched the boy emerge from a forest of blue-skinned adults to take his place at the elder's side. The boy looked at him impassively; his hands clasped together in front of him as he took his place next to the Gorrlock elder. Allen scanned the crowd and quickly found Anadar watching with wide eyes as he clutched the light brown garments of a beautiful Gorrlock woman, which Allen could only assume was the boy's mother. Anadar appeared just as shocked by Theoxim being called forward as Allen was.

"This one," the elder said, resting his left hand on Theoxim's right shoulder, "has volunteered to provide test in such capabilities."

"He is but a child," Allen protested, his eyes never leaving Theoxim's.

"Yet he stands your superior in the use of Mystica," the elder countered.

The events of the first trial were still quite fresh in Allen's mind. The clash of steel that held him but a moment from death rang vividly in his memory. He'd had great concern for the danger in which that trial had placed both participants. How could any of these people, especially the old man apparently charged with leading them, knowingly place a child in that type of danger? If the abilities he had exhibited in Mystica had manifested out of some sort of defense mechanism, Theoxim could be facing mortal peril in volunteering for this task.

"I refuse to allow this," he announced. "What little accomplishments in Mystica I have brought to life have not been of my volition. Control remains outside my grasp. I cannot leave to chance that Theoxim might be injured by that lack of control."

The elder's already severe features turned more so as a scowl spread across his face. "The choice does not fall to you," he said with condemnation. "You can take the test presented you or be gone with naught to show for your efforts!"

A sinking feeling of trepidation enveloped him. What was he to do? He didn't want to spare the older brother one day, only to accidentally kill the younger the next. But if he refused to participate he would fail in his promise to Sarah, and he would certainly never see his mother again. In the end it was the hard look in Theoxim's eyes which convinced him to resign his protest. With a small nod Allen lowered his gaze and accepted the old man's terms.

"Then it is settled," the Gorrlock elder announced. "You know what to do, child."

A moment later, Allen found himself alone in the circle with the boy who was to be his opponent. The boy unclasped his hands, upturned his palms as they raised to his side, and ignited flames in either one. He slowly, deliberately, pulled his hands together, combining the flames as his hands met in front of his torso.

"You must only survive," Theoxim said, and he cast the fireball directly at Allen's chest.

Instinct took over. Diving to the side, Allen narrowly avoided a direct hit as he rolled to safety. That safety, however, was short-lived as another green ball of light barreled toward him. He ducked to the left, causing the ball of liquid light to deflect off his right shoulder pad. Abandoning all hesitation, he rose from the ground and began to run the perimeter of his would-be arena, brushing the flames from his armor as blue faces blurred past him. He knew he should probably be trying to catch the fireballs being hurled at him, or block them, or at least attempt to nullify them, but he just couldn't bring himself to make a move that might endanger a child. The flames were flying at an alarming rate and he was surprised at the level of skill such a small child could was exhibiting in such a deadly skill.

As Allen continued to evade the onslaught of emerald light impacting to every side of him, he noticed that the boy wasn't moving from his spot at the other side of the circle. He surreptitiously watched his opponent as he rolled once more to the left to avoid being set ablaze by a new attack. It seemed to be taking an immense amount of concentration for Theoxim to maintain his effort. The ball of light exploded in the dirt behind him as he stood once more, kicking sparks and dust in all directions as it impacted. He wasn't entirely sure how this test was supposed to be demonstrating his own skill in Mystica, but then again he wasn't really fighting back. He glanced once more to Theoxim to find him sweating slightly, whether from exertion or the heat of the flames he couldn't tell, though the boy was still standing in the same place.

Pulling himself to his feet once more, Allen paused for the briefest of moments to scan the crowd in search of Pythor for some clue as to what he was supposed to do. It was in that instant that a large ball of burning energy impacted him square in the chest, sending him sprawling to the ground and setting his chest plate ablaze with emerald light. He was only vaguely aware of the roars from the crowd as he rolled in the dirt in an attempt to extinguish the flame. With great repetition fireball after fireball found its mark directly behind him, forcing him to continue rolling away from the constant attack. Theoxim seemed to be taking this challenge far more seriously than Allen.

When Allen found his path blocked by the blue legs of spectators, another fireball found its mark, this time on the bare portion of his left arm. He screamed in pain, immediately rolling in the opposite direction to plant his left arm in the dirt in order to suffocate the flame. The acrid smell of burning flesh filled his nostrils as he found his feet again. Clutching the wound, he leaped away from another attack, the flame catching him in the ankle this time. He was completely outmatched and he didn't even have his shield with him to block the assault.

Ducking under a rather large burst of green light, he let his eyes follow it to the point of impact. As all-consuming as the task was, he still found himself concerned that a stray fireball might accidentally injure one of the spectators. This one in particular flew directly at the woman standing over Anadar, who caught it with minimal effort and extinguished it in a matter of a couple seconds. The ease with which the attack was nullified impressed him, causing an idea to formulate in his mind. All at once he stopped running. He decided that if he was indeed the chosen one that he should be able to replicate the effect, and nullify an attack aimed at him. Perhaps that was all they were waiting to see him do. Perhaps he needed only stave off impending death using Mystica to accomplish the deed.

He stood his ground, held his hands up defensively, and braced himself. He noticed as he did so that Theoxim was yet standing in the exact same spot he had been occupying for the entire conflict. The boy was beginning to look tired as he cast the next assault; sweat traced curving paths down his face and arms from nearly every pore. As the glowing, green ball of light closed in, Allen brought his hands together in preparation to catch it. He let himself go, pushing all his concern to the side in deference to concentrating on the task at hand. The flaming ball of light scorched his palms as it impacted them. He could feel the flame eating his flesh as he attempted to extinguish it as he'd seen Anadar's mother do a moment before. Allen's eyes slammed shut in pain as he threw himself to the ground and planted his fists in the dirt. Pulling them up free, he stared down at his charred skin through blurred vision.

It wasn't until several moments later that he realized that the attacks had stopped coming.

When he looked up, Theoxim was kneeling on the ground in much the same fashion as he was. The boy was looking at him with tired eyes, sweat dripping from his chin. In the next moment, that fatigue turned to resolve as the boy brought his feet back underneath him. Theoxim expelled an exhausted breath and ignited his palms once more. Allen knew he had but one chance. Up to this point he had been keeping his distance from the boy's attacks. If he could move in close, he might reduce the likelihood of Theoxim's willingness to use an attack which was clearly designed for distant combat.

With all his strength Allen pushed himself up from the ground. Granules of dirt dug painfully into the burned flesh of his palms as he did so. When at last he'd reached his feet, he charged at the boy. Mild fear and confusion registered in Theoxim's eyes at his change in tactics. It seemed almost panicky the way the flames came at Allen now. Since he was already burnt and in pain, he ignored the barrage of green light as it bounced off his armor. When the gap had been completely closed, he grabbed the boy's wrists and despite the shooting pain which erupted in his hands as he did so, held fast.

With his opponent neutralized, he looked up at all those watching. "It is done!" he announced. "This contest is over!"

Murmuring broke out all around and Allen let go of his opponent. Now that the contest was over, the adrenaline rushing through Allen gave way to nerves and the pain in his burns intensified. He could feel every heartbeat throbbing in his blistering skin as the elder pushed his way back into the circle. The old man moved to Theoxim's side at once, leaning down to check on the boy's condition. Once he seemed satisfied with the boy's welfare, he rose to his full height, locking his gaze on Allen.

"You were unable to block, deflect, or otherwise call Mystica to your aid," the old man stated gravely. "You have failed the second trial."

The words registered in Allen's ears, but he found himself in utter disbelief at hearing them. This couldn't be happening. Theoxim had said he need only survive . . . and he quite clearly had. How could he have failed the second test when he wasn't given its parameters? It hardly seemed fair that he should be made to face mortal peril and still have to determine on his own what was expected of him. His disbelief quickly shifted to rage as the old man's words rang in his mind again and again.

Before he could voice his own protest on the matter, however, Pythor emerged from the many faces to his left, his jaw set in determination. "The decision is unjust," the Krathantor said as he approached those in the center of the spectators.

"You dare challenge decision given by authority of one who holds station above you?" the old man said in outrage.

"I take directive solely from the God-King," Pythor countered. "I have been outside your command since the day this armor was given me. I now hold my own authority and I say the decision is unjust. This one," he said, gesturing to Allen, "clearly survived the test."

"Yet he did so absent the qualifying conditions to pass the trial," the elder retorted. "You know as well as I that the second trial was put in place to test connection to Mystica. He exhibits none."

"Then let the demonstration presented upon his arrival stand as proof," Pythor challenged. "All present watched as he shed fatigue of his own accord, calling Mystica to his command in his greatest time of need. It has long been said that the connection made between Mystica and the chosen one would be unlike that to which any are accustomed. I say in that act he proved the statement true."

Allen shook violently as he looked to Pythor with gratitude, though whether more from pain or anxiety he couldn't say. He looked back and forth between the two figures of Gorrlock authority for what seemed an eternity. Although they were silent, the furtive glances being passed among all present spoke a great deal about the interest and concern shared by all as they awaited the old man's answer.

At long last the old man huffed an irritated sigh of resignation from his nostrils. "So be it," he said. "It is the final trial which will truly determine whether he is the chosen one." With that he placed his arm around Theoxim and escorted the boy through the crowd, away from where he'd nearly lost his life.

As the Gorrlocks began to disperse, Allen fell in step behind Pythor. "Gratitude for coming to my aid," he said.

"Save it," Pythor replied. "We must place our attention to your respite, for one day hence do you face the final and most onerous trial; one in which there can be no outside aid."

As he followed Pythor over to the Triclopians to begin the healing process, his mind was full of worry about what his blue-skinned companion's last remark could possibly mean.

36

BRAVADO

THE TINGLING IN ALLEN'S FLESH lingered well beyond the healing ritual in which Ithaniel had removed the burns from his conflict with Theoxim, and echoed still as he stood at the mouth of a great cave the following day about to begin his third and final trial. He rubbed his left arm absently as he stared into the darkness, considering the task set before him. Allen found it odd to know that the wounds were no longer there, yet ghosts of the pain left in their wake remained long after they'd healed.

When he'd awoken that morning, he'd opened his eyes to find both Pythor and the so-called honored elder standing over him. The sight had left him feeling mildly violated as he shook the last vestiges of sleep from his mind.

"Rise from your slumber," the old man said. "The task set before you this day will be long in the completing."

The old man had said no more while Allen had brought himself fully awake and dressed in his leather armor. He had followed the two Gorrlock authority figures out to the center of the village again once he was dressed, very aware of all the eyes on him as they moved to their place beneath the statue of Paragus. Allen stared up at the visage of the ancient deity and wondered if, in His premonition of Allen's arrival, He had foreseen this very moment or if the knowledge had come in fragments. He supposed it didn't matter, yet a small part of him wished that he could speak to the man, if only to ask exactly why he was the one 'chosen' to fulfill the prophecy and how he was to accomplish such a thing.

Once more the entire village of Gorrlocks surrounded them, the elder raising his arms to call everyone to attention. This time, however, he did not address the crowd, but Allen directly. "You face the final trial this day," he announced in a grave tone. "In order to accomplish the task, directives given must be followed with explicit care.

"Up to this point a propensity to ignore the rules given in deference to your own ideals has been exhibited. Continuing along this pattern will bring great peril to more than just oneself in this final trial. The point cannot be given enough stress." The old man paused a moment to let his words sink in, only continuing when Allen nodded that he understood. "The prize for seeing this task to completion is that which you seek: the Sword of Sythika. You travel a short distance up the mountainside to the cave of Naphiticus. Once inside, dangers will be yours alone to face; none are permitted to aid in the task."

Allen glanced around briefly to gauge the reactions of those present. Unlike the previous couple of days the mood of the crowd today was somber, almost to the point of reverence. Even the children in attendance were watching with wide eyes as the elder continued to give him direction. He looked to Pythor and was encouraged with a nod to return his attention to the task at hand.

"Once inside, the path forward will be illuminated. You must journey to the chamber in which the sword is kept. If your identity as the child of prophecy is not false, true test will present itself in the form of a beast which is said to guard the sword. If, however, you are not the child of prophecy the sword will pass judgment, removing the breath your from body. Either way your life is the price for successful exodus.

"Should the beast be revealed, there is but one method of escape: you must kill it." The old man paused once more in his instructions, eyeing Allen meaningfully as he continued a moment later. "In this there can be no negotiation, no debate. You must kill the beast with the Sword of Sythika to gain passage back into the light of day, for it will not cease its attack until it is one with Sythika. You are clear to your purpose?"

Allen stood in mute shock for what felt like a very long time. It seemed no matter how hard he tried to avoid it this old man was bound and determined to make a killer out of him. Allen didn't believe himself capable of such a thing, even when pressed to the point of his own survival hinging on it. As he stood there, staring at the weathered features of the Gorrlock elder, his mind raced to find any way around this particular stipulation. Surely murder couldn't be the only method through which the final task could be accomplished. He refused to take the life of any living creature if he could help it, even one referred to as a beast. There was always another option.

The hesitation must have shown on his face because the elder snapped him out of his evasive train of thought with a stern remark.

"If the terms presented cannot be abided, return from whence you came!" the old man stated firmly. "Failing to adhere to these directives with exacting purpose will bring great danger to all, not just yourself. To master the blade of death one must be willing to administer it! To hold such a weapon absent clear purpose will bring only disaster! In wielding the legendary weapon you will hold Sythika itself in your grasp! If proper respect is not given to the task, all around you face certain doom! Are we of a singular mind in this?"

The look in the old man's eyes as he reiterated his instructions was wild, almost desperate. He clearly believed that the only way to retrieve the sword was through taking the life of an innocent creature. Allen wasn't quite ready to admit that he had but one option; if there was a way to obtain the sword without killing, he would find it. As he considered the old man's words, he could not think of a single situation in which taking another's life was the only viable solution. The one thing of which he was certain was that he needed to face this trial; he needed to obtain the sword for Sarah's and his own freedom. It was that thought alone that coursed through his mind and steeled his nerves as he nodded in agreement to the old man's words.

At seeing Allen nod in agreement, the tension in the elder's features slackened noticeably, though he still seemed to be on edge. "Good," he said with relief. "Should you find success in the task set before you, we shall rejoice prior to returning to the surface of Datheron."

"You would return to Datheron?" he asked in alarm.

The elder eyed him in startled confusion. "There may be those that choose to remain behind, yet with our charge seen to completion reason to do so would falter. We have lingered upon Sythar these countless generations toward a singular purpose: the guarding of the Sword of Sythika. To not be present to bear witness to the change brought about by its reemergence would be a crime against our efforts."

For some reason the thought of the Gorrlock population joining him back on the surface of Datheron had never occurred to him. But what the old man said made perfect sense. Why would they stay here if the only reason for which they had travelled here in the first place was no longer among them? Even though he had not really established any kind of rapport with this old man, or the rest of his people for that matter, the idea of any of them being present to witness his betrayal by handing over the sword to Luziaph left a strong feeling of guilt lingering in the pit of his stomach. Perhaps it was because he had developed such a strong connection to Pythor in his time on Sythar, but Allen had the same sinking feeling in his gut that he experienced every time he'd lied to his mother and been worried about being caught in the lie.

"You find the news troubling?" the old man asked.

"No," he lied. "My thoughts but dwell upon the task at hand and the welfare of the one left behind as I set upon this journey. I long to see her once more and hope the day brings success, that I might be able to do so."

The old man seemed to accept his half truth and had sent Pythor to escort him to the cave. The journey had only taken about an hour or two, the trail having wound around the side of the mountain. Now, as Allen stood at its entrance, he could not see the village below. The mouth of the cave was positioned facing away from those that guarded its secret. If he looked off to his left he could see light smoke drifting up from beyond the edge of the rock-face, but he could not even hear the activity which accompanied it below.

Pythor had not said a single word on the trip up the mountainside, and had only offered a nod and a clap on the shoulder for reassurance before departing and leaving him to face his destiny alone. Allen wasn't really sure how long he stood there, just staring into that blackness before he finally mustered the courage to enter. He wasn't even entirely sure the decision to do so had been completely conscious, but at some point he simply began moving forward until the darkness swallowed him.

A short distance into the cave, when he was far enough in to be completely immersed in the darkness around him, but not yet far enough that he could no longer see the entrance behind him, a light sprang to life on the wall to his right in front of him. The light was weak at first, but grew stronger the closer he got to it. Watching the fixture as he moved closer, it brought to mind the lights he'd spent so much time with in Malacus' basement. The way they just sprang to life, seemingly of their own accord, left a small pang of sorrow lingering in his heart. He still found it difficult to believe that Luziaph had killed the old man who had offered shelter and instruction to him in his first days away from Earth, whom he had learned was supposedly the God-King of Datheron in his younger days. He felt as if he would be betraying more than just the Gorrlocks of Sythar were he to hand over the Sword of Sythika to Luziaph. He was certain that Malacus would forbid this course of action if he were alive to know of it.

When he'd reached the point at which he was standing directly next to the light fixture on the cave wall, Allen paused a moment to look around. The entrance behind him was smaller than his thumbnail would be if he were to hold his hand out, away from his body in comparison. The blackness ahead was so complete that he couldn't see beyond the twenty feet or so in which the light offered a little relief and sight of his surroundings. Knowing that he was quite literally moving forward into an area of total darkness, surrounded on all sides by thousands of tons of rocks and minerals, was one of the creepiest feelings he had ever experienced. There was no sound, save his heavy breathing and the beating of his heart pounding in his ears. In the many challenges he had faced in his life, he'd always been able to find some sort of strength with which to proceed, some way in which to reassure himself. In this task he could find none. It left him feeling completely naked to his surroundings. Pushing the fear back as best he could, he pulled the sword at his side from its scabbard with his right hand and clutched the shield on his left tightly before advancing. In the confined space of the cave, the sword sent a chilling ring echoing off the walls around him. His heart raced all the more at hearing it and he found himself hoping that whatever lay ahead hadn't heard the noise.

With deliberate care Allen placed one foot in front of the other slowly as he proceeded forward, away from the shelter of the light. He could only hope another one would reveal itself the further he travelled. About ten paces beyond the light fixture, it began to dim. It was as if his presence were the power source from which it produced its shining embrace. A few feet beyond that, as the light reached about half its capacity, the tunnel began to slope downward slightly. At the sudden change of incline he nearly lost his footing. He dropped his sword as he stumbled forward and reached for the cave wall to regain it. A loud, grating noise echoed all around as the sword clattered away from him, down the path ahead. For a very long moment he just stood there, listening as the eerie silence of the cave once again reclaimed dominance. His heartbeat thudded against his eardrums in violent cadence, his eyes wide, as he waited for danger to emerge from the darkness ahead.

When nothing happened after what felt an eternity, Allen slowly released his grip on the wall and crouched down in an effort to see where his sword had landed. In the looming blackness all around, he could not see it anywhere nearby. Refusing to release his shield, he began to crawl around with his one free arm in a desperate search to reclaim his one chance at self-defense. Panic consumed him as he frantically felt around in the dark for his missing weapon. As he continued downward the light behind him began to fade in earnest. It was near total blackness again and he still hadn't found his blade. In a final desperate effort he decided to stand up and grope his way along the wall to the next light in hopes that it would reveal the sword's location.

Just when the light behind him was about to fade from existence completely, the next sprang to life up ahead, if only marginally so. Allen could see it a goodly distance away, and realized immediately that it would be too far ahead for him to use its light to locate his sword. For quite some time he stood there considering his options. He wondered if he should just go back to the village to ask for another sword. The trip would only take an hour or so there and an hour or so back, he rationalized. But by the time he got back it would be near noonday, and what if returning to the village empty-handed was all they needed to proclaim that he wasn't in fact the child of prophecy? What if they refused to allow him another chance to come back up to the cave? He wondered silently why they hadn't just offered him some type of torch with which to see his surroundings. In the end, however, he decided he couldn't risk going back if it meant he might be denied reentry into the cave, so he pressed forward, reminding himself that he was here to lay claim to a sword, and that it was that blade which he was required to use to kill the beast.

For what seemed like hours Allen pushed on through the darkness. He had lost track of how many lights he'd passed as he'd continued his journey toward the chamber which held the sword. Each light was spaced just far enough from the other to begin to illuminate just as the other one was nearly extinguished; it had made for a nerve-racking expedition. The lights in the bowels of the palace of Vardiston reacted in much the same manner as these, but they were far closer together than these in the cave. He was certain that the trip would not have taken nearly as long had he been given proper lighting to see the path ahead. The convenience of electricity was one he greatly missed since leaving Earth.

After a while the path leveled off again. He only had to follow it a short distance, passing but another half a dozen lights, before two lights sprang to life in front of him. Each one was set opposite the other on the cave walls. As he neared them and their brightness grew, he saw that they revealed a doorway. He quickened his pace slightly, hoping that he'd reached the end of his treacherous journey through the dark.

Standing directly between the two lights, he noticed that they were set in the doorway itself. Though their light only penetrated so far, it was easy for him to see that the doorway opened into a very large chamber. He had made it. Taking a deep breath, he stepped forward through the doorway and into what lay ahead. Only a couple of steps later lights on all sides began to slowly illuminate the vast chamber. Allen counted six lights high up and running along the edges of the ceiling in a symmetrical pattern. They started out dim at first also and grew ever brighter the further into the chamber he moved. Though they never got quite as bright as the ones in the tunnel, they were much larger and seemed to react sympathetically to his presence just as all the others had. By the time he reached what he felt must be the center of the chamber the light had reached a level in which he was far more comfortable.

Allen stopped and glanced around to his surroundings. The heart of the cave was enormous. If there had ever been stalagmites or stalactites, they had long since been cleared away and had not reformed. As he looked around, the chamber seemed to him almost man-made. The walls were smooth and led up into a dome of sorts, and the floors, while not paved at all, were of a much smoother consistency than the tunnel through which he had travelled to get here. He was relieved to see no sign of a beast anywhere.

And then he saw it.

Directly ahead of him, roughly fifty yards away at the top of a short staircase, rested a small shrine. A statue of a large half-beast, half-human-looking creature stood holding in its grasp a very elegant-looking scabbard, from which he could see an ornately designed golden hilt protruding. Without even realizing that he was moving, the distance between him and the shrine began to close. The closer he got the more detail he could make out in both the statue and the sword to which it held fast. The beast-like creature had four arms, at the end of which were large three-fingered claws. A row of horns trailed back from its primal brow over the crown of its head, accentuated by large fin-like ears. It wore a vicious snarl on its face, bearing fangs that appeared as if they could tear through steal. Large bat-like wings extended from its back, below which could be seen a long, spiked tail. It was nearly twice his height and appeared almost as intricate in detail as the statues in the palace of Vardiston. The way it stood there, staring down in challenge to any who would dare approach it, left him feeling as if he were bearing witness to something from mythology.

Once close enough, Allen let his eyes wander from the menacing visage which guarded the sword, to the artifact itself. The golden hilt was simply crafted, yet somehow regal in appearance. The pommel bore a strong resemblance to a rounded arrowhead and led into a simple wire-wound hilt, spun in gold. The sword's cross-guard came out to both sides with points arcing both upward, toward the blade, and downward, away from it; the latter being slightly smaller than the former. In the center of the cross-guard a jewel as black as anything he had ever seen extended to a point partway up the center of the blade, also laced in gold. The scabbard had been fashioned to take this notch into consideration and shared the simple, yet extravagant design of the hilt.

Allen could hardly believe he was here, on the moon of a world on which Gods could be forged, staring at a blade of legend which had once belonged to the original God-King. The thought occurred to him that this sword had been resting here in wait for thousands of years. Considering the time-shift between this world and his own, he wondered just how long it had been here in respect to the flow of time on Earth. Could it have been here since the time of Earth's infancy? Such thoughts filled him with awe as he stood there, staring at the blade for a very long time.

After a while, however, he reminded himself that he was here for a reason and that he needed to claim the blade and be away so that he might rescue Sarah from the torment of Luziaph's patronage. With a final, furtive glance at the massive creature which held the scabbard in its grip, he reached out for the hilt of the legendary blade. His own hand seemed to move forward in slow motion, his actions coming with great hesitancy. Recalling the words of the Gorrlock elder, that should he not be the true child of prophecy the sword would judge him and make him one with Sythika, he paused a moment as his palm came within an inch of the hilt. The realization hit him that this could very well be the last thing he ever did, the last thing he ever saw, leaving Sarah alone to fend for herself. No. He couldn't afford to think like that. In that moment Allen chose to embrace all that he'd been told about who he truly was, that he was the child of prophecy. He decided then and there that, if for no other reason, Sarah needed him to be the chosen one; he accepted himself for who he was, so that he might claim the sword as his own absent the risk to his life in doing so.

All at once Allen gripped the golden hilt firmly in his hand.

In that moment, a surge of energy burst forth, rushing through him and filling the great chamber with a resonant humming. For the briefest of moments he was pulled inside himself while the hum echoed all around. He recognized, without knowing how, that the burst he had just experienced was a precautionary measure put in place to keep any but the true child of prophecy from taking the sword from this place. In that moment it became clear to him that he was the one Paragus had foreseen, that his life had always been leading him here. The feeling was as disquieting as it was awe-inspiring.

The humming slowly grew louder, more severe, causing the chamber to begin to shake. As all around him began to quake in response to his grip on the sword, the statue began to crack apart. The hands of the beast crumbled away, releasing the scabbard and allowing him to back down the steps away from the statue. He watched with fascination as the tremors grew stronger and pitch black smoke slowly emanated from the fractures in the statue. Not wanting to be caught unaware by whatever was happening he tore off his old scabbard and clipped the new one to his baldric in its place.

Taking a deep breath, he released the Sword of Sythika from the scabbard which had kept it confined for so very long. It announced its reemergence into the world with a ringing unlike anything he'd ever heard before. It almost sounded like a howling of relief when mixed with the noise already filling the chamber. He stared at the weapon in his right hand, its blade as black as the tunnel he had traversed to get here had been. Light trails of blackened vapor dripped from its edges, making it seem almost eager to inflict its will on any who would challenge it. This was clearly a weapon of great power and danger, one which demanded respect from any who would dare to master it.

The statue was crumbling in pieces when he finally managed to look away from the blade. The black oozing smoke began to swirl around the room with violent urgency. He spun in place, one step at a time, as he frantically tried to follow the smoke's progress. It moved with greater and greater speed until it finally began to culminate in a single location and take shape. He watched with his shield held high in front of him, his new sword held at the ready, as the smoke became solid directly in front of him, blocking the one and only path out of the chamber. The transformation seemed to all at once take forever and happen so quickly that it left his mind reeling. Before he knew it a massive beast stood in front of him, much larger than the statue had been. It looked less human and more bestial now that it had been released. It had six legs and stood on all of them as an animal would. Its spiked tail lashed around behind it as it took in its surroundings and recognized its own cognition. The spikes which trailed back from its brow followed a path down its back to the point at which its massive wings extended from its back. It had leathery skin and tufts of hair set around large spikes which protruded from what would be considered its elbows had it still appeared at all human.

The beast exhaled a low, powerfully guttural breath when it realized who stood before it, its muscles quivering with anticipation. Allen thought he saw its eyes drift briefly to the sword in his hands. With deliberate purpose it took a couple of thunderous steps toward him and lowered its head to meet his gaze. The beast's eyes were as black as the blade of Sythika. It grunted at him and a moment later ripped his shield in half with its powerful jaws so quickly that he didn't realize what had happened until he'd staggered back to balance and looked down at his left arm.

Realizing that what was left of his shield would do him no good Allen tossed it to the ground behind him and placed both of his hands upon the hilt of his sword. He took a couple of cautionary steps backward, never removing his eyes from the beast. He struggled to think of how he could overcome this situation. The Gorrlock elder had told him he needed to kill this beast to gain passage back into the light of day. Looking at the creature now before him, he was unconvinced a single blade of any type would be enough to kill it. In a move of desperation, he swiped the sword in the beast's direction. It backed away at the motion, if only slightly. Seeing how aware the creature was of the blade, and noticing that its eyes kept darting back and forth between him and it, Allen began to swing it at the beast as he attempted to inch his way toward the exit. Even as fearsome as this creature appeared to be, he had no desire to kill it; he would be content to trap it in this cave for another thousand years.

And then it came to him. Why should he have to kill the beast? Why couldn't he just trap it in here so that it had no way to follow him?

With that idea in mind, Allen kept swinging the blade, inching his way toward the exit. The beast, however, must have realized what Allen was doing because it lunged at him the next moment, forcing Allen to dive away from his only route of escape. He rolled as he hit the ground, bringing his feet back underneath him as quickly as he could manage. He looked up just in time to jump backwards, once again narrowly avoiding being caught in those massive jaws. A large snapping sound echoed around the chamber and his heart raced in in his chest when he realized just how close to death he'd come yet again. He would need more than just the sword to keep the beast at bay if he were going to escape.

In that moment something inside Allen's mind clicked. He understood the purpose behind the first two tests. If he could harness Mystica into some type of offense, he might be able to keep the beast at a distance with a measured attack. He might likewise be able to use Mystica to collapse the cave once he reached the exit. Allen let go of his doubt and gave in to that deeper need. He imagined a green flame springing to life in his left palm and a moment later watched as the very air above his upturned hand compressed and ignited. Elated that he had finally succeeded, he nearly lost control of that emerald fireball before he had a chance to release it at his target. Reigning in his excitement, he leveled the flame at the beast and commanded it to attack.

The beast flinched as the flame burst on the right side of its face. It didn't appear to have done any damage at all. The beast turned its gaze upon him and filled the chamber with a roar that left his ears ringing in earnest. Not wanting to lose what he considered to be the upper hand, he called another fireball to purpose, this time concentrating on making it more powerful. He released it with force, aiming once again at the beast's face. This time, however, the beast opened its massive jaws and swallowed the flame whole. A low rumbling came from deep within the beast which sounded very much like muffled laughter to Allen upon extinguishing the threat. Flames appeared to have absolutely no affect on the beast; it just swallowed the fire as if it were an appetizer. Perhaps that is why they sent me in without a torch, Allen thought to himself.

Allen dodged another lunge, and then another, jumping higher and further than he thought himself capable in order to escape becoming the beast's next course. He wondered for a small eternity what he was to do if flames had no impact on the beast's defenses. As he dodged from side to side, leaping and rolling to avoid being eaten, he desperately searched every corner of his mind for a way out of this predicament. And then it came. If he could generate the emerald flame by imagining it to life, he might be able to do the same with something else he'd seen demonstrated . . .

He recalled seeing Rexim charging his fist with electric energy the day they'd first arrived on Sythar during a short-lived conflict with Pythor, and pictured himself replicating that effect. He forced the need he felt to survive to do his bidding, using his will to generate a spark in his hand. It came slowly at first, and he was nearly caught off-guard by a swipe from one of the beast's talons while he concentrated on bringing his thoughts into existence. But a moment later he succeeded, casting a blindingly bright stream of liquid light at his aggressor with deadly intent. The bolt of lightning sent the beast bouncing hard off the far wall of the chamber and left it convulsing for a moment after it thudded to the ground.

It worked! Allen let out a whoop of victory at the accomplishment.

The moment of excitement was short-lived, however, as the beast arose a moment later, letting out a shriek of its own. Ignoring the panic in his heart, Allen charged his left fist once more and cast another bolt at the enraged guardian of the sword. The beast saw the attack coming this time and, with a mighty thrust of its wings, launched itself upward to escape the attack. The electric assault missed the creature by a wide margin, punching a hole in the wall where the beast had impacted only moments before. The entire chamber shook with the force of that blast.

Allen may have failed to hit his opponent with the second attack, but seeing the hole left in its wake gave him an idea. He looked up to find the beast somehow clinging to the ceiling with its massive claws. Once again he charged his fist with electric energy and sent a bolt tearing through the air toward his enemy. This time, however, he did not aim for the beast directly, but the section of the ceiling to which it clung. When the bolt impacted, he was already running toward the exit. The beast screamed and he nearly lost his footing as the chamber began to quake from the impact of his blast.

When he reached the doorway, Allen turned around to find the beast struggling angrily to dislodge a boulder from on top of its right wing. It howled in fury at him. Allen sheathed the Sword of Sythika and took a deep breath. With great effort and concentration he cupped both his hands six inches apart and called upon Mystica to fill his palms with lightning. He allowed the energy to surge forth and fill his hands, growing in intensity. Tendrils of electricity licked his fingers, desperate to be loosed on his target. Taking careful aim, he unleashed another bolt of white-hot fury at the ceiling directly above the beast. With thunderous force great chunks came crashing down on the beast's head, pinning it to the floor. Allen took several more steps backward and unleashed another charged shot at the doorway to the cave. He could practically feel the whole mountain shake as the tunnel began to collapse, concealing the chamber from which he had retrieved the sword.

Allen expelled a deep breath of relief at having seen his task to completion, proud that he hadn't needed to kill to do it. Now he just needed to gain passage back to Datheron so that he could rescue Sarah and take her home to Earth. He didn't look back once as he rushed through the tunnel toward the light of day.

37

DEBATE

A STIFF NUDGE TO THE RIBS woke Sarah from her restless slumber. Ever since learning of Luziaph's duplicity a few days prior during the confrontation with Gharr, her mind had been ignited with worry. Dreams had come to her only with the greatest of difficulty, her thoughts seemingly in permanent overdrive. When sleep did finally find her, visions of she and Allen being marched to the execution block tormented her to no end. Sometimes her father was there to witness it; at others it was Allen himself which held the axe above her throat. Those dreams in particular left the deepest wounds, as she was unclear why Allen would ever do such a thing, even if only in a nightmare. She did the best she could to shake such haunting thoughts from her mind as she opened her eyes to see who could be standing over her, waking her in such a rude fashion.

"You are summoned," Gazianna said in a hardened voice.

Sarah stretched the sleep from her aching muscles and rolled to a sitting position, propping herself against a wall. She squinted up at her blue-skinned companion, noting not only the tone in which she'd spoken but the haunted look in her eyes as well. The only times she had heard such a tone come from the woman had been immediately following one of Luziaph's fits of abuse; something which happened far too frequently in her opinion. She made a gesture meant to inquire why she was being summoned.

"It is not yours to reason why," Gazianna answered. "We but do as commanded in this palace. Now rise and bring yourself to purpose. Luziaph awaits."

Although Sarah found the manner in which Gazianna was addressing her to be odd, she did as she was told and brought herself to her full height. Once she was on her feet Gazianna looked her over, brushing some of the wrinkles out of the same drab garment she had worn during her entire stay on this planet.

"This will not do at all," she said in a tone somehow laced with concern and indifference. "Come; we shall need you to be clean."

She fell into step as Gazianna quickly marched away from the small room which had been designated to her for sleeping. When she finally caught up, she tapped Gazianna on the shoulder and gestured to the best of her ability a question regarding Gazianna's last remark. In all her time in this palace, she had never been told she needed to be clean. She'd long ago passed the point at which she felt disgusting in her own personal hygiene and would be glad for the chance to cleanse herself, but was nervous to remove the protective clothing Zorthos had provided ever since Malacus' passing. Even though the garments were becoming a little worn and wreaked of body odor, she knew what sort of protection they offered, not to

575

mention the memories she associated them with, and didn't want to be parted from them.

Gazianna glanced at her, looking her up and down as they moved. "Luziaph has demanded that I make you presentable," she said, bringing her eyes back in front of her. "You are to be properly bathed in preparation of the day's events."

Such a proclamation only filled Sarah's mind with more questions. She desperately wished she could give them voice. While she had grown somewhat used to being unable to speak to those of this world, the uncertainties left behind from her lack of ability to communicate was something which she still found difficult to accept. But she had come to learn when it was best to not ask questions and just follow Gazianna's lead. So, rather than continue the arduous task of communication, she kept silent and fell in tow behind Gazianna as they moved at a quickened pace through the palace corridors.

A short time later they stood in front of a large arched doorway, through which Sarah had yet to tread. Gazianna pressed her palm to a plate at the side of the door and it slid open, revealing a large bathing area beyond. In the center of the room was a large wading pool of sorts. Sarah could tell as she stared down from the edge that the water was no more than waist deep. The pool itself appeared to be fashioned in a large, elliptical in design and had steps on one end leading down into the water. There were exotic-looking plants lining the outer walls of the room, except on one side where a small window opened overlooking the eastern side of the courtyard and on the opposite wall where a large, full-length mirror trimmed in a golden pattern was placed. Next to the mirror was a low, stone bench she assumed was there for the purpose of dressing oneself; the mirror in place to inspect one's appearance after doing so.

"Remove your garments and use water to wipe the dirt from your body," Gazianna instructed. "I shall wait just beyond the door."

Sarah quickly clutched Gazianna's arm before she could escape into the hall. She did her best to convey that she needed help bathing. When Gazianna only stared at her in confusion, she gestured for the Gorrlock woman to follow her over to the dressing bench. She paused in mid-step when she saw herself in that full-length mirror. She looked herself up and down in horror. She looked awful! Her hair was matted together in places and poked out awkwardly in others. Her face was covered in dust and dirt, and she appeared as if she had never even heard of make-up. Dark circles dominated large spaces directly below her eyes and she couldn't help but notice a blemish or two forming on her chin. The shabby-looking attire in which she was dressed made her scream inside; it was mired in wrinkles and said absolutely nothing good about the sense of fashion on this world or any other. Having seen her own reflection at last, she suddenly questioned how Allen had even recognized her when they'd been reunited and why he'd been willing to embrace her so readily.

She glanced over to Gazianna through blurry vision.

The woman sighed in annoyance. "Yes, your unsightly visage is what prompted the need for cleansing," Gazianna said harshly.

Sarah stared at herself several moments more before turning from the ghastly image of what she'd become on this world. She stepped over to the dressing bench and motioned for Gazianna to follow her. When Gazianna only stared blankly at her, she held her arm out toward the Gorrlock woman and tugged on the sleeve of her tunic to indicate that she needed help undressing.

Recognition dawned in Gazianna's eyes. "You jest," she said with incredulity. "Are you so helpless that the task of bathing requires aid?"

Knowing that she had no real way to argue the point, she simply nodded. Gazianna shook her head in frustration as she set to the task of helping her disrobe. The tunic was only an inch removed from her flesh when she lost her balance and began to topple forward. Sarah clutched at Gazianna's arms for support as she fell. She was swept up by swift hands and was able to sit down on the bench a moment later.

With one hand on her bare shoulder and the other on her tunic, Gazianna looked at her with surprise in her green eyes. "These garments are adaptive," she reasoned aloud. "You have no tolerance for the gravity of this world?"

Sarah struggled mightily just to nod her head.

At this point, Gazianna seemed to understand Sarah's plight and offered no more protest. She simply focused on the task of helping Sarah through the strenuous ordeal of bathing. When Gazianna made a move to take the necklace from her neck, however, she couldn't help but cling to it desperately, vigorously shaking her head. The blue-skinned woman, startled by the sudden reaction at first, shrugged a moment later and finished the task of removing her clothing, removing her own garb as well and patiently helping her into the water; once immersed, paying particular attention to washing the knots out of her hair. Although she hadn't quite established the rapport with Gazianna that she had with Malacus, Sarah still felt more comfortable having her help with the process than she did the old man. While he had never come close to being inappropriate in the task, it was just awkward in comparison to have an old man helping her bathe when compared to the assistance of someone she considered to be more of a peer; not to mention the delicate attention

Gazianna showed in her efforts was nearly as soothing as if Sarah had been able to do it herself.

With the task complete, Gazianna helped her back into the dirty clothes which acclimated her to the intense surroundings, offering relief from the crushing pressure of the very air around her. Once completely redressed, she stood in front of the mirror once more to reassess her appearance. She still didn't look as good as she knew she could, but it was a far cry better than when she had first seen her reflection. Her hair was still wet and clung to the back of her neck, soaking through the back of her tunic, but at least it was straight. She still had no make-up to hide the blemishes on her chin, but at least her face wasn't plastered in dirt. If only she'd been given the option to wear something else.

"That will have to do," Gazianna said from behind her, as she too stared into the mirror. "Now come; Luziaph yet awaits our arrival."

Sarah placed her hands into her pockets to make sure that the seeds were still there. At this point she only kept them as a reminder of the kindness the old man had showed her, but the idea that they might be taken from her or had fallen out of her pocket during the bathing process worried her in the extreme. Relieved to find them exactly where they had always been, she fell into step behind Gazianna.

When the doors to Luziaph's chambers slid open, Sarah was surprised to see a wide diversity of people already inside, all of which were evidently awaiting her arrival. All eyes immediately looked past Gazianna and fell upon her as they entered and slowly made their way past the series of gruesome statues. Sarah counted five others standing near the throne wearing full suits of armor denoting their station as Proctus. Among them she easily recognized the furry visage of Gharr, who cast a look of intense trepidation at her as she approached. Among the others, all of whose armor was the same brilliant silver as Gharr's and Luziaph's, she noticed that none of them were of the same species as the two Proctus with which she'd dealt so far; two of them were males the same race as Gazianna, while the others appeared to be just as human as she was, one male and one female. Off to the side, behind the Proctus of this world, stood roughly a dozen others in lesser suits of armor which resembled closely the one she'd seen upon Allen before his departure; as well as a few select others dressed in white robes with silver trim. Based on the severe-looking weapons the ones in the armor had clipped to their belts, she assumed them to be military leaders or body guards from the various regions of Datheron. The sight of them all here at once left a bad feeling lingering in the pit of her stomach; she saw no scenario in which this could bode well for her.

When they got within half a dozen paces of those in attendance, Gazianna gestured for her to stop where she was, between the final two statues at the end of the walkway leading to the throne. She clasped her hands together in front of her, watching with insecurity while Gazianna stepped away to take her place at Luziaph's side. Feeling completely abandoned, she kept her eyes on her toes, but could feel everyone else's lingering upon her as she stood there completely exposed to their judgment.

"This is the girl?" she heard a male voice ask. "She is pleasing to the eyes."

The remark left her feeling even more exposed. She found herself wishing Allen were here at her side. He would never let anyone leer at her that way. She missed him terribly.

"She is meek," she heard a female voice say. "Regardless of origin, she could not possibly pose a threat to any of this world. Look at her. She is malnourished and bears the countenance of all who serve."

"Physical appearance is not the factor in question here," a low guttural voice retorted; she recognized it at once to be that of Gharr. "The girl hails from Earth! She was witnessed speaking in alien tongues in the market square of Abendroth! That should be enough to pass judgment upon her!"

"And how is truth in the statement to be measured when none can translate her words?" Luziaph countered smoothly. Once again the three-eyed lunatic surprised her by coming to her defense.

"At what point did yours become the voice of reason, Triclopian?" a new, deep voice asked.

There was a long pause before Luziaph responded. "You would do well to mind your tongue while in my province, Gorrlock!" he finally bit back. "I have ever spoken from a place of reason. It is prejudice that clouds the truth of this from your mind."

"Enough!" Gharr growled. "Pointless bickering will gain us nothing, nor is it the purpose for which we gather this day! Long has it been known that one day a child of Earth would walk among us. In the past, caution has always given way to the reckless endangering of our world! When the way of life is about to be stripped from comforting embrace, what must be done has never been in question! Why do we now stand apart when the mere threat of that end yet stands before us? I say the girl's life is forfeit!"

"And I say duty to uphold law, not chaos should win the day!" Luziaph countered angrily. "Long have my people suffered for no crime, save hatred and prejudice! I will not sit by and allow this girl to be executed absent proof of the crime to justify such punishment!"

"And how exactly might such proof be obtained in the absence of translation?" Gharr asked defensively. "Cause to believe she hails from the fabled world of prophecy has been given. The populace rises in panic at the thought that one from Earth yet dwells among them. I say we prove their trust in the authority granted us by turning her over to the hands of Sythika!"

"And if proof of such a thing can be given, I shall perform the act myself before a crowd of spectators," Luziaph answered.

At hearing that remark, Sarah's head jerked upward involuntarily to find Luziaph's third eye on her, while the others lingered on Gharr to his right. The male, human Proctus was the only other one watching her, and noticed her reaction to the claim. Recognition dawned in those calculating brown eyes as they roamed over her entire form.

"Why not just ask her?" the human Proctus suggested. "Olyphatarian may not fall from her tongue, but she clearly understands it."

All at once every eye there fell upon her. A feeling of great panic inundated her as the others considered the suggestion. She looked to Gazianna for some kind of support, only to find rigid panic in her eyes as well. How could she have been so careless? Perhaps it would have been better not to wear the necklace at all times, after all. In that moment she realized that she'd never wanted anything as much as she wanted Allen to burst through the doors behind her, sweep her up in his arms, and carry her away from this nightmare.

"What brings you to such conclusion?" the lone, female Proctus asked.

"A moment ago," he answered, "when Luziaph made comment toward intent of carrying out the order of execution, she bore a look of recognition. She bears it still.

Gaze upon the panic in those beautiful eyes. She understands our words, even if she cannot speak them."

Terrified that her secret had been discovered, Sarah's eyes darted amongst those now watching her. Slowly, ever so slowly, she attempted to take a step backward only to find her feet planted firmly to the floor before she could take a second. She couldn't move. Sarah noticed as the human male eyed her that his right hand was slightly raised as if to hold her in place.

"You see?" the human Proctus said. "She moves to flee this situation. She knows we collaborate to decide her fate. Tell us, girl, is it true that you hail from Earth? A simple nod of the head will prove sufficient."

Sarah stood there, unable to move, unable to even think, for a very long moment while all around her awaited a response she didn't dare give them. She could swear she saw the slightest hint of a smile on Luziaph's lips while the silence grew.

The male, human Proctus tilted his head toward Luziaph without taking his eyes off of her. "You possess mastery over the mind," he said. "Make her give answer."

Luziaph hesitated a moment before he replied. "While it is true that the mind is but playing ground to my every whim, it is a delicate craft. That I cannot understand the form in which her thoughts come prevents me from issuing a direct command. I cannot 'make' her do anything."

The human Proctus straightened his gaze. "Pity," he said. "That would have made it so much easier, yet alternative motivators will offer the same end."

With a slight gesture of his hand, her body suddenly went completely rigid. Her arms were pulled straight out, away from her torso and she was slowly lifted from the ground by an invisible force. The panic already consuming her was intensified as, in one swift motion, she was lifted far above all present, dangling in mid-air and tilted at an angle so that her hair draped past her face and swung across her eyesight. As hard as she struggled against it, there was nothing she could do; she was completely at the mercy of this man.

"Perhaps now answer will come with greater ease," the male, human Proctus said. A mischievous grin twisted the corners of his mouth. "What say you? Do you hail from Earth?"

"Release her, Brucivus," the female Proctus commanded.

"I will once I have the answer I seek, Aldythia," Brucivus replied, placing minor condescension into the pronunciation of her name. "Now, tell us," he reiterated, bringing his attention back to her, "is it true that you hail from Earth?"

Sarah's entire body convulsed as she lost control of her emotions. She watched as a single, hot tear escaped her right eye and drifted to the floor below her. It seemed to take forever for that droplet of moisture to splatter on the ground below. She didn't dare answer the question; she may as well ask them to kill her. She hovered there for what seemed an incredibly long time, debating what to do in her mind, a small part of her hoping that if she delayed long enough that the doors of the throne room might burst open to reveal a savior. As she hung there her eyes moved unconsciously to the only person in the room with whom she found even minute comfort: Gazianna. The blue-skinned woman's emotions echoed her own, her eyes full of liquid concern.

Once again, Sarah's unconscious response had betrayed her. Brucivus glanced over his shoulder, noting the connection between the two women. "How intriguing," he said. "There appears to be a connection between your handmaiden and the girl in question, Lord Luziaph. I wonder how you might respond to request made toward the purpose of exploiting such connection?"

"You have my permission to bring thought to life," Luziaph answered with minimal hesitation.

Sarah found herself back upon the floor far quicker than she would have liked, her extremities slamming loudly on the hard ground. After being all but dropped from such a height, she came to her feet only with great difficulty. Her palms, knees, and the left side of her hip ached horribly from the impact, but they didn't feel broken. After being suspended in the air against her will, unable to do anything to prevent it, a task as small as bringing her feet underneath her seemed a triumph, but felt very awkward.

When she'd finally reached her full height once more, she found Brucivus' eyes lingering on her still, a wicked gleam consuming them. A moment later he extended his left arm, and in one swift motion sucked Gazianna from across the room into his grasp. As his fingers tightened around her throat he drew the short sword from his belt and placed the tip of it against Gazianna's sternum.

"Hesitation may come when your life is all that hangs in the balance," Brucivus said in a taunting manner. "But what shall be your response when it is the life of one close to you that is the price for indecision? What say you now, girl? You understand the words we speak, do you not?" When she brought her gaze to meet Gazianna's, Brucivus bellowed another command. "Do not look to her! It is a simple question demanding simple answer! Does comprehension of our tongue meet your ears?"

Sarah trembled in shock as the reality of the moment sunk in. If she did not answer the question this man would kill the only friend she had on this world outside of Allen, and he would do it in front of her. Yet as soon as she answered the first she knew the very next question would be regarding her origin, an answer that would get herself killed long before Allen had a chance to resurface and win their freedom. She wished that she could tell them that she was from Earth and that she intended to return there as soon as possible. Why wasn't that a viable option for these people? And why wasn't Luziaph speaking up for her now the way he had only moments ago? How could he let this man threaten to kill someone as close to him as Gazianna, a woman who tended his every whim? When it came right down to it, Sarah asked herself what Allen would do in this situation. She realized that he would die rather than let a friend fall in his place. She couldn't allow this man to kill Gazianna for the crime of being her friend.

With a heavy heart and tears trailing down her face, she nodded her head.

A self-satisfied grin slowly twisted the features of Brucivus' face. "There," he gloated, looking to all the other Proctus. "You see? She can understand our words!" As he brought those ruthless eyes back to her, he dug his fingers into Gazianna's throat a little more and applied the slightest bit more pressure to her solar plexus with the tip of the blade. "Now . . . Let us come to the heart of the matter. Do you hail from Earth?"

Sarah could feel herself nodding again, but was in such a daze that she wasn't entirely sure it came from conscious effort on her part. All present gasped in unison and began to murmur amongst themselves. Above all others, she heard Gharr' voice bellowing his triumph.

"There!" the furry Proctus howled. "She admits it! What say you now, Luziaph? The girl openly admits to coming from Earth!"

Luziaph raised a hand to call for silence. It took several moments for all present acquiesce entirely. Once he was certain he had the attention of everyone, Luziaph let out an exaggerated sigh. "It seems there is no other option," he said in a tone of false disappointment. "That the girl truly does hail from Earth calls for the ultimate punishment. Spread word of this day's events, for one day hence I shall cast her in stone and shatter her for all to see."

38

SACRIFICE

ALLEN HELD THE SWORD OF SYTHIKA high above his head. The entire Gorrlock village surrounded him, their eyes full of fear and admiration. Even the Gorrlock elder stood mute, his eyes unable to leave the blade held aloft. The vapor which drifted so lightly from its sharp edges was just as black, just as disquieting, in the light of day. As he stood there reveling in his moment of triumph, the sea of blue skin surrounding him began to slowly fall to their knees one by one; though whether in reverence for the artifact Allen now held above them or because he had proven himself to be the child of prophecy after all, he could not say for certain. It was as invigorating as it was humbling to be at the center of such a reaction. Even Pythor gaped in awe at what Allen had done.

The scene continued like this for quite a while before the elder finally found his feet and slowly approached Allen. "You have done it," he whispered with fascination. "You must tell me . . . how did you slay the beast? What did it look like? I must know every detail of how you came to claim the Sword of Sythika as your own!"

There was a rabid look in the old man's eyes as he stared, unblinking at the pitch black blade. Allen couldn't help but wonder what inspired such a covetous countenance. Had he never before even seen the sword?

He lowered the sword and slid it home, letting the clicking sound of it locking into the scabbard break the elder's focus on it. "You stare as if you have never laid eyes upon the blade which you hold in such high regard, the very blade for which your people have sacrificed countless lifetimes. How can that be so?"

The Gorrlock elder's eyes drifted lazily from that which he had been concentrating so hard on to meet Allen's calculating gaze. The old blue-skinned man had never appeared as aged as he did in that moment. Allen swore he could see a hundred lifetimes flooding their way to the forefront of his mind, plainly visible in his weathered features as the he regarded Allen with something bordering regret. It was as if the weight of all his ancestors was finally being lifted from his shoulders in a single, decisive moment.

"Come," the old man said in an exhausted tone. "I will share stories of old with the child of prophecy."

The entire village moved collectively from where they had met him at the foot of the mountain trail and gathered underneath the larger-than-life statue of the original God-King. The sun was well on its way toward the horizon, casting orange hues on the clouds it was hiding behind. The very air above the desert floor wavered as if to greet the sun back home as Allen moved in tow with the others. Showing no emotion but relief, the Gorrlock elder plopped himself to the ground and leaned against the base of the statue before beginning his explanation. He and all the others followed suit, sitting as one around the sculpture of Paragus.

"To understand the magnitude of this accomplishment," the Gorrlock elder began, "certain aspects of history must be brought to light. Countless centuries ago, when Paragus first came to Datheron, ours was a culture quite primitive in nature. It is said that no real form of government yet existed, that the population consisted of but six sentient species. Numbers of diversity have since swelled greatly, but in the beginning there were but six: Gorrlocks, Triclopians, Saurothians, Voldehydes, Dracomites, and Humans."

Allen silently wondered to himself what a Dracomite looked like. He knew he'd met members of all the other species, but he had absolutely no idea what a Dracomite was. No one had ever mentioned one or pointed one out to him, so he had no point of reference. Had he seen one in passing and not realized it? Had they since become extinct? Curious as he was, and still replaying in his mind his bout with the beast, he decided not to interrupt the elder; making a mental note to ask Pythor later to elaborate on the subject.

"Of these six," the elder continued, "Gorrlocks were the first to completely accept Paragus as their lord and master, the first to swear undying fealty to his command. It was this that earned them the station of elite body guard, this that made them his chosen race."

"But Paragus Himself appears to be human," he interjected, nodding up to the stone visage of whom the elder was speaking.

"And yet it was Gorrlocks which accepted his rule first," the old man countered patiently. He waited a moment, as if to see if he had any other objections before continuing. "For this Paragus honored our ancestors by naming the bravest and the strongest of us to be agents and protectors in His name, providing chosen few with special armor crafted by His own hand. This armor," the old man stated, gesturing to Pythor as he did so, "contains within it properties which greatly amplify any skill, heighten any strength of the wearer. It was from this act that the Krathantor were born.

"Throughout His thousand year reign, the Krathantor remained favored for their loyalty. As infrastructure grew and government took shape, the sight of black and gold armor became synonymous with the word of Paragus. It was we whom He sent in His stead to enforce matters of law and the accompanying punishment. When rule over the entire world was secured, it was members of His elite Krathantor that were chosen as His first ambassadors of what is now the six major regions of Datheron.

"As the years passed, society grew strong under His rule. None dared question His word and it seemed prosperity would remain for all time . . . Until crisis surfaced in the form of six Orbs of Sythika."

As the elder continued his story, Allen remembered that he'd heard much of the same story from Malacus, though he found it interesting that those of the Gorrlock tribe recounted Paragus' rule as prosperous, when Malacus had told him that He was known for His brutality. He listened well while the Gorrlock elder shared the details of Paragus' initial failure to contain the threat of the orbs, that solving the problem was considered only a partial victory as it had robbed the original God-King of his immortality, not to mention his sanity. He also found it interesting to learn a new detail that Malacus had either neglected to mention, or did not know about its resolution. According to the elder's version of events, Paragus never destroyed the orbs of Sythika. The old man elaborated on a method through which the original God-King had contained the orbs of concentrated Sythika by encasing them in shells of concentrated Mystica, effectively counteracting their effects and preventing them from causing anymore damage.

"Am I to understand," he asked, "that the orbs of Sythika yet remain somewhere upon the surface of Datheron to this day?"

The Gorrlock elder nodded. "The vaunted orbs remain hidden beyond the knowledge of any who yet draw breath. It has been passed down that clues to their hidden locations were left behind, but they too remain well hidden." The old man paused a moment before continuing, watching him ponder this new information. "Following upon the heel of seeing the crisis abated," the elder continued, "Paragus made discovery that the presence of the contained orbs proffered great change upon the world He had fought so hard to forge in His image. Others began to slowly grasp the secrets behind His god-like abilities."

"Pause a moment," he interrupted again. "Am I to understand that the presence of the Orbs of Sythika was the catalyst upon which the current state of life for Datheronian's was set into motion?"

The old man expelled a mildly irritated sigh. "The telling of a story is taxing in your presence," he said. "Have you ever been made aware of such a thing?"

Allen lowered his head. "Once or twice," he answered sheepishly. "Apologies; I only seek understanding."

"Yes." The Gorrlock elder breathed, a little defensively in Allen's opinion. "Though it is not common knowledge among the populace of Datheron, to those closest to Paragus it was explained that the sympathetic relationship between His Armor of the Gods and the Orbs of Sythika, counterparts of immense power in measure, created the unique aura from which the learning of all godly abilities was generated. Such a realization forced Paragus

592

to establish academies wherein newfound abilities could be learned and mastered at His discretion. The Arena Games, which to this day remains a source of entertainment to all of Datheron, was established to provide opportunity for any willing to test their mettle.

"As time passed, those who could command godly powers grew in number. Paragus gathered His most faithful, to whom He had granted the most knowledge on manipulating Mystica, appointing them to be headmasters of academies in each of the six regions of His local empire. The duties of the Krathantor grew as well. They were required to aid in the training of any who sought knowledge on the subject, as well as being required to travel to other worlds under the influence of Paragus to the purpose of maintaining order. Events moved away from even the God-King's control as time cast him from its favor and the ravages of age slowly took him.

"Near the end of His life cycle, it is believed by most that Paragus lost control over His mind. Some considered Him to be mad. Visions of future events came to Him in earnest showing him things outside the understanding of most. One such vision revealed a shadowy figure claiming the Sword of Sythika as his own and using it to end the reign of Paragus. It was this premonition which inspired the hiding of His legendary blade upon the surface of Sythar, far beyond the reach of any upon Datheron. With this goal firmly in mind, He gathered a few of His most trusted, commanding them to accompany Him to this moon and remain here to protect the blade even beyond His passing into the hands of Sythika. He shared the location of the sword with none but His most trusted Krathantor; not even His closest advisor, Abendroth, knew where the vaunted blade was hidden."

Allen recognized the name at once; Abendroth was the name of the city in which he had traveled with Malacus to acquire ingredients to revive Sarah from her coma, the city in which he had been arrested and taken to Luziaph. Just hearing the name sparked harsh feelings in his heart. It occurred to him that the statue in that city, near to which those fateful events had taken place, might very well be crafted in the image of the man about whom the elder now spoke.

"It was Abendroth, however," the elder continued, "which discovered Paragus gasping for breath in His bed chamber following His evening meal. The man, a human, gathered servants from all over the palace to the purpose of locating one who might be able to spare the God-King from His suffering. It was then that Paragus first spoke the words of your prophecy, claiming vengeance upon the one who had poisoned Him once He returned from Sythika. To this day none know who bears responsibility of the act which destroyed the original God-King.

"Following the event which stripped Mystica from Paragus' flesh, society upon Datheron nearly crumbled. Paragus had named no successor. It was assumed by most that any who could claim the Armor of Paragus as their own would be named the new God-King, inheriting dominion over the entire world. Many of the most powerful attempted such a thing, bartering their own lives in the act. Of all who made attempt toward equipping the Armor of the Gods, none survived. When it became clear that none could safely wear the armor, it was suggested by a Gorrlock that the solution was obvious; only his most powerful, most faithful Krathantor could claim position over the whole of Paragus' empire.

"Such a remark nearly sent the world into civil war. Infighting among the Krathantor brotherhood ensued, each one bickering for their own right to claim supremacy. While those that had once enforced laws set example of weakness in the form of avarice, the rest of the world

594

succumbed to chaos. All was nearly lost until Abendroth stepped forward making suggestion that a final, decisive tournament be held to determine to whom total dominion should be granted."

The Gorrlock elder rested his head against the statue at his back, letting his eyes wander as he seemed to lose his train of thought. He paused for several moments, expelling a deep sigh before continuing. "Once a new God-King emerged, the brotherhood which had once stood so strong disbanded. Some remained loyal to the rule of the new God-King, but most fled to join those who still held to final request of the original. It was these events which brought the majority of our ancestors to this place. During the countless generations which followed, those who have remained here have kept their eyes to the horizon which would reveal the child of prophecy. An elder, such as myself, being granted final authority over administering the trials as well as the entire collective knowledge of those who came before."

Allen reflected on all he had just learned. Though he was eager to expedite his return to Vardiston and Sarah, the elder's last remark had piqued his curiosity. "You possess all the knowledge of your predecessors?" he asked with incredulity. When the elder simply nodded, Allen decided he needed to know how such a thing was possible.

Before he could, however, a great rumbling began to shake the whole village. All present, including the two Triclopians who had seemed content to remain silent through the course of events over the last few days, began to panic. Everyone rose to their feet, looking around and clutching one another as the quaking intensified. When a deafening explosion burst from roughly halfway up the mountain, many screamed and ran toward the desert. A great shrieking echoed all around as chunks of the mountainside tumbled toward the village.

The Gorrlock elder grabbed Allen's arm fiercely, a wild look of panic in his black and red eyes. "You let the beast live!" he accused angrily. "You fool!"

Before he could respond to the statement another shrieking cry filled the air, announcing the beast's emergence from the cave high above them. Allen watched in horror as its wings caught the air beneath them and it began to soar in circles around the mountain which had entombed it for so very long. It cried in anguish as it cut a path through the air above them, swooping down toward the Gorrlock village. It landed with thunderous force on top of the elder's domicile and bellowed its rage as it located him among the scattering crowd. Tendrils of black vapor trailed from the beast's skin, moving slowly at first as it lowered its head to gaze directly at him. A guttural rumbling echoed all around and the black mist began to swirl around its master, culminating and compressing in a single point as the beast opened its massive jaws. In a moment of sheer terror the beast loosed the pitch black energy it had gathered in its mouth, sending a burst forth, which seemed to cut reality in half as it moved furiously toward him.

Allen felt himself bounce off a wall to his left and looked up from the ground in time to see the burst of black energy come to an end, leaving a trail of destruction in its wake exactly where he had been standing only moments before. Vapor as dark as midnight wafted up from the ground in a path that cut a line down the center of the village. Villagers cowered behind the walls of their homes as another shriek filled the air.

He followed the path of destruction to its end and saw the statue of Paragus was laying on the ground in pieces; although chunks of it were conspicuously missing, as if completely erased from existence.

Allen's nerves shook as he pulled himself to his feet. He had only just escaped his previous conflict with this creature. Now it was more than just his own life that was at risk. He looked around at the village as remorse crept into his heart. He felt wholly responsible for the danger the villagers now faced.

As if in response to the turmoil engulfing him, the elder roughly shook Allen's shoulders. "Do you see?" the elder yelled at him. "The fault in this rests upon your shoulders! You allowed the beast to live, placing more than just your life at risk in the act! Had reflexes betrayed me you would be dead this very moment!"

Allen's eyes lingered on the elder and nothing as all around him fell into chaos. The elder shook him again. "Find your senses, or see all around you come to an end! Only the Sword of Sythika can kill the beast! Go! Protect that which foolish arrogance has placed in danger!"

With a stiff nudge from the elder, he was pushed out into the open. As he looked around, Allen saw all were watching him to see what he would do. But he could find no sign of the beast. He looked to the sky just in time to see the beast diving from above. Instinct alone saved him as he dived to the side and rolled away from the talons of the beast. As he brought himself to his knees, he gathered a ball of electric energy between his hands. Perhaps such an attack would slow the creature down as it had in the cave.

Allen paused just before unleashing the attack on the ravenous aggressor when he noticed something which all but stopped his heart in his chest. There, in the grasp of those vicious talons, lay Anadar's mother. She fought against the beast's grasp for only a few moments before going forever limp. When the beast realized that it did not have Allen clutched firmly in its grasp, it tossed the lifeless body of the Gorrlock woman carelessly to the ground far below as it continued to swirl overhead.

As much as he hated to admit it to himself, Allen was beginning to think the elder was right. Perhaps he should have just killed the beast; none of this would be happening if he'd only followed instructions and destroyed the guardian of the sword before he'd left the cave. Had he heeded the words of the old man, Anadar's mother would still be alive. The grief he felt over such a cataclysmic mistake began to overtake his resolve.

Pythor must have sensed Allen's hesitation because he began calling to all the other villagers for support. "To arms!" he cried. "We must not meet Sythika this day! Attack!" With his heart aching, Allen watched as Pythor ran over to the Gorrlock elder. "Remove that which binds Mystica from obeying my command!" he pleaded.

It was at this point that Ithaniel finally decided to get involved. "Not a chance!" he yelled in protest as he rushed to intercept the elder's raised hands. "Luziaph gave explicit instruction! The Triaga must not be removed from the head of the criminal!"

The Gorrlock elder turned an irritated stare at the Triclopian wizard as another shriek cut through the air above. "Current circumstances would demand otherwise," the old man retorted.

Ithaniel firmly grabbed the elder by the wrist, leaning in as he spoke. "I will not allow it," he said in a challenging tone.

"So be it," the elder replied. In one swift motion the old man forced the Triclopian to relinquish his grasp and sent the three-eyed aggressor flying through the air, already being consumed by emerald flames before the body landed several meters away. Without another word the elder turned to Pythor and pressed his palms to the

Triaga upon his head. The echoing click of success which rang through the air as the Triaga fell away could be heard even over the panic and violence all around them, if only dimly.

With the task done, the elder turned to him. "That," he said resolutely, nodding to the smoking body of Ithaniel behind him, "is how you do what must be done! I did not wish to kill him, yet he left me little recourse given current circumstances. Now, abandon what you believe to be right and cling to that which is necessary!"

Allen turned from the elder's gaze just in time to dive out of the way as the beast swooped down for another pass, spitting death at the village beneath it. The ground shook as the attack impacted behind him. When he brought his eyes back to assess the damage this time, he found several of the Gorrlock's homes split apart and more blue-skinned bodies scattered about and unmoving. Black vapor drifted up from each corpse, appearing as if their souls were fleeing their bodies before his very eyes. It was then that Allen noticed that all of the black vapor trailing back to a single point of origin: the beast.

Allen took another look around at all the destruction that had come from his indecision and something inside him snapped. He may not be able to undo what had already been done, but he could stop the beast from spreading more havoc.

Turning his gaze back to the beast resting once again atop the elder's home, he reached down and ripped the sword from its scabbard with fierce intent. The same odd ringing announced the sword's arrival and the beast howled in unison. "If you want the sword returned," he challenged, "then come and claim it from me!"

The beast let out a low snarl and Allen got the feeling that it had understood him. With a mighty thrust from its wings it hurled itself toward him with frightening speed. He drew the sword back, gripping it with both hands he braced himself for the oncoming attack. As the beast swooped in low, opening its claws in preparation to snatch him from the ground on which he stood, Allen threw himself forward into a roll, slashing at the creature's underbelly as he moved. He felt resistance as the pitched-black blade made contact and he narrowly missed being ripped open by the beast's talons. The guardian of the blade bellowed in pain as it swooped upward and away from what had just pierced it.

Allen brought his eyes up to see the creature spiraling overhead in an awkward pattern higher than it had previously been flying. He started when he heard Pythor's voice coming from behind him; he hadn't realized the man was that close. He brought his gaze around to see both Pythor and the Gorrlock elder standing close by.

"Wound has been inflicted by the Sword of Sythika," Pythor said in amazement. "Why does the beast yet live?"

"The beast has grown stronger since escaping the confines of its chamber," the elder answered. He turned a judgmental look of reproach upon Allen. "Such is the reason behind previously given warning to kill it prior to exodus. I fear it will take more than minor wounds to bring it to rest now."

Allen silently castigated himself; things just kept getting worse for him. Why couldn't anything ever be easy? He shuffled his fingers along the wire-wound hilt, considering his options. Slowly, a plan began to take shape as he watched the beast circling overhead. He turned to the elder, hoping that his assumption was correct.

"Word of possessing the entire collective knowledge of your predecessors was mentioned," he said. The elder nodded and he proceeded. "What skills does such knowledge afford you?"

"A great many," the elder replied. "Come to plain words."

"Can you call lightning to your aid?" he asked. The old man nodded again and relief flooded through Allen. "Then call it now and see the beast plummet from above! I will lay in wait leaping upon its back once it is grounded, toward the purpose of plunging the sword to its hilt in the beast's back!"

With no hesitation the Gorrlock elder raised his hands above his head, placed his palms together and summoned an electric charge large enough to cut a tree in half. The burst of light shot upward, cutting the sky in two with its force. The beast expelled its loudest shriek yet as the bolt hit its mark, forcing the creature's wings to lock up, sending it plummeting in a downward spiral toward the village. It crashed into the ground with thunderous force and slid to a stop several meters from the point of impact.

Seeing his moment of opportunity, Allen charged forward and leaped high through the air. He landed on the beast's back and nearly stumbled from the momentum he had used to reach his destination. The beast's muscles quivered violently under his feet, though whether from the bolt of lightning or from its crash-landing he couldn't say for sure. Gathering his balance, Allen stepped forward, bringing himself to a stop between the beast's massive wings and raised the sword over his head with both hands, blade pointed downward. It occurred to him that he was about to take the life of a living creature and he paused. It was in that moment of hesitation that the beast regained enough of its faculties to rise slightly and buck him from its back.

As Allen flew through the air over the beast's head and into its line of sight, the blade slipped from his grip. He threw his hands in front of him in an attempt to protect himself from the stiff ground as the sword disappeared from his peripheral vision to his right. He hit the ground, and the wind was forcefully driven from his lungs. As he rolled to his side, struggling to take in air, he chastised himself for missing yet another opportunity to end the beast. A moment later he looked up to see the monster leveling its glare at him and opening its massive jaws. That same black vapor began to gather in the beast's open mouth and Allen knew he had made his last mistake.

Then, seemingly out of nowhere, the Gorrlock elder landed upon the creature's back, slamming his palms to its head. It tried to buck the old man as it had Allen, but the Gorrlock leader held fast. The beast twisted and thrust itself in every direction it could, trying with obvious desperation to free itself from the old man's grasp. As it spun in place and swiped with its tail, the beast's movements became ever slower, ever more rigid. It let out a cry of anguish as its skin slowly began to change color and consistency. The old man was casting the ancient creature in stone.

Allen's awe, however, quickly turned to concern as the attack began to rebound on the old man. He was sure the stubborn old fool knew what was happening, but refused to relinquish his grasp. The entire village collectively began to hazard glances from their hiding places at the awe-inspiring scene. In a matter of moments, each of which felt like a small lifetime, the twitching and fighting slowly came to a stop. When it was over everyone present gazed up at a new statue which now stood in the very place in which the image of Paragus had once dominated the village. Atop the back of the beast stood the Gorrlock elder, wearing a look of eternal pain and concentration, forever frozen in place with the unmoving guardian of the Sword of Sythika.

The villagers slowly began to emerge and gather around what was left of the man who had been their leader, who had sacrificed himself so that they might live. Tears of loss and relief filled the black and red eyes of the survivors.

Children wept as they clung to their parents. Even Pythor, who had never exhibited much in the way of emotion, wiped a tear from his right eye as he too stared up at the immortalized visage of the day's tragic conclusion.

A sudden scream and commotion behind him, caused Allen to jerk his head to the left. There, not twenty-five feet away, was Rexim, clutching the Sword of Sythika in one hand and a Gorrlock woman in the other.

The Triclopian had a look of wicked desperation on his face as he addressed all present. "I have it!" he yelled. "The blade of legend is mine and it shall be my actions which alter the course of history!" All three eyes found Pythor. He pulled the Gorrlock woman close, raising the blade within inches of her throat. "Open the warp gate back to Datheron or see her share in the fate of the others lost this day!"

After the traumatic events of the last few days, Allen could scarcely believe that anyone would be as cruel as to take advantage from a situation that had none. He was reluctantly beginning to understand Pythor's misgivings about Triclopians. First, Ithaniel had tried to prevent adding a pair of experienced hands to the battle and now Rexim appeared ready to kill a defenseless woman to take that which he had not earned. Although he knew that the actions of the few could not truly condemn the many, these two Triclopians had set a very poor example of their race's disposition in the face of adversity.

Pythor stepped forward casting a look of pure hatred at Rexim. "Release the woman, Triclopian!" he spat. "You are outnumbered and will yield no victory from your current course of action."

Rexim pulled the woman's hair fiercely, exposing her throat ever so slightly more to the blade which was held a scant few inches from it. "Do as commanded or see her meet Sythika!" he threatened.

For a very long moment Pythor just glared at Rexim, considering his options. Allen looked around to find that same look of hatred in the eyes of all around him. He couldn't really blame any of them for feeling as they did. They had all just experienced a very tragic set of events, losing their leader and all his knowledge and guidance in the process. After a moment's consideration, he realized that he couldn't hold it against them if they chose to hate him too for his role in the day's events.

He brought his eyes back to Rexim and his hostage just in time to see the woman elbow her three-eyed captor in his side and vanish from sight. Rexim seemed just as startled by the sudden evasive maneuver as Allen was. An onslaught of green fireballs tore the Triclopian apart an instant later. The Sword of Sythika was thrown clear and slid to a stop several feet away. Allen stared down at a man who had only moments before been breathing in horrified amazement, no longer certain he wanted anything at all to do with special abilities if this was the price for obtaining them.

A moment later the blackened blade flew through the air past him, landing firmly in Pythor's right hand. The entire village paused as the Krathantor turned to him, gripping the sword tightly in his hand. To Allen, the man seemed unclear as to what he should do now that he had the sword in his possession.

After a very long moment of tense hesitation, Pythor held the sword out to him hilt first. "Now you have seen a Triclopian's true nature," he said, the words oozing contempt as they fell from his tongue. "You must reconsider your previous agreement with Luziaph. Do not bring regret to the act of returning the sword to your possession."

Allen cautiously reached out and took the sword from Pythor, immediately sliding it back into the scabbard at his hip. He looked around again to find every eye in the village on him, watching with a wide variety of emotion and uncertainty to see what he would do. He suddenly found himself very conflicted about handing the sword over to Luziaph upon their return. He realized it would be very selfish of him to cast aside all these people had sacrificed, to ignore their vigilance in guarding the legendary blade just to gain freedom and passage back to Earth for him and Sarah. It would be as if he were spitting at the feet of their collective efforts if he didn't consider how such a decision would affect them, not to mention the rest of Datheron.

He turned back to Pythor. "What is the custom of this world for honoring the dead?" he asked.

"A short ceremony which involves little more than reducing what remains to ash," Pythor replied. "For those who have earned more in the eyes of the many, a statue is erected in their image to be viewed in remembrance for all time."

Allen nodded, turning to the rest of the Gorrlock villagers. "And following the conclusion of such ceremony is it the intent of all here to return to Datheron at my back?" Every single Gorrlock nodded their head in unison. "Then let us honor those lost this day and reemerge upon the soil of Datheron together, that we might see your sacrifices be not in vain!" He looked to Pythor once more. "Can I rely on your assistance in seeing this course to proper conclusion?"

Pythor's only response was a smile and a stiff clap on the shoulder. Together, in silence, they set to the task of gathering those fallen to begin the Gorrlock approximation of a funeral. Allen knew that once it was done the real conflict would begin.

39

EXODUS

SARAH'S LIFE WAS ABOUT TO END. The realization of that left her feeling no less desperate, no less terrified the next morning. Upon hearing Luziaph announce that he would turn her to stone and shatter her in front of an entire crowd of spectators, her knees had buckled causing her to collapse in front of the Proctus of Datheron. She could still scarcely believe that it had happened had been able to get no sleep that night. Her mind had raced all night, and raced still in search for some way out of this situation. She ached to be able to plead for her own life, but as incapable as she was of speaking the native tongue, she couldn't tell them that it was Allen that was the chosen one and not her even if she wanted to . . . as desperate as she felt, she had actually considered the option at some point during her restless evening alone.

What galled her most about the whole thing was that she now knew herself to be just a pawn in Luziaph's twisted play for supremacy. The creepy, three-eyed despot knew very well that it was Allen and not she that was the one spoken of in the prophecy as he had been the one to send Allen to the moon of Sythar to ignite it. She realized too late that Luziaph had been manipulating events all along, that having the other Proctus show up at his doorstep eager to see the one from Earth put to death had been exactly what he wanted; his words on her behalf had never been altruistic, just a part of the plan. She shuddered to think of what the man had in store for Allen when he finally did return.

What filled her thoughts the most, however, during her final night among the living, had been her final words to Allen. As uncertain as she had been even in the moment of speaking them, she was now glad that she had given in to the urgency she had felt. He may not have made it back in time to rescue her, but at least she had told him how she felt before she died. Even that thought came as little comfort though when weighed against what lay in store for her.

Rather than being put back in the small room which had been her sleeping quarters for the rest of her time in the palace of Vardiston, she had been escorted down to the holding cells. Now that it was known that she came from Earth, she was being treated like a criminal, just Allen had been. She had cried so much after being left there that she was sure her face was still red and her eyes were puffy. Although she knew it would do her no good, she couldn't help but blame herself for where her life had gone and would quite literally end. If only she had insisted more vehemently that they not give in to Allen's incessant curiosities, she might this very minute be on her way to work or attending a class at the local community college. Even that thought, however, came as little comfort when she admitted to herself that Allen would have gone without her, leaving her to console his mother and wonder for the rest of her life what had happened to him.

At some point Gazianna had showed up, pressing her hand to the plate outside the holding cell releasing the field which kept her contained. With eyes full of regret the blue-skinned woman stared down at her, gesturing with a nod of her head that the time had come.

Sarah pulled herself to her feet, not entirely certain where the strength to do so was coming from. As she stepped through the threshold, taking a couple steps toward the exit of the detention wing of the palace, she noticed Gazianna seemingly lost in thought as she stared at the holding cell she had occupied all night. In absolutely no hurry to begin the day's events, Sarah waited while the woman considered something which left her looking almost haunted.

"This one was his also," Gazianna said in a low, mournful voice.

Numb as she was, the remark took a moment to register completely in Sarah's mind. She glanced to the pillars which made up the holding cell and then back to Gazianna when the woman finally removed her eyes from what seemed to be tormenting her.

When Gazianna brought her eyes to Sarah's, they were already filling with tears. "I have failed him," she said in a shaky voice. "He asked but one thing of me and I could not do it. Araset risked all to include me in his scheme for freedom, petitioning my release alongside yours. How I long for such to become reality." The tears were flowing freely down her cheeks now. "When he returns to find you one with Sythika he will hate me . . . and once Lord Luziaph has that which he seeks he will destroy me for entertaining such thoughts as freedom."

Sarah wouldn't have known what to say to the woman even if she could speak the language; all she could do was stand there and listen. She watched as an internal struggle quite obviously raged through the only companion

608

she'd had on this world in Allen's and Malacus' absence. As compassionate as she normally considered herself, she was having difficulty bringing herself to care at the moment. Again she asked herself what Allen would do were it him in this situation and not her. After a moment she reached out and took the Gorrlock woman in her arms, embracing her as a sister would when the other needed comfort. Going rigid at first, Gazianna looked almost assaulted by the gesture of kindness. Sarah would have found it sad that the woman trembled so at even the slightest touch of comfort had she not been so numbly preoccupied by her own plight.

When she released Gazianna, the blue-skinned woman was looking at her with whirlwind of confusion on her face. "Is such the custom on Earth when one is brought to tears by grief?" Gazianna asked. Sarah nodded her head mechanically. "How different your world must be . . . I think that I would have liked to see Earth before Mystica flees my wounded flesh."

An instant later Gazianna's countenance had shifted back to the stony visage it always was. She wiped the tears from her cheeks and nodded for Sarah to follow her without a word. If not for the tremendous weight hanging over her, clouding her every thought, she might have thought it were any other day in the palace of Vardiston.

The journey through the palace corridors had been one of the most arduous tasks she had ever faced. Just lifting one foot in front of the other took tremendous strength, her knees threatening to buckle with each passing step. She watched surroundings she had grown relatively familiar with pass by with new eyes as she marched ever onward toward her own execution. How could this alien world, these strange accoutrements and decorations be the last things she would ever see? Even the sunlight cutting into the corridors through the elevated windows seemed somehow tainted, as if it were taunting her that it would still be here even after she'd gone.

All too quickly they reached the main entry hall of the palace. She could see all of the same Proctus gathered near the exit, watching her come into view as if she were a tasty meal they were about to consume. While most appeared passive or complacent, Luziaph in particular seemed to be enjoying the moment. She could tell he was struggling immensely to keep the smile off his lips and out of his eyes. Brucivus eyed her with something bordering hunger and pity, as if she were the juiciest steak he'd ever sacrificed to feed his dog. Sarah found it extremely tragic that she couldn't even verbally condemn these zealots for what they were about to do to her.

When they reached the end of their journey Gazianna bowed her head to Luziaph, stepping aside to allow him access to Sarah. Light reflected harshly off his bald head as he looked down at Gazianna in contempt. "We shall discuss your weakness immediately following the conclusion of that which will return our world to civility," Luziaph said, the words oozing off his tongue as if it made him sick to even address her.

Then he turned his attention to Sarah. "As for you, take solace in knowing that the sacrifice made this day is sparing countless lives. You do this world a service in accepting your fate and passing into the arms of Sythika. From such passing will come the strength and comfort for all to remain secure in life as it is known here."

Knowing that she stood no chance in a physical confrontation with any of those so willingly bringing her life to an end, and that she couldn't even verbally dispute the act, Sarah responded in the only way she felt herself able. She raised her middle finger, passing it by each Proctus' face one by one and let it linger the longest in front of Luziaph.

A look of astonished confusion passed among the Proctus of Datheron. "What do you suppose is the meaning of such a gesture?" Brucivus asked.

"It matters not," Luziaph replied without hesitation. "Let us move to purpose and see the minds of our subjects returned to ease."

The doors scraped slightly as they opened, seemingly of their own accord. The light of day hit her so suddenly that she flinched at the intrusion as if it were offensive. She hadn't even noticed the guards at her back until one of them forcefully nudged her to move into that light. She heard the crowd before she could see them, the collective rabble coming in every form, from cheering to angered cries of hatred.

When her eyes finally adjusted, she stared out at a sea of alien diversity indignantly with loathing in her heart. The spectators gathered at the bottom of the stairs which led to the entrance of the palace and spread all across the entire courtyard and through the gates at its edge. This entire planet was barbaric and all of these people and creatures had shown up to revel in her execution. She hated them. She found herself, against her own nature, hoping that Allen truly was destined to destroy them. As tormented as she felt, however, she refused to give them the satisfaction of seeing her cry, of witnessing her beg for her life.

When all of this world's leaders had gathered above the crowd and she stood next to Luziaph, the Triclopian leader put one hand on her left shoulder and raised his other for silence. "It is with heavy hearts that we gather this day," he yelled for all to hear. "Rumors of one from Earth walking among us have not been exaggerated! Set your eyes upon the one of which you have heard such rumors whispered! She stands before you this day, ready to face punishment befitting her crime! Admission of guilt that she does in fact hail from the fabled planet of Earth was given before the Proctus of every region upon Datheron one day past! No hesitation came in the decision made to stand as one before you, our minds set toward a singular purpose, upon this discovery!"

When she glanced out at those in the crowd, Sarah saw faces of every type she could imagine, as well as a great many she never would never have been able to fanthom. They gaped at her with every expression of shock and horror conceivable, some even covering the eyes of their children as they did so. Sarah had never felt so exposed, so singled out in her entire life as she did in that moment. Unable and unwilling to endure the gawking hatred of those who had shown up to watch someone die, she closed her eyes and shook her head slowly as Luziaph continued to embellish the details of how she had come to be on Datheron, how Luziaph himself had sought her out to determine the validity of a rumor he'd somehow heard before anyone else. He told the crowd that he had only kept her presence at his palace in confidence out of the interest of justice, until he was able to be certain that she did truly hail from Earth, stating that the truth had cleared his conscience as to what needed to be done. The crowd roared with delight when he announced that she would be killed in the same manner as his predecessor; that she would be shattered in front of them all and that in doing so he would be restoring their world to balance.

With her eyes tightly shut Sarah let her mind drift to thoughts of home. She thought back to when she had first met Allen, recalling that in the beginning she hadn't wanted anything to do with him. It had bothered her to see her father dating someone less than a year after her mother had passed away and she had wanted to turn all of that frustrated anguish on the boy with whom she was being forced to spend time. But he had been so patient, so understanding, such a good listener that she had eventually found herself enjoying the evenings when their parents would get together. Even though he was a couple years younger than she, there was something about him which set him apart from other boys his age and older. Even then she had known that he was unique, that he was special . . . that he was meant for great things. She ached at the thought that she would never again set eyes upon him. She admitted to herself in that moment that if this was her role in his destiny that she was glad to at least have known him. If she had to be the catalyst that set this chain of events in motion for him then she would willingly walk toward her own death; she loved him enough to die for him.

Despite her best efforts, tears were flowing freely down her face when she finally opened her eyes again. The crowd occupying the courtyard was cheering loudly at Luziaph's last remark. She had been so lost in her own memories that she hadn't heard what he had just said, nor had she noticed that he had released her shoulder and taken to pacing the stage as he addressed the spectators.

Evidently finished with his false narration of the events leading to this point, he turned all three eyes upon Sarah. With a wicked look in his eyes Luziaph took a deliberately slow step forward, raising hands slowly toward her head. "Brace yourself for the end," he said with obvious delight.

The vision had awoken Allen abruptly, filling him with a panicked sense of urgency. His entire body was drenched in sweat and his heart raced painfully in his chest as he sat up from the hard ground. After helping perform the funeral rites for the fallen Gorrlock villagers, not to mention the stress of the trials, he had had great difficulty getting to sleep. The plan had been to get a few hours rest and collectively set out for Datheron at first light. But after what he'd just seen, he knew they could not wait until morning to depart. With frightening clarity he had watched as Sarah was paraded in front of the entire city of Vardiston, within the walls of the palace courtyard, and shattered to pieces after being turned to stone by Luziaph. He might have thought it was just a particularly intense nightmare had the vision not gotten more vivid after he awoke.

At once Allen lept to his feet and began running around the village, screaming for everyone to wake up. He had never experienced such a thing and didn't know how common of an occurrence it was for one learning to use Mystica to have visions, but he didn't dare take the risk that it wasn't real. Something deep inside Allen told him that he needed to get back to Sarah before it was too late. He hoped with everything in him that it wasn't already.

Slowly the entire village came alive, most looking distraught or offended at being woken so quickly after they'd fallen to sleep.

Pythor grabbed Allen firmly by the arm as he ran past shouting for everyone to rise from their slumber. "What seizes your senses to raise us from dreams in such a manner?"

"A vision has come to me in the night!" he answered, doing nothing to hide the desperation in his voice.

The remark seemed to have shaken all that remained of the sleep in Pythor's eyes. "A vision?" he asked incredulously. "Are you quite certain?"

Allen nodded, realizing a moment later that most of the village was already crowding in around them. Quiet murmuring began to break out at hearing him admit to having a vision. Allen shook his arm from Pythor's grasp and reiterated his desire to be away immediately.

"Pause a moment and tell me of this vision," Pythor replied firmly. "From what reason does haste become necessity?"

"The vision was of a betrayal at the hands of Luziaph!" Allen exclaimed, doing nothing to shield the irritation in his voice. "The truth of Sarah's presence has been revealed! She faces death absent my protection!"

Startled by what Allen had just told him, Pythor glanced around to the villagers crowding in around them as he considered something. A moment later his countenance shifted to one of steely resolve. "And what is it you intend to do to prevent such outcome?" he asked in a tone bordering on accusatory. "Would you now hand over that which Luziaph seeks in the bargain? Would you put the lie to promises made to my people in the wake of sacrifices made that you might bring validation to their efforts?"

Low murmuring broke out among those surrounding them. After a moment Allen even heard a voice several rows back ask the meaning in Pythor's question. He had been hoping to avoid any of these Gorrlocks learning the truth of his original intentions for the Sword of Sythika, but could see that was no longer an option. As much as he didn't want to, he knew that the truth had to come to light. He admitted to himself that sometimes it was even deserved and necessary despite how it would make one look in revealing it. In this situation there were things far more important than his pride.

Turning to address the onlookers Allen gave himself over to what needed to be done. "Let me raise the burden of truth from weary shoulders," he called out loud enough for all to hear. "When first I embarked on this journey, my intentions were not as pure as I allowed you to believe.

615

The Proctus of Vardiston, a Triclopian, holds the woman I love against my purpose in coming here. Bargain was struck that I retrieve the legendary blade for which you have sacrificed for centuries . . . that I hand it over to him in return for her release and safe passage back to Earth."

Angered mumbling filled the night air as the words of his would-be betrayal came into the open. He let them bicker amongst themselves for a few moments before raising his hand to call for silence. "I will admit to complacency toward the fate of this world in the moment when such agreement was made. Yet it is a path my heart will no longer let me travel. I no longer seek to abandon my fate; I only wish to spare the one I love from the hands of Sythika. A vision has awoken me in the night showing me the circumstances of her demise! If we do not depart for Datheron immediately I fear it to be a reality fast approaching! Please," he begged the onlookers. "I cannot bear to lose her."

"And what about our loss?" called a voice from deep within the crowd. Blue bodies slowly shuffled aside as the one who had spoken the words pushed his way to the front. When they finally parted Allen saw Senjin emerge, pulling Theoxim and Anadar with him. "This one lost his mother this day to destruction left in the wake of your decisions," Senjin accused, gesturing to Anadar. "Theoxim and I lost more. There now stand none to whom we can turn for guidance . . . and that is not withstanding the entire knowledge base of our culture being removed from our grasp in a single moment due to your hesitation. He was as a father to all of us . . . the title bearing more truth for Theoxim and myself than for the rest. Why should we hasten our departure from that which is all we have ever known to save one who inspires poor judgment in he who is said to be child of prophecy, yet cannot do what must be done even as all around him bends to chaos?"

Murmurs of agreement at Senjin's questioning approach filled the air. Allen looked around, knowing that he was far outnumbered in his desire to save Sarah. Even Pythor offered no words of defense or encouragement when Allen's gaze finally found him. "You are not wrong," Allen said at last. "I have given cause to doubt my word and my conviction. I cannot expect your aid in this matter, nor do I require it. I know that I do not have the trust of the Gorrlocks behind me. I have not earned it. But before decision is made, know this . . . the road I have been set upon has inspired great change in me. I no longer seek to turn tail and flee from it. I intend to embrace it and see Luziaph suffer for transgressions committed in the name of order!

"Stay behind if you must, but a wise man told me not one day past that to remain here as the blade is carried toward destiny would be a crime against your efforts. So you have lost a great deal this day; all the more reason to galvanize and see this course to conclusion! Do not let the sacrifices made so that you might have this opportunity be in vain! I do not ask your assistance in the battle that is to come. I will face Luziaph alone. But the choice as to who stays behind and who follows forward must be made now! With or without you I depart to see it done! Choose."

While the others discussed amongst themselves what he'd just said, Allen turned to Pythor in quiet desperation. "Consider the same," he said to the only friend he had in this hostile crowd. "Your assistance in what is to come is not required, save for the warp gate needed to return to Datheron. I would not hold it against you if decision to remain with your people were to take precedence over that which plagues me."

Pythor let out an amused harrumph. "As if I would ever abandon the opportunity to teach proper lesson to that Triclopian vermin! I return to Datheron at your side to see his rule come to an end and to free my brothers from bondage."

Allen couldn't help but smile at Pythor's remark. "We lose precious time," he said.

Turning to the villagers surrounding him, he raised his voice once more. "The time has come! We must depart at once! Those who chose to follow are welcome . . . those who choose to remain behind will be missed."

Without another word, he turned and marched from the crowd, Pythor at his side, only stopping long enough for them to put on armor and gather weapons. Allen was pleased to see that most of the village had decided to accompany them to the surface of Datheron. Only a select few decided to stay behind, Senjin's heated argument inspiring those few to remain at his side. It upset Allen that Senjin could hold such a grudge toward him, especially when he had spared his life in the first trial, but he couldn't afford to dwell on it. Sarah needed him. His goal was firmly fixed in his mind.

They'd only traveled a short way into the desert before Pythor placed his hands to the sand beneath his feet, summoning the gateway back to Datheron. Allen watched intently, hoping that his supposed unique understanding of Mystica might allow him to see how it was done so that he might replicate the effect one day, allowing him and Sarah to return back to Earth. But even as closely as he'd watched, the process made absolutely no sense to him. With other things he had somehow understood, without knowing how, what was happening. But as he watched Pythor open the passageway ahead that same understanding eluded Allen. He couldn't help but wonder how Pythor was able to purposely plot where the gateway would send those who stepped through it.

Even with the warp gate open wider than he had seen it before, allowing two or three to pass through at once, it had still taken quite some time before everyone was through.

The deep black of the night sky had already begun to shift to a dark blue, highlighted most prominently along the horizon, by the time he and Pythor were all that remained on Sythar. With a final nod to the Krathantor, Allen briefly relived the moment which had begun his journey before stepping into the light. Even though he had experienced it twice before, the initial shock of pain which came with passing through the gateway still momentarily stole his breath. His vision blurred completely and the feeling of falling at great speeds rushed through him. Then all at once the discomfort dissipated and his vision slowly began to return to normal. It surprised him to feel the distinct atmospheric difference of this world when compared to the one he had just left behind. The gravity alone took several moments of readjustment, but he found the distinct aura of this world invigorating.

Allen felt the gateway close behind him as he rose to his feet and checked the sword at his hip to make sure it had survived the trip. He looked around to take stock of where they had emerged. He was surprised to see that the sky on Datheron was much the same shade of dark blue it had been on Sythar; with the shift in time between the two worlds he hadn't quite known what to expect. In the distance to his right he could make out the silhouette of a city; a city he thought he recognized. A short distance in front of him the road exiting the city passed before him, leading toward the horizon at his left.

He turned to Pythor, who appeared mildly disoriented as well. "What city is that?" he asked, gesturing to his right.

With only a perfunctory glance Pythor answered, "Abendroth."

Realizing exactly where they were, and recalling just how long it had taken him to reach Vardiston the first time from this point, Allen began to sprint north, away from Abendroth, just south of Vardiston. He didn't even bother to see who was behind him as he ran. Being this close to Sarah again, and yet so far away, filled him with a renewed sense of urgency. He had to reach Vardiston as quickly as he could.

He pushed on through the night, running until his lungs burned and then walking until his breath returned to him, only to push himself harder the next time he took to foot. He was pleased to learn that the entire group of Gorrlocks had followed his lead without question and ran as he ran. He couldn't explain why, but having them behind him made him feel more confident as he marched toward a conflict he now knew to be inevitable. He knew that it was more morbid curiosity than loyalty which inspired them to do so, but it still felt somehow empowering to have them at his back as he marched toward his goal.

By the time Vardiston came into view the shroud of night was long gone. Allen had pushed himself to his limits and beyond to make it here as quickly as possible. His muscles now ached to the point of feeling like he commanded jelly to move him forward. He was surprised to find the streets of the city packed beyond capacity and found it more than difficult to push his way through the throng in his weakened state. Had Pythor not been there to exploit the station he held, made obvious to all by his black and gold armor, they might never have been able to push their way to the palace. Even as it was, the streets were so crowded that it took great effort to make room for the Krathantor and his legion to pass by.

When they finally pushed their way into the courtyard of the palace, Allen saw Luziaph and several others attired in shining silver armor standing on stage. It was difficult to make out most of them between the sea of heads in his way, but after a moment he finally saw her. Sarah was alive. Luziaph had just finished saying something about bringing the world back to balance and was moving toward Sarah with his arms raised toward her head.

This was it; the moment from his vision. Sarah was about to be turned to stone and destroyed . . . and he was at the edge of the crowd, too far away to do anything to stop it.

40

ANIMUS

"WAIT!" ALLEN SCREAMED at the top of his lungs. "Do not touch her!"

Every eye in the crowd scanned the area for who could possibly be protesting the punishment about to be witnessed, those closest to him zeroing in immediately and casting him looks of moral outrage. As the crowd slowly parted to let him through, Allen saw a mixture of emotion coming from those on stage. Sarah's eyes went wide with relief and gratitude, while the others looked just as confused and outraged as the rest of the spectators. Only Luziaph appeared conflicted by his sudden emergence.

He pushed his way to the steps and moved to the top of them with purpose, casting a look of judgment on all who got in his way. When he finally reached the top step, two Triclopian guards stepped forward to prevent his access to the stage. He glared at them for a moment before turning his ire toward Luziaph. "Command them to step aside," he demanded, looking directly at the Proctus of

Vardiston. All three of Luziaph's eyes immediately fell upon the sword at Allen's hip growing wide with greed.

"Who in the name of Paragus is this?" the Voldehyde Proctus bellowed. "Guards, remove this man to the detention wing of this palace at once! We will deal with him after the proceedings!"

"You will do no such thing!" Allen fired back. "For you move to end the wrong person; the one you seek stands before you now! I am the child of prophecy!"

All at once the crowd of spectators erupted in discourse. The moment was electric, the very air full of energy and tension. Even those on stage—who were quite obviously the Proctus of the five other regions of Datheron based on their armor—stood in mute shock at hearing his words of defiant confession.

"Silence!" the Voldehyde Proctus barked. "How are we to know that this is not a desperate ploy to spare this one from the hands of Sythika? You could just be claiming such a thing in a foolhardy attempt to sacrifice your life in her place!"

Allen cast his calculating stare at the beast-man, eager to shut him up with the evidence he had obtained upon Sythar. He pushed his way past the two guards onto the stage, gazing out at the gathered masses before bringing his eyes back to the Voldeyhyde. "I am the child of prophecy," he repeated, making sure his voice was loud enough for all to hear. "I come from a planet known as Earth, born from a union which included a man from this world and a woman from Earth!" He turned his eyes to the crowd once more, "My father is the current Arena Champion: Zorthos!"

Gasps of horror and amazement filled the air. Allen could tell that his proclamation had inspired immediate fear in all present, including the other Proctus who were watching him warily now. "And if that is not proof enough for you, feast your eyes upon proper evidence of my claims!" He drew the Sword of Sythika from its scabbard, the same strange howling ring echoing loudly and filling the air as he did so. He held the blackened blade high above his head for all to see. "Behold, I have awoken the vaunted Sword of Sythika from its slumber!"

At seeing the blade of legend held in his grasp, and hearing the name of it spoken aloud, panic ignited among the crowd. Many began pushing their way toward the exit of the courtyard. Allen brought his eyes back to the stage and found Sarah on her knees, shaking and crying with relief. The gathered Proctus of Datheron had taken a collective step backward, watching the blade as he lowered it to his side. Even Gazianna's eyes were wide in astonishment and seemingly unable to move from the pitched-black blade in his grasp.

"I stand before you now for reasons far greater in number than have already been mentioned," he yelled for all those still present to hear. "I come bearing news of treachery of the highest order! This man . . ." He said, raising the tip of the sword to point at Luziaph, "bears responsibility for all which led to this moment and all that follows in its wake! It was by his hand that I was set upon the task of retrieving the sword of legend! It was his coercion which forced desires of returning to my home with naught but the woman I love in my arms from reality! Let it be known that it was his avarice which ignited the prophecy you all fear so!"

Everyone present, including the other Proctus of Datheron, cast horrified looks of betrayal at Luziaph. The Triclopian glanced surreptitiously in all directions before addressing the accusation. "He lies!" Luziaph yelled defensively. "I would not so blatantly, nor so willingly endanger the fate of this world!"

"And yet the words which fall from his tongue are not false," a new, deep voice echoed from above.

Allen looked up with the rest of those in the courtyard to see the silhouette of two men descending from the heavens. They moved slowly toward the audience from above as if gravity bowed before their will. When the light finally shifted enough to reveal who had spoken, Allen gawked at the ornately designed golden armor, etched in silver trim, as the two men came into view. Reflected light danced off the shoulder pads and breast plate of the God-King, Rhenngoth, as He lowered Himself toward the ground below, ushering Zorthos at His side with a casual wave of His hand. The people parted, granting a wide berth as their supreme ruler planted His feet firmly upon the ground at last.

Allen was surprised to see, now that they were both in full view, that Rhenngoth appeared to be several inches shorter than Zorthos. Despite the obvious difference in height, however, the Gorrlock God-King cut an imposing image, clad in the golden armor which denoted His station and wearing a white travelling cloak intricately trimmed in gold. His black hair was far shorter than Pythor's and had a defining widow's peak. He also wore a well-trimmed goatee which came to points along either side of his jaw bone. He had those same black and red eyes as all Gorrlocks, eyes which had locked intently upon Allen long before both feet hit the ground. But it was His presence more than His appearance which inspired such awe. Even Allen, as enept as he was in the use of Mystica, could feel the energy this man possessed radiating from Him as if it were more than He could contain. All around him had already fallen to one knee and lowered their heads, with the exception of the other Proctus upon the stage, and Allen felt inclined to follow suit.

Before he could, however, Rhenngoth's eyes shifted from him to Luziaph. "My ears were met with most troubling news recently," the God-King said. "Zorthos approached me on bended knee confessing in great detail the truth of all his transgressions, the most prominent of which coming in the form of patronage of a child from Earth. This might have been enough for execution had it not been coupled with tales of duplicity and conspiracy from within the walls of Vardiston. His words spun in detail intention of a certain Proctus to ignite the prophecy rather than presenting proper discovery to me as the law demands. Clearly," He said, turning his gaze once again on Allen, "such detail has not been exaggerated."

Allen bounced his attention back and forth between Luziaph and Rhenngoth feeling the tension mount with each passing second. He briefly glanced to Zorthos in an attempt to gauge some type of reaction to the situation, receiving nothing but a slight nod in return. He watched as Luziaph mentally struggled for some way to regain the control he'd had only moments ago; he didn't need telepathy to see the panic so clearly evident in all three of Luziaph's eyes.

It was in that moment of panic that the attack came with frightening speed, catching him off-guard. Luziaph moved toward him at a blinding pace, reaching for the sword as he drew near. Allen knew that he shouldn't have been able to even see the attack coming, that it was the same unique understanding of which the Gorrlock elder had told him allowing him to watch as Luziaph slowed time to his advantage. Although he could see what was happening, his reflexes weren't sharp enough to prevent the shoulder block which sent him flying or the twist of hand which placed the Sword of Sythika in the Triclopian Proctus' grasp.

He landed hard on the ground at the feet of a female spectator. She screamed as he bounced off the ground in front of her, rising from her knee and taking a cautionary step backwards. The woman, a human, looked down at him with revulsion, as if just being near him might make her guilty of treason as well. Allen looked up from his place on the ground to see even the other Proctus on stage scatter now that Luziaph held the legendary blade of death.

With a supremely wicked grin on his face, Luziaph held the black blade high for all to see. "It is mine!" he exclaimed, bringing all three of his eyes to meet Rhenngoth's. "It is mine and now prophecy bends to my will! No longer must I be forced to endure a place at your feet! With this mighty blade balance shall be restored and your rule will come to an end!"

Allen watched in horror as Luziaph turned his head toward Sarah, still on her knees upon the stage behind him, while Rhenngoth seemed content to watch how things would play out from among the crowd. With deliberate intent the Triclopian shifted his body and raised the Sword of Sythika behind him in preparation to strike. It was in this moment of great need that something clicked in Allen's mind. He leaped to his feet and burst forward in a single motion, commanding time to obey him as he moved to intercept the strike which would end the woman he loved. He glanced around for a weapon and noticed that the only one present capable of following his movements was the God-King, Himself. A fraction of an instant later, he called a sword to his grasp from a scabbard at the hip of one of the local guards standing just beyond the stage. With but an instant to spare he'd thrust that blade between Sarah's horrified face and Luziaph's down stroke. The clatter of steel on steel impacting seemed to somehow shatter Allen's dominance over a moment in time, bringing everything around him back into focus.

With a look of utter disbelief consuming his features, Luziaph's eyes found Allen on stage, holing that which had prevented his moment of victory. "How did you . . . ?" Luziaph stammered.

"You will not harm her," Allen stated. "I will not allow it."

Luziaph leaped several feet backward and threw himself into a fighting stance. "You were always fated to die by this blade," he goaded. "It matters not if you meet your end before the bitch at your back!"

He stepped more completely in front of Sarah, gesturing with a wave of his hand for her to back up. He said nothing as he raised his own weapon to a ready position. As he watched Luziaph size him up, Allen did his best to shake the worry and doubt from his mind. For a fourth time in as many days he found himself in a life-and-death situation before a crowd of spectators. He mentally shook himself, doing his best not to focus on the eyes all around him but on the fact that it was this three-eyed man who now stood between him and his objective to return home to Earth.

In a flash Luziaph thrust himself forward, bringing the sword in his grasp up to follow suit and narrowly missing his target. Allen twisted his stance accordingly, lifting his own blade to parry the attack. Everything around them distorted as he struggled to keep up with the blinding onslaught of Luziaph's lightning-quick attacks. He knew that they were once again moving within an instant in time and wondered, as he deflected blow after blow, if the clatter of their confrontation sounded like machine gun fire to those bearing witness.

Frustration showed plainly on Luziaph's face as he threw strike after strike, only to come up empty as Allen deflected each. The man was expertly trained in swordplay and had a mastery over the skill he was employing which

Allen could not match. It was everything he could do to block or deflect each incoming attack. Despite his best efforts to the contrary, he knew that Luziaph was in control of this conflict. With each overhead strike and thrust, the Triclopian Proctus pushed him back. The man had evidently abandoned his disbelief of Allen's capabilities in the interest of winning the battle.

Allen dodged to the left, the black blade of death missing his face by a margin of inches. He could feel the fatigue of his long journey to reach Vardiston in time taking its toll; his reflexes were beginning to betray him. Though he knew the battle had likely only been a few seconds to those viewing it, it felt to him as if he had been fighting for hours. He needed to mount an offensive strike of his own, but it was everything he could do keep Luziaph's attacks at bay. In a moment of desperation he thrust his own blade at what he believed to be an opening in Luziaph's defenses, only to have it meet the air as Luziaph side-stepped the attack. Luziaph brought the Sword of Sythika around in a back-handed motion and Allen threw himself backward to avoid it. Blinding pain shook him as the world came back into focus once more.

Allen lay upon the ground gasping for air, feeling as if the entire world were crushing him. He lifted his head enough to see a solitary drop of blood fall from the tip of the black blade in Luziaph's right hand. The world spun as he glanced at the three inch gash at the top of his left bicep. Light trails of black vapor wafted away from the wound. He felt as if he might vomit if only he had the strength to do so. He was only vaguely aware of Luziaph's shouted gloating as the clouds in the sky wavered in and out of focus.

He had failed. He was dying.

The thought of failure swirled through his mind with unrelenting dominance. He knew now why they called the legendary weapon the "blade of death". As minor as the wound on his arm was it was slowly stealing his life. Understanding of what the black vapor was came to him; it was the presence of Sythika itself which seeped from the gash, from the very blade which had caused it. The wound was slowly poisoning the Mystica still in his body; he could feel his life slipping away. As he lay there, a lifetime of good and poor choices alike raced through his mind, the most predominant of which was the tragic nature of his and Sarah's relationship. He had spent far too long being afraid of sharing his feelings with her, realizing only too late that he would never have her. The worst realization came in knowing that she was now defenseless and would be just as dead as he was as soon as Luziaph finished his arrogant monologue.

As if from nowhere, Allen saw a blurry shadow looming over him. It placed something in his mouth and told him to chew. There were three of them. Whatever it was tasted somehow familiar as he mashed them with his teeth, like a candy he had once eaten as a child perhaps. He chewed the candy into a fine paste, swallowing its juices. Slowly his vision began to return to him. His breathing was coming easier. He rolled his head to the side and watched with fascination as the gash on his left arm began to close itself. With each passing second he felt more and more revitalized, until he felt whole again at last.

As cognition completely returned to him he realized his head rested in Sarah's lap. She was staring down at him, her eyes expelling tears in earnest. Her sobs turned into quiet chuckles of relief when she saw him looking back at her. She lifted him from her lap and threw her arms around his neck from behind, clinging to him with strength he didn't know she possessed.

"I thought I'd lost you," she whispered in his ear. He could feel the warmth of her tears cutting a wet path down his own face as she clung to him.

Allen reached up and clutched her arm firmly to show her that he was okay. "How?" he asked with a genuine lack of understanding. "How did my wound heal?"

"The seeds I had in my pocket," she answered. When he tilted his head toward her and gave her a look of confusion, she elaborated. "I got them from the bush the night I got bit. That's actually, probably, why I got bit. When Zorthos said they had tremendous healing properties, I got greedy and walked up to the bush to get some for myself. I was only able to get three, but they've been in my pocket ever since."

He let out a laugh of relief and disbelief; a laugh which drew the attention of those still in the courtyard. There was a collective gasp as he brought himself back to his feet. The look of disbelief in Luziaph's eyes was priceless. The three-eyed man gaped at Allen as if he were literally witnessing a ghost's reemergence into the world of life.

Sarah stood as well, grabbing his right wrist in both her hands. "What are you doing?" she whispered frantically.

Allen glanced over his shoulder at her with a half-cocked smile. "I'm going to get my sword back," he replied in English with a wink.

She looked at him apprehensively for a moment and then released his sword arm. "Just don't lose this time," she said in a mock-playful tone; though her eyes still betrayed the concern in her heart. "I don't have my baseball bat and I'm all out of those seeds."

He grinned at the reference and then turned his eyes toward Luziaph. "You have something which belongs to me!" he challenged, shifting his speech back to Olyphatarian. "I would see it returned!"

As he stood there taking in the reactions of all present, Allen noted just how revitalized he felt. Not only had the dendegayra seeds healed his wound, they had filled him with a surplus of energy. He couldn't ever recall feeling this strong, this energetic. A quick glance at his surroundings showed a proud smile on the lips of his father, a look of intrigue on the face of Rhenngoth, and apprehension on the face of nearly every other person or creature present.

Luziaph took stock of Allen's appearance, all three of his eyes scanning every inch of the boy who should have died. His gaze lingered on the arm that, only moments before, had had a mortal wound upon it. Luziaph's shock quickly turned to outrage. "So be it!" he spat, rushing toward Allen, once again bending time to his will. With the Sword of Sythika drawn back in his right hand, Luziaph burst forward with alarming speed, his left hand stretched out toward Allen.

Allen let his instincts take over. With thoughts of his victories upon Sythar rushing through his head, he raised his own left hand toward Luziaph, matching the speed of his adversary's approach. Contemplative recollection turned to deliberate intent as he charged his fist with electric energy. Luziaph didn't even have time to register a reaction to the counterattack before Allen unleashed a powerful blast of blinding light at the man. The burst of energy hit with such force that it sent Luziaph flying backward through the air, knocking the Sword of Sythika from his grasp as he landed hard on the ground.

His chestplate smoking, Luziaph fought to master his twitching muscles enough to sit up and reach for the blade on the ground to his right. As his hand was within inches of the weapon Allen summoned it away from him. The legendary blade spun through the air, coming to a stop only as his right hand found the hilt and gripped it tightly.

Luziaph screamed with rage and Allen's entire world exploded.

Allen's vision blurred into blackness and his brain felt as if it were melting from within. He no longer knew what was real and what wasn't as he watched images of Sarah and his mother being torn apart by skriff hounds. All of a sudden he was ten years old again and watching his mother sobbing behind closed doors over the loss of her wayward husband. Sarah was walking down an aisle in a gorgeous white dress toward her ex-boyfriend Tommy, who held a large handgun in his right hand in plain view for all to see. Allen was engulfed in flames while Brad and the others beat him into submission with flaming fists. Zorthos was laughing as he cut out Carol's heart with a black-bladed butcher knife. Malacus exploded into a pile of rubble, a look of terror on his face. Gazianna cried tears of blood as she lay at the feet of Luziaph, who wore the golden armor of the God-King and held the Sword of Sythika in preparation to strike at the blue-skinned woman at his feet. Pythor stabbed him from behind, whispering in his ear that he would do the same to everyone Allen cared for once he destroyed all evidence of his existence. . .

With tremendous effort Allen pushed against the haunting visions consuming him. Somewhere deep down he knew that they were all false images of his darkest fears. As he struggled to claim dominance over them— putting absolutely every ounce of will he could muster into the task—he could feel Luziaph's presence slowly receding. Allen pushed harder. His senses slowly returned to him and he could feel something warm dripping from his nose and ears. Darkness became blurred light as color returned to the world around him.

He felt a hand upon his scalp even before he could see the triumph in Luziaph's eyes. The Triclopian Proctus howled in victory, laughing as Allen's entire body began to go rigid. He tried to raise his arms to his defense, only to feel his joints cracking from the effort. His vision began to slip away again and he knew that Luziaph was casting him in stone. The mental assault had only been intended to prevent him from being able to fight back while Luziaph moved in to play his trump card. As Allen searched his mind frantically for a way to escape death, the image of the Gorrlock elder sprang to the forefront of his thoughts. He recalled witnessing this very attack rebound on the old man as he had attempted to turn the beast to stone. He knew that if he could muster the strength to once again replicate that which he'd witnessed first-hand he would at least be able to take Luziaph with him.

With that thought in mind, Allen placed all his concentration into recreating that moment. He watched the scene over and over in his mind, pushing with all his might against the forced transformation his body was undergoing. He mentally gathered the minerals consuming his flesh and pushed them back toward their point of origin. When he had reclaimed enough control over his faculties to do so, he raised both his arms to grab hold of Luziaph's right wrist. With a final push of will, followed by a concussive burst of energy which filled the air with thunderous force, he removed the Triclopian's hand from his head; with the connection severed, the attack rebounded entirely upon Luziaph.

Taking several steps backwards on wobbly legs, Allen gaped at what he'd just done. His head hurt tremendously as he looked up and down at the statue of the man who had once been Proctus of all Vardiston. Luziaph's right arm was forever outstretched toward an invisible opponent, that same look of painful concentration immortalized on his face as the Gorrlock elder had had in death.

Sarah's arms wrapped tightly around him from behind and he could hear her weeping as he looked to his right to see astonishment on every face in the crowd. Not a sound was made now that the conflict was over. Every man, woman, beast, and child gaped at him in stunned silence while Sarah clung ever tighter. Even the God-King and all His subordinates were at a loss for words, though Rhenngoth seemed far more intrigued than amazed.

With a quick, almost listless gesture from His right hand, the God-King forced the statue of Luziaph into the outer wall of the palace, where it shattered to bits and left a minor crater where it had impacted. "The memory of his treachery will not be immortalized in stone," Rhenngoth stated flatly, but loud enough for all to hear. He then floated toward the stage with a graceful fluidity that Allen doubted even an eagle could duplicate, landing in the very place where the sculpture of Luziaph had been only moments before. His feet on the ground once more, Rhenngoth cast an authoritative stare at Allen that nearly made his knees buckle.

Now that the supreme ruler of this world stood before him, Allen could see definite creases forming along the man's forehead, and at the corners of His eyes and mouth. Although He looked much older when viewed this close, Allen had to admit that He looked pretty good for a man who had supposedly held this world in His grip for nearly a millennium. But it was the power radiating from Him that intimidated Allen the most. It was as if the man, Himself, were one of those cosmic forces beyond understanding that Malacus had told him about.

"Though your presence represents a great threat to my world," Rhenngoth continued, "you have done it a great service in destroying Luziaph. The Triclopian has ever been a problem, only rising to power by killing his predecessor in a contest of wills. A debt is owed to your efforts and I would see it paid before I depart. Speak your desire and see it fulfilled."

His eyes wide and his mouth slightly agape, Allen turned to look at Sarah. Her lips were trembling into a small smile and tears still streamed down her face as she stared back at him.

"I love you, Allen," she said in a shaky voice.

"I have always loved you, from the moment we met," he replied with a smile on his face and in his heart..

She nodded and returned his smile. "Let's go home," she whispered into his ear.

He turned back to the God-King, hoping that his moment with Sarah hadn't been taken as a slight against the man's generosity. "I know that such is forbidden," he said, "but I would not place this world in further jeopardy. I would see myself and the woman I love returned to the world from which we hail."

Rhenngoth's face was unreadable as he responded. "I fear such is the one request I cannot grant," He said. "For doing so would create imbalance among the populace by discounting laws which have been in place for countless centuries." Allen's hopes deflated as the God-King continued: "The law as it has been written places he who is able to best a Proctus in mortal combat into the vacant seat of power. You are now counted among those at my beck and call, bearing the title of Proctus of Vardiston. I cannot allow you to return to Earth under current circumstances."

Allen's world stopped in that moment.

He couldn't believe what he had just heard. He couldn't help but feel as if his entire journey to Sythar had been for nothing.

As crushing as Rhenngoth's news was it took several long moments for the remark to register and several more for him to find the presence of mind to reply. "I . . . what?" he stammered. "Surely the statement is a jest."

Even to his own ears it sounded as if he were pleading.

"I do not jest when matters of the law are involved," Rhenngoth retorted firmly and with a harsh undertone. "You now stand Proctus of Vardiston, regardless of desire, and as such will have a great deal to learn about the laws which you will be expected to enforce. If desire to return to Earth yet remains, I will grant the opportunity to earn such reward in the Arena Games. Place yourself among other contestants and win title of Arena Champion and I shall see you safely back to Earth. Be warned, however, as such contests are often to the death and entry into such places title of Proctus at risk. Should you fall in the attempt, whoever defeats you will take title of Proctus as prize for their victory. Know prior to making decision that such outcome is coveted by many." Rhenngoth paused a moment, seemingly to let His words sink in before adding, "Put words to another desire and I shall see it granted."

Allen stood in mute shock of his own as he gazed at those among the crowd. A great many looks of uncertainty met him as he scanned the faces in the audience, searching his mind for anything else he could possibly want. He desperately wanted to change the God-King's mind, but a quick glance back at Him told Allen that to even attempt further protest would warrant a response he didn't want to experience. It wasn't until his eyes found Zorthos that he was finally able to come up with a request he thought the God-King might consider suitable.

"If request to depart this world cannot be granted," he said meekly, bringing his eyes back to Rhenngoth, "I would see Zorthos absolved of his crimes, the weight of them to be forgotten by all."

Rhenngoth was silent for several moments as He considered Allen's request. With a look of great reluctance upon His face, the God-King nodded. "So be it," He said, turning to face the citizens of Vardiston. "Let it be known that Zorthos, Arena Champion, bears the title of fugitive no more!" He brought his powerful gaze to meet Zorthos'. "I leave the responsibility of teaching him what is expected of all Proctus upon your shoulders," He stated with authority. With a final look of appraisal at Allen, Rhenngoth was lifted from the ground by an invisible force and disappeared into the sky in a blur of motion.

41

DENOUEMENT

ALLEN HATED THE ARMOR he was forced to wear as Proctus of Vardiston. Although it had specifically been crafted to fit him, it was far bulkier and heavier than the leather armor he had grown accustomed to in his time with Pythor. It had taken great effort just to move around in it the first couple weeks since its completion, and even though he was more used to it now that he'd been wearing it a while, he still found it quite cumbersome. Sarah said it made him look powerful . . . and sexy. He was still getting used to her being so flirtatious with him, too; though he was rather enjoying that particular transition.

   After Rhenngoth had flown away from the scene that was to be Sarah's execution, an awkward silence had dominated the entire courtyard. Every eye there had found him and refused to move. He wasn't sure if it was out of fear of who he was or in fascination to what they had just witnessed; though he was inclined to believe the former. Assuming at the time that they had been waiting for him to give some type of declaration in regard to the station to which he had just been appointed, he had offered words to those gathered of his intention to live up to their expectations. They had responded to such a claim with the same anxious silence which had so dominated them throughout most of his conflict with Luziaph. It wasn't until Zorthos strode up to the platform, telling the masses to disperse at once, that he had begun to feel marginally more comfortable.

As his first act as Proctus of Vardiston Allen had found Gazianna and granted her freedom from the bonds of servitude, though he told her she would always be welcome to stay at the palace as a guest. It was in that moment that he'd seen the first real show of emotion come from the woman. Her green eyes swelling with tears, she had thrown her arms around him and didn't let go for quite a while. When she had finally released him she'd insisted upon staying at his side to help him adapt into the role of a leader. He had only agreed on the condition that she take the title of advisor.

Although the outcome of that day's events hadn't met his expectations—not by a long shot—he did his best to adapt and make the best with what he had. He had ordered the gruesome statues Luziaph had so loved removed from palace grounds. He really didn't care where they ended up, but he refused to have such macabre decorations remind him of the man who had put them there, or the acts of violence from which they were created. He had also ordered Borograth and Sepharus released from the private incarceration chamber, had the Triagas removed from their heads, and had returned their black and gold armor. Pythor had thanked him for his kindness and offered to teach him more in the ways of Mystica some day before leading the Gorrlock tribe from Sythar to find new lives upon the surface of Datheron.

As positive of a turn as his life seemed to have taken since retrieving the Sword of Sythika, however, there was still a definitive sadness which loomed over him like the shadow of great storm cloud. He still missed his mother horribly and felt great regret that she had no idea what had become of him. The more he learned of this world, the more time he spent here, the more he came to truly understand his father's position and the difficult choice he'd had to make so long ago. Bitter feelings still lingered toward the man in his heart, but they were waning with each passing day.

Upon learning of what had happened to Malacus, Zorthos had insisted upon travelling to the place which had been his home; a place, Allen had learned, in which Zorthos had taken refuge many times while hiding from his status as fugitive. He'd insisted upon going with Zorthos and paying his respects. The destruction which met their eyes as they arrived had been difficult to witness. Malacus' cabin had all but been blown to pieces, the shattered remains of the old man's body strewn about haphazardly in the main living area. Nearly all of Malacus' belongings on the upper level of the domicile had been completely obliterated in his conflict with Luziaph. Both he and Zorthos were relieved to find that the lower library was completely intact. Zorthos nodded absently at his suggestion that they move the contents of the library to the Palace of Vardiston for safekeeping, so that he could continue to study his great grandfather's teachings. Neither man said a word as they set to gathering the pieces of what remained of Malacus, and dug a hole in which to bury them in the front yard near the banks of the small lake. Allen had gazed out at the waters of that lake, recalling that that had been the first place he had seen the old man.

Allen asked Zorthos about the tree which sprang from deep within the water at the center of the lake and was surprised to learn that the fruit of the tree contained a unique property which all but halted the aging process. That, Zorthos explained, was how Malacus was able to live as long as he had without succumbing to the hands of Sythika. As they covered the shattered statue with dirt, Zorthos explained that the tree only fruited once a year and usually only bore one or two fruits. He told Allen that such a tree was rare even on the Planet of the Gods, which was why it rested at the center of a lake full of deadly challenges which were put in place to prevent any but the most skilled from reaching its branches.

On their return trip home their conversation, sparse though it was, turned to the subject of Allen's mother and how much they both missed her. Zorthos related stories of what she had been like in her youth, while Allen shared stories of how she had changed since Zorthos departed. He told Zorthos about how Carol had switched her major at college to the study of law in hopes that she might someday locate him and be able to find a loophole which would allow him to return and maintain citizenship in the United States. Zorthos grew very silent at hearing all the details of how tormented and determined she had become in his absence.

Upon returning to Vardiston, Zorthos told him that he would once again be leaving for a while. Rather than allow himself to be affronted by the news, Allen had wished him well and given him a very awkward goodbye hug.

When the man finally resurfaced nearly two weeks later, he was clean-shaven and carrying a rather large unsightly mirror under his left arm. It had intricately carved golden edges and reminded him very much of the mirror which had always hung on the wall of his mother's living room and had always looked so out of place. With but a gesture from his hand Zorthos had motioned for Allen to follow. Sarah had joined them as they traced the all-too-familiar path to the throne room.

Zorthos mounted the mirror on the wall. Once he seemed satisfied with its position and height, he turned to Allen with a rare smile upon his lips.

"Come," he said. "I have brought a most welcome surprise. But tell no one of it," he added a moment later, casting a furtive glance at the entrance to the room.

Uncertain what could possibly be so special or welcoming about a tacky duplicate of his mother's mirror, he stepped forward skeptically. Once he and Sarah had gathered around him, Zorthos closed his eyes and placed his hands to the edges of the mirror's frame. The man's lips moved in some sort of rhythmic pattern and then the mirror began to glow. The image being reflected began to waver and shift until it presented an all-together different image. Allen gaped in amazement as he watched his mother sitting upon the couch in her living room. She seemed to have aged quite a bit since he'd seen her last; he silently wondered how many Earth years had passed since he'd left.

For a long time no one said anything; they just watched her sitting there, looking alone and utterly miserable. Allen couldn't help but notice the sad look upon his mother's face reflecting in Zorthos' countenance as well. For the first time Allen's heart was breaking for his father's loss as well as his mother's

Finally, when Zorthos seemed to have had his fill of watching, he called Carol's name. She started and glanced around for a moment before shrugging and resting her head once again against the back of the couch. Zorthos encouraged Allen and Sarah to join him in trying to get her attention. It took several attempts, Carol looking as if she thought she were losing her mind before she finally looked up at her own mirror and saw them staring back.

She stood from the couch and cautiously approached the mirror, her facial features shaking with disbelief. Her chin quivered as she reached her hands toward them from another world. She opened her mouth and took several more steps toward them, but no words came out. Her eyes darted back and forth between the three of them in utter bewilderment; she seemed certain she was going mad. She blinked again, a lone tear falling against her left cheek.

"Allen?" she called at last, her voice shaking tremendously.

"Hi, Mom," he answered with a smile, tears filling his eyes. "You aren't going crazy, I promise . . . It really is me."

Tears escaped her control as she finally gave in to what she was seeing; the look on her face said that she didn't care if she was going crazy as long as she got to see her son.

"Oh, my goodness!" Carol exclaimed. "Allen! My baby! And Zachary? And Sarah? What happened to you? Where have you been all this time?"

With his own vision swimming in the emotion of the moment, he cleared the lump forming in his throat. "It's a very long, very difficult to believe story," he began. "You may want to sit down . . ."

Coming soon from
Idea Creations Press

THE
ARENA
OF THE
GODS
A.M JOHNSTON

For more information visit:
amjohnstonauthor.com

A.M. JOHNSTON

IC Idea Creations Press

Want to have future control of your work? Our Publishing Options give you the control where you want it and need it. Do the writing and allow Idea Creations Press to do the rest. Choose the best price for your budget, or travel all the way to superior publishing options. Order TODAY and receive a FREE Amazon Kindle version of your book listed in the Kindle store on Amazon.com. Check out our publishing options at:

www.ideacreationspress.com.

Please contact us on any options you don't understand.

We would love to publish your book if it teaches positive morals and values. It can be a fun read, too, but ultimately, good must triumph over evil; readers must be left with a positive message. Generally we publish:

Middle Readers
Young Adult Fiction
Nonfiction
Self-Help
Guidebooks
Christian Fiction

General Fiction
Women's Fiction
Historical Fiction
Mysteries
Westerns

If your book doesn't fit in any of the genres or categories listed above, know that we are still open to hearing about your project. As long as the book follows the guidelines listed above and does not include bad language, adult oriented material (erotica) or excessive blood and gore, we would like to hear from you.

Although we are not a Christian publisher, we subscribe to Christian values, and feel like a great book doesn't have to include negative 'world views' in order to be accepted by readers.

Call us today for your FREE evaluation
(385) 529-5935
authorsupport@ideacreationspress.com
www.ideacreationspress.com

www.ingramcontent.com/pod-product-compliance
Lightning Source LLC
Chambersburg PA
CBHW050118030726
47505CB00007B/1930